AIDUEL'S SIN

Daniel T. Jackson is a fantasy enthusiast, with a love for fantastical worlds and thrilling adventures. After the critical success of his epic fantasy debut novel, *Illborn*, Daniel has continued the awe-inspiring story with the publication of book two, *Aiduel's Sin*. With *The Illborn Saga*, he hopes to create the next classic fantasy series.

Daniel is married with four children, and lives in the United Kingdom. He also loves hiking, cycling, piano and volunteering for good causes. *Aiduel's Sin* is his second published novel.

AIDUEL'S SIN

BOOK TWO OF THE ILLBORN SAGA

DANIEL T. JACKSON

Copyright © 2023 Daniel T. Jackson

The moral right of the author has been asserted.

Apart from any fair dealing for the purposes of research or private study, or criticism or review, as permitted under the Copyright, Designs and Patents Act 1988, this publication may only be reproduced, stored or transmitted, in any form or by any means, with the prior permission in writing of the publishers, or in the case of reprographic reproduction in accordance with the terms of licences issued by the Copyright Licensing Agency. Enquiries concerning reproduction outside those terms should be sent to the publishers.

Matador
Unit E2 Airfield Business Park,
Harrison Road, Market Harborough,
Leicestershire. LE16 7UL
Tel: 0116 2792299
Email: books@troubador.co.uk
Web: www.troubador.co.uk/matador
Twitter: @matadorbooks

ISBN 978 1803135 915

British Library Cataloguing in Publication Data.
A catalogue record for this book is available from the British Library.

Printed and bound by CPI Group (UK) Ltd, Croydon, CR0 4YY
Typeset in 10.5pt Adobe Jenson Pro by Troubador Publishing Ltd, Leicester, UK

Matador is an imprint of Troubador Publishing Ltd

*To Mum, Dad, Ian and Kate. Thank you
for so many years of love and support.*

Cast of Characters from Illborn

The Illborn

Allana dei Monis.
Lord Arion Sepian, the Hero of Moss Ford, the Butcher of Moss Ford.
Corin of Karn, the Chosen of the Gods.
Priestess Leanna Cooper, the Angel of Arlais.

Western Canasar and Septholme

Charl Koss – experienced and tough adviser to the Sepian family.
Duke Conran Sepian – former ruler of Western Canasar, father of Arion. Died following the selfish actions of Allana.
Lord Delrin Sepian – older brother of Arion, left Western Canasar to fight in the Holy Land.
Duke Gerrion Sepian – eldest brother of Arion, became ruler of Western Canasar after his father's death.
Lady Kalyane Sepian – formerly Lady Kalyane Rednar, now wife of Arion.
Lady Karienne Sepian – Arion's younger sister.
Captain Menion Thatcher – captain of the guard for Septholme Castle.

Andar – Other

Commander Arnas Roque – lead instructor at the Royal Academy of Knights.

King Inneos Pavil – monarch of Andar, close friend of the late Duke Conran Sepian.

Duke Jarrett Berun – head of the House of Berun, rival and enemy of Arion at the Royal Academy of Knights. He encountered Allana after she fled from Western Canasar.

Lord Lennion Rednar – second son of the House of Rednar, friend of Arion from the Royal Academy of Knights, brother of Lady Kalyane Sepian.

Queen Mariess Pavil – wife of King Inneos.

Prince Sendar Pavil – second son of King Inneos, friend of Arion from the Royal Academy of Knights.

Prince Senneos Pavil – eldest son of King Inneos, heir to the throne.

Arlais and the College of Aiduel

Priestess Amyss – Leanna's room-mate and closest friend at the College of Aiduel in Arlais.

Sister Colissa – head of the healers and the hospital at the College of Aiduel in Arlais.

Priestess Corenna – one of the teachers at the College of Aiduel in Arlais.

Elisa Cooper – mother of Leanna.

Senior Priest El'Patriere – abusive leader of the College of Aiduel in Arlais. Leanna became his enemy after she reported his actions, and he later arranged for her arrest.

Jonas Cooper – father of Leanna.

Senior Priestess Maris – priestess in Arlais who linked the actions of Aiduel's Guards to the event of the Great Darkening.

Karn and Bergen

Agbeth – Corin's wife, who travelled with him to the far north after he was banished, but who suffered a grievous head injury in an attack following their return to Karn.

Akob – Corin's father, and one of Corin's key advisers in the Karn clan.

Blackpaw – a mighty beast called a felrin, which Corin tamed in the far north during his banishment from the Karn clan.

Clan Chief Borrik – former clan chief of the Karn, who was killed by Corin in mortal combat.

Kernon – Corin's older brother, who bullied Corin when they were growing up.

Marrix – one of Corin's key advisers in the Karn clan.

Clan Chief Munnik – clan chief of the Borl.

Clan Chief Rekmar – former clan chief of the Anath, who was eaten by Blackpaw on Corin's instruction.

Aiduel's Guards and the Holy Church

Archprime Amnar – Head of the Holy Church in Andar.

High Priest Comenis – leader of the Holy Church in Arlais. Was at Leanna's pyre.

High Commander Ernis dei Bornere – leader of the Aiduel's Guards military order in Arlais. Sentenced Leanna to burning on the pyre for being an Illborn.

High Commander Evelyn dei Laramin – leader of the garrison of Aiduel's Guards in Septholme. Arrested and tortured Allana, who later murdered her.

Sergeant Monliere – Aiduel's Guard who was responsible for Allana's imprisonment.

Nionia dei Pallere – initially a friend of Allana, later responsible for Allana's imprisonment. She lied to Arion about Allana's fate.

Archlaw Paulius the Fourth – Head of the Holy Church, based in the Archlaw's Palace near Sen Aiduel, in Dei Magnus.

High Priest Ronis dei Maranar – high priest in Sen Aiduel, who was murdered by Allana after he assaulted her.

Other

Caddin Sendromm – mysterious traveller who murdered a young boy with apparent powers, several years earlier, and is now aware of Leanna.

Cillian Maddoc – young boy with apparent powers, who was murdered by Caddin Sendromm.

Emperor Jarrius El'Augustus – leader of the Elannis Empire.

Prince Markon El'Augustus – heir to the throne of the Elannis Empire, who was defeated and wounded by Arion, but was miraculously healed by Leanna.

Seilana dei Monis – mother of Allana, died of the Wasting Sickness.

Sern Maddoc – father of Cillian Maddoc, who was murdered by Caddin Sendromm.

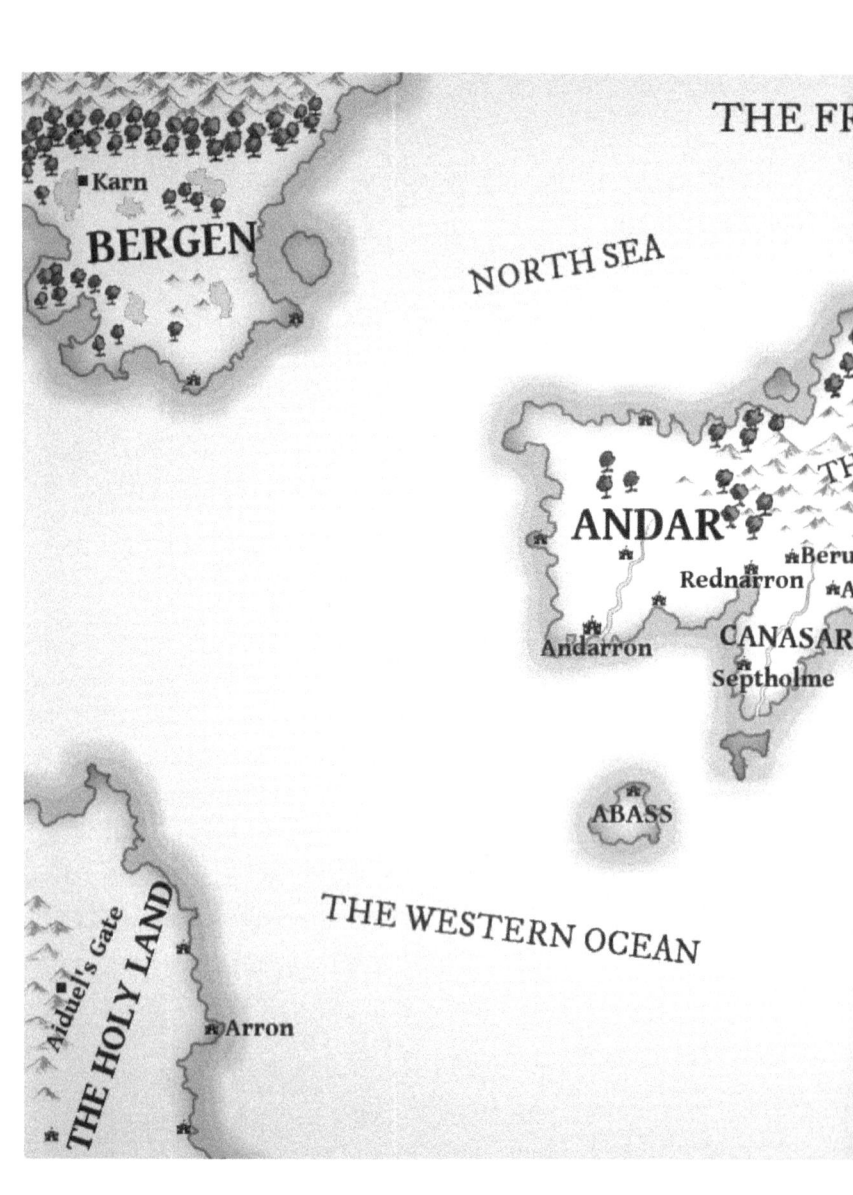

Prologue

Caddin

Year of Our Lord, After Ascension, 749AA
(several months after the Great Darkening)

Can a destiny be shaped, or does the first trickle of fate flow unerringly to the precipice of a distant future outcome?

Caddin Sendromm was not thinking about this question as he waited inside the Archlaw's Palace, within a sumptuous antechamber which belonged to the illustrious leader of the Holy Church. Instead, he was staring at his reflection in the polished marble floor, and was speculating about the possible nature of the encounter which lay ahead of him.

In most circumstances, Caddin was able to disregard any hinted sense of nervousness or anxiety. Indeed, after the many horrors of his childhood years, he was usually capable of suppressing such trivial emotions. At this moment, however, he was feeling particularly ill-at-ease.

His hand moved down to his side and his fingers clenched, but the familiar form of his mace was not there to provide comfort. It had been confiscated upon his arrival at the palace, at the same time that his robes had been thoroughly searched. No outsider was to enter these sacred grounds, or to come into the presence of His Holy Eminence, bearing anything which could be used as a weapon.

Lord Aiduel, thought Caddin, *make my thoughts and actions true, and please don't let me make a fool of myself.*

His gaze shifted towards the closed wooden door in front of him, which was ten feet in height and was decorated with an elaborate carving of The Lord Aiduel On The Tree. Four armed soldiers flanked this sealed entrance, all wearing the bright red cloaks and sashes which identified them as members of Aiduel's Guards, the fast-growing military order.

Caddin knew that the head of the Holy Church, His Eminence Archlaw Paulius the Fourth, might be waiting in the room beyond that doorway. Soon, Caddin expected to be called through to meet this esteemed individual, this man who was Aiduel's Mortal Voice on Angall.

Caddin's summons had arrived two days earlier, in the form of a hand-delivered letter. The message inside had consisted of a single sentence, instructing him to attend the Archlaw's Palace at noon on Sixth-Day, by order of Paulius himself.

Early on Fifth-Day morning, Caddin had therefore left his post at the College hospital of Sen Aiduel, and had walked northwards from the city for twenty miles. He had spent the night in a dormitory on the outskirts of the vast walled complex which surrounded the palace, before arriving at the magnificent central building this morning.

It was only then that a palace official had warned him that he should prepare himself for a personal audience with the Archlaw. The official had not offered any further explanation, leaving Caddin with this lingering and unwelcome sense of unease.

The imposing door opened inwards as Caddin was reflecting upon this, and a middle-aged man came into view within the doorway, attired in modest grey robes. Caddin had seen this man's visage on many paintings in the preceding years, and he immediately stood, then bowed low.

'Your Eminence,' he said.

The Archlaw was of medium height, with thick black hair flecked with spots of grey. He gestured with his hand towards the room behind him.

'Please, Priest Caddin, come join me,' he said. His voice was refined and sonorous, and the underlying accent clearly revealed his Elannis origins.

Caddin did as instructed, pacing across to the open door, and entering an audience chamber which was both large and opulent. He was surprised to see that there was no one else in the room.

An ancient and ornate desk sat in the room's centre, and Paulius gestured to a chair in front of that desk. Caddin seated himself, before hearing the door swinging shut behind him, again sealing the chamber. He was dry-mouthed as the Archlaw took a seat on the other side of the desk.

'Priest Caddin Sendromm. Welcome to my palace.'

'Thank you, Your Eminence,' said Caddin. 'It's a great honour to be here, and to meet you.'

'Please, be at ease, Priest Caddin. You're probably greatly vexed as to why I've called you here today, and I'll come onto that in good time. But let's talk together first, not as eminent Archlaw and humble priest, but as simple men, for just a few moments.'

'Yes, Your Eminence.'

The Archlaw leaned forwards with his elbows on the desk, his hands steepled together. 'What an interesting journey your life has taken, Priest Caddin, to lead you to your current position in the priesthood. You have a background which I would describe as unique.'

'Your Eminence?'

'Yes, unique. I know a *lot* about you, Priest Caddin. More than you would probably want me to know. How you grew up as a gutter-rat, an orphan, after your parents died when you were eight. How you were forced to scrounge for food and had to fight to stay alive on the streets of Elannis City. How you had no family or home but somehow survived on those streets for five years. All of that *is* correct, I presume?'

Caddin frowned. The years in Elannis City were a period of his life that he did not like to think about or talk about. Only a handful of people had ever been told that story.

'Yes, Your Eminence.'

'And you escaped that life by enrolling in the Elannis army. As I understand, you were only thirteen years old, but you passed for sixteen given the size of you.'

'Yes, Your Emin-'

'Don't worry, you don't need to keep confirming, I know that all of this is true. My people have done their... *research*. You then served in the army for fourteen years, and throughout a number of wars. You attained the rank of Commander, a most significant achievement given your background. Even more notably, you were awarded the Emperor's Star, for an act of extreme heroism.'

Caddin nodded in confirmation, growing more uncomfortable.

'Tell me about that,' ordered the Archlaw, his stare unrelenting.

'There was a fortress in a mountain pass, Your Eminence, during the First Patran War. I was given four hundred men and told to hold the pass, to let no one through. But when he gave the order, my superior didn't know that the enemy's main force intended to cross that route. We... held our position, until a relief force came.'

'You're too modest, Priest Caddin. Too modest. The story I've heard is that your force held back an army twenty times its size, and that you're reputed to have personally killed... *hundreds*... of men. That you were one of only eight survivors.' Caddin did not respond, feeling embarrassed, but the Archlaw continued, 'Were you really that deadly, Priest Caddin Sendromm? Were you truly such a lethal killer?'

Caddin paused, unsettled by the direction of the conversation, before answering, 'Yes, Your Eminence. I was. But I renounced that life, after I left the army.'

'But you also lost your second family during those years? Your wife and-'

'Forgive me, Your Eminence,' interrupted Caddin, 'but I don't want to talk about that. Please, may we not?'

The Archlaw stared at him for a few seconds, with brows narrowed, before saying, 'Very well, I'll not question you on that then. May I otherwise proceed?'

'Of course, Your Eminence. Please excuse me.'

'So, as I understand it, following the end of the First Patran War eight years ago, and the award of the Star, you were granted a boon. A chance to ask for a reward. And the Elannis army's deadliest killer surprised everyone by asking to be given a religious education, and to be trained as a priest. May I ask why?'

'I wanted peace, Your Eminence. During and after the war, I was… tormented. I'd done horrible things. *Many* horrible things. I couldn't sleep. I hated myself. And I'd… *lost everything*. But I found a sense of peace, and a chance at salvation, in the words of The Lord Aiduel and in the Holy Church.'

'And I understand that your new-found faith also helped you to control your drinking?'

Caddin gulped, shocked by how much the Archlaw knew about his personal history. 'Yes, Your Eminence. For a period, before I embraced a life of service to Aiduel, I was close to becoming a drunk. After that, I put it aside. I haven't touched alcohol since I joined the priesthood.'

'I know that, Caddin, and your abstinence has been a credit to you. Forgive me, it must be very disconcerting to have your past laid out like this by a stranger, particularly when that stranger is *me*, and I can only imagine the horrors that you've witnessed. The tragedy that you've experienced. But, as you say, you found Aiduel, and all of the reports from your religious training paint you as a diligent and devout novice. And then, after you were ordained, you joined the Order of Saint Helena. Yes?'

'Yes.'

'Again, why?'

'Because it was a chance to make amends, Your Eminence. To heal people, to find some redemption for all the… pain, I'd caused.'

'And has it? Made amends?'

'A little. Not completely, if I'm honest. I'm not sure if anything ever could.'

'And how strong is your faith, Caddin?'

'Strong, Your Eminence. It is the central pillar of my life now.'

'And you are completely without family, yes? No parents, no brothers or sisters, no… others. No one?'

Caddin grimaced, feeling awkward. 'No, Your Eminence. I have no family.'

'And what about close friends? Who would miss Priest Caddin Sendromm, if he were to leave Sen Aiduel, and were to never return?'

Caddin felt confused. 'Well… there are colleagues, at the hospital. At the College. But who would miss me? Really miss me?' He frowned once more, recognising the truth as something cold and numbing. 'No one, really.'

'That's what I've been told. Which, along with your background, is why I believe you may be perfect for what I need. What the Holy Church needs. And now, I have a vital question for you, Caddin.' The sudden gravity of the Archlaw's tone matched that of his expression. 'Would you be prepared to give up your current life, and to devote your future, perhaps your entire future, to the service of a vital mission for me and for the Holy Church?'

Caddin paused for a number of seconds, digesting the unexpected question, and feeling a sudden thrill of excitement. 'Devotion of my future? To what mission, Your Eminence?'

'I talk, Priest Caddin, of something which is perhaps the most important holy quest that I could ever give to you. Something which could truly offer you *redemption* and *salvation*.' The Archlaw's voice had taken on a more passionate and strident tone as he said these last words. 'But it would also mean the end of the life you currently know. However, I'm not prepared to offer any further details, until I have your answer and your commitment.'

'I'm sorry, Your Eminence, but if I don't say "yes", then what?'

'Then I'll tell you no more, I'll bid you to depart in the Grace of Aiduel, and you and I will never meet again, Priest Caddin. And, perhaps, for a long time afterwards you'll be haunted, wondering what I was going to say, and whether you turned in the wrong direction at the most important crossroads of your life. So, your decision, Caddin. Will you decline and leave, or will you answer "yes" to my question, and make your commitment to me?'

Caddin's eyes narrowed as he considered his response. It seemed that this answer could possibly define the rest of his life. But, in honesty, what did he currently possess which he would care about relinquishing? That he would mourn to leave behind? Nothing. His life in the Church had failed to seal the wounds in his soul. In consequence, when he finally answered, his response was resolute.

'Yes, Your Eminence. I will. I'll make my commitment to you.'

The Archlaw continued to scrutinise him, silent for a few seconds, and Caddin felt as if the other man was peering into his heart and soul. Evaluating and judging him. Making a decision.

'Very well. I believe you,' said Paulius. He placed his hand onto a worn, leather-bound tome which rested on the desk, then pushed the book towards Caddin. 'But swear it to me. Before The Lord, and on the Holy Book. Swear that you'll serve me faithfully, and will keep everything that I'm about to say to you secret, to be spoken about only to me or to others to whom I may direct.'

The soldier still lurking within Caddin responded instinctively to the authority within the instruction. It further solidified his commitment to his decision, and he placed his hand forwards onto the tome.

'I so swear, Your Eminence. Before The Lord, and on the Holy Book, I swear that I'll serve you faithfully and will keep what you say to me secret.'

The Archlaw nodded in confirmation, then said, 'Very well, then we shall proceed. Were you in Sen Aiduel, Caddin, for the Great Darkening?'

'Yes, Your Eminence, I was.'

Caddin could clearly remember the awful moments, months earlier, when the sun had disappeared and the capital had been cast into darkest night in the middle of the day. He could recall the traces of anxiety that had touched him as the world had turned to black around him, and the screams of the city's panicked citizens had begun.

'And what do you think it meant?' asked Paulius.

'I don't know, Your Eminence. Some people believe that we were being judged. And that Aiduel had turned away from us, that day, as a result of our sins.'

'A sensible thought, that. Sensible. But *not* correct.'

The Archlaw opened a drawer in his desk, and extracted an old and yellowing scroll. He placed it onto the desk surface and gestured towards it, making no effort to untie its strings or to unroll the aged parchment.

'This document is a letter, Caddin, which is usually locked away in my personal vault. It is my single most important possession, so you'll please excuse me if I don't invite you to touch it or to read it. It was written by my predecessor, Bohemius the Second. He wrote it for his successor, as one of his first acts of office, as I in turn have already produced a copy for my eventual successor. The only two people who've ever read this *particular* scroll are me and Bohemius. But the document itself is a copy. A copy of another document which is much, much older, and which was written by an altogether different hand. A letter which has been copied by hand by Archlaws from the Year of Ascension onwards, and which has only ever been read by Archlaws. Would you like to know what's in the document?'

Caddin swallowed, his face masking his inner excitement. 'Yes, Your Eminence, if it serves you to tell me?'

'It does, in part. The document is a *warning*, Caddin. It refers to the event of the Great Darkening. Predicts it. And it tells of what that event will be a precursor to.'

'It does?'

'Yes, it does. Something has been born into this world, Caddin. Something powerful and evil. Something *Illborn*. They are in human form, but they're *not* of our kind.' A hint of passion had crept into the Archlaw's voice as he had said this, but the man then paused, and seemed to take control of his emotion before continuing. 'I don't know where they are, Caddin, or who they are. But I *do* know that there are five of them. And unless I find them and stop them, unless *we* find them and stop them, this letter prophesies that they'll shatter the Holy Church and the faith, and will drown the world in blood and war.'

The hairs on the back of Caddin's neck were standing up, as he asked, 'What would you have me do, Your Eminence?'

'It's not a question of what I would have you do. Priest Caddin. It's what the original writer of this letter would have us both do.'

Caddin gulped. 'And who wrote the letter, Your Eminence?'

Paulius held his gaze, his face grave. 'Aiduel, Caddin. The Lord Aiduel wrote the letter. Before He Ascended. And now, this terrible matter, of which He warned us long ago, has come to pass.'

—

Sometime later, after the Archlaw had described Caddin's mission at length and had gifted an ancient and precious object, the head of the Holy Church again steepled his hands in front of himself.

'You've heard everything that I've had to say, Caddin. Perhaps you understand now why we've met alone like this, and why I swore you to secrecy?'

'I do, Your Eminence,' said Caddin. 'I understand.'

'I am fully aware that I have a choice,' said the Archlaw, 'as to how brutally I act to stop this evil. If I wished to be ruthlessly effective, and damn the cost, I could issue a proclamation now to order the faithful to kill all of the newborn children of Angall. Every child born across the span of a year. And by doing so, I might also find and kill these Illborn. But then, even assuming that people would obey me, which they wouldn't, it would be me who becomes the monster. Me who fulfils the prophecy of destroying the faith and drowning the world in blood. And before The Lord, my conscience cannot allow me to do that. That is why I choose this alternative. For now.'

'I understand, Your Eminence,' said Caddin. 'I'm honoured that you've chosen me for this.'

'Only a handful of people in the world know of the matters that I've discussed with you today, Caddin. You'll recognise that this knowledge could do great damage to the Church and to the faith, if shared carelessly. As such, now that you've heard my secrets, swear to me again that you'll serve me faithfully. And be in no doubt that if you break your vow to me, I'll not hesitate to excommunicate you, and your eternal soul will be condemned to reside in the unending darkness.'

'I swear to serve you faithfully, Your Eminence.'

'Very well. Remember the things that I've told you today. And always keep the medallion on your person, at all times. One day, if you find that which I need you to find, it may save your life.'

'I will remember, Your Eminence.'

Caddin could feel the small, silver medallion which now hung from the chain around his neck. The medallion's unembellished metal surface was cold against his flesh, but was it possible that he could sense an energy washing through him, emanating from the ancient object?

'And don't ever forget the markers you must look for, and what you must do if you encounter one of *them*,' continued the Archlaw. 'Henceforth, you're no longer ordained, no longer a priest. You have my sanction and dispensation to become whatever you need to be, and to commit whatever action or violence is necessary, in the pursuit of your mission. From today, you are one of *my* Disciples.'

Caddin nodded. The hairs on the back of his neck were still standing up. Redemption, which he had sought for years, appeared at last to have been given an attainable form.

'I am, Your Eminence. Your Disciple. Thank you.'

'Thank me with your deeds, not your words, Disciple Caddin. Now, go forth from here in the Grace of Aiduel. Relinquish the life that you have known. Help me to find the *Illborn*, and to kill them – every last one of them – before it's too late. Help me to save the faith, and to save our world.'

Part One

—

Strangers and Secrets

—

*Year of Our Lord,
After Ascension, 769AA – 770AA*

1

Arion

—

*Year of Our Lord,
After Ascension, 769AA*

Arion Sepian stood at the quayside in Septholme, feeling uneasy. He was watching the final boatload of red-cloaked soldiers being rowed across the harbour waters, to the ship that would soon be taking them far away from his homeland. As Arion waited, the hazy setting sun was drawing closer to the horizon in the west, silhouetting the hulking transport vessel which was anchored in the centre of the harbour.

The orders from King Inneos Pavil had arrived at Septholme Castle just a week earlier, and had been relayed immediately to the nearby garrison of Aiduel's Guards. All members of that religious military body were ordered to evacuate their fortress outside of the town, and to leave the country of Andar as soon as possible. Western Canasar forces had already taken possession of the stronghold.

I won't be sorry to see them go, thought Arion, as he placed his hand onto the hilt of the sword at his waist. *But Lord preserve us, does this mean that everything that we've achieved is now unravelling?*

'On a personal level, Lord Arion, I feel glad to see the back of those red-cloaked bastards,' commented Captain Menion Thatcher, keeping his voice low. 'But I don't like what this could mean for Western Canasar.'

Arion glanced across at the bald-headed and rugged officer, who was standing alongside him. The two of them had grown much closer, on both a personal and professional level, since Arion had returned home to lead the Army of Western Canasar. Today, Thatcher had commanded the company of Andar soldiers which had escorted the garrison of red-cloaks to the harbour.

'You read my mind, Captain,' Arion said. 'This is bad news. And I don't know where it's going to end.'

By the Lord, none of us do!

Much had changed in the three months since the war with Elannis had ended, and since the day when Arion had saved the life of Priestess Leanna of Arlais.

Arion was well aware of the ongoing deterioration in the relationship between the Andar royal family and the Holy Church in Sen Aiduel. Initially, King Inneos had been enraged by the Archlaw's failure to emphatically condemn Elannis's invasion of Andar. Subsequent to that, the Church had also refused to punish the imperial royalty who had instigated the invasion. That latter decision appeared to have finally pushed the monarch of Andar to this breaking point, whereby he had expelled Aiduel's Guards from the country.

Given Arion's knowledge of the negotiations which had led to the arrival of the red-cloaked soldiers, he understood how significant this decision could come to be. Arion's father, the late Duke Conran Sepian, had brokered a peace deal almost two years earlier, and the status of Aiduel's Guards in Andar had been a vital component of that peace. However, in the absence of the wise counsel which the duke had provided, Inneos had now ripped out that building block.

We already expected that war would be coming again, Arion thought. *But maybe it'll be coming sooner than we could have imagined.*

'Makes a man want to send the troops back to the castle,' added Menion Thatcher, interrupting Arion's thoughts, 'and find a… lively tavern, with a like-minded friend, and some *other* company.'

Arion raised an eyebrow in response to Thatcher's words. Arion's wife, Kalyane, was expecting him tonight. She had cornered him earlier in the day, to implore him to return for an evening meal alone with her, and Arion had agreed. He knew that he should be getting back to her, and to the overdue conversation which was undoubtedly coming.

He was fully aware of this as he reached a decision, and then grimaced.

'It does indeed, Menion. It does indeed. Very much so.'

―

Six hours and many tankards of ale later, Arion was settled comfortably into the corner of a lively tavern named *The Hungry Gull*. The hostelry was a short distance from the Septholme waterfront, in the northern quarter of the port. It was a sprawling building running the entire length of a lofty, narrow alleyway.

In the time since Arion and Thatcher had arrived, the sun had long since set, and Arion knew that it would now be chilly in the autumnal air outside. Inside, however, the roaring fire made the tavern cosy, and the main taproom was packed, with a raucous atmosphere. The warm thigh pressing against Arion's leg was also helping to raise his temperature.

This was a place which Arion had frequented in the year before he had enrolled at the Royal Academy of Knights. It was a destination which he had ventured to in his teenage years to meet women, including the memorable encounter that had led to the loss of his virginity. However, after chastisement by his late father, he had avoided establishments like *The Hungry Gull* for over two years.

That period had now ended. He had not consciously intended to seek out the refuge of a tavern, but he had been easily persuaded when Thatcher had first made the suggestion, a handful of weeks earlier. Arion now felt as if he was becoming a regular again, and that he and Thatcher were staking an implicit claim on this discreet corner booth.

'And Arion, here, he led the charge, with me close behind,' said Thatcher, gesticulating drunkenly as he did so. 'You've never seen anything like it. One thousand five hundred cavalry charging. Most incredible moment of my life. The bastards must have shat themselves when they saw us.'

The audience for Thatcher's story was the pair of women who were sharing the cosy corner space with him and Arion.

'And you've never seen anyone fight like this guy,' Thatcher added, tipping his tankard towards Arion as he spoke. 'You know, I can look after myself in a battle and I had my share of kills that day. But this man here? Fucking unstoppable. My good friend, the Hero of Moss Ford!'

Arion forced a grin as Thatcher continued to recount his tale of their exploits, and their female companions made appreciative noises in response. However, despite this external veneer of merriment, Arion could sense himself edging towards the maudlin again. Thatcher's reminders of the killing at Moss Ford were not helping his mood.

He could feel the woman who was sitting to the right of him – *was her name Astri?* – shifting her position to press her upper body more intimately against his arm. He was also aware of her hand sliding onto his thigh, under the concealment of their table. He knew that he should act to remove it, that he should get up from here and go home to the castle and to his wife. Instead, he did nothing, and made supporting comments as Thatcher continued to regale the two women with tales of the war.

Thatcher had clearly paired himself off with the tall brunette who had draped her leg across his knee. On each of their recent visits, the captain had ended the night by hiring himself a room on the tavern's upper floor, and the same outcome looked likely tonight. No doubt leaving Arion to once again take a solitary and drunken walk back through the town to the castle, in the early hours of the morning.

By the Lord, I should be getting home! I'll already have enough trouble to face.

The young woman to Arion's right was petite, with a voluptuous body. She was also pretty, with lustrous black hair, although her looks were not even remotely comparable to... *the other person in his thoughts*. However, there was some physical similarity there. A sense of familiarity which was leading him to contemplate a first betrayal of his wedding vows, and an unleashing of his frustration onto an eager partner.

The hand on his thigh moved again, sliding higher, accompanied by a whispered and low-class voice which said, 'The things you've done. Why don't we go upstairs for a while, and leave these two to chat? I promise you that I'll make you *my* hero tonight, and you'll leave here feeling very happy.'

Arion stared at his tankard, as he felt his body respond. He had already had far too much to drink, and he could not possibly be thinking clearly. He knew that he should get up. Decline her offer. Leave here. Go home. Attempt to sort out the confusions in his head which had led him here, and try to start to make things right with Kalyane.

He looked again at the attractive and willing woman beside him, feeling a confused mixture of guilt, excitement and agitation.

However, when he finally answered, he shook his head and said, 'No. I don't want to do that. I have to go home.'

It was past midnight when Arion left *The Hungry Gull*. He had resisted Thatcher's encouragements to stay, and had ignored the parting insult from the young woman whom he had abandoned.

He paused for a few moments in the alleyway outside of the tavern, exhaling as he became aware that his thin jerkin was unsuitable for the chilly night air. He shivered in reaction to the cold, then set off towards the end of the alley, before turning left onto a more prominent thoroughfare.

As he walked along this dark and largely deserted street, he could feel the cold air working to dampen the effects of the alcohol. He was also starting to reflect on his actions of the evening, and his ability to feel shame and remorse was beginning to assert itself. He knew how close he had come to betraying his wedding vows.

By the Lord, what am I doing? What do I hope to achieve by this?

How would he be able to look Kalyane in the eye? The early months of their marriage had been troubled enough already, without adding this guilt to their other problems. Just two days earlier, the tensions brewing between Arion and his wife had bubbled over, culminating in their first heated argument.

That quarrel had concluded with Kalyane in tears, saying, 'How am I meant to make things right between us, if you won't ever share anything with me? And how am I meant to know what's wrong, if you don't answer any of my questions?'

Arion had shrugged in response to that.

Lord preserve us, what am I meant to say to her?

He knew that at the root of their early issues were the feelings that he possessed for Allana dei Monis. Every time that his wife had tried to engage with him since his return from Arlais, he could feel this hidden truth of his unfaithful thoughts creeping into his mind, inhibiting his responses and poisoning their interactions. Much as he was trying to, he could not disregard the cold thought that, if Allana were still alive, he would want to be with her. Not Kalyane.

His wife had already sensed that he was concealing something vital from her, and was holding some essential part of himself in reserve. Her challenge about this had led to their quarrel.

Added to that, he had been unwilling to explain to her why his dreaming sleep was so restless. Why he was jolted from his slumber on so many nights, shouting out in fear and horror.

And, perhaps most significantly, he had been unwilling to share the reason for his headlong flight to Arlais on their wedding night. To tell her the truth of that meant revealing to Kalyane not only what Priestess Leanna was, but also what *he* was. And he was not ready to do that, not in the way that he had been able to open himself up to Leanna.

The reason for that was clear to him. Arion and Leanna were now forever connected by sharing a difference, and the secret of that difference. Indeed, their connection had been magnified a hundred-fold in those timeless minutes at the pyre. Those moments when he had witnessed the almighty power which she possessed, and had helped to save her by somehow sharing his energy with her, thereby helping to facilitate her miracle. His actions at the pyre offered him a fragment of redemption for his separate failure to save Allana.

But Kalyane was on the outside of all of that, and Arion had not been able to convince himself that his wife should be a party to those secrets. She was his wife by law, but she was not like him, not in the way that Leanna was.

Leanna of Arlais. The Angel of Arlais!

Thinking of the name served to conjure the priestess's image in his mind. Blonde-haired and radiant. Angelic. They had achieved only fleeting moments of eye-contact in the aftermath of the pyre, before the crowd had swarmed around her, sweeping her away from him.

Arion had been deep within a country which despised him, and he had been exhausted by his immense release of energy into Leanna. Therefore, as she had been swept out of view, he had taken the difficult decision to flee. There had been no opportunity to speak to her, and to implore her to return to Andar with him, as he had wanted to. But she had written to him afterwards, had told him of her ordeal, and had named what they were.

Illborn. They were both Illborn, whatever that was.

Somehow, thinking about Leanna made him even more ashamed of his actions on this night. How would the priestess judge him for his flirtation with potential infidelity? Strangely, he felt that it would be even worse to suffer her disapproval in respect of his illicit temptation, than to incur the opprobrium of his wife. And that made him feel even shoddier.

So, how would he be able to face Kalyane? In answer to his own question, he would no doubt act in a manner in accordance with their recent exchanges. Feeling guilt, but concealing his secrets behind a blank facade. Frustrating her with a lack of response to her questions and pleas, and watching her distress grow.

He was not savouring the thought of their next encounter. Not at all.

—

These thoughts were still running through Arion's mind when he first became aware of the noise of footsteps upon the cobbles behind him. Two pairs of light treads, which were close.

Arion was walking along a curving and narrow street off the main thoroughfares of Septholme, taking an oft-trodden shortcut back to the castle. He was ascending along a steadily climbing route which was lined along both sides with tall terraced properties. At this hour, the street was otherwise deserted, and none of the shuttered buildings showed signs of activity inside. Only the half-moon crescent in the sky was lighting his way.

Arion glanced back, and he noted that two men were walking together, perhaps twenty paces behind him. They were attired in the manner of Andar fishermen, both moving with a stumbling gait which was suggestive of drunkenness. Nothing about their posture or appearance indicated that they were a threat, but they had nonetheless managed to draw closer to Arion while he had been lost in his thoughts. Out of caution, he increased his pace to put distance between himself and the strangers, not wanting an encounter with cutpurses or thugs at this time of night.

The narrow, climbing street curved further to the right. To Arion's alarm, three more men came into view, a further thirty metres ahead of him. Two were standing to the fore, spaced a couple of metres apart in the centre of the cobbled road, while a third and much larger man was a few paces behind that pair. Both of the foremost figures were facing broadly in Arion's direction, and he noticed that their right hands were positioned out of sight. Their faces were also concealed by the deep-hooded cloaks that they were wearing.

Arion placed his hand onto the hilt of his sword.

By the Lord, this feels like a trap!

He was not about to walk casually into the midst of the three men in front of him. Instead, he decided to test his suspicions about the individuals to his rear. He stopped suddenly on the left of the street, and glanced back. His concerns were seemingly founded, because the pair of trailing men also stopped at a distance of thirty paces.

The two closest strangers on the path ahead of Arion now started to walk in his direction. Their right hands remained hidden from view.

'Come no closer, any of you!'

Arion's bellow rang out loud along the enclosed terraced walls. He rotated his body a half-turn, such that his peripheral vision now covered all of the men around him. Upon hearing Arion's shouted warning, the two men to his fore stopped at a distance of fifteen metres away.

Arion scanned the buildings to either side, searching for ways to exit this narrow street. However, on both sides ran unbroken lines of lofty terraces, offering no obvious escape route. He could try to bang on a door to seek sanctuary, but he would have insufficient time if the intention of these strangers was malign.

Although the two men who were closest on the road in front had ceased all movement, the taller and bulkier individual to their rear now strolled forwards. This cloaked and hooded figure stopped at least ten paces behind the others, and said, 'Lord Sepian? Lord Arion Sepian? Be at ease, sir. We mean you no harm.'

The man's voice was deep, with a peculiar accent which sounded foreign, but which might have been an affectation.

Arion drew his sword, before assuming a two-handed defensive pose, and responding, 'If that's the case, then you all need to back away from me. Now. Don't come any closer, or I *will* attack you. Move away!'

The five strangers were motionless after hearing this, and Arion could sense their coiled tension. The threat here was real. This group intended to attack him.

In response to this perceived danger, he was thrilled to experience a familiar crackling of energy inside, which coursed through and wrapped around his limbs. It invigorated him instantly with strength, speed and stamina, and washed away any trace of drunkenness within him.

This awakening of power was accompanied by the familiar words which he welcomed as a herald of his prowess and vitality.

STRENGTH. VICTORY. GLORY.

His abilities had always become available when needed, and this was the first such time that he had absolutely required them since the day of the pyre. His senses were suddenly more alert, and they were now locked onto the men around him. Time was slowed down, magnifying his perception of every minor movement that the surrounding group made.

Within this heightened state of alertness, he heard the largest stranger shout, 'Now!'

The reaction of the other men was immediate. The pair to the rear gracefully unsheathed swords, which must have been concealed on their backs. The closest two men in front took a step forward, at the same time that their hidden hands emerged into view. They were both holding one-handed crossbows, which they aimed and fired in unison, directly at Arion.

Their movements were precise and agile, and their shots were accurate, aimed at the centre of Arion's chest. For any other man, any slower man, the bolts would have skewered into their target. But Arion's unnatural reactions saved him.

He lurched his frame backwards, feeling the hiss of the two projectiles as they whistled past. One was less than three inches from his chest as it shot by, whilst the other was so close that it traced a line across the front of his jerkin with its fletching.

The instant that the bolts had whipped past him, Arion charged towards the crossbowmen. At that same moment, he could sense the two swordsmen to his rear commencing their own sprint to try to close on him. Arion intended to dispatch the pair of bowmen first; he had no intention of fighting swordsmen while a crossbow quarrel was aimed at his back.

As he hurtled forwards, he took note of how efficiently his assailants were moving, and he knew that he was not facing street thugs or cutpurses here. By contrast, a group of highly skilled men – *assassins?* – were attacking him on this street.

As testament to that, the two bowmen were moving apart from each other, even as they worked to urgently reload their crossbows. Arion knew that he would not be able to reach both of them with his sword from the same standing position. He would have to choose a target, and then leave himself potentially exposed to the other.

He selected the bowman to the left as he closed, swinging his sword in a feint towards the man's neck. The bowman reacted quickly, attempting to parry this attack with the stock of his weapon, but Arion had anticipated this, and turned his blade at the last moment to instead cut into the man's wrist. The attack sheared through the limb, sending a hand and the crossbow it was clutching spiralling away. Immediately, Arion planted his feet to shift direction and to spring to his right, towards the other bowman.

That man had reloaded his crossbow in a smooth and efficient manner. However, Arion's movement brought him back within close proximity before this enemy could target him again. Even as the bowman's arm was moving, Arion was stabbing his sword forward into the man's chest. The bowman stumbled backwards against a terraced house, before Arion reversed his blade across the man's neck, sending a splatter of blood flying across the cobbles of the street. The dead foe collapsed sideways, his crossbow dropping from his hand.

Kill them! Kill them! Kill them! Take your victory!

Arion could hear the two swordsmen who had been trailing him drawing closer. Closest of all, however, was the third of the untouched combatants, the apparent enemy leader, who was now the sole figure blocking Arion's escape route ahead. This hooded individual was stalking forwards, holding a hefty two-handed greatsword in an overhead strike position. He was at least as tall as Arion, and appeared ox-like in build.

Arion was brimming full of energy, and he stepped forward to meet this assault, planning to dispatch this adversary quickly.

The opponent wielding the greatsword swung his weapon in a furious arc downwards, aimed at Arion's head. Arion instinctively moved towards a high counter position, readying himself to parry the mighty blow and then launch into a lethal counterattack.

But time sped up again.

In an instant, the world shifted from a state in which Arion's opponents were moving at a snail-like pace around him, to one in which the sword swing of the enemy leader was suddenly viper-fast. Arion's sword deflected the overhead attack of his opponent's heavy weapon, but when steel met steel Arion found himself rocked backwards under the force of the strike. He staggered slightly, losing balance.

The enemy leader shifted his angle of attack, launching a sweeping follow-up which Arion barely countered. Arion was shocked to realise that his superior speed and strength had close to deserted him, in the midst of this mortal combat. He was now facing this adversary without any advantage, and the threat of death seemed much more potently real than it had mere instants earlier.

Relying on his years of training as a swordsman, Arion parried another powerful thrust. He counterattacked with a slash towards his opponent's neck, which was blocked, but he used the momentum of the attack to rotate around his adversary. As he separated and adopted a two-handed high guard position, Arion could see that the hooded leader was now placed between himself and the final two enemies, who were arriving to join the fight.

Both of the new arrivals were also wielding their swords in a two-handed stance, and they spread out to either side of their leader. Fortunately, the street was too narrow for them to easily step around Arion, to encircle him. Arion took a deep breath, readying himself, and feeling fear.

Lord preserve us, what's happening?

'Butcher of Moss Ford,' said the enemy leader. His tone was now taunting, his accent still peculiar. 'The man with the unnatural powers. What's up? Have they stopped working?'

Arion stepped backwards. What had affected his abilities? It was as if most of the energy which he could normally draw upon had just… drained away. Then he sensed it, coming from the enemy leader. Some kind of aura, some void, which was leeching Arion's power. Neutralising it, or weakening it so much that it was barely detectable. Was it something in the man's possession, or the man himself?

'I thought you might be one of them,' the hooded leader said, as the three opponents stepped forwards in unison. 'And I think I was right.'

The three were spaced apart from each other as much as possible in the street, all of them adopting a defensive posture, with swords raised. They had witnessed how lethal Arion had been against their two colleagues, and none of them were being careless.

But Arion was deeply concerned. He trusted in his own martial skills, but the enemy leader was dangerous, and the stance of the other two men also suggested that they were well-trained. Without the enhancement of his powers, could Arion survive a prolonged exchange of blows against all three attackers? If he allowed them to re-engage with him now, he doubted that he would able to disengage. That left him with little choice. Attack, to try to finish them all, or…

He shifted his grip on his sword's hilt, then hurled the weapon at the central adversary. Without waiting to see the result, he turned and started to sprint away from his assailants. He heard a curse, followed by footsteps moving in pursuit of him.

After seconds of this flight, the world crackled into life again, and Arion's powers returned. His speed picked up immediately, and his feet pounded along the narrow, cobbled street, drawing closer to the main road back up to the castle. If he could reach that thoroughfare, then there might be other people around. Get there, and his chances of survival would be much greater.

As he drew closer to the junction at the end of the street, he felt something whistle past his ear, and he realised that he had almost been impaled by another crossbow quarrel. He reached the corner with the main road, careered to the left while still running at full tilt, and then proceeded to charge up the hill towards Septholme Castle.

He did not look back as he sprinted up this road, the sanctuary of the castle drawing ever closer. However, with his speed and stamina fuelled by his rekindled power, he doubted that anyone could have kept up with him.

Only when he reached the castle entrance, and saw Andar soldiers approaching him with concern, did he turn around to check behind him. No one was there, or could be seen on the road below him.

He felt his power draining away naturally, this time, and suddenly felt out of breath, his chest heaving. He had survived, and escaped, but he was deeply alarmed. He had brushed close with death, back on that street. Very close. And it had been no accident, no chance encounter.

Someone had come here to kill him.

—

The three patrols of Andar guardsmen that went out into the town that night, one of which was led by Arion, failed to find the gang of attackers. Within the secure midst of a group of twenty armed soldiers, Arion returned to the scene of the assault. However, the only traces of the event which remained were the smatterings of blood on the cobbles, in the spots where he had struck the two bowmen. Otherwise, the place had been cleared, including the removal of the casualties and the severed limb. The act of so thoroughly clearing the scene of their crime reinforced to Arion that he had been dealing with professional killers.

By the time that he finally returned to the castle, much of the night had passed, and he was exhausted. He found himself a spare cot in the guards' barracks to sleep in, rather than disturbing Kalyane at such an early hour.

He sank into a much-needed sleep, but awoke in a dishevelled and still weary state less than three hours later, forced out of slumber by his recurring dream. It had become yet more troubled recently, always leaving him with a lingering sense of half-remembered violence. Had he also heard other words, spoken by the figure in the Gate, and had those words been a precursor to the violence? He was frustrated that he could never properly recall the full experience of the dream after waking.

As he was pondering this, a guard arrived to inform him that he had been summoned to the Great Hall of the castle by his older brother, Duke Gerrion. A hangover had also surfaced, and Arion was blinking sleep from his eyes and feeling sorry for himself as he crossed the castle courtyard to the main keep.

Upon arrival at the Great Hall, he was dismayed to see that Kalyane was also there. He would have to face his older brother and his wife at the same time.

Duke Gerrion Sepian, young ruler of Western Canasar, was sitting upright in the high chair on the dais at the far end of the hall. His face expressed an emotion somewhere between anger and impatience.

Kalyane was pacing in front of that chair, her fingers fiddling with her long auburn hair. She did not cease her pacing or move to greet Arion, although her green eyes locked onto his, expressing hurt. He dropped his own gaze, finding it difficult to meet her stare.

'Ah, you're here at last,' said Gerrion, his voice business-like as usual. 'I've received a full report from the Sergeant-at-Arms. Five attackers, of unknown origin, trying to kill a member of the Sepian family on our own streets. We can't tolerate this. I've ordered the town gates sealed until further notice, and any ships which seek to leave port are to undergo inspection before being permitted to depart. Ten patrols of guardsmen are also going through the town, as we speak, entering properties. If this group is still in Septholme, we'll find them.'

'Thank you, brother,' said Arion. 'Apologies for not organising that myself, but I desperately needed to sleep.'

By the Lord, please don't ask me what I was doing on that street, at that time. Not in front of Kalyane.

Gerrion continued, oblivious to Arion's silent wishes. 'Thank Aiduel for your skills with a sword, Arion. Otherwise, as I understand it, we could all be in mourning today. But what I don't understand is *this*. An attack after midnight. Two attackers following you. Three waiting for you. A quiet, deserted street with no side exits. A trap. Like they knew that you were coming. But how could that be, and what were you doing there?'

Arion blushed, aware that Kalyane's gaze would be fixed upon him. 'I was… drinking. In the Northern Quarter. They must have guessed which route I'd take back to the castle.'

But even as he said the words, he realised that it was not true. They had not guessed, they had *known*. He had taken that same route back after every evening in *The Hungry Gull*. Anyone who might have been trailing him in the past few weeks would have known how often he visited the tavern, and exactly what route he would follow to get home. Springing that trap would have been of no great difficulty, on such a careless target.

'Drinking!' exclaimed Kalyane, sounding frustrated. She was clenching her hair in both hands. 'Didn't I say so, Gerrion? He had promised to be here, with me. But again, he was… out… drinking! Drinking, and doing Lord knows what else!'

Arion felt squalid for the upset that his choices were inflicting upon his wife.

'Please be calm, Kalyane,' said Gerrion softly, before frowning at Arion. 'The *Northern Quarter*, you say?'

Gerrion was aware of the past antics of Arion's youth, and Arion blushed again when he noted the sudden comprehension in his older brother's regard. Arion hoped that he did not appear as guilty as he was suddenly feeling.

'Yes,' he replied. 'The Northern Quarter.'

'Kalyane says this isn't the first time you've returned to the castle in the early hours, drunk, Arion. It's something I was vaguely aware of, but I hadn't appreciated how frequent or serious it had become. I understand that this has become a very regular activity for you, brother, since the war ended. Now, please understand me, no one is more grateful for what you did for Western Canasar than me. No one. But I can't tolerate the continuation of what you've been doing recently. That kind of behaviour is not an acceptable example for a senior member of this family to set, as you well know. Not at all acceptable for someone who has the position and the authority that you have. And, frankly, it's a poor way to treat your wife.' He gestured towards Kalyane as he said this. 'And certainly, it cannot and *will not* continue after this incident, brother. Not least, because there could still be a gang of killers somewhere in this town, who've marked you for death. Am I understood on this?'

'Yes, brother, of course,' said Arion, feeling ashamed.

'But we have to find them,' said Gerrion. 'Find out who they are and who paid them to do this. Find out whether this is attempted retribution by Elannis for what you did at Moss Ford, or simply an attempt by them to eliminate a dangerous enemy.'

'Yes, of course,' said Arion, nodding as he replied.

However, he was remembering the severe diminishment of his abilities, mid-fight, and the hooded man's taunting words. Why and how had Arion's powers been so weakened by the stranger? And the man had specifically referred to Arion's possession of those powers, as if he had known about Arion's secret. How could that be possible? Arion's mind was churning about whether this attack could somehow be connected to *what* he was, rather than who he was. Could it be connected to the fact that he was an Illborn?

Gerrion was scrutinising him. 'There's something you're not telling me, Arion. What is it?'

'Nothing, brother.'

'Not telling us something!' said Kalyane. 'Of course. Why should we expect today to be any different?'

Gerrion leaned forwards, before asking, 'Is this attack somehow connected to your journey to Arlais? To the priestess they're calling the Angel of Arlais?'

'No, Gerrion,' Arion replied. 'Nothing to do with *that*. It feels to me like the most likely reason *would* be attempted revenge by Elannis. One of the attackers called me "the Butcher of Moss Ford" during the fight, which certainly points towards them being agents of the empire.'

'Yes, I was told that,' said Gerrion, but he maintained his scrutiny of Arion's face.

'But we won't know for sure unless we capture the surviving attackers,' added Arion, his eyes imploring his older brother to change the subject. 'Let's find them, then interrogate them.'

Gerrion leaned back, looking dissatisfied. 'Very well, Arion. I won't challenge you on this. For now. Because I trust you. But I'll say again, do *not* repeat this action. Your excursions out of the castle at night-time end *now*, and you and everyone else in this family – including you, Kalyane – will be accompanied by guards if we leave the castle in the day. Arion, you as much as me will appreciate the peril that Western Canasar could be in, now that we've expelled Aiduel's Guards. We'll all have to deal with the consequences of King Inneos's… impulsive decisions. More than ever, I need your strength alongside me now, brother, if we're to survive this.'

'Yes, Gerrion. You'll have it. I promise.'

'Well, in that case, I'll share with you both the news that I received yesterday. The king has summoned me to Andarron in three weeks' time. He's summoning all of the dukes of the great houses, for a council at the Royal Palace.'

'What for?' asked Arion.

Gerrion looked concerned. 'The summons doesn't say. But I fear that our king is about to make his next big decision, his next grave mistake, and that he wants all of the heads of the noble families gathered in one place to announce it.'

Arion frowned. 'Mistake? You don't possibly think that he's going to announce a split from the Holy Church in Sen Aiduel?'

'I don't know that,' said Gerrion, 'and I hope not. But I fear it. Fear it greatly. And believe me, I'll be leaving for Andarron with a heavy heart. I'll want you to travel there with me, Arion. I think that rulings may be announced there that will affect everyone in this family, and in the country, and I'm going to want you alongside me in the aftermath. But if the king does announce that he's breaking the country off from the authority of the Holy Church, then there *will* be war with Elannis, and probably Dei Magnus too. And possibly civil war, within Andar. We both know that Western Canasar will bear the brunt of any second Elannis invasion, which is why none of us can afford for you, my brother, to end up dead in a gutter after a night of drunkenness.'

Arion nodded in response, now silent and feeling even more ashamed of his actions. In the last three months, since Allana's death and Leanna's salvation, he had allowed himself to become self-absorbed and self-indulgent. However, if what Gerrion was saying was true, then it was clear that the current period of peace might be but a fleeting respite.

Knowing that, Arion was resolved that he needed to stop feeling sorry for himself. He needed to stop obsessing over Allana and Leanna. Needed to stop thinking about all of the death at Moss Ford, and to stop drinking. And he must try to make things right with Kalyane, through both his words and his deeds.

As if echoing those thoughts, Gerrion said, 'Now, leave me, brother. Go back to your quarters with Kalyane. Clean yourself up and get some sleep. And finally, Arion, apologise and make amends to your wife. That's an order.'

2

Allana

—

Year of Our Lord,
After Ascension, 769AA

'How dare King Inneos do this, Lana!' said Duke Jarrett Berun. He then shook the recently delivered letter, which was clutched in his hand.

Allana dei Monis looked up from her seat within the duke's private chambers of Berun Castle. Her eyes focused upon the imposing form of her lover, but she otherwise did not respond. She had already learned that when Jarrett was in this kind of mood, it was better to listen for a while to allow him to vent his frustrations.

'As if the expulsion of the Guards wasn't enough of an insult to the Archlaw,' Jarrett continued. 'Now, I'm being summoned to Andarron, and for what? So Inneos can tell me that he was right to expel them, despite the damage that he's done to the Church. Or, perhaps, he'll announce some new insult to my religion? The man will have us all excommunicated before he's finished!'

He was prowling back and forth across the room as he spoke, and as Allana's eyes followed him, she allowed herself a shiver of self-satisfaction. The young duke was a bull of a man, his giant body rippling with muscles, the power of his physical form a mirror of the power of his position. And he was hers. All hers. Within three months, she had ensnared him completely.

Almost completely, Lana, she thought, correcting herself. *But not totally. It would be total, if not for her.*

'*Our* religion, Jarrett,' she said, judging that now was the right time to speak. 'This will also affect me. It will affect everyone.'

He appeared contrite as he replied, 'Yes, Lana, our religion.'

'But you're right,' she continued, saying what she knew he wanted to hear. 'It *is* an insult to the faithful, the things that King Inneos has done and may yet do.'

So convincing and serious, Lana. You always are, when he talks about religion.

In the last three months, she had become more outwardly devout, in a calculated reflection of her pious young duke. She prayed with Jarrett multiple times a day, and she was always careful to support his moral and religious stances. However, that had not stopped her from being secretly delighted when she had heard about the expulsion of Aiduel's Guards.

'But what am I to do, Lana?' Jarrett asked, the heat now gone from his tone.

Allana set down the sewing which she had been working on, and stood up to approach him. He ceased his stalking across the room and turned to regard her, his face sombre. When she reached him, she put her hand onto his cheek, and the solemnity of his expression melted away as her flesh touched his. She could sense his sudden desire for her, even in the midst of his turmoil.

He wants you just as much as the first time, Lana.

She had seduced him on the very first evening after they had met, three months earlier, following her escape from Western Canasar. After their initial encounter at the borders of his region, he had invited her to accompany him to his fortress in southern Berun, and had later asked her to dine with him. At the end of that evening, she had set in motion the course of events which she had been following ever since.

—

'And so, Lana, I must wish you a fond good night.' Jarrett Berun had stood up as he had said these words, at the end of the dinner in his private quarters.

Allana had remained seated. After the traumatic events of the preceding days, she had resolved that she did not want to face the coming night on her own.

'Must you, Duke Jarrett?' she had asked.

'Yes, of course. I must go to pray, and your rooms will be ready by now. I'll call someone to escort you there.'

Had she detected a hint of blushing on his cheeks, as he had answered her?

For all of that day, Allana had been assessing the opportunity that the young duke represented. She had secured his invitation to accompany his party, based solely upon their initial conversation and on how attracted he was to her. And the invite to his southern fortress and to dinner had been achieved purely through her natural charms, without her needing to engage any of her other… *abilities*.

But she had concluded during dinner that he would be unlikely to take the next step by his own volition, although she had been able to sense the desire held captive within him. His sense of religious propriety, so evident in his earlier conversation, would act to inhibit him. He would need to be *pushed*. And this might be her last opportunity to be alone with him like this.

'Yes, my Lord,' she had answered. 'But do you *want* me to be escorted out of here?'

As she had said this, she had welcomed the sensation of a slowing down of time around her. Invisible tendrils had gently eased out of her mind, and had snaked sinuously towards him. This had been so different to the awful use of her ability earlier that day, when she had bludgeoned control of two Aiduel's Guards on the field beside the road. This time, it had been an occasion for finesse, for subtly penetrating his will and directing it as she chose, rather than smashing her way through to it.

'Of course, I must.' His voice had contained a tremor, as he had replied. 'I would not impugn your honour by asking you to stay. And, of course, my religion would not allow-'

She had made intimate contact with his mind for the first time as he had been saying that. He had stopped speaking as she had started to softly caress his senses, stimulating pleasure within him. She had then begun to whisper silent words to him through the connection which she had formed.

You want me, Jarrett. You want me, so badly. And you can have me. But only if you do what I want. What I need.

'What?' His voice had been strained as he had said this single word, and his pupils had become dilated as she had felt the response of his lust stirring inside of him.

She had stood up as he had said that, and had moved around the table towards him. She was attracted to his physical form, and her own arousal had been building in response to the pulsing connection between them. She had then placed her hand onto his cheek, softly.

'Those things don't matter, Jarrett, if you want me, and I want you.' That was the first time that she had addressed him so informally. 'And I want you, Jarrett. Tonight. Do you want me?'

She had watched him gulp. Twisting tendrils within his thoughts had been sending continuous whispers of pleasure throughout his body. She had been able to sense the victory within him of desire over propriety, and she had felt a sense of triumph when he had finally answered.

'Yes, Lana. I do.'

To Allana's surprise, that had been his first time with a woman. But ever since, she had been a regular visitor to his sleeping chambers. Each night that she spent with the young duke served to enhance her subtle control over him, and was an escape from the torment of sleeping on her own.

He was undoubtedly in love with her, and his newly discovered lust meant that he was all too willing to commit the sin of sex outside of wedlock, despite his piety. Indeed, he was becoming a talented lover, although he did not arouse the same incomparable passion which... *someone else* once had.

'I know that you'll find a way to do the right thing, Jarrett,' Allana said now, with her hand still on his cheek. 'For the Church, for the people of Berun, and for *us*.'

Her words and her touch acted to calm him. 'I will, Lana. Before The Lord, I will. King Inneos assumes that House Berun has no options but to follow him in these matters. That I'll be meek and compliant. But there are things developing. Other choices presenting themselves. Offers of meetings. Mother has received many messages, recently.'

'Has she?' asked Allana. 'From whom?'

He hesitated before replying, looking awkward. 'In time, when things become clearer, I'll tell you. But Mother has asked me to keep it confidential. I shouldn't even be saying this much, really.'

'Then don't, if it makes you uncomfortable.' She knew that she could force him to give her the information, but she had no desire to use her powers on him today. 'I'd never ask you to betray the confidence of another person.'

'Thank you, Lana,' he replied, and it was clear that he approved of her statement. 'But I can't help but feel frustrated with what's happening in this country right now. All these important decisions are being taken, all these insults to the Church are happening, and I'm just meant to watch and nod! But not for much longer, I swear!'

Allana's hand was still on his cheek. 'Please be calm, Jarrett.'

'But what if he takes the decision to break us off from the Holy Church in Sen Aiduel, Lana? What then? Anyone who obeys will be excommunicated by the Archlaw. Excommunicated! How can we be expected to keep our oaths to Andar, if we're turning our backs on The Lord's own Holy Church, and are destined to lose our path to the afterlife?'

She paused before responding, choosing her words carefully, then said, 'You'll do what is right, Jarrett, according to your conscience and your religion. You're a great man. A man born to lead lesser men. You will listen to your conscience, you will pray to The Lord, and you will seek guidance from the Holy Book. And then you will act. Because that is what great men do. And whatever that decision is, I'll be beside you, supporting you, because I trust you to protect me and to keep me safe. As you will keep all of the people of Berun safe.'

You sound so convincing and pious, Lana.

'Thank you, Lana. You always seem to know what to say to make me feel calmer. And it makes me guilty that I keep all these secrets from you.' He exhaled loudly, and looked a little sheepish. 'There are other matters that Mother's involved in, which I need to share with you. She's advancing her efforts to find me a bride. Correspondence has started with eligible families and matters are progressing. That's as much as I want to say, for now, but it would be dishonourable of me to keep it from you.'

Allana kept the disquiet that she felt in reaction to this away from the expression on her face. If Jarrett secured a bride from a noble family, then Allana was in no doubt that Jarrett's mother, Dowager Duchess Sillene Berun, would seek to banish her from the duke's life. Allana would then lose all of the security and protection which Jarrett provided.

That old hag Sillene will try to take all of this away from you, Lana. You know she will, unless you can prevent it.

But the uncertainty that was stirred inside her by Jarrett's revelation was not visible to her lover, and instead she smiled.

'That's a worry for another day, my love. For now, let's talk of happier things, and please know that I'm here to support you.'

———

She was visited by the recurring dream that night, back in the confines of her own small, private room within the castle. She awoke from the dream in pitch darkness, covered in perspiration, with her sheets kicked away from her. Her heart was beating fast.

She moved to turn towards Jarrett, to seek his comfort and to try to return to sleep as quickly as possible, before realising that tonight she was alone.

Go back to sleep, Lana. Please, just go back to sleep!

But she knew that her plea would be to no avail, and that there would be little more rest tonight.

The dream had awakened her, but soon other imaginings would start to creep into her mind within the darkness of the room. This was why she hated sleeping alone. Already, she could feel a trembling beginning in her fingers.

Her recurring dream had continued to haunt her sleep on a regular basis throughout the three-month period that she had been with Jarrett. However, its nature had become even worse since she had killed Evelyn dei Laramin. It made Allana wonder whether her unleashing of darkness that day had broken an invisible seal inside of herself, and had made her more receptive to the horror which lurked in the hidden recesses of the dream?

Once again tonight, in the aftermath of waking, she could recall the shining avatars of light. The winding path on the side of the mountain. The ethereal Gate, and the blinding, magnificent figure within, with a single finger raised. But in addition to these things, there were other flashes of memory now. Glimpses of terror and violence at the end? Of something awful being done to her?

Both of her hands were now shaking, as the aftermath of the dream began to merge into other terrible thoughts. Was it suddenly harder to breathe, as if there was a cloth on her face? As if water was pouring through that cloth and into her mouth, and she was drowning?

Her eyes were open, but she was in darkness, and there was no one beside her to comfort her. No one to protect her. Unless someone actually was there, lurking unseen, and ready to hurt her again? Ready to drown her? Ready to burn her?

It's not real, Lana. It's not real. You're on your own, that's all. You're not back there. They can't hurt you again.

Her heart was pounding, and she tried to force herself to think of other things.

'Jarrett's here. Arion's here.'

She spoke the words aloud, having discovered that this mantra had helped to soothe these panic attacks on prior lonely nights. If either of the two men had been with her, then she would have wanted them to take her in their arms, and to shield her from these memories.

Imagine they're with you, Lana. Holding you, and keeping you safe.

Jarrett had witnessed her traumas at night-time, and it always helped to have him beside her, to comfort her afterwards. However, she had never told him – had never told *anyone* – about what had happened to her in the fortress of Aiduel's Guards. She still struggled to even think about her humiliating ordeal, and she certainly did not want to discuss it with someone else. What words could she possibly use to articulate what had happened to her and how it made her feel? Better to bury it inside.

Anyway, a disclosure of her sufferings might result in a need for other explanations, such as why she had been held captive in the first place, and what she had done in order to escape. Jarrett did not need to know about any of those things. In particular, he would never be told about the murders of Evelyn dei Laramin and her associates.

'Jarrett's here. Arion's here.'

You can't tell him the truth, Lana. Not while his mother's here, anyway. She'd use it against you.

Jarrett had been given a sanitised version of Allana's history. He had been told that she came from Sen Aiduel, and that she had left there after the death of her seamstress mother, in search of her missing father. After that, he understood that she had lived in Septholme as a seamstress, until she had fled to Berun during the war.

There were many other secrets that she was keeping from him. Foremost amongst these was the existence of her powers, which she could casually use on him without any memory on his part. Nor had she told Jarrett anything about her interactions with the Sepian family, including the affair with Duke Conran Sepian, or the manner of the older duke's death. And her encounters with and feelings for Arion Sepian had been kept entirely to herself.

'Jarrett's here. Arion's here.'

Allana thought about Arion now, in the darkness of the room, as her chest heaved and her fingers trembled. He had married someone else, at a time when he had promised that he would wait for Allana to contact him. He had completed his betrayal, by giving himself to another woman.

You promised to stop thinking about that, Lana. About his lies.

The way that Jarrett occasionally talked about Arion made it clear that he despised the young Sepian noble. As such, Jarrett would also never be told that Allana had once been overcome with passion, and possibly love, for his hated rival. That she had been prepared to run away with Arion and to devote her life to him, and that she had been stunned when he had abandoned her on a deserted trail at the outset of a war. And of how this desertion had turned into crushing betrayal mere weeks later, when Allana had heard of Arion's sudden wedding to another.

'Jarrett's here. Arion's here.'

Up until then, even after she had become ensconced as Jarrett Berun's lover, she had been teetering on the edge of writing to Arion, to try to reunite with him. She had been on the brink of taking a quill and ink, and putting her unresolved emotions down onto paper, despite the risk if such words were discovered. However, the news of Arion's marriage had quashed those intentions. She had felt physically sick when she had found out, through a casual comment which Jarrett had made to her. She had taken herself off to be alone, and had wept for hours.

Stop thinking about him, Lana. He doesn't deserve you. Your future is with Jarrett.

But, if that was the case, why did she continue to repeat Arion's name alongside Jarrett's, in a mantra intended to subdue her panic? And why was it so easy to imagine him being beside her on the bed? Almost too easy.

However, those thoughts could not assuage her current anxiety, here in the darkness of the night. Her breathing was still fast, her heart was pounding, and her fingers continued to tremble. And it made her ask a question which she could not answer.

Why must you feel this panic and terror, Lana, every single night that you're alone?

—

The following day, Seventh-Day, Allana was in the church in the main central square of the town of Berun, waiting for the Holy Day service to begin. On this occasion, she was not at Jarrett's side.

The duke was seated in the front row of the pews set out in the austere building, and the only other person sharing that row with him was his mother, Dowager Duchess Sillene Berun. Allana was sitting four rows back, on a pew reserved for retainers of the Berun household. The dowager tolerated Allana's presence in the castle as her son's mistress, but Allana was forbidden from being at the duke's side whilst in this holy building.

Allana glared at the older woman's back.

If she wasn't here, Lana, everything would be so much easier.

Sillene Berun was in her early fifties, and was a hefty woman, who was several inches over six feet in height. Upon seeing her, it was clear who Jarrett had inherited his physical attributes from, although the woman's form was all flab. The dowager duchess was sitting close to her son, with their arms and shoulders almost touching. Allana could see the woman leaning over occasionally, whispering words into Jarrett's ear, and she felt a tinge of jealousy.

Allana hated the haughty old shrew. The dowager was a nasty bully, who used her size and status to intimidate those with less power than her, including Allana. Just that morning, Allana had seen Sillene viciously beating a servant boy. It had not been the first time that she had witnessed the dowager assaulting one of the castle retainers, but she had still been shocked by how the flabby woman had repeatedly slapped the small child's face.

Allana could vividly remember her first encounter with Sillene, after she had accompanied Jarrett and his cavalry back to Berun Castle. By then, Jarrett had already become infatuated with her, and he had promised to give her private quarters within the castle keep and a role as his personal seamstress.

—

Just a few hours after Allana's arrival at the castle, Sillene Berun had appeared at those private quarters.

Allana had been taking delight in gaining her own safe space again. The room which Jarrett had provided was cosily small, with dark stone walls and a high glass window, and was plainly furnished with just a bed, dresser and basin.

Allana had been in the midst of unpacking her few possessions when Sillene Berun had opened the door without knocking. Allana had been startled by both the unexpected intrusion, and also by the massive figure who had stalked into the room, towering over her own petite form.

'So, you're the whore who my son has taken for a mistress?'

Allana had been taken aback by the rudeness of the introduction, and had barely contained her annoyance as she had managed to reply, 'I'm not a whore. And you are?'

'Dowager Duchess Sillene. This is *my* castle, girl. You'll address me as "My Lady", or I'll give you a beating you won't soon forget.'

Allana had felt herself bristling. After her experiences with Evelyn dei Laramin, she had vowed that she would never again allow someone to physically abuse her. Indeed, in her final encounter with the Dei Magnun High Commander, she had released a latent power within herself which she believed could crush any such future attempt.

However, on this occasion she had opted to lower her eyes, and had calmly said, 'Yes, my Lady, my apologies. Yes, Duke Berun has asked me to return here with him.'

The woman had scowled, looking down at Allana through narrowed eyes.

'Well, I knew it might happen, eventually. Even though his piety was telling him not to, I'd told him that he needed to get himself some experience before marriage. And his own mother can't teach him *everything*. But look at what he's chosen. Something common, and there's hardly anything to you.'

The hefty woman had leaned over Allana, clearly savouring her height and bulk advantage. She had then placed a chunky hand onto Allana's upper arm, squeezing the flesh beneath thick fingers.

'Pretty enough, I suppose,' the dowager had continued, 'but I would've thought that he'd have picked himself a woman with some meat on her, for his first.'

Allana had said nothing, but had felt the anger building in herself again.

'And a foreigner,' Sillene Berun had continued. 'Clearly from Dei Magnus with that accent. You wouldn't dare to be a spy, would you, girl?'

'No, my Lady. I was a seamstress, who fled Western Canasar during the war. The duke encountered me on the highway.'

'Just a little commoner, picked up off the side of the road then. Well, if you *are* a spy, I'll soon know. I'll have people watching you girl, and they'll also be watching anyone you have contact with. So, be warned.' She had then paused for a handful of seconds, glowering at Allana. 'Well, I'll find you at another time to set out the rules by which I'll tolerate your presence in this castle, girl. However, be in no doubt, whatever my son says, that you will only be here for as long as *I* allow you to remain here. My boy loves me, and if I insist that you leave, you'll be gone. And if you do anything to hurt him, well, you'll also be gone. But in a different way.'

—

Allana was still thinking about this as the holy service started, and as she continued to glare at the older woman's back.

She acts so holy and righteous here, Lana. But it's all a pretence. She's so false and horrible.

The rudeness of the older woman had not abated since their first meeting. Allana had subsequently discovered that the dowager duchess was from Elannis City, and that the woman was a cousin of the Emperor, on his mother's side. The royal bloodline at least partly explained the large woman's haughty sense of superiority.

As the holy service continued, led by a dour priest with a droning voice, Allana joined in with the recitals. However, she was soon bored, and her mind was wandering.

You could ask Jarrett to go riding tomorrow, Lana.

Despite the problems that the mother presented, having the role of mistress of the young duke had given Allana far greater liberty than she had ever enjoyed in Septholme Castle. She was able to roam freely around both the castle and the bustling town of Berun, and she rejoiced in her new-found freedom.

However, horse-riding had become the activity which she enjoyed the most. Jarrett had taken her to the castle stables during her first week there, and had ordered a stableman to instruct her in the fundamentals of horsemanship. Once she had mastered the basics, Jarrett had accompanied her on a number of rides into the surrounding Berun countryside.

Allana loved it. The countryside around Berun was beautiful, full of rolling hills and verdant pine forests, and the foothill mountains of

The Horns sometimes came into view in the distance. When it was just Allana and Jarrett together, looking back towards Berun Castle and the surrounding town from some distant viewpoint, she could let herself escape into the fantasy that she was the Duchess of Berun. That he was her husband, and that this land was hers.

The day before, they had gone riding together for many miles. Allana was letting herself drift into the calming solace of the memory of this, as she joined in with the chanting of the final recitals.

As she did so, her eyes moved back onto the form of Sillene Berun, and she remembered what Jarrett had told her. The dowager duchess was going to try to take away Allana's life here. Even now, the older woman was plotting to bring a wife for Jarrett to the castle, at which point Allana would be replaced and removed. She would lose her home, her privileges and her protection as Duke Berun's mistress.

There would be no point in Allana trying to plead with the dowager to stay in the castle, since nothing would change the nasty woman's mind. The only two people who could prevent this from happening were Jarrett, or Allana herself.

Jarrett was clearly in thrall to his domineering mother, and Allana doubted that her lover would be able to stand up to Sillene if their wills clashed. Of course, Allana could coerce Jarrett to resist his mother's attempts to find him a bride. However, given the older woman's apparent dominance over her son, that would not feel as certain or final for Allana as just stopping Sillene directly.

That felt like the better option. If Allana wanted to keep this life, then she would need to act to halt the schemes of the dowager duchess. Without such action, she would risk losing everything that she had gained here.

As she was thinking this, the holy service finally concluded. With that conclusion, she realised that she had a question to answer and a decision to make.

To protect what you have here, Lana, just what exactly are you prepared to do?

—

Over a week later, on First-Day morning, Allana was standing in the courtyard of Berun Castle, amongst a crowd of servants and retainers. They had gathered to watch the departure of Duke Jarrett Berun on his journey to Andarron. Dowager Duchess Sillene had insisted that the duke's departure be marked with appropriate pomp and formality, and most of the castle retainers had been ordered to attend.

The duke had donned his resplendent black armour with gold engravings, which he had been wearing on the day when he had first encountered Allana. A luxurious fur cloak was wrapped around his shoulders, to protect him against the chill on the roads ahead. To Allana's eyes, he looked handsome and dashing.

Sixty Berun cavalry were to accompany the duke on the overland ride to Rednarron, from where he would be taking a ship for the remainder of the journey to the capital. Those cavalrymen were also gathered in the courtyard, and were all now mounted. Allana suppressed a smile as she observed that the noise of whinnying horses was undermining Sillene Berun's desire for a dignified atmosphere.

Allana had not seen a great deal of Jarrett since early on the preceding Sixth-Day. The young duke had never wanted Allana to sleep in his chambers on the two nights which sandwiched Holy Day, leaving her at those times to the risk of suffering alone in the darkness. Jarrett had also spent much of Sixth-Day daytime and evening sequestered away with his mother and senior advisers, planning his approach to the council called by King Inneos.

Allana had attended Jarrett's room early that First-Day morning, to steal some final private moments with him.

'I'll be waiting for you, my love,' she had whispered, between kisses. 'May The Lord be with you on your journey.'

He had smiled upon hearing that, and had replied, 'I do this for The Lord, Lana, but also for *us*.'

Looking at him now, as he mounted his horse, she realised just how deeply she would miss him. He had been adamant that it was not appropriate for his mistress to accompany him to the Andarron council, and Sillene had strictly forbidden it. Therefore, Allana's attendance alongside him had never been a feasible option, and he would be away from her for weeks. She was dreading being on her own for every night throughout that period.

After Jarrett had joined his cavalry, the dowager duchess approached her son again. He leaned down towards her, and again Allana felt a bite of jealousy as she saw the older woman whispering secret words to him, and the duke smiling in return. Sillene Berun was wearing expensive robes this morning, and her hair was assembled in an ornate bun, which made her look even taller.

The dowager then turned to face the crowd, and called out, 'All hail our brave and noble lord, Duke Berun! He goes forth from here to a great council in Andarron. He carries our love, but also a great burden. The burden to protect the people of Berun, the Holy Church, and the faith. All hail our heroic lord and his men with our cheers, as he leaves this castle. May our support sustain him on the long and difficult journey ahead. All hail!'

There was more passion in the woman's voice as she said this than Allana had ever before witnessed. In response to the last words, the retainers of Berun Castle started to cheer. Duke Berun then turned his horse, and began to ride out of the castle courtyard. His face was stoic as his cavalry followed him.

Allana's stomach was churning as she watched him depart under the raised portcullises. Jarrett would be away from the castle for weeks. During that period, Allana would have no one to help her to keep the tormenting thoughts at bay, each time that she tried to return to sleep. No one whose presence would help her to deter the panic and trembling, as she lay alone in the dark.

Even more significantly, Jarrett was Allana's primary protection against Sillene.

If only she was going with him, Lana.

Jarrett had told Allana that his mother was not accompanying him on the trip, due to the difficulties of the journey. That left Allana exposed to any nasty whims of the dowager duchess during the duke's absence.

As if to confirm this thought, after the last of the cavalry had exited through the castle gateway, Allana turned to find Sillene Berun standing near to her. The woman was staring at her intently, as a cat might regard a mouse. Allana gasped and took an involuntary step backwards, and she saw a hint of malice in the smirk which appeared on the dowager duchess's face.

'My Lady?' asked Allana, her voice hesitant.

'Nothing, girl,' replied the older woman. 'But he's gone now, isn't he? I bet you're thinking about the fact that he's no longer here to shield you from me. Aren't you?'

Allana was unsure how to respond. However, before she had time to resolve this, the dowager turned and strode off. Allana was left to once again glare at the hefty woman's back, feeling suddenly uncertain and unsafe.

You can protect yourself now, Lana. Remember that.

3

Leanna

—

*Year of Our Lord,
After Ascension, 769AA*

The wooden bowl lifted into the air, seemingly of its own accord. At one moment, it had been connected to the sturdy beech table beneath it. In the next, it was floating two feet higher.

Leanna concentrated, exerting subtle pressure against the whittled edges of the round object. As the vessel began to rotate perfectly within a fixed position, she allowed herself a smile of satisfaction. More pressure, and then the bowl was spinning faster, with several rotations each second. Next, she would-

Her concentration was shattered as a hand reached under her armpit from behind, and tickled her there. With that interruption, her control over the small object was broken, and it spun away across the room. It thudded against the far wall, before bouncing and rolling back across the floor.

Leanna sighed in mock indignation, but then smiled as she heard a feminine giggle from behind her. A small red-headed form leaned over her shoulder and kissed her on the cheek.

'Gets you every time! You should be more careful with that, you know. Could cause an accident.'

'Amyss! I was practising!'

'And you and I both know that you should be resting, given the day that you're going to have today.' Amyss moved around into view, and took the seat at Leanna's side, before entwining her fingers with Leanna's. 'Seriously, Lea. Sometimes, you have to take it easy. You might burn yourself out.'

'I know,' said Leanna. 'Take it easy. You tell me that every day! Rest. Sleep. Eat. But I'm still going, aren't I? I haven't burnt out just yet! And I need to learn how to do this, Amyss.'

Ever since the events at the pyre, over three and a half months earlier, she had been able to move objects with her mind. She had practised in the intervening period, and she was gradually becoming stronger, and more capable of moving heavier items. However, her efforts were still a world away from the miraculous experience of the pyre, when she had been bolstered by Arion Sepian's presence and energy.

Amyss ran her thumb across Leanna's palm, softly caressing it, and said, 'I know you do. And I look forward to when you can float my breakfast across the table to me, and massage my feet from the other side of the room. But until then, please will you give yourself an occasional minute to rest. They're already waiting for you at the hospital. Colissa said to come whenever you're ready.'

'I understand,' said Leanna, before taking a deep breath. 'I suppose we'd better go then.'

―

Shortly afterwards, they departed together from their private quarters within the College of Aiduel in Arlais. They started to move towards the hospital, which was near to the entrance of the walled complex.

They were trailed by four of the eight guards who had been standing sentry around Leanna's quarters. These soldiers were all wearing white cloaks with two red spots on the shoulders, a basic uniform which signalled loyalty to the Angel of Arlais, and membership of the militia. In recent weeks, Leanna had been accompanied by such protectors at all times, given the growing belief that retribution might be looming.

Leanna nodded in acknowledgement towards the lead figure amongst these guards, a hard-looking man in his thirties. His name was Lorth Dormer, and prior to the events of the pyre he had been a captain of the guards on a merchant wagon train. Dormer had been in Arlais on the day of the pyre, and had witnessed Leanna's miracle. Afterwards, he had renounced his prior career and had offered his services to protect her.

He had been the first to do so, but his action had been witnessed and subsequently repeated by many younger citizens of the city. Dormer was now the leader of the newformed militia, which had assumed responsibility for protecting Leanna and the College of Aiduel. They had also taken over the vacated fortress of Aiduel's Guards, after the survivors of that burned and decimated order had been driven from Arlais.

'Look, Lea,' said Amyss, pointing. 'It's going to be another busy day.'

Leanna peered towards the long queue of people who were outside of the hospital entrance. Over one hundred had come today, a number of whom would be severely ill or wounded. However, many more of those present would instead be pilgrims, who had travelled in the hope of meeting the Angel of Arlais.

Lord Aiduel, she thought, *please help me to heal those people who need me.*

In response to Amyss, she said, 'Well, you take care that you don't wear yourself out.'

Amyss smiled and replied, 'You take care, too.'

With Leanna's consent, Amyss had appointed herself as Leanna's personal secretary, and she was now the gateway to the Angel of

Arlais. Amyss would screen everyone in the hospital queue, and any pilgrims or people with minor ailments would be asked to leave. They would be told that they might be able to gain sight of Leanna if they attended the Seventh-Day service at Arlais Cathedral.

Leanna watched as Amyss and a pair of the militia guards walked in the direction of the waiting line. It appeared to be comprised of the usual assemblage of sizes and ages, although Leanna's eyes were drawn to a very tall and burly man, towards the back end of the queue. This individual was hooded, and he was facing in Leanna's direction.

She was not sure why this particular person drew her interest, and she would have liked a few moments to indulge her curiosity. However, there was much to do, and she moved towards the hospital entrance. She passed by another four militia guards as she entered, and the silent Lorth Dormer followed her inside.

Over the following hours, Leanna met with only ten of the people from the queue outside. These ten individuals had first been approved for access to Leanna by Amyss, and then by the hospital's lead healer, Sister Colissa. Each of the ten had been deemed serious enough cases to receive the healing which only the Angel of Arlais could provide.

Three of the patients had broken bones, and four had severe cuts and lacerations, with the remainder afflicted with illness and disease. In each case, Leanna seated herself beside the individual, receiving a hint of their pain via her ability to sense emotions. Since the pyre, she had become more capable of controlling the degree to which she experienced these external feelings, and she could almost dull them to nothing, if necessary.

With each patient, Leanna slipped into the trance that was now so familiar to her, that comfortable state of existence which seemed to slow down time, and which brought the patient's affliction into view within a river of dark colour. After that, she used her Aiduel-given powers to tear the illness out, or to mend what was broken. And by doing so, she healed them. With every occasion that she accomplished this, she was growing stronger, and her powers were becoming more refined. More capable of achieving miraculous deeds.

But still, the activity depleted her. She knew that the last two to three efforts of each day were never as precise as the first, which is why she had limited herself to a total of ten patients per day, across First-Day to Sixth-Day. By the time that she had aided ten people she was exhausted, but was left with a satisfied feeling that she had done something worthwhile.

After the final patient had departed that day, Leanna closed her eyes in prayer.

Lord Aiduel, thank you for giving me the strength and ability to help these people. And please let me help others, tomorrow.

She was disturbed by Sister Colissa's hand on her shoulder, as the older healer said, 'You look shattered, Leanna. You should go home and rest.'

Leanna smiled, wearily. 'Amyss keeps telling me the same thing. But these people won't all heal themselves, Colissa.'

'We maintained this hospital before we were blessed with you, Leanna. And we can survive without you for a few days, if we must. But you've done holy work again today, Angel of Arlais.'

Leanna huffed with mock exasperation. 'Oh, not you too, Colissa. Please don't you call me that, too.'

'I only use the name because it fits so, Leanna. Now get yourself home, get some rest, and let Amyss take care of you.'

―

That night, Leanna lay in bed, with Amyss in her arms.

The two of them shared a private cottage within the College complex, which had been granted to Leanna in the days following the pyre. The property consisted of two bedrooms, plus a living and kitchen area, and an alcove for prayer.

Throughout each day, novices attended to take care of cooking, washing and cleaning. Leanna and Amyss were therefore rarely in the cottage in the daytime without other company being present. But in the evening, after the eighth hour prayer service had concluded, it was just the two of them again. In those night-time hours, both the cosy property and Amyss became Leanna's sanctuary.

'How long do you think that things can stay like this, Amyss?' she asked.

'What? With me in your bed with my head on your chest, and your arms around me? Hopefully forever.' As the small priestess answered, her emotions of love were like a torrent, flowing ceaselessly into Leanna.

'Don't tease me. You know what I mean. With the College and Arlais like this. Seeming like we're cut off from Aiduel's Guards, from the Holy Church, and from the rest of Elannis. It doesn't feel as if things can go on like this for much longer.'

'I don't know, Lea,' said Amyss, and her tone was now more serious. 'At some point, Aiduel's Guards will return in force. You know that, I know that. Everyone in Arlais knows it. And it might be enough to overwhelm the militia and change everything again, for the worse. But until then, can we please just enjoy… being together?'

Leanna kissed the top of Amyss's head. 'Yes, let's enjoy it.'

Lord Aiduel, please keep her safe, and please protect all of the people of Arlais.

In the months since the pyre, Leanna's relationship with Amyss had progressed to a deeper level of intimacy. What had happened since then had been initiated by Amyss in the aftermath of that fateful day, and was a progression of the kiss that they had shared.

A couple of days after the pyre, Amyss had come to Leanna and had shyly said, 'I thought I was going to lose you, Lea. I couldn't bear it. And since… you survived, I haven't been able to stop thinking about what it would have been like if I'd lost you. So, I've made a decision, Lea. I want to be with you. Beside you. In whatever capacity makes you comfortable. With no requirements or expectations of you. But I want to commit myself and my life to you.'

The words had been said in private, the smaller woman's voice wavering as she had spoken. In response, Leanna had wrapped her arms around Amyss, and had whispered, 'For as long as you want to stay beside me, Amyss, I shall feel privileged to be with you.'

Since then, to the eyes of the outside world, Amyss had become Leanna's personal secretary, administering to the many demands on Leanna's time. However, in their secret world within the cottage, their relationship was more intimate than that. The Holy Church might perceive the way that they held and kissed each other, in the privacy of their bedroom, as sinful and wrong. However, after the events of the pyre, Leanna no longer believed that The Lord Aiduel would condemn their actions, and nor did she condemn them herself.

The transformation in her relationship with Amyss had been just one of the many changes in Leanna's life since the miraculous day at the pyre, when she had survived the intentions of Aiduel's Guards to burn her alive. It was an event which she still did not fully understand, other than that The Lord Aiduel had intervened to prevent her death.

He had called Arion Sepian to travel all the way from Septholme as part of that intervention. Then, following Arion's arrival, He had channelled awesome power through the two of them, such that Leanna had been able to survive the conflagration whilst bathed in a golden halo. But more than that, she had borne the marks of His Suffering, and she had bled in the places where He had once bled on The Tree.

And then, at the end, Leanna had unleashed previously unimaginable quantities of power and the pyre had exploded. The wood and the flames had shot outwards, an act which might have caused untold suffering to hundreds of innocents, given the size of the crowd which had surrounded her.

If that had happened, she would still be haunted now. But The Lord had again intervened, and all of the flames and debris had been targeted towards a specific group of people. Towards the forces of Aiduel's Guards, who had imprisoned her and had led her to the pyre. And towards Senior Priest El'Patriere.

It had caused grievous damage and death for those particular people, for which she felt great guilt. However, the targeted nature of the explosion had convinced her that The Lord had chosen those who were deserving of His righteous justice. Her guilt was therefore lessened, knowing that The Lord had used her as His vessel for His chosen act on that day.

The greatest confirmation of that was the person beside her. Amyss had been metres away from the pyre at the time of the explosion, standing with Leanna's parents, but all three had suffered nothing worse than a few aching muscles after the force of the explosion had knocked them from their feet. They had been untouched by flame.

As Leanna was thinking about this, a stray thought slipped into her mind. 'There was a very large man in the queue today. Near the back. Hooded. Who was he?'

'Hmmm, let me think,' said Amyss. 'I think I know who you mean. He didn't give his name though. Said he was a pilgrim, and he wanted the honour of seeing the Angel of Arlais. We sent him away, of course, and said you'd be at the Cathedral on Seventh-Day, if he wanted to attend service with you. Why do you ask?'

'I'm not sure. He just caught my attention. He wasn't from Arlais, then?'

'Not Arlais. Not sure where he was from exactly. He had a funny accent, like a mix of places. He seemed nice, very friendly, though I remember now that he smelled of alcohol, like he'd been drinking.'

Leanna was not sure why she had asked about him, but she was feeling tired, and closed her eyes. She hugged Amyss, and then slipped contentedly into sleep.

―

When Leanna awoke later that night, stirred from slumber by her recurring dream, Amyss was still in her arms.

Leanna opened her eyes, staring into the darkness, feeling agitated as usual by the visions within the dream which now seemed so familiar. The avatars of light. The winding path. The Gate.

But had she heard other words, new words, spoken by the figure in the Gate before she had awoken? Terrible words, which had come after that figure had raised a single finger? She strove to recall what had been said, but the detail of the memory was not there.

However, it was once again confirming to her what she now believed to be true; ever since the unleashing of energy at the pyre, she was seeing further into the dream. Deeper. Soon, she hoped that she would be able to comprehend and recall everything that was happening.

But until then, she had many other more prosaic matters to worry about, and she needed her rest. She closed her eyes, and sleep soon claimed her again.

―

Two days later, on Seventh-Day, Leanna was to attend Holy Service at the Cathedral of Arlais.

Prior to her salvation on the pyre, she had only occasionally attended services at the cathedral. However, in the aftermath of that event, the clamour from the people of Arlais to see their 'Angel' had become overwhelming. Leanna had therefore resolved to make a public appearance at the main Holy Service at least once per week, which seemed to satisfy the faithful of the city. However, she was rendered uncomfortable by both the size of the crowds in the city centre, and by the chanting of her new moniker.

That morning, she was walking through the city towards the cathedral, within a contingent of over fifty people. Half of these were militia guards, tasked with keeping any crowds back from her, and the remainder were priests and novices from the College. At Leanna's side was Amyss, with Lorth Dormer also never more than a couple of metres away, his hand on his sword hilt whilst his agitated gaze roamed around them. He clearly did not enjoy that she did this.

A few streets from the cathedral, Leanna met up with her parents, Elisa and Jonas. They both looked nervous, as they often had recently when accompanying her on the latter stages of this procession, but she could also feel their immense pride that she was their daughter.

When their group reached the central square of Arlais, which was edged on one side by the splendid cathedral building, Leanna could see a crowd of hundreds. This mass of people was cheering, and many were wearing white cloaks with red spots on the shoulders. The militia started to clear the way through this raucous crowd, creating a pathway perhaps five metres wide whilst maintaining a protective circle around Leanna.

Lord Aiduel, please keep me humble, and always remind me that I'm but a vessel for your will.

Leanna proceeded with her colleagues through the centre of this channel. The emotions emitted from the crowd were unrelentingly positive, and their cheers were expressive of joy and veneration. However, every time that she experienced this assemblage of noise and people, it brought back darker memories of the terrible walk through a comparable massed throng, on her way to the pyre.

Leanna stepped carefully along the open pathway through the crowd, as she had on that other day, feeling the beating emotions of the gathered masses washing across her.

JOY. LOVE. AWE. JOY. LO-

Abruptly, the emotions disappeared. Leanna stopped walking, feeling shocked. She had learned how to subdue any external emotions, such that if she now elected to, she could barely feel them. But this was different. They were gone. Completely absent. The noise of the crowd was receding in turn, reaching her as if from the end of a distant tunnel. And she felt different, as if something had been drained from within herself.

Her surprise must have been reflected on her face. Amyss paused and looked at her with concern, and Lorth Dormer hurried towards her, saying, 'Priestess Leanna. Please keep walking.'

Leanna shook her head, then looked to the side.

She noticed the hooded man immediately. He was less than three metres away, two of the militia standing between her and him. He was very tall and burly and, despite the hood, she could see that he had grey hair and a grey beard, with a wide nose and ruddy cheeks. She felt certain that he was the same man who had been standing in the queue at the hospital, earlier that week.

Her gaze found his, and she stared into bloodshot eyes. For moments, those eyes held hers, with no reverence or deference in his regard. The expression on his craggy face was enigmatic, but she experienced an immediate pulse of fear. She instinctively felt that the loss of her ability to sense emotions was connected to this man. Something about him. Something dangerous.

Then she glanced down and spotted the object held in his right hand. A mace. A lengthy weapon, the solid metal end lowered down towards the floor, resting on the cobbled surface.

Lorth Dormer must have noticed where she was looking, because he moved to interpose his own body between Leanna and the stranger, and shouted, 'You! Back off!' He then gave a gentle push on Leanna's arm, and to Amyss urged, 'Get her moving! Get her inside!'

These actions snapped Leanna out of her befuddlement, and she proceeded to move urgently along the cleared pathway to the steps at the entrance of the cathedral. Within moments, the emotions of the crowd were washing over her again, and the sensation of being drained had evaporated. When she had half-climbed the cathedral steps, she looked back towards the area of the crowd where the stranger had been, hoping to get a clearer look at him.

But he was gone.

Shortly afterwards, Leanna was sitting on a pew inside the cathedral, waiting for the appearance of the acting High Priest of Arlais.

When the man who was going to lead the Holy Day service appeared, he was flanked by two junior priests, who helped him to climb the steps to the pulpit above the altar. Leanna felt a tinge of sympathy as she looked upon this senior figure, who was attired in his holy vestments. Even from ten metres away, she could hear the strained wheezing from his damaged lungs. She could also observe the severe burn scarring which covered the entirety of his face, some of it hidden by the eyepatch which he was wearing on the left-hand side.

However, despite the severity of the wounds, she knew that she could only feel half-hearted sympathy. If she was being honest with herself, it could never be wholehearted, given the nature of the man.

Lord Aiduel, please aid in the ongoing recovery of Senior Priest El'Patriere, and help him to walk on a brighter path under your light.

The Holy Church in Arlais had been left reeling by what had happened on the day of the pyre, and its leadership had been devastated.

High Priest Comenis had not been struck by any of the flames and wood which had exploded out from the fire. However, Leanna had discovered afterwards that the senior churchman in Arlais had suffered a heart attack following the explosion. He had collapsed, red-faced and breathless, and had died unnoticed as the crowd had swarmed around him.

High Commander Ernis dei Bornere of Aiduel's Guards had perished almost instantly, his entire body being consumed by flame. His fate was now talked about as justice for all of the people who had been executed by fire, on his command, since Aiduel's Guards had arrived in Arlais.

That left Senior Priest El'Patriere, the man standing at the pulpit today. Until the day of the pyre, he had been the Senior Priest of the College of Aiduel, but he was now the acting High Priest of Arlais. The exploding timber and flame had not consumed El'Patriere, as it had consumed dei Bornere. Instead, his burns had been restricted to the face, neck and chest areas.

On the evening following the pyre, Leanna had come upon El'Patriere in the College hospital. The Senior Priest's face had been a blistered mess, with red pustules formed across the skin, transforming the previously handsome visage into a hideous mask. He had been awake when she had arrived at his bedside, and his chest had been heaving with every wheezing breath. One eye had been sealed shut, but the other had opened as she had come close, and Leanna had realised who it was.

She had been exhausted by that point, having already healed many surviving Aiduel's Guards who had been victims of the explosion. But she had still been able to feel El'Patriere's emotions, pulsing outwards.

PAIN. PAIN. HATE. PAIN. PAIN. HATE.

Any sympathy which she might have felt for the man's agony had been dampened by his malevolence. Nonetheless, she had reached her hand out, and had used her remaining traces of energy to heal him as best as she could. Her effort had reduced his pain, and had lessened the raw intensity of his burns. However, she had been unable to repair his damaged features, or to restore sight to his melted eye. She had been too depleted by then.

The next day, when she had returned to the hospital, El'Patriere had gone. He had moved to take over Comenis's quarters at the cathedral, and had assumed leadership of the Holy Church in the city. Since then, he had not had any involvement with the College of Aiduel.

Priestess Corenna had taken on some of El'Patriere's old duties, and Sister Colissa had continued to run the hospital, after Brother Perrien had been ordered to depart. But when a final decision on a College matter now needed to be taken, everyone turned to Leanna.

Looking upon El'Patriere now, as he stood on the pulpit, Leanna knew that she should feel more pity for the man. His face was disfigured beyond repair, and he had lost his left eye. El'Patriere had clearly taken pride in his handsome looks, but the ugliness of his soul was now matched by the hideousness of his face, an outcome for which he clearly blamed Leanna.

Lord Aiduel, please show him the way to forgiveness.

As Leanna listened and participated in the Holy Service which then followed, it was clear that El'Patriere's voice and throat had also been affected. He had once spoken in tones which had been refined and melodious, but his voice now felt strained and sometimes croaking in nature.

At the end of the service, Leanna expected El'Patriere to wish them all to, 'Go in the Grace of Aiduel.'

But instead, he smiled and said, 'Holy faithful. Before you all leave, there is a herald here. A messenger who has travelled to Arlais on behalf of His Eminence, Archlaw Paulius. This herald would deliver a message, publicly, here in this holy place. A message addressed to our living miracle, Priestess Leanna, our beloved Angel of Arlais.'

Leanna shuddered upon hearing the pretence of sincerity within the latter words. If she had not known the vehemence with which El'Patriere detested her, she might almost have believed him.

El'Patriere continued, gesturing as he spoke. 'Now, please welcome the Archlaw's Herald.'

A diminutive and rotund man approached the altar. He was dressed in religious vestments, and was holding an ornate and formal-looking scroll, which he unrolled as he moved onto the pulpit. When he started to speak, his voice was booming, echoing off the cathedral walls.

'This is an open letter from His Eminence Archlaw Paulius the Fourth, leader of the Holy Church, Aiduel's Mortal Voice on Angall. It is addressed principally to Priestess Leanna, beloved Angel of Arlais, but is intended to be heard by all of the faithful of Arlais. I shall be repeating this message in the town square at noon today, and for each of the next five days, so that all of the citizens of Arlais may hear it. Copies of this letter shall also be posted in all public spaces across the city. Now, hear the illustrious words of His Eminence, Archlaw Paulius.

'To Priestess Leanna of Arlais, the Angel of Arlais, Aiduel's Holy Healer, Worker of Miracles, and she who was saved by Aiduel's Own Hand from the unjust fire.

'I, Archlaw Paulius the Fourth, am writing to you now, to offer my apologies, my veneration and adoration, and my pleas for reconciliation.

'You have been done a great wrong, dearest Priestess Leanna, my beloved Angel of Arlais. You, and all of the people of Arlais, have been done a great wrong, at the hands of a man who purported to act in the name of the Archlaw and the Holy Church, but who acted only upon his own foul urges. You have all suffered at the hands of evil, but by Aiduel's Grace you have emerged unscathed. You, Leanna, have been delivered from the flames as a worker of miracles, and tempered by that fire into a stronger, purer, sanctified and holy steel.

'The Order of Aiduel's Guards in Arlais, to my everlasting shame and regret, was tainted by the command and influence of a man who I now understand had lost his mind; High Commander Ernis dei Bornere. He corrupted their holy mission, the seeking out of evil heretics, into his own personal and insane pursuit of power. In the course of that mad and unholy pursuit, he placed the single most important person in the recent history of the Holy Church onto a pyre, where he intended to burn her alive.

'Only by the Hand of Aiduel, and by His Divine Judgement against this depraved evil, were you saved from the flames, and was dei Bornere incinerated in an act of The Lord Aiduel's retribution. But, by this act we can all be thankful, for He revealed you to us, and unveiled the miracle of your existence to the world.

'And I, Archlaw Paulius, can now recognise and understand the mistrust dei Bornere's actions must have created within you and the citizens of Arlais for the Holy Church, and of my benevolent love for you all. But such lack of trust is deeply misplaced, I assure you. Please believe me when I say that the actions of dei Bornere were carried out without my instruction or knowledge, and I was as appalled as anyone there when they were finally reported to me.

'I have prayed to The Lord Aiduel for His and your forgiveness *for my lack of oversight and control over these heinous deeds. I long for nothing more now than to see the Angel of Arlais, and the city of Arlais, brought back into the loving embrace of the Church. For us all to be united again, in our love for Aiduel, for the faith and for the institution of the Holy Church.*

'As part of that reconciliation and reunification, you will soon be able to welcome a new replacement force of a thousand Aiduel's Guards to your wonderful city. Indeed, I have already dispatched this new contingent to you. By the time that you hear these words, they will have already arrived at the port of Boralais, and will soon be travelling onwards to Arlais. This force is uncorrupted by the insanity which gripped Ernis dei Bornere, and is headed by my esteemed colleague, Archprime Meira dei Corsi, third most senior member of the High Council.

'She and they have two purposes in coming to Arlais. Firstly, to bring the city of Arlais back into the fold of the Holy Church, by helping to free it from the scourge of vigilante elements who have taken possession of the fortress of Aiduel's Guards. And secondly, to find and offer their protection to you, Priestess Leanna, Angel of Arlais, and to form your honour guard on a return journey to Sen Aiduel.

'To Sen Aiduel, centre of the Holy Church, where you will come into my presence, where the Angel of Arlais shall stand before Aiduel's Mortal Voice, and I will venerate you. I shall recognise you as a Living Saint, the first person to be recognised as such for hundreds of years. And you shall take your position on the High Council of the Holy Church, as is befitting of a figure of such illustrious reverence.

'Please be assured of my everlasting goodwill and respect, Priestess Leanna, and I shall await, as your faithful servant, the moment when we may kneel together, and may join together in blissful devotion to The Lord.

'Archprime Meira shall be at the vanguard of your escort. She and a small support group will approach the city in advance, to prepare the way for the thousand Aiduel's Guards who follow in their wake. She would like a meeting of peace with you, Priestess Leanna, within the sacred and sanctified walls of Arlais Cathedral. My herald shall provide the details of this.

'I hope that you will receive the Archprime with all of the humility and love with which I have written this letter, Priestess Leanna. Please take my word that The Lord Aiduel has deemed that Arlais shall once again return into the fold of the faith, as a shining beacon of hope, and that the name of Leanna, Angel of Arlais, shall live in the Glory of Aiduel for evermore.

'May The Lord Aiduel forever walk with you all in the light, and keep you from the all-consuming darkness.

'And may you all go in the Grace of Aiduel.'

Having concluded these words, the herald's tone of voice altered, and he announced, 'Thus ends the letter of His Eminence Archlaw Paulius the Fourth, Head of the Holy Church, Aiduel's Mortal Voice on Angall.'

Upon completion of that statement, the herald stood back, and El'Patriere came forward to announce his own parting words to the congregation, notifying everyone to disperse. As he concluded, Leanna could not perceive if the acting High Priest was smiling or grimacing, behind the contorted mask of his scarring.

However, her own heart was beating fast. She looked across at Amyss, and the concern on the petite priestess's face mirrored her own. They both knew what the herald's announcement truly meant, and that it reflected the matters that they had speculated about, just a few nights earlier.

Aiduel's Guards were returning. The Holy Church had signalled its intention to reclaim the city of Arlais.

And to claim Leanna, too.

4

Corin

Year of Our Lord,
After Ascension, 769AA

Corin's army was spread out across the open plain, a massed force of warriors which was more numerous than he once could have imagined possible. From the low hillock upon which he stood, he was able to survey the bustling formations of this Chosen army, whilst also watching the ranks of the enemy drawing closer.

He could feel goosebumps rising on the back of his neck. It made him recognise that he was excited by the prospect of the coming conflict, despite the better side of his nature. In a reflection of this stirring of darker emotion, Blackpaw also stirred from a crouching position, a few metres down the hill. The felrin stretched its thick forearms whilst extending its claws, transmitting emotions of bloodlust back through their shared connection.

Corin welcomed the creature's hungry craving, letting it feed his own building anger. He knew that this was a time to subdue his natural instinct for peace, and to embrace his latent fury. Soon, he would need to release all of that accumulated rage. Soon, he would need to kill. He recognised just how much he had changed, since the time when the death of a single person might have paralysed him.

Clan Chief Munnik of the Borl, who was standing alongside Corin on the hill, chose that moment to comment. 'I never dreamed that I'd see a host of this size gathered, in my lifetime, Chief Corin. Four tribes, fighting together, for a common cause. The Gods are with us today! This will be a bleak day for the Renni, and a great one for the Chosen clans.'

Corin turned to regard the man, and nodded. Munnik was taller and stockier than Corin, but red hair was a feature which was common to both of them.

'It will, Chief Munnik,' Corin said, 'but let's avoid this becoming a needless slaughter. I want this ended quickly, and as bloodlessly as possible. If our men can engage and weaken them, then I'll break their spirits and I'll force them to surrender.'

On the plain before them, the allied warriors of Munnik's Borl clan were positioned on the left side of Corin's Chosen forces. The men of that northern tribe were all armed with their traditional long spears, and their own left flank was protected by the meandering river which ran alongside them.

The Qari tribe, neighbours of the Borl who fought with traditional axe and shield, were positioned on the Chosen army's right flank. Behind the main Qari line were a score of senior warriors of that clan, including their chief, who were all mounted on horseback. Horse riding was something that had been unknown to Corin, until a few weeks earlier. Seeing men on the back of beasts still fascinated him now, even if Blackpaw's relative proximity made the horses skittish.

In the centre of the extended Chosen army formation was a blended mix of Karn and Anath warriors. Corin had insisted that the two forces were to be intermingled for the coming battle, rather than forming separate groups. He was satisfied by how quickly the old animosities were being extinguished after he had quashed the violence between them, and they would fight together today as allies. Corin hoped that the sharing of such deeds would act to strengthen the ties of kinship which he was attempting to create.

In total, hundreds of warriors were gathered here, to fight as the Chosen army. It was a vast body of men, greater than any force in the recent memories of the Karn. And this army was led by him, Corin of Karn, the so-called Chosen of the Gods.

'I look forward to seeing you and the felrin fight together,' said Munnik, after a few seconds. 'But you are right. Let's not waste our people's lives here.'

Corin nodded, noting again that the other man was the most reasoned leader that he had encountered, amongst any of the tribes. Munnik had played a key role, alongside Corin, in the forging of the alliance between the four clans that were assembled here. Munnik had been receptive to the idea of peace at his very first meeting with Corin, and their relationship had grown stronger after a second successful meeting together.

Munnik had subsequently introduced Corin to Chief Quan of the more distant Qari, and the three leaders of the clans had discussed at length how they might co-operate and ally. Corin could well remember the fateful day when he had made the proposals which had led to this alliance.

—

'We would hear your thoughts then, Clan Chief Corin.'

The words had been spoken by Munnik, six weeks earlier. The leader's expression had been as serious as his tone, after he had concluded a long and considered speech.

Corin had nodded as he had prepared to answer, looking as solemn himself as the formal situation had demanded. He had been seated in the Clan Hall of the village of Karn, flanked by his senior advisers, Akob and Marrix. To one side of them had been Munnik and two of his own people, and opposite had been Quan of the Qari, also accompanied by two senior clansmen. At Corin's insistence, everyone in the room had been unarmed.

'Thank you, Chief Munnik, for your honesty,' Corin had said. 'And thank you also, Chief Quan, for the open words you've spoken. As I've said from the outset, Munnik, I want peace between us. The days of the endless raids led by the likes of Borrik and Rekmar have passed. If I have my way, they'll not return. They'll never return. But as I've said before, no one should mistake this desire for peace as weakness; Rekmar made that mistake, and he ended up as dinner for a felrin.'

'Rekmar was a fool, Chief Corin.' This had been stated by the lanky Quan of the Qari, his long hair hanging to his shoulders. 'Munnik and I are not fools.'

'That is clear to me, Chief Quan. You're both wise leaders of your clans. Leaders of proud clans, with great histories. But despite that, I know from your words today that both of your tribes are threatened. That you lose too many young men. The Renni grow stronger, and threaten your lands, and won't rest until both of your peoples are crushed. You *need* this peace with the Karn and Anath, in the lands to your west, as much as I want it.'

Munnik had inclined his head, as if conceding the point without voicing it. 'We are here, that is true.'

'But I don't think it's enough for you to have peace with us, brave chiefs,' Corin had continued. 'To face the Renni, and to win, you need more than peace. You need alliance. Need the men that the Karn and the Anath can bring to your assistance. Need the power and terror that the Chosen of the Gods and my felrin can deliver.'

Munnik and Quan had exchanged glances, before Quan had replied, 'The Qari and the Borl have been allies for a long time now. Together, we believe we can hold the Renni. Hurt them as much as they hurt us. But to defeat them, with just our two clans? The cost would be too great. That is why we've agreed to seek your help in this.'

'And I want to help,' Corin had answered. 'But I can't spend the blood of the Karn and the Anath without something in return. Something lasting. I want to create something in these lands which will endure. Which will protect. And whether you both believe you can agree to my conditions will depend on whether or not you believe I'm actually the Chosen of the Gods. Whether the felrin and my powers mark me out as someone who's been chosen, and who great men can choose to follow.'

'Follow?' Munnik had repeated, sounding cautious.

'I seek to build an alliance of clans, Chief Munnik and Chief Quan. An alliance of Chosen clans, who will trade together, will intermarry, will share ideas, and who will protect each other under threat. Imagine the possibilities, for peace and strength! Each of these clans will retain their own chief, great men responsible for the leadership of their clan and its people. But there will be only one leader of the overall alliance, one Chosen, who each of these great men will recognise as their leader.'

'And that man would be you, Chief Corin?' Quan had asked.

'Yes, it would. I am the Chosen of the Gods. I believe that. And I think that you believe it too. Join with me. Join with the Karn and the Anath in a Chosen Alliance. You will both still rule, but we'll become like kin, blood-brothers between clans. Do this, and *then* I will bring my armies and my power to stand alongside you. And to remove the threat of the Renni, forever. That is the choice which I offer to both of you today. Peace, and order, or an endless cycle of war and death. It is for you to choose.'

—

There had not been an explicit agreement in that meeting, but Corin believed that was the day when he had persuaded the two leaders. After weeks of subsequent deliberation and discussion within and between their clans, the two chiefs had accepted Corin's proposal. They had agreed to bend their knee to Corin, in return for the permanent vanquishing of the Renni clan threat against their people and lands.

As a result, they were gathered here today, on this chilly autumnal morning, about to fight alongside each other. Corin peered across the plain as the Renni forces assembled into position. The enemy warband was sizeable, and Corin estimated that they were a larger single clan than even the Anath had been. However, the Renni forces appeared to be outnumbered by more than two to one by Corin's own army.

Corin had already attempted to initiate discussions with the enemy chief, to encourage a bloodless surrender, but this had been rebuffed. Marrix had also attempted to deliver a final message earlier that day, offering negotiations of peace. However, he had returned swiftly after being intercepted in the land between the opposing forces.

Upon his return, Marrix had approached Corin and had said, 'The messenger of the Renni states that Chief Buljuk will not come near to you unless he's surrounded by an army of his kin, all baying for your blood. He says that he's heard of the fate of Rekmar of the Anath, and that he'll not be the second fool who falls for the evil tricks of a dirty shaman.'

Corin had nodded upon hearing this, deliberately allowing the insult to further feed his anger. He knew by experience that the more furious he got, the stronger his powers would become. Indeed, he could feel his bloodlust echoing back and forth between himself and Blackpaw, magnifying and strengthening with every passing moment.

However, his words were cool as he announced, 'It is time. Go to your men, Munnik, as I will go to mine. Advance on my call. And may the Gods deliver us a glorious victory.'

The Borl leader did as instructed, and Corin descended the short distance down to the combined ranks of Karn and Anath. Blackpaw stalked at Corin's side as he walked, and the lines of his warriors parted naturally before the two of them. Corin's face presented a calm exterior to those around him as he passed by his clansmen. However, his thoughts and those of Blackpaw were merging into one seething vortex, both of them poised to release the rage contained within.

Corin could also sense the tension within the warriors of the Karn and Anath around him as he reached the front of their lines. The forces of the Renni clan were again visible from this position, the enemy arrayed across the flat plain in an extended line two-men deep. From this perspective, the Renni numbers looked more evenly matched, and Corin knew that many of his own warriors would be thinking that today they would see their final sun.

Corin took a deep and long-drawn breath. Blackpaw at his side was crouched on its lengthy front limbs, coiled and ready to explode forwards. Corin's men were silent, all eyes now on him, waiting for his movement. Corin allowed himself a moment to think about Agbeth, and her fate, as a reminder of why he needed to do this. Why he needed to be prepared to dispense violence to deliver peace, and order, for all of those who chose to be within his protection.

Finally, he raised his chin and screamed.

All of the force in his chest and lungs was put into that scream, releasing all of his frustration about what had happened to Agbeth. The sound carried over his own lines and across the field towards the Renni. A moment later, Blackpaw added its own voice to the cry, its fearsome call overpowering Corin's. All of the Karn and the Anath then joined in, the whole war party screaming out their bloodlust, before the cry extended into the ranks of the Borl and the Qari.

And then they charged.

Corin and his company had travelled less than ten metres before their war cries were echoed along the ranks of the Renni, who also started to pour forwards.

The distance between the opposing forces was closing in mere seconds. Blackpaw could have bolted forward into the Renni line first, but Corin instructed the beast to stay close to him, and to protect him.

As he raced forward, Corin was focused on the centre of the enemy line. His ability to control others was feeling accessible and powerful, fuelled once again by the rage which simmered between himself and Blackpaw. Invisible tendrils were poised hungrily within his mind, ready to strike and control.

Just moments before the opposing ranks of warriors crashed together, Blackpaw surged ahead. The beast smashed into the enemy line directly in front of Corin, the impact sending a number of the Renni flying backwards. The felrin then started to savage the foes around it, in a whirlwind of deadly shredding and rending.

The screaming which resulted from this preceded a bone-shuddering clash as the opposing lines collided. Body was slammed against body, weapon against shield, axe against flesh, and there was an audible exhalation across the battlefield of released tension and aggression.

Corin was untouched by the immediate melee; as a result of Blackpaw's vicious assault, a gaping hole had opened up in the middle of the Renni line, and no enemy warriors were in Corin's close proximity. Blackpaw's beastly rage was beating across the link with Corin as the creature tore and eviscerated the unfortunate victims within its reach, further widening the breach in the enemy's ranks.

Corin breathed deeply, seeking focus within the twin tumults of the raging battle and his seething emotions. Time then decelerated about him as he accessed his powers, and the chaos of the battlefield was transformed into a slow and graceless dance of weapons and pain.

FEAR. CONTROL. ORDER.

The unlocking of his powers was once more accompanied by these words, and multiple invisible connections surged outwards from his mind. Seeking targets – *victims* – within the Renni.

Corin's powers were growing with every usage, and none of the targeted Renni warriors could resist him. Each time, the hidden tendrils surged against an enemy victim, seeking entry, and then shredded their willpower and resistance as easily as Blackpaw's claws might have torn open their bare flesh.

STOP! STOP! STOP! STOP! STOP!

It started with a handful. Then ten. Then twenty. But all around Corin the warriors of the Renni were rendered immobile, often while in the midst of mortal combat with Chosen adversaries. And as the Renni fighters' muscles locked in place, with either axes ceasing to fall towards their exposed opponents, or shields failing to rise to protect themselves, the Chosen army took advantage.

In the centre of the battle, significant numbers of Renni warriors started to die. And still, Corin felt the tendrils of his power extending further, drawing more of the Renni into his embrace, and shattering their resistance.

Corin's fury was transformed into power, and he felt vividly alive. His energy was feeding Blackpaw, and the felrin's corresponding bloodlust was energising Corin further. Blackpaw was now unleashed, charging along the rear of the Renni line in a feral frenzy of clawing and biting which was sending terror through the enemy ranks.

The battle continued to rage about Corin in slow motion, with weapons clashing and slicing, and injured men screaming. To Corin's alarm, a thrown axe whistled past his head, missing him by inches. It reminded him that he was not invulnerable, and that he could also lose his life here.

By now, Corin had taken control of over forty of the Renni. These paralysed targets had proven easy victims for their Karn and Anath opponents, and Blackpaw's actions were further decimating the Renni numbers. However, Corin was at the limit of what he was capable of within such a chaotic battlefield. A significant number of the enemy were fighting on, and too many warriors of the Chosen army were losing their lives.

Corin knew that he needed to end this, before the losses suffered on both sides were too great. He believed that the resolve of the Renni would be wavering as they witnessed the paralysis being suffered by some of their kin, and the resulting casualties. All they needed now was a forceful push.

He therefore bellowed a message from his mind which pulsed out across the battlefield. It was heard by every man there, but was focused upon each of the Renni.

FEAR ME! FEAR THE CHOSEN OF THE GODS! SURRENDER!

Corin repeated the same words over and over, bombarding their thoughts with this relentless command. He needed to break them. Needed to crush their collective spirit to fight, before the death toll in this place became catastrophic.

Blackpaw's chilling shriek was also repeated at that moment, and then Corin shouted, his voice somehow booming across the plain, 'I am the Chosen of the Gods! Surrender, or die!'

This proved to be the breaking point for the remaining Renni warriors. All along the battlefront, the Renni threw down their weapons and fell to their knees in terrified surrender.

The battle was over.

Sometime later, all of the surviving Renni warriors, with the exception of one, had been gathered into a circle. Their weapons had been confiscated, and they were being guarded by the victorious armed warriors of the Chosen clans.

Clan Chief Buljuk of the Renni stood alone, having emerged alive from the battlefield with only a minor cut on his forearm. Buljuk was an impressively robust-looking man, in his early fifties, with thick arms and a barrel-chest, and hair which was tied up in a topknot. At this moment, the Renni chief was frozen in place under Corin's control, with his jaw clamped shut such that he was rendered unable to speak.

The scene bore similarities to another encounter, almost four months earlier, when Clan Chief Rekmar of the Anath had also stood alone. Rekmar had subsequently met his excruciating end in the jaws of Blackpaw.

Indeed, Corin had instructed the felrin to prowl in front of Buljuk, just paces away. The Renni leader's message prior to the battle had indicated that he had no intention of falling foul of Corin's powers. That message, and the way that Buljuk's eyes were locked upon Blackpaw, indicated that the Renni chief was aware of the grisly demise of Rekmar. Blackpaw was staring unerringly at Buljuk, and was sitting upright, drool dripping from its red maw.

The key difference today was that Corin felt no personal animosity towards the Renni leader. True, the man and his tribe had acted as aggressors against clans with whom Corin had sworn alliance. However, there was none of the raw need for vengeance which Corin had felt towards Rekmar, none of the black grief over Agbeth which had driven Corin's grim choice on that day. Buljuk had not taken direct action to harm a member of Corin's family, and therefore Corin did not intend to end the man's life in the same horrific way that he had ended Rekmar's. However, as he approached Buljuk, he had not still not decided what the defeated chief's fate would be.

'I'm going to release my control over your ability to speak, now,' Corin said, in a low tone that only Buljuk could hear. 'I want you and I to be able to talk, Clan Chief Buljuk. But be aware that I can just as easily silence you again.'

He transmitted the instruction to the Renni Chief, who gasped as his mouth opened. Buljuk stared at Corin, but did not say anything.

'You are defeated, Clan Chief Buljuk,' said Corin. 'Your clan is defeated.'

'You tell me what I already know.' The man's voice was flat and emotionless.

'Then you also know what happened to Rekmar of the Anath.' Corin's gaze darted to Blackpaw, then back onto the Renni Chief. 'If you doubted what I am before today, do you still doubt it now?'

'You have powers. I saw that today. I heard it today. I feel it now. But that proves nothing.'

Buljuk's body was still locked in place, although Corin could feel that the man was trying to flex his arms against the invisible bonds which held them.

'I am Chosen by the Gods, Clan Chief Buljuk. You couldn't have been sure of that. But you must know it now, surely? I can control men and beasts. A felrin follows me. And I could order you to your death, right now. But I mourn the losses amongst your people today. I sought a peaceful agreement between us before the battle, and I don't want further death and bloodshed. I want peace, Buljuk, between the clans.'

'Peace is for cowards and weak men.' Buljuk hawked phlegm in his throat, and then spat forwards, though not in Corin's direction. 'Why do you tell me these things?'

'Because no one else needs to die here today, Buljuk. Kneel to me. Accept my leadership of you and the Renni. Agree to end your conflict with the Borl and the Qari, and join the Chosen Alliance. Let your people become part of five clans, working together to bring peace between us.'

Buljuk's eyes narrowed as he regarded Corin. 'I would still be Clan Chief of the Renni?'

'Yes, if you swear your oath of loyalty to me, before the Gods.'

'Then you'd be able to tell me what to do.'

'I would only encourage you to do the things which protect us all, and which make us all stronger. And would insist that you fight alongside us, when necessary, and don't fight against us.'

'But I wouldn't be clan chief, not really. Weak men like Munnik and Quan might accept this way. Not strong men like Buljuk.'

'You *would* be clan chief, Buljuk,' said Corin. 'You would have all of the honour and responsibility of that position, like Chief Munnik and Chief Quan do. The day-to-day running of the clan would continue to be yours. You would just have to accept my overall leadership over all of the clans, as the Chosen of the Gods. That's the only way that I can ensure peace between us all.'

'No.'

'Please, at least consider it.'

'No.'

'Then you'll not kneel to me?'

'I said no! What now, you feed me to the creature?'

Corin ignored the question, feeling irritated. 'You'd prefer to die, rather than surrender any part of your control over the Renni?'

'I'd rather die a free man, than live as a snivelling dog, trailing behind your ankles in fear and yapping every time that you throw me a small bone. Until today, I've been a great leader of a great clan. And I'll die that way, rather than become your slave, Corin of the Karn. So, if you're going to kill me, then fucking kill me. Our talk here is done.'

Buljuk's eyes faced forwards, away from Corin. The man looked frightened, but resolute about whatever fate was coming to him.

'Done?' repeated Corin, feeling frustrated.

He was then silent for a number of seconds, as he considered the matter. It would be of little challenge to murder Buljuk, and then to cow his people into fearful submission. To kill them one at a time, if necessary, until they were forced to appoint a leader subservient to Corin. However, Corin did not want a repeat of what had happened with Rekmar.

After an extended silence, Corin eventually stated, 'No. It's not done. Not yet. I'm not going to kill you, Buljuk. Enough people have already died here today. And I'll not keep you as a prisoner, either. I'll not cage people. Therefore, I must banish you, and any blood relatives you have. You force me to send you south, out of Renni lands.'

Buljuk was silent for a number of seconds. Corin could see the man's mouth twitching, and could observe his brows becoming furrowed in agitation. Eventually, Buljuk looked up towards Corin, and he stated, 'Not my relatives. Just me.'

'No. If you're banished, I can't have lingering hatred against me from your family. If you leave, they must all leave. Every generation. Immediately.'

There was another silence, before Buljuk added, 'They'll not all survive banishment. I have grandchildren. Just babies. And my mother, who can barely walk. There are rumours of death and war in the south, and winter's close. Leave them out of this, please.'

'It would be tragic for your family to suffer,' said Corin, his voice remaining stern though his heart was beating fast. He was bluffing, and he had no intention of banishing anyone who would not be able to survive the winter. 'But it's the choice you make, if you refuse my offer. And it's your choice, and I offer it to you again, Chief Buljuk. Kneel to me, swear an oath of loyalty before the Gods, and remain chief. And by doing that, you'll have status, and will know peace, and will protect your family. Or decline my offer, and see you and all of your kin escorted out of Renni lands today, never to be allowed to return. But I *am* done talking now, and this is the last time that I'll make this offer. Now make your choice. Will you kneel, or do you seek banishment, for you and your family?'

Buljuk looked up at Corin again. His certainty from moments earlier had been replaced by anxiety.

Eventually, the man said, 'Very well. I will kneel.'

—

Later, Corin was seated beside an evening fire, looking out across the joint celebration feast being held by the warriors of the victorious clans. Clan Chief Munnik was sitting alongside him, with an ale tankard in hand. For a number of minutes, there had been a comfortable silence between the two of them.

The surviving Renni were still being held under armed guard. Tomorrow, they would be freed, to return home under the continuing leadership of Buljuk. The Renni leader had knelt before Corin on the plain in front of his men, and before the Gods had sworn an oath of loyalty.

Clan Chiefs Munnik and Quan had already been given authority to resolve the aftermath of the battle, and to ensure that the Renni clan co-operated within the new alliance. The Renni warband had been devastated, and in the short term they were cowed, but Corin feared that there might be more trouble still to come. However, he trusted that Munnik would deal with the defeated clan in a fair and balanced way, despite the long-held enmity between the Borl and the Renni.

Corin perceived that Munnik was the person who could grow to become his true second-in-command, in the organisation and control of the expanding Chosen territory. Corin recognised and valued that Munnik was considered and deliberate in his actions, and lacked the hot temper of many of their fellow clansmen. And Munnik had great experience, being almost twenty years Corin's elder.

As Corin was thinking about this, Munnik finally broke the silence by stating, 'We all witnessed what you did today, Corin. You and the felrin. How you somehow made all those enemies freeze in place, so that they became easy prey. How you talked directly into our minds, and terrified us all. I'd heard the tales about you, and I believed them, otherwise I wouldn't have staked our clan's future on the decision to follow you. But still. To see it with our own eyes. Hear it with our own ears. Like a god walking amongst us. Chosen. There've been doubters amongst the Borl and the Qari, about the decisions we've made to follow you. But I think those doubters will make less noise now.'

Prior to these words, Corin had been feeling melancholy, but this lifted his spirits. 'Thank you, Munnik. This was as much your victory today, too. The alliance of our clans couldn't have come to be, and we couldn't have assembled here, without you. Even more importantly, you've ensured that your clan are safe from the Renni. And I thank you again for your support for me.'

Munnik reached a hand out, and placed it onto Corin's shoulder. 'There are other rumours circulating now, you know. Another name the men are calling you, other than the Chosen of the Gods.'

'Is there? What now?'

'Some of them are claiming, in the midst of their drinking, that they walk in the company of a god reborn. That there is a God in the West, and his name is Corin of the Karn. That he is Mella himself. Reborn.'

Corin laughed. 'A God in the West? I'm no god, Munnik, I can assure you of that. That I'm the Chosen of the Gods? Yes, that's true. The Gods gave me these powers, in the far north, and they visit me in my dreams. But claiming I'm an actual god, and not only that but that I'm Mella Reborn? I don't think I'm ready for taking that title, Munnik.'

Munnik laughed in return, and slapped Corin's back in a friendly manner. 'The question is not whether you're ready for that, Chief Corin. But whether you're already *becoming* that, to the men who follow you.'

—

The next day, Corin and the men of the Karn and the Anath were travelling together, returning in the direction of their villages.

Corin was in better spirits, and was feeling satisfied to see that the warriors of the two clans were intermingling as their warband returned home. The battle with the Renni had been their first experience of being blood brothers, of wielding their axes against a common enemy. It had been another significant opportunity for them all to recognise that their similarities far outweighed their differences.

The themes of unity and brotherhood had been central in Corin's mind that morning. Before everyone had departed, he had made a final speech to the gathered companies of warriors, offering words which he hoped would help to unite and inspire them.

'We are five clans now,' he had stated, before the assembled warbands. 'Five clans united under the Chosen Alliance. Karn. Anath. Borl. Qari. And now Renni. I am the Chosen of the Gods, chosen to lead this alliance. And you are all now Chosen warriors, within Chosen clans. And our clans will work together, to protect each other, and to make every one of us stronger. To protect our women, children and elders. To stop wasting the blood of our young warriors on needless raids.

'Now, let this word go out to all other surrounding clans. An attack against any one of the Chosen clans is an attack against *all* of us. We'll defend our lands, and our people, with all of our strength, and we'll destroy any aggressors. The time of raiding and conquest against these lands is over. We'll stand together, and we'll end it.

'But let this also be known. Spread the word to neighbouring clans and tribes. Any clan who wishes to join this alliance, and whose clan chief and people will accept my leadership, will be welcomed as kin. And they'll then enjoy our joint protection, and the trade and friendship that there will be between us. The Chosen Alliance will not end with just five clans. We can grow yet stronger, and there will be order, and *peace*, across this land. I am Corin of Karn, the Chosen of the Gods, and before those Gods, I swear it!'

The conclusion of the speech had not drawn cheers or hollers, but Corin knew that he had been heard and understood. They had listened to his words, they had felt his power, and they would follow him.

Agbeth had been the first to use the title "Chosen of the Gods", and although Corin had initially been reluctant to embrace the moniker, he now understood its power. It was the same point which Munnik had made the night before. Corin's titles, and his claims to power, allowed all of them to feel like they were becoming part of something bigger than petty clan rivalries. Something *destined*. And it allowed proud and strong men like Munnik and Quan to have a rationale for accepting his leadership, and for yielding what had once been unfettered power. Agbeth had seen that potential first, and her inspired words in the aftermath of Borrik's defeat had facilitated this.

Gather them.

Those other words, once spoken into an echoing void by a voice which had sounded like Agbeth's, now came into Corin's mind as he reflected on these other matters. That is what he had heard, as he had lain crying beside Agbeth's dying form. Gather them.

And he, Corin of Karn, the Chosen of the Gods, was gathering them. Gathering the clans.

Open the Gate.

He did not know where the Gate was, this place which had haunted his dreams for over two years, and which continued to trouble his sleep. But it must be in the far north. In the mountains at the end of the world, where the Gods resided. If he was to find it, he must travel there at some point. Sometime soon. Must travel further north than any living man had ever been, in order to find that Gate.

And claim the power.

What power? Powers beyond those which he already possessed? The power perhaps to restore Agbeth to what she had once been?

If there was any power in the world that could possibly return *his* Agbeth to him, then he would do all of the things which the voice had said in order to claim it, though he did not know for certain what the words meant. And indeed, in his heart, he knew that for Agbeth he would be prepared to do and sacrifice *anything* which might be required.

Agbeth.

Thinking about his wife, and her fate, suddenly soured the good mood that he had slipped into. It reminded him of what he had once had with her. And reminded him in turn of what he had lost, which more than offset what he had gained or might gain in future.

It was time to return to the village of Karn, and to the fractured soul of his wife. And to the ghost which lived in her. Time to return to the anguish which he knew would await him there.

5

Arion

―

Year of Our Lord,
After Ascension, 769AA

Arion stood alongside his brother Gerrion as the Sepian family galleon, *Star of Canasar*, entered the waters of the grand harbour of Andarron. The ship was passing slowly between the mighty, whitewashed stone walls which ran along either side of the harbour mouth. Newly installed trebuchets, scorpions and ballistae were clearly visible on those seaward walls, many of which were aimed towards the narrow passage of water through which the Sepian vessel was now sailing.

The two brothers were at the prow of the boat, holding onto wooden railings as their ship rocked in the choppy sea. Icy, wintry winds from the west blew across their faces, misting their breath.

'So, here we go, Arion,' said the older brother. 'Into the hornets' nest. I wish that just once I could visit this place without the threat of invasion looming over me.'

'I know,' said Arion, nodding. 'In fact, better that we didn't have to come here at all.'

'Or, at least, that father was with us,' replied Gerrion. 'I know that we're coping since his death, but this is one of the occasions when I truly wish that he was still with us. Advising us, and giving his private counsel to Inneos.'

'Can't you speak to the king in private, Gerr?'

Gerrion shook his head. 'No. Father had the king's ear in a way I can never hope to, given our age difference. If he were here, Father would've already been told what the king's intentions are, and would have privately advised against any poor decisions. I'm going to hear whatever Inneos has to say at the same time as the other dukes. And too late to try to change his mind, other than in public.'

There had been no news or intelligence about what King Inneos was going to announce. During the week-long journey by sea, Gerrion had speculated that the noble houses might have been summoned to discuss a change of law, or to explain the expulsion of Aiduel's Guards. Another possibility, more ominous, was that the king might be gathering his dukes for a council of war. But the elder Sepian brother kept returning to the alternative which he felt was the most likely; King Inneos intended to announce that Andar was breaking off from the Holy Church in Sen Aiduel.

'But I still trust that you'll be able to influence him, Gerr,' said Arion. 'Even if it's in public.'

Gerrion shrugged, before saying, 'I'm not so sure.'

Their galleon was turning towards the long quay which bisected the Andarron harbour. As the ship closed with the quay, Gerrion said, 'You're to stay with me for the next two days until the council, Arion. The dockside area here is even rowdier than Septholme's, by reputation. Before The Lord, there's no way I'm letting you head out at night into this city, to get up to whatever it is that you get up to, and expose yourself to another assassination attempt.'

'I've no intention of going anywhere, Gerr,' said Arion. 'Just planning to stay near you until the Council begins.'

He still felt ashamed of his actions of three weeks earlier, and he understood the need for his brother's caution. The Septholme garrison had not tracked down the team of assassins in the aftermath of the attack. One badly decomposed corpse had been found after a week, stuffed into a barrel, which Arion had identified as one of the two bowmen. The rest of the attackers had vanished, and had not been found despite extensive searches by Andar guardsmen.

Arion was still worried about the way that his powers had diminished to almost nothing during the course of the attack. After Moss Ford, he had begun to believe that he was close to invincible, but he knew now that he was vulnerable to at least one enemy. Could that person be intending to come after him again?

'And there'll be no drinking in our inn, either,' said Gerrion, as their ship drew alongside the quay.

'I understand, Gerr,' said Arion. 'And as *you* know, I've kept my promise and I've not been drinking. Don't worry. I'm not about to start again here, with everything else that's going on.'

Arion had not touched any alcohol since the night at *The Hungry Gull*. Kalyane had made that a condition of forgiving him, and he had agreed to it as part of his attempt to reconcile with her.

'Good,' said Gerrion. 'We'll head to our inn as soon as we can. I've a local agent to meet later, to see if we can glean any more information. Lord knows, we need it.'

―

Gerrion had reserved an entire upper floor in a rich tavern in the merchant quarter of Andarron, just half a mile away from the Royal Palace. Arion and his brother each had their own room, with a third room stuffed full with their accompaniment of guards and retainers. Two guardsmen were also permanently on duty in the corridor outside of their quarters, which gave Arion a sense of security when he reached his own room.

That first night, he was tired from the journey, and he settled down to sleep easily. The entire next day of waiting was then uneventful, and yielded no new information about the king's intentions.

However, on the second night in the tavern, for the first time in several months, Arion was visited by a very different type of dream…

—

He was sprinting up a spiralling stone staircase, in murky, candlelit light. He was moving urgently, his feet taking three steps at a time. It was disconcerting to be bounding upwards like this, without any discernible control over the motions of his body.

His focus was on reaching the top of this narrow spiral of steps. There was a dim light at the top, glimmers shining through the open door which now came into view. He somehow knew that he had to move faster, and that he was running out of time.

He charged through the doorway, and emerged into a corridor which was illuminated by occasional candles in sconces on the walls. It took a moment to register where he was in the flickering half-light, and then it came to him; the Royal Palace of Andarron. He had been here before, and he recognised the lavish paintings and decor which adorned the corridor walls. But where in that palace?

Then he realised. This long passageway ended with the private chambers of the two princes, Senneos and Sendar. He had been here once, as a guest of his friend.

At that moment, he noted that he was gripping a sword, and there was blood on the blade. Feeling more urgency, he started to sprint down the corridor. Through windows on his left, he could see that it was night-time outside, with hundreds of scattered lights illuminating the vast skyline of the city of Andarron.

And then the sounds reached him.

Fighting. The noises of battle. Swords clashing and men cursing. He remembered that the princes' bedrooms were located around a cul-de-sac at the end of the corridor, and he raced in that direction. He reached their rooms, as the sounds of conflict increased in volume and intensity.

Two figures, Andar guardsmen, lay dead in twin pools of blood on the corridor floor. The facing doors to either side of these victims were both open. He could remember that he had once visited the room on the left; Prince Sendar's room. But the noise of fighting seemed to be coming from the right.

He paused for a moment, his heart beating, and raised his sword. He then moved towards the open doorways…

―

When he awoke from sleep, his heart was pounding and he felt restless. The vivid quality of the dream was instantly recognisable.

He had experienced three other dreams of this nature; the boats on the beach at Fort Lennis, the armies crossing the river at Moss Ford, and the dream of Leanna approaching the pyre. Each of those dreams had come to pass, and had been proven to be prophecies of what was still to come. However, with hindsight, he realised that the visions had cast shadows over the future truth. He had misinterpreted the precise meaning of the latter two dreams, almost fatally in Leanna's case.

He considered preparing and arming himself, then dashing to the castle. He was already out of bed and was getting dressed before he noticed that the half-light of dawn had crept into the bedroom. This observation acted to soothe his sense of urgency; the events in the dream had taken place in the darkness of night-time, and if it was an occurrence of this past night, he could do nothing about it now.

More likely, the dream was another premonition of an event which was still to come, in the midst of another night. There was going to be an attack on the palace, which appeared to target the two heirs to the throne.

He would need to speak to Sendar.

―

Later that morning, at eleventh hour, Arion and his brother arrived at the Royal Palace of Andarron, for the council convened by King Inneos, ruler of Andar.

The two of them were escorted through to the same great meeting room which Arion had visited two years earlier, when he had first met the senior members of the royal family. On that occasion, Arion had still been a cadet at the Royal Academy of Knights, and his late father, Duke Conran, had been a crucial participant in the meeting.

The room was bustling with far more people this time. The grand table had also been enlarged in size; Arion could see three seats at either end, including a larger central throne at one of those ends. Along each side, eight chairs had been set out.

Arion followed behind Gerrion as they moved into the room, and he was relieved to see his brother heading in the direction of Duke Kalion Rednar, Kalyane's father. Standing with the portly duke was Lord Ronian Rednar, the eldest son and heir of that noble house.

After initial greetings, the elder Rednar eyed Arion in a friendly manner and said, 'Ah! My son-in-law. I hope that you're treating my daughter well?'

'Yes, of course,' replied Arion, hoping that he was not blushing.

As Gerrion then started to talk with Duke Rednar, Arion took stock of the other attendees in the room.

There were many important people there already. He first noted Archprime Amnar, head of the Holy Church within Andar. She was accompanied by two other individuals attired in holy vestments, the three of them clustered together in apparent nervous conversation.

Arion felt a jolt of dark emotion as his eyes moved to Amnar's right, and he spotted the enormous figure of Duke Jarrett Berun. Almost two years had passed since their last encounter, and Berun appeared to have become even bulkier, his dark beard thicker on his jaw. Seeing his rival again reminded Arion of the personal animosity which had existed between them at the Academy. He could also not forget that Berun had deliberately refrained from providing assistance to Western Canasar during the Elannis invasion.

Jarrett Berun was talking with a short and skinny man in his fifties, who had thinning, grey hair and a neat goatee beard. Arion did not recognise this individual, whose clothing was flamboyant and clearly expensive.

'That's Duke Orlen Condarr, head of the House of Condarr,' stated Ronian Rednar, who had moved alongside Arion. 'No surprise to see the devout brotherhood talking together. No doubt we'll be hearing his views on the expulsion, before too long.'

Arion nodded whilst scrutinising the elegantly dressed man. Condarron was the major city halfway along the coast between Andarron and Rednarron, and traditionally there had been close connections between the Berun and Condarr houses. House Condarr was reputed to be the second wealthiest of any of the noble families, after the Pavils themselves.

Arion and Ronian proceeded to talk together for a few minutes. During this time, they also identified the leading members of the relatively minor Dunark, Cendun and Rowarth noble houses. Between them, these families controlled the more remote northern and westerly territories within Andar.

The chatter in the room was interrupted eventually by a resounding shout from a palace retainer, who was standing by the main entrance door.

'His Royal Majesty King Inneos, Her Highness Queen Mariess, and His Highness Prince Sendar!'

The three members of the ruling Pavil royal family entered the chamber, their arrival being accompanied by a trailing off of any lingering conversation. Arion was reminded anew of the graceful beauty of the queen as she crossed the room, although he forced himself not to stare.

His eyes then found and locked with those of his friend Sendar, but the prince had a sour expression on his face and swiftly looked away. Arion knew that he would need to catch-up with his former room-mate before leaving here, although he was not yet sure how he would broach the subject of the dream. He also wondered where Prince Senncos was.

King Inneos paused a couple of metres from his own oversized chair, and stated, 'Nobles, friends, lords and ladies! Please, take a seat, we've much to discuss.'

The three royal family members seated themselves at one end of the table, with Archprime Amnar and her two colleagues taking the other end. The other attendees, two from each noble house plus two royal dignitaries, claimed all of the remaining chairs. Arion was seated at the end of the table's length, with Gerrion on his left, and the three Holy Church attendees on his right. Arion glanced across at Amnar, and he could see droplets of perspiration on the petite woman's forehead.

When everyone was settled in place, Inneos began to speak. 'Friends! My countrymen of Andar. Thank you all for being here today. We meet, at my behest, but sadly not in pleasant circumstances. As you'll all be aware, these have been unsettling times recently, and I'm afraid they could possibly become much more difficult in future. That's why I wanted to call you all here. Firstly, to explain why I took the recent action I did with Aiduel's Guards. And secondly, to talk about what the future now holds for us all, in relation to the Holy Church.'

Jarrett Berun was sitting on the opposite side of the table, and Arion noted his rival frowning in reaction to the last words.

'The decree against Aiduel's Guards,' continued Inneos, 'expelling their forces from this country. Why did I order that, you may ask? Why antagonise the Archlaw and the High Council of the Holy Church? I'll tell you why. *Elannis invaded us, and received no meaningful censure from that Church!* Their troops crossed our borders, burned our villages, took our stores, and killed our people, and they received no punishment!

'Before that, during my lifetime, Elannis has invaded and conquered Patran. They've invaded and conquered Sennam. And each time, the High Council in Sen Aiduel finds a reason to excuse their actions and to forgive them. However, if the people of Andar were to strike against Elannis, if our troops were pouring across *their* borders and killing *their* people, how quickly do you think the Archlaw would then issue an edict to condemn us? How soon until we'd receive a threat of excommunication?

'It pains me to say it, but we live in a world where there's no impartiality from the Holy Church in Sen Aiduel. The High Council and the Archlaw care about Dei Magnus and Elannis. The interests of Andar have been disregarded repeatedly, and will continue to be disregarded until we're all vassals of the Archlaw and the Emperor!'

Lord preserve us, thought Arion. *He's shouting at us all!*

The king's voice had been rising in volume throughout his speech, reaching heated levels by the end. He was interrupted by Duke Orlen Condarr, who was sitting two places away from Jarrett Berun.

'We should be careful of such talk in public, Your Majesty,' said the well-dressed man, in a soft and calm voice. 'As we all know, the Archlaw and the High Council are Aiduel's chosen mortal agents in this world. He acts through them, and they carry out His will. To question their actions openly like this, and to assign base partisan motives to those actions, could be deemed… blasphemous, by some.'

'We're not in public, Orlen,' replied the king, his voice frosty. 'You're attending a meeting of my senior nobles and advisers, and are in my palace, and everything said here will be kept as confidential or otherwise as I want it to be. And I'm stating truths, not blasphemies! But I'd warn you, *Duke*, not to interrupt me again until I've finished. You'll get your opportunity to speak here today, but only when I say so. Is that understood?'

Arion watched Duke Condarr bend his head in apparent silent deference, the man's expression unreadable. However, at the head of the table, Arion could clearly perceive the discomfort on Sendar Pavil's face. Once again, Sendar's father was sounding petulant.

'As I was saying,' continued the king, 'we live in a world where Elannis may attack us without fear of retribution, but we may not strike back. Two years ago, the Emperor of Elannis threatened to claim sovereignty over Western Canasar, with the support of the

Archlaw. As part of that discussion, my friends, we were again threatened with excommunication! But we rebutted that claim, although the hefty price for doing so, negotiated by my great friend, the late Duke Conran Sepian, was the acceptance of Aiduel's Guards.'

As the monarch said this latter part, he inclined his head in the direction of Gerrion, who nodded in return.

'We did not want Aiduel's Guards in numbers in this country,' said Inneos, 'but we accepted it as part of a settlement to preserve unity with Archlaw Paulius and the Holy Church in Sen Aiduel. We made *all* the concessions, in an attempt to preserve peace and trust. However, the invasion by Elannis, and the refusal of the Church to censure or punish, has shattered that peace. It has destroyed the fragile trust between us.'

Inneos paused and stared around the room, his lips pursed together, his eyes seeming to search for objection to his statements. Everyone else remained silent, mindful of the admonishment which Duke Orlen Condarr had received moments earlier.

'*That* is why I ordered the banishment of Aiduel's Guards from these lands!' shouted the king. 'If I'd done nothing, they'd have seen me as weak, and I'll not show weakness to that bastard Paulius!'

After Inneos said this, there were gasps from the four Berun and Condarr attendees, and noises of dismay from Amnar and her colleagues. Arion looked along the table and he could see Queen Mariess leaning in to whisper something to the red-faced king, while placing her palm onto her husband's arm. However, Inneos shook her hand off and he moved his head away.

By the Lord, he looks so petulant again!

Archprime Amnar spoke up, her voice hesitant. 'Your Majesty. Please excuse me, but we have many devout people in this room. Please, may we keep this discourse civil?'

Inneos glowered at her from under furrowed brows, and Arion wondered whether the monarch was going to explode in an outburst of fury at the diminutive woman.

However, after a few moments Inneos nodded politely. In a calmer voice, he said, 'I wrote to the Archlaw at the time of my decision. I explained that once we witnessed suitable punishment against Emperor Jarrius and Prince Markon, we'd be receptive to the reinstatement of Aiduel's Guards. My explanation and rationale for this request was entirely fair and reasonable.

'Indeed, I summoned you all here today to explain that decision, and to have a more general discussion about our future military and religious plans as a nation, including how we might respond to the growing threat from Elannis. That was my original intention for this meeting. However, as I'll explain, the Archlaw's response to me has changed *everything*.

'His answer came three days ago, almost as quickly as messengers could possibly have delivered it. He must have decided his response within days, if not hours. And, as I said, that response has changed everything. The Archlaw has issued me with an ultimatum; reinstate Aiduel's Guards throughout the country of Andar, within thirty days, without any condition or restriction imposed, or every member of the Pavil family is to be excommunicated. *That* was his answer to me. He will not punish the leaders of Elannis, for their great crimes. He will not threaten *them*. No, none of those things. But he threatens me! He would punish *my* family!'

There was silence for a few seconds, and Arion was surprised when Jarrett Berun asked, '*Just* the Pavil family, Your Majesty? Not the other noble houses?'

The king glared at Berun in response, as Sendar Pavil replied, 'Yes, Jarrett. Just the Pavil family.'

'That's irrelevant though,' added Inneos. 'The Archlaw has finally crossed a line which I've been fearing he might cross for many years now. He seeks to make himself pre-eminent to my authority as monarch, within Andar. He doesn't ask this thing of me. He *demands* it. He *orders* me. And he claims the authority to expel me and my family from heaven, and from Aiduel's Holy Light, if I don't bow down to his wishes.'

'He *has* that authority, Your Majesty,' stated Duke Orlen Condarr in a low voice. 'Over me. Over you. Over all of us.'

'So says he,' replied Inneos.

'So says holy scripture!' barked Condarr, his voice more heated this time.

'Stop trying to undermine me!' shouted the monarch. 'I'm King of Andar, not you. Now let me finish!'

Arion observed as Duke Condarr leaned back in his chair and folded his arms, following which the small duke glanced towards Jarrett Berun.

Inneos continued speaking, his voice still raised. 'The Archlaw's letter to me, this *ultimatum*, has brought to a head a matter I've been considering for three years now. That I've been thinking about and preparing for, for all of that time. I was dissuaded by honestly given counsel the last time I considered this, two years ago. But no more.

'I'll no longer answer to the whims of the Archlaw, the High Council and the Holy Church in Dei Magnus. This country will no longer be beholden to an institution which is in the pocket of Elannis and Dei Magnus, and which has an interest in seeing Andar decline and fail.

'Therefore, I'm proud to declare my ruling that, as of Seventh-Day this week, the Holy Church of Andar will no longer recognise the authority of Sen Aiduel. Or the High Council. Or the Archlaw. As of Seventh-Day, the Holy Church of Andar is to become a separate institut-'

'That's sacrilege!' bellowed Duke Condarr, as he stood up. 'You have no authority to do-'

'Silence, Orlen!' Inneos shouted in response, as he also lurched to his feet and slammed his fist down onto the table. 'Shut your fucking mouth and sit down! I have *every* authority. The Holy Church of Andar *is* to become a separate institution. Archprime Amnar will become the senior religious figure within that Holy Church, and the new Head of that church shall be whomsoever reigns as the monarch of Andar.'

'You appoint yourself to this role?' asked Condarr. 'You'd make yourself Archlaw as well as a king?'

The small duke's tone was derisive as he said these words. Arion's heart was beating fast as he waited for the next explosive outburst from Inneos.

Lord preserve us! It feels like there's going to be violence here!

'Your Majesty, is there no hope of reconciliation with the Holy Church?' said Gerrion suddenly, before Inneos could react to Duke Condarr's insulting tone. 'No route through this which might secure peace, like we achieved two years ago?'

Inneos focused his eyes towards Gerrion, but the monarch then shook his head, his tone more conciliatory. 'I'm beyond words of reconciliation and peace, Duke Gerrion. We've tried that, and in return they've abused our goodwill, yet again. If not for your brother here, our Hero of Moss Ford, we could've lost Canasar already. But he proved to us that every Andar man is worth three of the enemy! Shall we choose this moment now, after crushing the Elannis armies, to show strength? Or shall we meekly bow our heads and await the countless humiliations which will follow? Shall we allow them to make us too weak to resist, when the crucial moment comes?'

There was silence in response, until Duke Rednar spoke up, his manner equally conciliatory. 'Your Majesty, I'm a simple man, with simple pursuits. I'm not an expert on religious matters, and I know little about the intricacies of holy scripture. Perhaps Archprime Amnar could explain to us *her* views on this, to clarify matters while we all adjust ourselves to this… *surprising* news. How such a thing as breaking off from Sen Aiduel might practically work, and what it might mean for our eternal souls?'

Queen Mariess nodded, then said, 'Yes, that sounds like a very good idea, Duke Kalion.' She again reached a hand out, and gently placed it over her husband's right forearm. 'Why don't we all listen to what Amnar has to say about this?'

The king flinched, then glanced across at his wife with an annoyed expression on his face. However, after a moment he stated, 'Very well, Amnar. Proceed.'

In the hour that followed, Archprime Amnar gave her views on the king's intentions, and she answered numerous questions from around the table. During this time, Amnar provided a number of explanations about the religious consequences of what they were doing. Arion noted that her stated opinions were generally consistent with what she had expressed two years earlier in this same room, at the meeting which Duke Conran had led. However, she withheld some of the stronger objections which she had shared then.

It was obvious to Arion that the dukes of Condarr and Berun were the most visibly upset by Inneos's plan. The comments of houses Sepian, Rednar, Cendun and Rowarth indicated that they were not openly opposed to the prospect, although none of them voiced support. The duke of House Dunark was silent throughout.

'And so, that's the ceremony we'll hold this coming Seventh-Day,' stated Amnar, as she concluded her final explanation of the expected process. Arion could hear a tremor in the woman's voice, and she appeared on the edge of tears. 'The monarch shall be appointed and recognised as head of this new Holy Church of Andar. Andar's institution of the Church shall thereafter no longer be subject to the instructions and orders from Sen Aiduel.'

There was silence for a number of seconds, before Jarrett Berun spoke up.

'I've heard all of Archprime Amnar's words,' said the giant duke. 'And I thank her for the detailed explanations that she's given. But – and I say this without disrespect to her venerable position – her words feel to me like they're just that. Hollow words. Her own opinions. Opinions, to cast off centuries of recognition of the Archlaw and Sen Aiduel. In my view, an equally valid opinion is that we'll all be excommunicated if we do this. That we'll be cut-off from the Holy Church, from The Lord Aiduel and from heaven. From Aiduel's Holy Light.'

Arion noted that there was no heat in the large duke's voice, just a trace of fear which seemed genuine.

'Amnar already covered that,' replied King Inneos. 'Our eternal souls are protected, Duke Berun. We're not turning our backs on or being cut-off from Aiduel or from heaven. We're merely removing ourselves from subservience to the High Council and in particular to the Archlaw. We'll not bow our necks to him any longer.'

'So you say, Your Majesty,' answered Duke Condarr, calmly. 'But it will be a personal decision for everyone in this room as to whether they accept Amnar's interpretation. And there will be uproar in the land. This is a terrible decision. A *terrible* decision. You must see that, surely? It will make this country a target for Elannis and Dei Magnus, and for anyone else who wants to take up arms for the Holy Church. Paulius will excommunicate us all and will declare a crusade against us. This decision will ruin every man and woman in this room. This country will fall. I beg you, King Inneos, please reconsider.'

'I second that. This should not happen,' stated Jarrett Berun, the crease of a frown on his forehead. He then looked around the table, his dark eyes focusing in turn upon Duke Rednar and Gerrion. 'We would be committing an awful sin against The Lord Aiduel. If others agree, then speak up now, please. Or let your silence forever rot within your conscience.'

Arion glanced towards Gerrion as Berun was making this statement, and he saw his brother make a small, almost imperceptible, nod.

By the Lord, just what is Inneos unleashing here?

However, before Gerrion or anyone else could object further, the monarch shouted, 'I didn't ask for a vote on this! I didn't ask for your opinions, or for your permission! I am your king, and you've all sworn fealty to me! I am talking to you to tell you what's been decided. You will all attend the Cathedral of Andarron on Seventh-Day, and you will all watch and support me as I'm anointed as the Head of the Holy Church of Andar.

'If Elannis rises up in response, then we'll smash them as we've already smashed them! One man of Andar is worth three of them! And then we'll be free of the Archlaw's malign influence, once and for all. And if any man here doesn't give me his support, he'll find himself rotting in a dungeon before I let him speak against me further!'

The king's face was red, and as the ruler said these last words his eyes were locked on Duke Orlen Condarr.

The small duke held the monarch's stare for a handful of seconds, but then merely bowed his head and said, 'Very well, Your Majesty. I've shared my views, and I'll state them no more. As a loyal subject of Andar and of the crown, I'll be there to witness your... ceremony, on Seventh-Day.'

This declaration set off a series of concurring statements from around the table, including from Gerrion and Jarrett Berun. As this was happening, Arion glanced across at Archprime Amnar.

This time, he noted that there was indeed a tear forming in her left eye.

—

After the meeting had ended, and the participants were beginning to disperse, Arion sought out Sendar Pavil.

Sendar's expression was as grim as it had been prior to the meeting, but the blonde-haired prince forced a smile onto his face as Arion drew near. He placed a hand onto Arion's upper arm, steering them both away from the other parties around them.

Sendar glanced towards the king, who was leaving the room, and then commented quietly, 'Not the outcome any of us were hoping for today, other than my father. If the intention of the Archlaw's letter and threat was to goad Father into taking reckless action, then it worked completely.'

'You think this is a mistake, too?'

'By the Lord, Arion, everyone around that table considers it a mistake. It's a disaster. Senneos and Father are barely speaking, and

Mother and I had a heated argument with him last night, trying to dissuade him from this course. This will bring war, and worse. We'll lose Angloss's support, and there's so much that's uncertain now. How quickly will the Archlaw and the Emperor move against us? Will we just be fighting Elannis, or will Dei Magnus join in too?' He then leaned in close to Arion, and while looking towards the dukes of Condarr and Berun, he whispered, 'And after today, can we even be sure that every noble house of Andar will stay loyal to the crown?'

'Really?' said Arion. 'I know I've made comments about Jarrett in the past, but do you really think that-'

'Who knows? But let's not voice further accusations in this room. However, we must all prepare for war, now. Father has made damn sure of that.'

Arion had never seen Sendar looking so agitated, and it made him even more uncomfortable about discussing his dream from the night before. However, the vision had suggested a potential threat against the two royal princes, and Arion knew that he must mention it.

'Sendar, where's your brother, Prince Senneos?'

Sendar's eyes narrowed. 'He's away from the city. He left following an argument with Father. Why do you ask?'

Arion blushed. 'I'm just worried. With these decisions being taken. That there could be threats against... the royal family.'

Sendar stared at him. 'There might always be threats against us. Do you have some specific information about a threat against us, Arion?'

'No. No, nothing specific. Just, with what just happened in here, you know.'

Arion felt frustrated; he could not talk about the particular details of the threat with Sendar, without mentioning that the source was his dream.

'Arion, I know you well, and I trust you. But you're lying to me right now. I can tell, because you're a very bad liar. You *are* aware of a specific threat against us. What is it?'

Arion was silent for a few seconds, considering. He could not in good conscience keep his knowledge to himself, but how could he explain it to Sendar without appearing crazy?

'You're right,' he said. 'There is something. But if I tell you, I need your promise that it stays between us. Please?'

'Unless I have to disclose it for the good of the kingdom, then yes, you have my word.'

'Well, do you remember at Moss Ford, how I anticipated the enemy's action?'

'Of course, yes, I do. Father has mentioned it multiple times in just the last few days.'

'I didn't just anticipate it. I dreamt it. In advance.'

Lord preserve us, I sound ridiculous.

Sendar had a look of incredulity on his face. 'Is this a joke, Arion?'

'No, no joke. If you doubt me, ask Gerrion. I told him, a few days before the battle. I sometimes have visions – *dreams* – of events, which happen in the future.'

Sendar's expression softened. 'Visions? Very well. Say I believe you, or just want to humour you. What exactly have you dreamt?'

Arion proceeded to tell his friend about the dream, including the details of the dead guards and the sounds of battle from the royal bedroom.

At the end of this, Sendar looked ill-at-ease, and said, 'And you say that this feels like the other dream? The battle at the ford?'

'Yes. Exactly the same.'

'And it means that you'll be here, when it happens?'

'I think so, yes, but I can't be sure. Me telling you this might even change how events are going to occur, or it might never happen. But look, please just indulge me on this. Double the guards on your corridor. Bolt your door. Keep your weapon near to yourself. Be alert. Please, do all of this for me.'

'And you say that my door was open, but that the fighting was in Senneos's room?'

'Yes, it was. At least, I think so.'

'Well, if that's the case, then we at least have some time before this threat might manifest itself. Senneos will be away in the country for at least a few weeks. And Arion?'

'Yes?'

'I'm still not sure whether I fully believe this. Therefore, please keep this between us, lest anyone thinks we've both gone mad. But I'll do the things you ask, and I'll warn my brother when he returns. If someone does decide to come for me and Senneos, then they'll not find us easy targets.'

—

Later that week, on Seventh-Day, Arion was amongst the throng of important nobles, clergymen, dignitaries and soldiers gathered inside the vast Cathedral of Andarron. Within the walls of that magnificent location, he bore witness to the elaborate ceremony which formally broke the country of Andar away from the religious dominion of the Holy Church in Sen Aiduel.

Throughout the ceremony, King Inneos sat on a throne in front of the ornate main altar, with rays of coloured light shining down upon him through towering stained-glass windows. A massive and ornate statue of The Lord Aiduel On The Tree sat on the altar directly behind the throne, and from a distance the king's chair and the statue seemed to merge into one.

Queen Mariess and Prince Sendar were standing near to the monarch, but the royal heir Prince Senneos did not appear to be in attendance. Archprime Amnar led the formal rites, her voice more confident and authoritative in this setting than Arion had previously witnessed.

At the end of the ceremony, Inneos left his chair and knelt before the Archprime, in front of the altar. The king loudly reaffirmed his devotion to Aiduel, and repeated his oaths of rulership over Andar.

After the monarch had concluded, Amnar stated, 'Before The

Lord Aiduel, I proclaim you Head and Protector of the Holy Church of Andar. May you lead us wisely, in the Grace of Aiduel.'

The Archprime finally placed a golden statue of The Lord Aiduel On The Tree on the monarch's neck, completing the ceremony. Coinciding with this action, a choir of voices at the front of the cathedral soared into song, proclaiming the completion of the momentous event.

As this happened, Gerrion leaned across to Arion, and whispered, 'Mark this moment, brother. Father will be turning in his grave, right now. We'll all be paying for Inneos's mistake, for years to come.'

Arion felt queasy inside after hearing these words, for he knew them to be true. Messengers would be riding forth from Andarron today, heading in all directions across the land, and spreading word of the deed. Eventually, that news would pass beyond Andar's borders, and would reach Elannis and Dei Magnus.

And after that, Arion felt certain, there would be a response.

6

Leanna

—

*Year of Our Lord,
After Ascension, 769AA*

In the aftermath of the Archlaw's letter, Leanna soon became aware that there was much consternation within the city of Arlais. The message of the Archlaw's Herald had been repeated to the crowds in the town square, and the announcement had also been posted onto a number of public buildings. Within a matter of hours, the words of the Archlaw were known to almost every citizen of the city. In response, there was a buzz of agitation across Arlais, as people discussed the meaning and the potential threat within those words.

The herald had also approached Leanna after the Seventh-Day service, and had given her a separate letter, adding briefly, "This is intended just for you."

The letter had read:

Dear Priestess Leanna, Angel of Arlais,

May Aiduel's Love be with you.

I shall be arriving in Arlais in the early hours of Fifth-Day, accompanied by no more than ten Guardsmen. I wish to arrive unnoticed and without fanfare, and to meet you at Arlais Cathedral at eighth hour that morning.

Please rest assured of my goodwill and good faith in our coming meeting. To start, I will want to discuss with you the arrangements for the peaceful entry to the city of the thousand Aiduel's Guards who will be travelling from Boralais. As part of which, I intend to outline the expected process for the reclamation of their property from any vigilante elements.

Following this, I would like to share more details about the great honours which the Archlaw wishes to bestow upon you, and to make arrangements for your journey with me to Sen Aiduel. After our meeting concludes, I will be returning to the camp of Aiduel's Guards, which by then will be on the south-east approaches to the city. I intend to give you time after the meeting to contemplate what we have discussed, so please do not worry that I will be requiring you to depart with me immediately. I will not insist upon that.

Please do not fear our meeting, Priestess Leanna, but if it puts you at ease, feel free to also be accompanied by ten armed guards. I think that our discussions will be more productive if conducted without the spectacle of crowds outside, so I would also ask for your discretion in sharing the details of the time of our meeting. Acting High Priest El'Patriere will be aware of these arrangements, and shall host the meeting for us within the sacred walls of the cathedral.

My heart and soul leap with excitement at the thought of meeting you, Angel of Arlais, and of soon being witness to your miracles.

Go in the Grace of Aiduel,

Yours with love and esteem,

Archprime Meira dei Corsi, Member of the High Council

—

As she lay in bed that Seventh-Day night, Leanna was still contemplating the implications of the Archlaw's announcement, and of dei Corsi's accompanying letter. Sleep was eluding her, and a restless Amyss was tossing and turning under the bedsheets next to her.

Eventually, Leanna announced into the darkness, 'I think that I must give myself over to them.'

Amyss's hand reached out to find Leanna's. 'You don't have to decide anything yet, Lea. We have until Fifth-Day to think about this.'

'They've brought an army, Amyss. They intend to claim me.'

Amyss was silent for a few seconds, before she said, 'The people of Arlais won't allow it, if you don't want to go. They'll defend you. You know that. The militia will fight for you. They'll all fight to keep you here.'

'I know they will. And that's the problem, isn't it? If I ask them to defend me, I'll cause even more deaths. Bad enough all the suffering that I caused at the pyre. But at least that was the choice of The Lord, acting through me. But if I bring an army of Aiduel's Guards down upon the city, that will be *my* decision. Risking other people's lives, just to protect myself.'

'After everything that's happened, Lea, this offer doesn't feel right. The Archlaw's promises don't ring true. I just don't trust them.'

'Nor do I.'

Lord Aiduel, please forgive me for doubting the words of the leader of your Holy Church.

'Then, please don't rush into giving yourself over to them, Lea!' implored Amyss. 'Please. But anyway, you don't have to decide yet. You – *we* – have until Fifth-Day to decide.'

Leanna could recognise the desperation in Amyss's voice, and she understood the priestess's reason for trying to delay a resolution.

By putting the decision off for another four or five days, Amyss could seek to preserve the fragile pretence that they could maintain their current life here.

Leanna did not have the heart to disillusion her companion. 'You're right,' she said. 'We don't have to decide yet. Please, come and hold me.'

Amyss slid across to do as she was asked. 'Whatever happens, Lea. Whatever you now decide. I'll be at your side. You know that, don't you?'

'I do know that, Amyss. And I thank The Lord that you're with me.'

'Then let's talk about this tomorrow. Tonight, we still have this. Here. Just the two of us. Together.'

—

The next day, Leanna arranged a meeting with a small group of her closest advisers; Amyss, Sister Colissa, Priestess Corenna and Lorth Dormer. The purpose was to discuss how they were going to react to the Archlaw's words.

'We all knew that this could happen, eventually,' Leanna stated, at the start of the discussion. 'We knew that at some point it was possible that Aiduel's Guards would return, and that the Church would reassert its authority. And now we face it. What do you all think that we should do?'

Priestess Corenna answered first. 'We must accept the Archlaw's words, Leanna, and we should welcome this approach. What other choice is there? His Eminence has spoken, and he's recognised the grievous sins committed by Aiduel's Guards. He's promised to protect you, and to make you a *Living Saint*. What an incredible honour for you and for this College! It will be a wrench for all of us to lose you from Arlais, but you *must* go to Sen Aiduel.'

Amyss could be heard to tut in response to this, but it was Sister Colissa who said, 'Your faith in the Archlaw does you credit,

Corenna. But we mustn't forget what Aiduel's Guards did to this city. What they attempted to do to Leanna. Are we really ready to see her handed over to them again? Are we ready to trust that they'll obey the Archlaw's instruction to act as Leanna's honour guard? That they'll protect her?'

'Absolutely not!' stated Amyss, her tone abruptly as fiery as her hair. 'I've no trust in that at all. They're all murderers!'

'You both talk as if we have a choice in this,' said Corenna, the plump grey-haired woman looking in challenge towards Colissa and Amyss. 'But a thousand Aiduel's Guards are coming towards this city. What would you have us do?'

'We could simply say "no" to their approach,' said Amyss. 'If Leanna was to decline their offer, do we really believe that Archprime dei Corsi would unleash a thousand soldiers in an attack against the city? That they might be willing to have that much bloodshed – of *Elannis* citizens – on their hands?'

'And if we do say "no", but they call our bluff, and decide to march upon the city, what would you then have us do, Amyss?' asked Corenna. 'Resist them? Fight them?'

'Yes, resist, if we need to,' said Amyss. 'Fight to the last person, if we need to, rather than put Leanna into their hands!'

'Amyss, please,' said Leanna, softly. 'You know that I'll never allow the people of this city to die on my behalf. That's my very last option.'

'Even if they all begged to defend you, Leanna?' asked Amyss. She locked eyes with Leanna as she said this, an unspoken plea in her expression. Leanna could feel the love and frustration pulsing out from the red-headed priestess.

'Even then, Amyss,' replied Leanna, her voice deliberately gentle.

'Please, may I offer my thoughts?' asked Lorth Dormer. Leanna nodded in assent, before the soldier continued. 'For me, this is a simple matter. I'll do whatever the Angel of Arlais asks of me, and I'll direct the militia to do whatever she asks of them. If that's to fight to the last man to protect her and the city, then we'll do that. If it's to disperse or surrender, if it ensures Priestess Leanna's safety, then we'll also do that. And if she tells us that she intends to go to Sen Aiduel, we'll seek to travel with her, to protect her.

'But I'd remind everyone, including the Angel, that Aiduel's Guards were going to burn her alive. In my opinion, it would be a naive mistake to walk with blind faith into their camp, and to trust only in their goodwill for protection. A fatal mistake.'

'But the Archlaw has offered his assurance of Leanna's safety,' said Priestess Corenna. 'And that assurance has been broadcast to every citizen of Arlais. And a senior member of the High Council is coming here, in person. If the Archlaw truly has malign intentions and plans to just kill Leanna, then why even make the announcement? Why not just attack us?'

'To be seen to be acting reasonably,' stated Sister Colissa. 'To provide cover for later intended actions. To get her out of this city, where she's protected, to a place where she's not. Nice words and promises don't mean that he intends to act in good faith either, Corenna.'

'And now your lack of faith in His Eminence Archlaw Paulius, the leader of our Holy Church, does you no credit at all, Colissa!' snapped the grey-haired priestess. 'The Archlaw, like all of us, has recognised that Leanna is a holy worker of miracles. And he wants to venerate her for that! *That* is why he's written the letter. Lest you all forget; the *Archlaw* leads our Holy Church, at Aiduel's behest. I therefore tend to work on the assumption that his actions are always done in good faith, but perhaps I'm just old-fashioned!'

'Please,' said Leanna, 'don't share cross words on account of this. I welcome all of your counsel, and I respect all of your views. And, of course, Corenna is quite right; we must not assume that the Archlaw is acting with bad intent.'

Lord Aiduel, please give me the wisdom to understand what the Archlaw's true purpose is.

'Thank you, Leanna,' said Corenna, appearing mollified. 'But anyway, if you and the others around this table have doubts, there will be an opportunity to ask questions of Archprime Meira dei Corsi.

Based on what her letter said, you don't have to decide anything in advance of Fifth-Day, or even then. Hear what the Archprime has to say. Consider her words. And if you need it, secure yourself more time to decide. *Then* make your decision.'

'I agree with that,' said Amyss.

'As do I,' said Colissa.

Lorth Dormer merely nodded.

'Very well,' said Leanna. 'Thank you all. I'll think on everything that you've said, but I believe that Priestess Corenna is correct. Before I make any decision, I must meet with Archprime Meira dei Corsi.'

—

Four days later, she was walking to Arlais Cathedral in the early hours of the morning, to do exactly that. Since it was not a Seventh-Day, there was far less activity on the streets approaching the holy building than she had recently become accustomed to.

Nonetheless, Leanna was still surrounded by a protective cluster of people, including Amyss and Priestess Corenna, who were accompanying her to the meeting. Lorth Dormer and nine other armed soldiers of the militia were also with them.

The streets were still gloomy at this early hour. At one point, Leanna glanced back to talk to Amyss, and froze when she spotted a figure on the street behind them, perhaps twenty metres away. She could see the outline of a tall, burly individual, whose features were indistinguishable in the poor light.

'Lorth?'

The militia leader looked back in response, at the same time that the unknown person slipped into a side-alley. Leanna turned away, then continued walking at Lorth's instigation, but she felt a chill of fear.

Lord Aiduel, please give me the courage to do this, and to stop jumping at shadows.

When they arrived at the main entrance to Arlais Cathedral, they encountered a waiting group of Aiduel's Guards. Seven members of the religious military order were standing at the top of the steps before the part-open cathedral doors. All of them were wearing the ominous red cloak and sash.

As soon as he spotted Leanna's entourage, one of these guards stated, 'The Archprime is already inside, waiting near the altar, accompanied by only three of our Guards. In turn, only three of these... *militia* may enter.'

Lorth Dormer looked ready to protest, but Leanna whispered, 'That's fine, Lorth. Lead the way, please.'

Seven of Leanna's party therefore remained on the steps outside, as Lorth Dormer led a group comprised of Leanna, Amyss, Corenna and two other militia guards, into the vestibule inside the cathedral entrance. As they emerged from this into the nave of the building, the Archprime's party was clearly visible in the open area in front of the altar.

This group included three red-cloaked guards, who were separated by several metres from two other figures. This latter pair were sitting within a circle of chairs, close to the altar. The first of these was recognisable as El'Patriere, here in his capacity as acting High Priest, whilst the other was a tiny and frail-looking female; Archprime Meira dei Corsi.

Leanna walked briskly up the centre aisle. As soon as dei Corsi noticed Leanna's approach, she raised herself carefully from her chair. She was an elderly woman, perhaps in her seventies, with a bony frame and a wizened, skeletal face. In the woman's right hand was a staff, which she appeared to be using as a walking aid as she moved a couple of hesitant steps in Leanna's direction.

The woman's face adopted a welcoming grin as Leanna drew near, and she announced, 'And here she must be!'

'Yes, Mother,' said Leanna, bowing her head with deference. 'Thank you for travelling all this way to see me. You do me a great honour.'

'Nonsense, child, nonsense! The honour is all mine! The Angel of Arlais, here in person before me! This old woman feels blessed to behold you. Truly blessed!'

'Thank you, Mother.'

'Here, child, take a seat. These old bones of mine can't stand up for too long.' The elderly woman gestured to the ring of chairs which had been laid out in front of the altar. 'And please, tell your guards to find somewhere away from us to stand while we talk, like I've already told mine. It's very unpleasant for us all, to have these soldier-types lurking over us.'

Leanna glanced towards Lorth, who nodded. He then moved to a place on the opposite side of the ring of chairs from the three Aiduel's Guards, but an equal distance away. Lorth's fellow militia followed him, gathering near the front row of pews.

As Leanna and her companions sat down, Leanna noted that El'Patriere had made no move to stand or to greet her, and that his single good eye was looking away from her and Amyss. Now that he was up close, she could clearly hear his wheezing breath, and could not fail to observe his fire-ravaged face.

'You know Father El'Patriere, of course,' said dei Corsi, speaking with a refined Dei Magnun accent. 'He's been telling me all about his enormous pride for his role in your ordainment, and also about the wondrous miracles he's witnessed you performing!'

Leanna in turn introduced Amyss and Corenna. Leanna knew that it would be difficult for Amyss to be in close proximity to her once-abuser.

Lord Aiduel, please protect Amyss and me from the false words and deeds of Senior Priest El'Patriere.

As their gathering then exchanged small talk, with the Archprime almost ceaseless in her gushing compliments, Leanna used her ability to sense the true emotions of dei Corsi and the Senior Priest.

From El'Patriere, who was speaking little, there was the usual seething hatred, concealed beneath a neutral expression. In contrast, dei Corsi emitted no such malign feelings, but there was also an absence of positive emotion to match her expressions of delight about meeting Leanna. The Archprime appeared to be internally calm, and Leanna therefore judged that the woman's exclamations of wonder seemed insincere.

After a couple of minutes, dei Corsi announced, 'But now, if you'll forgive me, I must move us onto the business of this meeting, Priestess Leanna. Please note that, though the words I'm going to use are my own, the sentiment is that of His Eminence the Archlaw. First, I must express our deepest regret over what happened here. Over the madness of dei Bornere. When the news first reached us in Sen Aiduel of the attempt to burn you alive, and the miracles of the pyre and the stigmata, we both wept. Wept that such an abomination of an act could have been undertaken, in the name of the Holy Church.'

As Leanna heard these words, and sensed no trace of sorrow within the Archprime, her instinct was that the woman was lying to her. That no such act of weeping had ever taken place. Indeed, dei Corsi was sitting alongside El'Patriere, the very man who had arranged Leanna's arrest, an irony which did not appear to trouble the elderly woman.

Lord Aiduel, please forgive me for doubting such an eminent member of your church.

'But, wonder of wonders!' continued the Archprime. 'Aiduel saved you, Leanna! He saved you, and He punished those who had sinned against you. And the Archlaw knew then that you had been saved for the good of the Holy Church! After allowing himself a period of self-chastisement and penitence, he came to his conclusion. That he must make amends for his grave misjudgement in appointing dei Bornere, by bringing you to Sen Aiduel.'

'So, Mother,' said Priestess Corenna, taking encouragement, 'you're saying that the actions taken here by Aiduel's Guards – the burnings, and terror, and interrogating the young – these were not done at the Archlaw's instruction?'

'Aiduel's Guards were looking for evil heretics,' answered dei Corsi. 'Of course, it never was and never would be their purpose to burn someone like the Angel of Arlais.'

Leanna could see Amyss frowning and she knew what her companion was thinking; the Archprime had not answered the question.

'But anyway,' stated dei Corsi, 'let me get onto the Archlaw's proposals, if you'll permit me?'

Leanna nodded, and then prepared to listen intently as the elderly woman continued.

—

For the next thirty minutes, Leanna listened as dei Corsi did most of the talking. The Archprime was cordial and eloquent throughout, but Leanna never escaped the sense that the woman's friendly demeanour was a facade.

In response to questions about what would happen to the militia and to the citizens of Arlais once Aiduel's Guards entered the city, dei Corsi was relaxed in her reply.

'We simply seek to restore the authority of the Holy Church, Leanna. If the city militia stands down and disbands, and offers no resistance to our reclamation of Church property – including the fortress and the College – then no further action will be taken against them.'

When asked what life would be like for the citizens of the city, after the return of Aiduel's Guards, dei Corsi said, 'Please, rest assured that the city and its people have no need to fear our return. The regime of burnings instigated by dei Bornere will not recommence. The Holy Church is immensely grateful to the people of this city for their role in protecting the Angel of Arlais, and we wouldn't contemplate punishment or revenge. We simply want to restore things to how they were, before dei Bornere arrived here.'

And in answer to Leanna's questions about what they wanted from her, dei Corsi spoke effusively. 'We want to take you to Sen Aiduel, Priestess Leanna, to meet and to be honoured by the Archlaw. We want to bestow every honour upon one who has been so touched by Aiduel. In front of a crowd of thousands, at the Archlaw's Palace, Paulius intends to declare you a Living Saint. We'll appoint you to join the High Council, Leanna, as its youngest member. And we want to build a new hospital in your name, one which will be a shining beacon of hope for all of Angall. In that place, our Angel of Arlais will heal those who were beyond hope, using her Aiduel-given power. It will be wonderful, child. Wonderful beyond imagining. It's bringing me close to tears, now, just thinking about it!'

Leanna could perceive why dei Corsi had been selected for this mission of apparent reconciliation. Leanna could easily have been swept along by the Archprime's soaring rhetoric and charismatic personality. However, the intensity of dei Corsi's words were never matched by the woman's inner feelings.

Leanna had also been dwelling upon another key point, ever since the herald had appeared at Arlais Cathedral. For an extended period, Aiduel's Guards had been hunting for heretics possessing abilities like Leanna's. Pursuing her age group, burning many unfortunate individuals, and interrogating thousands of people. Following which, having found Leanna, they had been prepared to kill her.

Prior to her planned execution, dei Bornere had named her *Illborn*. He had said that the Archlaw had been visited by The Lord Aiduel, and had been given a holy mission to find and kill these Illborn. A mission which Aiduel's Guards had embraced with fervour. However, according to dei Corsi's narrative, all of that was to be forgotten now, and ascribed to the delusions of a single madman. Leanna was instead to be revered.

Eventually, Leanna could no longer contain this thought, and she said, 'Thank you for your kind words, Mother, and for the generous proposals by the Archlaw. But will you please help me to understand something?'

'What's that, child?' asked dei Corsi, smiling warmly.

'Who are the Illborn, Mother? And why does the Holy Church want to kill them?'

Leanna could sense that Amyss and Corenna were staring at her, the latter with an expression of puzzlement. Leanna had spoken about this with Amyss, but it was likely to be the first time that Corenna had heard the term. El'Patriere also appeared to shift in his chair, suddenly interested.

Leanna observed that dei Corsi's mask of congeniality seemed to slip a little, as the woman answered, 'The Illborn? A strange name. Who told you that word, child?'

'Dei Bornere, Mother. He told me that much, but little more. Perhaps you could tell me more, please.'

Dei Corsi's calm exterior returned. 'I cannot. I know nothing about it, Leanna.'

'Dei Bornere said that the Archlaw had been visited by The Lord Aiduel. That Aiduel ordered him to find the Illborn, and to kill them. That I'm one of them, which is why he tried to burn me.'

Dei Corsi laughed derisively. 'What drivel the man spoke! Lunacy! Perhaps, if this had actually happened, you might expect that the Archlaw would have mentioned it to me? Which he hasn't! Dei Bornere's words are a nonsense, child. It's a term I've never heard used before, the rantings of a madman. Nothing more, I assure you.'

As dei Corsi was speaking, Leanna could sense a sudden turmoil of emotion within the woman, and Leanna knew that she was being lied to. Dei Corsi recognised the term Illborn, although she was bluntly denying it. And if the woman could lie about this, so calmly and confidently, how could Leanna trust any other assurance which the Archprime had given? Whether those assurances were about the protection of Arlais and its citizens, or Leanna's own safety, she felt certain now that dei Corsi's promises were built on sand.

Lord Aiduel, please give me the wisdom to make the right decisions in the face of lies.

'Thank you for that assurance, Mother. Now, please excuse me for my next question. It will seem rude, but I must ask it. May I ask it, Mother?'

'Proceed, child,' said dei Corsi, and her fixed smile had returned.

'There is no polite way to say this,' said Leanna. 'Particularly, after hearing you speak today. However, there are some who believe that if I give myself over to Aiduel's Guards, they will kill me. Quietly and discreetly next time, somewhere away from here. And that I'll never set foot in Sen Aiduel. What would you say to reassure them, Mother?'

A frown appeared on dei Corsi's face, before an image flashed into Leanna's mind. A foreign image, coming from another. Seeing herself, but through some other's eyes. In woods at night. Struggling. Held down by two Aiduel's Guards. A knife raised. Slashed downwards...

Lord Aiduel, what is this? Am I seeing dei Corsi's thoughts?

Leanna was left reeling from this pictured scene, as dei Corsi calmly replied, 'I should say, Priestess Leanna, that those people should learn to have more faith in the words of-'

The Archprime's reply was interrupted by an echoing clang, which sounded like the main door of the cathedral being slammed shut. This was followed by another reverberating noise, which could easily have been the internal crossbar of that door being dropped into place.

As a confused expression appeared on dei Corsi's face, a panicked shout rang out from Lorth Dormer.

'It's a trap!'

Leanna's head turned towards the militia leader, and she was shocked to see that Dormer and one of his companions were drawing their swords. The third militia soldier was slumped on the floor beside them, with what looked like the fletching of an arrow sprouting from his back. A pair of hooded figures, both clad in dark leather, were charging towards the two standing militiamen.

At that moment, Amyss screamed. The petite priestess was facing in the opposite direction, and Leanna spun around, expecting to see the trio of Aiduel's Guards bearing down upon her. But instead, one of the red-cloaked soldiers was also prone and bloody on the floor, while the remaining two were locked in combat with a further pair of leather-clad assailants. Blades whirled and clashed in the air as the newcomers ferociously attacked the Archprime's bodyguards.

Leanna turned again, feeling panic. Lorth Dormer and his surviving companion were retreating towards her under a flurry of attacks from the unknown assailants. At the same time, Leanna witnessed El'Patriere pushing himself up from his chair. The priest started to scuttle breathlessly past the altar, his apparent target a small wooden door at the far end of the chancel.

'What's going on here?' demanded dei Corsi. Her voice had lost none of its authority as she rose to her feet, and she spoke as if she could end the violence using force of will alone. Louder, she called, 'I said, what's going on-'

The words were cut short as a crossbow quarrel abruptly sprouted through her neck. Dei Corsi's confident mask finally vanished as she took note of the missile emerging through her throat, before her eyes rolled upwards and she collapsed forwards. Priestess Corenna started to scream, reaching for the fallen Archprime.

'Leanna, run!' shouted Amyss, and she grabbed hold of Leanna's arm, attempting to pull Leanna in the direction that El'Patriere was taking.

Before Leanna could react, one of the leather-clad men cut down his Aiduel's Guards adversary, and then started to charge towards her. In the instants that followed, Leanna glimpsed that one of this attacker's hands wielded a sword, and the other carried what appeared to be a crossbow. She watched in horror as the man raised the crossbow up, aiming it directly towards her chest. From just metres away, she heard a click as he pressed the trigger of the weapon.

DEVOTION. SACRIFICE. SALVATION.

The words exploded within Leanna, unleashed as the indignant scream of an angelic choir. In an instant, the immediate area around her was ablaze with golden light, wreathing her body in a cocoon of shimmering colour. Time decelerated, and the crossbow quarrel which had been fired was somehow spiralling towards her with such sluggish momentum that she was able to observe its approach. It was a perfectly aimed killing shot, heading directly towards her heart.

Lord Aiduel, please protect me!

Without any conscious action on Leanna's part, the missile was deflected away, blocked by her dazzling shield of light. The rebounding quarrel skidded harmlessly across the stone tiles of the cathedral floor.

The voices of furious angels were still bellowing within Leanna's mind as she observed her surroundings through the lens of this holy, transparent veil. All of her senses were suddenly hyper-alert, and she was completely aware of the motions of everyone in her vicinity.

El'Patriere, who was now several metres away from Leanna, was moving with laboured breath towards the door at the end of the chancel area. Closer still was Priestess Corenna, who was crouching down over the limp form of dei Corsi, outside of the cocoon of light. At that instant, Corenna jolted in shock as a crossbow bolt buried itself into her chest, and Leanna could feel the precise moment that unexpected death claimed the elder priestess's body.

Lord Aiduel, please protect us all!

Amyss was still beside Leanna, still tugging on Leanna's arm. The golden veil of light had also now flowed around the red-headed priestess, enveloping her small form. Amyss's frantic cry seemed to be distant, as if Leanna was hearing the words from deep under water.

'Leanna! Run!'

Even as Amyss shouted this, the man who had fired the bolt at Leanna drew closer, now with his sword raised. Before he could strike, Leanna lifted her hand up towards him. Without any conscious awareness of what she was doing, a rush of power shot out from her palm towards the man. It was an instinctive manifestation of what she had been practising with small objects, but this time, it was magnified a hundred-fold.

This blast of power impacted with the rushing form of the attacker, and sent him hurtling backwards with his feet lifted from the ground. He flew several metres through the air, before his body crunched hard against the cathedral wall.

Leanna could then finally react to the urgings of Amyss. With the petite priestess's hand still clutching her wrist, the two of them started to chase after El'Patriere towards the possible sanctuary of the chancel doorway. As they moved, they were still bathed in the golden cocoon of light, and sounds of the ongoing melee and violence were echoing from behind them.

El'Patriere was several paces ahead of Leanna and Amyss. As he reached the door, Leanna witnessed the scarred priest glancing back and taking note of who was following him. El'Patriere then ducked through the small arched doorway, and slammed the door shut behind him.

'Please-'

As they reached the doorway and as Amyss uttered this despairing plea, Leanna heard the snick of a bolt being slid into place. El'Patriere had sealed off his place of refuge, and Leanna and Amyss were trapped in the corner of the chancel.

Amyss started to bang against the door, and was imploring the Senior Priest to let them in. Leanna knew already that this was a futile request, and she turned around to face whatever was behind her.

With despair, she witnessed Lorth Dormer falling to a tall attacker, as a lengthy sword was thrust through her protector's body. Dormer had been the last man standing amongst the militia bodyguards, and a leather-clad body on the floor near to him suggested that he had not surrendered his life cheaply.

In the same moments, the last surviving Aiduel's Guard was slain on the opposite side of the cathedral. The remaining two leather-clad assailants then turned towards Leanna, and started to move in her direction. This pair met in front of the altar, stepping over the corpses of Corenna and dei Corsi, before facing Leanna. She raised her gold-wreathed hand towards them, her heart pounding with fear. She was attempting to ward them off, though she had no idea of how to repeat what she had done just seconds earlier.

Then she spotted another figure, who was moving swiftly along a side aisle, heading towards her and the two leather-clad attackers.

This new male arrival was burly and was several inches over six feet in height. He was also hooded, wearing a thick leather jacket. In his right hand, he was carrying a massive and deadly looking mace, whilst on his left arm was a gleaming metal shield, which was raised before him as he approached.

A hint of a thick grey beard was visible beneath the hood. Leanna was suddenly certain that this was the man who she had seen outside the cathedral, on Seventh-Day. The stranger who had been gazing at her with bloodshot eyes, at a time when her powers had somehow disappeared.

And she realised then that this man had arranged all of this. He had known that she would be meeting here. And he had come here, with accomplices, to kill her.

The memory of how her powers had faded five days earlier, when in this man's presence, caused a rush of fear and doubt. Indeed, as he drew closer, the golden light around Leanna seemed to flicker and weaken.

Lord Aiduel, please stay with me! Please don't abandon me now!

'Leanna, he won't open the door!' cried Amyss. She sounded close to tears, her voice child-like and terrified. She was hammering her palm against the wood. 'Please! Help us!'

Leanna shifted position, so that her body was shielding Amyss's smaller form. The pair of leather-clad assailants had taken two steps closer, just a handful of paces away from her, at the same time that this new stranger was also approaching them from behind. Leanna could feel that the golden cocoon around herself and Amyss was continuing to lose strength. Dimming, gradually. And then it failed. Their protection was gone.

As this happened, the two leather-clad assailants turned away from Leanna, and they faced the stranger as he drew close to them. Leanna expected to see the two men moving apart for the arrival of their leader, to allow him through to complete her murder.

But instead, sudden violence ensued. The two leather-clad attackers launched themselves at the stranger in unison, their blades cutting deadly patterns in the air. With astonishing speed and grace for such a large man, the mace-wielding figure whirled his body and weapon sideways to evade one opponent, and used his shield to block the incoming sword-attack of the other. He then continued his unbroken spin to smash the steel head of his weapon into the jaw of the smaller of his two adversaries. Blood splattered across the tiles in front of the cathedral altar, as the victim's features were destroyed and his body was hammered backwards.

Leanna tried again to resurrect the golden barrier, but there was next to nothing within her to call upon. She was depleted. Drained, or abandoned by The Lord. All she could do was to watch, helpless and confused, as the hefty bearer of the mace ended his rotation, and squared up against the last of the leather-clad attackers.

Lord Aiduel, please save us.

This remaining assailant was carrying a knife in one hand, and a lengthy sword in the other, which he had used to cut down Lorth Dormer just moments earlier. The man was poised on the balls of his feet, now keeping his distance from the mace-wielder. Circling warily, and jabbing with his sword.

Leanna watched as the two adversaries both stepped to their right, biding their time in a tense mirroring of movement which lasted for seconds. But when the attacks came, it seemed instantaneous, and the men launched themselves at each other in a flurry of movement and deadly metal. The sword and knife could be seen to be slicing furious shapes, the metallic clash of blades against shield resonating inside the cathedral. It seemed inevitable that the bearded man was going to be sliced by one of the bladed weapons.

But then the mace head connected against the wrist of the other man's sword arm. Leanna heard a loud crack, followed by the clanging sound of the sword bouncing away. Seconds later, the mace crashed through a desperate block with a knife, and smashed into the forehead of the leather-clad fighter. The front of the man's skull was suddenly missing, and he collapsed without protest.

Leanna felt her stomach turn at the sight, but she controlled herself and continued to watch the grey-bearded stranger with the mace as he started to check around himself. She observed, not knowing what else to do, as he placed his shield onto his back, and stalked towards the nearby figure of another leather-clad assailant. This latter man was prone and moaning, and was trying to crawl away. The mace crashed down again, and the man's attempt to escape was ended.

'Lea...'

Amyss's voice was timid as her hand slipped into Leanna's. The banging of her palm against the door had ceased.

'My powers have gone, Amyss,' Leanna said. 'Get behind me.'

As the burly man with the mace now started to walk towards them, she knew that it was true. She could feel almost nothing of her powers. Whatever this man was, whoever he was, he had it within him to remove Leanna's abilities. As he reached the dead form of the last man he had fought, he stooped down. He appeared to rip a chain off the neck of the corpse, before pocketing whatever item he had taken.

When he stood upright again, he finally faced Leanna, and she watched as he pushed the hood down from his head. Revealing grey hair, grizzled beard and ruddy cheeks. The mace was still gripped, held at his side, and clumps of flesh and hair appeared to be mashed against its end.

Leanna forced herself to stand up straight, to face the man. If she was going to die here, and The Lord Aiduel was to allow it, then she would not cower.

'If you are here to kill me,' she said, astonished by the lack of tremor in her voice, 'then do it. But I beg you, please spare this priestess.'

The man remained in place, without further forward motion. His chest was heaving, and he appeared to scrutinise her, with an enigmatic expression on his face. When he responded, it was in a deep but breathless voice, and his words were not at all what she had expected.

'My name is Caddin Sendromm, Priestess Leanna. And if you want to live beyond this day, you must come with me.'

7

Allana

—

*Year of Our Lord,
After Ascension, 769AA*

To Allana's surprise, for the first fortnight after Jarrett Berun had departed for Andarron, she was not in any way harassed or bullied.

During that time, she had only two brief encounters with the dowager duchess, Sillene Berun, when they passed each other by chance in the corridors of Berun Castle. On both occasions, the dowager glared at Allana as she walked past, but made no attempt to engage in conversation. Allana therefore began to wonder whether she might have overestimated the threat that the older woman posed. Perhaps Sillene Berun was still plotting to remove Allana at some point, but the woman appeared to have little interest in initiating trouble whilst her son was away.

Allana spent a large proportion of those two weeks alone, trying to stave off boredom. She occupied a significant amount of time on seamstress activities, making clothes for herself within the confines of her small room. At other times, she either wandered into the town of Berun, or explored the castle and its grounds.

While she was exploring the town, staying within the areas frequented by the merchant middle classes, Allana was becoming more confident that she was no longer being followed. In the early days in Berun, she had often sensed that eyes were upon her, possibly connected to the dowager duchess's threat to have her trailed. However, that feeling had now faded. Perhaps the older woman had by now dismissed the notion that Allana might be a spy?

On more than one occasion, Allana passed by the building which she understood housed the Berun postmaster. In the second week after Jarrett's departure, it was increasingly piquing her interest. That was the place from where she would be able to send a letter, if she chose to.

Back within the castle, she was allowed free rein. Although she was presented as a seamstress, everyone knew that she was the duke's mistress, and there were few places that she was prohibited from exploring. However, it also meant that the castle retainers were uncomfortable spending time with her. She had still not made any friends or acquaintances amongst them, and the women in particular seemed to keep their distance from her.

With so much free time on her own, Allana discovered that she relished standing on the highest ramparts of the castle, as she had once also enjoyed being on the battlements of Septholme Castle. She felt a sense of contentment and peace whenever she was peering out over the surrounding countryside, despite occasionally experiencing a touch of vertigo.

Berun Castle stood on a tall promontory of rock above a small lake, overlooking the town, and the highest battlements of the weathered fortress allowed expansive views in all directions. To the north, rolling hills morphed gradually into the distant mountain range of The Horns, while to the south-east, open fields covered the expanse before the wide waterway of the Canas River.

However, Allana found her eyes drawn most often to the west and south-west, looking out across the lands of Berun and Andar. Sometimes, when she stared in that direction, she could imagine that she could feel something pulsing, far away.

It's just your imagination, Lana. Forget about it.

—

In Jarrett's absence, Allana's established routine therefore made the daytimes tolerable. However, the hours of darkness were awful.

At night, she continued to be stricken with the recurring dream and its lingering memories of horror. Panic attacks would then follow in the aftermath of waking, which would leave her anxious for hours afterwards. It sometimes helped to rouse herself and light a candle, but then she would be alone with her thoughts until dawn. And even though she tried to direct those thoughts in any direction but that of her imprisonment and torture, it was still a time for darker reflection.

One of the events which she reflected upon was the murder of Evelyn dei Laramin and her red-cloaked associates. In order to save herself, Allana had utilised her power to force two of the Guards to attack their own colleagues.

But of even more grim fascination was what she had inflicted upon dei Laramin, when she had poured an unseen darkness out of herself into the Dei Magnun woman. All of Allana's blackest emotions and most bitter experiences had coalesced into an almost tangible form, and had then been unleashed as a torrent into her sadistic tormentor.

It had crippled the High Commander. Had forced her to her knees, with her hands clutching her head, and forlorn screams emerging from her mouth. All of the fear and horror which Allana had ever felt, whilst on the run or being tortured, had been condensed into a stream of agony which had washed around and through the mind of dei Laramin.

Following which, Allana had swept a knife across the woman's throat, terminating the High Commander's life. In some ways, that act had been a mercy. Allana had released the woman prematurely from her suffering, and from the terror residing within the blackness which had entered her.

This raised a number of questions which still nagged at Allana in the night-time hours, several months later; what would have happened had she not slashed dei Laramin's throat? What would have come to pass if she had continued to let the horror course through the older woman, unchecked? How would it have ended?

Allana did not know, but she was aware now that the pouring of those dark emotions into dei Laramin had not cleansed them from her own body. In the days afterwards, she had realised that the darkness had returned to her, and she was certain that it was now once again lurking within her, ready to be accessed and used again in future. That thought made her feel both powerful and uneasy.

Allana also had much time to ponder on one of the last things which dei Laramin had said, in the minutes before her death…

'…*you're one of them, aren't you? One of the ones we've been looking for.*'

Those words had been consistent with dei Laramin's interrogation of Allana, back in the fortress. The High Commander had asked about dreams and powers, as if Aiduel's Guards were searching for a number of people. The questions asked had seemed to mirror Allana's own abilities, and the professed powers of Arion Sepian. Aiduel's Guards were searching for the likes of Allana and Arion, and that could not be a good thing.

Arion Sepian again, Lana! she thought, on the night this occurred to her. *Why must your thoughts always return to him?*

—

After two tormented weeks had passed of sleeping on her own, she was once more awake in the middle of the night, and her thoughts were again lingering upon the young Sepian noble.

'Arion,' she whispered to herself, as she watched the flickering patterns of candlelight on the wall. She had been sweating and trembling earlier that night, racked with anxiety, but now she was feeling calmer. Her hand slid down onto her lower stomach, circling there, and she closed her eyes.

You're whispering his name again, Lana. Not Jarrett's. What's wrong with you?

With every day that had passed since Jarrett had left, she was fully aware that she was devoting increasing amounts of time to thinking about Arion Sepian. She desperately missed Jarrett's physical presence at night, but it was becoming so much more natural to picture Arion in her mind. And to wish that it was him, not Jarrett, that she was with.

In some ways, it frustrated her that she was still fixating upon the young Sepian lord. After such fleeting encounters, he had no right to retain such a possession on her attention. Yes, she and Arion were different to everyone else, and shared secret dreams and powers. And yes, he *had* helped her to escape from Septholme, and she had felt differently when close to him – *more alive* – than any other person had ever made her feel.

But he had abandoned her, at a time when he had promised to flee with her. And afterwards, he had not waited for her to contact him, as he had also promised, but had instead married another woman. Lady Kalyane of House Rednar! Another *noble*, of course. He had so brazenly betrayed his solemn pledges to Allana; promises which, at the time, had burrowed into her soul.

Why did he have to do that to you, Lana? You were intending to reunite with him, until he did that! Why did he have to betray you?

She knew that she should forget about him and embrace a future with Jarrett, but there were lingering doubts which undermined the strength of that conviction. Arion was just so beautiful in her memory, and so overflowing with breathtaking power. It was easy to recall his image now, to imagine being with him, and to feel her breath quicken and her temperature change for different reasons.

If she wanted to seek out a reason to forgive Arion's actions, she could perhaps recognise that she had also broken her implied pledge that she would write to him. Maybe he would not have married if he had been certain that she was still alive? But it had happened so quickly, and he had given her little chance!

But could he still be thinking about you, Lana, despite his marriage? Wondering where you are and wishing he was with you? How would he react, even now, if he was sure that you're still alive?

It was such a tantalising thought.

Now that she was no longer being followed, it would be possible to make contact with Arion by writing to him. She could still act to *make* him think about her again, and to regret his decision to marry. It was entirely her choice.

However, what would she say? And did she want to send such a letter, given that writing to him could open up connections to her past? She had already lost everything in her life, twice before. First, when fleeing Sen Aiduel. Then later, when she had fallen within a few short hours from being mistress of a duke to a tortured prisoner in a grim fortress. Dare she risk what she had gained as the lover of Jarrett Berun, by reforging her contact with Arion?

But he's so perfectly handsome, Lana…

Arion's image was at the forefront of her mind as her hand moved lower down her body. Within moments, her more logical deliberations had become an afterthought.

—

Allana's thoughts about Arion lingered throughout the following day. Finally, after much fraught procrastination, she entered Jarrett's chambers to take possession of a quill, inkpot and sheet of parchment. Upon returning to the privacy of her own room, she wrote out a simple message:

Dear Arion,
I am alive.
Allana

After writing the letter, she stared at it for a number of minutes. Three brief words, but what reaction would they elicit within him?

She thought about writing more. Writing about where she was, and *who* she was with. Hurting him in the same way that she had been hurt when she had found out about his marriage. But she could not bring herself to put the quill back on the paper. If he still cared about her, that single sentence would be enough to allow her to invade his thoughts; to make him think about her, as she still thought about him. And if she decided subsequently to do nothing further about it, there was no information in the letter which he could use to trace her.

She folded the parchment, concealing the message within. She then stared at the folded document for a number of minutes, agonising. Before she had even realised that she was doing it, she was writing out the addressee; Lord Arion Sepian, Septholme Castle, Septholme, Western Canasar. Minutes later, she had sealed it with wax.

Then it would be a simple matter of walking into the town, to the offices of the postmaster, and handing the sealed letter to him. That was all that she had to do. After which, she and Arion Sepian would be reconnected. Somewhat.

She stared at the document in her hand, sitting there for perhaps twenty minutes. Eventually, she moved to the large dresser in her room, and she slipped the folded parchment into the bottom of a drawer, beneath a variety of clothing.

She would decide at another time.

—

Later that day, with the letter still unsent, Allana returned to the castle ramparts to watch the sunset. She was on the highest section of the western wall and was again looking westwards.

It was a relatively mild evening, with a gentle breeze blowing against her back. There was a lovely peacefulness about being up here at this time, wrapped in her fur cloak, even though she could feel the temperature dropping with every passing minute. Only a pair of circling guards shared the quiet of these upper battlements with her.

She spent almost an hour in that spot. By the time that she finally left the battlements and headed back towards her own room, barely a quarter of the sun remained above the horizon.

She anticipated an evening on her own in the private but chilly sanctuary of her quarters, working on embroidery under candlelight. But when she opened the door and saw a bulky figure already inside the room, she recoiled. Dowager Duchess Sillene Berun was seated on Allana's bed.

Stay calm, Lana.

'Lana,' said the older woman softly, with none of the usual venom in her voice. 'I've been waiting for you.'

'My Lady,' replied Allana, feeling cautious. The dowager had not entered Allana's private room since her first hostile visit.

'Come in and close the door.'

'Yes, my Lady.'

Allana slipped into the room, shutting the door behind herself. A single lit candle stood on Allana's dresser, illuminating the space in a murky half-light. Next to the candle was the parchment letter, with its waxed seal broken.

Sillene stood up and moved to within a couple of paces of Allana, looming over her. Several moments of silence passed, before the dowager spoke again. 'He told me to leave you alone, do you know that?'

'My Lady?' Allana's gaze flicked back to the letter.

'The duke, my son. He knew that I'd want to come after you during his absence. To bully you and belittle you. And he *ordered* me to leave you alone.'

'He did?' Allana's heart was beating fast in her chest. The other woman's hefty form swallowed the space in the small chamber.

'Yes. He's a young fool, and he'll soon learn to lose these notions, but I do believe that he's in love with you. He was very urgent and insistent in his instructions that, in his absence, you're to be protected.'

'I don't know what to say, my Lady. I have… deep feelings for the duke, too.'

'Yes. And even though I haven't liked you, your feelings for him have appeared to be sincere. Which is why, even though he's to be married, I've not taken action to remove you sooner. That's one reason. The other is that I thought you were harmless. And so, these last two weeks, I've been scrupulously obeying my son's orders and have left you alone.'

'Erm… thank you, my Lady.'

You're in danger, Lana. Get ready to use your powers, if you need to.

'Yes, he's in love with you. Which is why your sudden departure will be such a blow to him.'

'My depar-'

A meaty fist thudded into Allana's head.

Allana saw only a fleeting glimpse of the woman's clenched right hand as it smashed into her temple. The force of the impact sent Allana crashing backwards. Her back slammed against the wood of the closed door, before she tumbled sideways to the cold floor, her shoulder also connecting solidly with the hard stone surface.

Allana rolled dazedly onto her back, in time to see the much larger woman lumbering closer, and leaning down over her. Allana raised her arms defensively across her face as she saw another fist crashing down. The blow connected against the flesh of Allana's upper arm, impacting in a way that would no doubt leave a nasty bruise.

'Yes,' said the older woman, breathing heavily as she planted a knee onto Allana's waist, and then placed her wide palm onto Allana's chest. 'Your departure. For that letter, whore. Although your body won't be travelling any further than a local pigsty. And those pigs will eat practically *anything*.'

'Please.' Allana's plea was barely a murmur. Her head was still spinning from the force of the first blow, and she was completely pinned under the weight of the much larger woman.

'You think I wouldn't be told that you'd taken a quill and ink from the duke's chambers?'

Sillene Berun raised her meaty fist again and thudded it past Allana's shielding arms, striking Allana's chest.

Allana felt the breath rush out of her body, and her next words were wheezed. 'The letter? I didn't… intend to send it.'

'A letter to the Sepians, to the leader of their military. You're a spy. I'd pretty much dismissed the possibility, but there you are. What is it? Code?'

'No, it's not-'

Another fist crashed down against Allana's arms as she defended her face.

'What is it then? You think you're the first spy I've caught, girl? First enemy of my family I've dealt with personally?'

Another punch, this time into Allana's stomach. A soft moan escaped from her throat as the blow impacted, and she was unable to find the breath to speak.

She then felt two sweaty hands wrapping around her neck, at the same time that she heard the dowager say, 'First woman I've choked to death with my own hands?'

Fat fingers closed around Allana's throat and started to clench, constricting her air passages. Allana reached up frantically with her own hands, trying desperately to release the grip from her neck, and digging her fingernails into the woman's flesh.

But it was to no avail, and the chunky hands remained on her throat. The dowager was panting above her, making an unhealthy wheezing noise as she attempted to strangle Allana.

The remaining air was leaving Allana's body, and her head felt like it would burst. She closed her eyes, seeing stars in her vision, even with her eyelids squeezed shut.

LUST. POWER. DOMINATION.

As she drifted closer to the breathless unconsciousness which would soon be followed by death, Allana's powers triggered without conscious thought, and she reached for the darkness within her. The darkness which she had used just once before.

She imagined it coalescing into her limbs, into her hands. Gathering urgently within her fingers. Hungry. Rapacious. Black, infected, vengeful, sinful. Eager to do her bidding. To find a new target. To be unleashed.

As the grip on her neck drew ever tighter, Allana released this unseen darkness. She let it pour forth, through the connection between her fingertips and the flabby forearms of Dowager Duchess Sillene Berun. Torrents of dark filth, ripping into the flesh and the mind of the other woman. Streaming into her. Ruining her. Carrying the stench of death and fire.

Allana's grip on the larger woman's arms, maintaining this flow of horror, was now as fixed as was the dowager's hold on Allana's neck. As the lack of air began to overwhelm Allana, she was dimly aware of the horrified screaming which had started above her. Screaming which seemed to echo endlessly, in unparalleled anguish and despair, as Allana herself fell into unconsciousness…

—

When Allana regained awareness, an unknown amount of time later, she was still lying on the floor of her chamber. Her throat ached, and her lungs felt raw. The room looked oddly distorted from this low perspective, the flickering candle on the dresser still illuminating the confined space. The wooden door to the room had swung open, and the thin edge of the door was pressing against Allana's hip.

Sillene Berun was nowhere to be seen.

Allana rolled onto her side, attempting to move herself into a position from which she could stand. Her body felt bruised and battered, both from the weight of the woman who had pinned her down, and from the pummelling force of the blows. She tried to take in a gulp of cool air, but coughed instead, her throat feeling tender.

She reached across to the wooden end of her bed, and used the bedpost to gingerly drag herself to a sitting position. From here, she could see the top of the dresser. The parchment was still there, in the place where she had spotted it when she had returned to her room. But where was Sillene Berun?

Then Allana heard the scream. It was a man's voice, caught in a sound of terror or agony. It came from somewhere outside of her room, not in the immediate vicinity but still close enough to be heard. Allana pulled herself to her feet, then staggered to the dresser. In moments, she had concealed the letter back in the drawer.

She looked back towards her door and noted that it was lopsided. Only then did she spot that its top hinge had come away from the wall, causing the door to tilt away from its frame at an angle.

A second scream echoed from somewhere inside the castle, more distantly. Allana looked at the open doorway and at the now murky corridor outside. She could try to push the door shut and bolt it, and then lock herself within this room until the following dawn. Conceal herself away until whatever was causing those screams was long gone from here.

But that would not answer the questions of how the assault by Sillene Berun had ended, or why Allana was still alive? And why the dowager had left her there?

You need to know what's happened, Lana. You must know, in case you need to flee the castle. Don't cower here!

She gulped again, feeling another wave of pain in her throat as she gathered her courage. She then moved cautiously through the doorway and into the corridor beyond.

—

A further two screams directed Allana's passage through the darkening keep. One was clearly female, while the second was of uncertain gender, but both sent terrifying echoes through the draughty corridors of Berun Castle.

Allana's hesitant progress was finally halted by a group of four servants in front of her; two men and two women, who were clustered together in the keep's main central corridor. Directly ahead of them, a guardsman armed with a halberd was facing away down the corridor, his weapon raised and pointed in that direction.

'What's happening?' asked Allana. She struggled to form the words, and she was certain that her neck was bruising up.

'Someone's gone crazy in the castle,' whispered one of the male servants, not turning his gaze away from the direction which the guard was facing. 'On the rampage. Killing people, all over the place.'

'Who?' asked Allana, but she already knew the answer.

It's Sillene Berun, Lana. What have you done to her?

'Someone said it's the duch-'

Another scream carried to their group from the corridor up ahead, interrupting the reply. The sound was accompanied soon afterwards by the guardsman saying, 'Fuck!'

Allana witnessed the man taking a step back, halberd still raised, as one of the servants also uttered the words, 'Fuck me!'

The group of servants were edging away from the guard, passing Allana. Then Allana spotted the form down the corridor. Coming towards them.

It was Sillene Berun. She was bulky, fat, tall, as ever before. But there was something wrong with the way that the woman was moving. Something very wrong. She was hunched over slightly, her neck seeming to roll as she walked, with her arms dangling down in front of her. Her fingers were scrunched into a claw shape.

The guardsman called out to Allana and the servants, without turning his head. 'Get the fuck out of here! All of you!'

The four servants were away down the corridor in an instant, feet beating against the stone floor in their terrified desire to flee. In contrast, Allana found herself to be frozen on the spot. She was mesmerised by the unnatural sight of the woman coming towards her.

The form of the duchess was drawing closer, causing the guardsman to take another step back towards Allana.

Allana could see now that Sillene Berun's mouth was hanging open. There were red smears across the woman's face, and her lips and jaw were also covered in gleaming red liquid. Blood. The woman's teeth were visible, bared in a rictus of fury at the guard in front of her. There was no trace of the haughty dowager duchess in her expression or in her eyes. She looked… wild. Feral.

What have you done, Lana?

'D-Duchess?'

The guardsman spoke again, not lowering his weapon. The only response from the approaching woman was a noise which sounded like a snarl, as her head still rolled oddly from side-to-side. She had come to within two paces of the tip of the man's raised halberd, and had stopped there.

'Woman!' hissed the guardsman urgently, directing his comment towards Allana. 'Get the fuck out-'

He never got to finish the sentence. The movement of the dowager, when it finally came, was terrifyingly fast. She was past the end of the raised weapon and upon the man in an instant.

Allana watched as Sillene Berun's right hand shot out to grab the guard's neck. At the same time, the dowager's other hand wrenched the halberd out of the man's grip, sending it clattering against the stone floor. With what appeared to be inhuman strength, the guard was then lifted from his feet and was slammed against the corridor wall. One. Two. Three times. More. The man's helmet came loose on the third such blow. After that, each subsequent crunch of his limp frame against the stone blocks was accompanied by a squelching sound, as the back of his head was smashed open.

Allana knew that the rational thing to do was to run from here, to get away from this violence. But she was rooted to the spot. Transfixed. And she remained there as she observed Sillene Berun embracing the lifeless form of the guard. The dowager put her mouth to the man's neck, and then bit out a sizeable chunk of his flesh. Tearing it out, between her teeth.

With that done, the large woman cast the guard's body aside, and turned to face Allana. She was just three metres away. Slivers of the man's flesh hung from the woman's mouth, and drool and blood were smeared on her chin. Sillene's lower arms were darkened, with a number of small circles on them which looked like burns, and her hands were still scrunched up like claws.

Allana met the woman's – *the creature's?* – eyes. They appeared feral and seemed to shine gold in the half-light, but Allana also sensed recognition there. Given the speed and ferocity with which Sillene Berun had moved mere instants earlier, Allana knew that if she had been any ordinary person, she would already have been killed.

But Allana was not an ordinary person. Not at all. Indeed, the powers that she possessed were *extraordinary*. And she knew that whatever Sillene Berun had become, and now was, *she* had created it. This was *her* doing.

This was the product of the darkness that was Allana's gift to unleash, and only Allana owned that gift. Sillene Berun belonged to her now.

You are better than her, Lana. Better than all of them. This is no longer her castle. It's yours. You deserve it, and she deserves this, after what she tried to do to you.

The gleaming golden eyes continued to be fixed upon Allana's stare, as the large woman swayed above the corpse of the guard.

Allana observed the thing that had been Sillene Berun for seconds longer. She realised that she was savouring this moment.

Finally, she whispered, 'Go. Leave me.'

—

The next day, Allana was walking back into the town of Berun, with a sealed document tucked into her dress pocket. Her destination was the office of the Berun postmaster.

In Allana's absence, Sillene Berun had eventually been captured late on the previous night by a team of terrified but determined guardsmen. Using a combination of nets, ropes and clubs, they had finally trapped the dowager and had subdued her. They had then dragged the feral woman into the most secure dungeon cell that they could find. None of them had been willing to dismember or kill the noblewoman, knowing full well what the consequences of such an action would be upon the duke's return. As a result, many had been injured in the process of her capture.

The rumours across the castle were that the large woman had gone mad, and that she had brutally killed twelve people in the process of her rampage. She was now said to be beyond any rational thought or speech, and was ranting and screaming within the cell where she was confined.

No one had witnessed the fight inside Allana's chambers. Nor had anyone seen the later encounter in the corridor, and there had been no witnesses as Sillene had meekly obeyed Allana's order to leave, like a whipped dog taking an order from its mistress. Only Allana had knowledge of either of those moments.

Allana was aware that she had been indirectly responsible for the deaths of another dozen individuals. Deaths that were in addition to the horrific corruption which she had inflicted upon Sillene Berun. But it would not serve any purpose to dwell upon this, or to suffer from self-recrimination.

You had no choice Lana, remember that. She was going to kill you, and your life is worth more than theirs.

In fact, it was not at all Allana's fault. Her actions had been undertaken in self-defence, in the midst of the dowager's vicious physical assault. Nothing more. Sillene Berun had caused all of the violence and death, and had suffered a terrible but necessary retribution as a consequence of her decision to attack Allana.

As a result of that, it was a happy and fortuitous outcome that Allana had also broken the person who had been the single greatest threat to her position within Berun Castle.

You survived, Lana. As you've survived before, and will survive again. You will always find a way to survive. Whatever the cost.

As Allana arrived at the entrance to the postmaster's office, she realised that she was in a good mood, and that she had been humming a tune to herself. She slipped the sealed parchment out of her pocket and looked down at it. The prior evening's events had at least ended her indecision on this particular matter.

It was time to let Arion Sepian know that she was alive.

8

Corin

—

*Year of Our Lord,
After Ascension, 769AA*

'Agbeth?'

Agbeth did not turn around in response, when Corin first spoke her name. The petite form of Corin's wife was sitting by the shore of the Great Lake, to the west of Karn. She was staring out silently over the lake's rippling waters. Furs were wrapped around her shoulders, protecting her from the cold winds blowing in from the north-west.

As usual, two of Agbeth's rotation of helpers were close by. Today, the first of her companions was Rilka, one of the elderly Karn women responsible for Agbeth's care. The second was Arex, a young warrior who was tasked with her protection.

Corin glanced towards Rilka, and asked quietly, 'How is she today?'

'It's a normal day,' replied the elderly woman, the many lines on her face evidence of her countless years as a clan healer. 'Neither too good, nor too bad. But right now, she's far away from us again.'

Corin nodded, then walked forward to sit down beside his wife, aware that her two companions were withdrawing some distance to allow him privacy. Agbeth did not acknowledge Corin or turn towards him as he joined her, and her wide-open eyes were fixed on some distant point on the lake. As Corin looked at his wife, at the slightly lopsided features which he loved so much, he wondered again about what she might be thinking when she was like this. What thoughts – if any – might be running through her mind? But her stare across the water was unblinking and unbroken, and offered no clues in response.

He placed his hand onto hers, and entwined their fingers together. Then he raised the back of her hand to his mouth, and kissed it. This place seemed to have become one of Agbeth's favourite spots. It was at the end of a small promontory of land which jutted out into the lake, and which offered a panoramic view of the waters north and south. It was not far from the place where Corin had once kissed Agbeth's cheek, a long time ago, on the night when he had first declared his feelings for her.

'I'm back, Agbeth,' he said. 'Back with you, for the next few days. Blackpaw's away hunting right now, but he'll return later to protect you. And I have news! We've won a great battle, and more peace for this land. We're achieving so much, so quickly. So much of what you and I wanted. I hope that you're proud.'

He then proceeded to tell her about the events of recent days, ever since the warriors of Karn had departed the village. She was silent throughout, neither acknowledging him or responding in any other way, and still staring into the distance. But he continued to speak because sometimes, when she re-emerged into more active engagement with the people around her, she had surprised him. Had startled him by remembering and repeating some of the things which he had said to her whilst she was in this *dream*-state.

'And so, we're five clans now, Agbeth,' he said, after several minutes of one-sided conversation. 'Five tribes, joined together. And they all call me the Chosen of the Gods. Your name. You'd laugh, but Chief Munnik told me that he's heard murmurings that I'm also being called the God in the West. Some are even saying Mella Reborn, if you can believe that?'

Of course, there was no response, and she continued to stare outwards. It still did not feel natural to spend time with her like this, in unresponsive conversation, but he was becoming more accustomed to it. And he was in her presence, and she was beside him, and that mattered. It meant something, even if today he could not share in the warmth of her personality.

It was so strange that Agbeth looked normal, and physically recovered, and yet she had not returned to who she had been before the assault by the Anath warrior. The long brown hair of Corin's wife had been brushed and tied into a bunch on the left-hand side of her head, covering the place where a club had struck her, four months earlier. There was still scarring in that place, and a small bald patch, but the position of her hair concealed the traces of the injury, and on the outside she no longer looked unwell.

But Corin alone knew the whole truth of it. Agbeth had been dying, on the very brink of death, or perhaps beyond, and he had *brought her back*. Somehow. And she had indeed returned, but she had come back to him less than whole. The Chosen of the Gods had used his unnatural powers and his force of will to drag his wife back into her life, whether or not she had been a willing recipient, and although she had returned, she had come back *changed*. Damaged. Broken inside.

In the four months since then, she was only occasionally aware and more alert. More often, she was like this, seemingly withdrawn from the world in spirit and awareness. In these periods, she maintained only some of the functions of a normal person. If she was given food and drink, she would consume it. If she was led somewhere, she would compliantly follow, only showing faint signs of resistance if she objected to the destination. However, she did not speak at all when she was in this state, and she demonstrated little visible reaction to the world around her.

Corin was uncertain as to the precise cause of her condition, and he doubted that it could be explained solely by the blow to her head. If that was the only reason, then why did she sometimes return to who she had been, before the injury? Why, for fleeting moments, did she seem to be healed again?

In the preceding months, he had spent many hours pondering and agonising about this. What if the true cause was linked to his own action, of using his powers to drag her back from the precipice of the afterlife? He had *forced* Agbeth to come back, and in doing so she had carried *something else* with her.

And now, there was another presence inside Corin's wife. The *ghost*, as Corin had named it. He believed that this other presence had followed Agbeth's soul, when he had called her back from the brink of death. It had journeyed with her, from wherever she had gone, and it now lurked within her mind, submerged and hidden.

But now was not the time to dwell upon that, while beside his wife in the late-autumn sunshine. Those thoughts were for the dark of night.

'The warriors have called for a feast tonight, Agbeth,' continued Corin. 'To celebrate the victory. And I've agreed to it, but I'll only go to it for a few minutes. After that, after Rilka has prepared you for bed, I'll come and hold you. And we can talk again. I'm so happy to return to you, my love.'

Was there a slight movement in her eyes for a second, a glance towards him? He was not sure, but he wanted to believe it, and he squeezed her hand again. He had accepted that he must receive with happiness whatever communication was still available to her.

He was with Agbeth, and that meant that he was home.

—

The clan feast was in full flow and was turning raucous when Corin departed from it, later that evening. An ale barrel had been opened and was being emptied quickly by the celebrating villagers, although Corin had not indulged at all. He had not drunk ale since returning to Karn from the north, and he doubted that he would ever again consume an alcoholic beverage. Part of him was afraid of how dangerous he might become, if he ever lost control of his senses.

As he walked back towards his home, Corin was able to reflect upon how much the village of Karn had been transformed in the months since he had become clan chief.

After repairing the fire damage from the Anath raid months earlier, the main subsequent improvement had been to the settlement's fortifications. A palisade wall and external ditch now circled the entire village, broken only by two gates at the eastern and western edges. These gates were now guarded by day, and sealed and guarded by night. In addition, Corin had insisted on four watch-towers being built at points around the perimeter, and his next task was to have an internal wooden walkway constructed all the way around the palisade wall. Karn would never again be the easy target for raiding that it had presented in the past.

The Anath village was also close to completing these improvements, and Clan Chief Munnik had been tasked with overseeing these changes to the villages of the Borl, the Qari and now the Renni.

Corin often found that when he was on his own, his mind turned to what he could do to improve the villages. It was not enough for the people of the clans just to fear him, or to revere him as the Chosen. He knew that he also had to demonstrate to them that he could make their lives better. That started with ending the raids and the killing, but he felt that there was so much more that he could achieve. That they all could achieve.

When he arrived back at his home, Rilka was already waiting at the entrance. The elderly woman smiled when she saw him.

'Thank the Gods, you're back,' she said. 'I was just about to send someone to run for you. She's ready for bed, and she's *awake*.'

Corin hurried into the wooden building, immediately looking for Agbeth. She was lying down on her side on the bed, facing towards him. And in her eyes, recognition. Awareness. Intelligence.

'Agbeth?'

He was lying beside her in moments, facing her, his hands clasping hers.

'Corin. Have I been… away… for long?'

He raised her hands to his mouth, and kissed them. 'Not too long, my love. I've been away from the village myself for a few days. And now I'm returned to you.'

'I was dreaming,' she said. Indeed, she still sounded sleepy.

'I know you were. Was it a nice dream?'

'I think so. I remember I was floating, like I was under water, far from the world. The surface seemed so very far away, and for so long I couldn't reach it. I could only watch.'

'Was something stopping you?'

'I'm not sure. I think… *he* was. The boy. He was somewhere close. Holding onto me, and I could hear him sometimes. Whispering.' There was a dreamlike quality to her voice, as she described this.

'Please tell me about him, Agbeth. Who is he? What does he want?'

'He doesn't know, Corin,' she replied. 'But he's scared.'

'Scared about what?'

'I don't know. *He* doesn't know.' For a moment after saying this she frowned, but this expression was quickly replaced by a lopsided smile. 'I just remembered something. I was with Rilka and Arex. And you. Did we sit beside the lake, together?'

Corin grinned in response, his heart swelling. 'We did. We sat beside the lake together. Near our spot. And we talked.'

'I think I remember you speaking to me. You won a battle, you said.'

'That's right! And now we have peace again, Agbeth. I can be with you again. We can live together, in peace.'

'Thank you, Corin. I'm so proud of everything that you're doing.'

'Rilka and Menni have been looking after you, when you are dreaming,' he said. 'They both say that you're getting so much better. So much stronger, now.'

'That's good.'

'How do you feel?'

'I feel… tired. Sleepy.'

Even as she said this, he could see that her eyelids were drooping and threatening to close. And he knew that if she slept, she would be unlikely to wake in this same state of awareness. She would in all likelihood return to wakefulness within her dream-state, staring past him into some unfathomable distance. Not recognising him, and not responding to him.

He blinked his eyes twice, trying to stop a tear from forming, and his lower lip was trembling.

'I'm so glad to be here, just with you, Agbeth. You and me, together.'

'Thank you, Corin. Thank you for looking after me. Despite… how I am.' Was she also crying?

'I love you, Agbeth. Please try to return to me. If there's any way you can, please come back.'

'And I love you, Corin. I wish I could stay with you, but I don't know how…'

Just moments after saying the words, her eyelids shut, and a swift change in her breathing told Corin that she was asleep. He pulled her into an embrace on the bed beside him, and kissed her forehead.

'Goodnight, my love.'

Then he lay there, holding her, and watching the dancing shadows cast by the candles in their room. Tonight, he did not intend to follow her into slumber, or to suffer from his own recurring dream. Instead, he would remain here in this bed for a while, with his arms wrapped around Agbeth.

Soon, he planned to close his eyes, and to make connection with her sleeping mind. And after that, he would try to speak with the ghost.

—

ARE YOU THERE?

The words were Corin's first transmitted thoughts, after invisible tendrils had slipped softly from his mind and had entered his wife's. No longer was there a great void within Agbeth's soul, and Corin could sense her presence, somewhere distant.

However, she was out of reach. Something impenetrable was keeping him away from her, and he was sure that she could neither hear or respond to him. Wherever she resided now, Corin could not follow, and she was lost to him again.

But Corin's words were not intended for his wife. They were a call to the ghost, which often seemed to surface after one of Agbeth's infrequent bouts of awareness.

I'm here.

The voice which gave this answer was that of a boy. Its accent was peculiar, and the sound seemed like a distant whisper from the bottom of a deep well.

WHO ARE YOU? HAVE YOU REMEMBERED YOUR NAME?

In the silence after Corin asked this question, he could feel the unknown presence drawing closer towards him.

I don't know. I can't remember.

WHAT CAN YOU REMEMBER?

I died.

Corin willed himself to remain patient. These were the same confused responses that he had managed to elicit in the past.

HOW DID YOU DIE?

I don't remember.

AGBETH SAID THAT SHE COULD HEAR YOU. CAN YOU REMEMBER AGBETH?

I do. She talks to me in her dreams. We…

The voice trailed off, without completing the sentence.

WHAT DO YOU TALK ABOUT?

I can't remember. I feel… lost.

AGBETH SAYS THAT YOU ARE HOLDING ONTO HER?

I don't want her to leave me in the darkness. Alone. She mustn't leave me.

WHY ARE YOU HERE? HOW AM I ABLE TO SPEAK WITH YOU?

Because we heard you. And you told us that we must come back.
BUT WHAT DOES THAT MEAN?
You told me that I had to come here. I had to. And now I'm trapped and lost. I don't know where I am.

In other circumstances, Corin might have felt some sympathy in response to the anxiety and confusion expressed in the childish voice. However, he had too much need for urgency; the previous encounters with this ghost had been fleeting.

HOW DO I HEAL AGBETH? ARE YOU DOING THIS TO HER?
I don't know. Please don't take her away from me!
HOW DO I SEND YOU BACK?
I don't know! You must… find the Gate? Don't hurt me. Please.
This was new. The presence had never mentioned that before.
THE GATE? WHAT DO YOU MEAN?
I'm sorry. I don't know what I mean. I don't remember.
WHO ARE YOU?
I don't know! I can't remember!
DO YOU KNOW ANYTHING?

Corin snapped this thought at the other, and he immediately regretted the hostility and anger that was contained within it.

The ghost did not answer, and in the prolonged silence which followed, Corin could feel the presence receding from him, as if it was fleeing. Soon, it felt distant, and ready to disappear.

However, as their interaction ended, three final and murmured words drifted across the distance to Corin.

I was murdered…

―

The next morning, Corin awoke early, with Agbeth still sleeping beside him. Several hours of the night had passed as he had communicated with the ghost, although to Corin their contact had seemed brief.

He lay on his side, watching Agbeth as she slept, and for an hour he was able to pretend that everything had returned to normal. He could imagine that she would soon waken, and would greet him with a smile.

But when she opened her eyes in response to the blossoming light of dawn, it was apparent that she was staring past him, into the distance. She had returned to her dream-state.

'I'm going to find a way to heal you, Agbeth,' he whispered, as he stroked her hair. 'I'm going to find a way. Before the Gods, I swear it.'

—

Later, Corin was walking across the village of Karn. He had left Agbeth in the company of her carers, because he intended to spend a day dealing with matters within the settlement.

A mid-morning meeting with his senior advisers had been convened in the restored Clan Hall. As Corin was walking there, with a returned Blackpaw at his side, he was intercepted by his brother Kernon.

'Corin. How is Agbeth?'

Corin looked up at his older and taller brother, and grimaced forlornly. 'Thank you for asking, Kernon. She's… still struggling to recover.'

'I'm truly sorry to hear that.'

Corin still found it unusual whenever he heard Kernon using Agbeth's given name, rather than her insult name. However, he had noticed a remarkable change in his sibling over the last few months, ever since Corin had killed Rekmar and had claimed the chiefdom of the Anath clan. Kernon seemed to have accepted that Corin was his leader, and that the days of bullying his smaller brother were over. Kernon also appeared to be embracing the glory that Corin was bringing to their clan, and the enhanced status that he could enjoy as the Chosen's brother. The old enmity between them was fading fast.

Corin nodded. 'Again, thank you. How can I help you, Kernon?'

'I hoped to get your permission for something, Corin. I'll raise this to discuss at the Clan Hall today, as you've insisted. But I wanted to speak with you first.'

'Permission for what?'

'For me and some of our younger Karn and Anath warriors to approach the Qari. To get horses, and to learn how to ride. I watched the Qari leaders at the battle, on horseback, and I was amazed by them. I'd like to learn.'

Corin forced a smile. 'That's a wonderful idea, Kernon. I was just thinking that same thing, yesterday. That the Qari must teach this to all of the clans. Let's talk about this at the meeting, but you'll have my support.'

Kernon grinned in response. 'Thank you, Corin. I won't let you down.'

Corin had been dwelling upon the possibilities that the expertise of the differing clans offered, ever since the battle with the Renni. How the spears of the Borl, and the horse-riders of the Qari, offered different options in battle. He had not yet fleshed out these thoughts, but he intended to return to them when he had the time.

After a moment of consideration, Corin resolved that he would share something with Kernon. A plan had been forming inside Corin's mind for weeks, and indeed he had been considering it further, that morning.

'I've been thinking, Kernon,' he said. 'Of something which I need to do when winter has passed. And I'd like you to be a part of it.'

'What's that, Corin?'

'I want to go north. *Far* north, further than Agbeth and I ever went. Perhaps as far as to the mountains at the edge of the world. Into the lands of the Gods. In a small party. Me, Blackpaw and a handful of others. And I want you to be one of that party, brother.'

Kernon's eyes widened. 'By the Gods! Yes, of course!'

'Good.'

'But why would you return there, Corin?'

Corin paused for a few seconds, considering an appropriate answer. 'I went to the north, Kernon, and the Gods visited me in my sleep. They chose me, and they gave me these powers. I think at some point soon I must return, to honour them. And to find a way to enhance my powers, and to…'

He did not complete the sentence, but he knew what he had been about to say. *And to save Agbeth.* To find a way to free her from her dream-state.

Corin could not help but turn to look towards the far north as he thought this, and his eyes took in the vast line of distant peaks which covered the horizon. In the next few months, as winter came upon them, his business would be here in the lands of man. Acting for the good of the Chosen people of the five clans. Caring for his wife. Gathering his people.

Gather them. Open the Gate. And claim the power.

The ghost had mentioned the Gate during their interaction, and that had resolved Corin as to what he would have to do. It seemed possible that he could obtain further answers by seeking out the ethereal archway of his dreams. And, perhaps, might he also find the power to restore Agbeth?

Therefore, in spring, he had decided that his attention would return to the north, and to the lands of Gods and felrin. Somewhere in that place, he hoped to find the Gate, and a way to cure his wife.

—

A week later, Corin was in the Clan Hall when he heard a bustle of noise from the central area of the village. It was a commotion equivalent to the day when he and Agbeth had returned to Karn, and a crowd had assembled to watch them.

Interested to understand what was happening, he donned his fur cloak and headed outside, where he saw that a large number of people were gathering. The villagers were forming a circle, in the centre of which were four Karn warriors, who surrounded and appeared to be escorting a woman.

The warriors were all well-known to him, but the woman was not. She was of average height, with a gaunt face, and looked to be in her late-thirties in age. Her hair was straight and shoulder-length, with a few streaks of grey showing amidst the black. She was wearing long and dark robes, which were unfamiliar in style, and she wore a sizeable backpack. She appeared to bear the weight of this pack by leaning on the tall wooden staff which she held in her left-hand.

Corin stepped closer to the woman, and he could see her grey-blue eyes scrutinising him, and appearing to appraise him. He also took note of the wooden object hanging from her neck; a strange carving of a man who appeared to be wrapped around a tree, with sticks in his shoulders.

Corin was about to greet her, but the woman spoke first, in a manner which was both fast-paced and unusual.

'And you must be Chief Corin of the Karn, the Chosen of the Gods.' She bowed her head. 'I've heard a lot about you, Chief Corin, and I've travelled long and hard to get to you before winter sets in. My name is Hellin of Condarron, and I've found you, and am delivered to you, by the Grace of The Lord Aiduel.'

Corin frowned as he regarded her, before he replied, 'The Lord Aiduel? Who's that?'

9

Leanna

—

*Year of Our Lord,
After Ascension, 769AA*

In the moments after the grey-bearded stranger had spoken, following his killing of the leather-clad assailants, Leanna was unable to summon a response. She was too stunned by the violence which had just taken place.

Amyss was standing upright, behind Leanna, and the priestess's hand was still gripping Leanna's as they stood in the corner of the cathedral chancel. However, Leanna could not sense any emotions from Amyss or from this burly stranger. Nothing at all. Her powers were still absent.

'Why should I go with you?' Leanna asked the man, as a noise which sounded like the chopping of axes came from the direction of the cathedral doors. 'I don't know you.'

'As I said, I'm Caddin Sendromm, Priestess Leanna. And we don't have time for this.' The man's voice was deep and rumbling. 'If you stay here, you'll die before this day is over. You *must* come with me.'

'How do we know that you don't mean us harm?'

In response, he looked at the bodies surrounding him and said, 'Because if I meant to do you harm, Priestess, you'd already be dead. But if you stay here, Aiduel's Guards will murder you before the day is out. I believe they'd been planning to get you out of this city peacefully, and then to kill you in secret on the return to Sen Aiduel. But now that this… *assassination* attempt… has led to dei Corsi's death, they'll cast off the shackles of pretence. They're camped just miles away, and they'll be attacking this city before night has fallen. If they find you, they'll murder you. I can keep you alive. Come with me.'

He moved a pace towards Leanna, still holding his hefty mace.

Lord Aiduel, please give me the wisdom to know the truth of this man.

'If they're going to attack this city, then I must give myself up to them, as soon as possible,' she said, glancing in the direction of the noise from the cathedral doors. 'I'm not going to be the cause of more bloodshed.'

A grimace appeared within the grey beard. The man took another step forward, and said, 'We *don't* have time for this. Come with me.'

'No. I must remain here.'

The man twisted his thick neck, looking annoyed. He then lifted the mace and pointed the chunky metal head towards Amyss, past Leanna's shoulder.

'If you don't come with me willingly, and *now*, then I'll kill this woman, who you seem so keen to protect. Then I'll knock *you* out, and I'll carry you out of here anyway. I'm not allowing you the choice of sacrificing yourself for the greater good today, *Angel of Arlais*. I'm going to keep you alive, whether you want me to or not. Now, last chance to save your friend. Follow me.'

Leanna stared into the man's eyes, and even without her powers she sensed that he was telling the truth. That he would not hesitate to murder Amyss, in order to get what he wanted.

'Very well,' she said. 'I'll follow you.'

'A wise decision. She must come, too.'

The next few minutes were a confused blur for Leanna. Within moments, she and Amyss were following Caddin Sendromm past an horrific tableau of bodies, before heading through a doorway set within the right-hand wall of the cathedral. Sendromm closed the door behind them, then led them down a steep flight of stairs to a murky, subterranean passage.

At the foot of the stairs, the grey-bearded man extracted a lit candle from an alcove in the wall. Leanna recoiled in shock when this movement of light revealed another corpse, which was just a few steps along the underground corridor. It was a leather-clad individual, whose neck was twisted at an unnatural angle.

'I spotted them following you,' said Sendromm, after noting where her eyes were directed. 'I followed them in turn, and found their route in here. This one happened to fall down these stairs just as he was about to fire his crossbow again. Now, stay close.'

He moved off, candle-holder in one hand and his hefty mace still clutched in the other. Then Leanna and Amyss were following him again, walking through subterranean tunnels which were illuminated only by the candle. Leanna was lost within minutes.

On a couple of occasions, as Sendromm moved a few paces ahead, Leanna thought about grabbing Amyss's hand and trying to flee. However, the grey-bearded man had the only source of light. There would be no chance to elude him within these tunnels, if they were stumbling blindly in darkness, and he might hurt Amyss in retribution. Leanna therefore dismissed the idea.

Lord Aiduel, please let me know what this man's intentions are. And please keep Amyss safe from him.

Eventually, the tunnel started to slope upwards. After feeling like they had been ascending for some time, Leanna spotted a source of natural light up ahead. When they arrived there, the passageway ended at a circular opening, perhaps three feet across, which appeared to provide access to the outside world. It seemed that iron bars had previously been in place to block this opening, but that these had been cut and twisted out of position.

Another leather-clad male body was splayed against the wall, a metre from the hole. The brutal manner of this man's death was suggested by a lengthy smear of red on the bricks above his bloody head.

Caddin Sendromm turned to Leanna and Amyss. When he spoke, his tone was both urgent and menacing. 'Now, both of you, listen very carefully. And make sure that you comply with everything I say, if you want red-head here to live. Outside this hole is a six-foot drop, down to a quiet alleyway at the rear of the cathedral complex. We'll be a couple of hundred metres away from the main entrance. Further down this street, I have a horse-drawn wagon. We're all going to drop out of this hole, and you're both going to walk quietly and compliantly to that wagon, and get on it. I'm going to be walking with red-head here-'

'Her name is Amyss,' said Leanna, feeling fearful for her companion. 'She's a good person.'

The man glared at her through lowered brows, but then continued, 'I'm going to be walking with *Amyss* here. Very close to her. And if either of you shout out, or try to run, then I'll snap Amyss's neck with my bare hands. In an instant. Is that understood, Priestess Leanna?'

'Yes,' said Leanna. 'Don't hurt her, please. I'm not going to try to run.'

'Very well. I'll lower you down first, Angel of Arlais. Then Amyss and I will drop down together.'

In the following seconds, Leanna stepped gingerly over the dead body and crawled into the circular opening. She could hear Caddin Sendromm and Amyss following her. At the end of the narrow tunnel, she could see the cobbled alleyway below. It was deserted in both directions.

Sendromm took hold of Leanna's wrist, and lowered her over the edge. By the time that their arms had extended fully, her feet were touching the ground, and he released her. Seconds later, the man's own burly form appeared, hanging with his lower half over the edge, his mace and shield both strapped to his back. Leanna watched as Sendromm also encouraged Amyss through the round exit, and then forced her to drop to the ground alongside him.

'This way,' the man ordered, his free hand clutching Amyss's arm and pulling her behind him.

Thirty metres down the alley, they came upon Sendromm's open-top wagon, which had a horse hitched to it. In the rear of the vehicle, there appeared to be a variety of goods, which were largely covered by a tarpaulin.

'Priestess Leanna,' said Sendromm, 'climb onto the wagon bed at the front. Get under the tarpaulin, and get changed. Take those robes off, and put on the clothes I've left under there. Then stay under the tarpaulin, out of sight.'

'You've planned this?' asked Leanna. 'You're kidnapping us? Abducting us?'

'Yes, I've planned it,' replied Sendromm, sounding irritated. 'But I'm trying to *save* you, you fool.' He then gave a meaningful glance towards Amyss, whose arm he was still clutching. 'Now do as I say, Priestess Leanna, for the sake of your friend. You, Amyss, I don't have any other spare clothes for you. But there's a blanket there, wrap that around you to cover your clothing. You'll be riding up front on the wagon alongside me, as surety for the Angel's good behaviour. And if we get stopped, I'm your *father*. Understand?'

Amyss nodded cautiously, then the three of them clambered onto the wagon, the grey-bearded man taking up the reins. Leanna found that there was a space perhaps five feet long and two feet wide at the front end of the wagon bed, nearest the driver's seat. She lowered herself into this confined area, lying down on her side. Sendromm then clipped the tarpaulin into place above her, closing off her view of the outside world. The clothes which he had referred to were bundled at one end of this space, near Leanna's head. After a moment's hesitation, she started to pull off her robes, and to get changed.

'Remember, Priestess Leanna,' Sendromm said, 'your friend is sitting up here, alongside me. I want total silence from you. No talking, no complaining. And if you shout out as we're travelling through the town, or in any way try to use your powers or do anything else to thwart me, then she'll be the first to die. Do you understand?'

'Yes,' said Leanna, feeling scared. She had no doubts about the stranger's capacity and willingness to deliver brutal violence.

Lord Aiduel, please protect Amyss and me from this dangerous man.

—

In the minutes after that, Leanna could feel and hear the wagon trundling through the cobbled streets of the city. She was now dressed in the clothes of a common-woman of Arlais.

Her enclosed space under the tarpaulin was cramped, and it soon became uncomfortable. Alone with her thoughts, Leanna was even more aware that her powers were still absent. There was a miniscule trace of something there, tantalisingly out of reach, but it was nothing which she could draw upon or use. Caddin Sendromm seemed to be able to extinguish her abilities as comprehensively as a candle-snuffer might put out a flame.

Lord Aiduel, how can he subdue these holy powers, which you alone have granted to me?

On her own in the confined space, Leanna's mind was also replaying images of the carnage in the cathedral. Despite her wartime experience with the dead and wounded, the remembrance of the sudden eruption of violence was making her feel queasy.

All those people. Alive one moment, then dead the next. Poor Priestess Corenna. Lorth Dormer and his men. Archprime dei Corsi. Alongside all of the others who had lost their lives in those brutal few minutes.

The only other survivor had been El'Patriere, who had somehow found the presence of mind to flee immediately. But Leanna could not help but feel suspicious; had it actually been presence of mind, or had he known what was coming, and been complicit in the attack? There was no certain answer to that, but the Senior Priest *had* deliberately slammed and locked the chancel door, with full awareness that he would likely be condemning Leanna and Amyss to death.

Lord Aiduel, please offer your salvation to the innocents killed today, and deliver your justice against the evildoers.

As Leanna lay there, feeling helpless, she was also worried that Amyss would try to do something reckless in an attempt to free her. She was therefore surprised when she heard Amyss say, 'I remember you, from the hospital. Who were those men, at the cathedral?'

'Quiet!' hissed Caddin Sendromm.

'I'm talking quietly,' replied Amyss, clearly addressing her comments to their captor. 'And for all of your threats, I see what you're trying to do. You want to get Leanna out of this city, and away from danger. I want that too, so I'm not going to cause you any trouble. I'm just a daughter on a wagon, remember? Talking to her father.'

'Be quiet.'

'I am being quiet. Who were they?'

'Very well, if it'll silence you,' said Sendromm. 'They were assassins. One of them is a man who'd been tasked to find and kill the Angel's kind. I knew of him, and I recognised him and his hirelings last week. I saw that they were tracking her.'

'Tasked by who?'

'The Archlaw. That's how I know that Aiduel's Guards fully intend to murder her, once they have her.'

'The Angel's kind, you said?'

'Enough, now. No more questions.'

'But how do you know all of this?' asked Amyss.

'Be quiet!' the man ordered. This time there was more threat in his voice, and Amyss did indeed fall silent.

After that, Leanna remained on the wagon bed, on her side, as the wagon continued to trundle across the town.

—

She had drifted into a daydream when she heard the voice of Caddin Sendromm again.

'We're approaching the city's western edge now,' he said. 'We'll pass through a guard point there. There's to be no talking as we approach it, other than by me. And remember, Amyss is *right beside me*.'

Leanna realised that at some point they must have travelled along streets that were close to the home of her parents.

Lord Aiduel, please protect them from whatever is going to happen to this city, in the coming days.

Shortly after, she could feel the wagon grinding to a halt, followed by muffled words which she believed had been spoken by a city guard.

'Yes, yes, that's right, friend!' said Caddin Sendromm. His voice sounded higher-pitched and more friendly. 'Fully loaded!'

There was more speech which Leanna could not discern, but she thought that she could hear feet walking around the wagon.

Lord Aiduel, please keep Amyss safe if they discover me!

'Yes, that's right, to Andar,' said Sendromm. 'Now that they've re-opened all of the bridges, I have a wagon-load of Arlais goods for them. This'll fetch some good prices, friend. Some money to be made right now, for a canny man. And even some for a less canny man like me!'

Leanna heard him laughing out loud, sounding like the most good-natured man one could ever hope to meet.

There was more muffled speech, to which Sendromm replied, 'Oh, this one is my daughter. Although she's shy, around handsome guards like you.' Another unheard question followed this, before Sendromm chuckled and said, 'Oh, *that*. Please, pay the weapon no mind, friend. It's my travelling companion, and keeps me safe on the road, sometimes. No need for a good fellow like you to be concerned by it.'

He chuckled once more, and his laughter was echoed by whomever had been doing the questioning. Moments later, Leanna could feel the wagon moving again.

They had left Arlais.

The wagon had been trundling along for another thirty minutes when the tarpaulin above Leanna was pushed back. Amyss's head appeared above the opening.

'How are you feeling, Lea?' she asked.

'Not so good, after everything that's happened. You?'

'Same. A bit shocked and numb. But he's done nothing to harm me.'

Amyss looked different, with her flame-coloured hair flowing loose and the blanket thrown like a shawl around her shoulders. She was not recognisable at all as a priestess.

'You can sit up, Priestess Leanna, if you promise to behave,' stated Caddin Sendromm. 'We're out in the countryside now, away from the city. But don't even think about trying to flee. You wouldn't get far, and then I'd have to tie you up and gag you, and put you back under there for the journey ahead.'

Leanna lifted herself to a sitting position as suggested, stretching her aching legs and back as she did so. She raised her head out of the open flap, and turned to look behind the wagon. The vehicle was moving them along a wide dirt road, steadily gaining distance from Arlais.

Leanna turned back to address their captor. 'You said to the guards that we're going to Andar. Is that true?'

'Yes,' said Sendromm. 'We need to cross the border into Western Canasar. I've heard that they've banished Aiduel's Guards in Andar now, so if we can cross the river, they won't be able to follow us.'

'We must go back,' replied Leanna. 'Not run away. Please. After dei Corsi's death, and without me there to surrender myself, the Guards could attack Arlais. You might be condemning hundreds of people to death.' There was silence from the burly man, and Leanna added, 'Please, turn this wagon around, and take me back. Please.'

'No.'

'But it's my choice to make! Why do you even care?'

'I care because I think I know what you are, Priestess Leanna. I care because even after just a short time of hearing about you, and following you, I know what decision you'll make. You'll meekly give yourself up, in order to save others. But this time, if you end up in the hands of those Aiduel's Guards, you'll die. And they won't put you on a pyre. You'll be murdered somewhere quiet, with a knife across your throat, away from the eyes of an audience.'

'You don't know that for certain!' said Leanna, feeling frustrated. But even as she stated this, a recollection came back to her. A memory of a fleeting moment in the meeting with dei Corsi, when a foreign image had flashed into Leanna's mind, as if she had witnessed dei Corsi's secret imaginings. Of Leanna at night, in woods. Pinned down, and about to be murdered by Aiduel's Guards.

'I *do* know it,' replied Sendromm. 'And so do you, priestess. And Amyss here certainly understands it. I think she's even supporting me now, hoping that I'll drag you to safety, rather than allowing you to offer yourself up for martyrdom.'

Leanna glanced towards Amyss upon hearing this. The smaller woman blushed and looked away, suggesting that Caddin Sendromm had indeed touched upon the truth.

Leanna felt herself growing angry. 'By whose authority do you have the right to kidnap me? To make my decisions for me?'

'I have the right of someone who's going to stop you from doing something stupid, girl. I think that your life may be worth more than a few hundred, or even a few thousand, other lives in Arlais, Priestess Leanna. You just don't understand that, yet. But I'm going to keep you alive, Angel of Arlais, for as long as I'm able to. I've already made that vow to myself. And now I'm making it to you. As such, I'm taking away your choice.'

'But my parents are there! They're in danger! Can we at least go back for them? Warn them?'

'No. Once I get *you* to safety, we can think about your parents. Not before.'

'Please. The hospital needs me! Colissa needs to know what's happened!'

'No. We're not going back, so stop asking. And calm yourself down! Don't force me to come back there and gag you.'

Lord Aiduel, please give me the strength to deal with this cold man!

Leanna tried to control her emotions. She took a number of deep breaths, watching the countryside pass by as they travelled in silence for a number of minutes. When she was finally calmer, she said, 'You mentioned earlier, when we were still in the city, that the Archlaw had tasked people to kill me and my kind. What did you mean?'

He sighed, before responding. 'Exactly that. The assassins were there today for *you*. Probably set on their task many years ago, independent of any current schemes of Meira dei Corsi, or Aiduel's Guards, or even the Archlaw himself. Foolish of dei Corsi's herald to announce where your meeting was going to be. The killers knew you were going to be there, and they'd found a route in to wait for you, before springing their trap. Lucky for you that I detected them. I followed them and worked out what they were planning, and you should be thankful that I was able to get to you in time.'

'But you said "the Angel's kind", earlier,' said Leanna. 'What did that mean?'

'You're different to everyone else, Priestess Leanna, but for a handful of others. I would hope that you're aware of that, by now?'

'A handful of others? What do you know about others?'

'That's a conversation for a time of my choosing, priestess,' he said. 'But you *are* different, and I'm going to keep you alive.'

'But how do you know all of this? Just *who* are you? And why aren't my powers working, when I'm near you?'

'More questions for another time. I'm here to get you to safety, Priestess Leanna, not to answer your questions.'

'I don't think he means to do us harm, Lea,' said Amyss, glancing at their large captor as she spoke. 'If he did, he would've done it already. I think he *is* trying to keep you alive.' She then looked up and met Leanna's stare. 'And he's correct, you *were* going to end up giving yourself over to them, no matter what doubts you had about your own safety. If I'm being honest, I'm glad that he's stopping you from doing it.'

Leanna folded her arms. 'So, I'm simply going to abandon my parents, and the people and the city of Arlais? And I'm to sit here, like a coward and a prisoner, until we cross into Andar?'

'Yes, Leanna,' replied Amyss, her hand reaching out to touch Leanna's arm. 'And I want you to. Is it so wrong for me to want you to survive, Lea? I'm not ashamed to say that I *want* him to keep you alive! And for good reasons, too. You're a miracle-worker! You heal the sick! You've been blessed by Aiduel, and His power flows through you. *That* is why you mustn't sacrifice yourself.'

'Amyss-'

'Please, Lea! I ask so little of you, but please, just this once, if you love me, do this for me! Come to Andar. Don't go back to Arlais, to martyr yourself. I couldn't bear to lose you again!'

Lord Aiduel, am I being a coward by not trying to escape? But how can I hurt Amyss by denying her this request?

'Very well,' said Leanna, after a few moments of contemplation. 'I won't resist further, Amyss, if you don't want me to. I'll accept this for you. But only if he agrees to let me help my parents.'

Amyss beamed in relief in response to this statement.

'You're in no position to bargain, girl,' stated Caddin Sendromm. 'This is my choice, not yours. However, after I've got you to safety, I'll try to do something to help your parents.'

'Thank you,' said Leanna.

'But to be clear, you're not out of danger yet,' continued Sendromm. 'I expect that matters in Arlais will have played out something like this; when the group at the cathedral doors finally managed to break in, they'll have discovered the murders there. And that you're missing, presumed kidnapped. Whilst the militia will start a hunt for you, the surviving members of Aiduel's Guards will return to their camp. And they'll probably be mustering already, to descend upon the city.

'Now, it's possible that everyone concentrates all their efforts within the city boundaries, and doesn't even consider that you could already be outside. But it's equally likely that one or both sides send out patrols in all directions. Including this way, to the west. We won't be safe until we cross the Ninth Bridge. So, you two keep your eyes in all directions, and if you see anything, you both get under that tarpaulin.'

Amyss looked worried as he said this, and she asked, 'How far to the border?'

'Almost twenty miles,' Sendromm replied. 'It'll be late-afternoon before we reach it. We'd best hope that no one is too clear-minded or organised, given the speed that this wagon moves. So, go join your friend in the back, Priestess Amyss, and stay low. We've a long way to go.'

Amyss clambered backwards to join Leanna in the small space at the front of the wagon bed. The two of them then hunkered down, with just their heads raised higher than the sides of the wagon, and they prepared for the long journey ahead.

—

The light was fading in the late-afternoon when Caddin Sendromm stopped the vehicle, and ordered Leanna and Amyss to lie down in the space under the tarpaulin.

'We're two miles from the river,' he announced. 'But I've spotted horse-riders in the distance, behind us. I want you both out of sight. And no more talking. No sounds at all.'

Leanna and Amyss arranged themselves on their sides, facing each other within the cramped area, their mouths just inches apart and their arms and legs entwined. Caddin Sendromm then dropped a sheet over the two of them, and they heard him re-arranging certain boxes to slide the edges forwards, further concealing them. Finally, the tarpaulin was clipped back into place, sealing them from the outside world.

Leanna could feel Amyss's nervous breathing against her face, as the wagon moved off again. It was getting darker outside as the sun was setting, and there was now very little light in their hiding space. For the next few minutes, the wagon continued onwards. Then Leanna heard the whinny of a horse, accompanied by the stamp of multiple hooves. Moments later, the wagon came to a halt.

This time, Leanna could clearly hear the drawling voice which called, 'Where have you come from, old man, and what's in the wagon?'

The accent was that of Dei Magnus.

Caddin Sendromm replied, 'Ah, good friends, thank you for your interest. I'm a merchant from Elannis City. Taking trade goods to Andar.'

'And you came from Arlais?'

'On this road, yes, of course I did, master,' said Sendromm. 'But I simply passed through there. I'm running late with this delivery. My customer's going to be docking my payment, if I don't get there soon!'

Leanna noted that Caddin Sendromm had once again assumed the persona of a good-natured citizen. She could also hear the whickering of horses, and the clopping of hooves, on either side of the wagon. There was certainly more than one person here. Perhaps several, surrounding them. She could also sense a quickening in Amyss's breathing, and she placed a hand forward onto the small priestess's cheek to try to calm her.

'Let's see your goods, then,' ordered the Dei Magnun, whose voice was now closer. It seemed that he was peering over the side of the wagon.

'Forgive me, good sirs,' said Sendromm. 'I'm but a humble merchant, but I'm not aware that it's in the authority of Aiduel's Guards to stop traffic on the highway, and to inspect it?'

'*Our weapons* give us our authority today, old man. Now, you'll get down from there and open up this wagon, so we can see what you're carrying. Or, we'll drag you off that seat, and then we'll open it up and do it ourselves. Your choice, merchant.'

'Forgive me, good sir, no offence was meant. Here, here.'

Leanna could hear Caddin clambering down from his seat, the burly man making a huffing and wheezing noise as he did so. Suddenly, there was a loud thud, accompanied by what sounded like the anguished squeal of a horse. This was followed by cursing, and a second howl of pain, this time from a person.

A frantic Dei Magnun voice shouted, 'Surround him!'

Leanna could hear Amyss whimpering in fear as there were several crashing sounds beside the wagon. Something then smashed into the vehicle's side, causing it to rock. Leanna's heart was beating hard as she listened to the repeated sounds which followed of metal bashing against metal.

Seconds then passed with more panicked cursing, none of which came from Caddin Sendromm, before there was a loud Dei Magnun plea.

'Please, no-'

A squelching noise. And then there was silence.

Moments later, Leanna felt and heard a figure climbing back onto the driver's seat, in front of them. The wagon then started to move again, slowly trundling forwards.

'They won't be completing their inspection,' announced Sendromm.

Shortly afterwards, the wagon stopped again, and the tarpaulin above Leanna and Amyss was pulled back. The night sky was now dark.

'Both of you, get up,' said Sendromm, in a gentler tone. 'There's something that you need to see.'

He shoved back boxes and other containers to clear space for Leanna and Amyss, who then raised themselves up.

'How far to go?' asked Amyss.

'Less than a mile to the Ninth Bridge,' replied Sendromm. 'This is the last high point before we descend back to the river. But first, look back. That way.'

He was pointing behind them. Leanna and Amyss turned at the same time, and the source of Caddin's interest was immediately apparent to Leanna. An orange glow, in the distance. Clearly visible, although many miles separated their current position and the source of that light.

'What is it?' asked Amyss, before realisation came to her, and she added, 'May The Lord preserve us.'

Arlais was burning. In the place where the city stood, there was an unmistakeable glare of flame.

There was silence for a number of seconds, before Caddin said, 'You can ride beside me now, as we cross the border, *daughters*. As long as you promise not to cause any trouble. But you must see that you cannot go back there.'

Leanna's mouth was dry as she observed the fate of her home city. She said, 'This is all my fault, Amyss.'

'No, it's not, Lea! That's not true! It's not! You didn't have a choice.'

Leanna was numb inside, feeling responsibility for all of the suffering that she feared must be going on there. And worry for her parents, and for the good people of the College. However, she knew that it was too late for her to change the fate of Arlais and its citizens. No good could be done now by returning to her home, and by offering herself up as sacrifice.

Lord Aiduel, please protect my parents, and Sister Colissa, and the people of the College and the hospital. Please keep them safe from harm.

'It *is* my fault, Amyss,' said Leanna, 'but the damage has already been done. I promise that we'll not cause you any trouble at the border, Caddin Sendromm.'

'Good,' he replied. 'Both of you, climb up here.'

After a few moments, as she and Amyss seated themselves alongside the burly man, Leanna said quietly, 'It's my duty to stay alive, to repay the people of Arlais for what they've suffered for me. But The Lord Aiduel will judge us all for our actions and choices here today. Particularly you, Caddin Sendromm.'

His face contorted into a sneer after she said this, and he replied, 'I've been damned by The Lord for longer than I care to mention, girl. Why should I care about one more act of sin?'

The wagon then started to move forwards again, rolling slowly along the dark highway. Travelling towards the border, and to the sanctuary of Andar.

—

The Canas River crossing proved to be uneventful, and they passed by the respective Elannis and Andar border guards with little threat or challenge. Leanna and Amyss were silent during the border inspection, while Caddin Sendromm engaged in amicable exchanges with the soldiers on the bridge.

The grey-bearded man kept the wagon rolling for hours more that chill night, taking them far away from the Ninth Bridge and its accompanying fortresses. They were following the wide River Road southward into Western Canasar. It was the same highway which Leanna had once travelled whilst in the company of the invading Army of Western Elannis.

Leanna and Amyss were huddled together, shivering beneath a shared blanket. After the awful spectacle of seeing Arlais burning in the distance, neither of them was in the mood for talk, and they travelled in silence.

They reached a tavern in a small roadside village in the middle of the night. Caddin roused the owner, and after a curt discussion and an exchange of coin, he secured two rooms; one for him, and a twin room for Leanna and Amyss.

After the two priestesses were safely ensconced in their room that night, Amyss put her mouth close to Leanna's ear and whispered, 'What are we going to do now, Lea? Should we stay with this man, or should we run away?'

Leanna frowned, considering. 'For now, I think we should stay with him, Amyss. For now, I think that we need him.'

—

The next morning, Leanna woke early. After dressing, she knocked on the door of Caddin Sendromm's room, ready to confront him.

His response was a grunted, 'Come in.'

As Leanna entered the room, the stale smell of alcohol was immediate and overpowering. Sendromm was lying down on his bed, fully clothed above the sheets, with his head propped up. His mace rested against the wall next to the bed's headboard, and three empty pitchers stood on the floor alongside the weapon. Sendromm's cheeks were veined and purple, and the eyes which he turned towards Leanna were bloodshot.

'You got drunk, last night?' she asked, struggling to keep the disapproval from her voice.

'Yes, I did,' he answered, his voice hoarse. 'And why not? I did myself a lot of killing again yesterday, Priestess Leanna. And when I kill, I drink. Always have, and old habits die very hard.'

Lord Aiduel, please help me to choose the right words with this man.

'I wanted to speak with you,' she said. 'But... I didn't expect to find you... like *this*.'

'If you're just here to judge me, then leave me be, girl. My head hurts too much.'

'That's not why I'm here.'

Sendromm yawned and then belched, before saying, 'Enlighten me, then?'

'I need you to go back to Arlais, to help my parents to get away.'

'I don't think so. Too risky.'

'You agreed that if you got me to safety, you'd do something to help my parents.'

'Yes. Something. But not that. And not now.'

'If you don't do it, I'll have to go back myself.'

'No, you won't,' he said, before yawning again.

Lord Aiduel, please give me the courage to stand up to this man.

'I will, and I won't allow you to stop me. And if you don't agree to do this, then I'll certainly refuse to travel any further with you. And I'll go downstairs to announce to anyone who'll listen that you've kidnapped Amyss and me.'

Leanna could hear her voice wavering as she said this last part. Making threats was against her nature, and she sensed that she sounded more frightened than intimidating.

In response, Sendromm forced himself to an upright position, then swung his legs down onto the floor. He glanced briefly towards his mace, then focused his eyes upon Leanna, with a fierce look on his face.

'Ah, so the virtuous priestess is prepared to play dirty, once in a while? Threatening me? Are you sure that you want to play that sort of game with someone like me, girl? Do you really want to put the lives of Amyss and all of those people downstairs in danger?'

Leanna swallowed, determined not to back down. 'I'm not playing a game. And you can just stop threatening me, too! I want you to go back to get my parents, like you promised. You must tell them that I'm alive and that they must come here. And you must help them to get away.'

Sendromm paused, suddenly appearing to be more alert and focused, before saying, 'Very well. Let's say I do that. What would you give me in return?'

Leanna frowned, feeling uncertain. 'What do you want?'

'Your oath, before The Lord, that you'll wait for me here, and that once I return, you'll remain in my company. For, let's say… a year. That you'll accept me as your protector for that time, and that we'll travel together. Oh, and that you'll not ask me questions about my past.'

Leanna paused, considering. The thought of travelling with this man for any length of time was not appealing, but he was her best chance to help her parents.

Lord Aiduel, please guide my decision.

'Why does it matter so much to you that we travel together?' she asked.

'My reasons are my own. But let's just say that I don't want to see someone with your… *talents*, end up with their throat cut, or with their head smashed in.'

His bloodshot eyes were locked upon hers as he said this, and she was not sure what to make of his last statement. She paused, considering.

'Three months,' she said, finally. 'I'll give my word to wait here, and then to remain with you for three months. But only if you swear that you're going to go to Arlais, and that you'll try to bring my parents back with you. And there are to be no more threats against Amyss. If you ever hurt her-'

'Six months,' he interrupted. 'And I promise not to hurt or to threaten to hurt red-head again. If you agree, I'll saddle a horse and I'll be on my way to Arlais within the hour. I'll go to your parents and, if I can, I'll bring them back with me. While you promise to stay here. Now, give me your oath. Before The Lord, and on the Holy Book.'

Leanna stared at him, hesitant about what she was committing to. Eventually, she said, 'Very well, I swear that if you return to Arlais to help my parents, I'll travel with you. Before The Lord, and on the Holy Book.'

Sendromm belched again, then said, 'There you go. That wasn't too difficult, was it? Now, tell me all about your parents and your home, so I know what I'm looking for.'

—

Sendromm departed that morning. He paid a local to keep watch over his goods, and set off riding southwards on his horse, this time without the wagon. He was planning to approach Arlais by a circuitous route from the Eighth Bridge, to avoid the highways that they had travelled on the day before.

He was gone for three days, during which time Leanna and Amyss remained in or close to the roadside tavern. They left the premises once, to procure some alternative clothes for themselves from a villager. However, apart from at meal times they otherwise remained in their room, and out of sight. They spent a lot of time trying to process the shocking events of Arlais Cathedral, but there were also long periods of silence as they waited for Sendromm.

Late on the third day, he finally returned and came directly to their room. He was grim-faced.

'Parts of central Arlais have been burned and destroyed,' he announced. 'And your parents are gone.'

'Gone?' repeated Leanna, feeling dizzy. Amyss moved closer, and put her arm around Leanna's back.

'Yes,' said Sendromm. 'The neighbours I managed to contact had not seen them since Fifth-Day morning. I had to be careful who I spoke to, because there's a nasty presence of Aiduel's Guards on the streets. But no one had seen them since the attack at the cathedral. Lots of people attended their house that day, apparently, after you went missing. And those who I spoke to think your parents went off to the College of Aiduel, to join the search for you. But they haven't returned to their home since then. Nor has your father been seen at his business.'

'And did you go to the College?' asked Leanna, with a tremor in her voice.

'No, it was impossible. Aiduel's Guards have taken over the College complex, and have also reclaimed their fortress. There were just too many of the Guards there to be able to get into the College.'

Lord Aiduel, what have I brought upon my parents? Please protect them.

'Did you manage to find anything else out?' queried Amyss.

'Nothing significant,' stated Sendromm. 'But if Leanna's parents are wise, they'll be in hiding now, and they shouldn't return to their home.'

'What do you mean?' asked Leanna.

'I observed your house. There were two Aiduel's Guards

stationed there, at the front entrance. No one had witnessed the redcloaks taking your parents, but if you or they return to your home, the Guards will be waiting.'

'So, what can we do?' queried Leanna, feeling helpless.

'With regard to your parents? Nothing more. If they're already dead, then there's nothing to be gained by you returning to Arlais.' Leanna felt queasy as Sendromm casually stated this. 'And if they're alive, I'm quite certain that they wouldn't want you to return and risk yourself, by looking for them. Anyway, in the short-term, it's too dangerous for you to try to find them, Priestess Leanna. Perhaps we can try to contact them again, weeks or months from now. But for now, you must do what I suspect they'd want you to do, and that is to stay alive.'

Leanna felt a wave of woe rising up inside, and the next moment she was crying, with her head buried in Amyss's shoulder. The petite woman pulled her into a hug.

Caddin Sendromm left them like that, holding each other.

—

The next day, Caddin had re-hitched his horse to the wagon, and they were preparing to travel again.

Leanna had shed many tears the night before, but had now regained her composure. As they were about to set off, she stated, 'I believe that you've acted in good faith, Caddin Sendromm, and that you've saved my life. As such, we agree to travel with you.'

He nodded, and said, 'Very well. But first, we must decide where we are to go.'

'I have a place in mind,' said Leanna. 'Somewhere that I must go to, and someone I must meet, before we do anything else.'

After she had explained this, they set off on the horse-drawn wagon, heading deeper into the lands of Western Canasar, and away from Arlais.

It was time for a reunion.

10

Arion

—

*Year of Our Lord,
After Ascension, 769AA to 770AA*

Arion Sepian was sitting within his bedroom chambers in the early morning, on the edge of his mattress. His chest was bare, and he was enjoying the site of his pretty wife getting dressed before him.

'And she admitted to me, she and Lennion have been writing to each other, ever since our wedding,' said Kalyane, who was pulling her dress over her shoulders as she talked. Her auburn hair was hanging down along her slim, naked back. 'She wanted to tell me first, so I could let you know, before any of us speak to Gerrion. But I think that they're quite smitten with each other!'

Kalyane was talking with excitement about Karienne, Arion's younger sister. Lennion was Kalyane's older brother, and Arion's close friend.

'I'm pleased for them both,' he said, feeling a mild sense of loss once Kalyane had covered her body up. 'But someone must talk to

Gerrion about it soon. He may still want Karienne to be matched with another house, for political reasons.'

'Someone?' said Kalyane, with amusement in her voice.

Arion shrugged. 'Well… not me, obviously. You know I've no talent for that kind of thing. But if *you* were to offer your services to talk to him, well… I think that'd be great.'

She laughed. 'Very well. But not just yet, my husband. Gerrion will already have far too much to think about in the next few days.'

They continued to chat as Arion started to dress, untypically at ease with each other, and Arion recognised that he was enjoying her company. He had arrived home from Andarron just the evening before, and she had greeted him warmly, as if she had resolved to put the difficulties of their early months of marriage behind them. That had been in accord with his own resolution on his homebound journey, that he would try to make things right with her. Given all of the problems that they were going to face as a result of King Inneos's actions, he did not want any more disharmony and upset within his married life.

They had spent the entire prior evening together, before retiring to their chambers at the end of the night to make love. Their relaxed banter this morning was clearly benefiting from the intimate moments that they had shared, just hours earlier.

As Kalyane was about to leave their chambers, she came forward to kiss his cheek, and said, 'Have a good day, my love. Be safe.'

'You too.'

He smiled at her as she left, then he moved to the bureau in the corner of his room, preparing to spend a dull morning catching up on reports. A bundle of opened parchments was piled on the centre of the desk, which would be the reports sent in by the various military garrisons scattered around Western Canasar. In Arion's absence, Charl Koss had been given permission to review these. Arion grimaced at the thought of the several hours of dry reading which lay ahead of him, but he knew that he would have to be familiar with the contents before speaking with the ever-diligent Koss.

To the right of the desk, there were two unopened letters. Koss must have deemed these personal, and had therefore left them alone. Arion broke the seal on the first of these, and was delighted as he recognised the handwriting as that of his brother Delrin. After the war with Elannis had ended, Arion and Gerrion had both written to their middle sibling, and this was his first response:

Dear Arion,

Hello again, little brother. Or should I say, Hero of Moss Ford, mighty leader of the armies of Western Canasar!

Seriously though, Arion, I'm proud of you. Gerrion waxed lyrical in his letter about your deeds in the war, and I'm honoured to call you my brother. To destroy an army of that size, and to save Western Canasar — what an achievement! I wish that I could have stood beside you on that day, to witness your exploits. Gerrion says that you personally defeated dozens of men, including the Elannis prince. Oh, what would we would give for a hundred like you, out here in the Holy Land!

And congratulations too on your marriage. I don't know Kalyane, of course, but if you and Gerrion both approve of her, then that is good enough for me. And we have long term allies in House Rednar, so no doubt Father would have approved too. I hope that you and Kalyane will have a long and happy life together.

I am still adjusting though to the idea that Father is no longer there, running our family. I am not ashamed to admit that I wept when I first read Gerrion's letter about Father's death. Despite the way that things ended between us, I still loved him, and I hope that he loved me, too. Gerrion will be a fine duke though — I think he has always had much better judgement than the two of us, ever since childhood!

Thank you also for the message that both you and Gerrion conveyed to me, that I am now reinstated to the family. That makes me happier than you can both know. But I will share with you what I have also written to Gerrion; whilst I am overjoyed to be reinstated to the family, I do not want to be Gerrion's next-in-line. My home is the Holy Land now. I will never return to Western Canasar permanently, and therefore it is only right (particularly after your feats in the war!) that you remain his heir until such time that Gerrion has children.

I am now a Knight of the Order of Saint Amena, and am progressing well. The last few months have seen less warfare (thank the Lord!), and there are rumours that Baladris is preparing his forces for an assault to try to take Aiduel's Gate itself. Better that he wastes his men's blood attacking the impregnable Holy City, than directing them at our forces in the Enclave!

I also have my own good news, brother. Shalina is pregnant. I will be a father, less than six months from now! Can you believe it? If it is a daughter, we will name her Meralynn, and a son Conran. Mother and Father will live on through our next generation of children.

Knowing that Shalina and I will soon be parents makes me more determined than ever to protect and preserve the lands of the Holy Church here, and to hold the enemy at bay. Although, with the recent conflict between Elannis and Andar, we are concerned that there will be insufficient recruits coming from Angall to maintain the strength of our forces.

Please let me know as soon as you and Kalyane have your own news to share, on the child front. I hope that Aiduel will bless you with children, as He has blessed us.

Take care, little brother. Please support Gerrion as he adjusts to the responsibilities of being the duke, and please protect your family.

Your loving brother,
Delrin

Arion felt a pang of sadness upon reading Delrin's words, and it made him realise just how much he still missed his elder sibling. He picked up and pocketed the letter, looking forward to sharing its contents with Gerrion.

He then turned his attention to the remaining unsealed document, casually breaking the seal and unfolding it.

When he read the short message within, his heart lurched in his chest and his mouth went dry. He felt breathless, and suddenly any thought of working through the pile of tedious military reports was gone. Along with that, the fragile equilibrium in his life, which a night of intimacy with his wife had helped to restore, was shunted back out of balance. All of this from three simple words, contained within a letter which he had never expected to receive.

Allana was alive.

―

In the hours that followed, the letter resulted in much agitation and pondering. He was giddy in reaction to the unexpected news, but he also felt a tinge of anger and frustration. If Allana was truly alive, then why would she only tell him that much, but no more? Why would she not share the details of where she was, and what she was doing? Why choose to torment him with that isolated piece of information?

It made him resent her a little, that she had chosen such a brief and impenetrable message. However, if her intention had been to burrow herself into his thoughts again, just when he was trying to put her memory aside, then she had succeeded.

Lord preserve us, must she haunt me forever?

As he drummed his fingertips against the surface of the bureau, he started to question both his own credulity, and the veracity of the letter. He could clearly recall the conversation with the Aiduel's Guardswoman, Nionia, who had assured him that Allana was dead. Had the woman deliberately lied to him? Or, if she had told the truth, was the writer of this letter someone other than Allana? Someone who was attempting to deceive him? There was no way to investigate; Nionia and her religious order had been expelled from the country.

But whatever the answer was, Arion was deeply unsettled again. After much consideration, he moved across to the hearth in his bedroom, with the letter still in his hand. He could simply start a fire, toss in the document, and then pretend that he had never received it. He could ignore its contents, and concentrate on the resolutions he had made on his homeward journey. To make his life right, and his marriage right.

He glanced down at the letter again, at its simple message, and then looked at the hearth. After a few moments, he tutted audibly at himself, and refolded the document. He returned to the bureau, opened one of the drawers, and hid the parchment in the midst of a pile of papers.

He would burn it later.

—

In the week that followed, he attempted to put the letter out of his mind, and to concentrate on the tasks that he needed to complete.

Just do my job, he told himself during moments of doubt, *and try to be a good husband*.

However, the message still lingered in the background of his thoughts. It created an undercurrent of unease, a disquiet which was only lightened when he was throwing himself into military preparations.

There was much to be done, in the aftermath of Andar breaking away from the Holy Church in Sen Aiduel. During their return journey by sea, Arion and Gerrion had discussed this at length.

Gerrion was to oversee the transition within Western Canasar to the Holy Church of Andar, and the elder brother threw himself into this task with vigour. Working with the local High Priest, he organised an immediate gathering of senior clergy, and established a plan of action and communication. The early reactions of the people of the region seemed satisfactory, with little visible discontent.

Arion and Charl Koss were tasked with preparing for a second invasion by Elannis. They planned to recruit more troops into their standing army, in addition to bolstering the training of the militias.

The defences on the river forts were also to be enhanced, and additional watchtowers were to be built along the length of the Canas River.

During that first week, Arion was impressed with the way that he and his brother were being supported by Kalyane. In Gerrion's absence, Arion's wife had taken over the running of Septholme Castle. She seemed determined to continue with this role, which allowed Gerrion more time to concentrate on religious matters and on financing the military. Arion found that he was admiring his wife anew; she was resourceful and clever, as well as kind and loving.

However, there remained a barrier between them. She did not know of his secrets, and he still could not bring himself to share that information. He could sometimes feel an unspoken tension about this when they were alone together, but for the moment at least she was content not to pressure him.

—

After Arion had been back home for over a week, news reached Septholme about the burning of Arlais. Gerrion summoned Arion and Kalyane to the Great Hall of Septholme Castle, where he shared the news with the two of them and Charl Koss.

'The information we have is that an army of a thousand Aiduel's Guards descended on Arlais,' said Gerrion. 'They fought against local militia, defeated them, and then set fire to parts of the city. Hundreds of citizens were massacred.'

'Murdering scum!' exclaimed Koss in response, the normally stoic adviser expressing a rare display of emotion.

'But why have they done this?' queried Kalyane. 'Why attack Arlais?'

She glanced across at Arion, as did the others. They could all remember his headlong flight there following the wedding.

'Our reports indicate that they'd come for the person known as the Angel of Arlais,' replied the duke, his eyes still fixed on Arion. 'The miracle-worker.'

'And... did they find her?' asked Arion.

'No one knows,' said Gerrion. 'She's disappeared from the city, that much *is* known. Whether she's in the custody of Aiduel's Guards, or is even still alive, is unclear. She's not been seen since the attack. It's probably safe to assume that if the purpose of Aiduel's Guards was to get her, then they succeeded.'

'Fucking red-cloaked bastards!' exclaimed Arion. He blinked his eyes twice, trying to force away the tears that he was worried might be forming there.

Lord preserve us, he thought. *Leanna! Why didn't you find a way to return to Andar with me, and to get away from those fanatics?*

'*Who* is she, Arion? Who is she to you?' asked Kalyane, her voice soft. 'Perhaps if you tell us who this woman is, we can help you.'

He looked at her, feeling distressed. He *wanted* to tell her. Wanted to tell all of them. But it was too much to take in, and he felt overwhelmed. First Allana's letter, and now *this*.

'Not now, Kalyane, please,' he said. 'I need some time alone.'

He moved away from her, though he could see the resulting look of distress on her face.

He left them before there was any opportunity for further questioning, and went out to the courtyard, where he picked up a sword. For a time, he lost himself in the simplicity of the motions of martial exercise. He concentrated on the graceful movements of his weapon, and tried to shut the fate of the two *Illborn* women out of his mind.

It worked, but only for a short time.

—

That night, he retired to bed with a sullen disposition, his thoughts still agitated. He had avoided his family for the remainder of the day, and he waited until he thought that Kalyane might be asleep before returning to his room. She was lying awake in the dark, waiting for him, but he rebuffed her attempts to speak. He knew that he was wounding her again, and he truly did not want that, but he could not help himself.

The next day, he returned to martial practice, and to his duties as military leader. He was doing his best to avoid anyone who might ask him awkward questions, and he attempted to distract himself with action. However, Allana and Leanna continued to trouble his thoughts for the entire day.

First, he had abandoned Allana, then thought her dead and lost to him. For four months, despite the insignificant period that he had known her, he had been in mourning. Then finally, when he had at last resolved to move on, she had been resurrected by three short words in a letter. A letter which taunted him by containing no other information. A letter which he could do nothing with, other than to conceal it in a drawer, feeling guilt and futility.

By contrast, he had helped to save Leanna. He had acted to do *something* to give her the energy to protect herself from the flames, and he had witnessed the miracle of the explosion of the pyre. But he had chosen to flee afterwards, and he had failed to ensure that she also fled her country. And now she might be dead, his past actions to save her redundant.

Why was he such a fool? Why had he not insisted that she return with him? Again, she had only touched his life for a short period. However, the thought that Aiduel's Guards had ultimately achieved what they wanted, and had murdered such a miraculous person, was making him both miserable and furious.

These thoughts continued to plague him for the rest of that day and night. The following morning, he headed back out to the courtyard to once again try to relieve some frustration through martial exercise. He was standing alone, with a sword in his hand, at the moment when he first felt the *presence*.

He immediately recognised what it was. An outside force was calling to him, a source of energy which was pulsing from inside Septholme. He could feel another person, one of his own rare kind, and they were somewhere close. Only Allana and Leanna had ever created this sensation within him.

The presence pulsed with power and vitality. It was vibrant and insistent, and was filling him with energy, making him feel as if the air was crackling around him. His senses became hyper-alert, attuned to every slight sound and motion. Accompanying this, invisible coils of energy snapped into place around every limb of his body. In mere instants, he was charged with intense power, speed and strength.

He sheathed his sword, and turned to face in the direction of the presence. He felt as if he had the sudden might to run straight through the castle wall, to take the most direct route to this new arrival. Instead, he paused, as conflicted thoughts were rushing through his mind.

Did he hope for this presence to be Allana? If it were her, it would confirm the news of her letter, but would also generate all of the turmoil which she had always ignited within him. What would he do, and how could he explain it to his wife and family, if Allana had indeed returned to him? But despite those concerns, the thought of reuniting with her made his heart thump with wild excitement. What would it be like to hold her again, after all of this time?

Or did he want this new arrival to be Leanna? The golden-haired priestess who was a living miracle, and a friend who was able to provide him with such a sense of peace. If it was Leanna, he would know for certain that she had been spared from the slaughter in Arlais. He would be able to rejoice that she was alive, and was at last safely away from the clutches of Aiduel's Guards.

He started to walk in the general direction of the presence. He crossed the castle courtyard, building pace, and by the time that he passed through the castle gate, he was sprinting. He recognised that he was heading out alone without armed guards, but he could not help himself.

He was suddenly brimming with so much energy and vitality that he had to let it out through this act of running. As he started to race down the hill from the castle towards the town, he knew instinctively that whomever *she* was, she was also travelling in his direction.

And then he saw her. She was moving up the hill towards him with a hurried step. At first, he thought that she was alone, but then he spotted two other individuals some distance behind her, who were of greatly contrasting sizes.

Energy pulsed out from her in waves, making him feel as if he could leap the last hundred paces to close the distance between them. Making him *want* to leap that distance. Making him remember the last time that he had felt like this, when he had allowed his own energy to flow into *her*, exhausting himself to save her life.

Then they were beside each other, and her dazzling blue eyes were gazing at him. Her mouth stretched into a radiant smile, and she looked as if she was about to say something. However, before she could do so, he had pulled her into an embrace, crushing her against his chest. After just a second of shocked pause, her arms wrapped around him and hugged him back. She chuckled, and a beaming smile spread across his own face.

They stayed there, like that, for seconds. He could feel the energy within her enveloping him, mingling with his and forming a cocoon around them. Holding her made him feel content and at peace. Once again, he was getting the sensation which he had experienced before when in her company; that they had been known to each other, at another time before this. Long before this.

'I never got to thank you in person, Arion,' she eventually said, not releasing her hold. 'For what you did at the pyre. But thank you.'

He felt happy, and he knew in his heart that he was glad that the Illborn woman who had come to Septholme on this day was her.

'Your being here, and alive, is thanks enough Leanna. It's thanks enough.'

In the moments that followed, Arion watched as Leanna waved back to her two companions, signalling that she was proceeding on her own. Arion noted that she was wearing a commoner's dress, rather than the robes of a priestess.

Before turning away to lead Leanna to the castle, Arion scrutinised her associates. One was a petite red-headed woman with delicate features, and the other was a hefty and grey-bearded man. This large male returned Arion's stare, looking surly, until Arion looked away.

Within the castle walls, Arion took Leanna to a private chamber, just off the central courtyard. When they were seated, he said, 'We heard about Arlais. I was very worried about you.'

Leanna nodded, and her expression was sombre as she said, 'We've heard more about what's happened, since we arrived in Andar. Aiduel's Guards claim that their actions are done in the name of The Lord, but Aiduel would never condone the evil that they've inflicted upon my city.'

'I'd heard that they were after you. Is that true?'

'Yes. Everything that's happened in Arlais, it's my fault.' She grimaced as she said that, and he felt a shift in the aura around her. A dark ripple across the usual serenity. 'They wanted me to surrender myself to them, but… *events*… transpired, that meant it wasn't possible. And now people have died, and my parents are missing. And it's all my fault.'

'I'm so sorry about what's happened Leanna,' Arion replied. 'And if your parents are missing, I can only imagine your worry. However, I struggle to believe that it was your fault.' When she did not respond, he added, 'In fact, I don't believe it, and I don't accept it. Aiduel's Guards and their leaders in the Holy Church are to blame, not you. This was their evil, not yours. I also don't believe that you'd still be alive if you'd surrendered to them. But how did you escape?'

'I escaped because of the man you saw out there. He's asked me not to speak about him, so I won't. But he got Amyss and me out of the city and the country.'

'Then he has my eternal gratitude.' She nodded, but did not otherwise respond to the comment. After a pause, Arion took a deep breath, and said, 'That day, at the pyre…'

'I know.' Her blue eyes were suddenly wide open, radiating excitement, as she shared the memory with him.

'It was a true miracle,' said Arion. 'I don't know what you did… no, what *we* did, or how we did it. But what happened to *you*, at the end, it was incredible. You *bled*, like The Lord, Leanna!'

'It was The Lord's miracle, Arion. I believe that The Lord chose to save me, and that you were the vessel for His action. I just wish that we'd not been separated afterwards.'

Arion nodded, remembering that day. 'It was impossible to get near to you, following the explosion. It was madness, with the crowd swarming around to protect you. I was exhausted from the journey, and also from what happened at the pyre, where it felt as if every last drop of my energy had flowed into you. And a lot of people there would've torn me apart, if they'd known who I was. So, once I'd seen that you were safe, I had to leave.'

'You did the right thing,' she said. 'But that didn't stop me from wishing I'd been able to thank you.'

'You *did* thank me, Leanna. You wrote to me. But… there was something that I hadn't told you. That I should have told you, that might've avoided you ever being put into danger.'

A wrinkle appeared on her upper nose. 'And what's that?'

'I'd dreamt about the pyre,' he said. 'I'd seen you walking towards it. I'd dreamt all of it before. But I thought it was about Allana, not you, so I kept it secret from you. And I let you return to Arlais. I'm so sorry.'

As he said this last word, he could hear his voice breaking, and he realised that he had been carrying the guilt of this for months.

She looked concerned, and she took his hand in hers, her voice gentle. 'You have *nothing* to apologise to me for, Arion. Nothing. I owe you my life.'

By the Lord, it's so good to hear that! Thank you, Leanna!

They talked some more after that, of matters of less consequence, until he returned the conversation to a more serious topic. 'That thing you told me, in your letter. That we're Illborn?'

She nodded. 'Yes, Illborn. That's the name which the commander of Aiduel's Guards said to me. And he said that we all need to die, because we're evil.'

Arion frowned, and said, 'But you're a priestess and a miracle-worker! Why would anyone ever call *you* Illborn or evil? What else did that commander say?'

'There wasn't much else,' she answered.

'But *why* are they hunting us?' asked Arion. 'Why do they want to kill us? Did he tell you that?'

'He said that The Lord visited the Archlaw. That the order to kill us came from Aiduel Himself.'

'I don't believe that, for one moment,' said Arion. 'Do you? But even assuming it's true, did the commander say *why*?'

'Just that we're heretics, and that we'll undermine the faith with our evil. No other reason, other than that we're these Illborn.' She then paused, appearing to think. 'Actually, there *was* something else, which I need to tell you. He said "you're the second that we've found, and you'll be the second to die". If what he said was true, then they've already killed one of us.' She paused, looking uncertain whether to proceed. 'Was it–'

'Allana?' responded Arion, shrugging. 'I truly don't know.'

He proceeded to tell Leanna the story of Allana's apparent death, followed by her mysterious resurrection through the letter he had received.

'If she's alive, Arion,' Leanna said, 'and wrote that letter, then why would she tell you that much, but no more?'

She sounded as sceptical about the source and intent behind the letter as Arion himself had been.

'I don't know,' he said.

Leanna locked eyes with him, and she looked troubled. 'How well do you really know this woman, Arion?' She lowered her voice. 'I mean, do you know for certain that she's a… *good* person?'

'Yes,' he answered. 'Well, yes, I think so. Well, I suppose I don't know her well enough, you know, to say it with total confidence. But I think she is. Yes.'

She frowned, before responding. 'Please promise me that you'll be careful, Arion. Please. I know that you're a good man. And I've never met Allana, so I've no right to comment on what kind of a person she is. But I *do* know that even though I struggle to properly sense your emotions, given the energy that always surrounds you, I can still feel a maelstrom of passions seething within you whenever we talk about Allana. She seems to unsettle you. She unbalances you completely.'

Arion grimaced, then said, 'Then you're probably sensing right.'

Leanna did not react to this for a few moments. Eventually, she said, 'And you are married to… Lady Kalyane, now?'

'Yes. For over four months.'

'How are you finding married life?'

'Difficult, at first, if I'm being honest.' He blushed, feeling sudden shame about his drunken nights in *The Hungry Gull*, and noting that Leanna was doing a studied impression of someone who had not noticed his discomfort. 'This last week? Better. A little. It's not her fault, it's mine. Kalyane's a lovely person, but there are so many secrets that I keep from her. About you. About Allana. My powers. The dreams. She knows that there's a large part of me which is concealed from her. She doesn't know what it is, but it hurts her. And then I resent myself for that hurt, and wish that she'd just leave it alone. And then I shut her out. Or we argue. Like I said, difficult.'

He realised that he had been babbling, and he could see that she was looking at him with sympathy.

'Amyss, who you saw outside, is my… companion. My *partner*.' She stared at him meaningfully as she said that. 'I once kept secrets from her, and it almost destroyed our relationship. Now, she knows everything about me. And it's such a release, Arion, to have just *one* person. One person, that you can be yourself with. That you don't have to hide yourself from.'

'But, what would you have me do, Leanna?'

'It depends. Do you trust your wife, Arion? Would you trust her with your life, and with mine?'

'Yes,' he said, without hesitation. 'Yes, I do. I would.'

'Then go get her, right now, and bring her here so that she can meet me. And in turn I'll go and get Amyss, to introduce her to you. And then we'll both share our secrets within that group of four people. About who we are. And about *what* we are. I'll understand if you don't want to talk about Allana, but share *everything* else, Arion. Unburden yourself, and release yourself from this weight and guilt that I can see pressing down on you. Let Kalyane in. Let her know and understand the good person that you are.'

He stared at her for seconds, thinking that if he had proposed this to himself it would have sounded too simplistic. That he would have dismissed the notion as fraught with too many problems. But when Leanna said the words, it just made sense.

'Very well,' he said. 'I will.'

—

In the hours after that, the four of them gathered in a private room in the castle, and they did exactly as Leanna had suggested. Arion shared the truth about himself with Kalyane, talking about everything except for Allana, and as he did so he felt a massive burden being lifted.

He observed the shifts in expression on Kalyane's face throughout their revelations; from initial unease, to scepticism, and eventually to fascination and wonderment. When Arion told her about the dream of the pyre on their wedding night, his wife exclaimed, 'So *that's* why you left me!'

In the short time that they spent together, he found that he liked Amyss, and he also witnessed Kalyane and the other women warming to each other as their conversation went on.

Eventually, Leanna stated that it was time for her and Amyss to leave, indicating that her large companion had secured discreet lodgings for them. She promised that she would visit Arion again over the coming days.

Just before the two priestesses departed, and as Amyss was talking with Kalyane, Leanna moved Arion gently to one side.

'I can sense emotions in people, Arion,' she said. 'Can sense them clearly, in almost everyone but you. And I can tell you that your wife is a good person, a loving person, and she loves you with all of her heart. That love cascades towards you, when the two of you are together. And I agree that you can trust her. Completely. Remember that, if Allana-'

'I understand,' he said, not needing her to voice the next words.

―

The next day, Leanna returned to see him.

At the start of this second meeting, she amazed Arion by demonstrating her new-found power to move objects. She raised up a chair with her ability, before swinging it in the air before him.

'It's not much, right now,' she said. 'Certainly, most of the time it's nothing like what I did at the pyre. But I'm getting stronger. And with you here, I feel like I could lift up every object in the room.'

Following that, they talked again at length, and after a while their discussion turned towards the assassination attempts against them. After Arion had described the attack against him, and the momentary loss of his powers, Leanna stated, 'That sounds familiar. The older man that I'm travelling with, he owns two objects – *medallions* – which can almost extinguish my powers.'

'Really?'

'Yes,' she said. 'One which he says he's owned for a long time, and one which he took from the body of a person who was trying to kill me. When I'm near to them, it's like my powers are almost useless. It seems like one of the people who attacked you might also have been wearing an object like that.'

'That would make sense,' said Arion. 'Has your companion told you how he came to own the first of those medallions?'

'No,' said Leanna. 'Not yet. He's very secretive.'

Arion grimaced, and asked, 'And has your companion let you know *who* might have carried out and ordered the attacks against us?'

'Yes. He believes that my attackers were part of an organisation of assassins and killers who've been acting for the Archlaw for a long time. It seems possible that your attackers might be from the same group. I think that they came after me because of the pyre, and people calling me the Angel of Arlais. Could they have come for you because of the stories of what you did at Moss Ford?'

'I suppose so,' said Arion, nodding. 'And this man with the secrets, your companion, do you trust him?'

She paused before answering. 'Strangely enough, but yes, I do trust him. He's a difficult man, and I know there are things that he's keeping from me. But he saved me from certain death during that attack, and if he wanted to harm me, he could've done so already. By contrast, he tells me that he's going to keep me alive, and I've made a promise to remain with him, for a time.'

'Have you told him about me, Leanna?' asked Arion. 'About the fact that I have powers too, and share the dream with you?'

She shook her head. 'No. Not unless you want me to?'

'No, I don't. But if he's protecting you, you must tell him that there were assassins in the town, recently. And that we never found them.'

'I will,' she said.

'But what's happening to us, Leanna? All of this. Dreams, powers, being condemned as *Illborn*. People trying to kill us. What does it all mean?'

'I don't know,' she replied. 'As I've said before, I believe that my powers are a gift from The Lord Aiduel, and that I'm to use them for His purpose. But I don't understand why that would mean that the Archlaw and others want to kill us.'

'Me neither. But if there's a purpose, what is it? Just what are we meant to do with these powers?'

'I'm not sure, Arion. I want to do good, in the name of The Lord. For me, that's my purpose.'

He nodded, but he was unconvinced by her response, and said, 'The answer *must* be in the dream. I keep questioning myself about what the dream means. It's been getting worse, over time, but I'm also remembering more now, particularly since the day of the pyre. For instance, I can recall that the figure in the Gate raises a single finger. What do you think that means?'

'Again, I'm not certain,' she said. 'I've thought that, maybe… only one is meant to approach the Gate?'

'Possibly. But… after that, I think that the figure in the Gate speaks to me, and then something awful occurs. But I can't remember what they say or what happens. Just flashes of memory. Afterwards, it makes me feel… angry, frustrated… sick inside.'

'I think you may be remembering more than me,' she said, softly, 'but I think I can remember that they say something, too. But I can't recall what it is.'

Arion frowned, then asked, 'And the Gate that we're seeing, do you think it could be real?'

'I've wondered that,' Leanna said. 'Many times. Whether it exists. Whether we could find it. Whether that would answer what's happening.'

'I've thought the same. But where would you start looking?'

'There's one place which feels more likely than others,' she answered. 'Although, I've been assured by a priest who I trust that there's no actual Gate there. And anyway, it's impossible to reach.'

'Where?'

'Aiduel's Gate, in the Holy Land.'

―

On her third visit to him, a couple of days later, Leanna said, 'I'm going to leave Septholme soon, Arion. My protector's concerned that I'm taking too much risk, by coming here to see you. He thinks people will be searching for me, and he was particularly concerned after I told him about the assassins. He wants me to go into hiding, and to stay away from any busy towns. You may still feel me here, in Septholme, for a while. But soon, I'll be gone.'

The news was a blow to Arion, but he accepted it. He enjoyed Leanna's company that day, and Kalyane also joined them for a while. Arion's relationship with Leanna was no longer a worry for his wife.

Later that same day, when Arion and Leanna were ready to part company, they pulled each other into a long-lasting hug. Once again, Arion experienced peace and contentment from the intermingling of their auras, as he held her in his arms.

As they separated, Leanna said, 'Until we meet again, Arion.'

'Until we meet again, Leanna.'

—

For a handful of days afterwards, Arion continued to feel Leanna's vibrant presence in the town, intermittently pulsing towards him from the distance. And then, one morning, it was gone.

In the days that followed, Arion was determined to live as a better person. At the forefront of this, his relationship with Kalyane was transformed. He could perceive the joy evident within his wife, now that she had finally broken through the barrier of his secrecy. And to Arion, too, it felt wonderful. As Leanna had said, there was someone at his side with knowledge of exactly who and what he was, and that person happened to love him with all of her heart.

A few days after Leanna had departed, Arion and his wife made love, and he was holding her in the moments before sleep.

'I love you, Arion,' she murmured, sounding happy and drowsy.

'I love you, Kalyane,' he replied. For the first time, he felt that he might be speaking true.

During the period until then, he had not extracted the hidden letter from his bureau, to look at it again. Nor had he spent any more time pondering why Allana might have sent it. However, he had not been able to muster the willpower to destroy it.

The day after he had professed his love to Kalyane, he came to a decision.

As soon as he was next alone in his chambers, he moved to the bureau and extracted the letter from Allana. He opened it and read the simple message one last time. Then he carried it over to the hearth in his bedroom, and held it above the fire.

After a few moments, he tossed the letter into the flames, and he watched it burn.

―

A number of days later, on a chilly and crisp winter morning at the dawn of the new year of 770AA, news of a Proclamation of Excommunication arrived in Septholme.

Arion first heard about this after Gerrion summoned all of the occupants of Septholme Castle to the courtyard. The duke then read out the full text, his manner confident but disdainful.

Archlaw Paulius had declared that if any citizens of Andar accepted the authority of Inneos's Imposter Church, then they were to be excommunicated. Only those who remained faithful to the Holy Church of Sen Aiduel would retain their future place in heaven.

At the end of this announcement, Gerrion stated, 'We have been told by the highest authority of the Holy Church in Andar that Paulius's statements are false. If we keep our faith in The Lord Aiduel, and if we continue to honour The Lord and the Holy Church in Andar, then our path to the afterlife and to heaven will be safe. We should dismiss these arrogant falsehoods, and we should ready ourselves for more imminent and tangible threats; the countries of Elannis and Dei Magnus.'

Gerrion's work with the clergy of the region had already done much to prepare the faithful of Western Canasar, and Arion observed with relief that the response of the castle retainers to the proclamation was muted.

Later that same day, Arion and Gerrion were standing together on the eastern battlements of Septholme Castle. They were peering beyond the vacated fortress of Aiduel's Guards, looking eastwards across their territory, in the general direction of Elannis and Dei Magnus.

'I can't help but feel that the life we've all known is coming to an end, Arion,' said Gerrion, sounding melancholy. 'This Proclamation is one more defining step on the journey towards a terrible war.'

'I know,' replied Arion, his voice grim. 'War is coming, brother. The key question is *when?*'

Gerrion looked across at him. 'Soon, Arion. It is coming soon.'

11

Allana

—

Year of Our Lord,
After Ascension, 769AA to 770AA

Two weeks after the onset of Sillene Berun's feral madness, Jarrett Berun arrived back at Berun Castle. The young duke had ridden hard to get home from Andarron, after receiving a message that his mother had gone insane.

Allana rushed from her chambers after hearing of his arrival, and she greeted a bedraggled Jarrett in the pouring rain, out in the castle courtyard.

After a brief embrace, he asked, 'How is she? Where is she?'

Allana adopted a sorrowful expression and a mournful voice. 'Jarrett, it's awful. Worse than you can possibly imagine. Please prepare yourself for what you're going to see, my love.'

A guard then led the two of them in silence as they descended to a torchlit corridor of the Berun Castle dungeon. Allana took hold of Jarrett's hand as they moved towards the end cell. As they drew closer, she could hear a ranting of unintelligible words, and she had to resist the urge to retch in response to the pervading stench of urine and faeces.

Jarrett's expression contained horror when he first looked through the bars of the cell, and observed the filthy condition of his mother. Sillene Berun was squatting in the corner of her enclosed area, her obese body only partially covered by her shredded clothing. She looked up at her son with a feral gaze which showed no sense of recognition.

Allana had visited this dungeon cell before, and she was already accustomed to Sillene's loss of humanity. However, Jarrett's voice sounded scared and bewildered as he uttered, 'How?'

In response to the question, the dowager raised herself up and approached the bars of the cell, her eyes fixed upon Allana. She then remained there, in an animal stance, with her arms hung loose before her and her teeth on display. Her body was swaying, and she was continuing to rant a stream of gibberish.

Better that she cannot speak, Lana, to tell her story. Better that only you will ever know what caused this.

'Can I go in to see her, Lana?' Jarrett asked. 'Can I hold her?'

'It's too dangerous, my love,' Allana replied. 'Please, you must not. She has… killed many people. You must not go within reach of her.'

'What has caused this?' asked Jarrett, sounding grief-stricken. 'How did this happen?'

'No one knows, Jarrett,' she answered. 'She just went… mad, one night. And she's not recovered.'

Jarrett sighed, before edging closer to the cell bars. He then lifted up his necklace of The Lord Aiduel On The Tree.

'Mother,' he said, with a tremor in his voice, 'look upon The Lord, please. Look upon Him and remember who you are.'

Sillene's only response was a snarling and hissing sound.

—

Jarrett remained in that place for an hour, praying to The Lord Aiduel as he watched the hulking form of his insane parent through the cell bars. Eventually, Allana placed a hand onto his bicep and softly steered him away.

That evening, she prayed with him in the castle chapel for over two hours, and together they entreated The Lord Aiduel and Saint Amena to make Sillene well again. Later, Allana sat with Jarrett in his quarters, with his head on her lap.

For a long time afterwards, she stroked his hair as he wept, and she promised to protect him and to keep him safe. At a time like this, when he was stricken by grief, she knew that he would be depending on her more than ever before. He would need her to act as a wife, not as a mistress.

Let him remember this, Lana. Just how much he needs you now that his mother is gone. Gone, and she's never coming back.

—

In the days and weeks that followed, Jarrett continued to grieve for his mother's condition, and Allana continued to support him.

Despite Jarrett's low mood, Allana was delighted to have her giant duke back with her, both for his ability to sate her physical needs, and for the comfort which he provided during the hours of darkness. The night-time terrors which Allana had experienced were greatly subdued now that she was back in Jarrett's bed and in his arms. She soon convinced her lover to allow her to stay with him every night, given how much she had been suffering in his absence. Allana was resolved that she never again wanted to sleep alone.

With Jarrett's physical presence restored to her, she was devoting slightly less time to thoughts of Arion Sepian. However, the young Sepian noble still lingered in her mind, and she often wondered how he had reacted to her letter. Would it have made him think of her and wonder where she was? Would it have made him wish that he was with her, rather than with his wife?

You are more beautiful than his wife, Lana, you know that. He must be thinking about you now.

She still sometimes found herself slipping into flights of fantasy, wondering how Arion would react if she wrote to him again and asked him to meet in secret and to run away with her. Would he do it, as he had once promised? And would she ever have the courage to leave the protection and security which Jarrett now offered her?

On one occasion, she sat down in private to write a second letter to Arion, to tell him more about how she felt. However, the words would not come. After staring at a blank parchment for a long time, she eventually put her writing materials away and returned to her life in Berun Castle.

In the weeks after Jarrett's return, Allana could see that her young duke was continuing to be agitated by the religious upheaval in Andar.

In between bouts of grief for his mother, Jarrett shared the details of the king's Andarron council. He described his appalled frustration at the decision to break away from the Holy Church in Sen Aiduel, and his deep concern for how the Archlaw might react.

At times, Jarrett appeared distracted and worried, and he was often locked away in rooms with his advisers, or was praying in the chapel. However, he still seemed unwilling to divulge all of his concerns to Allana. For a while, she was content not to force the issue.

That all changed on the first day of the new year of 770AA, when news of the Archlaw's Proclamation of Excommunication arrived in Berun.

At the end of that day, Jarrett and Allana went to pray together in the chapel. Jarrett rose to his feet after their final prayer, and he was looking sombre as he stared at the altar. He was still clutching his copy of the proclamation, which he had received that afternoon.

Allana stood up beside him, remaining silent. Despite Jarrett's warnings in the preceding weeks, she had still been shocked by the Archlaw's announcements.

Archlaw Paulius had excommunicated the entire Pavil family, for gross heresy against the Holy Church and the one true faith. King Inneos was described as the Imposter, and the new Holy Church of Andar was derided as the Imposter's Church. The Archlaw also threatened excommunication for anyone else in Andar who chose to follow the breakaway religion.

Allana could see how deeply unsettled Jarrett was, even though he had been expecting the proclamation. As he turned away from the altar and strode out of the chapel, she followed in silence. She was being patient, but she was determined to understand everything that was troubling him.

As if hearing her thoughts, Jarrett turned to her and said, 'Let's go to my chambers, Lana. There are urgent matters that we must discuss. In private.'

When they were back in his rooms, he pulled two chairs together and took her hand in his. His expression was still grave.

'I'm worried, Lana,' he said. 'This proclamation means that we're all running out of time, and things are not going to stay as they are for much longer. I must stop keeping secrets from you.'

'What is it, Jarrett?' she asked, feeling alarm.

'There is some good news in this,' he said, as he gestured towards the document. 'Excommunication won't apply to anyone who continues to observe their devotions towards the true Holy Church. I can't tell you how relieved that makes me, because that's exactly what we're going to do.'

'Of course,' she replied.

'However,' he continued, 'the Archlaw is also threatening to declare a crusade, unless Sen Aiduel's authority is restored. I'm certain that isn't going to happen, so there can be no doubt now; it's only a matter of time before Paulius calls for a crusade against King Inneos and the Imposter Church. And I'm certain that call will be answered by Elannis and Dei Magnus. There will be a war.'

'Another war? When?'

'I can't be certain, Lana, but it must be coming soon. Within months, possibly weeks.'

'What will it mean for us, Jarrett?'

'It means we're going to have to choose a side,' he said, his voice grim. 'There's going to be no way to avoid this war, for us or for Berun or for anyone else in Andar. Every noble house and their people will have to choose between fighting for the Archlaw and the Holy Church, or fighting for their king and country against that church. There's going to be a civil war, and we're going to be invaded. And Berun will be on the front line of that invasion.'

Allana shivered, before asking, 'And what are you going to do, Jarrett? Have you decided?'

He stared at her, his expression sombre, then he nodded. 'I have, though I want your support and approval, Lana. Inneos has forced an awful decision upon me, but I must put my religion before my country, and I can't remain loyal to a heretical king. In good conscience, I will not recognise the Imposter Church and suffer excommunication from the only true Holy Church. And when the call for crusade comes, I'll be ready to answer it. I've prayed to The Lord, and I know that I must do this.'

After that, he went on to outline the secret discussions which he had become involved in. This included details of the clandestine correspondence and negotiations which had been instigated by his mother, prior to her madness. As Jarrett explained all of these matters, two significant realisations dawned upon Allana.

First, if there was a war, and the Holy Church was victorious, then Aiduel's Guards would be free to return to Andar. And, with their return, she might once again find herself in great danger.

Second, if Jarrett followed this course of action, then the Houses of Berun and Sepian would be on opposing sides of the pending conflict. If she was at Jarrett's side, they would soon be at war with Arion.

That night, Allana struggled to sleep. Even though Jarrett was beside her, she teetered on the verge of a panic attack, with her heart pounding and her chest feeling tight. She was running through possible scenarios and outcomes in her mind, and they all seemed awful.

If she stayed with Jarrett and he was on the losing side of the coming war, he would be ruined, and Allana with him. She would once again lose everything.

However, a victory for the Holy Church could also be disastrous for her, because Aiduel's Guards would then be able to return, perhaps in far greater numbers and with even more power. Would they then hunt her and imprison her, if they found out who she really was? And would they torture her again, before burning her on a pyre?

You can't allow them to get you, Lana. Not ever.

Another option which she pondered was that of running away from Berun, and heading as far westwards as she could get. And that caused her to revisit the possibility of writing another letter to Arion Sepian, to try to persuade him to run away with her. This idea suddenly seemed less fanciful.

However, what if she were to abandon Jarrett to flee from here, but Arion did not join her? If that happened, then once again she would have lost everything, and she would be forced to face the world and the panic of night-time on her own.

What are you going to do, Lana? What are you going to do?

She felt anxious throughout the night. However, before dawn arrived, she had come to an initial conclusion. She was resolved that she would need to reveal more about herself to Jarrett, if there was to be any hope of a future with him.

The next morning, she spoke to the young duke as soon as he awoke. He was on his back in bed, and she was resting naked against him, with her head on his chest.

'I've been awake all night, Jarrett,' she said, her voice serious. 'I've been thinking about what you told me.'

'And what have you been thinking?' he asked, his tone equally sombre.

'That I'm terrified about what's going to happen. Do you really have no choice in this, Jarrett? Are you truly decided that if this holy war comes, you're going to fight against Andar?'

'I'm absolutely certain about my decision, Lana. My faith tells me that I must do this. But even if that were not the case, I can't face the alternative for Berun.'

'What alternative?' she asked.

He gently moved himself out from underneath her, and sat up to face her. She rolled onto her back, displaying her naked body to him, and she could sense the reaction of his desire despite the gravity of their conversation.

'If I were to stand with Andar and the Pavils on this,' he said, 'then Berun will be in the front line of the war, facing an invading army the likes of which Andar has never seen. Not only would I then be betraying my faith, but my army would likely be slaughtered, and Berun will fall. If I choose that option, I'll be dooming my eternal soul, *and* my people and this land. And our future together. I can't do that, Lana.'

Allana was silent as she considered his words. She knew that she could compel him to change his mind, if she chose to. However, the disastrous consequences which Jarrett had outlined seemed to render that option equally unattractive. Instead, she arched her back and stretched her arms out across the bedsheet, and once again she could feel his lust for her mounting inside him. It was time to share some of her secrets.

'Could you ever forgive me Jarrett, if I've told you a little lie about who I am, and if I've done something bad in the past? Something which wasn't my fault, but which means that Aiduel's Guards might arrest me and kill me, if they return here?'

In the aftermath of his shocked reaction to that statement, she shared her true name. She then proceeded to tell him about the events of the murder and flight from Sen Aiduel, and her imprisonment in and escape from the fortress of Aiduel's Guards in Septholme. Of course, she told him a version of that story which varnished the truth in her own favour. She brushed over some of the more gruesome events, and entirely omitted any details about her powers and her interactions with the Sepian family.

At the end, she said, 'And that's why, if your actions mean that Aiduel's Guards might return here, and in greater numbers, then I'll have to run away. As soon as possible, because I dare not stay, Jarrett. I'll have to leave you.'

After her final words, he did not speak for several seconds. His expression was hard to interpret, but she could still feel the desire beating inside of him as he stared at her.

Finally, he said, 'No.'

'No?' she repeated.

'No. You're not leaving me, Lana. I'm not losing you, too.'

He has lost his mother and his father, Lana, and he desperately needs you. That gives you power.

'But how can you expect me to stay, after what I've done? If this war happens, and Aiduel's Guards realise who I am, they'll arrest me. They'll *kill* me, Jarrett.'

'You mustn't leave me, Lana.' There was now a hint of pleading in his voice. 'Please. I forgive you for whatever you've done, and I love you, with all of my soul. And I'll find a way to keep you safe.'

'But how?'

'Right now, I don't know. But give me some time, please. Hours, days, that's all I need. Just don't leave me. I'll find a way.'

She looked at him, at his muscular form and earnest expression, and she could feel his need for her burning throughout his body. He was suddenly desperate to please her, and she liked having that power and control over him. She felt her own desire rising to match his own.

'I believe you Jarrett.'

Give him time, Lana, and then you can decide.

After that thought, she reached a hand up onto his arm and pulled him down towards her.

—

Two days later, Jarrett invited Allana to go horse-riding with him, and she happily accepted. Their destination was a gently-sloping hill to the north, which rose out above a sprawling pine forest, and which offered unbroken views back towards Berun Castle.

It was a chilly but beautiful winter day, the sun in the clear sky above having melted the morning frost by the time that they set off together. Allana was soon delighting in the freedom of riding, although she quickly noticed that Jarrett was unusually quiet and pensive.

After they had reached the hilltop and had dismounted, Allana took a moment to savour the view across the lands back to the castle.

'It's so beautiful here,' she said, her breath misting in the chilly air.

Jarrett did not reply, and in puzzlement Allana turned towards him. The expression on the young duke's face was unfamiliar; he appeared both excited and bashful.

'What is it, Jarrett?' Allana asked. 'What's wrong?'

'I've had another letter,' he announced, and abruptly clasped her hands in his. 'I wanted to bring you out here, to somewhere special, to… share this news with you. Two senior foreign leaders are travelling in secret to come here, to arrive in a month's time. They're visiting to finalise matters in relation to our mutual… *objectives*.'

He proceeded to tell her about who those visitors were going to be, before adding, 'But this is our opportunity, Lana! I think I'll be able to use this meeting to free you of all of your worries.'

'What do you mean?' she asked. 'How?'

With an excited voice, Jarrett then outlined his plans to her. As he did so, Allana started to smile. It was clear that the duke had thought things through in detail, and Allana could quickly perceive that the coming encounter with the foreign leaders might shape her entire future.

When he had finished, Jarrett said, 'I hope now that you can see how much I'll fight to protect you? How I never want to lose you?'

'I do, Jarrett.'

'But these are serious people, Lana, and I've been in agony for these last two days. If I'm to do this, then I need something back from you. I need two promises from you.'

'What promises, Jarrett?'

'First, you must promise me that you won't ever leave me, if I secure these things for you.'

'I promise. If you get this for me, and I feel safe, I promise I won't leave.' She maintained eye contact as she said this.

Better to make the promise for now, Lana. You can decide later whether or not to keep it.

'And second,' he said, while suddenly kneeling down before her, with the beautiful wintry landscape of Berun directly behind him as he stared into her eyes, 'you must promise me that when this coming war is over, you will become my wife.'

Four weeks later, Allana was waiting in the Grand Hall of Berun Castle, on her own. A fire was blazing in the great hearth of the hall, helping to soften the deep cold of winter within the draughty room.

Allana was sitting on an ornately engraved chair, which was in the centre of the dais at the end of the hall. She was dressed in the finest gown that she owned, one that revealed an eye-catching amount of bare chest and cleavage. She was fully aware of the chill in the air, but she wanted to ensure that Jarrett's visitors would feel desire for her, in case any intervention was necessary to secure the day's outcome. Enduring a little discomfort would be more than worthwhile, for that.

The chair that Allana was seated in had once belonged to the dowager duchess, and it was positioned alongside the duke's own grand chair. In the last few weeks, Sillene's seat and the status which it represented had been claimed by Allana. Opposite these chairs, two further seats had been placed for their guests. Close by, a table had been set out, which was loaded with a sumptuous display of food and drink.

Jarrett had been informed minutes before that his two visitors had arrived in the courtyard outside. He had gone off to greet the arrivals, leaving Allana on her own for a few minutes.

This is your opportunity, Lana. Today, you can secure everything that you deserve.

As she was thinking this, the main doors to the hall opened and Jarrett entered. He was followed by two men, both of whom were hooded and wearing nondescript robes. Jarrett turned to close the door after them, and then he walked towards Allana. The two newcomers followed him, both pushing down their hoods as they did so, while Allana stood up to greet them.

'Your Highness, Your Eminence,' stated Jarrett, gesturing towards the table as he spoke. 'Please, take off your travel robes and help yourself to whatever food and drink you desire. It must have been a difficult journey in this weather.'

The two men appeared to be in their late-fifties or early-sixties. They were each of average height and were dwarfed by Jarrett. The first was handsome for his age, with a stocky build, grey hair and a neatly trimmed full grey beard. Allana noted the way that this individual's gaze drifted over her figure, and she sensed with satisfaction that he was a man of strong appetites. The second arrival was scrawny-looking, with a gaunt face and oversized eyes, and her immediate assessment of him was that he contained no equivalent hunger.

As the two men drew close, Jarrett announced, 'Gentlemen, please may I introduce Allana. She has full awareness of our discussions and has my complete trust. Allana is my companion and my adviser, and we're to marry.'

Allana forced herself to refrain from smiling as he said this. She had accepted Jarrett's proposal of marriage.

She could see the two newcomers exchanging glances in reaction to the announcement. She curtseyed to them both, noting how the grey-bearded man's eyes were devouring her form as she did so.

Jarrett continued, gesturing towards this admirer. 'Allana, please may I introduce His Imperial Highness, Prince Lorrius El'Augustus, brother of His Imperial Majesty, Emperor Jarrius El'Augustus.' The man nodded his head in reaction to this. 'And our second illustrious guest is His Eminence, Archprime Runus Kohn of the High Council.'

'Your Highness, Your Eminence,' said Allana. 'I am Allana dei Monis. It's an honour to meet you.'

She observed Archprime Kohn raising an eyebrow in response to either her words or her accent. She suspected that he might have recognised her full name.

Prince Lorrius simply nodded again then turned to Jarrett, before glancing towards the four chairs. 'It *has* been a long journey, Duke Berun, and I look forward to sitting down to rest my legs. But first, may I say how distressing it is not to be able to see my cousin Sillene here. When I heard of her illness, it upset me greatly. Such a tragedy.'

'Yes, Your Highness,' replied Jarrett. 'A great tragedy. Mother's illness came on very suddenly, while I was away in Andarron. Sadly, her mind is… not what it was.'

Jarrett doesn't need her any more, Lana. He only needs you.

'A great woman, your mother,' said Lorrius. His accent was refined but Allana also found it to be a little oily. 'Always formidable, and not one to suffer fools. And so sad that you were away at the time. Another matter to blame that idiot Inneos for, eh?'

Jarrett acknowledged the comment, and then the two men made small talk for a handful of minutes, after they had all moved to the chairs. Runus Kohn was silent during this exchange, his expression dour. To Allana, it appeared as if the man had no taste for social niceties, and just wanted to get onto business.

Eventually, Kohn cleared his throat and said, in a voice that was as sullen as his demeanour, 'Lorrius, please. We've travelled a long and perilous way for this *clandestine* gathering. I, for one, would like to get started.'

'Very well, Runus,' said the Elannis prince, before sitting forwards in his chair and adopting a more serious manner. 'I'll start then. We all know why we're here, Duke Berun. And from our correspondence of recent weeks and months, and your acceptance of this visit, we believe that our minds are set on a similar course. That our interests are aligned. In simple terms, our purpose in being here is to discuss the following objectives, and the means to achieve them. First, the removal by force of the House of Pavil from the throne of Andar. Second, the instatement of a new monarchy to this country, being one which is more closely... *bound*, to Elannis and Dei Magnus. Third, the restoration of the one true Holy Church throughout this land. To ensure that there is no possible confusion about our intent, is that also your understanding, Duke Berun?'

In response to this, Jarrett nodded, then said, 'Agreed. That is also my understanding of the purpose of this meeting.'

With those words, Allana knew that Jarrett was committing himself and his people to treason against the Andar crown.

'Good,' said Lorrius. 'To be clear, I'm here as the representative of my brother, Emperor Jarrius, and I have his authority to negotiate and agree matters within certain boundaries, on behalf of Elannis. Archprime Runus is here as representative of the Archlaw and the High Council, and carries equivalent authority on behalf of Dei Magnus. You can therefore have assurance that what we agree here today, if we state it as residing within our authority, will be supported by our nations. I trust that this is also clear, Duke Berun?'

'Yes, it is,' replied Jarrett. 'And of course, I have full authority to speak on behalf of the House and territory of Berun.'

'Very well,' said Lorrius. 'Let's get to business. First, we can discuss the *how* of what we want to achieve. Then, Duke Berun, we can discuss the *conditions* for your involvement which you've alluded to within your correspondence. Are we agreed?'

Again, Allana watched Jarrett nod in response to this, and then the discussions began in earnest.

—

Two hours later, the three men had covered a lot of ground in their conversation. Allana had contributed only minor amounts to the exchange, but she had stayed because she wanted to be present when Jarrett set out his requirements. She needed to witness whether he was successful.

'That concludes our strategy discussion, Duke Berun,' stated Prince Lorrius, who had been the most dominant participant in the conversation. 'To summarise, now that we've established where Prince Markon is being imprisoned, and have the means to free him, your co-operation will form the final element of our plan.

'Once we've acted to free Markon, Elannis will also be free to act, and that will trigger everything else. The Elannis army and the Dei Magnus navy will both be ready to move by then, in overwhelming force. The Archlaw and the High Council are in turn primed to issue the Proclamation of Crusade once Markon is safe. And under the assault of our combined land and naval forces, alongside the unrest to be stirred following the proclamation, Andar and the Pavils will soon be reeling. The rebellion of the Houses of Berun and Condarr will be the final essential piece, which will ensure the complete collapse of the Pavil reign.'

'All understood,' said Jarrett, his tone neutral.

'Very well,' replied Lorrius. 'And so, we come on to the question of the *price* of your assistance in these matters, Duke Berun. Please share with us these conditions, which your letter referred to.'

Before Jarrett started to reply, he glanced towards Allana. She nodded and smiled at him, trying to show encouragement. There was no going back now.

This is your opportunity, Lana. Your chance to wash away the past.

'I will start with some… *personal* matters,' stated Jarrett. 'In the context of what we've just discussed, these may seem trivial to you. But they're deeply important to me and to my betrothed Allana, and I'd ask you to receive them as such.'

As Jarrett mentioned her name, Allana felt Prince Lorrius's eyes upon her again. The Elannis royal clearly relished the sight of her physical form.

'To begin,' continued Jarrett, 'I've already mentioned that I intend to marry Allana. However, it can create problems if a member of the nobility marries a… non-noble. And also, there are some other issues. But these are problems which could be easily resolved by a member of the High Council.'

'Go on,' stated Archprime Kohn, his eyebrow raised up again.

'Well, Allana has disclosed to me that she was involved in an unfortunate incident, a number of years ago. High Priest Ronis dei Maranar, of Sen Aiduel, was killed in an incident which involved Allana.'

For the first time, Allana observed what appeared to be an expression of interest on Kohn's face, as he regarded her again and exclaimed, 'I *knew* I recognised that name! Dei Maranar, of course!' His dour expression then returned. 'Anyway. Continue.'

'Allana has been pursued by Aiduel's Guards as a result of this matter,' said Jarrett. 'At one point, they imprisoned her, but she escaped, and there were deaths involved, of a number of soldiers from that order.'

'This is all very interesting, but what do you actually want?' Kohn asked.

Allana's heart was beating fast, as her past crimes were spoken about in the open. Jarrett had prepared in detail to discuss these matters, and Allana had reinforced and confirmed what he was going to ask for. However, she was still nervous.

'I want full absolution and pardon for Allana,' replied Jarrett, 'by the High Council of the Holy Church, for *any* crime she has committed, or might have committed in the past. And guarantees that Aiduel's Guards will never again take any action against her. I can't offer my assistance and support for your actions, if the end result will be Aiduel's Guards returning to this country and threatening my future wife. Particularly, after hearing stories about the recent carnage in Arlais.'

Kohn shrugged. He then turned to Allana and said, 'As Duke Berun suggested, it's a trivial matter. Very well, you're absolved by the Holy Church and by the High Council of any and all past crimes, and I'll personally ensure that Aiduel's Guards will take no future action against you. I'll put that in writing today. It will be conditional of course, Duke Berun, on final agreement to your co-operation with our plans.'

'Of course. Thank you,' said Jarrett.

He's agreed to it, Lana! You won't have to hide for the rest of your life!

'What else, Duke Berun?' asked Prince Lorrius. The royal appeared bemused by the nature of the conversation.

'Secondly, I mentioned that Allana is not from the nobility,' replied Jarrett. 'That's not strictly correct. You recognise the surname, Your Eminence?'

'Yes. Dei Monis,' said Runus Kohn. 'I'd been wondering about that.'

'Allana is the daughter of Seilana dei Monis,' continued Jarrett. 'Seilana was the daughter of Baron Ullren dei Monis. Seilana was disowned by the family after she became pregnant with Allana, out of wedlock.'

'Another interesting tale,' stated Kohn. 'But again, please tell me what you want, Duke Berun.'

'I want Allana to be reinstated to the title which should be her birth-right. I want the dei Monis family to recognise her. I want her to become Lady Allana dei Monis, such that I'll be marrying a woman of the nobility.'

'But she's illegitimate,' stated Kohn. 'She has no right to that title.'

Jarrett's mouth was set into a hard line. 'She is a child of the dei Monis family, but I don't want to get into discussions about legitimacy. As I said, this is a trivial matter to Elannis and Dei Magnus, and to the Holy Church, in the context of the issues which we've been discussing. But it *is* a matter of great significance to Allana and to me, particularly in light of the matters I'll come onto. Therefore, I request it, whether she has the right to it or not.'

Kohn frowned for a few seconds, clearly considering, before responding, 'Very well. I can't confirm this right now, because I'll need to secure the acceptance of the dei Monis family. But I'm close to certain that I *will* obtain that acceptance. Again, it's conditional on your compliance, Duke Berun. And, to be clear, she'll gain no rights to property or inheritance. Subject to that, your future wife will be *Lady* Allana dei Monis, and will be formally recognised as a member of that family.'

'And therefore,' said Jarrett, 'our marriage will have the blessing of the Holy Church, and the Imperial Family, yes?'

'Agreed,' stated the other two men, sounding somewhat confused.

He's done it, Lana! He's achieved so much for you!

'Thank you, gentlemen,' said Jarrett. 'You'll be pleased to know that concludes my *personal* requests. Now, I have two more substantive requirements.'

'Very well,' responded Lorrius. 'Please proceed.'

'If the plans which you've set out, Prince Lorrius, are to come to pass,' said Jarrett, 'we all understand how pivotal Western Canasar is going to prove to be. Indeed, how significant it was last year, in thwarting Elannis.'

'Yes,' said Lorrius. 'An ugly affair for my people.'

'And in what is to come,' said Jarrett, 'the Houses of Andar will either be for the Pavil family and the Imposter Church, or they'll be against them. The House of Sepian will undoubtedly support Inneos.'

'We know that,' stated Lorrius.

'Well, there's no love lost between the Houses of Berun and Sepian. In fact, there's hatred between us. After this has all been concluded, and when the supporters of Inneos have fallen, there will be lands to be redistributed. I'll pledge to make no claim on the lands of Rednar, Cendun, Rowarth and Dunark. Those provinces will be for Elannis, the Holy Church and House Condarr to apportion. However, I insist upon claiming possession of Western Canasar, for House Berun.'

Lorrius's face was grim, and he shook his head. 'Elannis will be supplying nine out of every ten soldiers in the coming war, Duke Berun. Western Canasar is a great prize, and we'll want to control the whole peninsula.'

'You'll be supplying nine out of every ten soldiers, Prince Lorrius,' responded the duke. 'But I'll be supplying the gateway to Andar for those armies. Western Canasar is my requirement. Let's not play games with each other here. I think that we both know that my request is a fair one, leaving several wealthy provinces for Elannis and the Holy Church to choose from.'

Allana was impressed with how calm and measured Jarrett sounded.

Lorrius glanced towards Runus Kohn, making eye contact as he appeared to consider, then the Elannis prince dipped his head in acknowledgement. 'Very well. House Berun may have Western Canasar, but only on the condition that the war criminal Lord Arion Sepian must be given to the custody of Elannis. He butchered our army at Moss Ford, he threatened the life of Prince Markon, and the Emperor has vowed that he'll die begging on his knees in our capital city, under an Elannis executioner's axe.'

Allana was upset by those words, but Jarrett opened his arms expansively and said, 'I would happily hand Arion Sepian and his entire loathsome family over to your custody, to do whatever you wish with them.'

You can't let that happen, Lana. Whatever else you decide to do, you can't let that happen.

'Very well,' said Lorrius, and his voice sounded weary. 'Then we are settled? We have an agreement?'

'There is one last matter,' stated Jarrett. His tone was neutral.

'Don't test our goodwill or push us too far, Duke Berun,' said Runus Kohn, although without any heat in his voice. 'But please, if you must, proceed.'

Jarrett then set out the last of his demands. Allana's heart was once again beating fast, as she listened to what he had to say.

—

Two days later, Allana was on her own and had returned to her private room. The illustrious visitors had departed that morning, and Jarrett was planning to spend the whole day overseeing drills and manoeuvres of Berun soldiers. Allana knew that she would not be disturbed for several hours.

On the dresser in front of her was a parchment, inkpot and quill, all of which she had retrieved earlier. As yet, the parchment was blank.

Allana was thinking about the momentous meetings from the prior two days. So many matters of great import had been agreed upon during those discussions. After much negotiation, that had included agreement to Jarrett's final demand.

Allana had subtly employed her talent of coercion in order to secure that last, incredible success. Prince Lorrius had been on the verge of conceding anyway, and he had only needed a little… *push* in private to get to a final agreement. Jarrett had otherwise presented a convincing argument.

Jarrett was so impressive, Lana. He's a man to be proud of, in so many ways.

With every day that had passed recently, Allana had seemed to become more committed to a future with Jarrett. She had accepted his proposal to wed, he had made her complicit in his secret schemes, and now he had achieved so much for her. There should be no doubt that remaining with Jarrett was the safest and best option for her future, particularly in the face of impending war. She knew that she should embrace becoming his wife, and then enjoy all the status, wealth and power that such a choice was likely to bring to her.

But she felt torn. If she was really so resolved to marry the young duke, then why was she sitting here in secret, staring at a blank parchment and agonising over what to do?

Because Jarrett can never make you feel the way that Arion Sepian did, Lana. He's not like you, in the way that Arion is.

That was the reason. Arion haunted her thoughts, far too much. And it was still not too late to attempt to reunite with him, despite all the impracticalities of such an action. The rational part of her knew that there were so many difficulties and so much that she could lose if she tried to do it. A life with Jarrett would offer her protection and status, whereas the alternative offered no such certainties. She did not even know if Arion still wanted her, after his abandonment of her and subsequent marriage. But, in her heart, she believed that he did.

However, she dared not return to Septholme. As such, she could only hope to run away with Arion if she took the step of writing to him again and arranging to meet somewhere else. Over the preceding days, she had been giving detailed consideration about what she would write and where she would ask Arion to meet. *If* that was her choice.

You're running out of time though, Lana. If you're going to do it, you have to make a decision today. You have to act today.

To add to her dilemma, there was the awful complication of Arion being hunted by Elannis. She knew that she still might decide to remain with Jarrett. But it would be one thing to make that choice, rather than taking the enormous risk of chasing a future with Arion Sepian. It was another matter completely to realise that Arion was to be hunted down and killed by the very people who Jarrett was plotting with.

In those circumstances, she could not just ignore Arion's fate. But if she chose to stay with Jarrett, what could she possibly do?

Would she be prepared to risk the successful outcome of Jarrett's plans, by warning the young Sepian lord? Or was there any other action which she could take?

She felt torn apart inside, and undecided about what she was going to do. However, the time for procrastination was over. She was resolved that she was not going to leave this room until she had made her decision, whatever that might be.

For an hour afterwards, she stared at the blank parchment. Her heart was pounding, as she thought hard about what she wanted her future to be, and who she wanted to be with.

Eventually, she picked up the quill, dipped it in the ink, and she started to write.

12

Corin

—

*Year of Our Lord,
After Ascension, 770AA*

'The... Lord... Aiduel... cast... down... the... I'm sorry, I don't know this word.'

Corin's head was hurting from this intensive session of practising his reading.

'Usurers. U-sur-ers,' said the missionary Hellin, delivering her response in her usual calm and patient manner. 'It means moneylenders. Someone who lends money but requires high interest rates.' Corin frowned, and was preparing to ask for further explanation, but she anticipated this and said, 'No more questions, please! You really don't need to know about that. Anyway, that's probably more than enough reading for today.'

'Thank the Gods,' said Corin, and he smirked. He had taken to using these words much more often recently, as gentle defiance of her persistent efforts to convert him to the ways of the man Aiduel.

'No, thank The Lord, Chief Corin!'

Corin suppressed a further smile, having become familiar with such stern responses across the winter months. He had spent a lot of time with the older woman, ever since her arrival in Karn just before the onset of winter.

She had introduced herself that first day as a missionary of The Lord Aiduel. She had informed Corin that she had once been a priestess in the overseas country of Andar, until she and others had volunteered to spread The Lord's Word throughout Bergen. She had heard about Corin of the Karn, the Chosen of the Gods, just days after the battle with the Renni. She had then travelled as quickly as she could to find him.

Corin had escorted her to the Clan Hall that day. He had listened to her story, and had asked her what she wanted. In response to this, she had said, 'I beg your permission to stay here with you, in Karn, for the winter. I want to teach you about The Lord Aiduel, Chief Corin, so that you and your people may forever walk in His Holy Light.'

Corin had replied, 'That doesn't really answer why the people of the Karn should shelter you, or feed you from our winter reserves. Or why I should listen to you when you talk about this man.'

'I wouldn't ask you to do that, Chief Corin, without something in return. And the something I can offer you is *knowledge*, from the lands to the east. I've heard much about how you're seeking to make changes in these lands. But if you're like the other chiefs I've met, you'll not have been taught letters or numbers. If you let me stay here, Chief Corin, as a missionary of Aiduel, then I'll teach you about numbers, and I'll teach you to *read*.'

Sometime after that, she had opened her backpack and had shown Corin the three aged, leather-bound books inside. Corin had been fascinated by the elaborate scribblings on the pages, and by the woman's explanation of how those patterns captured and contained a range of stories and knowledge. Knowledge of a world far away from Karn.

'And in return for my lessons,' Hellin had finished, 'all I ask is that, for a few hours each week, you'll also let me tell you about the teachings of The Lord Aiduel, from this book here.' She had patted the cover of the largest of the three tomes. 'This is the Holy Book.'

Corin had been trying to conceal his excitement, wondering about the secrets hidden on the pages of the three books.

He had eventually replied, 'I'm Chosen by the Gods, and I'll always honour the Gods for that reason, but I agree to your proposal. You will teach me letters, and numbers. In return, I'll listen when you talk about this *man*, Aiduel.'

Ever since then, they had spent an hour together each day. The middle-aged woman had become Corin's teacher, and he had learned a lot. From the outset, Corin had relished the world of knowledge which was opening up to him, and Hellin had expressed astonishment about his speed of learning.

Corin could now add and subtract numbers in the thousands, and he had used this skill to calculate how many people now lived within his domain. The answer was over two thousand.

More significantly, he could also now interpret the previously meaningless scribblings on the page. He had read from each of Hellin's three books, including the one that she called the Holy Book. In Corin's opinion, this latter tome was a confusing combination of a story of the man Aiduel's life, and also a record of the things which he had said. Hellin often quoted those latter statements, in regular conversation.

So far, Corin had only read selected short passages from the book, and that had been undertaken *very* slowly. However, from this and from Hellin's descriptions, he was beginning to form a picture of the man Aiduel, and he liked him. This Aiduel had come from close to nothing, and he had risen to be a leader. He also seemed to have been fair, and caring, for most of the time, but had been utterly ruthless when necessary.

Corin could not help but notice the similarities between the man Aiduel and himself. Certainly, Aiduel was also described as possessing special powers. However, some of Aiduel's purported actions sounded preposterous, and far beyond Corin's abilities.

In one story which Hellin had read out loud, Aiduel had raised up all the water from a lake and had cast it onto a city of sinners, to wash away their foulness.

Corin had laughed upon hearing this, and had asked, 'Did this man Aiduel use that power on the well, when he needed a drink?'

The comment had earned him a glare followed by a reprimand.

Hellin insisted that the stories of this man Aiduel were true, and she stated that he was worshipped throughout all of the lands to the east. She regularly reiterated that her mission was to try to convert the people of Bergen, including Corin, to the path of The Lord.

One night, Corin had challenged her on this, and had said, 'But he's just a man. We worship the Gods. Banta. Cint. Mella. Karo. So many others. *You* worship a man.'

'He was a man who became a god,' she had replied. 'The only true God, Our Lord.'

'The Gods are the Gods. In our lands, a man cannot become one.'

She had stared at him, then had smirked. 'So says Corin of the Karn, the man they call Mella Reborn, the God in the West.'

Corin had been unable to respond to that.

—

The winter had otherwise been a productive one. Corin had encouraged the sharing of resources between the five Chosen clans, such that none had suffered shortages during the most difficult season of the year.

In those periods when the weather had been milder, he had also spent time at both the Anath and Borl villages, and he could feel their acceptance of him growing.

Even more significantly, two more clans, the Kelma and the Milni, had become part of the Chosen Alliance. Both of these had received word of Corin's invitation to join the growing group in return for accepting his leadership. In addition, a further three clans had made overtures to start discussions in the spring, although this had not yet progressed. Corin could perceive that his objective of peace was coming to fruition.

A handful of weeks earlier, however, he had encountered a potential dark cloud over that vision. He had been in discussion and negotiation with Clan Chief Dorlan of the Kelma. Corin had been asking about the Kelma clan's motivation for joining the alliance, when the wiry chief had first mentioned rumours of a collection of barbarous clans to the south.

When Corin had enquired further, Dorlan had replied, 'We've been told that they've swept over clan after clan. Killing their men, and taking their women and children as slaves. I've heard the name Kurakee mentioned, although for my people it's only rumours of horrible things done to clans we don't know. But if they do come north to our lands, Dorlan doesn't want the Kelma to stand against these Kurakee alone.'

After hearing this, Corin had sent out scouts to the south, to find out more about this unknown tribe. None had yet returned.

Other than this point of unease, Corin could be satisfied with what he had achieved during the winter. The Alliance had developed, and Corin had gained much knowledge from the missionary Hellin. However, despite the importance of these things, Corin's foremost consideration had been to plan for his expedition to the far north, to try to find the Gate of his dreams.

The planned journey had been growing in scale, ever since Corin had announced it to the senior warriors of Karn, and later to the chiefs of the Chosen clans. Even though Corin wanted a small travelling party, it had soon become a matter of honour for each of the four founding clans to have someone on the expedition, to accompany Corin. He had agreed to this, with Kernon already allocated that role for the Karn themselves. The missionary Hellin had also asked to come, which he had accepted, because he wanted to continue his lessons with her.

All of the parties who were going on the expedition had been told to assemble at Karn in a week's time, at the start of spring. The journey to the north would then depart. Corin had also informed all of the chiefs that he expected to be away for up to two moons. During that time, Clan Chief Munnik of the Borl would be standing in Corin's place.

What had started in Corin's mind as a mission to restore Agbeth, had become an event of great significance for all of the clans. Many of them truly believed that he was going to find the Gods, which made him feel uncomfortable and slightly fraudulent. He knew that his real mission was to find a Gate, not the Gods, but he had kept that from his people.

—

Corin was thinking about these things, walking through Karn with Blackpaw at his side, when he saw the young warrior Arex sprinting towards him from the direction of the lake. Corin guessed immediately as to what the youth's hasty arrival must mean, which was confirmed when Arex called out, 'Chief, she's awake!'

The young warrior reversed direction as soon as he had said this, and Corin set off running in pursuit of him. Corin knew that Blackpaw had also picked up an understanding of the message through their shared connection, and the beast started to lope alongside him as he ran.

Corin could sense Blackpaw's excitement mirroring his own; he had often been able to feel the creature mourning Agbeth's absences since her injury, in its own unique way. It had been four weeks since her last short bout of lucidity, one of only three such instances across the long winter, and it seemed that the gap between each was growing longer.

They arrived at the lake within minutes, the winter ice now gone from its glassy waters, and Corin was panting heavily when he got there. Although he possessed powers and had been altered by the connection to Blackpaw, he had never fully overcome his natural physical frailties. However, when he saw Agbeth sitting on the promontory of land beside the lake, looking towards him and smiling, his fatigue was disregarded.

Blackpaw beat him to Agbeth. Corin watched the beast surging ahead to reach her, and it dipped its head when it arrived. Agbeth rose to her feet, and she reached out and rubbed her hand into the fur of the felrin's neck. Corin felt a burst of the creature's happiness washing through their connection, and he was smiling when he reached his wife.

In the moments afterwards, he and Agbeth embraced. Their arms clasped around each other, with her head on his chest, and Corin hugged her tightly. He was trying to convey to her, in the fleeting moments that they might have, just how much he still loved her. The warrior Arex had withdrawn, as had Agbeth's carer, but for Corin they were anyway forgotten. Blackpaw had also retreated a couple of paces, but Corin could feel the beast's contentment at seeing its family become whole again.

It was Agbeth who broke off the hug, her gaze fixing upon Corin's face while their arms remained around each other.

'I fight, Corin… I have to fight so hard for this,' she said. 'To pull my way back to the surface, and to you. I think I'm sinking deeper, and further away, as time passes. But there are things I must tell you, while I still can.'

He heard the urgency in her tone. They both knew that these encounters could end abruptly and with little warning. 'Then tell me, please.'

'Yes, but be ready to hold me up, if I… *go away*, again.'

'I will.'

'You are going north? I remember you speaking of it. Telling me.'

'Yes.' He lowered his voice. 'To find the Gate. To find a way to make you better.'

'You must take me,' she said. 'You must take *us*. *We* both think so.'

'What has he said?'

'Just that. You must take us.'

Corin's mind was churning, and he was thinking rapidly, aware that he might not have the time for questions. 'But how? It's a hard journey. It will be difficult for you to travel, while you're…'

'You'll find a way. You always do. But you must take us.'

'What else did the boy say? Does he remember who he is?'

'No.'

'Did he say *why* I must take you?'

'No. I don't think he knows. But please promise me that you'll take me, Corin. Remember, long ago, you once swore that you wouldn't leave to seek out the Gate, without me.'

'I'll take you, Agbeth. By the Gods, I swear it. I'll find a way to take you.'

'Thank you. I think… we should sit.' Her voice was sounding sleepy. 'Will you sit behind me, with your arms around me?'

'Yes.' He gulped.

They did as she said. He seated himself on the floor, facing out towards the lake. She settled into the space between his thighs, and leaned back against him, following which he wrapped his arms around her, and kissed the back of her head. The movement of a massive form then told Corin that Blackpaw had come closer, and the felrin lay forwards, with its neck and head resting across Agbeth's lap. Corin watched as Agbeth's hand returned to lazily stroking the beast's fur, and he could feel its contentment.

Agbeth had fallen silent, her head resting back against Corin's chest. Her breathing soon told him that she had descended into sleep and was once again lost to him. He remained there, holding her in his arms, with Blackpaw's weight pressing down across his leg. Agbeth's hand was still on the back of the creature's neck, in the place where it had been as she had drifted into slumber. Corin moved his own hand there, and started to stroke Blackpaw's fur.

He looked down at the beast, which had closed its eyes and also appeared to be sleeping. Another plan was already forming in Corin's mind as he stared at the dozing creature.

Later that day, Corin attempted to contact the ghost inside Agbeth again, but without success. The contacts with the presence during the winter had been as infrequent as Agbeth's periods of wakefulness, and they had also continued to be vague and frustrating. The ghost's revelation that it had been murdered had not yet unlocked any new pathways to the truth of who Corin was speaking to. Nor had he gained any further insight as to why this presence had taken up residence within Agbeth's soul, other than that it had come on Corin's command.

In contrast to the irregular contacts with the ghost, Corin's recurring dream had remained a frequent visitor during the winter months. It came to him again that night, eventually forcing him from his sleep in a state of agitation.

The image of the Gate was in his mind afterwards, as it had been for so long. He would know that magnificent archway of the Gods for certain, if he came upon it in the far north.

He also believed that he was seeing ever more of the dream, with the passing of time and with the use of his powers, although he could not retain clear memories of the final moments. However, he had a lingering and growing suspicion that the figure in the Gate spoke to him towards the end, and that these words triggered the remembered flashes of violence which followed. Violence which was done to him? To his frustration, the precise detail of what was said and done would never stay with him after waking.

As he lay in the darkness, thinking about this, it added to his sense of resolution about what he was doing. He *needed* to find the Gate. Following that, he believed that many other answers would also be revealed.

—

Over the subsequent days, the preparations for the journey to the north were being finalised. The day after Corin had spent time with Agbeth beside the lake, he went to visit the village blacksmith. He discussed his detailed requirements in relation to an idea which he had, and gave instructions that his request was to be worked on immediately, to be ready before the end of that week.

After that, he set about issuing orders for the running of the Chosen territory, for the period while he would be away. Clan Chief Munnik was due to arrive two days before the departure date, to give him and Corin ample time to discuss and resolve matters.

Corin was therefore surprised, three days before he was due to depart on the journey north, to be told that Chief Quan of the Qari had arrived in Karn. After being informed, Corin headed out to meet the lanky Qari leader.

As Corin approached, Quan was pushing his long, matted hair back behind his shoulders. Quan and three of his clansmen had dismounted, and had hitched their horses near to the entrance to the village.

Corin greeted the arrivals, before adding, 'Chief Quan, I'd not expected you today.'

Quan nodded, then grimaced. 'Chief Corin.' He then gestured to a young warrior, who was next to him. 'This is my nephew, Charrek. He'll be the member of the Qari who'll accompany you on your great mission.'

Corin nodded to Charrek. The muscular Qari was even taller than his uncle, with hair which hung below his shoulders. He looked to be of a similar age to Corin.

'Well met, Charrek,' said Corin. 'But you look troubled, Quan. What is it?'

'Munnik advised that I should ride to you as soon as possible,' replied Quan, 'to get here ahead of your next visitors, and to warn you. As such, we've ridden hard, first from Qari, then from Borl.'

'What visitors? Warn me about what?'

'A warband of eighty warriors arrived in Qari. We believe that they're now on their way here, to Karn. They call themselves a name that we've heard recently, spoken by the Kelma. They call themselves the Kurakee.'

—

Later that day, thanks to Quan's advance warning, Corin was prepared when the Kurakee party arrived within a mile of Karn.

Based on the troubling rumours that he had already heard, Corin had no intention of letting these strangers view the village and its fortifications up close. He had therefore hastily assembled a war party of sixty warriors. He intended to intercept the Kurakee on a dirt trail, hundreds of metres from the settlement.

Corin positioned himself in the centre of the path, with Akob, Marrix and Kernon in close proximity behind. The other warriors of the Karn were spread out around them. Everyone was armed and armoured, including Corin. Blackpaw was at Corin's side, and was standing upright to its full eight feet in height, with claws extended.

Corin had ordered Quan to remain in the village, such that the Kurakee would not be alerted that Corin had been forewarned. However, Corin had listened intently earlier as Quan had detailed the demands which the Kurakee had made of the Qari. Corin felt that he was ready to respond and to react.

He watched as the sizeable party of foreign warriors approached on foot. These newcomers moved in an unhurried fashion, with an apparent arrogant swagger, as if they did not care that Corin faced them with a warband only slightly smaller than their own. The Kurakee all had heavy beards and long hair, and they carried axes and shields. However, of most note was the number of markings which the men had on their faces and arms, as if patterns had been coloured into their skin. On their faces, these patterns and the thick beards acted to obscure their features, and made them appear more fearsome.

As they drew closer, Corin noted that the Kurakee were staring at Blackpaw, some with apparent uncertainty. The felrin was a surprise to them, at least.

When the strangers were twenty paces away, Corin shouted, 'Halt! You are in the lands of the Karn, of the Chosen Alliance! State your purpose for being here.'

The individual at the front of the group was burly and fat, with probably the heaviest beard of any of them. He responded to Corin, his voice rough and his tone dismissive.

'We're the Kurakee. And we're here on behalf of Warlord Kurune of the Kurakee. We've not come to talk with pissy-little boys in the road. We seek your leader, the one known as Corin of the Karn, the Chosen of the Gods.'

Corin heard the Karn warriors around him bristling in response to this, but he controlled his own temper, and said, 'I am Corin of the Karn, the Chosen of the Gods, and you're fortunate that I don't always kill people who insult me. Now state your purpose.'

He already knew what was coming, but this exchange was necessary.

The fat Kurakee sneered before responding. 'The Chosen of the Gods? You? Fuck your shitty Gods and their choices then! I am Brune of the Kurakee, brother of Warlord Kurune. I bring my brother's words to the clans in the north.'

'Then speak them.'

Corin's anger was rising. In response, he heard a low growl from Blackpaw's throat. Corin observed as the stranger Brune's gaze darted to the beast, and for a moment the man lost a trace of his demeanour of confidence.

'Know this!' the Kurakee warrior then called out. 'The Kurakee are coming! Kneel before us or die! Over eighty clans now fall within the domain and rule of Kurune, Warlord of the Kurakee. Over eighty tribes now kneel to our clan, the greatest in all of Bergen. Axes beyond number fight on Kurune's order. We've conquered the south, soon we'll have the west, and next we'll take the north. All of the lands of Bergen shall kneel before the Kurakee!

'In two moons' time, at Spring's Heart, the great Kurakee horde shall come to the north. The clans of the north, including your *Chosen* clans, shall be ready to kneel to us, and to accept our demands and offer us tribute, or we'll wipe you out.'

'Bold words,' replied Corin, affecting a casual air which he did not feel inside. 'And what does your Warlord Kurune demand of us?'

Brune turned his head, and spat into the grass beside the dirt pathway. 'If you're ready to lay down your arms and surrender, we'll be lenient. We'll take only our first tribute. One in every four of your livestock. One in four of your young warriors, for our warband. One in four of your child-bearing women, including any of your married women we choose, for our men. One in four of your children, as slaves. And one in four of your elderly, as sacrifices to *our* Gods. After that, there'll be annual tributes.'

'Is that everything?' asked Corin.

'No. We'll also take your chiefs and their families as slaves. Afterwards, every clan is to have a Kurakee chief and will follow Kurakee ways. And we require your head to be delivered to us, Corin of the Karn, separated from its body.' He then glanced at Blackpaw again. 'Along with the head of this beast. Word has travelled of your… powers, and Warlord Kurune won't let you get anywhere near to him in person, to attempt harm. But in your honour, he'll mount your puny skull next to the skulls of his other enemies, on the walls of his shit-house.'

Corin had no doubts that the words were intended to provoke, and he could hear angry cursing and muttering from the Karn warriors around him. He knew that some of them would want to launch into attack against these Kurakee, as repayment for the insults and threats delivered. Corin himself would have relished releasing Blackpaw against them, or unleashing his own powers upon them. But he had picked up on key words. *In two moons' time.* Long enough, unless Corin did something rash to expedite their intended invasion. He was therefore outwardly calm, as he asked his next question.

'And if we don't accept your terms?'

'Then the Kurakee will still come, at Spring's Heart, and we'll take what is ours to take. And as you watch all of your villages being burned, your men and elderly being killed, and your women and children being raped, then you'll wish that you'd accepted our demands. And given your tribute when you still had a chance.'

'And if we accept your demands? I'm the leader of many of the clans in this region. If we accept, can we assemble all of my people, all of the clans, here, in one place in Karn, for the tribute?'

'If your people kneel to us, then yes, the Kurakee will accept that. The Kurakee horde will come to this place, first. Have your people assembled, so that we may take our offerings, and then the Kurakee will not need to kill you all.'

'I understand,' said Corin.

'Do you have an answer for Kurune then, Corin of the Karn?'

Corin paused. He knew what he truly wanted to say, but he could not perceive an advantage to saying it. Instead, his response was measured and controlled.

'The Chosen peoples will await the arrival of the Kurakee. I can't give you a definite answer today, without speaking with all of my chiefs, but you can tell your Warlord Kurune that I'm minded to agree to his demands. That includes what you've said for me, if it will save my people. But tell your brother to come *here*, where we'll all gather, if he wants to collect his tribute from the north. And now, if you and your party want to live to deliver this message back, you'll turn around, and you'll leave my lands.'

The fat Kurakee spat again after listening to this, then began once more to shout, spittle flying from his lips as he did so.

'Know this! The Kurakee are coming! Kneel before us or die! These are the words of Kurune, Warlord of the Kurakee! The Kurakee are coming!'

The burly warrior continued to repeat these words as he and his party turned and started to walk away. Corin was frowning as he watched them leave. He recognised with grim certainty that if Brune had spoken true, and the Kurakee were indeed coming, then the Chosen Alliance was in grave peril.

Corin also understood that he and his people would have only two moons to prepare for this new threat. A period which he had previously intended to devote towards an expedition to the far north, in order to seek the Gate and a cure for Agbeth, before it was too late.

He would have to decide what to do. And at that moment, it was a deeply unappealing choice.

Interlude One

—

*Year of Our Lord,
Before Ascension, 60BA*

—

Interlude 1

Aiduel

—

*Year of Our Lord,
Before Ascension, 60BA*

His name was Aiduel, and he did not resist when they bound him to the tree.

Coarse rope had been wrapped and knotted about each of his wrists and ankles. His captors now yanked these cords tight around the thick trunk, stretching his limbs out sideways and forcing rough bark into the flesh of his shredded back. He heard a ripple of laughter from the gathered crowd.

He was clad only in a dirty loincloth, and sweat glistened on his bare skin. The thick foliage of the mighty tree cast him in shade, but the day was baking hot, and he allowed his head to slump forwards in apparent exhaustion. Let them all think that he was broken and defeated; they would soon learn otherwise.

He had been beaten and tortured in the preceding days, and his body was now torn, bruised and deliberately unhealed. During those torments, he had permitted himself to suffer, to bleed and to scream.

However, before this day was done, the bleeding and the screaming would be suffered by others.

They had once feared him. They had been afraid of the coming of *Aiduel the Conqueror* and his armies, descending upon them from the far lands of the west. But instead of arriving with an avenging host at his back, he had appeared in their city as a man alone and unarmed. And they had seized him.

They believed now that his spirit was shattered and that he no longer posed a threat to them. In their arrogance, they had roped him and dragged him to this place to end his life, as a public spectacle for their vulgar gratification.

There were thousands of the elite of the city in this crowd, all of them gathered within this vast, enclosed parkland in the wealthiest suburbs of their capital. The assembled citizens, in various states of recline and undress, were spread out before him across an extensive lawn in the centre of their park. This pristine, grassy area was enclosed by a spectacular ring of soaring trees, and interspersed amongst those trees, almost as tall, were the almighty statues of the Twelve. The false deities of these truly godless people.

Aiduel himself was bound to the most majestic and towering of all of the trees, and he was facing towards the masses. Aiduel's tree stood alone, inside but away from the encircling wall of statuary and foliage.

He knew that many of the bloated spiders who sat atop the web that was the Angallic Empire would be in this place today. For centuries, their empire had brought misery to millions, and this ancient city was its avaricious heart. And these assembled families had wrapped themselves around that heart, and they gorged upon it.

They gathered in this place each Seventh-Day, to celebrate their ascent to the pinnacle of wealth and power. While assembled here within this arboreal palace of sin, they indulged in shameless debauchery and delighted in the ritual humiliation of those who had dared to stand against them. Even now, brazen excesses of gluttony, fornication and slave-rape were taking place before Aiduel's eyes, and he felt contempt.

He noted that the imperial archers were marching into place before him, and he counted ten in total as they approached with regimented precision. All of these would-be executioners were male, and all were attired in burnished-gold, gaudy, ceremonial armour. The half-score of bowmen formed a line, no more than twenty paces away from his tree.

He could hear the excited chatter building amongst the gathered assembly as they spotted this group of marksmen. This babble turned to applause as a lavishly dressed figure appeared before them, a man who was turning and waving to acknowledge and return the adulation of the masses.

Aiduel could feel the darkness of this man who they all recognised as their emperor. Every web has a single, dominant spider, and this approaching individual was the manifestation of everything that was loathsome about the Angallic Empire. Aiduel could touch the corruption inside the approaching corpulent, bronzed figure, and he felt an urge to immediately drown the man in his own horror. But not yet. Let the monster have his moment. Let all of this be witnessed and *remembered*.

The emperor raised his hands to silence the crowd and then began to speak. 'We have before us the coming *Conqueror*,' he said, whilst gesturing towards Aiduel. 'And yet, I do not believe that we are *conquered*!'

There was widespread laughter at this. The emperor then proceeded to agitate his audience, building them into a growing frenzy by listing a series of real and imagined crimes committed by Aiduel and his followers. The man's words both fuelled and fed upon the crowd's hate, and his cunning twisting of the truth made them feel like their animosity was valid. Just. Righteous.

HATE. KILL. HATE. KILL.

The dark emotion of the audience beat outwards, and Aiduel gathered it to himself, relishing it, offering himself just cause for what he was planning to do. There were of course many in the gathered throng who did not share the hate; slaves, servants and those few within the system who longed to be free of it. Aiduel took note of every one of these. *They* would be spared.

However, most who were present were revelling in the filth of their power, their wealth, and their domination over their slaves. And he marked them all.

But even as he continued to be bombarded by the bitter emotion of the crowd, one single and contrasting call stood out amongst all of the others.

LOVE. WORRY. LOVE. WORRY. LOVE.

This emotion came from outside of the ring of trees, and he refrained from looking in her direction.

I will survive this, Amena. There is no need to worry.

He could feel his wife, somewhere close. Today, the Disciples had been ordered to put aside their medallions and to remain outside of the ring of encircling trees. They were to be the witnesses of this event, and indeed Josia had been chosen to write the chronicle for the future. But to keep them safe, Aiduel needed to know where they were, and to be able to speak to them, at all times. The medallions which he had created would have been a hindrance to this.

'We can come, and we can give our enemy war,' he had said to the Disciples, prior to leaving the conquered island of Abass to come to this place. 'And if that happens, we all know that we'll win. Eventually. But better that we give their people something else. A moment. An event. A symbol. Something that they'll draw inspiration from, as they cast off their shackles and rise up. A humiliation of their oppressors, within the beating heart of oppression's power. We all know where the Angalls will take me to kill me, and it's there that I'll rip the head from the beast. There that I shall create that symbol. One which will endure, for the longest time. I know this because I have seen it, and I have lived it, within my dreams.'

The emperor had finished talking, and the game of execution was about to begin.

Ten archers. One hundred arrows. And the nature of the game? How many such arrows could they fire into a man's body, one-by-one at intervals, without the victim succumbing to death? How many times could these supremely skilled marksmen pierce flesh whilst avoiding a killing shot?

It would be a marvellous spectacle for such an assemblage of the greatest of Angall. A true demonstration of their power to crush any threat against them. They would pin him against their tree, and they would eventually kill him, while their false gods bore witness.

The first arrow took Aiduel in the right shoulder. He had seen it coming, of course, had watched its slow spiral towards him. And perhaps he had subtly directed it and had let it pierce him, too. But that did not prevent the excruciating agony as it went straight through flesh and bone and pinned that part of his upper body against the tree. He allowed himself to experience his suffering and again to welcome it as the crowd cheered in response to the impact. Pain was a bridge to mortality, and there would be healing later.

Two arrows.

That was what he had agreed, what Amena had made him promise. Originally, he had wanted six. However, his wife had withheld her consent, and she had garnered support from all of the other Disciples to ensure that he changed his mind. He had acquiesced to this protest, as he had promised them that he always would whenever they voiced unanimous objection to his plans. It was another means for him to retain his connection to mortality, and to avoid a descent towards tyranny.

The second arrow struck him, this time through his left shoulder, in a mirroring position. He again savoured the burst of pain as he heard the masses cheering raucously.

His entire upper body was pinned against the tree now. His arms were still outstretched to either side by the ropes, his legs also spread uncomfortably. Blood was pouring from both of the arrow wounds, running down his bare chest and stomach in separate streams and staining his loincloth.

There would be no more arrows.

He raised his head at that moment and looked up to the sky, to his right-hand side. Thinking. Focusing.

He could feel the Gate, in the distance. Even from here, separated by a vast ocean, he could sense it and touch it. In the place where he had found it. In the place where it had found him and had changed him, after he had been willing to pay the awful cost.

And he reached out to it now, drawing its power unto himself.

He was aware of the gasps and curses as a radiant glow began to form around his body, bathing him in golden light and forcing many within the assembled masses to cover their eyes. He was also alert to a third arrow bouncing off the shield of energy which now cocooned him, and to the agitated shrieks of the emperor, who was cajoling the imperial marksmen to finish their job.

The colour of the parkland had changed in these moments, with verdant greenery becoming pale under the brilliance which now pulsed from his form on the ancient tree. Turbulent winds suddenly whipped through the foliage in the encircling ring of trees, bending the trunks of the greatest and tearing the lesser from their roots.

Along the perimeter of this enclosed area, the statues of each of the Twelve now shattered, exploding a hail of rock and rubble into the air which showered onto the unworthy below.

Many of the assembled were starting to scream in panic, and were hastening to their feet. But they were trapped here now, within a vortex of wind which whipped around the outside of their open parkland.

Aiduel cast off his ropes as if they were no more than string, and he pulled the arrows from his body, healing the residual wounds and torn flesh as he did so. The bowmen came rushing forwards in attack, but tendrils of darkness swept at them, delivering death, and their bodies crumpled as one.

Then Aiduel strode forward, closing towards the many terrified spiders who were about to lose their place on the web. And the web itself. He pointed his arm towards the emperor, and a surge of energy pulled the bronzed, fat figure into the air, dragging him away from his guards. For a handful of moments, horror was inflicted upon the squealing man, until Aiduel ripped him apart.

It was time for vengeance. It was time for justice. It was time for a renewal of the world, and a purging of sin.

He unleashed his power.

Part Two

Invasion and Discovery

*Year of Our Lord,
After Ascension, 770AA*

13

Leanna

—

*Year of Our Lord,
After Ascension, 769AA to 770AA*

In the weeks following her arrival in Western Canasar, Leanna's life was again transformed. She had returned to relative anonymity, and was no longer revered as the Angel of Arlais.

The journey to Septholme had been undertaken at Leanna's insistence, despite Caddin Sendromm's initial misgivings. Visiting Arion had helped to distract Leanna from her hurt over the events in Arlais, including the disappearance of her parents.

Having lived her whole life in a relatively flat inland city, Leanna had found it exciting to visit the coastal town. It had been fascinating to experience the bustling port, with its winding streets leading up from the harbour to the mighty castle sitting atop the hill.

She also felt that she had done some good there. Arion had appeared to be tormented and unsettled when she had first arrived at the castle. In contrast, he had seemed more at peace when they had said farewell.

Unlike Leanna, Caddin had not enjoyed being in the busy coastal town. Leanna still did not understand who Sendromm was, or what his reasons were for deciding to protect her. However, with every passing day, she was becoming more convinced that he was sincere in his resolution to keep her safe from harm.

In Septholme, she had noticed how diligently the grey-bearded man watched over her, scrutinising anyone who came too close. She had already witnessed how lethal he could be when tested, and it gave her a reassuring sense of security.

After a number of days, Caddin had insisted that they depart from Septholme. Once Leanna had mentioned the attempt on Arion's life, which might have involved Elannis assassins, the burly man had become deeply nervous about who else might be in the town. About who else might see them and recognise Leanna.

They had departed a handful of days later.

—

In that first week after their flight into Western Canasar, they travelled on the roads without interference, with Leanna and Amyss both adopting the clothing of a common-woman. From the outset, their cover story of a father travelling with his daughters seemed to be accepted without remark. Caddin's peculiar accent was suggestive of a man who had journeyed far and wide.

In those initial days aboard the trundling wagon, Leanna and Amyss often talked together in hushed tones. In contrast, their grey-bearded companion continued to rebuff their efforts to make conversation with him.

On one of those days, Amyss turned to the burly man and asked, 'Who are you, Caddin? Are you a soldier? A merchant? And your accent's funny? Where are you from?'

In response to this, Sendromm said, 'Leanna, tell your friend about our agreement. About how I don't like questions, and don't intend to answer them.'

Amyss huffed. 'You agreed that with Leanna, not with me. Very well then, at least tell me these things. How did you recognise those attackers in the cathedral? And how did you know that they were hired by the Archlaw? And you talked about the Angel's kind. How do you know all of these things? Are you an Aiduel's Guard?'

Sendromm said, 'You can always walk behind the wagon if you won't shut up. But no, I'm not a member of that order.'

One matter which Leanna had become determined to understand was why her powers did not work when she was near to him. On the second day of travel, she raised that subject.

'We're remaining with you, Caddin, as I promised,' she said. 'And you choose to tell us very little about yourself, which I also agreed to. But I must understand something. My powers are diminished to close to nothing when I'm near to you. I can feel them, somewhere distant, but I can't access them. Please tell me why.'

Sendromm stared at her, appearing to consider her question whilst holding the reins of their moving wagon.

'Very well, if it will give me some peace. I own a medallion – actually, *two* medallions now – which I wear around my neck, and which protect me from people with powers. The man I killed in the cathedral also possessed one, which I took after I'd killed him. So, now I own two, possibly more than anyone else in Angall. If I keep these close to me, I'm not at risk from your powers.'

'What are these medallions?' Leanna asked. 'Are there lots of them? And how did the first one come into your possession?'

'There aren't lots of them. And how I own it is my business. Just know that your powers will be greatly diminished while you're near me, so if you need to use them, get away from me. And also know that I'll never take my medallion off, so don't even think about trying to use your abilities on me. Understood?'

Leanna pressed him for more information that day, but as with so many other questions asked of him, he clammed up and said nothing more.

—

After they had departed from Septholme, they stopped at a hostelry which was miles to the south of the town. At dinner that evening, Amyss initiated a conversation about what was to happen next.

'So, here we are,' the petite woman said. 'An odd group, if ever there was one. So, what do we do now? Travel from tavern to tavern, watching our secretive protector get drunk every evening, until he runs out of money?'

'I've plenty of money, girl,' the burly man replied. 'More than you know. That's not an issue.'

'Yes, but what now?' Amyss questioned, turning to Leanna. 'What are we doing here? Where are we going to go, and what are we going to do? We were priestesses, Lea, doing important work, but right now we're just-'

'Staying alive, girl,' Sendromm interrupted, his tone dismissive.

Leanna could sense an argument brewing.

Lord Aiduel, please supply me with the words to persuade them both.

'I need to stay here in Western Canasar, Amyss,' she said. 'Close to the border. After some time has passed, I'll need Caddin to return to Arlais, to look for my parents again.'

'We'd be better to get far away from Elannis,' Sendromm replied. 'Northern Andar, somewhere remote.'

'No,' said Leanna. 'If I leave Western Canasar, it will feel like I'm giving up on my parents after just one attempt to find them. I'm not willing to do that. I'll need you to return to Arlais to look for them. Maybe more than once.'

'It's a bad idea,' said Sendromm. 'More chance of people recognising you here. We should go somewhere far away.'

'To what purpose? I've lost *everything*, other than Amyss and my own life. I'll not go to some far-flung place, then act as if my parents never existed, as if I've already forgotten them. I agreed to travel with you, Caddin, but I didn't agree to be led wherever you want to go. If you want to stay in my company, then you need to accept this.'

Sendromm frowned, then shrugged as if in acceptance.

'But what are we going to do, Lea?' asked Amyss. 'Just sit in a wagon all day, and a tavern room all night? Until when?'

'It's safer to keep moving,' said Sendromm.

'I understand that,' said Leanna. 'But Amyss is right. Doing what?'

The grey-bearded man stared at her for a number of seconds, as if he was considering something. Finally, he said, 'Leanna, you were a healer, yes? Even without your… miracles, you've been taught medicine?'

'Yes, that's right.'

'I was a healer, too, once,' Sendromm stated, with a wistful tone to his voice. 'A long time ago. A good one, too. I journeyed to remote places, tending to people. I still have my old tools and a store of herbs in the wagon.'

Leanna and Amyss stared at him, dumbfounded, and for one of the first times he looked almost embarrassed.

Lord Aiduel, what other secrets does this man carry?

'Perhaps we could do that?' Sendromm added sheepishly.

―

As a result of that discussion, for the following weeks of winter, Leanna and her companions started to travel around Western Canasar.

Throughout that time, Sendromm directed them towards more remote settlements. At each location, they would offer healing services to people who otherwise had no access to a local healer, and Caddin would attempt to sell some of his accumulated wares.

For the first time since her role as an army healer, Leanna was outside of the cloistered environs of a religious establishment, and she was able to travel with relative freedom in a new country.

Therefore, despite the trauma of her flight into Western Canasar, she experienced a sense of liberation. It was clear that Amyss felt the same. The petite woman appeared to be quietly rejoicing that they had both survived, and that she was still with Leanna.

They all agreed that it was too dangerous for Leanna to use her powers. They were therefore reliant on their collective medical knowledge and conventional remedies, and Leanna was soon surprised by just how experienced Caddin Sendromm was. The man's healing knowledge surpassed her own, and she assessed that he was even close to Sister Colissa's level of expertise.

Leanna observed that Caddin was like a different person when he lost himself in medicine and healing. One who seemed more genuine, and less reserved and curt. It was clear that Sendromm had indeed lived a life like this in the past, possibly for a long time. He was comfortably familiar with the process of arriving in a new settlement, and then encouraging people to spread the word to the surrounding areas that a healer had arrived.

He also seemed oblivious to inclement weather. This was in stark contrast to Leanna and Amyss, who would huddle together under a blanket as they journeyed.

On their travels, they aimed to stay in a single location for a handful of nights at a time, taking two bedrooms in the better taverns that they came across. Once inside these establishments, Caddin advised Leanna and Amyss to stay in their bedroom other than for meals, and to remain out of sight during the evenings.

However, Sendromm often then spent his own evenings in the main drinking room of the tavern, always with his mace by his side. In the middle of each night, Leanna would hear him stumbling up the stairs and past her room. The following morning, he would emerge bleary-eyed, reeking of sweat and alcohol.

Despite his drunken indulgences, on most mornings Sendromm would insist on finding a place outside to train with his mace, sometimes for as long as an hour. After Leanna and Amyss had witnessed this a handful of times, it renewed their speculation that he must have been a soldier. The grey-bearded man could wield the hefty weapon, either single or two-handed, with an impressive grace and strength which belied his bulk and age.

It added to their confusion about who and what he was.

―

In the early days of their wanderings, news about the Archlaw's Proclamation of Excommunication came to the village where they were staying.

When they first heard of this, Amyss appeared to be the most upset and concerned, but Leanna found herself to be surprisingly unperturbed. The events of the last year had damaged her loyalty towards the Holy Church, and she no longer received the Archlaw's words with blind faith.

Instead, she could fortify herself with the knowledge that The Lord Aiduel had saved her on the pyre and that she retained her abilities; if Aiduel had truly turned away from her, she would have also lost those powers. She no longer believed that the Archlaw would be able to sever her connection to The Lord and to heaven, with mere words on a piece of paper.

Caddin Sendromm shrugged, after Amyss raised the subject at dinner.

'This proclamation doesn't bother you then?' Amyss asked.

'No,' said the burly man. 'I'm damned by The Lord, so Paulius and his laws can't touch me.'

'Why do you always say that, Caddin?' asked Leanna, wishing that just once she could sense the man's emotions. 'That you're damned by The Lord. Just what happened to you?'

He shrugged again, before saying, 'I was born, that's what. And what happened afterwards is my own business, girl.'

After that, he refused to say any more.

―

As the weeks passed, Amyss was growing increasingly frustrated about Sendromm's secrecy. Following one of the burly man's mace-training sessions, after they had returned to travelling on the wagon, she challenged him again.

'You were obviously a soldier,' she said. 'Why won't you just admit it?'

'Because my past is my concern, not yours,' said Sendromm.

'Which army were you in? When did you leave? Why do you own a medallion that stops Leanna's powers? And how do you know so much about Leanna's kind?'

The grey-bearded man gave an exasperated sigh.

'How can you ever expect us to trust you,' added Amyss, sounding annoyed, 'or, ever *like* you, when you refuse to tell us anything meaningful about yourself?'

'I don't want *you* to trust me or like me,' the man replied. 'I want *Leanna* to allow me to protect her.'

Amyss tutted in response to this. Later that day, once she and Leanna were in the privacy of their bedroom, she again raised the question of whether they should run away from their male companion.

'I don't want to do that,' said Leanna. 'Sometime soon, I'll need him to return to Arlais for me, if I'm to have any chance of finding my parents. And anyway, I've given him my oath.'

Leanna was able to persuade Amyss with this reasoning. However, she knew that her answer had not articulated *all* of her own motives for wanting to stay with the secretive man.

Some part of her believed that her loyalty to Sendromm was about more than just the promise that she had made. Her instinct was telling her that she had been meant to encounter the grey-bearded man, and that it was The Lord's will that she should continue to travel with him. She did not know why she felt like this, but she wanted to trust that instinct.

Lord Aiduel, I hope you will help me to understand these feelings, and soon.

—

The recurring dream continued to trouble Leanna during these travels in Western Canasar.

She was certain now that the figure in the Gate spoke to her before the commencement of violence, but she still could not retain the memory of what was said. However, she felt sure that the words were not benevolent, and she was becoming more convinced that they were a trigger for the ensuing horror. She needed to find a way to remember.

On a couple of nights, after waking from the dream, she also believed that she could feel a faint, distant *pulsing*. It teased the hidden recesses of her mind, in some ways a pale imitation of what she could feel when near to Arion. It made her wonder if she was still sensing the young noble, somewhere far away.

To her surprise, sometimes the dream did not invade her sleep for several consecutive nights, which was the longest undisturbed period that she had experienced since the early days at the College of Aiduel.

This puzzled her until Amyss speculated whether the dream could be impacted by Caddin's medallion. After that, they realised that Leanna had not been visited by the dream in any inn where her bed rested on the other side of a wall from Caddin.

Amyss suggested that they ask Caddin for the second medallion, so that she could wear it and keep Leanna free from troubled sleep, but Leanna declined. Even though she had come to fear the repeated torment of the dream, she felt that she needed to comprehend its secrets, and she did not want to be cut-off from it.

Lord Aiduel, you have given me this dream, alongside the gift of my powers. It is therefore not for me to make the choice to be rid of it.

—

One night, Leanna awoke in the darkness hours for another reason.

Amyss had gently shaken her awake. The petite priestess placed a finger on Leanna's lips, and whispered, 'Listen.'

At first, Leanna was confused, uncertain what she was meant to be listening for. Then she heard it. Sobbing, from Sendromm's room on the other side of the wall.

'He's crying,' whispered Amyss. 'But listen to what he's saying, if he speaks again.'

Leanna did as was instructed. For a number of minutes, she listened in the darkness, hearing occasional weeping noises. Her eyelids were heavy, and she was close to drifting back into sleep when she finally heard Sendromm speaking.

'Why are you turned away from me? I thought that this might change things. What else must I do? Am I never to see them again?'

His speech was slurred and he sounded drunk. Leanna listened for a few minutes longer after that, still struggling to fight off sleep. She heard Sendromm's last two words as she finally fell back into slumber.

'I'm sorry.'

The next morning, after discussion with Amyss, Leanna decided to approach Caddin. She found him in an area of open ground behind their hostelry, where he looked ready to begin his martial practice. As Leanna drew close, she could see that his eyes were again bloodshot and that his expression was guarded.

'Caddin, may we speak?' she asked.

'What is it?'

'Last night... we heard...'

His brows furrowed. 'You heard a drunken man, that's all.'

'We heard you say certain things. If you-'

'I was drunk and that was private,' he said, his tone unfriendly. 'That's enough.'

'If you want to speak to us... about whatever upset you. You can, you know that don't you?'

'I said, that's enough!' he snapped. 'Now leave me alone!'

He turned his back to her and raised the mace outwards to his right, gripped in one hand. He held it there for a number of seconds, and she could see the thick muscles in his neck, shoulder and arms straining to maintain the position.

Leanna walked away, feeling frustrated. Later that day, Amyss tried to explore the same subject, but with an equal lack of success.

—

Throughout the winter evenings, Leanna and Amyss had many hours to spend in tavern bedrooms together. They often used this time to try to train and develop Leanna's abilities.

Now that she was no longer using her powers to heal the sick at the College of Aiduel, by the end of each day Leanna was brimming with energy. In the privacy of their room, once Caddin's medallions were downstairs in the bar area and out of range, Leanna would practise.

She would use her ability to lift a range of objects selected by Amyss, and would then manipulate each item in the air. Most nights, they would start small, with Amyss placing a selected object in front of Leanna. Amyss would then gradually increase the level of challenge.

Leanna could sense that her strength and stamina were building, the more that she used this power. One night, after a succession of ever-larger objects, Amyss pointed towards Leanna's bed and said, 'Go on. Lift that.'

Leanna concentrated on the heavy wooden construction. She could feel herself straining, pushing invisible, ethereal fingers through and around the object. Focusing all of her will towards moving it. Unconsciously, she raised her arm outwards and upwards, lifting her limb in a mirror of the movement that she wanted the inanimate object to make.

The bed started moving. Gradually shifting, and raising from the ground. Its slow ascent was marked by a whirl of dust and the scurrying of a spider away from a shadowed area which had become exposed. Leanna could feel herself straining, as the bed continued to lift upwards. Two inches. Four.

'Go on, Lea!' exclaimed Amyss, laughing as she watched. This laughter was matched by emotions of wonder and love which were radiating outwards from the petite woman. 'You're glowing!'

Leanna realised that she was, and that her golden aura had returned. She gently lowered the wooden bed back down to the floor, in the exact same spot where it had been moments earlier. As this happened, Amyss clapped her hands together and made a cheering noise. This sound was accompanied by more emotions of unreserved love, which were cascading towards Leanna.

Lord Aiduel, thank you for the gift of her love.

'You're amazing, Lea,' Amyss said more softly, as her emotions continued to flow between them.

LOVE. WONDER. LOVE. DESIRE. LOVE.

Leanna's reaction was instinctive, and the same ethereal fingers which had been encircling the bed just moments before now reached out towards Amyss. This was the first time that Leanna had consciously tried this with another person. The fingers swirled around the red-headed woman, reaching beneath her clothes and caressing her skin with feather-soft touches.

Leanna heard Amyss gasp, at the same moment that a more intense and raw emotion was emitted by her companion, to accompany the wonder. Arousal. It was then such a simple matter to manipulate the invisible fingers. To envelop Amyss's entire body, and to gently raise the petite woman until her feet were several inches from the floor. Leanna then floated Amyss across the short distance which separated the two of them.

Leanna grinned as she heard her companion giggle in response to this sensation of flying, and she watched Amyss's arms opening wide as the power brought her close. The small priestess was still elevated as she entered the golden aura surrounding Leanna, and as her arms closed around Leanna's neck in a soft embrace.

Amyss's excitement was then matched only by her love and desire, as the two priestesses started to kiss.

—

Leanna and her companions spent the frostier winter weeks in the most southerly parts of Western Canasar. As strange as their life was, Leanna was beginning to savour an element of routine within it. She felt a peacefulness that she was no longer the Angel of Arlais, and had returned to being just Leanna.

However, as the weather improved and as spring approached, she was becoming increasingly restless for news about her parents. She told Caddin that she wanted him to make another journey into Arlais, to spend more time searching for her mother and father.

'I'll do it,' said Sendromm, his face solemn. 'And you have my word that if I can bring them back, I will. But after that, I want us to go to northern Andar.'

They therefore travelled back towards the first tavern that they had stayed in, to the south of the Ninth Bridge. By the time that they returned there, it felt like they had been living in exile in Western Canasar for a long time.

Shortly afterwards, Caddin departed alone on horseback in the direction of Arlais. Leanna and Amyss were left to wait at the tavern, feeling both hope and fear for the news that Sendromm might bring. While they waited, Amyss returned to the question of what their future might hold.

'You agreed that we'd travel with him for six months, Lea,' said Amyss. 'What do you intend after that time has passed?'

'I don't know,' Leanna replied. 'I can't decide that until we find out about my parents. But, if there's no news this time, perhaps we *could* go north? We could carry on healing people, at least for a while. I'm learning a lot, and I can see that you're learning, too. Perhaps we could have a life here, in Andar, in obscurity? And then,

I can try to understand more about the purpose that Aiduel has for me.'

'And would we stay with Caddin after six months has passed?'

'I don't know,' said Leanna. 'Perhaps only if he tells us everything about who he is and what he knows.'

'He's done something, Lea, in the past. Something bad, that he's ashamed of. He knew of those assassins, so he's clearly dealt with some bad people. And he's proved he's a killer, too. I think that's why he won't tell us anything, because he's so ashamed of his past.'

Leanna only nodded in return.

Lord Aiduel, if that's the case, please give him the courage to speak the truth, and to ask for forgiveness.

—

After just over two days had passed since his departure, Caddin returned from Elannis. When he arrived back at the tavern, his presence was alerted to Leanna and Amyss by the sound of heavy feet clomping up the stairs. After a hurried knock on their door, he entered their room, clutching a rolled parchment in his hand.

'Get your things,' he said. 'We have to leave. Now.'

'What?' asked Leanna. 'My parents?'

'No positive news. Not seen, not heard of, not returned. Your home is still being guarded and your father's business has been boarded up. And there's no way to get into the College, which seems to have become an extension of the Aiduel's Guards' fortress. I'm sorry, but the only mention I've seen of your parents anywhere is on *this*.'

He then unrolled the parchment in his hand and held it up for Leanna and Amyss to see. Leanna blanched as she scanned the contents. Printed on the document was an inked portrait of a face, with the hair painted golden-blonde and the eyes painted blue. It was a remarkably lifelike and realistic image, which was immediately recognisable as herself. She read the words below the picture:

Our saintly Priestess Leanna, the Angel of Arlais, has been stolen from us. Kidnapped by heretics.

The Archlaw and the Holy Church will offer a reward of 10,000 crowns for her return to the safe custody of Aiduel's Guards. May The Lord restore our Blessed Angel to us and to her devoted parents, with your help.

'I'm told that they've searched every house in Arlais and the surrounding region, looking for you,' said Caddin. 'And these posters are everywhere.'

'It mentions my parents,' said Leanna, feeling despair. 'Does that mean that they have them?'

'It might not mean anything,' said Caddin. 'It tells us nothing about whether your parents are dead, or captive, or alive and free. I think that they've been mentioned in case you read this. To induce you to return, to try to save them. But there's nothing you can do for them now. We must leave, as soon as possible!'

'Why such an urgency to leave?' asked Amyss, sounding fearful.

'There's a bad feeling in Arlais,' answered Sendromm. 'Rumours, that they're about to invade again. And things didn't feel right at the Elannis border. The way that the soldiers at the Ninth Bridge were acting.'

Leanna paled, before asking, 'Invade Western Canasar? Again? But how is that possible?'

'Not just Western Canasar. Andar. The whole of it. We might be just weeks – even *days* – away from the start of a massive war. We have to get away from here and travel north and west. Urgently.'

'But my parents-'

'Forget your parents, Leanna! We can do nothing for them. This is about keeping *you* alive.' He brandished the parchment again. 'You can be damn sure that every member of Aiduel's Guards has a copy of this. We've got to get out of Western Canasar and as far from the border with Elannis as possible. No arguments. Now get your things. We leave in twenty minutes.'

After saying this, he bustled out in the direction of his own room. Leanna and Amyss looked at each other for just a few seconds, then started to pack.

—

Shortly afterwards, they were riding on the wagon, heading northwards along the River Road. The temperature today was more clement, but there was a steady drizzle of rain which was soaking their clothes and the highway.

Caddin Sendromm looked more anxious than Leanna had ever seen him, with his mace resting against his thigh. On a couple of occasions, she observed him reaching inside his clothes to touch what she assumed was his medallion.

'Where are we going?' asked Leanna.

'We go north until the Ninth Bridge, then we turn towards the west,' stated Sendromm. 'Then we get past Rednarron and travel north from there. Head for somewhere remote.'

'You look worried, Caddin,' stated Amyss.

'I am worried. If Elannis invades, this whole region will be engulfed in war. And if the Elannis regular armies flood into Andar, then I'm sure that Aiduel's Guards will also follow close behind, and they'll be searching for Leanna. We have to get away from the bridges as quickly as possible, and get out of here.'

Leanna understood Sendromm's concern.

Lord Aiduel, please forgive me for abandoning my parents, but we must go. I promise that I will try to find them, one day.

If Elannis invaded this land, it seemed clear that Aiduel's Guards would also return. And if they did, the Archlaw's military order would once again be hunting for Leanna, and they would have her portrait in their possession.

She had to get out of Western Canasar.

14

Arion

—

Year of Our Lord,
After Ascension, 770AA

It was a Fifth-Day morning, near the end of winter. Arion was in the midst of inspecting the defences on the northern town walls of Septholme, when he received an urgent summons to attend his brother's chambers. He turned away from his examination of a recently installed ballista, and set off back towards the castle.

As he walked down from the battlements, accompanied by a handful of guards, he could feel satisfied about the town's readiness for any future conflict. New defensive weaponry now lined the landward walls at intervals, and the garrison was stronger and better-drilled than ever before.

By the Lord, we're going to need it!

Several weeks had elapsed since the Archlaw's Proclamation of Excommunication. In that time, the coldest days of winter had begun to pass, and the promise of the renewal of spring now beckoned once again.

Throughout this period, the aftershocks of the severing of the Holy Church from Sen Aiduel had continued to reverberate across Andar. Indeed, there had been riots and protests in several provinces, although these had been quickly and forcefully subdued. Western Canasar had avoided any such difficulties, having been fortified by Gerrion's preparations and by its citizens' dislike of Elannis.

Arion had remained focused on completing preparations for the impending war. His and Gerrion's efforts to recruit more troops into their army had become more intensive during this time, and he believed that they had made Western Canasar as ready as it could possibly be. However, the urgency of Gerrion's summons now gave him cause for concern. Indeed, when Arion arrived at his brother's chambers, he could immediately perceive the young duke's sombre mood.

'What is it, Gerrion?'

'I've just received awful news, brother. Awful news. Markon has escaped from his captivity. There was a raid of some sort, and he was freed. There's a manhunt going on, but no one has found him yet.'

'Lord damn it!' Arion exclaimed. 'They should have locked him in the deepest dungeon of Andarron, not held him prisoner somewhere secret!'

'I know, but it's too late for that now. We don't know how he was found, and I fear that treachery was involved, but we both know what his escape means, Arion.'

'Yes?'

'Andar no longer holds the Emperor's son. We no longer possess an imperial hostage. And the most significant obstacle to Elannis attacking us again has just disappeared.'

Arion nodded, feeling grim. War was now inevitable.

―

At the end of that day, as Arion tried to drift into sleep, he was still feeling agitated about the news of Markon's escape. And that night, as he tossed and turned in restless slumber, he experienced a dream which had visited him on only one prior occasion…

—

…and then the sounds reached him.

Fighting. The noises of battle. Swords clashing and men cursing. He remembered that the princes' bedrooms were located around a cul-de-sac at the end of the corridor, and he raced in that direction. He reached their rooms, as the sounds of conflict increased in volume and intensity.

Two figures, Andar guardsmen, lay dead in twin pools of blood on the corridor floor. The facing doors to either side of these victims were both open. He could remember that he had once visited the room on the left; Prince Sendar's room. But the noise of fighting seemed to be coming from the right.

He paused for a moment, his heart beating, and raised his sword. He then moved towards the open doorways…

—

The next morning, he was deeply unsettled, and he was trying to decide what to do. This dream had almost slipped from his memory in the intervening months, given everything else that had happened. But now it had returned, and it raised a number of questions. Was it prophecy? And did it mean that he had to act on it with urgency?

He was soon pacing around the castle courtyard, agonising over what action to take. Did the recurrence of this dream mean that he would need to travel to Andarron and to the Royal Palace? Or would it suffice to send a message by bird to Prince Sendar, to give him warning? Arion was unsure, but each of the prior visions had shown him events which he had ultimately experienced in person.

He would have to make a choice, and quickly. However, this time he did not want to face the decision on his own. He resolved to seek advice from Gerrion and Kalyane, and he turned around, ready to head to the Great Hall.

He then noticed that a young castle retainer was coming towards him. This man said, 'Lord Sepian?'

'Yes?'

'There's a letter for you, my Lord. I was going to deliver it to your chambers. Or would you prefer to have it now?'

The youth was clutching a sealed parchment in his hand.

'I'll have it now,' said Arion, feeling curious. The servant passed the letter to him, and Arion turned it to read the writing on the outside. He knew instantly who the writer was.

Allana.

Arion's heart was beating fast as he retreated to a private area and broke the unmarked seal on the parchment, before reading the letter. Last time, her brevity had tormented him, making him wonder why she had not said more. On this occasion, her words flowed in a torrent. And, as his eyes devoured every word on the page, he knew that his equilibrium was being shattered once again.

Dear Arion,

You have been in my heart and in my thoughts ever since that day when we first met, and since that night when you saved me from Aiduel's Guards.

Please forgive me for the mystery of my last letter to you. When I wrote that letter, I did not yet have the courage to let you know where I was. I was worried that Aiduel's Guards might return, and that they could still find me. But I just had to let you know that I live. And now, I cannot wait any longer to tell you how I feel, as I dare to hope that you share those same feelings for me.

Thanks to you, I escaped from Western Canasar. But I did not remain in Rednar, because I feared that I was still being pursued. I travelled all the way to Andarron, where I now write this letter, and dream of you being here beside me.

I understand now why you had to leave me that night, and I apologise for the way that I acted when we parted. I appreciate the importance of everything that you had to do. Just like everyone else, I have heard the tales about the wondrous Hero of Moss Ford.

But I also remember the connection that there was between us. The way that I wanted you, and believe that you wanted me too. Even now, sitting here as I write this, I yearn for you Arion. I want to be with you, and to feel you, and to become one, joined together in every intimate way possible. We are like each other. We bring each other to life, and I believe that we are meant to be together.

That night, when you rescued me, I had already decided that I wanted to spend my life with you. That I love you, which sounds crazy even as I write it, given how little time we have spent together. But I know it to be true. We are unique, you and I, and no one else will ever make me feel the way that you do. I truly believe that we can find a way to live together in joy and ecstasy, away from the troubles of the world. I hope that you feel the same; that you want me and need me, too.

If you do feel the same, then come to me, Arion, and be with me. I am staying at The King's Boar tavern in Andarron, in the Merchants' Quarter. I will stay here until the 5th day of Springdawn. If you come to me before then, I will know that you feel the same as me, and we will be joined together. If not, I will accept that my feelings are not reciprocated. I will then leave here heartbroken, and I will disappear from your life forever.

Yours with love and hope,
Allana

—

'And that's why I must leave immediately, to go to Andarron,' finished Arion, later that day.

Even as he concluded the statement, he could see that Gerrion, Kalyane and Charl Koss were looking at him with worry.

Gerrion hesitated before responding. 'Why don't you just write to the princes to tell them about the dream, Arion? It concerns me massively for you to be away from here, even for a couple of weeks. War could be declared at any time.'

'I've already written a warning letter to Sendar, Gerrion. With your permission, I'll send it by bird as soon as this meeting's concluded. But you know how my dream worked at Moss Ford. *I was there!* Whatever's going to happen in Andarron, I know that I need to be there, at the palace, as soon as possible. This was a prophecy. My presence could be vital, and I don't think that sending a warning is going to be enough.'

Arion was aware of how persuasive and plausible he sounded, despite his concealment of a significant personal motivation for the journey.

'The thought of you leaving here worries me, too,' said Kalyane. 'But if you feel that this is the right thing to do, then I trust you and support you, Arion. The Lord knows, your judgement on Moss Ford couldn't have been any better.'

Arion nodded at his wife in thanks, trying to mask the guilt from his face as Allana dei Monis's promises lingered in his mind.

'I've a bad feeling about this, Arion,' stated Charl Koss. 'A very bad feeling. Particularly the timing, given Markon's escape. But I also trust you in this, if you say this dream is like the other ones. But I think you should give Gerrion your word that you'll spend no longer than a handful of days in Andarron. Do whatever you have to do there to protect the princes, and then return. I can oversee military matters here for a short time, but we can't afford for you to be away for much more than two weeks.'

'That's all fine, of course,' said Arion.

'And you say that you've written a letter for Sendar, to warn him?' asked Gerrion.

'Yes.'

'Saying what?'

'Setting out the details of the dream again which, as I've said, I'd already told him about. And also telling him that I think it's going to take place soon, so he and Prince Senneos need to take extra care.'

'Very well. I'll also trust you in this, Arion,' said Gerrion. 'Send the letter immediately by bird, then commandeer a fast ship from the harbour on my authority, and go to Andarron. But as Charl says, don't linger there. We need you back in Western Canasar as soon as possible.'

'Thank you, Gerrion,' Arion replied. He was trying to suppress any feelings of shame which were threatening to arise, now that he had achieved what he wanted.

Allana's letter was tucked away in an internal pocket of his jacket. Hidden and secret.

—

He departed from Septholme later that day, at dusk, during a high tide.

Kalyane was the last person who he was to say farewell to, before crossing the gangplank to the sleek merchant vessel which had been commandeered for the journey.

'Take care, my husband,' she said to him, with her hand on his cheek. 'Do what you need to do, then please return to us.'

He was looking down into her emerald-green eyes, still trying to ignore the guilt that was causing his stomach to churn.

'I will,' he said. 'As soon as possible.'

'I love you, Arion.'

'And I love you.'

Those were the last words that they shared. After that, she kissed him on the cheek, and he boarded the ship.

—

The five-day journey to Andarron seemed to stretch out interminably, with only the merchant crew of the ship for company.

During the daytime, with very few other distractions, Arion's thoughts were once again consumed by Allana dei Monis. He read her letter over and over, digesting every word and nuance, cradling the parchment close to his body so that no one else could see his secrets.

He was uncertain about what exactly he was going to do after he reached the city, and he was aware that there were elements of Allana's story which did not make sense; why had Aiduel's Guards declared her dead, and why had she set such a tight deadline for him? However, it was easy to disregard such logic amidst the tumult of passions which her words stirred.

In the daylight hours, Arion was still trying to persuade himself that the reason he had declared for his journey was the truth. That he needed to get to Andarron to answer the call of his prophetic dream, and to save the two princes. Leaving his family and his homeland, at a time of great need, could be justified by that worthy cause alone. He had no reason to feel guilty.

True, if as part of this same trip he could visit *The King's Boar* tavern to finally resolve matters with Allana, then that would be convenient. But just a convenience. Nothing more than that. He would notify Allana that they could not be together, and then he would travel on to the palace.

That was the justification he could use to try to reassure himself as to why he had not told his family about Allana. The existence of the Dei Magnun woman was just so trivial in comparison to the fate of the royal princes, and knowing about Allana would have worried them unnecessarily. Particularly Kalyane. It had been a kindness to continue to keep Allana and the letter completely secret from his wife, to avoid further worry. He had simply been trying to be a considerate husband.

In the daytime, that all sounded plausible to him, if he ignored the guilty whispers in his mind. But at night, alone with his thoughts in his bunk, he was confronted with the truth.

Lord preserve us, I know the true reason that I'm making this journey. And it shames me.

He had no clear idea of how precisely he would react when he saw Allana again. But he knew that he wanted to hold her, and to kiss her, and to lie with her. To be with her. He wanted it – *needed it* – desperately, to the exclusion of all other considerations.

And he also recognised that, if Allana wanted the same things, all of his self-deluding lies, told under the light of the sun, would be exposed for the sham that they were. As would his wedding vows, and his shallow declarations of love to Kalyane.

To add to Arion's waking torments, the recurring dream continued to trouble him on the voyage. It would wake him from sleep, and would leave him feeling restless within the confined spaces of his bunk. His thoughts would then once again turn to Allana dei Monis, and to what awaited him in Andarron.

One night, in the darkness of his cabin, he thought that he could feel a pulsing sensation, teasing at the edges of his mind. In some ways, it was similar to what he could feel when near to Allana and Leanna. However, in comparison it was very faint, and was barely discernible.

He concentrated on this for a few minutes, wondering what it might be, until he turned onto his side and fell back into slumber.

He arrived in Andarron at nightfall, five days after departing Septholme. As he disembarked from the swift vessel which had transported him, he was aware that his priority should be to travel to the Royal Palace, to find Sendar.

However, there was no way that he was going to pass through the Merchants' Quarter, on the way to the palace, without first visiting *The King's Boar*. For most of the journey across Andarron, the two destinations required the same route, so Arion set off in that direction.

As he crossed the city, he quickly became attuned to a certain restlessness in its streets. More than once, he noticed large groups of men and women gathered outside courtyards or on street corners, some of whom were talking in agitated tones. The members of these gatherings appeared to be ordinary citizens rather than soldiers, but Arion was concerned to notice cudgels and clubs in the hands of some.

Each time, he gave these groups a wide berth, and his hand shifted towards his sword if anyone appeared to be wandering too close. It was making him recall the night of the assassination attempt in Septholme. Even though no one could have anticipated that he would be coming here, he still felt uneasy.

There were very few noises of boisterous excess coming from any of the city's taverns, which was unusual now that darkness had fallen. Indeed, as Arion passed into the Merchants' Quarter, he soon noticed that many premises had been closed, and a number had guards stationed outside.

He also noticed something else. Or rather, the absence of something; he could not sense Allana anywhere close. There was no trace of the pulsing presence which had alerted him to her proximity on prior occasions, and that did not make sense, given the size of the Merchants' Quarter. He should have been able to sense her by now.

By the Lord, I may have arrived when she's elsewhere in the city, that's all. Calm down!

He stopped a couple of passers-by to ask for directions to Allana's tavern. After wary glances, he was given instructions which allowed him to press on through the darkened streets. Soon after, the establishment came into sight. It looked expensive, with an extravagant painting of a boar wearing a crown on the sign hanging outside.

Two large men, both armed with cudgels, were blocking the entrance doorway, but after a glance at Arion's attire they parted to let him through. However, Arion could still not sense Allana, which meant that at the current time she would not be in the premises.

As he entered the main room of the tavern, Arion observed a number of well-dressed people turning to regard him. He could sense their wariness of him, that same undercurrent of unease which he had been feeling since entering the city.

He crossed to the tavern bar, and addressed the stocky and well-groomed middle-aged man who was serving there.

'Hello,' Arion said, 'I'm looking for a woman who is staying here.'

The man's eyes shifted to the front entrance, then back to Arion. 'Strange night to be looking for a woman, lad. What's her name?'

'Allana dei Monis.'

The man frowned, then shook his head. 'We don't have anyone here with that name. You sure you've got the right place?'

'Yes. This is *The King's Boar*, yes?'

'It is, lad. This is my fine establishment, Lord bless it.'

'Her name's Allana. Might use Lana.' Arion raised his hand up. 'She's short, about this tall. *Very* beautiful. Long, dark, wavy hair. She told me that she'd be staying here, until the 5th day of Springdawn.'

'Sorry, don't recognise the name. Definitely don't recognise the description.' The man glanced around the tavern room as he said this. 'Not had anyone like that staying here in recent weeks or months, as far as I can remember. And I've a good memory for faces. Particularly the pretty ones.'

Arion turned away, grimacing. He could not sense Allana. Certainly not here, and not even in the wider city. No sensation of her presence, at all. Did that mean that she was truly not here? That either she had come and then departed, or that she had never even been here?

From what the tavern owner was saying, the latter sounded more likely. Arion suddenly felt embarrassed and ashamed by his giddy imaginings of the last few days, and by his flight from home in response to Allana's summons. He had rushed recklessly towards their reunion, but it could not have been any more anticlimactic. He felt like a fool.

And a separate and awful idea was emerging. Had he been manipulated to come here? Was it possible that neither of the letters which had purported to come from Allana were real? In which case, was he being set up by someone? And could that manipulator be the same person who had tried to kill him, months earlier?

With that thought, he placed his hand onto the hilt of his sword, and scrutinised each of the other occupants of the tavern. None appeared suspicious, but he was not ready to relax.

The tavern owner had been watching Arion, with a sympathetic expression on his face. The man gestured to the tavern windows, which showed the dark street outside, and finally said, 'You appear a little uneasy, young man, and Lord knows, I can understand why if you're worried that your woman is out there tonight. But I can see that you're a man of wealth, and you look like you can take care of yourself. Why not pull up a chair and spend tonight with us in the old Boar? There's safety in numbers on a night like this.'

Arion frowned. 'A night like this? Why, what's going on?'

'You mean you haven't heard? Where've you been this last day, lad? Head in a barrel?'

'Heard what?'

'It's the worst possible news, lad. Elannis and Dei Magnus have both declared war on us. And not only that, but old Paulius has called for a Holy Crusade against Andar, too. News came out just yesterday.'

'By the Lord!' exclaimed Arion. 'I've just got in from the sea. I hadn't heard.'

Lord preserve us! War, and I'm here in Andarron, on the other side of the country to Western Canasar. To my family. What have I done?

'You've gone white, lad. Look, you take a seat, and I'll pour you a mug of ale. You spend the night in here with us, and we'll all keep each other safe from those mobs.'

'Those mobs? I saw people gathering. What's it for?'

The tavern owner shook his head, looking solemn. 'There's been trouble brewing in this city for months, ever since we broke off from the Holy Church. But the rumour is it's all coming to a head tonight. There's talk of rioting. Mobs marching on the palace. Even some calling for the overthrow of the Pavils-'

Arion was away from the bar and sprinting out onto the darkened street, before the man had any opportunity to finish his sentence.

Once he was back outside and running towards the Royal Palace, Arion was even more attuned to the aura of menace in the city. The gangs on the streets were growing in size, forming a mob, and more of them were walking in the direction of the palace. Several members of these groups were carrying flaming torches, and an assortment of weapons were visible.

Arion was picking side-streets to try to avoid these gathering crowds, and he could hear chanting in the distance. Stray words carried back to him.

'For the Archlaw!'

'For peace!'

As he ran, the night sky was black above him, and he recognised the connections with the scenes in his prophetic dream. Would this be the prophesied night when the royal princes were going to be attacked? Would Arion soon be sprinting down a palace corridor with a bloodied sword in hand, heading towards their royal chambers? He had to reach the palace, to know for certain.

He was trying to ignore the twisting sensation in his gut that told him that he had been played by someone. By a person who somehow knew about Allana. Had they written the letter to deceive him into leaving Western Canasar, just as Elannis and Dei Magnus were about to declare war? Even now, the enemy could be assaulting the defences on the Canas River, and the forces of Western Canasar might be mustering to try to defy them.

However, he was on the wrong side of the country, almost a week's journey away by sea. Unable to fulfil his duties, to lead his people, or to protect his family. And not, he knew, because he had been compelled to come here to save the royal princes. Not really. He was in this place because of his lust for Allana dei Monis. Because, from the moment that he had read that letter, he had been unable to think about anything else other than being with her.

He was a fool, but he could still try to make things right. Perhaps he was indeed meant to be here, despite the deception? He needed to get to the palace, to save Sendar and his brother. Then he would sprint back to the docks and would embark on an immediate return journey to Septholme. He could make this right and be a hero again. Somehow.

He was coming closer to the border of the royal estates which surrounded the palace, and it was becoming more difficult to avoid the crowds on the streets. He emerged onto the main thoroughfare which led to the gated entrance to the royal grounds, only to find that it was jammed with people.

There was a crowd of thousands between Arion and that entrance. He could see a line of Andar soldiers in the distance, their royal blue tabards identifiable in front of the palace gates. However, their thin blue line looked fragile relative to the angry mob which was massing in front of them.

Arion knew that he needed to get into the palace as soon as possible, but there was no way that he would be able to gain access through that front gate. He headed off again into the side-streets, trying to reach the border of the royal estate, but at a point well away from the main entrance. Chants were still carrying to him from the mob.

'Down with Inneos!'

'For the Holy Church!'

Eventually, Arion emerged from the side streets and into a wide road which ran parallel with the high stone wall which enclosed the palace estates. The palace gates were two hundred metres away, and he could see the mob tussling with the line of soldiers there. The masses were pushing the thin wall of defenders back, accompanied by more angry shouts.

Arion had a growing sense of alarm that the events of his dream were going to happen imminently. He needed to enter the royal grounds and get into the palace urgently, to intervene in whatever was about to take place.

He looked up at the wall next to him. It was three times his own height, possibly twenty feet high, and there were no obvious handholds to use to climb it.

By the Lord, I need to get over this. Just jump it!

The thought was instinctive, as was his action afterwards. He sprinted towards the tall stone barrier, the air seeming to crackle around him, and he launched himself upwards.

STRENGTH. VICTORY. GLORY.

He was unsure whether either of his feet had touched anything on the way up, but then his hands were gripping the top of the wall. In an instant, he had pulled himself up onto the ledge of the barrier. He looked down from this elevated position, feeling wondrously alive.

Lord preserve us! How did I manage that?

There was no time to ponder this. Two hundred metres away, the mob appeared to have over-run the thin line of guardsmen, and were assailing the gates. They might soon enter the palace grounds. The princes were in danger!

Without thinking about the consequences, Arion launched himself in a leap from the top of the wall. He landed on both feet with an audible thud, which seemed to shake the ground. He then set off sprinting again, dashing across the hundreds of metres of royal gardens between the wall and the palace. His senses were hyper-alert, and the air continued to crackle around him. At one point, there was a shouted challenge from a pair of guardsmen as he sprinted past them. He did not pause, and he could soon hear their breathless sounds of pursuit.

But his focus was on the palace. Specifically, he was targeting an entrance which he knew was on the same side of the building as the princes' chambers. As he drew closer, he could see two Andar guardsmen blocking this entrance. These two men had spotted Arion's rapid approach, and they were attempting to draw swords as he charged towards them.

'Halt!' shouted one of these guards, but Arion ignored him. There was no time now for delay and rational explanation. He had to get into the palace, to save the princes. Urgently. Nothing else mattered.

He was shocked at how quickly he closed upon the two guardsmen, as the world seemed to blur around himself. Before he could consider just what he was doing, he punched the upper part of the sword arm of the nearest man, whose blade was only halfway out of its scabbard at that point. There was a bone-shattering crunch and a scream, and the man's arm fell limp at his side.

Arion then felt the arms of the second guard close around him from behind, wrapping on his neck, as if the man was attempting to grapple him to the ground.

Arion wanted to free himself as quickly as possible. It seemed a simple thing to wrench those two arms outwards, accompanied by a ripping noise and a scream, and then he twisted around and hurled this second guard. The man sailed through the air over a distance which was unbelievable, perhaps twenty metres. He crunched to the ground as he landed, and did not move again afterwards.

By the Lord. I feel so strong. So fast. So powerful.

The first guard was cowering on the floor away from Arion, his good arm reaching across to hold the limb which had been shattered.

'Please, mercy!' begged the man, with terror in his voice.

Kill him, kill him, kill him, kill him. Take your victory!

Arion drew his sword, looking down at the pleading guard. At the same time, he realised that the pair of guardsmen who had been pursuing him were drawing close. Both were charging towards him with drawn swords, both looking ready to dispense violence. A subdued part of Arion's mind screamed that he did not want this encounter, but he was being threatened. They wanted to kill him.

What happened afterwards took mere seconds, and again seemed to pass in a blur. However, by the time that Arion had finished, this pair of attackers were lying dead at his feet. He turned back towards the man with the broken arm, only to realise that, at some point in the brief combat, a sword point had also entered this man's neck.

Killing him, and leaving no witnesses to what Arion had done.

But he had no time or inclination to linger. He needed to get to the princes. He barged through the palace doors and into the corridor beyond, and after looking around he found what he was searching for; a spiral staircase at the end of the corridor.

As he ran into the stairwell, he at last recognised where he was. He had been in this place and in this moment before, in the midst of his prophetic dream.

He started to sprint up the stairs. He had to save the princes, to be a hero once again.

15

Allana

—

*Year of Our Lord,
After Ascension, 770AA*

Allana was beside Jarrett, near the western entrance to the Tenth Bridge, when she first spotted the ranks of the Elannis Imperial Army emerging onto the eastern side of the crossing.

'It's begun,' said Jarrett, a breathless quality to his voice.

'There's no turning back now,' Allana responded, to which the young duke nodded.

But in truth, Lana, you've been committed to this from the moment that you made your decision.

It was the middle of the night, with torches flickering along the walls of the two opposing fortresses which flanked the wide waterway. This uncontested river crossing was to be made without ceremony, and with as little noise as possible. Allana understood from Jarrett that sixty thousand soldiers of the Imperial Army would cross into Andar on this night, using this southernmost bridge of the Canas River in Berun as their entry point.

Allana watched as the Elannis army crossed the stone span towards her. At the head of the approaching column of troops, three men were riding on horseback. Behind them, all others were on foot, marching in uniform ranks eight men across.

Allana was also on horseback, on a grey gelding, alongside Jarrett on his black stallion. They were waiting to greet the three leaders of the approaching forces. Jarrett wanted to be seen from the outset by the arriving army, and he had requested that Allana be at his side. People needed to get used to observing her beside him in public, to normalise the idea that she was going to become a duchess and ruler. To emphasise this, she had chosen to wear her most sumptuous riding attire, a combination of red satin jacket and riding trousers, which clung to her figure.

These common soldiers will look upon you and think that you're a beautiful member of the nobility, Lana. As you now are.

Near to Jarrett and Allana, forty soldiers of Berun flanked the bridge on either side, all of them holding halberds in an upright position. These twin lines of troops ended at the open portcullis beneath the western fortress, at the point which marked the entry into Andar and Berun territory.

The three leading men on horseback now approached Jarrett and Allana's position. As they drew close enough to allow the flaming torches on the fortress walls to illuminate their faces, Allana recognised two of the horsemen; Prince Lorrius and Archprime Runus Kohn.

'Your Highness, Your Eminence,' said Jarrett, his voice pitched low. 'Welcome to Berun.'

'Duke Berun,' replied Lorrius, tilting his head in acknowledgement as he reined in his horse. He then raised his hand and the trailing column of troops also halted. '*Lady* dei Monis. We thank you both for the welcome. May I also introduce Lord Bornhaus, High Commander of the Elannis Imperial Forces.'

Allana suppressed a smile as she heard her new title being announced by the Elannis royal. Just two days earlier, confirmation of her place in the Dei Magnun nobility had been received.

'The armies of Berun are ready,' said Jarrett. 'Once your troops are crossed and assembled, we're ready to move.'

'I expected no less, Duke Berun,' responded the prince. 'We are also ready. Runus carries the Archlaw's Proclamation of Crusade, which shall be read to the armies tomorrow, and announced in all of the major cities of Andar over the coming days. And I carry the Declaration of War signed by the Emperor and the High Council, for which the same announcements shall also take place.'

'Then everything is in place, Your Highness,' said Jarrett.

'Almost everything,' replied the prince. 'Runus has a *small* favour to ask.'

'A favour?' repeated Jarrett.

'I have a force of eight hundred Aiduel's Guards,' said Archprime Kohn. 'They're under my command, and are waiting to the east of the bridge. I wish to bring them into Andar, for purposes of retribution, and to search for someone.'

Allana shuddered when she heard these words.

You knew that they were going to return at some point, Lana, though you never expected it to be so soon. But you no longer have to fear them. Do you?

'Searching for whom, Your Eminence?' she asked, wondering whether it was connected to Arion. Her heart was suddenly beating faster.

'Oh, don't worry, it's not you,' responded Kohn. 'I'm asking purely out of courtesy, and it's of no consequence to the agreements we've made.' His tone hardened as he said this last part. 'May I bring my Aiduel's Guards force across, Duke Berun? I'll tell you more tomorrow, but I'll be offended if you refuse my small request.'

Jarrett hesitated for just a moment, then responded, 'Of course. They may cross.'

'Very good,' said Prince Lorrius. 'In that case, Duke Berun, please will you and Lady Allana ride alongside us, so that we can all lead the armies of Elannis into Andar.'

Jarrett nodded and said, 'I would be honoured, Your Highness.'

He and Allana circled their horses around to face westwards. Their group then set off, crossing under the raised portcullis and into the tunnel through the western Tenth Bridge fortress. Thousands of soldiers, marching in uniform procession, were to follow behind them.

—

That night, Allana, Jarrett, Lorrius and Kohn rode ahead with a cavalry escort, travelling towards the prepared encampment where the combined Berun and Elannis forces would muster. They were trailed by the slower-moving Elannis infantry, which was marching on foot to the same destination.

Allana and Jarrett had agreed that she would travel with him for the duration of the upcoming campaign. Allana had not been willing to be left behind in draughty Berun Castle, being forced to face the panic and terrors of countless night-times on her own. She was resolved to remain physically close to her future husband, particularly in the hours of darkness.

Jarrett had not taken much convincing to allow her to accompany him. The young duke had been unable to face being parted from her again, such was his need and desire for her.

As she and Jarrett settled down to sleep, inside a luxurious tent within the encampment, Allana was thinking about what she might witness in the coming weeks. Jarrett had outlined that the combined Elannis and Berun armies would invade Western Canasar on multiple fronts. There would then be a decisive battle when their overwhelming force would crush the Sepian armies. Finally, they would march upon and conquer Septholme.

'And once we have Septholme, their most significant town, we own Western Canasar,' Jarrett had explained. 'After that, the rest will surrender.'

Jarrett fell asleep quickly. On their camp bed beside him, Allana lay awake, imagining more about what was to come. What would it be like when she returned to a conquered Septholme?

She was envisaging a scene in her mind; all of the retainers of Septholme Castle gathered in the castle courtyard, as she was presented to them. Each of them remembering her, and recognising how far she had risen in just a matter of months. The men bowing and desiring her, the women curtseying and envying her. All of them cheering her arrival. It was a pleasant image.

You'll be a beautiful and powerful duchess, Lana. None of them will be able to threaten you, or hurt you, like in the past. And they'll all grow to love you.

Hopefully, Duke Gerrion Sepian would also be there to witness her return. Perhaps she could watch him being transported to a prison cell, in the same manner that he had once so casually imprisoned and condemned her? And perhaps Arion's wife could also accompany the deposed duke to the castle dungeon?

The only shadow over this vision was the concern about what would happen if Arion was still there. What would Allana do if she had to face him again? She hoped that she had done enough to remove him from Septholme and Western Canasar, but she could not be sure.

She had finally decided, in her private room weeks earlier, that she was going to stay with Jarrett and become his wife. No one could offer her greater security and status than the young duke, particularly in the face of the coming war.

Having made that decision, she had thought long and hard about how to act to save Arion's life, without betraying Jarrett's schemes. And she had been very satisfied when the idea of the fake letter had come to her.

It had been an emotional experience when she had finally picked up a quill to write that letter. Her writing had started as a scheme, a device to persuade him to leave Septholme. However, as the words had flowed from quill to paper, her missive had come close to transforming into something more. Her words of love had been too passionate, too ardent, too easy to write.

And other visions had come into her head; of riding away to Rednarron herself, and of finding a way to get to Andarron.

Imagining what it would be like to be waiting for Arion at *The King's Boar*, that tavern in the capital city which Jarrett had once spoken of. And whether, if she met with Arion and became his lover, she could convince him to run away with her, like she had once almost begged him to.

But then the words had been written, the letter concluded, and she had taken a grip on herself. She was choosing to remain with Jarrett, and the only outstanding decision had been one of *when* to send the letter. Not too early, such that Arion would have opportunity to travel to Andarron, recognise the ruse and then return. Nor too late such that he would catch wind of the invasion prior to leaving. All of which only mattered if the words in the letter would lure him away from Septholme, in pursuit of her. That was what she hoped for now, such that she would not need to face him as his family fell into ruin.

He'll want you, Lana, and he'll travel for you, so he won't be here when Western Canasar falls. You've done a good thing. You've saved him.

—

Allana dreamt of the Gate that night, and she was once again assailed by images that were vivid and disturbing.

When she awoke, with her heart pounding and her hands trembling, she was feeling something beyond her usual horror and fear. She was full of anger. In fact, anger was too tame a word; fury was her dominant emotion, a fury that was touching upon the darkness which lurked inside her.

She knew that she had seen further into the dream, though again she could not form a clear memory of what she had witnessed. Had she heard other words, spoken by the figure in the Gate? Had those words been followed by awful violence and death? And had she been betrayed at the end by one of her shining companions?

Her face was suddenly feeling heavy, as if a sodden cloth was covering it, and her breathing was becoming fast and erratic. Were

Aiduel's Guards now somewhere close by, preparing to imprison and torture her?

Shut those thoughts out, Lana. Shut them out, please! Try to sleep.

She turned towards Jarrett, pushing herself against his side as he slept on his back. His muscular arm moved to pull her into an embrace, holding her close against him. She rested her head against his chest, and she could immediately feel her breathing slowing and the shaking in her hands subsiding.

'Thank you, Jarrett,' she whispered, and she kissed his chest.

Jarrett will protect you, Lana. Against Aiduel's Guards. Against anyone. And if he doesn't, you'll protect yourself.

She *would* always protect herself. Indeed, with every usage of her power she believed that she was growing stronger. Ever stronger. More capable of stopping anyone from ever again hurting her. More capable of *surviving*.

Evelyn dei Laramin and Sillene Berun had both been taught that lesson. One was dead, and the other was now an insane monster. That was the price which they had paid for being a threat to Allana's life. That was the price which would be paid by anyone else who dared to threaten her.

The memory of Sillene acted to further soothe Allana, as she thought about their last encounter. On the morning prior to leaving Berun Castle, an impulse had led Allana down the steps to the underground dungeon, to visit the feral dowager.

Allana had silently approached the bars of the woman's cell. Initially, Sillene had been curled up on her side, with legs bunched into her chest. But under Allana's scrutiny – *and sensing the connection between them* – the woman had turned her head. The dowager had then raised herself to her feet and had moved to the bars with that sinister lurching motion, with back hunched over and arms dangling downwards.

Allana and the older woman had held each other's gaze, the latter with jaw hung open to reveal her teeth. Allana had been taken aback by the further physical changes which had occurred in the dowager.

Sillene's eyes had taken on a golden hue and her teeth, particularly her canines, had grown longer. But the most significant change had been the hair on the woman's face and body. Soft, downy hair – *fur?* – everywhere. Allana had realised then that whatever she had done had not stopped wreaking its ruin and corruption upon the woman.

What will she look like, Lana, when the changes have ended?

The memories and the question made Allana smile, and she noticed that she was no longer frightened in the darkness. She snuggled herself tightly against Jarrett's side, and she soon fell back into a peaceful and contented sleep.

—

Allana and Jarrett rose early the next morning, and prayed together. Jarrett led the prayers, first beseeching The Lord for His support in the coming campaign, then making his usual plea for the recovery of his mother.

When the two of them later left their tent, which had been pitched on top of a small rise, Allana could see that the military encampment had been transformed. The night before, there had been approximately five thousand soldiers of Berun camped in a relatively small area. Now, perfectly straight rows of Elannis tents stretched into the distance.

The entire Elannis army had crossed the bridge and had arrived in the camp overnight. The enormity of the massed forces was staggering to Allana.

'Impressive, isn't it?' said Jarrett. 'Sixty-five thousand soldiers gathered here. And with camp followers, maybe eighty-five thousand people in total. I doubt that either of us will ever see a bigger gathering.'

Allana rotated on the spot, absorbing the sight of the whole encampment around her. There was a lot of activity in the Berun tent areas. By contrast, the Elannis camp seemed much quieter.

'It's amazing,' she said. 'So many tents! But what happens now, Jarrett?'

'I'm to take part in a council of war with my commanders and the Elannis leaders this morning, whilst their soldiers are resting. After that, there'll be speeches, following which the army will split and we'll march to war.'

'It's going to split?'

'Yes. Half will accompany our Berun armies, marching south through Western Canasar. The other half are to invade Rednar, and will aim to join up with the armies of Condarr.' There was a sombre look on Jarrett's face as he was speaking, and he sounded subdued.

'And how are you feeling, Jarrett?' asked Allana. 'Now that this moment has come, and you're soon to go to war?'

He grimaced before responding. 'I still regret that Inneos has forced me to do this, Lana. That we'll be killing men of Andar. But now that I've chosen a side, I won't stop until I've won, and I've claimed my prize.'

She placed a hand onto his arm. 'You're acting for the Holy Church and for the cause of good. Always remember that.'

'I do,' he said, as he nodded. 'And I also won't forget that once Septholme has fallen and Western Canasar is ours, I'm going to marry you, Lana. That's all the incentive I need. Now that you're raised to the nobility, there's nothing to stop us.'

'You know how much I want that, Jarrett.'

You do want that, Lana. You do.

As they continued to talk, she was turning to peer around the camp. After a few moments, she spotted something which made her breath quicken. In the distance, a figure wearing a red cloak and sash was moving between tents. Then another, and a third. Aiduel's Guards, in an area of the encampment which must have been set aside for their soldiers.

She had not encountered any of these red cloaks since the day that she had murdered Evelyn dei Laramin. Seeing that hated uniform was a shock, and it again reminded Allana of some of the High Commander's last words.

Allana was one of the people who Aiduel's Guards were looking for.

They can't touch you now, Lana. They can't hurt you again. They can't!

But she still shuddered as she looked at them, and a new and worrying thought occurred to her; could Nionia dei Pallere, the keeper of Allana's murderous secret, be somewhere within that encampment?

Allana certainly hoped not.

—

Jarrett returned two hours later. By then, Allana was standing outside of their tent, which was already being taken down. This process was being repeated across the camp, and there was bustle everywhere.

'We're close to ready,' stated Jarrett, after kissing her. 'But we'll have to separate soon. As I said, during the daytime I'll need you to travel towards the rear of the line with the camp followers, rather than alongside me. But I'll assign five guards to you for the duration of the journey. I trust that's acceptable?'

Allana nodded, having already agreed to this. 'Of course, Jarrett, yes.'

'We'll be assembling the troops soon, for the reading of the Proclamation of Crusade and the Declaration of War. Then we'll move out. But I brought something for you, which I thought you'd find interesting.'

He passed a scroll across to her.

'What is it?' asked Allana.

'Remember how the Archprime said last night that Aiduel's Guards are going to be searching for someone? Well, this is the person.'

Allana unrolled the parchment, feeling intrigued. Printed on it was a portrait of an attractive young woman. The image was just black ink lines, apart from the long hair, which had been painted golden-blonde, and the eyes, coloured blue. Under the printed drawing, there were a number of words:

Our saintly Priestess Leanna, the Angel of Arlais, has been stolen from us. Kidnapped by heretics. We think that she may be in Andar.

The Archlaw and the Holy Church will offer a reward of 10,000 crowns for her return to the safe custody of Aiduel's Guards. May The Lord restore our Blessed Angel to us and to her devoted parents, with your help.

'They must really want to find this woman,' said Jarrett. 'Hundreds of these scrolls have been distributed to the soldiers. And just look at that reward.'

'Who is she?' asked Allana, feeling a trace of unease.

'I understand that she's a priestess, a miracle-worker from Arlais, who's blessed by The Lord. It's said that she has the power to heal the sick, and there's a story circulating that she bled from stigmata, and that The Lord saved her from a flaming pyre!'

'A pyre?'

'Yes. I'm told that she stood in the middle of a blazing fire and was unharmed. Imagine that, to have been granted such protection by The Lord! From the sound of it, she's a truly miraculous woman, and I'd be honoured to meet her. And Aiduel's Guards think that she's in Andar.'

Allana looked at the picture again, narrowing her eyes as she stared at the image of the other woman. Her heart was beating faster as she considered the implications of Jarrett's words. Could this young priestess, who looked so pure and innocent, possibly be another who was like Allana and Arion? Someone else who possessed powers?

Allana did not like the thought of that; she had imagined that she and Arion were a unique pairing. What if this woman had powers which were greater than Allana's own?

You are unique, Lana. Unique! There's no one else like you.

Allana scrutinised the portrait once more. Even though she now felt a little uncertain, she could take some solace from the fact that this woman's beauty did not compare to her own. This Priestess Leanna was pretty, yes, if someone was attracted to that type. But certainly not beautiful like Allana was.

'Can I keep this, Jarrett?' she asked.

'Yes, of course. They're everywhere. Every company in the army must have a copy of this, and there's already chatter amongst the men about the size of that reward. Trust me, if this lady is in Western Canasar, someone's going to find her and rescue her.'

As Jarrett was finishing this statement, they were both distracted by sudden cheering and shouting from the Elannis encampment. They turned and saw a flurry of activity there, and Allana spotted a small group of horsemen riding through that camp. One of them was carrying a banner which she could only barely discern from this distance, which displayed a pattern of a blazing sun, with a hawk in front of it.

The cheering and shouting were also now transforming into a more recognisable single word.

'Markon! Markon! Markon!'

Allana asked, 'What is it? What are they shouting about?'

'Their prince has returned to them,' Jarrett replied. 'He's arrived just in time. Prince Markon El'Augustus has returned to lead the armies of Elannis.'

―

Towards the end of that morning, the full might of the combined armies had gathered in formation. Sixty-five thousand soldiers were mustered on the outskirts of the camp, in full armour, arrayed in perfect formation. Most of them were wearing the imperial yellow of Elannis, but a significant minority wore the darker Andar blue of Berun.

The soldiers were facing towards a temporary stage, which had been erected for the occasion. Allana was observing from a position somewhat removed to the side, but with a clear view.

In the minutes that followed, the gathering witnessed a rousing and passionate speech from Prince Lorrius. The Elannis royal announced the declaration of war, by his country and Dei Magnus, against Andar and its heretic king.

Archprime Runus Kohn then gave a much drier speech, reading out verbatim the Archlaw's Proclamation of Crusade against the Imposter Church and the state which supported it.

Jarrett also then spoke, his words aimed at his own countrymen. He talked carefully about the need for alliance between Berun and Elannis, and announced his unequivocal support for the Archlaw's Crusade. His manner of speaking sometimes felt awkward to Allana, but it was clear that the duke's words were heartfelt and considered.

After Jarrett had concluded, Prince Markon took to the stage, amidst a rapturous reception from the soldiers of Elannis.

Allana was soon unable to tear her eyes away from the tall, blonde-haired royal. Markon spoke confidently, with a natural charisma that had been lacking from Jarrett's own effort. The prince was very handsome too, his good looks only enhanced by his supreme self-assuredness, which had to come from his birthright.

Allana had met powerful men before. Indeed, she had already shared a bed with two dukes of immense wealth and influence. But neither Conran or Jarrett could match the power of the man on the stage. One day, Prince Markon El'Augustus *would rule half the world*, as Emperor. Perhaps more. And someday, could there be a woman beside him? An empress?

There was something intoxicating about such imaginings, and she shivered.

You've chosen to be with Jarrett, Lana. And he'll keep you safe. Should you be greedy for more?

Prince Markon brought his speech to an end on a serious note. 'Soon, we shall leave here. I shall travel southwards with half of this army, commanding the Western Canasar campaign alongside Duke Berun and his forces. Lord Bornhaus shall lead the remainder of the army westwards with Prince Lorrius, into our Rednar campaign.

'But before we depart, let me remind you again why we're all here. We are devoted servants of the Church on its holy crusade, but we also stand together to right a great wrong. Ready to remove a stain on the honour of Elannis and on the Army of Elannis. A stain on my own honour, in fact.

'Through their devious tricks last year, the Andar armies of Western Canasar humiliated us at the Battle of Moss Ford. Such a devastating defeat would be hard enough to bear. But Lord Bornhaus has told me how Lord Arion Sepian, the Butcher of Moss Ford, then allowed our surrendering troops to be massacred in the aftermath of the battle.'

He paused after this, to allow a few moments for boos and jeers from the assembled Elannis forces, before continuing.

'Lord Bornhaus has also told me of how Arion Sepian and his brother Duke Gerrion Sepian then threatened to kill me, their prisoner, and indeed *all* of our prisoners, if our remaining armies didn't surrender. How they threatened to chop me up and return me to my father, *your* Emperor, in pieces.'

More boos greeted this, but the prince held up a hand to settle them, impressing Allana with how expertly he was manipulating the crowd.

'It was an act of deep dishonour which should shame them but instead shames me. *Shames* me until it's avenged in the glorious name of the Emperor and the Empire! On this coming campaign, we shall avenge all of those insults and that butchery. We shall raise the standards of the Imperial Sun and the Hawk, and we shall claim Western Canasar and Rednar. We will conquer Andar, and we will overthrow the Imposter and his Imposter Church!

'Now ready yourself to leave. We march and we ride to glory. For the Emperor, and for the Empire!'

By the end of this speech, Markon's voice had lifted to heights of passion. As he concluded, he raised his fist high. This action caused thunderous cheering and hollering to break out amongst the ranks of the Elannis army.

Allana kept her eyes on the man on the stage, and her heart was beating fast.

—

Later that day, Allana was waiting towards the back-end of the combined Berun and Elannis army column, which was preparing to move southwards. Jarrett was apart from her, riding near the front of the column.

Allana was on horseback, once again savouring that she was outside, and that she could enjoy her new skill of riding. Four of her allotted Berun guards were alongside her. Before Jarrett had departed, she had been thrilled to hear him instructing those guards to address her as, 'My Lady.' It would be exciting to hear those words whenever they spoke with her.

She was also close to a horse-drawn carriage which Jarrett had assigned to her, along with a driver and a fifth guard. She was grateful for this; there were dark rainclouds to the south, and she suspected that she might be transferring into the comfort of that carriage later.

As she waited, she took a few moments to reflect upon how much her life had changed. Soon, this column of soldiers would cross the border from Berun into Western Canasar, and she would return to the land where she had lived for two years. She had left that place as a fugitive with few possessions, who had just committed murder to secure her escape. Now, less than a year later, she would return as a noble and as a future duchess, accompanied by an all-conquering army.

As she continued to wait, Allana reached into the pocket of her satin jacket, and extracted the scroll which Jarrett had given to her. She unrolled it, and looked again at the face on the parchment.

She is called Leanna, Lana. And they have named her the Angel of Arlais.

She lifted the document and showed the picture to her lead guard, who was a boyishly-handsome officer in his mid-twenties called Connar.

'Have you seen this?' she asked.

'Yes, my Lady,' he replied, nodding. He gestured to the other soldiers. 'We all have. 10,000 crowns! I'd very much like to find her.'

Allana nodded in return.

'So would I,' she murmured, as she stared at the image of the blonde-haired woman. 'So would I.'

16

Corin

—

Year of Our Lord,
After Ascension, 770AA

Corin and his party reached the edge of the Great Forest as the sun was beginning to set in the west. They had decided to end their day of travel there, and to make camp.

Their intended sleeping place was at the side of the river which flowed southwards from the forest, where Corin and Agbeth had also camped almost three years earlier. The trees of the forest towered skywards just a short distance away, emphasising the immensity of the deep woodland that Corin's party would be travelling through in the coming days. Indeed, it also reinforced the scale of the journey which lay ahead of them.

It had been three days since the encounter with the Kurakee, and since the warrior Brune had set out his appalling demands. Three days since Corin had resolved that he was still going to undertake the expedition to the north, despite the deadline presented by the Kurakee threats. Today had been their first day of travel away from Karn.

As the group set about establishing camp, Corin took a moment to observe the individuals who had been chosen to accompany him on this expedition. Nearest to him was Blackpaw, the beast extended upright to its full height. Blackpaw had spent the whole day in this stance, walking on its two hind legs, rather than adopting the four-legged lope which gave it much greater power and velocity. Indeed, Corin had never before seen the beast moving with such ponderous care.

The reason for that solicitude was carried on Blackpaw's back; Agbeth rested there. She was seated within a harness and frame, made from metal and leather, which was attached to Blackpaw's muscular shoulders and chest. The device had been Corin's idea, as a way to safely bring his wife on this journey without slowing the whole party down. Right now, Agbeth was leaning into Blackpaw's body, her head against the back of the creature's neck. Her eyes were open, but her stare was vacant and distant. For now, she was lost to Corin.

Corin transmitted an instruction to Blackpaw, telling the beast to lower itself down. Corin and two others then worked together to remove the harness device, and to undo various leather straps in order to safely extract Agbeth.

One of Corin's two helpers was Arex, the young Karn warrior. As soon as Arex had heard that Agbeth was going on the journey, he had volunteered to stay by her side as her protector. The other person assisting was Menni, a young Karn woman in her early twenties, who was the elderly Rilka's daughter. Menni had volunteered to be Agbeth's carer during the weeks ahead, given that the journey would be too arduous for her mother. Menni was attractive and outgoing, with ginger hair which was long and braided.

Close to them, Hellin of Condarron had already taken off her backpack. The missionary was the oldest person amongst the group, being in her late-thirties in age. However, she appeared to be robust and strong, and Corin was confident in her ability to keep up with their pace. Hellin had made it clear to Corin that she would earn her position in the expedition, beyond her tutoring role. Indeed, at this moment she was moving off to start collecting wood for a fire, for which Corin was thankful. It was early spring, but there was a definite chill in the air.

The other four remaining members of the group were its more hardened warriors. The first of these, representing the Karn clan, was Corin's brother Kernon. The second, chosen from the Anath, was a black-haired and stout fighter in his late-twenties, called Nethmar. This individual carried a two-handed great-axe, which was only slightly smaller than the weapon which had once been wielded by Borrik Greataxe himself. The third, representing the Borl, was a spear-carrying and burly warrior in his thirties called Rennik, who was the younger brother of Chief Munnik. And the last, chosen on behalf of the Qari, was the lanky and long-haired Charrek, nephew of Chief Quan.

All four of these warriors also carried a bow and a quiver full of arrows. Alongside Blackpaw and Corin, they were going to be responsible for keeping their party fed in the weeks to come. Corin was satisfied to see that the four warriors from different clans were working together amicably to establish the camp. He had also enjoyed listening to the friendly banter between them as the group had walked north during that day.

After the encounter with the Kurakee, Corin had decided almost immediately that he was not going to change his plans to travel to the mountains at the end of the world. To the lands of the Gods. Now that the weather had improved, he had to attempt to do *something* to heal Agbeth.

The only condition that he had set upon himself was that he was going to give them a maximum of forty days. Twenty days for the outbound journey, and twenty days to return. If they did not find what he hoped for within that period, then their expedition would be a failure, and he would have to attempt to find a cure for Agbeth at another time. But either way, he wanted to ensure that he would be back in Karn for at least a fortnight before the Kurakee's stated deadline arrived.

After the encounter with Brune and his party, Corin had tasked Akob and a company of sixty warriors with tracking the Kurakee warband to the edge of the Chosen lands. Akob had later confirmed that this had been done.

The following day, Clan Chief Munnik had also arrived at Karn, and Corin had assembled Munnik and Quan, along with his other advisers, for a council about the Kurakee. At that meeting, Corin had instructed his senior clansmen as to how to prepare for the Kurakee horde. Corin had been thinking about this from the moment that the meeting with Brune had ended, and his instructions had been very explicit.

Corin had placed Munnik in overall charge during his own absence, and he felt confident that the Borl leader would implement his plans effectively.

Corin had ended that council by saying, 'You all know what to do. I'll be back within forty days, and I'll be here to lead you when the Kurakee return. But we must be ready. Do as I say, undertake the preparations that I've set out, and we *will* be ready.'

—

In the days that followed, Corin and his party travelled through the vast woodlands of the Great Forest, following the river to the north.

Corin had tasked the four hardened warriors with driving the pace of travel of the group. The four clansmen did this with enthusiasm, while still managing to fulfil their shared hunting responsibilities. By the time that the party made camp each evening, Corin was satisfied by the distance covered but was wearied by the relentless trek through the dense woodland.

Throughout this period, Agbeth was lapsed into her dream-state, with Arex and Menni attending to her diligently. Corin noted an equal attentiveness and care within Arex towards Menni, and he wished the young warrior well in his pursuit of the Karn woman. Corin gave them space to talk as they travelled.

The person who Corin therefore found himself walking alongside most often, and also speaking with regularly, was the missionary Hellin.

One day, as their party was spread out over a distance of fifty metres, the dark-haired woman leaned in to him and said quietly, 'So, what are we really going north for?'

'I'm sorry?' replied Corin, feigning confusion.

'Whenever anyone asks or has asked you about this expedition, you state that you're going north to honour the Gods. That we intend to travel into the lands of the Gods and to pay our respects. But you're always a little vague. And I think that I know you well enough now, Chief Corin, to spot when that vagueness is deliberate. Your people have complete trust in you, and they always accept what you say at face value, without question. But I… listen to your words.'

Corin frowned. 'And what do you hear?'

'That you're not saying something. Not telling us something. For instance, why you've brought Agbeth.'

'Agbeth's my wife. I want her with me. That's my choice.'

'Or, what are we looking for? What do you hope for us to find in the lands of the Gods?'

'I'll know when I get there.'

'I think you already know, Chief Corin. And I think I can guess at the true purpose of this journey.'

He glanced across at her. He knew that she was intelligent and perceptive, such that flat denials would achieve very little.

'Humour me then,' he replied. 'What's the true purpose of this journey?'

Hellin pointed towards Blackpaw and Agbeth. 'Agbeth. Agbeth is. I think that you believe that you can cure her. Can make her better. That something in the north will allow you do that.' She paused. 'Am I right?'

He did not respond to her for a few moments. Finally, he said, 'By the Gods, you must be bored. Your mind appears to have too little to do. Perhaps you should seek answers from your man Aiduel, who seems to know so much. Then you won't need to be a nuisance to me, with all of these questions.'

'That's not an answer,' she replied, frost in her tone.

'I know,' he said, smirking. 'It's not.'

—

After five days of travelling through the forest, and latterly ascending an arduous slope, the group reached Corin and Agbeth's old home beside the lake. It was late-afternoon when they got there, and Corin gave the instruction that they were to set up their camp early that day. He wanted to spend the night in the place that he loved.

He felt a bittersweet poignancy as he peered around the lakeside area where he and Agbeth had lived for two years. This isolated place had been their home, and they had shared many happy moments here. Corin had taken the difficult decision to leave, in fear of what another freezing winter might have done to Agbeth's health, but that decision had in turn led Agbeth to the place of her head injury. Corin could also sense a mix of emotions being emitted by Blackpaw, as the beast roamed around this once-familiar location.

Corin was satisfied to see that the lean-to was still in good condition, and he resolved that he and Agbeth would sleep in their old home that night.

Whilst the warriors and Blackpaw used the remaining daylight hours to head out to hunt, Corin took his lesson with Hellin. The only book that she had carried on this journey was the Holy Book itself. For this lesson, Hellin was attempting to teach Corin about the events of The Lord Aiduel On The Tree.

After some time reading about this, Corin was confused. 'This man Aiduel, he had the power to move things, didn't he? With his mind?'

'Yes,' she said, sounding wary.

'So, why didn't he make the arrows miss him?'

'The Lord gave Himself as a sacrifice, to save us all,' she said, patiently. 'To show that, even though He was a God, He too was prepared to suffer for the salvation of His people.'

Corin was not satisfied by this response. He pointed at the carved wooden statue which was dangling around Hellin's neck.

'I don't understand how being shot with an arrow in the shoulder would save his people?'

Hellin's mouth was drawn into a thin line, and Corin supposed that he might be pushing her too far. 'Well,' she replied, 'there's a lot you don't understand, yet. But only by His sacrifice were we all saved.'

'So, why did they shoot him in the shoulders, then? Why not the heart? Or the forehead?'

'The Lord Aiduel walked in the light. His faith protected him.'

'So, he steered the arrows?'

Her eyebrows were lowered, and she glared at him and said, 'Are you trying to treat me like a fool, Chief Corin?'

'No, I'm sorry. I want to understand these things. If it were me and I had those powers, I'd steer the arrow. That's all I'm saying. To somewhere less dangerous.' A thought then occurred to him. 'How did he die, then, this man Aiduel?'

'He didn't die. He Ascended. To Heaven.'

'What?'

'He Ascended. He ceased to live in our world, and He became Our Lord, watching over us all and guiding and protecting us.'

'What? How did he do this? Where?'

'He returned to the place where He had come into His powers. Aiduel's Gate. And it was there that He Ascended. He-'

'Wait, stop there,' Corin interrupted, his mind suddenly alert. 'Aiduel's Gate? Aiduel's *Gate*? What's that?'

She looked at him with bemusement, noting the sudden excitement in his voice. After that, she proceeded to tell him about what and where Aiduel's Gate was. He listened. *Very* carefully.

That evening, he and Agbeth were sitting beside their lake, with his arm around her. He had chosen the precise spot where, long ago, they had so much enjoyed being together.

He had hoped that returning to this place might also trigger a return to lucidity for her. However, her gaze as she looked out across the water was unfocused and vacant, and he knew that she was not truly present there with him.

He was thinking about his conversation with the missionary Hellin, from earlier that day. And a place called Aiduel's Gate. Hellin insisted that the name Aiduel's Gate was a *metaphor* – some complicated term which Corin had no interest in – and that it had nothing to do with an actual Gate. But given what he already knew about this man Aiduel, and the similarities between the two of them, Corin was not so sure.

What if the man Aiduel had seen a Gate, similar to the one in Corin's recurring dream? What if that had given him his powers, like Corin had gained powers after seeing the ethereal archway in his own dreams? Perhaps that was why Aiduel had given the place such a name.

It was an intriguing thought.

Corin was pinning his hopes for this expedition on locating the Gate in the north, in the lands of the Gods. And on finding a way to heal Agbeth there.

But if the Gate was not there, he had an alternative possibility now. *Aiduel's Gate.* A place far to the south, described by Hellin as being in a land where the sun blazed with a heat that was beyond Corin's imaginings. A place which Hellin said had never witnessed snow, and which had little water. It sounded ridiculous and fantastical to Corin, and horrible too.

As he was thinking about this, he turned his head to the south and faced in the direction where this Aiduel's Gate might be. Was it his sudden imagination that he could feel something out there, a vast distance away? Something alive and powerful?

His speculation was interrupted as he heard Agbeth murmur, 'Tonight. Speak to him. Tonight.'

He turned towards her, feeling excitement, but was dismayed to see that there was no suggestion of alertness in her features. She was still *away*, her mind and soul still absent in her *elsewhere* place. She had surfaced just long enough to deliver those brief and simple words. However, her message had been clear.

Tonight, Corin would once again try to speak with the ghost.

—

After darkness had fallen, Corin was lying down beside Agbeth inside their lean-to, remembering the many nights that they had spent inside this small structure. It seemed cramped now, after months in the comparative grandeur of the Karn chief's home.

Agbeth had already settled into sleep, and the camp had become calm outside. Corin could hear the reassuring sound of Blackpaw snoring loudly in its old spot outside the entrance. The noise of two members of the party chatting in low tones also carried to Corin from some distance away, as he readied himself for the night ahead.

Agbeth was also snoring, albeit more lightly, when Corin first eased into her mind. Once again, he knew that her soul was somewhere locked away from him, unattainable and separate. He took a few moments to prepare himself, before calling out with familiar words.

ARE YOU THERE?

This time, the response was quicker, and there was an immediate sense of the presence.

Yes. I was waiting for you.

As before, Corin could hear the distant voice of a boy who possessed a strange and melodious foreign accent.

YOU WANTED TO SPEAK TO ME?

Yes. I think we're getting closer.

CLOSER TO WHAT?

There was an extended pause after this question, and Corin was relieved when the next response finally came.

I'm not sure. But it feels… like something else. Something familiar. It calls to me. Draws me… closer, to the surface. You must keep going, please.

Corin felt a trace of suspicion upon hearing this response.

IS IT THE GATE?

The Gate? I don't know.

WHO ARE YOU?

I don't know. But I can remember… some things. I'm starting to remember.

REMEMBER WHAT?

My dogs running in a field. My sister walking beside me…

The final words trailed off, and then there was another period of silence. Despite his eagerness to interrogate the presence, Corin was trying to stay patient, to avoid scaring it away. He asked his next question as gently as he possibly could.

YOU TOLD ME THAT YOU'D BEEN MURDERED?

Did I?

YES. YOU SAID THAT YOU WERE MURDERED.

Oh.

Another pause.

I think I was.

WHO KILLED YOU?

There was silence for a long time after that, as if the presence did not want to dwell upon the question that Corin had raised. When a response finally came, there was more awareness in the other's voice.

Do I know you? I think I know you. I think that's why I came when I first heard you. But I don't know why.

I DON'T KNOW YOU.

Did I do something to you? Something bad?

I THINK YOU'RE DOING SOMETHING TO AGBETI, NOT TO ME!

Corin could hear the frustration in his last delivered thought. He instantly regretted it, knowing that such moments of anger had pushed the ghost away during past interactions.

I'm sorry. I don't want to remember any more.

Corin had an immediate sense that the ghost was again receding from him.

DON'T GO! I'M SORRY TOO. DO YOU KNOW HOW I CAN HEAL AGBETH?

There was no answer to this. The presence had departed, and it was time for Corin to leave Agbeth's mind.

He would need to ponder the ghost's strange answers the next day, and he would try to make some sense of them. However, he could clearly recall one statement that the presence had made, early in the conversation.

They were getting closer to something. And they were to keep going.

—

The next day, the party left the lake and continued to head northwards. After just a few miles, Corin realised that he was in territory further to the north than he had ever been.

To the best of his knowledge, no one from amongst any of the clans had ever come this far. No man or woman had ever set foot in the places that they now walked upon. From amongst their group, only Blackpaw had explored the lands to the north of this.

Corin was walking a few paces behind the felrin and its passenger Agbeth, with the missionary Hellin alongside him. As they trekked through woodland beside the river, the older woman raised the subject which they had been discussing the day before.

'When I talked about Aiduel's Gate,' she said, 'you got very interested and excited. May I ask why?'

'You may.'

He heard her huff with exasperation. 'And will you answer me?'

'Probably not. It's between me and the Gods.'

'Perhaps I have knowledge from the east that will be able to help you, if you tell me. Aiduel says that *he who does not search, shall never find.*'

He considered her words, then looked around, checking their distance from the rest of the party. She spoke the truth; she possessed much knowledge that he did not.

'Very well. But swear on your man Aiduel, that this is only between me and you. Only Agbeth knows, other than me. No talking about it to the others.'

'I swear on The Lord Aiduel that I will keep what you're about to tell me secret.'

'Very well. I'll hold you to that, Missionary Hellin. I have a dream, one that comes to me most nights now. In that dream, there's a golden… magical, shining Gate. An archway. In the dream, this Gate is high on a mountain. I believe that what I'm seeing is an entrance to the Land of the Gods. And I also believe that if I can open that entrance, open that… Gate, I'll gain more powers.'

She was looking at him with a quizzical expression. 'And you think that this Gate is in the north? In the mountains?'

'Yes. Possibly.'

'And if you gain these powers? Then what?'

'Then I'll try to heal Agbeth. And I'll protect my people from the Kurakee.'

Hellin nodded carefully and then said, 'I thought so.' After a pause, she then hesitantly added, 'How *old* are you, Chief Corin?'

'Almost twenty-one summers,' he replied. 'Why?'

'No reason.' Her expression masked whatever she was thinking.

'Very well, I've told you. Now share your knowledge with me. What do you know about this matter? Did your man Aiduel also find a Gate?'

'No, sorry. I already told you that. The Gate referred to in Aiduel's Gate was just a-'

'Metaphor!' Corin finished, and then tutted. 'By the Gods! You easterners and your useless knowledge!'

—

For the week after that, Corin's party continued to travel north. They were climbing steadily for much of this time, and were gradually closing the distance to the range of mountains at the end of the world. The mighty peaks of this vast mountain range, which had seemed merely large from the perspective of Karn, now started to impose themselves with enormity over the looming horizon. A significant part of these mountains was covered in snow.

As the group progressed, the terrain around them was also changing, with the trees and woodland growing sparser, and loose rocks and scree becoming more prevalent on the ground. Corin vaguely recognised some of the terrain through which they passed, from sights he had seen through Blackpaw's eyes when the beast had returned to the north, two summers earlier.

The river which they had tracked all the way from Karn became increasingly difficult to follow, with sheer cliff walls making it close to impassable in places. Indeed, two day's north of Corin and Agbeth's lake, the group took the reluctant decision to abandon the river in order to follow an extended crevice through a rockface.

In the journey that followed, Blackpaw's presence was essential. Corin was certain that, without the felrin as part of their group, they would have faced a disaster of dead-ends and turning back on themselves. Thankfully, Blackpaw had been in these lands before, and the beast was familiar with this route to the far north. It often steered the party through narrow ravines and along sheer rock-faces which they otherwise would have avoided. The creature also knew where to find the next source of water. However, even with Blackpaw as guide, the going had become much more difficult, and their progress was slow.

The temperature had also dropped despite the spring month progressing. Many of the party were commenting that it was harder to catch their breath, and some were suffering from headaches. There was noticeably less amiable chatter amongst the group as they trekked onwards.

Food sources, either from hunting or foraging, were also becoming scarcer. On a couple of occasions, the party had to stop early in the day, and then was reliant on Blackpaw's efforts to hunt on their behalf.

Corin was aware of the dwindling number of days until his self-imposed deadline for turning around. Twelve days had now passed since they had departed from Karn, which gave him eight remaining days to either find what he was seeking, or to abandon his quest.

But now that they had come this far, he was increasingly torn. He knew that he had a duty to return to defend the Chosen peoples against the Kurakee. However, after travelling such a distance, he could not bear the thought of potentially getting within a day or two's travel of his objective, and then prematurely abandoning his quest.

Corin knew that he was not the only person thinking about this. A day later, he was approached by Rennik. The experienced Borl warrior had become the unofficial senior member and leader amongst the warriors in the party.

'We are thirteen days north, Chief Corin,' Rennik said. 'Do you think we're near to what you seek?'

Corin grimaced. 'We are drawing nearer to… something, Rennik. How near, I can't be sure.'

'Will we turn around in a week's time? I fear that food is going to become harder and harder to find out here.'

Corin looked directly at the man. 'I'll decide then. And we'll find food. We'll find a way.'

—

Agbeth had not re-emerged from her dream-state throughout these latter stages of the journey, and nor had Corin been able to make any more contact with the ghost inside her. However, despite his concerns about the looming deadline, he continued to feel intuitively confident that they were heading in the right direction. He still believed that they were getting closer to the lands of the Gods and to the… *something else*, which the ghost had spoken about.

The connection between Corin and Blackpaw was becoming more dynamic and active than ever as the days passed. These were the creature's lands, the domains where it had lived most of its life. Corin could feel the felrin's memories being rekindled by features in its surroundings; a kill it had once inflicted here, a chase there. He often saw remembered images of a gloomy cave with a low ceiling, where he assumed that Blackpaw had once lived. During its life in the south, the creature had pushed these memories aside as it had become tamer. But being here, amidst the remote wilderness where it had long resided, was bringing these recollections back.

As they travelled ever further north, Corin was noticing something else too. Something which he had not previously noticed in all of the time that he and Blackpaw had been together, and had been connected. There was a part of the felrin's memories which was concealed from Corin. Something about its life in the far north. A closed-off and submerged segment of the creature's consciousness, which was hidden from Corin, and from the felrin itself.

Corin could understand how he had not detected this previously; the beast always lived in the here and now, and it focused its attention on the present. Rarely when with Corin had it thought about its past life, or the years before Corin had become its master. There had therefore been no trace of concealment for Corin to identify. But here, returned to the north and amongst terrain which evoked its past, this fragment of memory which was sealed from both the felrin and from Corin was more readily apparent.

And Corin believed that it related to something which was still ahead of them.

—

On their seventeenth day out from Karn, in the mid-afternoon, Corin was walking beside Blackpaw. Their party was trekking along the centre of a bowl-shaped valley, which threaded through the surrounding snow-capped mountains. Corin could sense a deep familiarity within the felrin towards this place, and he perceived that the location was well known to the creature. Accompanying this sensation, the image of the cave was flashing more regularly through Blackpaw's mind. A dark, murky place, with a narrow and low entrance. But it was also a location which suggested comfort to the beast.

Corin was wondering about this sense of recognition at the moment when the felrin slowed down and then came to a halt. Agbeth had been sleeping against the creature's back, and she stirred restlessly as Blackpaw stopped moving.

They were standing at the bottom of a dip, with gently sloping and dusty rises to either side of them. There were no remaining trees in this valley, only dry grass, scrub and occasional thorny bushes which held little greenery. Scattered throughout the valley was a jumbled assortment of rocks and boulders; some as small as a fist, and a number which were several times taller than a man. The group had been winding its way slowly through these obstacles.

After Blackpaw halted, the beast remained in an upright standing position, as it had been for so much of the last month. It towered over all of the people around it, and Corin could see the creature rapidly turning its head from left to right. The felrin's snout was moving, and it was sniffing the air.

Corin could also feel its alarm; a sudden fear for the safety of Agbeth and Corin.

'Everyone, halt!' hissed Corin.

The group reacted to his call and to the concern in his voice.

Rennik and Charrek were at the front of the party, whilst Kernon and Nethmar stood at the rear. Hellin, Arex and Menni gathered in the centre, close to Corin and Blackpaw.

There was a moment of silence, before a wailing screech echoed out across the valley, sounding as if it was several hundred metres to the south, behind them. Corin recognised the cry instantly, as did all of the other warriors in the group. Within moments, every man there was brandishing a weapon.

The noise sounded like Blackpaw. It was similar to Blackpaw's own call, and yet was still alien. It was the cry of a felrin.

Corin could see that Kernon and Nethmar were stepping back towards him. They were moving cautiously in response to the sound, with their eyes facing in the direction of the screech. Corin could also hear Blackpaw growling in response to the noise, and could feel the creature extending all of its claws.

Then a second shrieking noise echoed along the valley, coming from somewhere to the north. From somewhere ahead of them. And then a third such cry, a haunting bellow from the west, which sounded closer. Finally, a fourth terrible call, from the east, which was also close.

All these sounds were the cries of beasts which were as yet unseen, but Corin was certain what these feral noises must mean; his party had entered the territory of a number of other felrin.

And they were surrounded.

17

Leanna

—

*Year of Our Lord,
After Ascension, 770AA*

Leanna, Amyss and Caddin journeyed north on the River Road, in the direction of the Ninth Bridge. An hour had passed since their hurried departure from the inn, following Caddin's return. They were travelling in worried silence, each of them soaked by an unceasing rainfall. Caddin's concern was palpable.

The skies above were a blanket of grey cloud, casting their surroundings into an ominous gloom. Leanna was hunched up on the wagon seat, looking out towards the Canas River as the waterway's surface was dappled by the heavy rain. There was little traffic on the road, and it was an eerie feeling for the highway to be so quiet.

It was therefore a surprise when Leanna spotted four riders galloping on horseback from the north, coming towards their wagon. As these horsemen drew closer, she could see that they were all wearing the blue tabard of the Andar military. Three of these riders galloped straight past the wagon, paying no attention to Leanna and her companions. The fourth reined in his horse on the highway ahead, and shouted, 'Halt!'

Caddin brought their wagon to a stop, as this last rider now walked his horse closer. An agitated look was on the man's face.

'Is something wrong, sir?' asked Caddin.

'Turn this wagon around and get out of here,' ordered the soldier. He glanced behind himself after saying this.

'What is it?' queried Caddin. 'What's happening?'

'We're being invaded again, that's what! We don't understand it, because there's been no activity at any of the bridges or on the river, but thousands of Elannis soldiers are in the north of Western Canasar, and they're coming this way. The whole lot of them might be just hours away. Cavalry scouts probably closer than that. So, if you value your lives, turn this wagon around and get the fuck out of here.'

After saying this, the man urged his horse back into a gallop, and set off past them to the south.

Caddin did as the soldier had instructed. In moments, their wagon was returning southwards. There was a grim look on Sendromm's face, and again Leanna observed the burly man's free hand reaching up to grasp his medallion. She looked back over her shoulder, staring towards the north.

There was no one else in sight there, but it seemed that there would be no way out of this land, in that direction.

Lord Aiduel, am I again to find myself in the midst of war in Western Canasar? Where should we go, Lord?

They would need to determine their destination, in due course. However, there was no doubt about what their immediate action needed to be. They had to get away from this place.

Far away, and as soon as possible.

—

Less than ten minutes later, Caddin turned the wagon off from the highway. He directed them onto a smaller trail heading westwards.

'Where are we going, Caddin?' asked Amyss.

'You heard what that soldier said,' the grey-bearded man replied. 'We can't stay on the main road. Elannis advance troops might appear at any moment.'

After just a handful of minutes of travel on this westward trail, the River Road and the Canas River both disappeared from sight. However, the small track they were on soon turned into a quagmire, making it difficult for the wagon to progress. Eventually, their forward movement ceased altogether, with the wheels of the heavily-laden vehicle sinking deep into the mud.

'Lord damn it!' exclaimed Caddin, after he had climbed down to inspect the problem. He was staring at the sunken rear of the wagon, shaking his head. 'Right, both of you get down. We'll need to continue on foot from here.'

'On foot?' repeated Leanna. 'What about the wagon?'

'We'll have to abandon it,' said Sendromm. 'I'll unhitch the horse, we'll carry what gear we can, but we leave the wagon here. Now get down, and take only what you absolutely need to. One bag each, maximum. We need to move fast.'

As Caddin worked to unhitch his horse, Leanna and Amyss gathered their possessions from the wagon. Within moments of climbing down onto the boggy trail, both of their dresses had become covered in mud at the bottom, and their feet were soon wet inside their shoes.

After he had released the horse, Caddin moved to the wagon bed and accessed a previously unopened container. Leanna observed as the man then proceeded to wear or equip the objects extracted from within. First, a gleaming chainmail vest. Then, a padded leather jacket which fell below his waist and added to his bulk. Next, a pair of knives were strapped to his belt, and gauntlets were slipped onto his hands. Finally, a burnished helmet and shield were hung from the horse's saddle. The last object extracted and placed onto the saddle was a length of coiled rope, before he strapped his mace to his back.

He handled all of these items with an efficiency which suggested that this had been done many times before.

'We've always thought that you'd been a soldier,' said Leanna.

He did not respond, but Leanna saw him glancing towards her and then Amyss, with a severe expression on his face.

'What is it?' she queried.

'We could move quicker if you and I are on the horse, Leanna,' he said. 'Riding, rather than walking. I'd have a better chance of getting you out of Western Canasar and to safety.'

'But what about Amyss?' asked Leanna. He shrugged in response, and she realised what he was suggesting. 'No, don't even think it.'

Sendromm looked across at Amyss, making eye contact. 'Perhaps Amyss should decide on that, and not you, Leanna. She understands that you're more important than her and that she shouldn't hinder your escape from here. Isn't that right, Amyss?'

Leanna glanced at her companion, and saw the crestfallen look on Amyss's face as the implications of Sendromm's words dawned on her.

Lord Aiduel, would he abandon Amyss with such little care?

'No, don't answer that, Amyss,' Leanna said. 'I'll only continue to travel with you, Caddin Sendromm, if Amyss is with us. If that isn't acceptable to you, then get on your horse and ride off. And Amyss and I will take care of each other.'

Sendromm snorted. 'You understand that you could be in real danger? And just how much having to walk will slow us down?'

Leanna glared at the burly man and said, 'I do. But we'll all have to walk. Amyss stays with us, and I expect you to protect her, too. Is that also understood?'

He twisted his neck, looking back at her with a dark expression. 'Very well. We walk, and she stays with us. But be in no doubt, Priestess Leanna, that we're in danger now. And if I ever need to sacrifice *her*, to protect *you*, I won't hesitate. You should both understand that.'

—

Shortly afterwards, Leanna watched as Caddin gave a last, mournful look towards his wagon and possessions. They then abandoned the vehicle and set off on foot, with Caddin leading the horse. All of them were stony-faced and silent.

They travelled like that for the remainder of the day, and Caddin was still urging them on as darkness descended.

They spent that night in a barn, sharing the space with their horse, after paying money to the barn's owners for an evening meal and a place to sleep. It was a chilly night, and Leanna and Amyss were huddled together against the cold. Their clothes were soaked through; they had taken off their outer garments to try to dry these, but they continued to shiver under their remaining damp layers.

Sendromm had wedged the barn door shut once they were inside. As Leanna was close to dozing off, she noted that he was sitting with his back against a haystack, facing towards the door. The handle of his hefty mace was resting against his leg. Leanna felt certain that he was going to sleep in that position.

—

Caddin roused them before dawn. They were soon back to trekking on the countryside trail, with the grey-bearded man leading the horse.

It continued to rain throughout the morning, and their journey westwards was miserable, travelling along a path which had turned into a bog. Leanna's feet were wet, the lower part of her dress was caked in mud, and all of her clothes were damp.

'Where are we going, Caddin?' she asked, early in the day. 'What's our plan?'

'I'm aiming to take us across Western Canasar, to the western coast,' he replied. 'Hopefully, we'll still have enough time to get out of the territory, northwards. If not, we'll have to head south.'

By lunchtime, the rain had finally stopped, and the sun was starting to appear from behind the clouds. The trail at this point was less muddy, with low drystone walls flanking either side of a wider, rutted path. Leanna had begun to feel in better spirits, and she was determined to ignore her rumbling stomach.

At that moment, a number of riders emerged from around a bend in the trail up ahead. These horsemen were only a couple of hundred metres to the west, and there was no opportunity to seek a hiding place. Leanna counted seven in total, all of them wearing yellow tabards which identified them as soldiers from the Elannis army.

'Fuck,' muttered Sendromm. The burly man slipped his helmet onto his head, before taking hold of his shield and gripping his hefty mace. He then turned to Leanna and Amyss. 'Stand behind me and this horse. Keep your heads down. Don't stare at them. Don't speak. And, if anything starts between me and them, both of you jump over this wall and *run* as fast as you can.'

Lord Aiduel, please watch over us.

As the riders came closer, Leanna and Amyss did as instructed, taking up a position with the horse in front of them and a drystone wall to their back. When the riders reined their horses in, Leanna lowered her head. She was remembering the poster which Caddin had brought from Arlais, upon which an image of her face had been emblazoned.

'Dressed for war, old man?' asked the lead rider, a short and stocky soldier with a reddish beard. The other riders had also noted Caddin's mace, their hands moving to their swords. 'And just who are you intending to fight?'

'No, no, no, sir,' said Sendromm, meekly. The grey-bearded man was hunched over slightly. 'There's no fight in me, sir. Just a man out in the country, wearing some old gear for comfort in troubled times.'

The man with the red beard gestured down the trail to the east. 'Where does this lead?'

'Through countryside, sir, back to the Canas River and the River Road.'

'Have you seen any Andar troops in these parts? Scouts? Gatherings of men?'

As the lead rider was asking this, one of the other men rode past him to the east on the trail, before circling back. The rest remained beside their apparent leader, in front of Caddin.

'None, sir,' replied Caddin.

Leanna was keeping her eyes down, but was trying to look over the withers of Caddin's horse. She saw the lead rider gesturing towards her and Amyss.

'Who are these two?' the red-bearded man asked.

'Just my daughters, sir. Travelling with their father.'

'Where to?'

'Not sure, sir. We'd heard word of… invasion. Not our business, sir, and Lord Aiduel bless your army, and bring you all success, I say. Just thought I'd get us out of this area.'

'These two are both good looking, Captain,' said the man who had ridden past, who was a swarthy individual. He had steered his horse to a position a few metres from Leanna and Amyss, alongside the wall, such that he had a clearer view of the two of them. 'Very good looking. Time for some rest and entertainment?'

The captain glanced towards his compatriot and smirked. He then looked back towards Caddin. 'This war's going to be a miserable business, old man. My lads trust me, because they know I look after them and let them take what joy's there to be taken. So, how much for us all to spend some time with your daughters?'

Caddin's voice remained meek. 'I'm sorry, good sir. My daughters are not for sale, for *that*, although I take no offence that hearty lads like you would ask such a question. Again, best wishes for all of your endeavours in this land, good gentlemen, and may you walk in Aiduel's Grace in the days and weeks ahead.'

Leanna observed a sneer forming on the lead rider's face as Caddin finished these words. The man then addressed his next statement to his fellow riders.

'I think the old fella's dismissing us, lads, with his fine words. I'm not sure that he understands that if our minds are set on this, he can either let us have our fun and earn himself a little coin, or we'll take it anyway, and he'll earn nothing. Are we in agreement on this, lads?'

'Yes, Captain,' came the response from several of the gathered riders.

There was a pause of seconds. Leanna felt her heart pounding, as she observed Caddin standing up straight and appearing to twist his thick neck. She tensed, sensing that they were on the cusp of terrible violence.

Lord Aiduel, please protect us.

'I think I understand well enough, *Captain*,' Caddin said, his voice suddenly deeper and full of authority. 'And what you suggest is behaviour which will dishonour the uniform you wear and the cause you represent. You address once-Commander Caddin Sendromm of the Eastern Elannis army, the Hero of the Siege of Accunder Pass, and a bearer of the Emperor's Star.' Leanna stared at Sendromm with surprise as he uttered these words. 'I served Elannis with honour, Captain, at a time when you would have been sucking on your mama's tit. And I understand what an honour it is to fight for the Emperor and the Empire. Now, please move your men on from here and leave my family in peace. Show respect to a man who long fought for the same cause as you, and let there be goodwill between us.'

'You were a commander?' said the captain, with hesitancy in his voice. 'You fought for our country?'

'Yes, Captain. I'm a veteran, of Patran and Sennam. Look into my eyes, hear my voice, if you doubt that. Fourteen years. One day, when you're a veteran, you'd not want your family to be mistreated by future soldiers, would you Captain?'

The red-bearded man looked uncertain, as if he was finding his earlier proposal unpalatable. Leanna tried to control her rapid breathing.

Lord Aiduel, please let them leave us alone.

Just as the captain was about to say something, the swarthy rider who was closest to Leanna announced, 'Her hair's damp, but I just realised that this one's a blonde, Captain.'

'What?' replied the officer.

'A blonde, like on the scroll. The reward.'

'Oh, right,' the captain said. 'Very well, I believe you, *Commander*. We've no business harassing an Elannis veteran. Let's have a quick look at your daughter, and then we'll be on our way.'

Leanna was uncertain about how to react, until Caddin turned sideways, and she heard him mutter, 'Remember what I told you to do.'

Lord Aiduel, please give us the strength and courage to survive this.

Leanna could feel that her limbs were trembling with fear. She could also see Amyss's hand shaking beside her. Both of them were poised for what might be about to come.

'I don't think so, Captain,' said Caddin after a moment. Leanna saw him shifting his body slightly, raising the mace and shield. 'Now, I'm asking you this politely, as one Elannis officer to another. Move your men along and let there be no trouble between us.'

There was menace in his voice, and Leanna noticed that a number of the riders reacted by placing their hands back onto their weapons.

'You need to watch your tone, old man, ex-commander or not,' said the captain. 'Now, I'll ask this one more time, and one more time only, or there will be fucking trouble between us. Tell your daughter to step out, round here, so we can get a good look–'

'Run!'

Caddin shouted the word at the instant that he sprang into action. Leanna caught a fleeting glimpse of Sendromm smashing his mace into the head of the captain's horse, then she was spinning around and leaping over the wall which bordered the trail. Amyss was beside her, the red-headed woman frantically vaulting the stone barrier at the same time as Leanna.

Then Leanna was running into the field beyond, into waterlogged ground. After just a few steps, her feet sank deep into the boggy surface. The frantic noises of combat were behind her, and she could hear screams of pain from both men and animals.

She glanced back after having travelled no more than twenty metres, and was dismayed to see that the swarthy rider had dismounted and was in pursuit. The man was less than ten metres from Leanna, and even closer to Amyss, who was struggling across the muddy ground.

Leanna pushed on, mentally urging Amyss to hurry, but the gap was closing between the pursuing soldier and the petite woman. There was no way that Amyss could outrun this man, who looked intent on violence.

From the corner of her eye, Leanna could see a ferocious melee taking place between Caddin and the other Elannis troops. It was clear that the burly man would not be able to help them with this pursuer.

As the swarthy soldier came within arm's reach of a desperate Amyss, Leanna realised two things. First, time had decelerated around her, throwing the chase into a macabre focus. Second, now that she was out of range of Sendromm and his medallions, her powers had blossomed into life.

DEVOTION. SACRIFICE. SALVATION.

The soldier's hand was just inches from grasping Amyss when Leanna acted. She raised her arm and invisible, ethereal fingers raced out towards the man, entwining themselves around his limbs. Forcing him to stop. Then lifting him.

The soldier screamed as his body was wrenched from the ground. He was dragged away from Amyss, his shrill cries mixing in with the ongoing groans and shrieks from the conflict on the trail. Amyss turned to see what was happening, and gasped as she witnessed what Leanna was doing.

Leanna lifted her arm higher, mirroring the actions of the invisible fingers which were clenched around the man. Raising him further from the ground. Ten metres. Fifteen metres. Higher still. She felt energy coursing within her, flowing down her arm, and then along the invisible connection to this hostile soldier. She was squeezing the man's limbs in a vice of ethereal power, and was once again bathed in a golden light.

Lord Aiduel, please guide me. How can I show mercy here, without endangering Amyss?

Leanna was intimately connected to the captive man through this stream of power. She could sense his fear pulsing outwards, but another image swept into her mind, unbidden. A ghastly picture of her and Amyss, held down by unseen hands. She shuddered, recognising that she was witnessing the man's sinister fantasies across their connection, and the darkness of that image triggered her next, instinctive, action.

She flicked her wrist, and the soldier was released from her control under a surge of force. He flew through the air, crossing over the field and the trail, and his body crumpled as it crashed into the thick trunk of a tree in the woods beyond. The man did not move after that.

Lord Aiduel, please forgive me.

With this threat removed, Leanna became aware that the sounds of combat from Caddin's direction had ceased. No one remained on horseback, and four of the Elannis riders' horses appeared to have trotted away from the area of battle. Nor was anyone standing beyond the waist-height stone wall.

Amyss was the first to react. 'Caddin? Caddin!'

There was no response from the other side of the wall, and Amyss began to trudge back across the muddy field, with Leanna following.

'Oh, Lord!' said Amyss as she reached the low wall and looked over, lifting her hand to her mouth.

Leanna exhaled when she saw the carnage in front of her. Seven bodies and three dead horses were spread across the floor. Caddin's horse was the only animal to still be standing in the midst of this aftermath of violence.

Leanna's eyes swept across the motionless figures, finding Caddin, who was collapsed on his back next to the Elannis captain. Sendromm's body was covered in blood, and it appeared that he had been stabbed in multiple places. The shield remained on his left arm, dented and battered. In his right hand, a long dagger was clenched, with his mace discarded close by.

Amyss was already crossing over the wall. Leanna followed, whilst trying to determine whether any of the Elannis soldiers still posed a threat. None of them appeared to stir.

They reached Caddin to find that his eyes were open, and that he still lived. He seemed to be trying to speak, but blood was bubbling from the corner of his mouth and no sounds were emerging. Beside him, the Elannis captain was dead, with multiple stab wounds visible across his body. The chaotic melee appeared to have ended with a close-up knife fight between Sendromm and the red-bearded officer.

'Heal him, Lea!' implored Amyss.

Leanna tried to focus, but in the presence of the medallions her powers were once again dulled to almost nothing. Caddin was staring up at her, the light fading from his glazed eyes.

'The medallions!' shouted Leanna. 'Get them off him and run away from me!'

Immediately, Amyss reached down to Caddin's neck. There was a snapping sound, and she pulled out a thin chain on which two coin-like silver metal circles were threaded. She turned away and then sprinted down the road.

Leanna sensed the precise moment when her powers sparked back into life. Time decelerated again, and Caddin's wounds sprung into view in a gathering of dark shadows. The grey-bearded man had been stabbed in six places across his limbs and torso, each of these wounds marked by a stain of darkness within Leanna's vision. But one area of blackness dwarfed all of the others; a blade had slid into one of his lungs. It was this damage that would see him dead in moments.

Leanna had once saved Prince Markon from an equally grievous wound, but that had been done while drawing upon Arion Sepian's energy. This time, she was alone.

But she was more powerful than she had been then. The Lord had blessed her with growing powers, which she knew had continued to build since the day of the pyre. Powers which she had trained and refined during the months in the College hospital.

Lord Aiduel, please help me to save him.

She felt energy surging within her as she focused upon the central damage in Caddin's body. She gripped the blackness in and around his lung with invisible fingers, then she tore it out as she healed and knitted the damaged flesh. Next, she concentrated on another wound, then another.

Power was flowing through her body, along her arm, and out across the invisible connection to Caddin. Resolving each of his injuries and restoring his body to what it had been before multiple blades had pierced it. Leanna was bathed in golden light, and she was dimly aware that Caddin's eyes were fixed upon her as she worked her miracle. His chest was heaving, but the froth of blood at his mouth had begun to subside.

There came a point where Leanna realised that Sendromm's physical wounds were healed. It was then that she identified another sickness within him. Something malignant, which was contained deep within his soul. A core of blackness, of intense sorrow and horror, akin to that which Leanna had once witnessed when she had acted to restore Amyss after El'Patriere's abuse. But this was thicker, darker and was burrowed even deeper.

Before she could stop herself, Leanna's hand had extended to Caddin's forehead, and she was searching for that darkness. Then she reached for it, with ethereal fingers digging deep, and what she saw there stunned her.

Memories, of a life of pain…

…a small child, standing beside the bodies of his two parents. Both of them victims of a terrible disease. But the boy did not know that, and he did not know what to do, other than to stay there beside them, hoping that they would wake up. He was holding onto his dead mother's hand, trying to blink the tears from his eyes…

…the same child, although some years later. Standing in an alleyway, knife in hand, panting hard as he stared down at the

bloodied corpse of a long-term abuser. At last, he was big enough to fight back…

…he had become something. A soldier. A killer. And there was a woman, whose smile lit up the world for him. A new life, with a new home. And a child? A daughter! He could be happy. He could know peace. Just one last campaign…

…a fortress, in the mountains. He was a leader of men, a dealer of death, but never before had it been like this. They swarmed upon him and his men, but he smashed them down. Again, and again, and again…

…a small cottage. Burned by raiders. Outside, two charred bodies. One large, one small. Black despair…

…he was a priest? A healer? It could not restore what had been lost, but it was something. And then, an unexpected invitation…

'Stop!' croaked Sendromm, as he lay exhausted before Leanna. There were tears in her eyes, as she dipped into this well of hidden sorrow. 'Please! No more.'

'I can heal you,' said Leanna, as she submerged herself further. 'I can take this hurt away.'

…inside a grand and lavish room. Listening to the words of another man. A recognisable man? The Archlaw? A sense of destiny…

…years of wandering. Wilderness years. Drinking. Healing. Searching. But seeking what? And then a shepherd. A coming storm. A farm. And a young boy, sitting at a table. One who appeared to be possessed of powers…

'No more!' This time there was terror in the voice as Caddin Sendromm's hand shot out. He gripped Leanna's wrist and forced her fingers away from his forehead. 'Get out of my head!'

The connection between them was shattered, and it left Leanna reeling. She had witnessed the darkness lurking within the burly man, but she had not been able to heal his soul, had not been able to draw the foulness out of him.

As the link was severed, Leanna's golden aura also faded. She was suddenly feeling woozy, and she swooned backwards. She realised that she was completely drained by her actions to save Amyss, and to heal Caddin.

She looked at Caddin Sendromm, and saw that he was regarding her with fear. There were so many questions that she wanted to ask him, so much that she needed to know, but then her eyelids drooped uncontrollably, and blackness dawned.

—

When Leanna woke up later, she realised that she was on the back of their horse, slumped forward in the saddle. Caddin was leading the animal on foot, and Amyss was walking beside her.

'Where are we?' asked Leanna.

'We carried on, Lea,' said Amyss. 'We're heading south now.'

'South?'

'Yes. We found another trail. Caddin says that it's too dangerous to try to head north.'

'We encountered Elannis scouts earlier,' stated Caddin. He sounded exhausted. 'And where there are scouts, the army is going to follow. It's too late to flee Western Canasar. I don't believe that it's safe to try to take you past their main army. So, we go south, as quickly as possible. And we try to stay off the main roads.'

Leanna remembered the things that she had witnessed as she had healed the grey-bearded man, and she said, 'Caddin-'

'I don't want to talk about it,' he said. She noted that she could no longer sense his feelings, and she realised that his medallions must have been returned to him.

Lord Aiduel, please encourage him to share his pain and to reveal what he knows to me.

'I saw,' said Leanna. 'So much of your life. The awful things that happened to you. And I saw you with the Archlaw, sometime long ago. How do you know him? And who was the boy?'

'I said, I don't want to talk of it.'

'But I do, Caddin Sendromm. I've thanked you before for saving my life in Arlais. And I thank you again now for what you did earlier, to try to protect us. But I'll not travel with you for much longer, unless you start giving me answers.'

'I must take you south,' he said. 'Away from this danger.'

'I could heal you, you know,' she replied. 'The Lord Aiduel could take away your pain, acting through me.'

'I don't want your healing. My... pain... is mine to bear.'

'The meeting with the Archlaw, was it connected to me? He looked young. When did it happen?'

'Stop asking me questions!'

He was turned away from her, still leading the reins of the horse, and she saw his shoulders hunch up.

'Then who was the boy?' pressed Leanna. 'Was he like me, with powers? What happened to him?'

There was no answer.

'You'll still not tell me more of who you are and what you know,' she said, 'after all the time that we've spent together? And after what I saw?'

Again, there was no response.

'Very well,' said Leanna. 'Take us south, and please protect us on the journey. For now, Amyss and I have need of you for that. And I want to return to Septholme, where we'll seek sanctuary with Arion Sepian. Get us to Septholme Castle, but then, unless you tell me the whole truth, your duty to protect me is done. After that, go wherever you will, and keep your precious secrets if you must. But I no longer want to travel with a man who's hiding something so vital from me.'

Caddin did not say anything further in response to this, and they continued on their journey, travelling in silence.

Later, Leanna was deep in thought, still considering their predicament as they travelled onwards.

Somewhere behind her weary party, the armies of Elannis were advancing southwards into Western Canasar. To the south, Septholme and its castle seemed a possible bastion of protection from these invading forces. That destination might also offer an opportunity to reunite with Arion Sepian, much sooner than Leanna had anticipated.

She was determined to carry through on her promise to Caddin. It was time that he either revealed all that he knew, or that they parted ways. She had always been aware that he was keeping secrets from her, but she had been prepared to tolerate that after he had saved her life.

However, now that she had seen glimpses of a remembered meeting with the Archlaw, and of an encounter with a boy who seemed to have powers, she could no longer accept Caddin's secrecy. What had the Archlaw said to him? Who was the boy, and where was he now? And how were both of those questions connected to Leanna and the other Illborn?

She would have her answers or she would send Caddin away, oath or not. And then she would entrust her future safety to Arion Sepian. Something which she now regretted not having done earlier, the last time that she had visited the young noble.

And so it was that Leanna and her companions journeyed south, long into that night. They travelled in fear, with uncertainty ahead, and with the threat of an invading army following somewhere behind them.

18

Arion

—

*Year of Our Lord,
After Ascension, 770AA*

Arion sprinted up the murky stone staircase. He was moving urgently, his feet taking three steps at a time, all of his focus upon reaching the top of this narrow spiral. There was a dim light at the top, glimmers shining through the open door which now came into view. He felt certain that he had to move faster, and that he was running out of time to save the princes.

He charged through the doorway, emerging into a lavishly decorated corridor which was illuminated by occasional candles in sconces. He had finally entered the long passageway which ended with the personal chambers of the two princes, Senneos and Sendar.

He was still gripping his bloodied sword as his feet started to pound along the corridor. The air continued to crackle around him as he moved, and he felt supremely strong. Through windows on his left, he could see the night-sky outside and the vast skyline of Andarron, which was revealed by the illumination of hundreds of scattered lights.

And then the sounds reached him.

Fighting. The noises of battle. Swords clashing and men cursing. He knew that the princes' bedrooms were located around a cul-de-sac at the end of the corridor, and he ignored other doors on his right-hand side as he hurried in this direction. When he finally reached the end of the corridor, he was not at all surprised to discover the two murdered Andar guardsmen, their bodies collapsed over spreading pools of blood.

The facing doors to either side of these victims were open. Prince Sendar's room was on the left, but the noise of fighting seemed to be coming from the right.

Arion paused for a moment, his heart beating, and he raised his sword. He then moved towards the open doorway of Prince Senneos's room, where he was greeted by a scene of chaotic melee.

Another two lifeless men were sprawled immediately inside the door to the large chamber. Both of them wore the uniform of Andar guardsmen.

Further back, in the far corner of the room beside an ornate four-poster bed, he recognised Prince Senneos Pavil, who was fighting alongside a black-shirted man. Arion was shocked to see that these two were in combat with another pair of Andar guardsmen, with a further three bodies scattered around them.

Arion's gaze then swept across to find his friend, Prince Sendar, who was nearer to the door. Another pair of bodies lay beside Sendar's feet, both slumped before a polished wooden bureau. The younger prince was under assault from a further two soldiers who were wearing the royal blue Andar tabard. Sendar was desperately trying to defend himself from twin attacks.

By the Lord! Traitors! They're trying to kill the princes!

Arion's immediate priority was to save Sendar.

STRENGTH. VICTORY. GLORY.

Again, the air sparked with energy as he launched himself into attack against the prince's two assailants. Arion's sword swept across and severed the head of the nearest attacker. As the second man turned, Arion swung his free fist in a ferocious uppercut, and he felt it thump against the bottom of this man's chin. There was a shuddering crack, the sound of a neck breaking, and the man toppled to the floor.

Arion turned towards Sendar, uncertain of what to do next. For a moment, the prince appeared dumbstruck, but then he seemed to regain control of his senses and shouted, 'Arion, it's a coup! A coup, by Senneos. Stop him!'

Arion stared at his friend, feeling suddenly bewildered, then turned towards the four figures who were fighting in the corner of the room. At that moment, Senneos's apparent ally in the black shirt cut down his direct adversary.

Sendar raised a finger and pointed it at this black-shirted man, who was advancing upon them. 'That one, Arion! Senneos's protector. Kill that one!'

Arion moved forward to intercept this individual, and their swords clashed in a blur of metal. The man was agile and very skilled, and he attacked without fear. However, he was not remotely fast enough for Arion's reflexes, or strong enough to withstand the flurry of bone-jarring strikes which Arion proceeded to unleash upon him. After Arion had finally beaten his opponent's sword aside, he slashed downwards, and severed the black-shirted man's sword-arm at the shoulder. Arion then reversed the sweep of his blade, and took the man's head off.

In the corner of the chamber, Prince Senneos had also dispatched his adversary. The older prince now raised his sword warily in Arion's direction. The only three people now alive in the room were Arion and the two princes.

'Disarm him, Arion!' commanded Sendar, from behind Arion's shoulder. 'He's tried to murder the king.'

'You liar,' replied the elder brother, as he glanced down in anguish towards the headless corpse of the black-shirted man. 'There's a traitor here, but it's not me! Defend me, Lord Sepian. I'm the heir to the throne, and this is a coup attempt by Prince Sendar.'

Arion adjusted his body position so that he could see both princes. He was unsure about what to do as he said, 'Sendar? What-'

'Disarm him, Arion!' repeated Sendar. 'He freed Markon! And he's poisoned the king!'

'That's a lie!' shouted Prince Senneos, but the older brother's words were cut-off as Arion moved in a blur towards him. Arion's hand was on the heir's sword-wrist before Senneos had any time to react. A fierce squeeze was followed by a twist, then the elder prince's sword was falling to the floor.

'Restrain him, Arion,' ordered Sendar.

Arion sheathed his sword. He then pinned the older prince's arms behind his back with a single hand, and held the heir in place with an arm around his neck.

'You seek to make yourself king?' hissed Prince Senneos, as his younger brother moved closer to stand in front of him. 'You would imprison me?'

'I seek to save Andar,' stated Sendar. 'I'm sorry, Senneos. But you're too weak to face what's coming, and too stubborn to abdicate.'

Arion was baffled. 'Sendar, what's going on?'

The younger Pavil ignored Arion. He continued to stare at his older brother, then drew a dagger from his belt.

'I'm sorry, brother, that it's had to come to this,' said Sendar as he lifted the weapon. 'But between Father's madness, and your weakness, our country is being destroyed. You've brought war on us, and freeing Markon was the act of a traitor.'

'Sendar, I just want peace,' said Senneos.

'So, you're confirming that you did it?' asked Sendar, sounding distressed. 'You arranged for Markon's escape?'

'Sendar, pleas-'

Before Senneos could finish his plea, Sendar buried the dagger into the stomach of his brother. Arion could feel the younger royal thrusting the weapon upwards, several times. Prince Senneos grunted in response to the first two thrusts, but then his head slumped forwards.

For a number of seconds after this murder, there was a look of anguish on Sendar's face. The prince then stared up at Arion, who was still holding the now-lifeless body.

'You ask what's going on?' said Sendar. His voice was cracking and there were tears in his eyes. 'Why, I'm resolving the succession, Arion, to try to save Andar. And thanks to you, it's done.'

—

A short while afterwards, Arion was following Sendar to the other side of the palace, to the suite of chambers which was shared by the king and queen. The events of the evening had left Arion feeling stunned.

As the two of them drew close to the antechamber of the royal couple's rooms, the prince stopped and turned to face Arion. His eyes were red and his cheeks were tear-stained.

'Thank you for what you did back there, Arion,' said Sendar, his voice low. 'I didn't expect Senneos to have so many guards with him, and I think I'd be dead now, if not for you. I don't know how you got here when you did, but I thank The Lord for your arrival.'

'What's happening here, Sendar?' asked Arion.

'I know that you're confused right now,' said Sendar. 'I'm still appalled myself at what I've just done. But know this. What we just did was necessary to save our country. Senneos intended to surrender to Elannis. He *must* have been involved in Markon's escape and Father's poisoning.'

'But why?'

'Because he's weak, and he wanted peace and reunification with the Holy Church, at any cost!'

'But you kill-'

'No more talk of that,' said the prince sharply, cutting him off. 'Remember, you and I are friends. Allies. When we go into this room, I need you to nod and to agree with me. Don't contradict me, don't undermine me and don't ever disclose what just happened, or I'll be forced to label you traitor. Do you understand?'

Arion grimaced, still feeling stunned by everything that he had witnessed. 'I don't understand. But I won't contradict you. I'm no traitor.'

'I know you're not. And... *thank you*, friend. Please remember, I'm – *we're* – doing this for the good of Andar.'

Sendar then strode away. The prince turned into the doorway of the royal couple's chambers, with a look of grief set upon his face.

'Sendar, what is it?' The question was asked in a lilting foreign accent, which Arion recognised as that of the queen.

Arion was following the prince towards the doorway as Sendar answered, 'We were too late, Mother. We've been betrayed from within. An attempted coup. And...' Sendar paused, then audibly sucked in air. 'My brother, Prince Senneos, is dead. Lord Arion and I killed his attackers, but we were too late to save him.'

Arion shuddered as he heard Mariess's anguished wail in response. He followed Sendar into the room, and his gaze immediately focused upon the queen. Her cheeks were flushed and her eyes were red, as if she had already been crying. A number of palace officials and courtiers were also in the room, gathered around her. All of them were in various states of grief, and now their own expressions of shock and distress at Sendar's news were added to the laments of the queen.

After a few moments, Mariess appeared to take control of her anguish. 'I have more dreadful news, my son. King Inneos, my beloved husband, your father, passed away just after you left us to find your brother. May The Lord Aiduel preserve both of their souls.'

Sendar gasped and seemed to stagger forwards, placing a hand out onto the shoulder of his mother. His forehead touched hers in what appeared to be a moment of shared, silent grief.

Arion observed as Mariess then stepped backwards, before she slowly lowered herself to her knees and bowed her head forwards. Everyone else in the room except Sendar started to copy the motion, causing more confusion for Arion. But realisation then dawned upon him and he too knelt down.

As he did this, he was beginning to recognise the impact of his latest prophetic dream. His own role in what had come to pass. And how he might once again have twisted future events by coming here.

The words that followed were spoken by Queen Mariess, her tone firmer and louder this time.

'King Inneos is dead. Long live King Sendar.'

—

During the night that followed, the Royal Guard mustered in force and drove the mob out of the grounds of the Royal Palace. Fighting then extended into the streets of Andarron.

Arion was not involved in any of these skirmishes. He was too dumbfounded by the many events of the day. Just minutes after Mariess had hailed the new king, Arion moved away to be on his own. He then sat for a long time with his head in his hands, staring down at the floor.

He was a reckless fool, a man who acted without thought or honour, and he knew that he fully deserved the shame that he was now feeling.

Starting from his arrival at *The King's Boar*, everything in the preceding hours had gone disastrously wrong. The first setback had been to realise that he had been duped, and that Allana was not there.

Then, he had heard about the declaration of war by Elannis and Dei Magnus. He had recognised that he had deserted his family and his home on a false pretext, and that he would not be there when they needed him most.

Following which, driven by a whirlwind of emotion, he had acted rashly in the midst of the events of the night. Watching the mob attacking the palace gates. Somehow making it over the towering wall into the palace grounds and then, in his urgent panic, killing four Andar guardsmen. In his race to be a hero, he had murdered four men who had only been seeking to protect the palace.

By the Lord, I massacred them! What have I done?

And then, worst of all, he had entered the palace in pursuit of his prophetic dream. And in coming to Prince Senneos's chambers, Arion had personally killed many of the heir's protectors. *He* had been the one who had tipped the battle in favour of Prince Sendar. *He* had been responsible for disarming Senneos, and then had stood and watched as Sendar had slain his brother.

Arion recognised that he had been central to the murder of the rightful heir to the throne. Indeed, at the moment of Senneos's death, the older brother might have already been king. Without Arion's intervention, Sendar would not have triumphed.

As such, it was not sufficient condemnation for Arion to accuse himself of betrayal, of being a liar who had been prepared to commit adultery. Above all of that, he was someone who, in the space of a grim night, had instead committed thoughtless murder. And regicide. He was a disgrace.

At some point in the night, he found an empty bedroom within the palace, shut the door behind himself, then lay down to sleep. Before slumber took him, he pictured the faces of his wife Kalyane, his brother Gerrion, and his sister Karienne.

And with tears in his eyes, once more he felt shame.

—

The next morning, Arion sought out the man whom he had once trained alongside at the Royal Academy of Knights. *King* Sendar Pavil. He found Sendar in the palace throne room, leaning over a long table, surrounded by a number of senior military officers.

Arion moved closer to the new monarch. Sendar appeared to be discussing tactics for the restoration of order in Andarron, while gesturing towards a map on the table. The king glanced up as Arion approached.

'Not now, Lord Arion,' Sendar said. 'This isn't a good time.'

'We need to speak, Sendar.' Arion stopped himself, realising who he was now addressing. 'Your Majesty, we need to speak. *Please.*'

Sendar must have noted the tension in Arion's voice, because this time he turned fully towards Arion. In a more welcoming tone, he stated, 'Very well, let's speak, friend.' Addressing the other figures around him, he added, 'Everyone clear the room. Leave us. And close the doors. We'll be no more than a handful of minutes, so wait outside.'

With some looks of puzzlement, the other parties exited the throne room, leaving Arion alone with the royal.

Sendar stared at Arion, the young king's expression now hard to read, and he said, 'Please say what you want to say, Arion. There are to be no secrets between us. But choose your words carefully and speak quietly.'

'How can you appear to be so calm and controlled?' asked Arion. 'The king and the royal heir, your father and brother, are both dead. And you know… what happened. What we did.'

Sendar grimaced. 'You have no idea what pain I'm in right now, Arion. How much I want to mourn them. But my focus is on saving this country. And after Father's death, we still have a chance. Father's hatred for the Archlaw had turned into a mad obsession, and he'd set us on a course to destroy Andar. We could never hope for reconciliation with Dei Magnus, or for more than neutrality from Angloss, with Father on the throne.'

Arion looked at Sendar, then said, 'So you… the king, too?'

'Nonsense. My father was the victim of an assassination by poison. And we've now found evidence to implicate the acquaintances of Prince Senneos in his murder. The very men who were killed in the melee last night. So, in effect, you and I avenged the king.'

'Really?' said Arion, knowing that he sounded sceptical.

'Are you suggesting otherwise, Arion?' asked Sendar, his tone suddenly colder.

'But what about Senneos? I was there!'

'Senneos wanted Father off the throne. It makes sense that he might have been behind the plot. But his idea of a resolution if he became king was abject surrender to Elannis and Dei Magnus, in return for the restoration of his eternal soul. He told me as much.' Sendar took a step towards Arion. 'Believe me, Arion, I loved my brother. But he had no backbone, and he would have seen us all become vassals of the Emperor before the month was out.'

'And that justifies-'

'Let me finish, please!' interrupted Sendar. 'We also think that his agents may have been involved in revealing where Prince Markon was being held captive, and that Senneos might have already betrayed us. Andar could not risk allowing my brother onto the throne. However, that fate was avoided when he was tragically killed in the melee, by the same traitors who poisoned Father.'

'But-'

'That's what happened, Arion! By the Lord, I used your letter to work out where Senneos had gone to hunker down after Father fell ill. And it prompted me to act, before Father passed away. To all intents, you sent me there, so how can you complain now? In me, Andar has someone who knows how to wage a war sitting on its throne. Please, stop being so self-righteous, and make a choice. Either you're for me, and will stand beside me in the war to come, or you're against me. Which is it?'

Arion exhaled loudly, feeling torn, and he was silent for a number of seconds.

'I'm for you, of course,' he replied, eventually. 'But I want to return to Septholme, Your Majesty, to lead the armies of Western Canasar.'

'You may. Soon. But not yet. I need you to stay for another day, to help me to put down the religious rebellion in this city. After that, you have my permission to go home.'

'Thank you.'

'Oh, and Arion?'

'Yes?'

'I'm more grateful than you can know for what you did last night. I know that you'll be suffering and feeling guilt. And believe me, what I... did last night, is causing me more pain than you can imagine. But

I know that we both did the right thing for the good of Andar. You might not believe that right now, but it's true. As a result of last night, we can still save our country. You are my friend, Arion, and I think you're the greatest warrior in this land. I need your support in what's to come. I need your strength, if we're to save Andar.'

Arion nodded, but without enthusiasm. 'You will have it, Sendar.'

'Thank you,' said the king. 'Oh, and there's one more thing I should mention.'

'What is it?'

'Do you know that your eyes were glowing last night, during and after the battle? They were golden.'

'They were?'

'Yes. But I won't tell anyone. Like everything else that happened in that room, this is the *last time* that either of us will ever talk about it. With each other, or with anyone else.'

—

During that day, Arion took control of several companies of soldiers. He was given responsibility for restoring order in the western districts of the city, although it quickly became apparent that fear of military retribution was quashing the enthusiasm of the rioters.

But more than that, the tragic news soon spread that King Inneos and Prince Senneos were both dead, rumoured to have been murdered by agents of the Emperor and the Archlaw. The mobs had been furious that the late king had led them into war, but Arion could see that the announcement of the two deaths was acting to dissipate and divert this anger. Any remaining rage was soon being turned against those residents of the city who were from Elannis and Dei Magnus.

During the course of the day, from certain viewpoints, Arion could witness the billowing sails of royal navy warships as they sailed out of the harbour mouth. He felt agitated to still be in the city, and he longed to be back on a fast ship, on his way to Western Canasar.

Towards the end of the afternoon, he returned to the Royal Palace, determined to obtain the new king's permission to leave. However, when he arrived in the throne room, there was again a cluster of people there. They were all assembled around a lengthy map of Andar, which had been laid out on the table.

Sendar was at the head of that table, and he gestured for Arion to come closer.

'We've received the most grievous news, Lord Arion,' the king said. 'We're all now debating how to react to it.'

'What is it, Your Majesty?' asked Arion.

'We now fear that the treachery which led to last night's uprising, and the murders of my father and brother, has deep roots throughout the Andar nobility. News has come to us by bird, from Rednarron and Septholme. The Houses of Condarr and Berun have switched sides. Those traitors are fighting alongside Elannis and Dei Magnus.'

'What?'

'And there's worse news. We've received word that Elannis troops are pouring into both Rednar and Western Canasar, from the lands of Berun. As far as we can tell, Duke Jarrett Berun has opened all of the bridges. The armies of Elannis have crossed the Canas River into Berun, and are moving through the Berun lands, unopposed.'

'Into Western Canasar?' asked Arion, as his heart was hammering in his chest.

'Yes, from the north. Tens of thousands. Whilst Rednar finds itself trapped between Condarr to the west and Berun to the east.'

'What news of Duke Gerrion's reaction, Your Majesty?'

'The duke has reported that he's mustering his troops as fast as he can, including drawing forces from the Canas River garrisons. He intends to march north to meet the threat as soon as possible.'

Arion felt sick inside. 'Your Majesty, I need to get onto a ship, and I need to go home. Right now.'

'I'd prefer you to stay and to join my armies, Lord Arion. To help me to crush Condarr before we face Elannis.' After Sendar said this, he appeared to take note of the tension in Arion's demeanour, before adding, 'But very well, if you must leave, then leave. Get to the harbour, and you have my authority to order the vessel which brought you here to take you home.'

'Thank you, Your Majesty.'

As soon as Arion had finished the sentence, he set off running.

—

He sprinted across the city, running without any shortness of breath and feeling the air crackling around him. He was dashing along as quickly as anyone else could have managed, sustaining this speed for the duration of the run.

He heard a number of people cursing him as he rushed past them, but he did not care. He had to get back onto a boat and return to Septholme. Maybe he would not be there for the first engagement, but if Gerrion could act to delay the enemy, Arion would be able to join the Western Canasar armies for subsequent battles. Perhaps for the key battle.

He could still try to make things right, and could yet atone for his error in coming here. He just needed to get onto that ship and get back home. Then he could protect his family and could once again be the hero to save Western Canasar.

As he reached the dockside area, however, he could hear horns blowing. They were sounding from the harbour mouth and from all along the city's seafront walls. He looked out over the harbour, towards the narrow entrance between the massive whitewashed walls on either side. And what he saw there appalled him.

A chain was being raised across the mouth of the harbour. Massive thickened metal links were rising out of the water, being pulled upwards by giant winches on either side. The Andarron harbour entrance was being sealed.

Arion looked out past the harbour mouth to the seas beyond, and what he spotted there was equally shocking; a massive fleet of foreign ships. Certainly, upwards of thirty vessels, their design and flags marking them out as Dei Magnun. The chain across the harbour mouth was being raised in response to this newly arrived threat, to prevent the assault on the city by the most formidable naval force in the world.

Arion stopped, suddenly feeling out of breath and stricken with panic. There was no way that he could now leave here by sea. No way that he could return home to Septholme, other than across the country, through Condarr and Rednar. Across lands which were now at war.

Once again, he cursed himself for his obsession with Allana dei Monis. He had abandoned his family and his people to the threat of Elannis and Dei Magnus. All for the sake of his infatuation with and lust for a woman whom he barely knew. And he had been played for a fool, for she was not even here.

And now he was trapped, at the start of a war, hundreds of miles from home.

19

Corin

—

*Year of Our Lord,
After Ascension, 770AA*

The cries of the felrin continued in the seconds after the beasts had made their presence known. Judging from the sound of their chilling calls, it seemed as if each of the creatures were moving closer. Rapidly.

Corin's party were bunching together, all of them peering outwards as they stood with weapons drawn. Corin was also scanning their surroundings, and he recognised that this was a particularly perilous location to be facing something as swift and agile as a felrin. There were too many huge boulders obscuring the view around them, and too many overhangs from which a deadly predator could launch itself at them from high above.

From where he was standing, Corin could see four points from which a creature could emerge just a few metres away. He knew that he might not be granted sufficient time to use his powers if a felrin was tearing towards him.

Corin could feel Blackpaw's bloodlust rising as the beast prepared to fight, but he could also sense its protectiveness towards Agbeth. The creature would be hamstrung in any battle by its need to keep Corin's wife out of harm. Corin reinforced that message to it; protect Agbeth, no matter what. Blackpaw was growling with menace, but it was not yet returning the cries of its felrin kin.

'Keep moving!' Corin shouted, making a decision. 'Try to find some open ground.'

The party did as he said, passing in single-file into a narrow passage between rocks ahead, before hurrying along the right-hand side of a massive and jagged boulder. Rennik and Charrek were at the front of their group; the former was carrying his spear, and the latter was wielding a one-handed axe. Corin was braced for a sudden attack, his senses alert for any sensation of a feral mind drawing close, but the group was still untouched as they emerged around the corner of the rock.

'Corin!' Rennik shouted. 'Up there!'

The Borl was pointing up the scree-laden slope towards an area of open space, which was perhaps fifty metres past their current position. The centre of this area was at least ten metres from the surrounding rocks, on all sides. It would give them slightly more time to react to a felrin's deadly approach.

Without waiting for Corin's response, Rennik was already heading that way, with Charrek at his side. The party hurried after the Borl warrior, while the threatening calls of approaching felrin still carried across the valley. As the group reached the centre point of the open space, they formed a circle, facing outwards. Kernon, Rennik, Charrek, Nethmar and Arex were to the exterior, all with weapons raised. Completing this external circle was Blackpaw.

Corin, Hellin and Menni remained in the centre, with Corin facing in the opposite direction to Blackpaw. He was using his connection with the beast to see through its eyes, at the same time as looking through his own. That way, he could keep watch on all directions at once.

However, he actually sensed the first of the felrin arriving, moments before he saw it. He could feel an alien and vicious mind, racing low on four legs through a crevice to the west. He could observe its progress through its own eyes, and could witness the moment when the circle of prey emerged into view…

STOP! STOP! STOP! STOP! STOP!

A grey-furred beast leapt out into the open higher ground above the party's position, at the same time that invisible tendrils ripped out of Corin's mind towards it, forcing his command upon it. He could feel the felrin's arms and legs seizing up, despite enraged resistance. The creature landed heavily on these paralysed limbs, before tumbling across the shallow slope down towards Corin's party.

This felrin was big, close in size to Blackpaw, and it was making a shrieking noise from its throat as it rolled. Rocks and scree were flying up into the air as it skidded over them, and Corin could feel the beast fighting furiously against the paralysing command. This was to no avail, and its momentum ended just paces from the group's circle. Rennik and Charrek charged towards the suddenly stricken creature.

Whilst this was happening, Corin observed a second felrin appearing around a rock from an easterly direction, witnessed through Blackpaw's eyes. He could feel Blackpaw tensing up and preparing to fight as the rival beast bounded forwards. However, Corin again intervened, sending a paralysing instruction to this new arrival.

This newcomer also fought against the command. It almost made it to their defensive ring on jerking limbs before it collapsed forwards, its maw snapping shut. Kernon and Nethmar launched into immediate attack against this beast, the blades of their axes glinting in the sun as they were raised high, before biting down deep into the felrin's flank.

Across from them, in Corin's own eyeline, Rennik was stabbing his spear into the other vulnerable felrin. This creature's limbs were jerking in response to each thrust, with claws extended, and Corin watched as one spasming rear limb almost caught the Borl fighter.

With each new wound inflicted by the Chosen warriors, the fury of the two restrained creatures was renewed, and their feral willpower struggled against Corin's control.

Corin could hear the cries of the other two unseen felrin drawing closer, at the same time that the first pair of attackers were straining to resist him. More distantly, he could hear the shrieking howls of yet more felrin, and his heart sank. He could certainly hold two of these creatures at bay, and possibly a handful more if he saw them coming. But with the speed at which the beasts moved, and the ferocious strength of their will, he doubted that he could keep his party safe from many more than that.

As he was thinking this, a third felrin appeared, leaping from the closest boulder to their north. Menni screamed as this beast launched itself towards her, and Corin saw Arex charging forwards to interpose himself between the creature and his clanswoman. Corin wanted to yell to the young warrior to stop, given that he had not yet gained control, but it was too late.

Even as Corin attempted to dominate the third felrin, it was taking another bound forward, claws pointed towards Arex. As Corin's command to cease movement became embedded, the beast's extended claws skewered the stomach of the young Karn warrior, and then it cast him aside as it jerked to a stop. Arex flew several metres down the slope, his body spinning. There was an audible crack as he landed head first against the hard ground.

Menni was screaming with panic as the third felrin became locked into place, under Corin's power. This time, despite its need to protect Agbeth, Blackpaw lunged forward and buried both sets of front claws into the neck of the prone beast close to it. Whilst Blackpaw's left claws then remained in place, skewering its rival, the right arm repeatedly lifted and stabbed downwards. Blood splattered outwards, coating Blackpaw's fur.

Kernon ran out towards Arex's limp body, but from the way that the young warrior's neck was twisted at an unnatural angle, Corin already knew the outcome before his older brother announced, 'He's dead.'

As Menni wailed in reaction, Corin shouted, 'Get back in the circle, Kernon!'

Two of the three felrin that had already assailed them were now dead, and the other was incapacitated. Corin was aware that the fourth felrin must be due to arrive imminently, but he could also hear multiple other cries from every direction. He knew that if they stayed here, they were doomed.

'Corin!' bellowed a frightened Rennik, echoing this thought. 'We can't fight this many!'

Corin was feeling panic for himself, for Agbeth, and for all of the lives around him. His eyes scanned their surroundings in desperation. What could they do? Where could they go?

Then a picture flashed into his mind, an image which was coming from Blackpaw. The cave. The murky place which Blackpaw had been remembering. The felrin was speaking to Corin, letting him know that its old home was close to here. But was it close enough to provide possible sanctuary? There was no time to ponder, so Corin transmitted an urgent command to the beast.

LEAD US THERE! PROTECT AGBETH!

'This way!' Corin shouted, as Blackpaw reacted and began to move off.

At that moment, another felrin streaked onto their open slope from the south, charging directly towards them. Corin's response was immediate, sending out tendrils to lock the creature in place, which caused it to tumble forwards in their direction. He could see Nethmar starting to move towards the stricken beast, raising his great-axe high.

'Leave it!' Corin ordered. 'Follow me! Follow Blackpaw!'

He did not wait to see the outcome. He turned away and then placed a hand onto Menni's arm, forcibly dragging the frantic Karn woman along with him, in pursuit of Blackpaw. The felrin was soon setting a fast pace, its head turning to check in all directions as it moved. Corin could see Hellin in his peripheral vision as he ran, the older woman panting hard in the thin air as she tried to keep up.

Corin could also hear other footsteps crunching on the rocky ground behind him.

The cries of multiple additional felrin now rang across the valley as Corin's group fled. Indeed, there were a number of shrieks to the south, in the place where the party had made their first stand. Within these noises, Corin felt sure that a human-sounding scream had also echoed outwards, but he could not afford to stop and check who was still with him. His eyes were focused on Blackpaw's moving form, as the beast carried Agbeth.

They were now running through a narrow and winding passage of rock, with high walls to either side of them. If they were attacked from above here, they would likely be finished. All that they could do was to keep running, despite lungs which were struggling to take in air. At one point, Corin heard another human scream some distance behind them, which was quickly drowned out by a cacophony of felrin cries.

After what seemed like hundreds of fraught metres of running through this passageway, they emerged again into a wider and more open space. The ground here was flatter, and strangely more verdant, with a greater abundance of vegetation and greenery. And the sense of recognition within Blackpaw's mind was resounding. Although the creature did not have language, Corin could recognise the thought which flashed into its mind. *Home.*

THE CAVE! LEAD US TO THE CAVE!

The felrin started to move off to the left in response to the instruction. Corin followed, while taking note of who else was still with him. First, there was Menni, whose eyes were red, as if she had been crying whilst running. Next was Hellin, who was white-faced and panting heavily. Then Kernon, facing away from Corin, with axe still raised. Finally, Rennik was at the rear, looking grim and tired. There was no one else.

'The others?' Corin called out.

'Nethmar attacked the fourth felrin,' responded Rennik, as they moved. 'We didn't see him again. Charrek chose to remain behind, to defend the passage and to slow them.'

The human screams which Corin had heard were now explained. He was feeling shocked by the loss, and his lungs were burning, when they finally reached a narrow crevice. This appeared to slope downwards for ten metres to a cave-mouth at the end. At last, it seemed that there was a possible sanctuary, even if it was just a temporary one.

Corin was ready to follow Blackpaw into this cave, but the beast halted abruptly, then released an almighty roar in the direction of the entrance. Despite the burden of Agbeth on its back, the felrin crouched forwards with claws extended.

The answering howl from the cave was immediate, following which a grey and white beast, with claws out and jaws wide open, came barrelling out of the cave entrance towards Blackpaw. The two felrin clashed in a melee of savagery, ripping and slashing, before Corin had any opportunity to intervene.

STOP! STOP! STOP! STOP! STOP!

Even while Corin was feeling panic that one of the attacker's claws might impale Agbeth, his command was taking effect on the grey and white creature, and freezing it in place. Blackpaw did not cease its own violence, however, and blood splattered against the crevice walls as Blackpaw's claws penetrated into the enemy creature's stomach, and its jaws clamped hard on the foe's throat. After seconds of this, and an audible crunch as neck bones were shattered, the now limp enemy beast was tossed aside. Blackpaw then dropped down onto all four paws, before crawling under the low cave entrance.

Corin watched as Agbeth's form barely cleared the ceiling of that entrance, and then he ushered Hellin and Menni to follow Blackpaw. Cries from the pursuing pack of felrin sounded ever nearer, and both Rennik and Kernon were still facing away from Corin.

'Come on!' Corin shouted. 'Inside!'

He then followed Hellin and Menni, crouching down to enter the cave. He remained hunched over as he passed through a narrow, low tunnel. This extended for three metres, before emerging into a wider interior cave area which was perhaps five metres across, with a ceiling which was only slightly taller than Blackpaw. The space was illuminated by the dim light from the entrance passage, which revealed a dirt floor that was covered in bones and detritus. The place smelled rank.

But for Blackpaw, this small space had complete familiarity. For a long time, this had been the creature's home.

Corin watched as Kernon and Rennik both emerged through the passage, each looking as panicked as Corin himself felt. Corin could sense an urgent frustration within Blackpaw as the calls and shrieks of the other felrin came closer. The beast had moved to the mouth of the passageway at the cave entrance, and had crouched down. Corin knew what Blackpaw wanted.

'Quick!' he shouted. 'We need to get Agbeth and the frame off Blackpaw's back, so it can fight!'

Corin and the others worked as quickly as possible to release the straps which were holding the carrying frame to Blackpaw. Corin's hands were shaking, such that the task seemed to take longer than ever before. But then Agbeth was released, and Corin was lifting her free and was holding her in his arms. Separately, Rennik pulled the frame off Blackpaw's back.

Blackpaw then took up a position blocking the end of the entrance passageway. Kernon and Rennik both moved to its flanks, with weapons raised. Blackpaw howled after a number of seconds. It was a chilling, shrieking call, which was piercingly loud within the confines of the cave. The sound seemed to announce that this place was Blackpaw's territory, and that it would fight any rival which dared to enter.

Within moments, the call was answered by a cry which sounded like it was a few metres away, in the crevice outside. Then a second shriek, which seemed only slightly further back. Then many others, in the surrounding territory. Terrifying cries from multiple feral and deadly creatures, joining together. Howls that seemed to blend into one continuous and discordant chorus of menace.

Corin sought out the closest alien mind and was preparing himself to paralyse it. He was feeling exhausted from the run and from the thin air, and was also stunned by the rapid succession of losses that their group had suffered. But he knew that he could stop this next felrin. And the one which might follow it. But after that, how many others could he hold at bay? And how could they ever get out of here?

It seemed as if they were in the heartland of the felrin, and the growing clamour of calls from outside the cave suggested that more of the beasts were descending upon them. All eager to kill, and eager to feed.

As Corin was considering this, and steeling himself for what was to come, he heard the startling contrast of a gentle and familiar voice speaking to him.

'Corin?'

He looked down at the small form in his arms, and stared into Agbeth's eyes. She was awake. Alert. Returned. Communicating with him.

'Agbeth,' he said, his voice wavering.

'Corin.' Her eyes were blinking, adjusting to the murky light. 'Where are we?'

―

In the minutes that followed, the survivors of the group were clustered within the foul conditions of the cave.

Twice during this period, another felrin had threatened to attack. On both occasions, Corin had initially paralysed the hostile creature and had then compelled it to leave. After the second approach, there had been no more immediate attempts to breach their sanctuary. However, they were not being left alone.

Throughout this time, Blackpaw was their guardian and sentinel, blocking the entrance. The beast was vigilant for outside threats, and Corin was also observing the entrance passageway through its eyes.

Rennik and Kernon remained poised at the creature's side, with their weapons ready.

Hellin of Condarron and Menni were crouched in a hollow at the furthest recess of the cave. The younger woman was sobbing, and the missionary had placed an arm around her shoulder.

Corin and Agbeth were standing between these two groups, in the centre of the small enclosed space. Corin's arm was around his wife's waist, holding her tight to him. As a result of him focusing his attention on protecting the group, he and Agbeth had not yet had an opportunity to speak.

From the lands surrounding the cave, there was a continuous stream of aggressive noise. It seemed that scores of felrin were howling and shrieking in an unbroken chorus of deadly threat. Corin had no real idea as to how many were actually outside and waiting to pounce. However, after a few minutes of listening, he guessed that it might be upwards of a hundred of the creatures.

He knew that he could not allow himself to feel hopeless about their predicament. He had to think and to find a solution. But it was beyond his powers to control that many strong-willed felrin. If his group was to leave the cave now, and to return to the open spaces outside, they would be swarmed upon and ripped apart. They had already lost three members of their party to the beasts in just a matter of minutes.

'Fuck!' cursed Kernon, his voice echoing around the small enclosed area. The despair in his tone echoed Corin's own thoughts. 'Fuck!'

'I'll think of something, Kernon,' Corin replied, trying to sound calm. 'Just give me some time.'

'*I* don't have time, Corin,' responded Agbeth. 'You and I must speak, before it's too late.'

He turned to face her, feeling guilty. 'I'm sorry. You asked where we are, Agbeth. We're in the north. The far north. Searching for the…'

He did not finish the sentence, but he looked at her meaningfully. The continuing calls of the felrin outside provided a chilling accompaniment to his words.

'I understand,' she replied, nodding. 'You brought me, like you promised. Those are felrin outside?'

'Yes.'

He saw her shudder, then she whispered, '*He* sent me back, Corin. These howls awakened him again, and drew us both to the surface. You must speak with him.'

'What did he say, Agbeth?' asked Corin.

'That you must speak with him. *Before* you leave this cave. He says we're close, to the thing he can sense. But you must speak to him.'

Corin could see that Agbeth's eyelids were drooping already, and he knew that he was about to lose her again.

'I will, I'll speak to him.'

'And he said a word, Corin. I don't know if it's a name. But he whispered it to me, when I last heard him.'

'What word?'

Her speech was slurring. 'Kellon. Kellon…'

'Kellon? Is that his name?'

But she was already lost to him, slumped forward within his arms. Corin inhaled deeply, then took a few moments to compose himself.

'What are we to do, Chief Corin?' asked Rennik. The warrior appeared to be trying to remain stoic, but his voice contained a tremor.

Corin released the breath he had held, attempting to find control. At least there was now something that he could *try* to do.

'This is what we're going to do,' he said. 'Hellin, Menni, try to move all these bones and filth to the end of the cave. Clear some space for me to lie down with Agbeth. Menni, please try to be strong. We'll mourn them all properly later, but right now you must be brave and quiet. Kernon. Please stay calm, brother. I need you to be a great warrior. Kernon and Rennik, you must support Blackpaw to guard the entrance. Don't take your eyes from that passageway. Don't let anything in. If anything gets past the three of you, we're all dead. Because for what might be a long time, I won't be able to use my powers to keep the other felrin away. I won't be here, with you, and I won't see them coming.'

'Then where will you be, Chief Corin?' asked Hellin of Condarron, the first words she had spoken since arriving in the cave.

Corin noticed that the missionary was scrutinising him, and that there was a fascination in her regard. The cries of felrin continued to carry from outside as he returned her stare.

'I'm going to lie down,' he answered, 'and I'll close my eyes. And then I'm going to speak to the Gods.'

—

The chorus of felrin shrieks faded into the background of Corin's consciousness, as he entered Agbeth's sleeping mind and sought out the ghost.

AGBETH TOLD ME TO COME. ARE YOU THERE?

Yes, I am. And we're close. I can feel it more clearly now.

The presence's voice was still that of a boy. However, it sounded less distant.

WHAT IS IT? IS IT THE GATE?

I don't know. But it feels so... old. You must go there.

BUT WE'RE TRAPPED. WE CAN'T LEAVE HERE.

Yes, you can. But you must listen.

LISTEN TO WHAT? TO YOU?

To the song.

WHAT?

Listen to their song. I can hear it. Can you?

WHOSE SONG?

They're all around you. Speaking to you. You must listen.

STOP TALKING IN RIDDLES! WHO ARE *THEY*?

There was an extended silence after this, and Corin privately cursed himself for allowing his temper to flare. But just as he was beginning to wonder if he had driven the ghost away, he finally received a response.

I can hear them. They're all singing. Telling a story. You must listen to them.

LISTEN TO WHO?

The ones who are singing.

Corin tried to suppress his annoyance and frustration.

WHO ARE YOU?

I can't remember. But... did I tell you that I was murdered?

IS YOUR NAME KELLON?

Kellon? That sounds... familiar. But I don't know. Have you forgotten, too?

FORGOTTEN WHAT?

Again, there was a frustrated heat in Corin's reply, which he immediately regretted. And after waiting and drifting for a further extended period, hoping for another response, he eventually conceded defeat and acknowledged that the ghost was gone.

—

When Corin opened his eyes, he was lying flat on his back, with Agbeth asleep beside him. The cave was almost in darkness, other than for a flickering of light from the entrance passageway.

Corin turned to look that way. Blackpaw was still hunched there, guarding the entrance, and its chest was heaving. Kernon and Rennik were both close to the beast, but they were sitting now, with their weapons across their laps. They had also cleared a space around themselves, free of the detritus of the cave. The chilling and continuous cries of other felrin still resounded throughout the lands outside.

'You are returned to us, Chief Corin?' The voice was Hellin's. She sounded subdued and scared.

'Yes,' said Corin. 'How long have I been gone?'

Rennik turned his head, and said, 'Three to four hours. It's night now.'

'That long? Really? Is that light from a fire?'

'Yes. We managed to start a fire, at the end of the passage,' replied Rennik. 'Using some of the waste from the cave. It's kept them away for a while. But it's almost burnt out, and then we'll be in darkness.' There was weariness and defeat in Rennik's tone.

'Have there been any more attacks?' asked Corin.

'Only one,' said Rennik. 'One of the beasts tried to come up the passageway, to gain entrance. Blackpaw stopped it. None since then.'

Corin's gaze moved to his felrin, which had its own eyes focused down the passageway. Through their connection, he could feel that it was in pain. There were claw scrapes across its chest and arms, and lacerations on its neck. It was breathing heavily, and it was clearly fatigued.

'Well done, all of you,' said Corin.

'What are we going to do, Corin?' asked Kernon. The older brother's voice also sounded despondent. 'Listen to how many there are. We're going to die in this fucking cave.'

The wails and shrieks of the felrin carried eerily through the darkness. It seemed that there were even more discordant voices now than there had been when Corin had gone into his trance. It was an unbroken wall of terrifying sound, made by a multitude of feral creatures. Beasts that all seemed to have gathered in this place in order to kill Corin's party.

'We're not dead yet, Kernon. I'll find a way to get us all out of this,' Corin said, with more confidence than he felt. 'The Gods told me to do something.'

'What did your... *Gods*... tell you to do, Chief Corin?' asked Hellin.

Corin saw little point in concealing the answer from them. 'They told me to listen to the song.'

'What song?'

'I don't know. But everyone be quiet, please. I must listen.'

They did as he said, and they all waited silently within the darkened cave, as Corin attempted to hear the song that the ghost had referred to.

He closed his eyes and tried to concentrate, but the only sound that came to him was that of the masses of felrin which had gathered in the areas around the cave. A multitude of shrieking howls that pierced the night air then blended into another such call. And another, and another, in an uninterrupted cry of threat and fear.

Corin felt both annoyed and concerned. How could he ever hope to perceive the melody of a song whilst trying to shut out the discordant cacophony that the creatures were making? He needed them all to shut up and to allow him some silence, even for just a few seconds.

He opened his eyes again, feeling frustrated, and was alarmed to find that Blackpaw had turned away from the cave entrance, leaving the opening momentarily unguarded. The creature prowled towards him, such that its face was mere inches from Corin's, the tip of its snout close to touching his nose. Blackpaw's golden eyes were fixed upon Corin. For just a moment, they appeared to possess an intelligence which Corin had never recognised before.

Through their connection, Corin again received a hinted sensation that there was a memory within Blackpaw which had been closed off from the beast, and also from Corin. Something that was sealed away and contained. Something which was now tangibly close to being opened and revealed to them both.

Then Blackpaw opened its jaws, and the felrin emitted its own piercing shriek. At this close distance, the noise pained Corin's ears and blasted back the hairs on his head. Blackpaw's cry joined with those of the creatures outside, and as the sound faded away it seemed to blend into the calls of the other felrin.

Those cries carried on, ringing out into the night sky, even as Blackpaw paused. And then, for the first time, Corin heard *it*. And once he had recognised it, he felt foolish that he had been oblivious to what was there. That it had remained unknown to him, for this long.

But he could hear it clearly now. The call of the beasts, given shape and form. Melody, entwined and hidden within the apparent discord. Harmony within the chaos, calling to his consciousness and beckoning him to join in with their chorus. And to hear their story.

It was the Song of the Felrin.

And it was beautiful.

20

Allana

—

*Year of Our Lord,
After Ascension, 770AA*

Allana watched with appalled fascination as the battle at the Sept River Bridge took place in the valley before her.

She was standing on a hill at the edge of a wood, over two hundred metres away from the river and from the fighting. Her four personal guards were around her, and they were also surrounded by many other camp followers.

Allana was feeling safe, despite her proximity to the battle. This sense of security was derived mainly from the fact that the fast-flowing waterway lay between this vantage point and the killing grounds. All of the fighting was taking place on the southern side of the Sept River, with only Elannis and Berun soldiers on this northern side.

'You still think that we're winning, yes?' she asked the lead guard Connar, who was by her side.

'Yes, my Lady. As far as I can tell, the battle's going very well.'

She could see that he was careful not to allow his eyes to drift downwards across her body, as he said the words.

Allana liked the young officer. He had spent a lot of time in her company in the last week, being attentive in his assigned role of lead protector as their army had moved southwards. He had been particularly diligent whenever their column had arrived at hostile Western Canasar settlements, passing through places which had been pillaged by the army. However, his attentiveness had now morphed into something else.

He yearns for you, Lana. How easily you've begun to consume his thoughts.

The desire that she could sense in him was ever-present and building. Occasionally, she would allow invisible tendrils to ease into his mind, and would then enjoy watching his unwitting reaction as she teased his body with sensations of pleasure. However, she would never partake in more than that, despite being flattered by his attention. Given her new status, it would not be appropriate to have any dalliance with common soldiery.

'Tell me what's happening, now, then,' she ordered.

'Well, if you look to the far side of the bridge, my Lady,' Connar stated, gesturing as he spoke, 'you can see that we've pushed the enemy back, and we've a spearhead of troops on the south bank. That's Duke Berun's banner, just there. If that spearhead can push a little further forward, then all of our men will be able to cross the bridge, and we'll slowly overwhelm them.'

Allana shuddered as she looked past the wide, arched stone bridge. Somewhere down there, Jarrett was in the midst of that maelstrom of battle. He had told her that he was going to be dismounted for the bridge advance, and she could not pick him out despite his extraordinary size.

He'll survive to return to you, Lana. And he'll be a terror in battle. What man could possibly stand against Jarrett?

Allana could see the spearhead to which Connar referred. A mass of yellow and darker blue tabards had fought their way onto the far bank of the river, expanding outwards from the southern mouth of the bridge. This growing cluster must have represented upwards of a thousand men, but they were facing an even greater number of the lighter blue of Western Canasar.

On the bridge itself and on the near side of the Sept, thousands more Elannis and Berun infantry were still waiting to cross. In addition, hundreds of yellow-clad archers were arrayed along the river bank, firing waves of arrows into the body of the Western Canasar forces.

However, despite the intensity of this battle around the bridge, the location of the fiercest fighting appeared to be two hundred metres along the river, to the west. Elannis and Andar forces were also engaged in combat there, on the meadows beside the southern bank.

'And over there?' Allana asked, pointing in that direction.

'Over there, we appear to be winning, my Lady,' stated Connar. 'You can see that the Western Canasar lines are being driven back by Elannis pikemen. And that Prince Markon's cavalry are starting to move around the enemy's exposed flank. It looks like we heavily outnumber them there. Possibly by three-to-one. I doubt that they have the numbers to both hold the bridgehead and to stand against Markon's force.'

'Very good,' Allana replied, still feeling mesmerised by the sights and sounds of the spectacle.

The noises which were carrying to her from the river were awful to listen to, though admittedly also exciting. She could hear a constant clash of metal on metal, accompanied by cries of pain and anger.

Did you ever expect to find war so thrilling, Lana?

She understood from Jarrett that the invading army, which comprised of almost thirty thousand men, had split a couple of days earlier. Half of this force, including the contingent from Berun, had stayed on the main highway towards this Sept River Bridge. The remainder had been led off by Prince Markon El'Augustus, to cross the river at the place called Moss Ford.

When Jarrett's half of the army had arrived at this bridge, they had encountered a defending force of thousands, which had been positioned on the south side of the water. Jarrett's orders had been to establish a defensive line on the north bank of the river, holding those enemy troops in place until Markon arrived, after which Jarrett's forces were to attack.

Prince Markon's army, with its recognisable hawk and sun banner, had appeared just before lunchtime. Allana believed that the Western Canasar defenders must have been horrified when they had seen such a large force approaching on the south side of the river. The ensuing, bloody fighting had now been grinding away for over three hours.

But Arion is not with them, Lana. Your plan must have worked.

She had been relieved when she had first seen the army arrayed on the other side of the river, and had not been able to sense Arion there.

For the duration of the journey south, she had been wondering whether she would begin to feel his presence. Would begin to feel that wondrous sensation of his power and aura, as they drew closer together. A sensation that would mean that she had failed in her scheme to remove him from danger.

However, when she had realised that he was not there, she had felt satisfaction. True, she had manipulated him to encourage his departure from Western Canasar. And yes, he might well be upset about it, at first, when she was not in Andarron to meet him. But later, he would come to understand how much he should be grateful to her, for her clever plan. They had both now acted to save the life of the other. It made them even, but also bound them closer together.

You have probably saved his life, Lana. One day, he'll thank you.

She realised that tendrils had unconsciously eased out of her mind as she had been thinking about Arion. They had started to toy with the senses of the young officer, Connar. She glanced across and saw him standing awkwardly, with a glazed expression on his face.

This man is a loyal soldier of Berun, Lana, but he's obsessed with you. He'd do anything that you ask of him, for just a promise of what he craves.

She severed the invisible connection, and heard the guard gasp as the stimulation of his body suddenly ceased.

Allana was about to comment, but she was distracted by a tide of activity on the other side of the river, on the western edge of the battle. She could see the masses wearing light-blue tabards shifting backwards, followed by a surge forward by Markon's imperial troops.

'What's happening?' she asked, pointing.

The young guard looked flushed, and his voice cracked as he replied, 'It looks like the enemy's lines have broken. They've either sounded the retreat, or they're routing.'

As he was saying this, Allana watched the wall of yellow Elannis tabards continuing to charge forwards, and it seemed that the Western Canasar soldiers were running away. Allana's eyes swept across to the bridgehead, where the forces in light-blue tabards were also now retreating. Thousands of Elannis and Berun troops were pouring across the bridge in pursuit, spreading out into the fight as they reached the other side. Allana hoped that Jarrett was still unharmed, in the midst of that activity.

'Have we won?' she asked.

'Yes. They're fleeing now. You can see that Markon's cavalry are chasing them, and our armies are coming together. We've definitely won.'

From the shifting sweeps of colour on the battlefield, Allana could perceive what Connar was describing. The Elannis infantry from the west was joining up with the forces at the bridge, while the men of Western Canasar were fleeing, running for their lives as yellow-clad cavalry pursued them. It was clear that victory had been secured.

Allana smiled, feeling exhilaration, her heart beating fast. She recognised that a number of men had died today, which was of course very sad. However, it appeared that a massive milestone had been achieved towards the completion of Jarrett's plan, which was much more important.

Just let Jarrett be unharmed, Lana. Then the day will be perfect.

—

Later that day, the mass of army followers crossed the river to set up a sprawling new encampment, a mile to the south. Allana was part of a long column which threaded its way through the aftermath of the battlefield. She kept her eyes lifted upwards throughout this process, focusing on a treeline on the horizon, and she did her best to ignore the dead bodies and anguished moaning which surrounded her.

During this time, a Berun officer found Allana, and notified her that the duke was alive and well.

In the early evening, Jarrett returned to their shared tent. He had removed his armour and was unhurt, except for some livid bruising on his upper left arm. After he pulled off his shirt to show her this, Allana almost pounced upon him. His eagerness matched hers as she dragged him with hunger onto their bed.

Afterwards, she was curled within his thick arms. As they lay there, he talked about the battle.

'I've proven myself today, Lana,' he said. 'Finally. I fought as part of the vanguard which crossed that bridge, and no one could stand against me. And The Lord was with me, lending strength to my arm and to our crusade. I must have cut down ten men, and I could see the terror in the eyes of those poor souls who had to face me.'

'I can believe it, Jarrett,' she said. 'You're a giant amongst men. No one should dare to face you, as you fight for The Lord's cause.'

As if a man of Jarrett's size and strength needs The Lord to help, Lana.

'And at the end, when they broke in the centre, it was my doing, Lana! Me and the men of Berun.'

'Was it? How?'

'I cut down their military leader. Charl Koss. He came at me as we were breaking through. Almost had me, if you'd believe it; he was fast and strong for an old bastard. And he took some killing, I was fighting for my life. But The Lord was with me, Lana. At the end, I shattered Koss's shield with one blow and almost chopped him in half with the next. After that, his men broke and ran!'

Allana shuddered, remembering the aged adviser from her time in Septholme Castle. Koss had once allied with Gerrion Sepian, to try to bully Allana to leave Western Canasar. But another time, in the moments before Duke Conran had died, had he not also offered to protect her from Aiduel's Guards? Best not to dwell on that. Either way, the old man was dead now, at Jarrett's hand.

Better him than Jarrett, Lana. Koss would never have accepted you as his duchess.

'He was a fool to fight you,' she said. 'And what about the Sepian brothers, Jarrett? Were they there? Did you capture or kill them?'

She heard Jarrett exhale. 'Pair of cowards. Arion Sepian, I couldn't see him on the battlefield. I want to face him, Lana. Face him in combat and make amends for... past insults. But he wasn't there, damn him. He must be hiding in Septholme.'

Good, Lana. You wouldn't want them to kill each other, would you?

'And Duke Gerrion Sepian?'

'I saw him fleeing on horseback, at the end of the battle. I was close to breaking through to him, when Koss came at me. Markon's cavalry are pursuing him though. We'll have him soon.'

Allana turned to kiss his chest. 'Western Canasar should be ruled by a duke who's a hero, Jarrett. Not by a coward.'

'I know. They should call me the Hero of the Sept River Bridge for what I did today.'

'They should,' she agreed, smiling to herself. 'You're truly blessed by The Lord, Jarrett. And after your great victory, what's going to happen next?'

'Tomorrow, we move southwards. We get to Septholme within days, and we take the town as soon as possible. Once we've done that, we can join up with the Dei Magnun navy. But before any of that, Lana, we've an important engagement tonight.'

'Tonight? What is it?'

'Prince Markon has invited us to dine with him in his tent.'

Allana felt a thrill of excitement as she heard those words.

Later that evening, the two of them were dining in the impressive tent which had been claimed by Prince Markon. This structure was in an elevated position, with its canvas open at one side, such that they had an unobstructed view of the vast military camp which encircled them. Allana's line-of-sight also included the teeming Aiduel's Guards' enclosure, which she was trying hard to ignore.

Allana had donned her red velvet riding outfit, which felt appropriate for a close encounter with the Elannis royal. Something feminine but not dainty, with material which drew attention to her curves. Within moments of meeting the prince, she had sensed a stirring of desire within Markon, which suggested that he was approving of her choice.

Allana was aware that the prince's attraction towards her had been growing throughout the course of the meal, particularly after the royal had finished two glasses of wine. However, Markon remained business-like throughout and was continuing to direct most of his attention to Jarrett.

This prince hides his desires well, Lana. Jarrett has no idea what his host has been feeling, during this meal. Or indeed, what you are thinking about.

Being in the company of this man, who might one day rule the world, offered an opportunity for an intoxicating fantasy. A teasing temptation, that there might be someone who could offer her even more protection and security than Jarrett. At the side of a future emperor, the likes of Aiduel's Guards would never again be able to hurt her. Even the Holy Church would not dare to threaten such a man and his empress.

However, there was no way that she could contemplate acting upon such fanciful thoughts right now, here and in these circumstances. And such a course of action would inevitably hold substantial risks.

You're committed to Jarrett, Lana. Aren't you?

She shivered, but neither of the two men noticed. She realised then that she had become distracted, but the mention of a certain name led her to focus on the conversation again.

'A pity we didn't face Arion Sepian,' Markon was saying. 'I long to see him in chains, and worse, for what he did to me and to my army.'

'I understand that,' said Jarrett. 'And we both have reasons to dislike Arion Sepian, Your Highness. He's faithless. He once attacked me, unprovoked, because he had a distaste for my own faith and piety. I long to avenge that moment.'

'He's a dangerous man though,' replied Markon. 'And from what little I saw of him, when we met, I also disliked him. He possessed an arrogance, and an anger which was barely contained. And he had no respect either, making threats to my men to cut me up. I've a debt to repay to him, for what he did.'

'I fully understand your upset for what he did to your army, Your Highness,' said Allana, attempting to reinsert herself to the conversation. 'I must admit though, that I'm a little confused about what happened to you. The story I've heard is that Sepian ran you through with his sword? And yet you sit here today, with no indication that you've ever suffered a wound? As healthy, strong and full-of-life, as any man I've ever seen.'

She had intended for her words to flatter Markon. However, from his grimace, she could see that she had stirred a painful memory.

'Sepian cut me down,' said the prince. He lifted his hand to sweep his shock of blonde hair back from his face, and his deep blue eyes fixed upon Allana as he replied. 'He thrust his sword into me and gutted me. I was a dead man, and would have bled out within minutes. However, I was saved by another, a miracle-worker, in a story which is less well-known. In the name of Aiduel, she saved my life and restored me to health.'

'A miracle-worker?' repeated Jarrett. 'Please, tell me more.'

'She used her powers to heal me,' said Markon. 'I'm told that she was bathed in a holy golden light, and that she knitted my flesh back together. The Holy Church says that she's been blessed by Aiduel and has worked countless other miracles. You may have heard of her? Priestess Leanna, the Angel of Arlais?'

Allana's mouth was dry as she listened to this.

The stories of her being a miracle-worker are true, Lana. She really does have powers. Is she like you?

'Isn't that the woman who everyone is searching for?' asked Jarrett. 'The one on the poster?'

'Yes, that's come to my attention,' replied Markon. 'There's a strong possibility that she may have been kidnapped and taken to Andar. Aiduel's Guards are accompanying the army to search for her. If my troops can assist in finding Priestess Leanna, I'll consider it a partial repayment of my debt to her, for saving my life. Indeed, you will have noticed that I've recently allowed the red-cloaks to be more... active, and independent. In their crusading activities in general, but more specifically in their search for the priestess. If she's captive here, we must find her and deliver her to their safekeeping. I owe her that. Truly, I've never met one so blessed by Aiduel.'

'May The Lord protect her, then, until we find her and bring her to safety,' said Jarrett, in a sombre voice.

'May The Lord protect her,' stated Markon, nodding in approval.

While the prince had been speaking about this Leanna woman, Allana had noticed that his desire for her had been fading away, as if he had become distracted by purer thoughts. She felt annoyed.

Must everyone be so obsessed with this woman, Lana? The things she can do are as nothing, compared to what you can do. You just choose to keep your powers secret, rather than showing them off to the whole world!

'Was she beautiful?'

She had asked the question before giving proper consideration to her words. She felt regret as soon as she witnessed the strange looks which Jarrett and Markon turned on her.

'Beautiful?' repeated Markon, frowning. 'Well, yes, I suppose so. But she's a priestess, so I'm not sure that's particularly important, is it?' He then smiled and added, 'What a very peculiar thing to ask.'

As he said this, Allana could feel the prince's attraction towards her waning further, and she secretly cursed herself.

She must have looked crestfallen, because Jarrett reached out to touch her arm, and said, 'No doubt not as beautiful as you, my love.'

Allana attempted a wan smile, but the expression did not reach her eyes.

—

The next day, the invading army was headed southwest, in the direction of Septholme. Allana was riding within the moving column, close to the rear, in the company of her personal protectors.

At mid-morning, a large mounted force of Aiduel's Guards started to ride past her. The red-cloaked soldiers were also heading southwards, with an open-topped wagon in tow. Allana's heart began to beat faster.

You don't need to fear them anymore, Lana. You were absolved by Kohn.

Despite that absolution, she still felt uneasy to be this close to the red-cloaks, and she watched them carefully as they passed. She was also wondering whether Nionia might be amongst them, but she did not spot the lanky guardswoman.

Allana had given much consideration as to what Aiduel's Guards were intending to do now that they had returned to Andar. She hated the idea that they would once again be free to commit their evil. She was trying to ignore the accusing voice inside which suggested that Jarrett's choices had led to this, and that she had supported his decisions in order to protect herself.

They would have come here eventually, Lana, whatever Jarrett had decided. It's not Jarrett's fault that they're here, and it's certainly not yours. It's not!

Later, just before midday, Allana's section of the column began to pass through a large village on the highway. This settlement appeared to have already fallen victim to the transit of the army, because several buildings were on fire, and it looked like it had been looted.

The location had also become a focus for Aiduel's Guards. Upwards of fifty of the military order were spread out around a green in the centre of the village, in front of a church. The red-cloaks were surrounding a cluster of several hundred villagers. It appeared as if the entire population of the settlement had been assembled, and Allana could see fear on the villagers' faces as they were addressed by a red-cloaked officer. A number of smaller children were crying.

Allana noticed several motionless bodies lying near to the feet of the officer. She brought her horse to a stop at the side of the highway, and signalled for her personal guards to halt as she looked more closely. One of the victims was a man who wore the vestments of a priest. This figure was slumped on his side, his eyes open and lifeless. Allana could see that his face was bloody and swollen, as if he had received a vicious beating.

Aiduel's Guards have beaten him to death, Lana.

She shivered, then heard the red-cloaked officer shout, 'All women under the age of forty and teenage girls, step forward. Line up along this line. Now!'

There was resistant murmuring in the crowd. However, after a number of armed Aiduel's Guards stepped closer to the surrounded villagers, the will of the entrapped group appeared to break. The younger women and girls started to move through the assembled crowd, lining up as directed. In total, perhaps sixty women and children had come forward.

'My Lady,' said Connar, with discomfort in his voice. 'We should be moving on.'

'Not now,' Allana replied. 'I want to see this.'

As she watched, two Aiduel's Guards began to move down the line. They were holding a document in their hand, which Allana recognised as the poster of the Angel of Arlais. As they passed each girl and woman, they either directed her back into the clustered villagers, or pushed her towards their officer. It quickly became apparent that those unfortunates who were selected fitted a particular type; younger, between late-teens and mid-twenties, and slim and tall rather than plump and short. All were blonde-haired.

After this process was complete, four young women had been separated into a small cluster near the officer. Allana heard the red-cloaked man shout, 'Right, get them onto the wagon.'

There was more protestation from the villagers, accompanied by pleading from two of the selected women as they were bundled towards the vehicle.

'What's happening, my Lady?' asked Connar.

'I think that they're taking these women, for... *questioning*,' she replied.

Even as she spoke the words, she could feel a mounting anger and darkness inside herself. This evil had been allowed back into Andar as a result of the Elannis invasion. How was Allana to know that these young women were not going to face what she had once suffered, in the terror of an Aiduel's Guards fortress?

These women need help, Lana. But there's nothing for you to gain by intervening here, so why do you feel that you must do something?

The answer came to her quickly.

Because you hate Aiduel's Guards, Lana. Hate them so much!

For seconds, as she sat there watching, she could sense the blackness inside of herself. She could touch it. It was calling to her, ready to be used to protect these women. To stop Aiduel's Guards from inflicting upon them what had once been done to her. To save them from the horror.

She shuddered again, then began to reach for the darkness...

At that moment, the officer of Aiduel's Guards turned around. For the first time, he took note of Allana and her protectors, and as he looked up at Allana she felt a jolt of shock. She recognised him.

She had met him just once before, in the courtyard of Septholme Castle, on a day which had changed her life. He had been a sergeant of the Guards accompanying Nionia dei Pallere, when Nionia had recognised Allana. It had been the encounter which had led to Duke Conran's death and to Allana's imprisonment. She could not remember this man's name, but she would never forget the hostile face.

'My Lady,' the officer said in a Dei Magnun accent, bowing his head. Then his brows furrowed and he added, 'Have we met before, my Lady?'

Any thoughts which Allana might have harboured about intervening in the fate of the four women were now gone. She just wanted to be away from here.

'I don't think so, unless you've been to Berun,' she replied, trying to disguise her own accent. She then turned to her guards. 'Come. We must move on.'

They started to ride away southwards with the last remnants of the column, unchallenged by the officer. Allana risked one backwards glance when they were thirty metres from the village green. The officer was still staring towards her, with a puzzled look on his face.

—

That evening, Allana was back with Jarrett, outside of their tent, in the latest overnight encampment.

Jarrett was in an ebullient mood. Earlier in the day, Elannis cavalry had forced the surrender of over five hundred fleeing soldiers of Western Canasar. Those soldiers were now being held captive at the southern end of the camp.

'We're just days from Septholme, Lana, and they're broken,' Jarrett said. 'I doubt that they have more than a thousand of their original army left as an effective fighting force, if even that. This campaign will be over in a couple of weeks, perhaps less. After that, I'll start to restore the true faith here, and I'll have a new duchy.'

'And a new duchess?' she asked.

'Yes, that too. Soon. I want us to wed soon.'

As he was saying this, a score of yellow-tabarded Elannis cavalry appeared in the distance, riding fast through the encampment in the direction of Markon's tent. Allana and Jarrett stood up to peer towards them.

Allana observed that one of the horses was being led, and that it appeared to have a body trussed up over the back. The black-haired head and the arms of the person slumped across the horse were hanging downwards. Other than bobbing with the movement of the animal, the figure was motionless.

'What is it, Jarrett?' she asked.

He was squinting towards the riders, who were halting outside Prince Markon's tent.

'I'm going to go closer to be certain,' he replied. 'But, if I'm not mistaken, I believe that The Lord has ensured that this campaign is as good as over.'

Allana looked again at the unmoving body on the horse, following Jarrett as he walked towards Markon's tent. It was now easier to see the trussed figure, given that the accompanying riders had come to a halt there.

And then Allana recognised the person who was slumped across the back of the horse, though she could not perceive if they were alive or dead.

It was Duke Gerrion Sepian.

21

Leanna

―

*Year of Our Lord,
After Ascension, 770AA*

Leanna felt relief when Septholme finally came into view to the south, visible from over a mile away.

The coastal town's tightly-packed buildings blanketed the mighty hill which climbed from the seafront, while the majestic fortress of Septholme Castle crowned that same peak. Imposing stone walls could be seen to surround the whole town, skirting the clifftops which ran on the landward side of the hill, and abutting with the defences of the castle at the highest point.

Arrival at the town's northern gate and wall would finally signify the end of Leanna's arduous journey south through the coastal areas of Western Canasar. Her party had been fleeing southwards for several days, ever since the bloody encounter with the Elannis scouts. Following that battle, Leanna had tied her hair up and had covered it with a makeshift headscarf. Since then, for most of the time, her party had steered clear of any major highways, fearful of who they might encounter there.

Even with this precaution, two days into the journey they had spotted another group of Elannis horsemen in the distance. Leanna's party had immediately hastened away from the trail that they were on, and had pushed deep into the surrounding woodland, fearful of pursuit. Thankfully, the Elannis cavalry had ridden away.

On another occasion, Leanna and her companions had encountered a larger column of refugees. The leaders of that group had described seeing dozens of Aiduel's Guards attacking a small village to the north. This news had caused Leanna to shiver with fear; it was clear that Western Canasar had become a very dangerous place, and that the entire countryside was at risk from the invaders.

Leanna's muscles were now sore from the prolonged exertion, her stomach ached with hunger, and she felt dirty. Amyss was in a worse state of exhaustion. At this moment, the petite woman was sitting on the back of their horse, leaning forwards. Caddin Sendromm was leading the animal, the burly man seemingly unaffected by the hardships of the last few days.

They had joined the main road to Septholme a couple of hours earlier, and they were no longer travelling alone. This highway was busy with other citizens of Western Canasar, a stream of refugees who were also fleeing from the approaching hostile armies. Septholme, with its garrison and high walls, was a destination which had become common to many of them.

Leanna was viewing the town as a sanctuary from the adversity of the last few days, and a place where she could hopefully eat a proper meal and find a bed to sleep in. She also continued to hope that Arion would be there, although she had become more doubtful about that as they drew closer. She knew that it was possible that he would be away from the town, leading his armies into battle again, somewhere to the north.

She would soon find out, one way or another. Once she reached Septholme, she would be able to sense him if he was still there.

'Look over there,' Caddin Sendromm said, breaking an extended silence. He was pointing to the west, out to sea.

It was a surprise to Leanna to hear him speak. Other than to comment on matters of practicality, Caddin had been withdrawn and sullen since Leanna had witnessed his hidden memories. On two further occasions she had offered to help him, and had asked him to divulge his secrets. She had also warned that she would insist on parting company at Septholme, if he chose to continue to conceal what he knew. Both times, Sendromm had offered no response other than an awkward grimace.

Leanna looked towards the ocean and quickly identified what Caddin was referring to. A line of tall-masted ships was visible on the choppy waters to the west of Septholme's harbour.

'I see them,' she said. 'What does it mean?'

'They're Dei Magnun,' he replied. 'Could be a blockade. If it is, there'll be no aid or supplies coming to Septholme by sea. Better that we avoid the town and keep heading south.'

Leanna stared at the ships in the distance for a few moments, considering her options.

Lord Aiduel, please help me to choose the right path.

She frowned at Sendromm, then shook her head and said, 'There is no "we", Caddin, while you hide the truth of what you know. This land and these roads have become too dangerous for me and Amyss. I'd rather be within that town, behind its walls, where I'll no longer have to rely on you.'

She returned her focus to the road ahead, and to the entrance to Septholme. Despite her warnings, the grey-bearded man seemed determined to keep his secrets. She and Amyss would therefore reach the relative safety of the town, and would travel to the castle. She would then say goodbye to their secretive protector.

Lord Aiduel, please give us the strength to reach our destination.

She carried on walking.

—

They were soon queueing before the northern gate to the town, awaiting their turn to be questioned by one of the dozen guards who were manning the entrance. Amyss had dismounted, and Caddin held the reins of their horse.

The walls of Septholme were even more impressive from this perspective. The towering fortifications started at the end of the harbour peninsula, then ran inland, intersected by the two square towers which flanked this northern gate. After reaching a further tower several hundred metres inland, the wall turned sharply, then followed the edge of the hill up towards the castle.

The entrance to the town was through an arched stone tunnel with open gates at either end, and several raised portcullises in between. The guards stationed here were questioning everyone at the front of the queue, and Leanna noted with concern that many refugees were being turned away.

When her party eventually reached the front, they were approached by an Andar soldier in his early thirties. This guard's face was dark with stubble, and the red lines in his eyes gave a suggestion of his fatigue.

He turned to Caddin and asked, 'What's your business here?'

Sendromm replied, 'We're refugees, sir, as you can probably see. Fleeing the invasion to the north. I'm bringing my daughters to seek refuge here.'

The guard's gaze moved across them, taking note of their dirty clothes and their meagre possessions. 'No food with you? No other provisions?'

'Just what you can see,' replied Caddin. There was none of the affability which Leanna had witnessed in Sendromm's previous interactions with soldiery. The grey-bearded man seemed dispirited and glum.

The stubbled guard frowned, and Leanna was becoming concerned that he would turn them away.

'I know Lord Arion and Lady Kalyane,' she said. 'In fact, I'm friends with Lord Arion. We intend to visit him at the castle.'

Lord Aiduel, please let us be allowed to enter.

'You know Lord Arion?' the guard said, sounding sceptical. 'You and half of Western Canasar know the Sepian family, judging from today's conversations. If you've no supplies, why should I let you into the town, in the midst of a war?'

'We're healers,' stated Amyss, calmly. 'All of us. And Father can fight. That's why.'

'Healers?'

'Yes,' said Caddin, with what sounded like forced enthusiasm. 'We're all healers, and two of us have experience in field surgery at war. If there's a battle coming here, there's plenty of people who might benefit from us being around. And if it comes to it, as my daughter said, I can fight.'

The guard frowned again, before gesturing to the tunnel. 'Very well. Carry on.'

Leanna exhaled, and they started to pass through the tunnel under the stone arch, between the two large towers. As they were emerging at the other end, she heard a disturbance of clopping horse hooves and shouting behind them.

She turned to see a group of four Andar cavalrymen galloping along the road from the north, urging people to get out of their way. These horsemen then reined in their mounts in front of the guards at the arched gateway. The lead rider was a rugged-looking bald man, who shouted with authority to the assembled guardsmen.

'We're defeated in the north, and routed! What's left of our army is in retreat, with Elannis and the traitors of Berun in pursuit. I must ride to the castle and deliver the news. Be ready for any of our surviving soldiers who make it back here. Get as many of them into the town as we possibly can, but be alert for enemy advance riders, and be ready to close the gates.'

'Come on,' stated Caddin, whilst pulling the horse and ushering Amyss away from the end of the tunnel. Leanna followed him just in time, as the bald-headed soldier and his colleagues urged their horses past them. The riders had left behind an agitated bustle amongst the gate guards and the waiting queue.

'We're inside, at least,' said Amyss. 'What now, Lea?'

'We go to the castle,' replied Leanna. 'But before we do that, Caddin, please walk away from me.'

'I'm not leaving yet,' stated Sendromm, his voice glum. 'I'll deliver you to the castle, at least.'

'No, not that,' said Leanna. 'For now, I just want your medallions to be away from me. Just go over there, please.'

Caddin did as instructed, and Leanna could feel her powers reigniting from their dormancy after the medallions were removed from her vicinity. And with the return of her power, she knew immediately that a major part of the reason for her journey here was in vain. She could not sense Arion Sepian. He was not in Septholme.

She paused for a moment, considering, and then said, 'To the castle, then. Let's go.'

—

The town was more crowded than Leanna remembered, although the lively street noises from her first visit had been replaced by an undercurrent of anxiety.

Upon reaching the higher approaches to the castle, Leanna was able to gain a much clearer view of the Dei Magnun naval blockade. The foreign navy could be seen half a mile out to sea, a fleet of ten ships which formed a formidable barrier arrayed around the port.

At the narrow mouth of the Septholme harbour, stretching between matching towers built at the tips of the north and south peninsulas, a massive metal chain had been raised from the water. Directly behind this, forming a secondary barrier within the waters of the harbour itself, was a row of ships which appeared to have been attached together. These were a variety of sizes, with one much larger than the others. It appeared that there was no way to enter or leave Septholme by sea.

As she neared the castle entrance, Leanna turned to face Caddin. In a gentle tone, she said, 'Have you changed your mind, Caddin? Are you willing to tell us everything you know about what I am and what my powers mean?'

The burly man stared at her. For a moment, it seemed that his face assumed a look of anguish. However, this was swiftly replaced by a grimace and he said, 'The events of my past are my own business. I've only tried to do good by you, Priestess Leanna. And I seek to continue to do good. But you leave me with no choice.'

'Is that a "no" then?'

Sendromm said nothing in response. His eyes looked down at the floor.

Lord Aiduel, how am I to help this man, when he refuses to help himself?

'Very well,' said Leanna, feeling troubled but resolved. 'You may leave us here, then. I want to help you, Caddin. To use The Lord's powers to *heal* you. I truly do. But if you insist on concealing the truth from us, then I can't trust you, and I no longer want your company. Do you agree, Amyss?'

'Well, you know I don't like this,' said the petite priestess, looking uncomfortable. 'But I suppose so, yes.'

Sendromm grimaced again and said, 'So be it. Let me see you safe in the castle, then you'll be free of me.'

Leanna felt saddened by his decision. 'That is your choice?'

'It is.'

The guards at the castle entrance were even less welcoming than those at the town gates. Indeed, they refused entry to Leanna's party, even after Leanna insisted that she was a friend of Lord Arion, and then implored them to mention her name to Lady Kalyane.

It was only following an hour of waiting that Leanna and her companions were finally allowed entry into the courtyard beyond. One of the guards acknowledged gruffly that Lady Kalyane had indeed recognised Leanna's name, and he offered to escort Leanna to the Great Hall.

Before she could accept this offer, Caddin Sendromm said, 'I'll take my leave now, then.' He patted the flank of his horse. 'I'm going to lead her to the stables, to see if they'll agree to stable her here. I'll take your things off her and give them to a castle retainer to watch for you. Then I'll go.'

'I'm sorry it's come to this, Caddin,' Leanna said, making no move towards the man. 'But I wish you well. May The Lord watch over you and bring you peace.'

Amyss was less restrained. She moved forward and wrapped her arms around the burly man's waist, then hugged him and said, 'Take care, Caddin. May you go in the Grace of Aiduel.'

Caddin reached out a hand. For a moment, it appeared that he was about to return the hug. However, he stopped his motion, and instead his large fingers pried her away from him.

Leanna and Amyss then moved away, following the guard. At the moment when Leanna felt her powers once again blossoming into life, she glanced back. Caddin was standing where they had left him, leaning with his forehead against the neck of his horse. One of his hands was stroking the animal's forelock, whilst the other rested on the coil of rope which still hung from the saddle.

—

Lady Kalyane Sepian was sitting at the table of the Great Hall of Septholme Castle when Leanna and Amyss were taken through to meet her. Troubled emotions were beating out from the auburn-haired woman.

FEAR. WORRY. FEAR. SORROW.

There were two others at the table with Kalyane; one was the bald-headed horseman who Leanna had seen at the town gate, and the other was a teenaged girl who appeared to have been crying. Sorrowful emotions were emanating from the girl, whilst the soldier seemed close to overcome with stress and fatigue.

Leanna observed that Lady Kalyane was making a determined effort to compose herself, after she had noted Leanna's arrival.

'Priestess Leanna, Priestess Amyss,' said Kalyane, 'come take a seat with me. You both look... as if your journey here has been hard. I didn't expect to see you two, of all people, today. Please excuse me if the guards have kept you waiting.'

'Please, don't concern yourself with that,' said Leanna. 'You must have so much to deal with. Thank you for agreeing to see us.'

As Leanna approached the table, the bald-headed man stood and said, 'My Lady, with your permission, I must take my leave. There's much I have to arrange.'

'Of course, Captain,' replied Kalyane. 'You may go.'

Following the man's departure, Leanna took a seat and said, 'I'd come to see Arion – sorry, *Lord* Arion – but he's not here? And I understand that there's been terrible news today?'

'He's not here, no. Just me and Lady Karienne,' said Kalyane, gesturing to the teenage girl. 'And you're right, Priestess Leanna, there's been much terrible news. Lord Arion is trapped in Andarron, on the other side of the country. He's not with us, when we need him most. And Captain Thatcher has just finished informing me that the armies of Western Canasar have been defeated and routed, in a major battle at the Sept River Bridge. The survivors are retreating here as we speak, pursued by armies of Elannis and Berun.'

'I can feel your grief, my Lady.'

'That's not all, I'm afraid. Thatcher has also informed me that a dear friend of this family, Charl Koss, has been killed. And my brother-in-law, Duke Gerrion, is missing. We fear that he's also dead.'

After Kalyane had said this, the girl Karienne made a sobbing noise.

'And there's no one else to help,' continued Kalyane, 'with my own family facing invasion in Rednar. I'll send another bird with this latest news, but I doubt they'll be able to come. Can you believe it, Priestess Leanna? An army of Elannis and Berun is descending on Septholme, to attack or besiege us. A wave of refugees is heading for the town. The harbour is blockaded by a large and hostile foreign navy. And *I* am in charge. I'd laugh at how ridiculous it is, if not for the grief that I'm feeling.'

Indeed, as the auburn-haired woman made this statement, there was another rush of emotions from her, to confirm the truth in her words.

Lord Aiduel, please deliver comfort and guidance to this good woman.

'Do you have any advisers to support you, Lady Kalyane?' asked Amyss.

'Just Captain Thatcher, now. He's the most senior member of the army who's returned so far. But he admits himself that he has no real experience of siege warfare. He'll do his best, I'm sure. But I have to decide whether I'm to surrender the town.'

'And what do you think you should do?' asked Leanna.

'I really don't know. I pray that Duke Gerrion is alive and is on his way back here, to take this decision away from me. But Gerrion was very explicit that no town of Western Canasar is to surrender, I know that much. And neither Arion or Gerrion would want me to surrender Septholme; it would signify the end of House Sepian's rule in Western Canasar, and Arion would never forgive me. But now that I face this awful reality, I'm also thinking about the people here, about the citizens and surviving soldiers. About how many of them will die, if we don't surrender. About my duty to *them*. I just don't know.'

'We've no experience of these matters, either, Lady Kalyane,' said Leanna, still sensing the woman's distress. 'But if you would like us to stay here to support you, and to hold you in our prayers at this difficult time, then we'll do so. And… I'm a healer. That may be of help.'

Kalyane looked directly at her and said, 'I would like that, Priestess Leanna. I remember your… *connection*, to Arion. You are very welcome to stay here.'

'Leanna, I've just had a thought,' said Amyss. 'Caddin… the things he did, the battle you said he took part in. He was a soldier. A very senior soldier. Could we ask Caddin to stay, and to help Lady Kalyane?'

Leanna turned to face her companion, uncertain whether Amyss was being serious. As she was about to reply, an abrupt realisation came, and the world seemed to lurch around her.

Caddin Sendromm. Standing beside his horse. Preparing to leave the animal behind. A rope in his hand.

His earlier statements of, *'you leave with me no choice,'* and, *'then you'll be free of me,'* were suddenly given a stark new meaning.

She was stricken with a terrible sense that something awful was about to happen. That it was already happening.

She jolted to her feet, and started running towards the castle courtyard, before anyone had an opportunity to ask her what she was doing.

—

She found him in the stables, his body hanging from the rafters.

One end of the length of rope was attached to the wooden beam which ran beneath the roof. The other was tied in a noose around his neck.

His face was covered by a hood, but the flesh on his neck was raw from where the coarse rope was cutting into it. At the end of his hulking form, close to a stool which had been kicked over and a mace which rested on the floor, there was the slightest twitch from his right foot.

Leanna started to scream for help as she ran to the hanging body. She wrapped her arms around his lower legs, clasped her hands together, and tried with all of her might to lift him. But he was too heavy, and she barely moved him, his body tilting slightly so that the rope stayed taut.

Lord Aiduel, Lord Aiduel, Lord Aiduel! Please help me!

She did not have sufficient physical strength to raise his form, and once again she could feel her inner powers being subdued by the medallions on his person.

Outwardly, she heaved with every fibre of muscle, whilst internally she strained with the entire residue of her willpower.

Desperation powered her efforts, as she strove to overcome the neutralising effect of the medallions.

Then, for the first time, there was something in reach. The slightest reaction. Whispers of ethereal fingers materialised, assisting her, and helping her to push. A shimmering of golden light started to wrap around their two forms, despite the close proximity of the medallions.

After that, it was easier to raise him, as the invisible fingers pushed at his now motionless body. It was not much, but she was achieving something; holding him up, just slightly, such that the rope was no longer completely taut.

Amyss and others found them that way. Two figures bathed in a pale light. Leanna was kneeling with her eyes squeezed shut in strain, and with her arms hugging the legs of the hanging form. Her hands were clasped together, as if she was praying.

Caddin no longer moved.

—

Later, Leanna and Amyss were sitting to either side of Caddin Sendromm's still form, in quarters which Lady Kalyane had granted to them.

For a long time, Caddin did not speak. A despairing expression was on his face, and the skin on his neck was raw from the grip of the rope. But he was alive.

Eventually, he said, 'Did you... look inside my mind? Did you get your answers?'

'No, I didn't,' said Leanna, gently. 'I won't force myself again, to where I'm not invited.'

'I'm sorry,' he said, his voice hoarse. 'For putting you through that.'

'Please, don't be sorry. I'm so sorry, Caddin, that you felt that you had no alternative but to do that. And... that, I'd not understood... your despair. Not fought harder to help you. I ordered you away when you were clearly desperate.'

'I deserved it,' he said. 'I'm a terrible person. I deserve to be dead.'

'No, you don't,' said Amyss, with passion. 'You keep telling us that you're a terrible person, Caddin. But you're not. You saved Leanna! And me! And you care for us both, though you won't admit it.'

The corners of Sendromm's mouth were turned down, but he just shrugged.

'Please, talk to us, Caddin,' said Leanna. 'I'm not going to invade your mind, and take your secrets, if you fear that. But please talk to us. We'll both listen, and we'll try not to judge you.'

'We're here for you, Caddin,' added Amyss, placing her hand onto his thick upper arm. 'Please talk. Then you can stay with us, for as long as you need to. Can't he, Lea?'

Leanna nodded.

The burly man turned his neck to look at both of them in turn. For a moment, his expression adopted that same reserved look which Leanna had witnessed so many other times in the last three months. Indeed, she thought that he was again going to shrug and maintain his secrets. But Sendromm then started to speak.

'I've kept my secrets, out of shame,' he said. 'Bad things have happened to me. In my childhood. In my life. Lots of bad things. And what you did… in my mind… it made me remember some of those things which have been buried deep inside. Some events which I've tried so hard to forget. But I'm not ready to talk about all of that yet.'

'Whatever you want to talk about,' said Leanna, 'we're with you, and we're here to listen.'

'I was a soldier once, as you know, and after that a priest,' stated Caddin. 'Surprised? Yes, I was a priest in Sen Aiduel, which is where I learned about healing. And it was there, over twenty years ago, in the months after the Great Darkening, that I was summoned to an audience with the Archlaw.'

'The meeting that I glimpsed in your memories,' said Leanna.

'Yes. And at that meeting, the Archlaw gave me a mission. A holy quest. A task to find five people who would be born with the potential for almighty powers. *Miraculous* powers, I now realise. People like you, Leanna.'

'To find us?'

'To be more specific, to find you all and to kill you all, in order to save the world and the faith.'

There was silence for a few moments after he had made this statement.

'But why?' asked Amyss. 'Why did the Archlaw want that? And how could… *killing Leanna* possibly save the world and the faith?'

'I can only tell you what was explained to me,' answered Sendromm. 'Paulius told me that the coming of these five had been prophesied, long ago. He named them *Illborn*, and said that they would possess unnatural powers and abilities. He mentioned traits such as prophetic visions, reading and controlling other's thoughts, and manipulating the world and the people around them. And he talked of a recurring dream. A dream about five people, who were walking up a winding mountain path, to reach an ethereal archway. A Gate, with a figure in it.'

Lord Aiduel, how can the Archlaw have known about this, before I was even born?

Leanna had never told Caddin about the particulars of her dream, although she knew that he was aware of her troubled sleep.

'You know that I dream,' she said.

'Yes, of course I do,' he replied. 'I describe your recurring dream, don't I?'

'Yes, and that scares me. Did the Archlaw say what it meant?'

'I asked, but he didn't answer. He just said that I would know them for certain, by the dream. And that they must be killed before they find the Gate that they dream about.'

'He said that the Gate is *real*?' asked Leanna.

'He didn't say that, as such. He just told me that you must all be found and killed, before you ever reach that Gate. But I suppose that it must be real and must be somewhere, if you are able to find it.'

'Did he say where it is?'

'No.'

'Could it be in Aiduel's Gate?'

'I don't know. He didn't say.'

'And did he say what will happen *if* we find that Gate?'

'Not everything,' said Caddin. 'But I understood that it would allow you to come into your full powers, and would trigger the destruction of the faith and the world.'

'But how can the Archlaw have known all of this?' interrupted Amyss. 'You said that the coming of these five had been prophesied long ago? Prophesied by who?'

'By The Lord Aiduel,' said Caddin. 'The Archlaw possessed a letter, which he said told of the Illborn's coming, Leanna. That you and the other four would come into the world after the Great Darkening. It was a letter which Paulius told me had been written by The Lord Himself, before He Ascended.'

Lord Aiduel, can this be true?

'The Lord?' repeated Leanna, feeling unsteady. 'I don't understand.'

'Paulius said that it was a letter which had been written by Aiduel before the Ascension, and was then passed down from Archlaw to Archlaw,' stated Caddin. 'Until it came to Paulius himself. He showed me the letter.'

'And this letter ordered the Archlaw to kill me? To save the world?'

'Yes, it did. To kill you, and all of the others, too. The Archlaw told me that the powers of the five Illborn will continue to grow. And that, if you find the Gate and come into your full strength, you'll destroy the Holy Church and will drown the world in blood and war. He told me that it would be his life's work to save the world and the faithful. That was the reason for the holy quest given to me and to others. That's the reason why Aiduel's Guards have now been set on that same hunt. As I said, to find you all and to kill you all. I think Paulius is becoming desperate.'

Leanna was dumbstruck.

Lord Aiduel, how could anyone ever believe that I would do such evil?

'So, you've been hunting Leanna's kind for over twenty years,' stated Amyss.

'Not for all of that time. The last few years… I have…' He paused, then did not continue.

'You said that the Archlaw showed you the letter,' said Amyss. 'Did you actually read it?'

'No, he didn't let me read the letter. He wouldn't even let me touch it. But he told me what was in it.'

'So, you have only the Archlaw's word for what's in that letter,' said Amyss, while giving a meaningful look to Leanna. 'And also, only the Archlaw's word as to who it was written by.'

'I suppose so, yes,' said Caddin. 'But there *was* a letter there. And it looked old. And the things it set out, the markers to look for, they've since been proven to be true. Including the dream. How could the Archlaw have known about that?'

'I don't know,' said Amyss. 'But the rest of it could all be made up, Lea. Don't believe it. You're not a danger to anyone.'

'It could be untrue,' agreed Leanna, appreciating Amyss's faith in her. 'But, at the time, you believed it, Caddin?'

'Yes,' he replied. 'The Archlaw spoke with such passion and sincerity, and I believed him with all of my heart and soul. I was convinced that my orders came from The Lord Aiduel.'

'And what if it *is* true, Amyss?' asked Leanna. 'What if the Archlaw *is* acting under the instruction of The Lord, and he and Aiduel's Guards want me and the others dead for a good reason? What if we *are* a danger?'

'We both believe that The Lord Aiduel gave you your powers, Leanna,' Amyss replied. 'If that's the case, then why would He also want you dead? It makes no sense.'

'I suppose not.'

Lord Aiduel, please reveal the truth to me.

'And the only person who might know for certain what's in that letter, and whether what he said to Caddin is true, is the Archlaw,' added Amyss. 'Unless you were to read the letter yourself, that is?'

'He keeps it in his personal vault,' said Caddin. 'He told me that much.'

Leanna paused, considering this, as another question occurred to her.

'Who was the boy, Caddin?' she asked. 'The boy in your memories, the one in the room?'

Sendromm looked downwards, and he avoided their eyes as he said, 'He was one of you. Perhaps even stronger than you, Leanna, because he was much younger – just a boy – and his powers still almost overcame the medallion. And…'

After a few moments of silence, Leanna said, 'Go on. What happened to the boy?'

'I killed him. I murdered him. Crushed his head in with my mace, and then smashed his body to pieces. Then I killed his parents, and I burned his body, left him charred and broken, like…'

'You killed them all,' stated Leanna, her voice flat. 'And you killed *him*, the boy. He was definitely one of the five? One like me?'

'Yes, I'm certain of that. And for many years since, I've known that what I did was wrong. That it was the worst mistake of my life. I now believe that the boy was meant to do something… *important*, something potentially world-changing. But I ended his life. And every single day, I wake up with the image of that boy's face in my mind, his words in my head, and I know that Aiduel has turned away from me. *I wasn't meant to kill the boy.* And now I try to pray to The Lord, Leanna, and there's *nothing* there. No one answers me. My action that day has damned me. I believe that I'm shut out from heaven, and that I'll never see…'

'Never see who?' asked Amyss.

'My wife and daughter. If they're waiting for me there. Can you guess the main reason why I'd managed to resist the urge to end my miserable life for the past decade?'

'Because those who commit suicide are barred from heaven,' said Amyss, softly.

'Yes,' said Caddin. 'Even though I'm damned, part of me has been clinging on to a hope that one day I might be forgiven. That I might be able to see them again. And so, I've often drunk myself into a stupor to forget what I am, and what I've done, and I've tried to ignore the voice that tells me I've nothing to live for. The same voice which urges me to end my cursed existence. And that's all that I've done, for more years than I care to count. But today...'

He fell silent again. After a few moments, Leanna said, 'What you did to the boy *was* wrong. But you did it for reasons that you thought were right. And you haven't killed me, Caddin. You sought me out and you *saved* me. Why?'

'Why?' he repeated. 'Months ago, I'd stopped in a tavern in Elannis. I'd bought myself the length of rope that day, you know.'

'To use to kill yourself?' asked Amyss.

Sendromm nodded. 'Possibly. Like today, I was on the very edge, and I'd even tied it in place on the rafters in my lodging room. And after doing that, I went downstairs to get drunk. I was thinking about how I had nothing to stay alive for, if heaven was anyway barred to me. But by pure chance, while I was drinking, a merchant sat beside me. He wanted to talk, and so I listened. And he told me a miraculous tale about a priestess who had lived through a blazing pyre. A woman who they were calling the Angel of Arlais.

'And after I'd listened to that man, I went back up to my room, and I thought about his story long into the night. And when the dawn came, I took the rope down from the rafters, and I decided to travel to Arlais, to see this miraculous priestess. And what do I find there? Not a doer of evil, no. Not a creator of misery and bloodshed. Not one who threatens to destroy the faith and to end the world, or who scares me like the boy did. But just a young woman who uses her powers to heal others. One who's dedicated to the faith.'

'Why didn't you come and speak to me?' asked Leanna.

'I was thinking about it. But you were a hard person to get near, with so many guards around. And anyway, what would I have said? But then I sensed that you were in danger. I could feel another with a medallion close by, and I knew that it meant that another like me was also nearby. And I could at last see a way to start to make amends. I set out to find the assassins, and I did, just in time. And I *saved* you, Leanna. That day in the cathedral, I kept you alive. A life for a life. I killed the boy, but I saved *you*.'

'You did,' said Leanna. 'And I've been ungrateful. Please forgive me.'

'There's nothing to forgive. But the next day, and ever since that first day with you, I've realised that I have a purpose. Protecting you gives me something to live for, and offers me the hope of salvation. Our time as healers, on the road… for the first time in many years, I felt… more at peace, although I was still too ashamed to answer your questions, even after you threatened to send me away.' He paused, and drew in a deep breath before continuing. 'I believe you are meant for greatness, Leanna. I honestly do. And whatever truth exists within the Archlaw's words, *I* no longer believe that *you* will ever do evil. The only thing I want now is for you to allow me to stay with you, to keep you alive. Please. Don't send me away. If you send me away, there's… nothing left.'

Lord Aiduel, please forgive this man, and relieve him of his pain and guilt.

'Thank you for telling us the truth, Caddin,' she said, after a pause. 'We'll have other questions to ask, some other time, but for now that's all that I wanted from you. And with that, you have my promise that you may stay with us. For as long as… we all need each other.'

'Thank you,' he said.

'Leanna could heal you, Caddin,' said Amyss. 'She could take away your pain. She once did it for me.'

'No,' he replied. 'I must hold this. I must remember.'

Leanna said, 'Very well, that's your choice. But if you ever change your mind, I'll be here.'

'Thank you,' he replied.

'But before we leave you, there's one more thing to ask,' said Amyss. She looked towards Leanna and raised her eyebrows.

'That's right,' said Leanna. 'Caddin, we need your help. If you don't think that you're ready for this, then just say. But if you think that you're able to, can you please help Lady Kalyane with the defence of this town?'

—

Over the course of the next two days, a continuing stream of returning soldiers and refugees flooded into Septholme. Most of these travelled from the north, towards the entrance at the North Gate.

During that time, Caddin appeared to be a man renewed, and he had accepted Amyss's suggestion to aid in the defences of the town. Lady Kalyane and Captain Thatcher agreed to meet with Sendromm, and after hearing of his military experiences at Accunder Pass, they gratefully accepted his assistance.

From then on, Caddin was often seen beside Thatcher on the battlements of the town walls, organising the defences. During a brief encounter inside the castle, Sendromm outlined to Leanna that there were two thousand soldiers in the defending garrison, including the remnants of the defeated Western Canasar army. This compared to an approaching force which was thought to be ten times larger.

Lady Kalyane appeared relieved to have access to Sendromm's expertise, in the midst of her other worries. Duke Gerrion had never returned, and Kalyane had still not heard from Arion since his last message from Andarron. On Leanna's second evening in the castle, she became aware that Kalyane had resolved to resist the invaders. The noblewoman was not going to surrender the town.

During the daytime, Leanna volunteered to help Septholme's healers to set up field hospitals, in anticipation of the coming bloodshed. Buildings were taken over for this purpose in the northern and southern quarters, and a third area was established in the courtyard of the castle. Leanna was prepared for what was to come. This time, she had decided that she would not refrain from using her powers when they were needed.

—

On the third day after her arrival in the town, Leanna was in the northern quarter field hospital when she heard a commotion from the northern wall. Intrigued, she set off in the direction of the clamour of agitated noise.

As she approached the North Gate, which was now closed and reinforced, she spotted Caddin standing on the battlements to the right of the gate towers. She climbed the steps up to those ramparts.

From the top of the walls, the source of the commotion was readily apparent. To the north of the town, but still hundreds of metres away, an army of thousands was emerging and spreading out across the fields. Travelling towards Septholme.

The arriving soldiers were split into three main groups of colours. The majority were clad in yellow, recognisable as Leanna's own countrymen. A smaller but still significant force was wearing an Andar-blue. Separate from all of these was a large body of red-cloaked cavalry, and the sight of so many Aiduel's Guards caused Leanna's heart to beat faster.

Following behind the countless ranks of soldiers was another visible and less regimented mass of people. Leanna knew that these would be the camp followers, including any healers. Could Sister Colissa and Leanna's other colleagues possibly be amongst that group?

Then Leanna felt the presence for the first time. It was pulsing from somewhere to the north, within that body of humanity which was coming towards the town. It was a powerful sensation, similar to what she had experienced at the Battle of Moss Ford, when she had first encountered Arion.

On that occasion, she had mistaken the nearby presence for The Lord Aiduel. She had believed that The Lord had come to her, and had watched over her, before the battle. This time, she suffered from no such illusions, even though she could feel her own powers already responding to the *other*. Growing stronger, as they had done before when near to Arion. The sensation was rejuvenating and energising her.

She peered northwards, trying to determine the source of this feeling, but it was impossible to be precise amongst so many thousands. But Leanna knew that a tide of invaders was about to crash against Septholme. They would attempt to wash over these walls and to swamp the town.

And somewhere, amidst that sea of humanity, she was certain that another had arrived, who was just like her. Another of her kind.

Another *Illborn*.

22

Arion

—

*Year of Our Lord,
After Ascension, 770AA*

The Battle of Condarr was to take place on flat grasslands within sight of the sea, under the damp embrace of a covering of grey mist.

Arion was on horseback, in command of sixteen hundred Andar cavalrymen. His assigned force was on the left flank of an extended line of soldiers who had given their allegiance to the newly crowned king, Sendar Pavil. This loyalist army had been mustered within days of the declaration of war by Elannis and Dei Magnus. In total, it now comprised a force of over thirteen thousand men, all of whom were wearing the royal blue tabards of Andar.

The front line of this army extended hundreds of metres from Arion's position, until it ended with the right flank touching the sand dunes beside the foaming sea. Arion could hear the sound of gulls cawing from the sky above, and he was certain that there would be a gory feast for the circling birds before the day was out.

His eyes were focused upon the enemy line, which was approximately three hundred metres away from him, across land covered in knee-high grasses. The forces of the traitor Duke Orlen Condarr were arrayed in a mirroring formation, but with their left flank touching the beach. The gauzy mist in the area was acting to drain the colour from the enemy soldiers, who were visible as an extended line of pale figures crowding the horizon.

Break them. Kill Orlen Condarr. After that, the way through Condarr will be clear.

'Fight your way back home, Arion,' Sendar had said, a week earlier, after Arion had returned from the blockaded harbour to the Royal Palace. 'Lend me your strength. Help me to win victories across Condarr and Rednar, so we can unite with our armies in Western Canasar.'

Arion had sent a message by bird to Septholme Castle after that discussion, notifying his family that he was unable to return by sea. There had been no response during his remaining time in the capital, and he had accepted the command of this cavalry force. Warfare at least offered the potential to vent some of the guilt which had arisen from his actions in Andarron.

He knew that he was ready to wound, maim and kill. Ever since the Andarron naval blockade had started, a frustration and anticipation had been building inside him. Frustration that he was trapped on the wrong side of the country, and was unable to influence events in Western Canasar. Anticipation that he would soon be able to make someone pay for this feeling of impotence.

These thoughts had persisted during the army's advance eastward from Andarron, into the province of Condarr. The House of Condarr had chosen to turn traitor, and to betray its country to Elannis and the Archlaw. By doing so, Orlen Condarr had cut-off Western Canasar and Rednar from the rest of the country, and had blocked Arion's landward route back to his home. Arion intended to make sure that the duke would pay a heavy price for that. If he needed to, he would clear the way back to Western Canasar on the strength of his own arm.

'I'll rip his fucking head off.'

'What was that, Lord Arion?'

This question was asked by Commander Amersson, previous leader of this cavalry force, who was now Arion's second-in-command.

Arion was embarrassed to realise that he had verbalised his last thoughts. 'Oh, nothing. Just thinking out loud.'

'We're honoured to have you leading us, Lord Sepian,' said Amersson. The man was of average build, in his late-thirties but with traces of premature grey in his hair and beard. 'With your presence in our company, the men feel confident. And I also have faith that The Lord Aiduel will support our cause today.'

Amersson's horse was alongside Arion's, close enough that Arion had already noticed a carving of The Lord Aiduel On The Tree, hanging from the man's saddle.

'Yes, very good,' Arion replied. 'But let's put our trust in the quality of our own skills and training, rather than rely on The Lord.'

I don't want to rely on The Lord Aiduel, but I certainly wouldn't object to having Leanna here beside me, to give me the power to win.

Arion could clearly remember how Leanna had bolstered his powers at the Battle of Moss Ford. How he had felt strength and vitality blossoming inside himself, which he had somehow shared with all of his surrounding troops. He would not benefit from that bountiful energy today, although he believed that he had grown independently stronger in the intervening time.

Nor would he have the advantage this time of planning a trap for his enemies; there had been no prophetic dreams of the coming battle, nothing to forewarn him of the outcome today. On this morning, he would have to rely on his wits and on pure military might.

At that moment, horns were blown at various points along the line, and the massed infantry of King Sendar's army began to advance in uniform and unbroken ranks. In turn, Arion heard Commander Amersson issuing an order, and Arion's body of cavalry also began to move forward, at a matching pace.

Arion watched the enemy forces directly across from his own position, which were shifting in reaction to the advance. His direct opponents were a large body of Condarr cavalry, which must have been assigned the same role as Arion's own horsemen.

I'm to protect the flanks of the main line, he thought. *Protect it from that cavalry. But where's the glory in that?*

Arion estimated that the opposing cavalry force had perhaps two thirds of the numbers under his own command. Despite the clear battleplan set out by King Sendar, Arion was determined to exploit this differential. Before too long, he would lead his men to engage that enemy cavalry, and he would turn the battle.

—

'We possess an overwhelming superiority of skilled, heavy infantry. If we engage them on this flat plain, just here, and lock them in position, then we'll aim to break them left-of-centre. We can then roll their line up towards the sea.'

The words had been spoken by King Sendar Pavil, the evening before, as a number of senior officers including Arion had gathered around a sketched map inside the monarch's tent. At the king's side had been a man identifiable by the black patch which covered his left eye; Commander Arnas Roque, the long-term lead instructor at the Royal Academy of Knights. Roque had volunteered to re-join the army.

'We estimate that they have six thousand infantry, and fifteen hundred cavalry,' Roque had added, his presence and voice as commanding as Arion could remember. 'Our own numbers are eleven thousand and two thousand, respectively. Therefore, we'll use the cavalry, under Lord Sepian's command, to protect our exposed left flank and to neutralise the Condarr cavalry. And we'll simply aim to insert overwhelming force on one point on their line, here, and then break and turn it.'

There had been a number of words of agreement from around the table.

'So, my cavalry force is not to charge?' Arion had asked.

'Only to react to manoeuvres from the Condarr cavalry, to neutralise them,' Sendar had replied. 'And only then, on the basis that you don't overcommit, and that you return to protecting our left flank as soon as you're able.'

'Then how are we to influence the battle outcome?' Arion had challenged.

'You hold our flank until the enemy line breaks, that's how,' Roque had answered. 'If they rout, we'll sound the call to pursue, and then you can unleash everything on their cavalry. But until then, stand firm and protect the flank.'

—

There had been much other discussion, but those particular exchanges had been the most pertinent to Arion's command today. He was still feeling dissatisfied with the orders which had been issued to him, despite his reluctant acceptance of them on the prior evening.

Arion's cavalry continued to walk their horses forwards now through the light mist, keeping pace with the advancing infantry line. There was a steady drumbeat sounding from within the loyalist lines, which was controlling the uniform advance.

The enemy infantry was holding a fixed position, arrayed behind a waist-height, crumbling stone wall which ran for much of their front. As the king's army began to draw to within a hundred metres, there was a response of arrow fire from the ranks massed behind that wall.

The Condarr cavalry also moved at this moment, some of them circling outwards towards Arion's force, then returning to the end of their line.

'It looks like they're trying to goad us, Lord Arion,' stated Amersson. 'Trying to lure us into a charge.'

Arion nodded. 'Sound the halt, now. If we're not to charge, I'll not walk us into a hail of arrows. We'll be close enough here to protect the flanks.'

Amersson carried out the command, and Arion then watched as the main body of the king's infantry closed with the Condarr forces. The sound of thousands of men crashing together was released as an angry thunderclap over the grey battlefield, and the killing started.

Arion's gaze was switching between the mass of bodies in combat along the low wall, back to the Condarr cavalry. On two separate occasions in the minutes which followed, the opposing horsemen manoeuvred in what appeared to be a prelude to a charge. Both times, Arion reacted by issuing commands for his own force to trot forwards, and to be ready to respond. After the second such advance, they were less than fifty metres from the front line of the battle.

The combat there was ferocious, with hundreds being killed or wounded within a short timeframe. In contrast, Arion and his troops were spectators, making no meaningful contribution to the victory. He tutted, then looked southwards towards the sea.

King Sendar and his mounted bodyguards were positioned behind the front lines, in advance of the king's reserves. Arion could discern the figure of the new monarch, who was gesticulating towards the line. Once again, Arion felt frustration at the battleplan issued by Sendar and Arnas Roque.

After thirty minutes of fighting had passed, the enemy front line had been pushed away from the low stone wall, and hundreds of the king's infantrymen had crossed over that small obstacle. However, Arion was certain that hundreds more must have already died. The enemy cavalry was still unengaged, but that body of horsemen was moving in another wheeling, threatening manoeuvre. Arion felt his patience break.

'That's it. No more waiting here,' he stated to Amersson. 'Sound the charge. We're going to charge them.'

'Lord Arion? But our orders were to-'

'Sound the charge! Now!'

'Yes sir.'

As Arion slipped his arm into his shield, Amersson issued the requested orders. Arion then drew his sword and raised it high. He could vividly remember the equivalent events of Moss Ford, when he had led a glorious cavalry charge.

In an echo of that moment, he shouted, 'For Andar! And for glory!'

Then they charged.

—

This time, there was no deep thrust into the exposed flanks of an unprepared infantry force. In contrast to Moss Ford, the enemy cavalry also galloped forwards, to meet Arion's assault head-on in a thunderous clash.

Within moments, Arion was lost in a whirl of bloodletting, his sword whirring and slicing about him.

STRENGTH. VICTORY. GLORY.

His powers were exploding into life. Once again, everything about him was crystallised into the most precise focus; colours were bolder, movements were slower, and details were sharper. The unfortunate enemies who engaged him were soon helpless in the face of his blistering speed and brutish strength.

He could also feel that his power was starting to flow out of himself again. As had happened at Moss Ford, his violent energy was soon being shared with the nearby men who fought for him. It was imbuing them with just a fraction of his own enhanced power and agility, but it nonetheless gave them an unnatural advantage, and it was driving them to greater levels of ferocity.

In the midst of what was cramped, close-quarters fighting, Arion was a relentless killer. He was soon at the point of a wedge which had driven deep into the enemy cavalry. After minutes had passed, he could see that opponents were trying to steer away from him, and he could witness the terror in their eyes as he cut a swathe through their ranks.

Kill them! Break them! Kill them!

He instinctively knew that his rage was being shared with his allied cavalrymen, while words from the enemy reached through to him in the midst of his killing frenzy.

'Look at his eyes! They glow!'

He paid no heed to such cries though, as he concentrated on the butchery at hand. He could again feel invisible coils of energy wrapped around all of his limbs, thick cords which fuelled his strength and which protected him. At one point, he felt a sword slice down onto his shoulder from behind, cutting through his chainmail vest to the flesh beneath.

But the blade then deflected away after barely touching the skin, his body seemingly shielded by the coils of energy. Arion swung his gauntleted fist around into the attacker, and felt satisfaction as the crunching impact flung the man backwards off his horse.

And still, he pressed forward into the reeling cluster of enemies, cutting down one after another. He was lost in a frenzied rage of combat and killing. In this moment, he no longer needed to feel ashamed of his actions in Andarron. He no longer needed to feel like a betrayer and a breaker of promises. In this moment, he was supreme amongst all of these men. Unique and unmatched. *Godlike.*

Kill them! Kill them! Kill them! Take your victory!

He could hear some of the enemy shouting, 'Kill his horse! His horse! Bring him down!'

Moments after that, spears were launched towards Arion and his mount. Arion was untouched, but at least one must have impacted the animal because it lurched to the side, forcing him to leap away as it fell. Arion rolled clear of the stricken beast, while his own men pushed forward on horseback to surround and defend him. They were shielding him from the enemy, while still fighting with their own enhanced power and ferocity.

But instead of gratitude, Arion felt annoyance at this constraining barrier of men. Again, it was an instinctive reaction to leap upwards and forwards. He jumped an unnatural distance and height, a leaping arc which no man in armour should have been capable of… and then he was over and past his own cavalry, setting upon the enemy again. He dragged a Condarr soldier from his horse, before wrenching and breaking the man's neck. He then vaulted onto the now riderless animal, and turned once again to face the enemy survivors.

But they were fleeing. The Condarr cavalry was breaking off from the fight, galloping away to the east.

Arion took stock of his position, rather than pursuing, and he realised that he had advanced far. His force was now a hundred metres to the rear of the main enemy line. Towards the sea, Arion could see Orlen Condarr's banner, surrounded by a cluster of mounted warriors.

Arion pointed his sword in that direction and cried, 'To me! To me! I want Duke Condarr!'

Soon after, he was leading another charge.

—

Some hours later, the battle was over, and Arion was once again on the side of the victorious army. The enemy force had been comprehensively defeated, and Condarr's soldiers had either been killed, captured or routed. Commander Amersson was leading the cavalry's pursuit of the fleeing enemy.

In the aftermath of the battle, Arion went in search of King Sendar, carrying an object wrapped in bloodied cloth in his left hand.

He found the king close to the sea, looking outwards. Sendar appeared unruffled, his armour undented, as if he had managed to remain clear of any direct combat. By contrast, Arion was coated in blood and gore. For a few moments, the new monarch just stared at him warily, with no sense of recognition.

'Sendar,' stated Arion, his voice hoarse. He had come down from the frenzy of battle-rage which had gripped him in the preceding hours, and he was feeling exhausted by the prolonged use of his powers. The end of the battle had been a welcome relief, for his energy had been close to depleted.

'Arion? Is that you?'
'Yes.'

Sendar frowned. 'By the Lord, look at the state of you!'

Arion dropped his bloody bundle at the feet of the new monarch, and uttered, 'A gift.'

'What is it?' asked Sendar.

'Condarr's head.'

'You killed Orlen Condarr?'

'Yes.'

The combat against Orlen Condarr's bodyguard had been brutal, although the small duke himself had clearly not been a fighter. However, he *had* been a traitor and an enemy, and that had given Arion just cause for what he had done. Had the duke thrown down his sword and begged for mercy at the end, after seeing the last of his personal protectors fall? Perhaps. Had Arion, lost in his ferocity, instead chosen to decapitate the small man?

Arion shuddered. He did not want to dwell upon the memory of that.

'Good that he's defeated,' stated Sendar, 'but I'd instructed that I wanted him capturing alive, if possible.'

'It was a battle,' replied Arion, his voice gruff. 'I was fighting for my life. And while he lived, there was a threat of him escaping and rallying his troops. But now he's dead, so that threat's gone.'

The young king frowned. 'Better that he would have lived, to give us a hostage to force Condarron to surrender to us.'

Arion shrugged.

'And your cavalry charged,' added Sendar after a moment, his tone suggestive of controlled disapproval. 'You'd been ordered to protect the flanks. Not to charge their cavalry and then their rearguard. You left our flank exposed when their cavalry regrouped. We lost a number of men as a result.'

Arion stared at the young king, with a coldness in his regard. This moment felt different to the events in the palace, where Arion had been a confused and subservient participant. Today, Arion had *ruled* the battlefield, while Sendar had merely watched and directed. Arion felt no need to cower or to apologise for his actions.

'It was a battle,' he said. 'I was reacting to events. And I won your battle for you. Like I won-'

He paused, deciding against finishing the sentence.

'Like you won, what?'

Like I won your crown for you.

'Nothing,' stated Arion, after a moment. 'But I expected thanks, not this. My men and I routed their cavalry, we turned their flank, we killed their leader, and we caused the morale in their main infantry line to collapse. That was all decisive. A simple thank you would suffice. But instead, I get this criticism.'

'Not criticism. Observation. Of commands not followed. Don't forget yourself, or who you're speaking to, Lord Arion. And I suggest that you address me as "Your Majesty".'

Arion stared hard at the monarch, considering. He was trying to resist clenching his fists. Eventually, he said, 'Very well, Your Majesty. Please excuse my actions, in the heat of battle. But, in the end, we won. So, what next?'

Sendar returned his gaze, neither of them being prepared to be the first to look away, and said, 'What next? First, we rest. We recover and mend as many of the wounded as we can, in the remainder of today. We hope for good news from the east. And then, we move on. Forced march through Condarr, and then onto Rednarron. We've no time to besiege Condarron, or to parley with Orlen's family. We have to try to join up with Rednar's armies and face the main body of the Elannis invasion as a single force, before it's too late.'

'Onto Rednar it is, then,' said Arion. After a pause, he added, 'Your Majesty.'

—

Later, after the sun had set, Arion was sitting alone within the overnight Andar army camp. He had scrubbed his body in the sea at dusk, but he could still feel the stain of blood and gore on his flesh. Could still hear the sounds of death and pain ringing in his ears.

Ever since his actions in the battle, it seemed that others were wary of him. Certainly, no one was approaching him to talk as he reclined on his bedroll. However, he was not particularly bothered by that; after the killing of the day, he wanted to be on his own. The sense of glory which he had felt after Moss Ford had not returned to him in the aftermath of this latest battle, and he still felt exhausted from his extended use of power.

There was a flagon of ale placed on the floor before him. He had taken it from a supply wagon thirty minutes earlier but had not yet drunk from it. However, for the first time in months, he had a strong urge to consume every last drop.

By the Lord, I was vicious today. An unstoppable killer. Is that what I have become? Is that who I am?

He had promised Gerrion and Kalyane that he would stop drinking. He had sworn it to them both, and he had steadfastly stayed true to that vow, ever since the night in *The Hungry Gull*. However, after the recent events of Andarron and the awful killing of today, what significance was there to one more broken promise?

Eventually, his hand reached out, and he grasped hold of the flagon. Slowly, he moved it to his mouth. Even then, he paused for a while, and the first gulp was the most difficult to take. After that, they came more easily.

—

The next day, the army was on the move shortly after sunrise, marching into the heart of the Condarr region. The morning was uneventful, with a challenging pace set for infantry soldiers who were still weary from the battle.

In the late-afternoon, Arion's outriding cavalry scouts were approached by a sole horseman, who was travelling towards them from the east. After a brief exchange, this newcomer was escorted towards Arion.

The man was middle-aged, with thinning hair, and was wearing the plain clothes of a commoner. However, he seemed vaguely familiar.

'Do I know you?' asked Arion.

'Perhaps, Lord Sepian. I'm a senior retainer within the household staff of House Rednar. I know you from your time at Duke Rednar's country estates. Morrul Fletcher's my name. Do you remember me, my Lord?'

'Ah, that's right. I do. But you're a long way from home, Morrul. Do you bring news from Rednar?'

'Yes, I've been sent by Duke Rednar to bring an urgent message to the royal army, my Lord. And I'm beyond relief to have found you. But the duke ordered me to only deliver my news in person to the king, or to whomever else is in charge.'

'Very well,' said Arion, 'come with me.'

Minutes later, the army column had been called to a brief rest halt, and Morrul Fletcher was standing in the midst of Arion, King Sendar and Arnas Roque.

After introductions, Fletcher said, 'The news from Rednar is dreadful, Your Majesty. We were invaded by Elannis forces entering our land from Berun. Estimated at over thirty thousand in total. Duke Rednar and his sons assembled our armies as quickly as possible, and we met them in battle twenty miles to the north-east of Rednarron.'

'And?' prompted Sendar.

'Our army was defeated, Your Majesty. We were badly outnumbered and were routed. Duke Rednar survived the battle, and retreated with our surviving forces to Rednarron, to prepare for siege. The duke ordered me to find you and to implore that you march with all haste to help his city. He instructed me to highlight the urgent need and to state to you that every single day might count, before the city is overrun. I carry a letter with the duke's seal, supporting these words.'

'Understood,' stated Sendar, his countenance grim.

'What of Lord Lennion Rednar?' asked Arion.

'I don't know, my Lord. I was dispatched on this journey by Duke Rednar as soon as he returned to Rednarron. I didn't see Lord Lennion after the battle. I pray to The Lord Aiduel that both of the duke's sons returned unharmed.'

Lord preserve us! The whole country's collapsing!

'How many soldiers are left to try to hold Rednarron?' asked Sendar.

'I'm sorry. Again, I don't know, Your Majesty,' replied the messenger. 'I left immediately after receiving Duke Rednar's instructions, and don't have that information. However, I do have other news. From Western Canasar.'

'What is it?' asked Arion.

'It's more awful news, I'm afraid,' said Fletcher. 'We received a message by bird before the battle. A message from Lady Kalyane, in Septholme.'

'Saying what?'

The man grimaced, looking awkward. 'Saying that the army of Western Canasar has been defeated, by a combined army of Berun–'

'Berun! Fucking Jarrett Berun! I'll fucking kill him!' Arion shouted, before noticing that Sendar was glaring at him. In a quieter tone, he added, 'Sorry, please carry on.'

Morrul Fletcher continued. 'A combined army of Berun and Elannis. And then... I'm very sorry, my Lord. Saying that Duke Sepian is missing since the battle, presumed dead, and that the leader of your armies Charl Koss is also dead. That the armies of Berun and Elannis are moving south through Western Canasar, travelling towards Septholme. And the port has been blockaded by the Dei Magnun navy. Lady Kalyane requested that Lord Lennion was to come to her aid with an army of Rednar, because she didn't know what to do. But... that won't be possible, of course.'

Arion felt numb inside as he listened to this series of disasters. His army had been defeated, in his absence. Gerrion was missing, possibly dead. Charl *was* dead. And Kalyane was alone, with only Karienne for support. All of them had been abandoned by him to this catastrophe. He could only imagine what Kalyane was enduring, facing that much adversity on her own.

'What are we to do, Sen-' He stopped himself. 'Your Majesty, what are we to do?'

Sendar looked rattled, but Arion could see that the new king was battling to master his emotions.

'Our armies in the east have collapsed,' stated the monarch, after a few moments. 'The future of this country now rests with this army, here. These soldiers, here. We must bypass Condarron, as we anyway intended, and must march on to Rednarron. If we can hold Rednarron and push Elannis back there, then we have a chance to gather more forces from the north, and to negotiate for a peace. To… offer Elannis what they wanted last year, and to try to reconcile with the Holy Church in Sen Aiduel. However, if Rednarron falls, then the entire country is open to the Empire. We must march faster and further, every single day. Every moment might count.'

'And what of Western Canasar?' asked Arion. 'And Septholme?'

'We can do nothing for Western Canasar now, Lord Arion,' stated the king. 'Our focus must be on Rednarron, and on holding the rest of the country together. I fear that Western Canasar is lost to us.'

'Am I understanding right?' asked Arion, with rising heat in his voice. 'You're suggesting that you're going to abandon Western Canasar, and give it to Elannis? After everything that we've done for this country and for the Pavils? You can't do that!'

'I am the king, Lord Arion, and you don't get to tell me what I can and can't do!' snapped Sendar. 'If I can save this country by holding Rednarron and by giving Western Canasar to Elannis, then be in no doubt; I *will* do that.'

—

That night, in the hours of darkness, Arion rode out of the army camp.

He was challenged by a pair of guards as he passed the borders of the encampment, on the eastbound road. However, after he highlighted his rank and status to them, he was permitted to leave without further question.

He was setting off to travel with little in the way of provisions. Some food, a flask of water, and his bedroll. Other than that, he possessed his clothes, armour and weapons. That would have to be enough. Morrul Fletcher, a household retainer, had been able to make it all the way from Rednarron to the western reaches of Condarr. That confirmed to Arion that the journey could be done, and now he was going to travel in the opposite direction.

In the aftermath of the meeting with the messenger, Arion had resolved that he needed to leave. He intended to journey alone across Condarr, Rednar and Western Canasar. He would return to Septholme, and he would try to make amends for everything that had gone wrong because of him.

By the Lord! I'm a deserter now, too, to add to everything else that I've done.

It was clear to Arion that King Sendar was viewing Western Canasar as already lost. The new monarch was going to offer the province to Elannis, as part of a peace settlement. There was no indication that Sendar was prepared to do anything to aid the territory.

As such, the only person left to save Septholme, and what remained of the Sepian family, was Arion himself. The journey ahead of him was going to be long and arduous. For much of it, he might be travelling on roads and through lands which were held by hostile armies.

But he was resolved now. He would return to his family, he would strive to reach Kalyane and his younger sister before Septholme fell, and he would do *something* to try to restore his lost honour.

Or he would die in the attempt.

23

Corin

---

*Year of Our Lord,
After Ascension, 770AA*

That night, within the confines of the cave, Corin heard the ethereal Song of the Felrin. Indeed, he spent most of the hours of darkness lost within the collective voice of the beasts outside. To the people around him, he appeared to be in a deep trance.

Visions came to Corin throughout the night, delivered to him through the melodies of the haunting Song, offering images of what had come before. Although the felrin did not have language, Corin realised that the shared memories of their race had been carried through the ages by this communal cry.

He knew that they were aware of his soul joining their Song, and that they recognised him. It relegated their hunger to break into the cave and to kill beneath a desire to be heard, and to be understood.

Corin sensed them welcoming the fact that they had at last found someone who could perceive and could interpret their memories. One who they recognised as akin to the man who had created their kind, many thousands of years earlier. One who could show them what they had once been.

As Corin experienced the stories hidden within that Song, in the midst of his trance, he learned much of their truth. Indeed, he witnessed the awful moments of the felrins' birth as a species, observing the event as if he was there and was watching it through countless frightened eyes. He experienced their horror, as if standing amongst the tragic victims who had suffered on that day...

They were clustered within a fenced-in enclosure, near to a place of great power, and they were terrified. Hundreds of men, women and children, all gathered together. The children were crying, but the surviving parents were too numbed by their losses, and they had little remaining hope with which to provide succour to their young.

These captives were the last of their people, the last survivors of the kingdom which had ruled these mountain lands in peace, for centuries prior. And they knew that they were doomed.

The cause of their downfall, and the reason for their terror, was currently stalking across a high platform which stood along one edge of the fenced-in area. It was a man, an individual who was tall and muscular, with long brown hair. This man's face was scarred from the day when one of their people had come closest of all to ending him, in an assassination attempt which had failed by the narrowest of margins. But it had failed, nonetheless.

The scarred man talked at the assembled prisoners for a long time, in a language which was unknown. However, his tone was completely recognisable. It was vicious. Merciless. Triumphant.

At the end of this speech, a name was shouted by the man. A name that was repeated by the hundreds of axe-wielding warriors who surrounded the enclosure.

Mella!

And then the scarred man raised his arms outwards and within moments… there was a sense of something unseen emerging from him. Something evil, a hidden aura of darkness, which was spreading hungrily down from his platform, expanding into the massed body of the people below.

It surrounded the captives, it embraced them, and then it invaded them. Any who were touched started to scream in agony. Within moments, the sensation of darkness had covered the entire mass of prisoners.

People were soon bunched over, with hands raised to heads. Their friends and family, whom they had clustered near to, and whom they had lived alongside and had loved, were forgotten. Each of them knew only the very personal and excruciating agony of what had been released upon them.

It was something which was hideous, rotten and corrupting. Something ruinous.

And then they were twisted and tortured, as their bodies were slowly broken, then stretched and reshaped. Their minds were assailed with unimaginable sufferings, they knew incomparable grief and woe, and their sanity was shattered.

And this suffering lasted for longer than any of them imagined that they could bear, even in their madness.

But when it was finally over, and the blackness was lifted from their now warped and misshapen bodies, they had become something new.

Gone from them was kindness, and compassion, and knowledge, and love. But these things had been replaced by new attributes. Strength. Ferocity. Hunger. A need to rend and to kill.

As they looked about themselves, in those first moments after their rebirth, they did not have a name for what they had become. That name would be given to them later, by others.

But they knew who they had to serve, without question or

remorse. Their god was the figure on the platform, who now gazed down at them. The one who had made them. The one who now owned their souls.

The one known as Mella.

And with this knowledge, they lifted their necks, and they collectively howled towards their tyrannical master.

It was a new dawn. And they were ready to be unleashed.

After surfacing momentarily from the lowest depths of this vision, Corin comprehended an awful truth. The first of the felrin had not been born. They had been *made*. Many thousands of years ago.

By one like Corin.

And that person's name? It was still embedded within their racial memory, and was resonant within the Song, remembered with fear but also with reverence.

Mella. One of Corin's Gods.

The first felrin had been people. Good people. They had chosen to oppose Mella, and he had ruined them. Following which, he had made himself a deity over them, and had forced them to serve him, for the duration of his life and thereafter.

Corin allowed himself a moment of anger, as a brief and controlled reaction to the abomination and evil that he had witnessed. He then slipped back into the trance. In the hours that followed, as he drifted within the currents of the Song's melodies, he was an appalled witness to many other scenes of horror and injustice.

He observed as the felrin race was used by Mella, delivering death and devastation on countless other peoples. He witnessed civilisations collapsing under the assault of the scarred man and his remorseless minions. He shared in memories of battles on an epic scale which he could barely comprehend, and of places which seemed hundreds of times larger than villages like Karn.

And he also saw others battling to hold back this tide of evil. Glimpses of men and women fighting together to eventually thwart the one known as Mella, and to force him back. Massive sacrifices being made to reverse Mella's gains.

Then finally, after years of fighting, the felrin could remember being driven from the lands of man. During this time, their race had continued to survive, despite their losses. They had bred and had spawned offspring; creatures which were shaped like them, but which had never known what it was to be human. But the memories possessed by their race had remained, and over time the Song had formed, and had outlasted their creator.

As the vision continued, Corin could ultimately see the day, many years later, when Mella's life had ended. The scarred man and his surviving followers had returned to the place where he had once come into his powers.

It was a clearing in a lush and fertile valley, surrounded by forests and snow-capped mountains, a place which Corin sensed was near to the cave in which his party was now sheltering. And it contained something which he was immediately in awe of. Something which Blackpaw had been forced to conceal, from both itself and from Corin, for all of the time that they had been together. Something which, like Mella, had been dying.

As he witnessed these last moments, seen through the eyes of the felrin, Corin could understand the dying god's language, and could comprehend his final order. It was a command which had remained embedded within the race of felrin ever since. Which had bound them within these northern wildernesses, for the passing millennia.

You must guard this place. Let no other approach, or know of it. Deliver death to them. And serve me, for all of eternity.

And with those words, Mella had trapped an entire species within these lands, for the many thousands of years which had followed.

―

The next day, shortly after dawn, Corin and his party emerged from the narrow mouth of the cave. They moved into the unprotected spaces outside.

Corin walked at the front of their group. Blackpaw was immediately behind him, with Agbeth once again carried on the creature's back. Corin's wife was awake, but she had returned to her dream-state. The other four members of their party emerged in a huddle, glancing around in fear, despite Corin's assurances.

And they were right to be fearful, under normal circumstances.

As he emerged into open space, Corin could see the masses of felrin on the surrounding rocks and slopes. Hundreds of the creatures, all facing in the direction of Corin's party, and all now silent.

The beasts had adopted various poses, with some standing and some curled up. Most were hunched forward onto their front paws, and all had their eyes on Corin. The closest were within five metres, just a second's lunge away from inflicting deadly harm. Corin could also see the forms of some of the creatures on distant cliffs and rocky outcrops. Each one of them was watching him.

He sensed that many of the beasts had travelled great distances overnight to arrive here. He believed that they had been summoned by the Song, and by his joining with it and understanding of it. This had allowed the felrin to recognise what Corin was. And, more importantly, to remember what *they* had once been.

Corin could feel the tension within his companions, and he could hear whimpering from Menni. In a low voice, he said, 'Everyone, just stay calm and near to me. They're not going to attack.'

Despite his assurances, he still felt uneasy; he was confident, but not *that* confident.

Corin could already discern the corridor which the creatures had formed for them. A space which was less than ten metres wide, and which headed through the ranks of felrin on either side, curling towards the north. A route which Corin was certain would take him to the place of his vision.

As his group began to advance cautiously along this channel, Corin again noted that the terrain ahead of them was becoming more verdant. Lusher grass and shrubs had reappeared on the lower slopes around them, and a line of pine trees came into view ahead, in the distance.

After Corin's group had travelled just a few metres, the felrin nearby raised themselves to a walking position, and started to shadow them. Soon, there was a massed pack of the creatures stalking Corin's group to either side and behind. Those on the more distant cliffs and outcrops were also moving.

Blackpaw had now come alongside Corin, and was walking upright, in order to carry Agbeth. Corin took encouragement from the fact that Blackpaw seemed relaxed, and appeared to be unconcerned about the risk of an attack.

Corin knew that his felrin had also heard the Song, and that the beast had shared in the experience of Corin interpreting that melody. The hearing of the Song had also freed those hidden memories which had been locked away in Blackpaw, ever since the felrin had left this place to travel south.

Corin now understood why the felrin race had never expanded out into the lands of man. After the time of Mella had come to an end, the descendants of the felrin had been set to guard this place. They had been bound to stay close to this remote location and to prevent others from coming near. Only the stronger-willed, like Blackpaw, had sometimes managed to escape from the compulsion to remain close to this place. But even then, only for short periods. However, Blackpaw's encounter with Corin, and Corin's overwhelming willpower, had given the beast the capacity to deny Mella's command.

But the rest were still captive. Corin felt pity for them, and outrage at the evil which had once been inflicted upon them. In the midst of these emotions, during the previous night, he had recognised that he could act to put right an ancient wrong. He had heard their plea.

Free us.

As such, at the end of the Song of the Felrin, he had made a promise.

A promise which was enabling Corin and his party to now walk unimpeded towards the place which the felrin had been bound to protect, for the remainder of eternity.

To the Land of the Gods, and to the place where the life of Mella had ended.

—

Their journey along the valley took Corin's party into ever more verdant territory. Within a mile, the surrounding terrain was transformed from barren rocks to dense pine forest, with a carpet of grass underfoot.

They passed into the once-distant line of trees and were soon trekking through thick foliage, which was formed from a combination of boughs and bushes. On a number of occasions, Corin passed over rows of shaped stones, which were half-buried in the ground in the spaces between the trees. These boulders were moss-covered and worn, but he sensed that they were the ancient foundations of the structures which had once stood in this place.

Throughout, Corin's party was shadowed by hundreds of felrin, the creatures moving silkily through the vegetation around them. The valley had flattened now but was curving to the right, winding through steep mountains on either side.

'Are we going to enter the Land of the Gods, Corin?' asked Kernon at one point, as he followed behind.

'I think that we are,' Corin replied. 'Be ready.'

They travelled through the forest for almost an hour, the dense foliage serving to make their progress awkward and arduous. They could not see more than a few metres ahead at any time, but the surrounding presence of the felrin helped to steer their direction of travel.

Finally, they pushed through a thicket of trees and emerged into a massive clearing, which was encircled by forest and mountains. A giant stone arch stood in the centre of that clearing, towering and majestic.

It was the structure which Corin had witnessed in his vision, during the previous night. The place where the god Mella's life had ended.

'By the Gods!' exclaimed Kernon and Rennik, almost in unison.

'By the Lord, this is incredible,' added Hellin. There was awe in the missionary's voice.

'It's so beautiful. Is this what you see in your dreams, Corin?'

Upon hearing the latter words, Corin glanced around, and he saw that Agbeth had once again returned to him. He smiled at her, feeling happy, and then turned his head to stare once more at the great edifice in front of him. Felrin were stalking past Corin's group, and were beginning to form a circle around the mighty structure. They were all still watching Corin.

The arch was enormous. It was comprised of two pillars of stone, which were perhaps thirty metres apart and were each several metres thick. These columns sprouted upwards from the ground, and stretched vertically into the sky. At the top, over a hundred metres high, the two pillars curved inwards and joined together.

The surface of the whole structure was intricately carved, with shapes which seemed to twist and contort before Corin's eyes, even if he tried to focus on a single spot. These carvings extended all the way upwards, providing the structure with a disconcerting sense of constant movement.

Corin was awestruck. The edifice represented a level of craftsmanship which was beyond his ability to comprehend. It was unfathomable to Corin as to how such an awe-inspiring structure could exist, other than that the Gods had built it.

But it was not the ethereal archway of his dreams.

'No, Agbeth,' he replied, eventually. 'This isn't it.'

First, this structure was showing signs of dilapidation, evidence of its apparent great age. In several places, there were gaping cracks running along the rock surface, and at the top great chunks of the structure were missing, as if collapsed away. These absences were mirrored by the mighty stone boulders which were scattered on the ground beneath the towering pillars.

It was also obvious to Corin that the surroundings of this arch were not the same as those of his recurring dream. The place which he witnessed in his slumbers was high on a mountain, not sitting within a clearing in a valley and surrounded by forested mountain slopes.

But of most significance, and only evident to him now that he had arrived here, was that this structure was not *alive*. He could feel an old power here, a dormant remembrance of what this edifice might once have been. However, it did not thrum with a vibrant and terrible energy, like the Gate of his dreams. Nor was a golden, blinding light emitted from it. In contrast, he could see straight through the space within the arch, to the valley beyond.

Corin sensed that this structure had once lived, and had shone with brilliant radiance, in the days of Mella. However, in his visions of Mella's final moments, Corin had witnessed only a faded glow, and he believed that the arch's light had long since been extinguished. He hesitated, trying to decide what to do next.

'Please will you get me down, Corin,' said Agbeth.

In response, Blackpaw knelt down low, and Corin and the others worked to extract Agbeth from the carrying frame.

After she was freed, Agbeth leaned in towards Corin. She placed her mouth close to his ear and said in a low voice, 'Right now, he's nearer to me than he's ever been, Corin. I could hear him whispering in my mind, as I came to the surface.'

'And what was he saying?' Corin asked.

'He said that we should touch the arch. That you should enter my mind, and we should touch it together. He said that he can speak to you here, without… without hurting me.'

Upon hearing these latter words, Corin felt a little uneasy. However, the ghost had been the one to draw his attention to the felrin's Song, which had saved their lives. Corin was therefore prepared to accept the instruction. He nodded, then he and Agbeth started to walk towards the structure, with their hands clasped together. The rest of Corin's party was following close behind.

Before them, the masses of felrin were now formed in an almost complete circle within the forest clearing. They were surrounding the arch, leaving only a narrow corridor for Corin's group to pass through. As Corin drew closer to the ancient structure, the felrin started to howl and to shriek again.

Just a day earlier, the collective cries had sounded terrifying and ghastly to Corin. However, this time he could discern their Song as he walked through the creatures' ranks towards the structure. His mind relaxed, and in moments his thoughts were again flowing within the hidden melodies and currents of their calls.

The visions and the memories returned to him as he stepped forwards. Once again, he witnessed the final moments of Mella's life. The one hailed by Corin's people as a god had passed on in this place, in the shadow of this edifice, at a time when the structure had also been dying. That moment was forever embedded in the memories of the felrin race.

But even with these visions playing in his mind, Corin strove to remain alert as he and Agbeth drew close to the vertiginous pillars of stone. He was trying to peer at the intricate carvings and inscriptions along the two great columns, but they still seemed to twist and shift before his eyes, and their meaning was indecipherable to him.

His prime focus as he approached the arch, however, was returned to his purpose for coming all the way to this remote place. Agbeth. He had travelled this great distance to find a way to cure her. To restore her.

He intended to place his hands with hers onto the surface of this ancient structure. He would enter her mind, and he would then see if any answers would be revealed to him.

The two of them drew alongside one of the pillars, Corin's hand still holding hers. He looked at her, and they both smiled. Corin felt happiness to again be reunited, but also trepidation about what was to come.

'I love you, Agbeth.'

'And I love you, Corin.'

Their gaze was still fixed upon one another as he formed a connection with her waking mind. He slipped inside her soul, this time with her full awareness and permission.

Then, together, they pressed their palms onto the stone surface of the ancient arch.

—

The moment that he touched the structure, the world around Corin disappeared. He could feel his consciousness becoming detached from his physical surroundings, and then it seemed that he was plummeting weightlessly through an endless spiral of brilliant colours.

In mere instants, fragments of myriad images had touched his mind, revealing old secrets to him. This had not been the first of these edifices, not by any means. Had there been other places like this, stretching back into the recesses of ancient time? Each burning bright with power for millennia, then fading away, to be replaced by another? Corin was granted fleeting and elusive recollections of such structures, a reel of memories displaying an unbroken line of descent, which left a question screaming in his mind.

Did all of this end with the Gate of Corin's dreams?

Before he could process his awe and wonder, however, Corin was jolted from this vortex of memory and colour, and he was returned to Agbeth's mind. To the spaces within her.

Immediately, he could feel the presence of the ghost. It was floating, tangible, somewhere close. The sense of it was more vivid this time; Agbeth had stated that the presence was nearer to her than it had ever been, and Corin knew this to be true.

Once again, Agbeth was not consciously with them, in the spaces where Corin and the ghost now lingered. Corin could sense her soul, somewhere distant, but again she was shielded from him. Locked away.

ARE YOU THERE?

Corin knew what the answer to that question would be, even before the presence responded.

Yes, I am. I can feel... echoes of a power here. It's bringing me to the surface... helping me to remember. And while I'm here, I can see both ways...

BOTH WAYS?

To you, at the surface... and the way back, to the place that you took us from.

The ghost's voice was still framed in the tones of a young boy, but it was more lucid and alert than it had ever been before. It was also close to Corin, surrounding him, rather than sounding like whispers spoken from the bottom of a deep well.

I WANT TO HEAL AGBETH. HOW DO I DO IT?

Heal her?

I WANT TO BRING HER BACK... TO HOW SHE WAS.

She was dead, when you summoned us. I think we both were.

Corin felt scared when he heard those words, as a confirmation of what he had done.

NO, BEFORE THAT! BEFORE HER INJURY.

I healed her injury, when we returned. I don't know how, but I did it, so we'd both survive. Her wound is gone.

BUT HER MIND! FOR SO LONG, SHE'S... NOT AWARE.

I think... we're both sinking. Going back. Soon, it will be too late.

TOO LATE?

We came back together. Two people, into one mind. One body. But it's wrong. It can't last. We drag each other down. It gets harder and harder to reach the surface.

WHAT CAN I DO?

Order her... to complete her journey. Let her die. While we're at this place, I can show her the way.

NO! YOU MUSTN'T DO THAT! I'M GOING TO SAVE HER.

Then I think we'll both die. Eventually.

NO. YOU MUST LEAVE.

I need to stay. I wasn't meant to die.

There was a certainty in the voice, as it uttered those words.

CAN I ORDER YOU TO LEAVE HER? CAN YOU LEAVE HER, AND GO BACK, WHILE WE'RE HERE?

It seemed to Corin that the ghost released a sigh. There was then a delay before a quiet response came.

Yes.

AND WILL IT HEAL AGBETH?

I don't know for sure. But you must not do that.

WHY NOT?

I feel... that you will need me. You all will. I think... I was meant to make things right.

WHAT DOES THAT MEAN?

You must order her to go back, and to die, to save yourself.

I DON'T UNDERSTAND!

Corin was feeling frustrated and confused, and his exasperation was expressed in this response.

I answered, when I heard you... because... I thought I recognised you, and there was something I was meant to do. To save you. To save all of you. I don't think I should go.

WHAT WERE YOU MEANT TO DO?

I don't know. I'm trying to remember. Gather them? Open the Gate? And claim the power? But this time...

The voice trailed away, as if in confusion.

WHO *ARE* YOU?

I want to remember... but... it feels as if Ma's wool blanket is around my memories... it's so difficult to see what I need to see.

After that, there was an extended silence. On a number of occasions, Corin could feel a surge of energy surrounding him, and he knew that the ghost was still there. He wondered if the presence was drawing any lingering traces of power from the ancient edifice, as it strove to find a way to remember.

Finally, Corin perceived that this process had ended and that the ghost was preparing itself. Eventually, it spoke.

My name was… Cillian. I think that there were five of us, once. I think I was meant to find you, and to make it right. But I was murdered.

FIVE?

I remember you now. I'm starting to remember all of us, and I can see us, too. Now look…

In the aftermath of those words, a succession of images flashed into Corin's mind. Images which might have been visions, or memories, or both. And as Corin witnessed these, he experienced a revelation which shook him to the very core.

He was not the only one of his kind.

Interlude Two

―

*Year of Our Lord,
Before Ascension, 54BA*

―

Interlude 2

Amena

—

*Year of Our Lord,
Before Ascension, 54BA*

Aiduel was weeping when she found him.

The corpses of the four children were spread out on the granite floor before him, sprawled in various poses of violent distress. The victims were two girls and two boys, all in their early adolescence. Red splatters of blood decorated the four, marking the work of the blunt instrument which had been used to kill them.

'Aiduel?'

As she approached her husband, Amena's voice was calm and gentle, but her heart was beating with alarm. In all of the years that they had been together, she had rarely seen him in as much distress as this. She could feel his power pulsing erratically, washing over her in almighty waves, despite the protection of the medallion on her neck.

'He killed them all, Mena,' Aiduel announced, his reddened eyes still fixed on the four dead children. 'He had nothing to gain from it, but he killed them all anyway, as a last act of spite.'

She placed her hand onto his neck, before replying, 'And now he's dead, my love. The last of the Angall tyrants, dead today. You've avenged these children, and you freed many others, when you killed him.'

Aiduel did not answer. Instead, he shuddered, then started to sob again. Amena moved around before him and pulled him into her embrace, allowing his head to rest upon her shoulder.

They were alone in the lavish personal bedchambers of the now-deposed Vizier of Sennam, in the heart of the city's oppressive fortress. After six years of relentless war, this remote location had become the final refuge of the surviving rulers of the dying Angallic Empire. Just hours earlier, Aiduel had shattered the walls of the dark-stoned fortress, and had led the assault to conquer this last bastion of evil.

As a result, the war was finally over. They should be celebrating now, relishing the end of years of campaigning and battle. However, the murder of the four young slaves seemed to have ruined Aiduel's sense of triumph.

Amena was confused. This was a grim scene, but she knew that her husband had witnessed much worse violence and death across the course of the last two decades. His current level of grief was therefore disconcerting.

'What is it, Aiduel?' she asked. 'Why are you so upset?'

'I killed them, Mena,' he answered, his voice lacking its usual vibrancy and authority. 'I killed all four of them. Am I any different to the Angalls?'

Amena glanced down at the children on the floor, feeling more confusion and uncertainty.

'You didn't kill them,' she said. 'The Vizier and his soldiers did it. You did everything you could to save them, my love, but we were just too late.'

'I killed them, Mena.'

His body was trembling as he wept against her shoulder, and she was stroking his sandy-coloured hair.

'I don't understand,' she stated. Amena was certain that she had never seen the four victims before. 'These children were dead before you arrived, Aiduel. And think of all the slaves, all the children, who have been saved today. Freed today. Sennam is free because of your actions. As is the rest of Angall and our homeland. The war's over, and we've won, all because of *you*.'

'I know,' he said, and he lifted his head from her shoulder, such that they were face-to-face. His gaze fixed upon hers, his dark, piercing eyes once again seeming to peer into her very soul. 'We've won, and you think I should be celebrating. *I* recognise that I should be celebrating. But now that it's finally over, I also recognise something else.'

'What, my love?'

'That everything I've done, everything *we've* done, it isn't enough. Nothing is enough. Nothing makes up for what I did at the start, when I claimed my powers. Nothing can make amends for my sin.'

Amena could perceive the depth of the distress held within him, as she gazed into his eyes.

'What sin?' she asked. 'What did you do? Stop talking in riddles, Aiduel. Please, speak plainly to me.'

'I've a confession that I need to make, Mena. Something which I need to share. Something that I've kept crushed within myself, for all the time that I've known you. Please forgive me for keeping this from you.'

'A confession?'

'Yes,' he said, his voice full of anguish. 'For so many years, I've been trying to make amends. Trying to do good, to offset a *single* terrible act. But no matter how hard I try to block the memory of it, it's been coming back to me in dreams, more and more. It tortures me.'

'I've seen your troubled sleep, my love.'

'And *today*, finding these dead children,' he continued, 'it's making me feel that it's all too much. I'll never escape from what I did, no matter what I achieve. I need to share my sin with someone, Mena, before it drives me to madness. I need to confess.'

As he spoke those last words, she could again feel the turbulent pulsing of the powers within him, making her worry that he might shatter the protections of the medallion which he had made for her. She placed a hand onto the side of his head.

'Don't speak to me of madness, my love,' she whispered. 'Please, be calm. If you wish to confess to me, then do it. But whatever it is that you've done, I'm going to forgive you, because you're a good man.'

He had stopped sobbing, and he now took a deep breath, his face solemn.

'Words are not enough for this,' he said. 'Put aside the medallion, Mena, and I'll *show* you.'

She nodded, stepping several metres away from him to the far side of the chamber. She then grasped the necklace and medallion, and removed them from her neck, before depositing them onto a wooden dresser. On the same necklace chain was a small wooden carving of Aiduel on The Tree, which more and more of their followers had taken to wearing in recent years.

After she had returned to him, he placed his hands onto her shoulders. She sighed when she felt him entering her mind, and she willingly accepted the intimate joining between them. Invisible tendrils connected the two of them, caressing her thoughts and creating feelings of pleasure within her.

The ease with which he penetrated her mind and soul served to remind her of how different he was to everyone else, despite his decency and humanity. How supreme he was. How godlike.

She shivered, and could see him watching her. He knew her every thought in this state.

Are you ready?

The question was asked without spoken words. In response, she nodded.

She closed her eyes, and it started. Visions began to play out in her mind, as if she was in another place, at another time, and was seeing all. She knew then that he was sharing his memories.

There was a winding path, on the side of a mountain. And in

what followed, she witnessed an inexorable ascent of that mountain, with four young companions. Two boys and two girls. Then she gazed upon an astounding vision of an awe-inspiring and ethereal archway, which caused her to gasp aloud in wonder.

However, shortly afterwards, she emitted a number of horrified screams. Four in total.

And each scream represented a death.

—

Later, she was wearing her medallion again. She was sitting upright, with Aiduel's head on her lap, and she was stroking his hair.

She was scrutinising his face, while his eyes were closed. And she was thinking about their life together, knowing that he had removed himself from inside of her mind. She was reflecting upon what she had witnessed in his vision, and was considering how it might colour her own memories of their lives and their marriage.

He had been a boy in his late-teens when they had first declared their love for each other. He had been two years younger than her, and had been struggling to reconcile himself with what he had become, and to the momentous duties which lay before him. She had been the first amongst his early followers to recognise the human frailty which still lived within their new god, beneath the facade of his almighty power.

Since then, it had always been her duty, and her privilege, to remind him that he was still a man. And to love him. She felt a sense of peace at that moment, as she recognised that today's revelation did nothing to change that. He was her husband, the man she had dedicated her life to, and she loved him.

'I understand now,' she said, finally. 'And I wish with all of my heart that you'd shared this with me many years ago. That you'd not carried this burden alone, for such a long time.'

He did not say anything, and she knew that he was fearing her judgement, and was bracing himself for her scorn.

After a moment, she added, 'As your wife, I forgive you, Aiduel. And as your Arch Priestess and Lawmaker, I absolve you of this sin.'

She heard him exhale loudly, before he asked, 'You do not condemn me? You do not turn away from me in horror?'

'No. Never, my love. You know everything about me that there is to know, Aiduel, and now I believe that I've seen your darkest secret. I forgive you for what you did, and I still love you as before for the good man that you are.'

'Thank you, Mena.'

'But...'

'But?'

'This confession ends with me, Aiduel,' she said. 'You've told no one else?'

'No. Never.'

'Then you must keep it that way, and we'll carry the burden of this secret together. I'll always be here to remind you that you're forgiven. But the others... you mustn't tell them. We both know that this could undermine so much of the good that we've done. It could destroy the faith.'

'I know.'

'Then forgive yourself, Aiduel, and let's leave this room.' She rose to her feet, and held out her hand to him. 'Come now, my love. Our people will be waiting to see you, and they'll be expecting you to give a victory speech.'

He stood up, taking her hand. 'They will. Thank you again, Mena. For everything.'

She leaned in close, kissing him on the mouth, and said, 'And thank you, my husband. My Lord, my God. We stand at the dawn of a new age. *Your* new age, Aiduel. You can remake this world as a better place. You can make amends for what you did, a thousand times over. It is time to put the past behind us.'

Part Three

—

Siege and Revelation

—

*Year of Our Lord,
After Ascension, 770AA*

24

Allana

—

*Year of Our Lord,
After Ascension, 770AA*

Allana could sense the presence pulsing towards her from within the besieged town of Septholme. Even though she was almost two hundred metres from the town's walls, and was outside the ring of invading forces which had encircled the settlement, she could still feel the *other*.

There could be no doubt that it was someone like her. Someone else with *powers*. Allana felt revitalised and strong, in a way that she had only ever experienced when in close proximity to Arion Sepian.

Which meant that the presence in the town was either Arion, or was the woman known as the Angel of Arlais. If the former, then Allana's scheme to remove the Sepian noble had failed. If the latter, then the famous priestess with powers was indeed within Western Canasar. And someone would soon be able to claim the enormous reward for her return to Aiduel's Guards, if the woman survived the coming days.

But whichever of them it was, Allana was certain that this other could feel her proximity, just as she could sense them. If it was Arion, how would he be feeling to have detected her again? Would his heart be beating faster, to know that she was once again so close? And if it was this Leanna, perhaps she would be as confused as Allana herself had once been, and would be wondering about the cause of the strange sensations within her body?

Do you think that Arion will want to come to you, Lana, if it's truly him? Would he be prepared to leave his family and his wife, just for you?

Allana had plenty of time to dwell upon these considerations, because she was bored. She was sitting outside of her and Jarrett's tent, within an army encampment to the north-east of the town. It was not exciting to be waiting in this fixed camp, and to be a redundant witness to the preparations for a siege. Even her fascination about this other person with powers was not enough to alleviate her boredom.

Three days had passed since they had arrived at Septholme. Three days in which she had been sitting around or inside her tent, or wandering within the boundaries of the camp. She was not participating in any of the constructive activities which were going on around her, and she felt useless.

Their sprawling encampment had already taken on an air of permanence. A large number of army followers were located within its perimeter, situated far enough away from the town and its bristling defences to be out of immediate danger.

Allana's location afforded a clear view of the northern and eastern walls of Septholme, and of the ring of earthworks which were being established by the invading army around the entire town. Jarrett had explained to her that the Dei Magnun fleet was completing this encirclement, as it blockaded the harbour.

Elannis and Berun soldiers were spread along the visible length of the encircling earthworks. However, the majority of Elannis soldiers were camped on the fields facing Septholme's northern wall. Allana understood from Jarrett that the main assault would come from that direction, if the town was not surrendered peacefully.

To the east of her position, Allana had already witnessed a bustle of activity as Elannis engineers were cutting down trees in the forest. These soldiers were building a series of large constructions which Jarrett described as siege engines. That work was ongoing today, with regular crashing noises in the distance which heralded the toppling of one large tree after another.

However, the sight to which Allana's eyes were drawn most regularly was to the direct south of her position, several hundred metres away. She had often found herself staring towards it since her arrival, and she felt unsettled every time. It was a squat and ominous structure, which was visible on a shallow hillside, facing across a valley to the far more impressive Septholme Castle.

This was the building which Allana had been taken to, after Gerrion Sepian had chosen to hand her over. This was the place where she had been intimidated, mistreated and tortured, by the monstrous Evelyn dei Laramin.

It was the fortress of Aiduel's Guards.

Her gaze now rested upon its grim walls. She knew that it would not help to keep dwelling upon the wretched things that they had done to her there. The way that they had treated her like filth. Had drowned her. Had burned her!

That's in the past, Lana, never to be repeated. Never!

But even the brief recollection caused her lip to tremble and a shudder to pass through her body.

Two days earlier, she had watched Aiduel's Guards reclaiming that fortress. It had initially been a relief to see a large number of the red-cloaked order departing from the main encampment. However, this emotion had been eclipsed hours later by intense unease, as she had witnessed wagonloads of captive young women being transported into the fortress.

Allana hated that those women were now inside the same dark walls which had once been her own prison. She did not like to consider what might be occurring inside.

She frowned as she spotted another wagon approaching the

fortress from the south. Again, there appeared to be figures squatting in the back of the trundling vehicle, as it turned into the grounds of the fort. Women with fair hair. In the preceding days, many other Aiduel's Guards had dispersed into the surrounding country, and it seemed that they were continuing to be busy in their search.

Why must they do this, Lana? The world would be a much better place if none of them were in it. If they were all dead!

She shuddered again, then turned her body such that she was facing away from the fortress.

Jarrett will be back soon, Lana. Until then, try to stop thinking about it.

—

'The stubborn woman has refused to surrender Septholme,' said Jarrett that evening, after he had returned to their tent. 'Despite all of our arguments, she says that she intends to defend the town, until the armies of Rednar arrive to defeat us.'

'And could that happen?' asked Allana. She was aware from Jarrett that emissaries of Elannis and Berun had approached the northern gate, earlier that day. Jarrett was describing the parley which had then taken place with Lady Kalyane Sepian, the woman who was Arion's wife.

'Of course not,' he said. 'Rednar's been overwhelmed, and Rednarron will be under siege. It might have already fallen, for all that we know. The garrison of Septholme is on its own.'

'And how did she react when she was told that her duke has been taken prisoner?'

After spotting Gerrion Sepian slumped over the back of an Elannis horse, several days earlier, Jarrett had soon confirmed that the young noble was still alive. Duke Sepian was now imprisoned within the fortress of Aiduel's Guards. The bitter irony of that was not lost on Allana, after the man had condemned her to torture in that very place.

'Our lead emissary says that she has a backbone,' replied Jarrett. 'He told us that when she heard the news, she appeared shaken, but that she soon composed herself and announced that it has no impact on her intentions. She states that she'll only surrender the town if she receives a direct order to do so from Duke Sepian, in person. She then informed our emissary that they've stored provisions for a long siege, and have the will to fight.'

Allana grimaced. Despite never having met this Lady Kalyane, she did not like her.

'She sounds arrogant,' she said. 'And foolish.'

Don't ask if she's beautiful, Lana.

Jarrett raised an eyebrow. 'I don't know about arrogant, because I wasn't there. But foolish, yes. A lot of people are going to lose their lives in the coming days, because of her.'

'So… if she was leading the discussions for the town,' added Allana, trying to adopt a casual manner, 'does that mean that Lord Arion Sepian is not there?'

'That must be the case,' replied Jarrett. 'Otherwise, it would have been his responsibility to lead the talks today. The coward must have fled.'

Allana took an involuntary glance in the direction of the town, towards the pulsing and vital presence.

If it's not Arion, Lana, then it must be the other one. This Priestess Leanna.

'He didn't dare to face you, Jarrett,' she said, trying to sound sincere as she spoke the words.

He nodded, and she saw his chest swell in reaction to her statement.

He's so easy to manipulate, Lana.

'So, what happens now, Jarrett?' she asked, trying to hide a smile.

'Our siege of the town starts in earnest,' he replied. 'They're trapped, with no means to get further supplies. But we're not going to wait for a prolonged siege and starvation. As soon as we've finished a ram for the gate and a number of siege ladders, we'll commence our assault. We massively outnumber the defenders, and it should be a simple matter to swarm over their walls and overwhelm them. We'll have this town conquered within days.'

—

Later, in the middle of the night, Allana was jolted from sleep.

She had been woken by her recurring dream, and the sense of half-remembered violence lingered upon waking. However, she was stunned to realise that she had also retained a new memory. After the single finger had been raised, words had been spoken by the figure in the Gate, in a voice which had swept over Allana like rolling thunder.

'ONLY ONE CAN CLAIM THE POWER…'

She trembled as fragments of that terrible voice echoed in her mind. More had been said afterwards, but she could not recall these further words, other than that she believed them to be a precursor to the violence which followed.

Only one can claim the power, Lana? Is that what you heard?

She turned onto her side, her body shaking further, and she realised that it would be impossible to return quickly to slumber. Panic was threatening.

'Jarrett's here,' she whispered.

She moved over to the duke, and felt his arm wrap around her in his sleep. It helped a little, but it was still becoming harder to breathe again, as if a damp cloth was restricting her airways. And did her legs suddenly feel painful, as if they were burning? As if she was back in captivity in the nearby fortress? She felt tears forming in her eyes.

'Jarrett's here.'

But the mantra was not working. The rational part of her recognised that seeing that bleak building again was reigniting her awful memories of torture. The additional terror caused by her memory of the voice in the dream was exacerbating this.

Tonight, even Jarrett's presence seemed insufficient to subdue her mounting sense of panic. Indeed, she was still shaking, and her chest now started to heave in silent sobs.

The things that Aiduel's Guards did to you are done and gone, Lana. They'll never touch you like that, ever again. You won't let them. It's the reaction of a child to cry about it, over and over. Stop thinking about it!

But her self-remonstration did not make the memories go away. Or the tears. Or her seething hatred for Aiduel's Guards, for what they had done to her.

However, the matter which remained foremost in her thoughts, as she fought against panic in the darkness, was the statement which she had heard in the dream.

Only one can claim the power.

—

The first assault on the northern walls and gate of the town was ready to commence, two days later.

Allana was able to observe events from a distance, as the army of Elannis assembled in orderly ranks on the lands before the town. In the centre of their forces was a lengthy triangular frame on wheels, beneath which an enormous tree trunk was hanging. There were also many ladders being carried, which had been constructed in the last few days.

Allana understood from Jarrett that various other siege equipment was not yet ready. Indeed, construction activity seemed to be continuing in the woods to the east. Jarrett had informed her that siege towers and trebuchets would take longer to complete, and that this first attack would rely on ladders and sheer weight of numbers. Jarrett expected the coming battle to be bloody, and Allana was relieved that her duke did not intend to participate in the assault.

Across from the Elannis forces, Allana could see that the battlements of the Septholme northern wall were bristling with men and weaponry. The defending soldiers were facing outwards in anticipation of the attack to come. Somewhere in the town behind them, Allana could feel the presence of the *other*, pulsing. The sensation seemed more vibrant today, and it was infusing her with energy.

Allana had invited Connar to stand with her again, so that she would have someone to answer her questions as the attack proceeded. After the triangular frame started to trundle towards the wall, pushed by dozens of soldiers, she pointed and asked, 'What's that?'

'That's the battering ram, my Lady,' he replied. 'They're advancing it to the gates, to try to break them down.'

'And will they succeed?'

'I don't know, my Lady.'

He was looking at her with an adoring expression as he replied, and she realised that she was tiring of his infatuation.

He's just a soldier, Lana. He lacks the required… power, to remain interesting to you.

A cluster of soldiers with shields raised high were surrounding the battering ram as it advanced. At a certain point, the siege engine and its protectors came into range of the defenders. A dark wave of missiles descended upon them, some of which were aflame. A number of Elannis soldiers fell under the barrage, and for moments the advance stalled, but others then rushed into place to keep the cumbersome ram rolling forwards.

Soon after, Allana witnessed the rest of the Elannis forces accelerating into a charge towards the walls. The defenders reacted with a further hail of arrows, spears and other projectiles which were fired and thrown from the battlements. The previously pristine Elannis ranks were soon splintered, leaving behind scores of bloodied bodies. A much less orderly mass of charging men then reached the base of the wall, at the same time that the battering ram arrived at the town gate.

Even from a distance, Allana could see the tall siege ladders being raised up by the attackers, and she was an excited witness as men began to ascend those ladders. Once again, despite her awareness of the suffering and death playing out before her, she found herself to be thrilled by the intense spectacle of men going to war.

She noticed then that the defenders were pouring something from the top of the wall, and a chorus of pitiful screaming was audible.

'What's that?' she asked. 'What's making them all scream?'

'It'll be oil, my Lady. Boiling oil.'

Allana winced at the thought, feeling even more relieved that Jarrett was not involved today. She could perceive that the attack up the ladders was already floundering. Very few men were making it to the height of the battlements, with most being attacked from above or having their ladder pushed away from the wall.

Despite these setbacks, the mass of soldiers at the base of the walls were continuing to attempt to ascend. Indeed, a few isolated clusters were managing to reach and fight atop the battlements. However, even these more successful attempts were soon cleared by the defenders.

At the northern gate, between two mighty defensive towers, there was even less apparent success. In the midst of a pile of bodies, it appeared that the siege ram was on fire. Allana was certain that she could hear cheering from the defenders in the towers.

At that moment, she felt the presence in the town pulse more strongly. There was a swift surge of power, but Allana felt as if an invisible hand had reached out and touched her, and had *taken* something from her. A trace of her energy. A mere trickle, but enough that she could feel its absence.

She recoiled. It seemed as if the *other* was near to that north gate. Either on the battlements or somewhere close behind.

Then there was another pulse, and a further rivulet of energy was drawn from Allana.

She felt sudden anger. 'How dare-'

'My Lady?' queried Connai, looking confused.

451

'Nothing,' she said, but she could still sense the connection. As if invisible fingers were touching her and were entering her body. Joining her to the other, through an ethereal bond. Drawing upon her energy. Somehow feeding upon her.

And violating her.

The assault on the northern walls ended sometime later. In Allana's estimation, its only achievement had been to leave hundreds of bodies and a burnt-out battering ram strewn on the land outside of the town.

Allana was in her tent, holding the poster of Leanna, Angel of Arlais, in her hands. She was staring at the image of the other woman, trying to reconcile the guileless face on the parchment with the violation of the preceding hours.

In truth, she was uncertain whether she was more angry or frightened. This person within the walls, this other who was like Allana and Arion, was somehow *using* her.

Allana felt tired and spent, as if much of the energy had been drained from her body. She had thought about trying to fight back, about resisting what this other was doing to her, but she had been unsure about what to do. If she was honest with herself, she had also been afraid of how this other might react to any attempt to stop this invisible, ethereal *touch*.

She was worried. This Angel of Arlais seemed so very powerful, to be able to do something like this. There had never been any sense that Arion had ever drawn energy from Allana, and Allana herself had never done this. Was this woman somehow more powerful than her? More skilled? More special?

Could she take it all if she wanted to, Lana? Is she a threat to you? Could she kill you?

Arion had only ever made Allana feel more alive, powerful and rejuvenated. Indeed, until this afternoon, Allana had felt similarly revitalised by this new person's presence. But ever since the assault on the town, there had been repeated bursts of power by the other, each of them incrementally draining more energy from Allana.

Even more confusingly, Allana could sense that the other presence was now as tired and depleted as she herself was. If this Priestess Leanna had indeed stolen energy and vitality from Allana, it did not seem that she had kept it for herself. She was using it for some unknown purpose, somewhere behind the walls of the town.

But whatever it was, Allana did not trust her. The other woman was taking what Allana was not freely giving, and this made her worthy of Allana's distrust and contempt.

This Leanna, Angel of Arlais, was a thief. And even worse, she was a violator.

How dare she do this to you, Lana. How dare she!

Allana looked at the image on the poster one last time, then crumpled the parchment within her hand and tossed it away. She would need to decide what to do to protect herself.

—

The drawing of Allana's energy continued intermittently into the evening hours, and she collapsed onto her cot that night, feeling exhausted. In the midst of sleep, the dream came to her again…

—

…He moves His hand, a summoning gesture, and once again her body takes her forwards. Seductive whispers of unspoken words assail her.

LUST. POWER. DOMINATION.

But then the gesture of His hand changes, and she is aware that something is wrong.

A single finger is raised. And she knows what she must do.

ONLY ONE CAN CLAIM THE POWER.

The words erupt from the Gate like rolling thunder, merciless and discordant, tasting and feeling like fire and ash.
KILL THEM TO MAKE IT YOURS. KILL THEM ALL!

—

She awoke gasping into the darkness, her chest heaving. She stared upwards, trying to contain her pressing anxiety.

Kill them, Lana. Kill them all. That's what you heard before the violence.

She recognised that she had retained even more of the words which had been spoken by the figure in the Gate, and she had remembered more of the dream. It felt like a revelation.

She wondered whether the presence of the woman Leanna could have somehow contributed to this? Allana did not know. However, as she struggled against the threat of panic, she was still thinking about those final words.

Kill them.

As she lingered upon this, her thoughts kept returning to the *other* inside the town of Septholme. The woman with apparently fearsome powers, who had drained Allana's energy, and had left her in this exhausted state. The woman who seemed to pose a possible danger to Allana's safety. And, perhaps, to her life?

Kill them all.

—

The next day, there was no equivalent assault from the forces of Elannis against the northern gate and walls. Instead, the focus of the invading army appeared to have returned to construction. From the woods to the east, there was a continuation of the felling of trees, and ongoing assembly of the massive siege engines.

In the land to the north of Septholme's walls, in sight of the defenders but out of range of archers, Allana noted that a different structure was being assembled. Something which had a raised wooden platform, with two vertical beams at either end, and a crossbeam between these.

Allana observed this latter construction process with interest. She was feeling much better today; her energy had recovered somewhat overnight, and her recovery was continuing this morning. There were occasional moments throughout the morning hours when she again felt power being drawn from her, but these were infrequent.

When Jarrett returned to her tent at midday, she asked him what the strange structure on the land in front of the northern walls was.

'It's a gallows,' he replied. 'For hanging someone by the neck.'

Allana grimaced. 'Hanging someone? Who?'

'Gerrion Sepian. We're going to send negotiators under another flag of truce, soon. And we'll tell them that unless they open their gates, lay down their arms, and surrender the town, they'll be watching their duke hang before sunset.'

'And do you think they will? Surrender?'

'I don't know.'

'So, you're going to kill him?'

'I don't think Markon has decided that yet. I suspect he'll decide later.'

Allana did not relish the thought of it.

Gerrion Sepian always hated you, Lana. But he still doesn't deserve this, surely?

Later, after Jarrett had departed, Allana returned to her place outside of the tent. Shortly afterwards, she saw a group of yellow-clad riders emerging from the fortress of Aiduel's Guards. As these riders drew closer, she could see that Duke Sepian was amongst them, with his hands bound. At one point, the young duke glanced across in Allana's direction, and she turned her head away, feeling suddenly embarrassed. However, in that brief moment, it seemed that he had recognised her.

The duke was soon led onto the raised platform of the now completed scaffold, which had a single rope hanging down from the crossbeam. Allana observed from a distance as a noose was placed around the neck of the captive, who was then left to stand in place. Sepian's hands were still bound, and he was facing Septholme.

Shortly after that, three figures emerged from the front of the Elannis ranks, walking towards the town with a flag of truce held before them. Allana watched as the three approached the walls, and then observed as a small wicket gate within the main gate was opened, to allow them entry.

She then waited, wondering what was going to happen next.

—

Sometime later, Allana observed the three figures re-emerging. The sun had passed its zenith during the period of waiting, and was now descending towards the western horizon.

Gerrion Sepian had been made to stand in place, on the gallows, for the duration of the afternoon. The noose had been around his neck for the entire time, and Allana wondered how the young duke would be feeling. Would his legs be shaking with fear? Would he be reflecting on how far he had fallen in just a matter of weeks; from duke of the town he now faced, to a condemned man standing on the gallows before it?

Allana could also identify the giant figure of Jarrett, looming close to the scaffold structure. He was alongside the tall, blonde Prince Markon.

On the town walls, thousands of people were visible, suggesting that the soldiers had been joined by many townsfolk. There was a palpable silence along those battlements, with none of the jeering or defiant gestures which had been prevalent in the preceding days.

Allana watched as the three emissaries approached Prince Markon, and she observed a shaking of heads as they exchanged words with the royal. The prince then turned to face the prisoner, addressing a further unheard message to the figure on the gallows. Allana saw Gerrion Sepian shaking his head in turn, appearing to reject whatever had been said to him.

From all of these observations and interactions, Allana could quickly understand what the answer from Lady Kalyane Sepian had been. The threat had been rebuffed. Septholme was not going to surrender. There would be no quick resolution to this siege.

And Duke Gerrion Sepian was going to hang.

25

Arion

—

*Year of Our Lord,
After Ascension, 770AA*

In the aftermath of his desertion from the army of King Sendar Pavil, Arion had been travelling on his own for two days.

After setting out alone on horseback in the darkness hours, he had covered a lot of ground on that first night. The next day, after a short rest, he had set out on an extended arc around the city of Condarron. He had chosen to sacrifice the most direct route to reduce the risk of encountering enemy patrols, and he had been journeying on country trails ever since.

He was now beginning to regret his decision to take the long way round. For these two days, he had been travelling through countryside which was a patchwork of anonymous fields and forests, interwoven with a winding maze of trails. He knew that he had been maintaining the right general direction towards Rednarron, although he had already lost significant time after twice being forced to backtrack. He was also uncertain whether he had yet crossed the border from Condarr into the province of Rednar.

The sun would soon be setting at the end of his second full day of lone travel, and he felt tired and hungry. During the prior night, he had slept rough, settling down on a bedroll on the dry banks beside a stream. It had been a broken night of sleep, which had been disturbed further by his recurring dream of the Gate.

He was certain that he had again heard words being spoken prior to violence in the dream. However, once more the memory of those words and the nature of that violence had eluded him after waking.

For much of this day, he had been feeling tense. A sense of urgency had been with him ever since the events at the Royal Palace, and he felt it again now. It was like fingers clenching around his heart, accompanied by an accusing whisper in his mind, which warned him to get back to Septholme before it was too late. He had a foreboding that terrible things were going to happen to his loved ones, if he did not reach them in time to make amends for all of his wrong decisions. Such anxiety had made his detours during the day even more frustrating.

He emerged now from an extensive woodland, and spotted a grand farmhouse and accompanying barn, several hundred metres away. From its size and whitewashed facade, it looked like the residence of wealthier farmers or landowners, and there was a flickering of firelight visible through the lower windows. Arion craved a proper meal, and did not want to sleep outdoors for another night, so he urged his horse on towards the property.

He heard the dogs before he saw them, their frantic barks sounding from the yard in front of the building as he drew nearer. Moments later, four men appeared from the front door of the property. Each was carrying a weapon, but they kept a careful distance from Arion.

'Be at ease,' said Arion hastily, raising his hand as he did so. 'I'm just a traveller, passing through. I'm no threat to you or to your families.'

'Be on your way then,' said the closest man, who was a short figure with a noticeable mass of facial hair. 'We don't want any strangers bringing trouble down on us.'

'I want no trouble either, sir. Just a meal, if that's possible, and somewhere to sleep. I'll pay.'

The hirsute man squinted at Arion. 'We don't know you, sir. And this isn't a good time for being hospitable to strangers. What's a lone rider doing out here, and who do you serve?'

'My name is Arion, and I'm a Knight of the Realm. I ride to Western Canasar, to return to my family there. My loyalty is to the king, to Andar, and to the duke of Western Canasar.'

The speaker frowned. 'And your thoughts on Houses Condarr and Rednar?'

Arion considered his response. If his answer upset them, they would be of little threat to him, and he would simply lose out on a place to sleep.

'Duke Condarr has turned traitor,' he said. 'Rednar are my allies, and I would happily fight for their cause.'

Arion watched as the four men exchanged quiet words with each other. There was some nodding, then the lead speaker announced, 'Very well, we'll not turn you away. My family are true to House Rednar, so we'll let you rest here. We'll get you a meal, and you can sleep in my barn, but I want you gone by dawn tomorrow.'

'That would be perfect, thank you,' said Arion, feeling relieved. 'Am I in Rednar, then?'

'You are. We're fifteen miles from the border with Condarr, but we're firmly inside Rednar territory. Although, from the reports that we've heard, so is most of the army of Elannis.'

—

Arion was thankful for the hospitality of the household that evening. He ate a hearty meal, and the hirsute farmer provided directions towards Rednarron.

Arion tried to glean more information, but he soon established that his hosts' knowledge of wider events was limited; they knew only that Rednar had been invaded and that Rednarron was under siege. Arion was relieved that they had not received any news of the city's fall.

Later, as he was settling down to sleep in the barn, his thoughts returned to a subject which had been troubling him; his role in the murders at the Royal Palace, and the madness of his actions in the hours before and during those events. He was still struggling to make sense of the fact that he had been there at all, and that he could have acted in such a rash way.

He was particularly troubled by the suspicion that he had been used by Sendar Pavil. Prince Senneos's protestations seemed too genuine in hindsight, and Arion now had worrying doubts about Sendar's possible role in his father's death. If Sendar *had* committed treason, then Arion had become his unwitting accomplice and saviour, by the reckless act of storming into the palace.

Once again, Arion regretted his foolish decision to travel to Andarron, after being lured by the false message.

By the Lord, if only I'd ignored that fucking letter!

The more that Arion considered the missive which had led to all of his current woes, the more that he returned to one of two conclusions. Either Allana dei Monis still lived, and had chosen to mislead him, or she was dead, and someone else had deceived him.

However, the only other people who could possibly have known that he had *any* interest in Allana were either Leanna, or the pair of Aiduel's Guards who had notified him that the Dei Magnun woman was dead.

He did not believe for one moment that Leanna could have been involved, which left the only possible suspects as the two Aiduel's Guards. And he could not see how they could have been aware of the intimate details which had been referred to in the letter.

Therefore, the most plausible conclusion was that Allana still lived, and that *she* had deceived him. If that explanation was true, then it also followed that she was responsible for luring him away from his home, his family and his wife. *She* was the one who had made him a betrayer and a king-slayer. And she had put him on the wrong side of the country, at a time when his land was being invaded. An action which had led to the death of Charl Koss and to the possible death of Gerrion.

At the start of each evening since the events at the palace, Arion had felt frustration and self-pity. But with each night that he dwelled upon his suspicions, his emotions were morphing into something else.

Something darker.

Sometime later, he finally drifted into sleep on his bed of straw. Once again, during his slumber that night, one of his dreams was far more vivid and intense than all of the others…

He was running down the hill from the castle in Septholme, towards the sea.

He could immediately sense that the situation was dire, with the acrid smell of smoke and fire present in the air. From somewhere nearby, he could hear screams amidst a ringing clash of arms.

His attention though was drawn to the waterfront. Out on the ocean, a line of Dei Magnun warships had bows pointing in the direction of the harbour, seemingly travelling in that direction.

But ahead of them, something was… shimmering, risen from the surface of the churning sea. An ethereal, golden wall of light, which was standing high above the frothing waves. It was radiant, vast and breathtaking.

Then he saw the monster. It was on the road ahead of him, much closer to the harbour. It was a beast; dark, inhuman and shockingly fast.

This creature was bounding towards the seafront and quay, and was causing terror amongst many townsfolk as it barrelled straight through them.

He was sprinting in apparent pursuit, rushing past a corpse which looked as if its throat had been ripped out. Then he spotted another of the beasts, also ahead. This one was leaping from rooftop to rooftop with unnatural agility, and its destination again appeared to be the harbour.

The ethereal wall of light seemed ever more imposing as he approached the entrance to the waterfront. He was drawing closer to the beasts, but they disappeared from sight as they entered the quayside area. Moments later, he could hear monstrous howls, followed by a chorus of distinctly more human screams.

It dawned on him then that these creatures were hunting. And, if so, it seemed that they had at last found their prey...

—

He awoke from this vision with his body drenched in sweat beneath his clothing. For a few moments, he struggled to draw breath. He had been unsettled by prior visions in his prophetic dreams, but this one had left him both bewildered and frightened.

By the Lord! What was I seeing?

It was still night-time, but he knew that sleep would elude him after what he had witnessed. He stood up, and started to pack his gear in preparation for leaving.

He had to return to Septholme, and he would need to take greater risks to get home sooner. That would include travelling on main roads to reach Rednarron as soon as possible, and he would have to circle closer to that city.

He was full of fearful apprehension. Something terrible was going to happen in his home town. Many people were going to lose their lives, unless he could do something to save them.

He needed to be there before it was too late.

—

After leaving the farm, Arion began to follow the farmer's directions towards the main highway to Rednarron.

He wanted to go faster than the steady trot of his horse, but he knew that he needed his mount to retain some reserves of stamina, in case he encountered enemy soldiers.

By the time that dawn had passed, he was journeying in a south-easterly direction, travelling through a gloomy forest. Eventually, he emerged onto the main road between Condarron and Rednarron, and continued in the direction of the latter. The farmer had estimated that it would be over a day's travel to Rednar's capital, once Arion reached the highway.

Arion had decided that he was going to risk travelling on this route in daylight, in the hope that the armies of Elannis were still bogged down around Rednarron. Once he got nearer to the city itself, he would need to find a way to skirt around any besieging enemy lines.

The highway proved to be quiet as he rode along it, and the weather was fair. He made good progress for the remainder of the day and did not encounter any Elannis soldiers. As he travelled, he had a lot of time to think about the strangeness of his latest prophetic vision, with its images of monsters and a golden wall of light.

He no longer trusted blindly in the visions, for they had been proven to be unreliable guides. Although some had served him well, and had given him an opportunity to prepare for events still to come, the dream of the palace had tricked him. It had obscured the truth to encourage him to a place where he should never have gone, and had led him to commit a series of shameful acts.

Furthermore, whilst none of his prior visions had been entirely transparent, they had at least retained a grounding in reality; boats on a beach, an army at a river, a woman on a pyre, and a battle in a royal palace.

But this latest dream had contained images which seemed utterly implausible. Shimmering walls of light rising above the ocean while nightmare monsters raced through the streets of Septholme. How could any of that be a vision of what was to come? Of something that he might face if he returned home? It was hard not to be incredulous, but it still worried him.

He was also thinking about his family as he travelled onwards. His thoughts often turned to Gerrion, who had gone missing. Did his brother still live, or had he fallen in battle? And if the latter, how would Karienne be coping with the loss of another family member?

But most of all, Arion was thinking about Kalyane. About the loving wife whom he had been prepared to betray in Andarron. What would he say to her if he made it home and was reunited with her? Would he confess to his misdeeds and adulterous intentions? Or would he carry his actions and lies as secrets within, to further compound his crimes and guilt?

In his heart, he wanted to tell her everything and to beg for forgiveness. Only by doing that might he try to do right by her and restore his honour.

However, if he failed to reach Septholme in time, none of it might matter.

After another short night of sleeping outdoors, Arion was back on the road the next morning. He was soon travelling along a series of rolling hills and valleys, again encountering very little traffic on the highway. The road seemed to be drawing closer to the coast, with the waters of the ocean appearing in the distance whenever he ascended from the depths of the valleys. He was again remaining alert, but he knew that in his haste he was taking a risk by staying on the main highway for so long.

In the early afternoon, as soon as he passed over the crest of another hill, he spotted the barricade blocking the road.

Lord preserve me! This means trouble.

Two wagons had been placed sideways across the highway, approximately one hundred metres away. Around those vehicles were standing upwards of three score of soldiers, with over a dozen horses hitched nearby. The uniform of the soldiers was the yellow tabard of Elannis.

In the distance behind them, a couple of miles away and at sea-level, was Rednarron. From this vantage point, Arion could immediately observe that the city was surrounded and besieged by an enormous army. There were visible flickers of flame and plumes of smoke rising from various buildings across Rednar's capital. The city appeared to be in deep trouble.

Arion took in all of these details in moments, before his gaze flashed back to the barricade. Unfortunately, the soldiers stationed there had observed him cresting the hill at the same time as he had spotted them. He could see an officer pointing, and other soldiers moving to their mounts. Trying to feign a casual air, Arion turned his horse around. He then directed it at a trot back the way he had come, quickly putting him out of sight of the Elannis soldiery.

As soon as he was concealed from view, he spurred his mount into a gallop, and started searching for a route off the highway onto fields or side-trails. He glanced backwards while turning onto such a trail and saw mounted Elannis soldiers cresting the hill.

He knew that they would continue to pursue him along this side-trail, and he would not be able to outrun that many horsemen for long without rendering his own mount useless.

As his horse galloped onwards, with the sound of pursuit drawing closer, Arion felt his powers crackling into life. Energy and strength rushed into his body.

After that, it became a question of when, and not if, he would stand and fight.

—

In the aftermath of the battle, he was once again covered in blood and gore. Despite his discomfort, he would need to continue on like this, since he would have no time to wash. Eight Elannis horsemen had pursued him along the trail, and eight corpses were now splayed around the small clearing where he had chosen to make his stand.

Yet again, his powers had saved him during the battle. One of the Elannis cavalrymen had shot a crossbow bolt into his upper back from close range, which had pierced Arion's armour but had not broken his flesh. For any other man, the quarrel might have been expected to rupture vital organs, leading to death, but Arion was unharmed.

He now picked out the healthiest looking two horses from amongst the Elannis animals, and quickly transferred his gear onto them. His own horse had become tired from the prolonged journey, and it was time to abandon it.

He was soon mounted up and riding away from the clearing, without making any effort to conceal the carnage left behind. He had no doubt that the Elannis soldiers at the barricade would later send out scouts to look for their missing colleagues. Once they found the scene of slaughter, they would conclude that their compatriots had been led into a trap, and massacred by a superior force. After that, it was possible that there might be another pursuit, by a much larger group.

Arion therefore recognised that he must depart this area quickly, navigating a route around the city and its besieging army. He estimated that he had already journeyed across almost two thirds of the land distance between Andarron and Septholme, to reach this point. However, his home was still distant, and the roads for the many miles ahead might be teeming with enemy soldiers.

He had no doubt that he could handle groups of eight without any great difficulty. But when would he reach his limit? At what point would he find himself outnumbered and overwhelmed, with his energy too depleted for his powers to continue to save him? Would it be at twenty enemies? That felt unlikely. But at fifty? A hundred? Possibly.

He did not know for sure, and nor did he want to find out. But he must follow this new trail now, and try to stay alert to threats. The borders of Western Canasar were his next goal. After that, he could finally focus on the journey through his homeland to Septholme.

He felt certain that he would have to fight again, and kill again, if he was ever to reach his destination. However, after the prophetic vision in his dream, of much greater concern was what he would face when he finally arrived.

26

Leanna

—

*Year of Our Lord,
After Ascension, 770AA*

Leanna was standing on the northern ramparts of Septholme, in the midst of thousands of other citizens and soldiery of the town. Amyss was close beside her, the smaller woman's hand resting casually on Leanna's lower back.

Despite Leanna's miracles of healing during the previous day, she had retained her general anonymity, and her presence here was not remarked upon. However, she could sense the crowd's collective anxiety about the event which threatened to play out before them.

The dark gallows had been erected on the lands outside of the town, two hundred metres away from Leanna's position. Two individuals were standing upon that raised wooden platform. One cut a forlorn figure; a man who was slightly built, with dark hair. He stood with his hands bound before him and a noose around his neck.

Duke Gerrion Sepian.

The other figure was burlier, and was standing beside what appeared to be a lever. From the murmurs which Leanna had heard, one pull of that lever would drop the duke to his death.

The pair had been standing like that for many minutes now, ever since the Elannis emissaries had returned to their own army. In the meantime, the sun was drawing low to the west, colouring the sky with an angry orange glow.

Lord Aiduel, please let them show mercy on this poor man.

The mood amongst the watching crowd was subdued, and word had spread that Lady Kalyane had again rejected the Elannis demands. She had apparently insisted that she would only surrender the town if her duke ordered her to, in person. The Elannis emissaries had not returned to the North Gate since their earlier visit, and it appeared that no such order had been issued by the captive.

Leanna's eyes focused upon Gerrion Sepian, wondering how he would be coping with this cruel ordeal.

Lord Aiduel, please give him the strength to endure this. Please help me to-

'I know what you're considering, Lea,' whispered Amyss, interrupting the thought. 'But even if you can, don't you dare try to intervene.'

Leanna was startled. She had indeed considered whether her powers would work from this great distance. Whether, should that lever be pulled, she would be able to hold the duke up. To save him, as she had saved Caddin.

'I'm not sure I could do it, Amyss,' she said, also whispering. 'Even with… the *other*, it might be too far.'

She could still sense the other of her kind, out there in the Elannis encampment; the same presence that she had been aware of ever since the arrival of the besieging army, almost a week earlier. Leanna stared in the *other's* direction, and her eyes once again found the figure whom she had identified earlier.

The woman was petite with long black hair, and was standing beside a large tent on a raised embankment, to the east of the gallows.

Even from this distance, Leanna felt sure that she could sense an aura of pulsating power which flowed and swirled around this individual.

Leanna was certain that this person was the *one*, the source of the vibrant sensation which tingled within her. The woman who was filling her with energy, and who had given her the strength to work miracles in the hospital.

Another one of the Illborn.

Allana.

—

The last few days had been fraught with tension, ever since the arrival of the invading armies from the north, and from that moment when Leanna had recognised the presence of another of her own kind.

Throughout that time, she had been aware of the constant energising proximity of this *other*. She had wondered briefly if it could be Arion, and whether he had been taken prisoner. However, she had not truly believed that to be the case, because something about this new presence had felt… *different*.

On the fourth night after the besieging armies had arrived, Leanna had been disturbed from her sleep. She had been awoken by an emotion of suffering which had beaten out from the other Illborn, even across the distance which separated them.

This other person had been in distress, almost close to panic. The feelings of sorrow and fear had shocked Leanna, and her ability to interpret them had confirmed her belief that the presence was not Arion.

Leanna had concluded then that it must be Allana, who Arion had once seemed to be so besotted with. Somehow, the young woman had become attached to the invading army.

Leanna had remained awake for the rest of that night, sharing in the woman's pain. In the darkness of her castle bed, with Amyss sleeping beside her, she had wished that she had been able to hold this Allana. And to comfort her, and to heal her.

In the days before the first assault on the walls, Leanna had continued to play a role in establishing the temporary hospitals in the town.

She had been aware during those tense days that parley was being held between Lady Kalyane and the emissaries of Elannis. Indeed, there had still been a lingering hope amongst the townsfolk of a peaceful outcome, although Leanna had known that the noblewoman was stalling for time.

However, on the fifth night of the siege, Caddin had visited Leanna and Amyss, and had announced, 'I think that they'll attack the North Gate tomorrow. Get the hospital ready, but stay well away from the northern wall.'

The following day, Leanna and Amyss had been in the northern field hospital, a building two hundred metres back from the North Gate, when the first assault had started.

Leanna had been able to hear screams and hollers carrying from the ramparts of the wall for twenty minutes, before any casualties had started to arrive at the hospital. The wounded and dying had then poured in, a tide of unfortunate men suffering from an assortment of cuts, breaks and occasional burns.

Leanna had decided to use her full healing powers, and she had forewarned the other physicians and healers about her abilities. This warning had been met with some sceptical looks, but that scepticism had later turned to awe as she had miraculously healed a succession of injured men.

She had mended breaks, closed cuts, and restored flesh. She had knitted wounds and had torn out the blackness of injury, under the ministrations of the ethereal fingers which were hers to control. It had not taken long for a crowd to gather in reverent awe around her, while she had tended to a succession of patients. As she had done this, they had all been illuminated by the radiant glow around Leanna's body.

'She is blessed by The Lord,' Amyss had announced often, with pride in her voice, 'and she does The Lord's work.'

Leanna had healed scores of wounded men over the course of the day, though she had not acted alone. *Allana* had helped her throughout those hours; revitalising her and feeding her with energy, such that she could perform Aiduel's holy work.

Leanna's powers had been enhanced while in the proximity of the other woman. But more than that, Allana's nearby presence had given Leanna access to a vast reservoir of energy. She had felt a connection with the other Illborn throughout that first day of battle, and it had provided Leanna with new reserves of power, even as her own resources were being depleted by the relentless stream of wounded.

By the end of that day, Leanna had felt exhausted and close to collapse. But without Allana, she would have been spent much sooner, and many more soldiers would have died. Only with the wonderful support of the other woman had Leanna been able to find the endurance to heal everyone who had passed through the hospital doors.

After her final act of healing, Leanna had put her hands together in prayer.

Lord Aiduel, thank you for the work that you've allowed me to do today, and for the lives that you've allowed me to save. And thank you for bringing Allana to this place, to help me in your holy work. Please watch over her and protect her.

—

Leanna was startled now to finally notice some movement in the area around the gallows.

She observed a figure whom she recognised as Prince Markon walking onto the platform, and appearing to address both Gerrion Sepian and the large man beside the lever.

Leanna drew in a deep breath as she watched. She also readied herself, still unsure how she would react if the body of Gerrion

Sepian were to drop. Almost unconsciously, she touched the pulsing connection with Allana.

Markon then stepped down from the raised platform. The burly man beside the lever moved and Leanna jolted. However, the man's movement was purely to reach across to Gerrion Sepian, and to remove the noose from around the duke's neck. The prisoner was then led down from the gallows.

The breath that Leanna released was accompanied by a similar exhalation from many in the crowd around her.

It seemed that Duke Gerrion Sepian was not going to die today, after all.

Later, Leanna was taking dinner in Septholme Castle. She was seated at the table in the Great Hall with Lady Kalyane, Lady Karienne, Menion Thatcher, Caddin and Amyss.

Kalyane was quiet as they ate, appearing distracted and pale. After noticing this, Leanna reached out and took hold of the other woman's hand.

'You made a difficult decision today, Lady Kalyane,' she said. 'A decision that must have been awful to make. But you did what you believed to be *right*.'

Kalyane took a deep breath. 'Thank you. I know that, I really do. And I know that if Gerrion had wanted me to do otherwise, he'd have told me to surrender the town. But... if they'd actually...'

She left the sentence unfinished, and Leanna could see tears forming in the emerald-green eyes of the noblewoman. In the preceding days, everything that Leanna had witnessed of Kalyane had reinforced her first impressions of Arion's wife. Arion was married to a *good* woman, who was in possession of deep reserves of inner strength. Leanna squeezed Kalyane's hand.

'They didn't, my Lady,' stated Menion Thatcher after a few moments. 'With our thanks to The Lord, Duke Gerrion still lives.

But… we think another attack may come tomorrow. Please, may we discuss?'

With Kalyane's consent, such a discussion was then led by Caddin. The grey-bearded man displayed an impressive understanding of every aspect of the city's defences, and he talked in an assured manner which contained none of his past belligerence. Leanna noted that Sendromm was completely sober, as indeed he had been for the entire preceding week.

Lord Aiduel, thank you for starting this man on his journey of redemption.

Leanna had witnessed a transformation in Caddin during the last week, ever since the cathartic events of his attempted suicide and subsequent confession. Leanna's powers had saved his life by raising the taut rope which had been strangling the life out of him, and now he was a man *reborn*. He appeared to have been given new life and purpose.

From those depths of despair, Caddin had re-emerged to engage with commitment towards the town's preparations for siege. Sendromm's expertise was such that Captain Menion Thatcher had effectively ceded authority to the older man.

'We also have good news, thanks to Priestess Leanna,' Thatcher now stated, catching Leanna's attention. '*All* of the men who were wounded in the first assault are now back on active duty. Every single one of them. Over eighty men, all healed to full health by the miracle of the priestess's work. We lost thirty men to death in that battle, but we've lost no one to injury, which is incredible. The toll on the enemy was much greater. If we keep that going, we may just have a chance.'

'It truly is a miracle,' stated Kalyane, turning towards Leanna. 'A miracle befitting of the Angel of Arlais. But *can* you keep it going, Leanna?'

Leanna met the woman's gaze. 'For as long as I have the strength, yes.'

Lord Aiduel, please give me that strength.

But she knew that she would not be able to do it alone.

The next morning, there was indeed another attack.

The flow of wounded on this day was greater, and the fighting on the northern ramparts sounded even fiercer.

Leanna was sorely beset from the outset, and the volume of casualties meant that she was not able to address all of the injured. Some of those with less serious wounds were left to be dealt with by other physicians, using more conventional means.

Lord Aiduel, why must we choose to inflict such suffering on each other? Why can't there just be peace in this world?

However, Leanna still healed scores of the wounded. She called upon her own reserves of energy, and was also thankful for the sustenance that she drew from Allana.

By mid-afternoon, the battle on the northern wall had been raging for three hours, and Leanna was close to exhaustion. The aura of the woman Allana also seemed dull and depleted. By this time, the field hospital was filled beyond its capacity, with every bed and area of floorspace taken up.

Leanna's forearms and dress were covered in blood. She stood up, moving away from a patient whom she had just pulled back from the brink of death, and she felt suddenly woozy.

'Lea, are you alright?'

Amyss was beside her, placing her arm around Leanna's back and waist, to hold her upright.

'I just need a rest, Amyss. A few moments.'

'You need more than a few moments. This is too much, even for you.'

'Just a-'

She was interrupted by one of the other physicians shouting, 'We've just had word from the wall. The attack failed again. The battle's over!'

There was a muted cheer from the people around Leanna, and she forced herself to stand up straight.

Lord Aiduel, please give me the energy to carry on, for just a little longer. Please help me to continue to save lives.

And for the rest of that afternoon, she did.

—

The next day, there was another massed assault. Once again, Leanna exhausted herself and Allana close to depletion as she attempted to heal as many as possible. Leanna repeatedly dragged the most severely wounded away from the clutches of death, whilst bathed in a halo of golden light.

In The Lord Aiduel's name, she was working countless miracles in the small field hospital. She could hear reverence in the voices of the injured men as they were brought before her, and it was clear that word had already spread throughout the army and the town about the hospital's angel of healing.

The northern walls held again, that day.

At dinner that evening, in Septholme Castle, Leanna was feeling physically and mentally drained. She wanted to close her eyes and sleep, but she forced herself to pay attention to Menion Thatcher and Caddin's report of the day.

'We've held them back three times now, my Lady,' said Thatcher. 'But we fear that soon we'll face our most difficult test. Despite Priestess Leanna's… miracles, we've now suffered almost three hundred deaths since these assaults started. We estimate that the enemy have lost at least six times that number, to death and serious injury. But we can't withstand many further losses of our own, whilst still maintaining the integrity of our defences.'

'Our forces in the entire town have dropped to roughly one thousand seven hundred,' stated Caddin. 'We've only five hundred men in total now manning the castle, the harbour, and the eastern and southern walls. However, even with us spread thinly in those places, we can only deploy one thousand two hundred men to the north wall. That's becoming dangerously low compared to the ten thousand which might come against us. And tomorrow's fight will be even harder.'

'Why?' asked Kalyane.

'Their siege engines are nearly ready,' replied Caddin. 'Two trebuchets, so they'll be able to start bombarding the northern parts of the town tomorrow. But worse than that, two siege towers also look close to completion, and a third is not far behind them. If they're not deployed tomorrow, they'll be ready the day after next. And believe me, it's much easier to hold off your enemy when they're climbing ladders, than when they're running off a tower ramp straight onto your battlements.'

Lord Aiduel, will things get even worse soon?

'What can we do?' asked Kalyane.

'To stop a siege tower, you have to prevent it from reaching the walls,' said Caddin. 'We'll have to use all of our firepower to try to bring those towers down or to set them on fire, before they reach us. But Elannis siege equipment is designed to take a hammering, so stopping them will be easier said than done. If their commanders are sensible, they'll wait until all three are ready, so we won't have the ability to stop them all.'

Leanna was listening intently to what Sendromm had to say, and she was dreading what might take place in the coming days.

'And do you think that we can be successful?' asked Kalyane, with a slight tremor in her voice. 'Can we hold?'

'I think we can hold the wall, yes, at least next time,' replied Caddin. 'But there'll be a bloody cost. And with every able soldier that we lose, it'll get harder. We need to know soon whether there's any prospect of a relief force.'

Kalyane looked directly at the burly man, holding his gaze for a moment, then she stated, 'Lord Arion will return to us. From what you've said, it would be prudent of me to start to think about a contingency plan, for what I'll do if the town falls. But I firmly believe that if we can hold out, my husband will return. He'll not abandon us.'

'But will he bring soldiers?' asked Sendromm.

'He'll return,' repeated Kalyane. 'That is enough.'

Leanna wished that she could share in such apparent certainty. She recognised that she was beginning to lose hope and was feeling helpless. Starting with the events in Arlais, she had witnessed so many deaths, so much suffering, and for what? Her efforts so far felt utterly futile. She could carry on trying to heal people, trying to use her powers to stem the gaping wound of this war, but it seemed as if that wound would just keep on growing with each renewed assault.

Elannis would continue to attack, until too many were dead or the town had fallen. That would be the end result, unless Leanna could find another way. Another solution.

Lord Aiduel, please help me to find a way to stop this.

Two days later, in the morning, Leanna was in the courtyard outside of the northern field hospital, with Amyss standing beside her. The smaller woman was clearly nervous about what the coming day would hold, and her hand had crept across to gently grasp Leanna's.

Leanna had slept poorly during the prior night, after being disturbed by the recurring dream. Once again, after awakening in her private room in Septholme Castle, she had been certain that the figure in the Gate had been speaking to her. She sensed that she was on the cusp of retaining those spoken words within her waking mind, but yet again they remained frustratingly out of reach.

She had awoken with Amyss's arm draped across her, the petite woman still asleep as she lay with her cheek on Leanna's chest. For once, Amyss had also been unsettled in her sleep, and Leanna had soothed her by stroking her long red hair in the darkness.

Despite the broken night's sleep, Leanna felt much stronger today. The prior day had passed without further assault against Septholme's walls, which had enabled her to recover from her last exertions of healing. The woman Allana had also continued to remain close to the town, which was helping to fortify Leanna with energy and vitality.

From this position outside of the hospital, Leanna had a clear view of the northern wall, including the towers at the North Gate. She could also observe the hundreds of soldiers lined along the wall's ramparts, all of whom appeared to be facing outwards.

The battle had not yet started, but she knew that it was going to be a bloody affair. Earlier that morning, Caddin had come to the hospital to tell her that he felt certain that all three of the siege towers were going to be deployed.

'And do you think that you'll hold the walls?' she had asked him.

'We've a good chance,' he had replied. 'But if it feels like we're being over-run, then I'll come back to the hospital to find you. Wait here for me. I'll keep you alive, Leanna, no matter what.'

'And Amyss?'

'And Amyss.'

'Then we'll wait for you, Caddin. Take care.'

He had departed after those words, looking resolute and without fear.

Leanna was also trying to maintain her own courage and resolve. However, it was terrifying to contemplate the defence on the walls failing, allowing the fighting to surge into the streets of the town.

'What are you thinking about, Lea?' asked Amyss.

'I'm not sure,' replied Leanna. 'Just that I'm scared. I don't want to have to face so much bloodshed, yet again.'

Amyss squeezed her hand. 'We're together, remember that. Whatever happens.'

Leanna turned to the petite woman. She could see the love in Amyss's eyes, and the equivalent heartfelt emotion was beating out towards her.

Lord Aiduel, thank you again for the gift of her love.

As a spontaneous reaction, she softly placed her hand onto Amyss's neck, and kissed the other woman on the mouth. Amyss responded, and for moments they embraced and kissed. They had always been careful to maintain the secret of their intimacy, displaying their physical passions only when behind closed doors. However, in the context of what might come today, such considerations seemed trivial.

When they broke off from the kiss, Leanna whispered, 'I love you, Amyss.'

'And I love you, Lea.'

Shortly after, as they continued to wait in the hospital courtyard, the noises of battle began to be heard from atop the walls.

Even from this distance, Leanna could hear the steady thrum of hundreds of arrows being fired by the defenders, and the louder metallic clang of ballistae as their spear-length missiles were released. Soon after, thunderous crashes could also be heard as rocks launched by Elannis trebuchets landed on buildings in the streets behind the wall. Each such alarming impact was accompanied by an exploding cloud of dust and rubble.

Leanna watched with increasing concern as there was a rush of movement on the battlements, and a resounding clash of metal and shouting which suggested that hand-to-hand fighting had commenced.

Then she spotted the two siege towers appearing into sight beyond the northern wall, the top of these mobile constructions taller even than the battlements. The towers did not look as if they had yet reached the wall, but Leanna could see that they were teeming with Elannis soldiers. Once these structures touched against the ramparts, many more would enter the fray. There would be carnage.

No amount of healing by Leanna would compensate for the blood which was going to be shed here today. For the lives that would be lost. And to achieve what? It was senseless slaughter.

Lord Aiduel, must you allow this to happen? What must I do, Lord?

The siege towers were trundling ever closer. As Leanna watched them with a sense of frustrated anxiety, a realisation sprang into life of what she could do. How she could stop this. For a handful of seconds, the idea seemed impossible, sheer madness, and she hesitated.

But she was brimming with energy. She felt strong and powerful, and was bolstered and rejuvenated by Allana's presence. And she felt capable of... *miracles*.

Lord Aiduel, thank you for showing me the answer.

She had once been unable to aid Arlais in its hour of need, following which many people had died. But today, it was within her power to do something. To save thousands of lives.

She came to a decision, then set off running in the direction of the northern wall, without pausing to explain herself.

She heard Amyss shouting in protest from behind her, but she did not stop. The surrounding world seemed to slow down as she ran, and her senses were suddenly alert and attuned to all of the horror on the looming battlements. But she was imbued with a sense of purpose; a sense that Aiduel was with her and that He was guiding her.

It was only two hundred metres to the North Gate and to a stone staircase leading up to the ramparts. However, as she ran that way, another arcing boulder crashed down against a nearby building, somewhere to her left. She ignored the earth-shaking impact and flying rubble and instead continued to run, reaching the foot of the gate's adjoining towers in little time.

Her whole body felt alive, vibrant, and infused with energy. The feeling was almost equivalent to her final, ecstatic moments on the pyre.

DEVOTION. SACRIFICE. SALVATION.

A choir of angelic voices burst into her mind, instilling her with even more power, and helping her to draw boundless more energy from the one beyond the walls. This sound of angels heralding the moment made her even more certain about the action that she was about to take.

The Lord Aiduel supported her intention.

The battlements now sounded of chaos. From this position, at the bottom of the tall stone wall, she could no longer see the siege towers. However, she judged from the clamour of shouts and screams above that these weapons of war had now reached the walls, and that the intensity of the fighting had escalated.

Lord Aiduel, please give me the strength and courage to do this.

She started to climb the steps up to the ramparts, feeling trepidation about what she would encounter when she reached the top.

'Leanna!'

She heard the plaintive cry when she was halfway up the stone stairway, and she turned to see Amyss in the courtyard below. The petite priestess was looking distressed.

Leanna raised her hand, palm forwards, and ordered, 'Stay there, Amyss! Do not follow me!'

Her tone of voice surprised her, sounding deeper than usual and somehow more fearsome, and she hoped that the other woman would obey. Leanna then returned to climbing the stairs, before finally emerging onto the battlements.

She was greeted by a chaotic sprawl of melee along the entire length of the northern wall, accompanied by endless beating emotions of terror and pain. In every direction, the blue tabards of Andar were mixed in brawling, brutish, close-quarters combat with scores of yellow-clad troops of Elannis.

Leanna could see frantic fighting where one siege tower had already reached the wall. A spearpoint of Elannis soldiers had charged across its upper ramp and onto the battlements. The second siege tower was just metres away, whilst the third could be seen ablaze and toppled, burning in the fields outside.

Directly in front of Leanna were several dozen Andar soldiers, standing with their backs to her. She judged that she was out of any immediate danger of being caught in the churn of combat, and she focused upon what she needed to do.

Energy was still surging within her, as much energy now as she had felt on the day of the pyre. She had been granted powers which extended far beyond the wonderful act of healing, she knew that. Additional powers that she had first discovered on that momentous day in Arlais, and which she had since honed and trained with the assistance of Amyss.

And now, in the magnificent, bolstering presence of the nearby Allana, she was ready to do The Lord's work.

Lord Aiduel, I am your devoted servant. Please help me to stop this madness!

Unlike at the pyre, this time she was able to control the release of energy. It began as a golden glow around her body, a shimmering cocoon of light which swiftly encased her form. This brilliant illumination had such radiance that the closest soldiers began to turn towards her, and were forced to shield their eyes.

As she unleashed more power, she witnessed the shimmering glow expanding from her body to reach the front of the ramparts. From there, it flowed rapidly outwards to the east and west, whilst also rising high above the heads of the fighting soldiers. By the time that its growth was finished, there existed a golden, transparent wall of light which cascaded from high above. It ran along the entire front of the northern battlements.

Leanna raised her arms heavenwards, in thanks to Aiduel.

Lord Aiduel, thank you! Together, we shall end this fight!

Wherever someone was touched by this ethereal shield, it forced them away from it, to one side or the other. In moments, the combatants began to realise that they could not pass through or strike beyond this golden light, and that it was impenetrable to both man and weapon.

The first siege tower still carried men on its staircases, who were now unable to cross the shimmering cascade of light to gain access to the battlements. As the second siege tower reached the wall, its passengers also found that they were denied passage to the ramparts.

Leanna felt alive and triumphant as she held this shield of light in place. Her golden cocoon protected her from threat, and she was attuned to everything that was taking place.

Yes, there were men of Elannis already on the battlements, and the fighting was continuing in all of those places. But the vast majority of the two opposing armies had now been separated, and would continue to be held apart for as long as Leanna could maintain this barrier of impenetrable energy. No more soldiers would climb onto the battlements from ladders or cross to it from siege towers. The fighting would be contained to that which was already taking place, and a vast number of lives would be saved.

With the aid of Allana, Leanna believed that she could hold this shield in place for hours more. She looked towards the encampment to the north-east, and her eyes immediately found the crouching form of the dark-haired woman who was sharing this bountiful supply of energy. Leanna could not discern Allana's features, even with her senses as heightened as they now were, but she knew that the woman was looking in her direction. And that she must be rejoicing at their joint achievement on this day.

Lord Aiduel, thank you for bringing Allana here, to this place, to help me to achieve this!

Leanna realised that Amyss was now standing beside her. The red-headed woman had ignored the instruction and had followed Leanna onto the ramparts. The small priestess smiled shyly, her expression full of awe, and Leanna beamed in response as her protective cocoon of light spread out to envelop Amyss in turn.

Leanna raised her hands into the sky, even higher, and she exulted. She was Priestess Leanna, the Angel of Arlais, and on this day, she was infused with indomitable holy power.

And in the name of Aiduel, she was using that power, *unleashing* it, for the cause of good.

27

Allana

—

*Year of Our Lord,
After Ascension, 770AA*

As she observed the shimmering wall of light above the battlements of Septholme, Allana felt violated and dirty.

She was sitting on the grass outside of her tent, scrunched into a tight ball, with her knees pressed against her chest. She wanted to close her eyes and to bury her face beneath her forearms, though she knew that this would do nothing to prevent the ongoing intrusion of the other.

How many more times must she do this to you, Lana? How many more times must you accept this violation?

Once again, the woman Leanna was drawing energy out of Allana's body. Energy which Allana knew was helping to power the other's deeds. It was as if invisible fingers had penetrated Allana and were stealing something vital from her, a steady stream of her essence being fed upon by the other woman.

The miraculous spectacle above Septholme was inescapable. A shimmering cascade of golden colour was falling from the sky along the entire length of the northern wall. On the ramparts of that wall, the silhouette of a woman was visible, who was standing inside a dazzling orb which all of the surrounding fighters had backed away from. This woman's arms were raised to the sky, as if in supplication.

Allana was certain that this was Leanna, the Angel of Arlais.

On the nearside of the wall of light, there appeared to be mounting confusion amongst the attacking soldiers about what was happening. Even from this distance, Allana could perceive that no one was passing through the golden barrier. The sound of fighting, so prominent just minutes earlier, was now fading out.

At that moment, Allana heard the whirring creak of a trebuchet arm being released, and she tracked a boulder as it arced towards the northern wall. This hefty rock impacted the shield of light perhaps twenty paces above the ramparts, but it did not pass through. Instead, it shattered against the golden barrier, before falling in deadly pieces onto the unfortunate soldiers below.

The sight of that failed boulder attack seemed to be the final confirmation for the assailing army that nothing could pass through this miraculous barrier. The Elannis troops on the siege towers and ladders now began to climb down and retreat, amidst scenes of confusion.

The wall of light continued to shine, radiant across the sky. It would no doubt be hailed as a true miracle, an extraordinary creation of the Angel of Arlais. In contrast, Allana's own role would remain unknown and unremarked.

Allana bent her head forwards and closed her eyes, resting her forehead against her knees. The ethereal fingers were still there, burrowing deep inside her, and taking from her. She tried once more to ignore them, as she had been trying to disregard them over the last several days, every time that she had felt this other woman leeching from her. But it was without success.

Instead, she focused upon her anger and her fear. She explored the depths within herself, and sought out that inner source of darkness which she had only used twice before. And she found it; still waiting, still hungrily lurking, still ready to protect her.

She is not the only one with powers, Lana.

She was losing all patience with the wondrous Leanna. Soon, if this priestess continued her violation of Allana, there would be a response. And this Angel of Arlais would discover that there would be a cost – a *severe* cost – for taking what was not freely given.

―

Later, Allana was curled into a ball on her bed when Jarrett returned to their tent.

'By the Lord, Lana,' said the young duke, as soon as he had closed the entrance flap behind him. 'Did you see that earlier? Please tell me that you did? We've been present at a true miracle today.'

'I saw it, yes,' she murmured. 'A true miracle. Thank the Lord.'

'I can't stop smiling, Lana,' he said. 'The Angel of Arlais, somehow here in Septholme and working a miracle before us. Even though she's currently a prisoner, and stopped our assault, I'm just feeling in awe. I'd heard the stories of the miracle on the pyre, but to see that today! Just incredible, as if Aiduel was amongst us, acting through her.'

'I'm happy for you, Jarrett,' Allana said, but her voice struggled to muster any enthusiasm.

She was deeply fatigued again. The Elannis army had eventually retreated back to their starting position, following which the golden wall of light had finally disappeared from the sky. By then, Allana had been exhausted, and she had been able to sense that the priestess had been in a similar condition.

But you didn't have a choice, Lana. That's the difference between the two of you.

Jarrett came to kneel at the edge of their bed, and placed his hand onto her arm. 'Are you feeling unwell again, my love?'

'Yes. Tired, and I have a headache. I just need to rest, Jarrett.'

'Is there anything I can do?'

Allana paused, considering this. 'Perhaps, let me take my guards and ride further away from this town, like I asked before. I think that I need to get away from here.'

'You know that's too dangerous, Lana. I'm fine with your guards escorting you around our camp, but any further out than that and I'd worry. There could be rogue bands of Andar soldiers in the surrounding countryside.'

'Then you're not helping me, Jarrett. In fact, you're making me suffer, by keeping me here.' She felt tears forming in her eyes.

'I'm so sorry, my love. But I can't allow you to put yourself in danger. Perhaps I can arrange for your horse to be readied for you tomorrow, so you can at least go for a ride around the camp? Would you like that?'

What use is that to you, Lana? Is he a fool?

She glared at Jarrett, then rolled onto her other side, facing away from him. For a few seconds she thought about coercion, about using her powers on him for the first time in a long while, to force him to obey her. But she recognised that she could not muster the energy. She was just too tired.

She then scowled as Jarrett began to quietly pray.

'Lord Aiduel,' she heard him say, amidst these prayers, 'please watch over and protect the blessed Angel of Arlais.'

Upon hearing this, Allana secretly clenched her fists.

—

The next day, there was no immediate renewal of the assault by the army of Elannis. The morning was punctuated by the occasional creak of a trebuchet as missiles were launched towards Septholme's walls, but there was no direct conflict.

Jarrett had left early to attend a meeting with the other leaders of the invading forces. He had indicated to Allana that they would be discussing how to react to the events of the prior day.

Allana was feeling refreshed, and she had accepted Jarrett's offer to have her horse readied. She intended to go riding in the camp later that morning, with Connar in attendance, but she was distracted before then when she noticed that Aiduel's Guards were busy on the land in front of Septholme's walls. They were building something in the area near to the gallows.

She watched the activity of the red-cloaked soldiers from outside of her tent, her expression masking her tightly-held hatred towards them. She tried to see if the officer that she had recognised was amongst their number, but she could not pick him out. Nor had she yet seen any sign of Nionia; perhaps the lanky guardswoman had returned to Dei Magnus.

At first, Allana was unsure of what the religious soldiers were doing, as they delivered wood on carts and began to stack it around a single raised pole and platform. But then it dawned on her; they were building a pyre. But for whom?

You're free of them, Lana. It's not for you, not this time.

Soon after, Jarrett returned to their tent, which provided an opportunity for her to ask questions.

'It's a pyre, Jarrett. What are they doing? Do they plan to try to burn her again?'

He shook his head. 'No, it's not for Priestess Leanna. Of course not, that was a terrible mistake. It's a pyre for a heretic, who's already in their captivity. They intend to use it, they say, to… *negotiate*, for the release and return of Priestess Leanna, to their safekeeping. Markon also seems very anxious to secure her return, and he doesn't seem at all angry about her miracle stopping our attack. He believes that the heretic defenders are forcing her to act on their behalf. She saved his life, of course, last year. Remember that?'

'Yes, I remember,' replied Allana.

'What a remarkable woman she must be. Once she's under our protection, I pray to The Lord that I'll have a chance to meet with her and to spend time with one who's so blessed by Aiduel.'

Must you constantly be reminded of how special she is, Lana?

'Yes, she's remarkable,' she said. 'So, what happens now?'

'They're going to send an emissary of Aiduel's Guards to the North Gate soon, who will announce that, unless the Angel of Arlais is freed, they'll burn this heretic.'

'Which heretic?' Allana asked. 'They're not going to drag out Gerrion Sepian again, are they?'

'Oh no,' replied Jarrett. 'They've already had their bluff called on that, and Markon isn't prepared to see *this* Sepian brother murdered, just yet. But Aiduel's Guards have several dozen Western Canasar women in their fortress, who have already confessed to witchcraft and heresy. And their intention is to burn one of these heretics every few hours, unless Priestess Leanna stops intervening in our attacks, and is returned to them.'

―

Later, Allana was outside and watching as a horse-drawn wagon trundled past her position from the direction of the Aiduel's Guards' fortress. The wagon was travelling towards the pyre on the lands in front of the northern walls.

At the front of the wagon was a red-cloaked driver, and there were two more soldiers of the religious order in the wagon bed at the back. These latter two were sitting to either side of a slim woman with long blonde hair, who was clearly their prisoner. In fact, *girl* might have been a more appropriate description for the captive, since she appeared to be little older than a teenager.

Allana watched the wagon as it approached the now finished pyre. She had no doubt that the prisoner would be horrified when she realised what was planned for her. Indeed, Allana was struggling to process and contain her own emotions.

This young woman, who was to be burned alive today, was likely an innocent who had been plucked from one of the villages of Western Canasar. Someone whose only apparent crime had been to be of a similar age and look to Leanna, the Angel of Arlais. This teenager had likely spent days in the Guards' dark fortress, suffering depravities which Allana dared not imagine, only to then be selected for this moment.

Had the girl signed a confession, stating that she was a heretic? Most likely. Would this have been obtained under torture and duress? Also, very likely. And now she was being led to this place, to be murdered in front of thousands of people.

Allana had only avoided such a fate as a result of her own refusal to surrender to her captors. And, of course, because she was in possession of unique abilities, which had enabled her to escape from that awful fortress.

But this girl had no such capacity to free herself.

They would have done this to you too, Lana, if you'd not escaped. If you'd not killed them first. This is what comes from being innocent and without power.

She felt appalled and sickened at the thought of what she was soon going to witness. But more prominent than either of these emotions, a fury was building inside of her. For the second time in two days, the darkness within Allana seemed tangibly within reach.

Once again, she could also feel the presence of Leanna of Arlais. On this occasion, the priestess was not using her own powers or drawing energy from Allana. By contrast, Allana was feeling rejuvenated and revitalised by the other woman's presence. Today, she felt *powerful*. This was adding to the sensation that her inner darkness was becoming more accessible, in reaction to her mounting anger.

The wagon now stopped, and the minutes which followed were a bleak echo of the scenes with Gerrion Sepian. But while the duke had remained stoic and silent, this prisoner struggled frantically as the red-cloaks dragged her onto the platform. She could be heard screaming for help as ropes were then tied around her arms, chest and legs, binding her to the central pole. The blonde-haired girl continued to beg for assistance for minutes afterwards, her head turning in every direction in search of a saviour, until those entreaties were finally replaced by silent despair.

Shortly afterwards, an emissary cloaked in red rode towards the town gates under a flag of truce. However, this figure returned alone within minutes, with nothing to indicate that he had achieved any success.

Allana believed that the Angel of Arlais was somewhere on the ramparts, watching what was taking place on the land outside. Allana also wondered about what role the woman had taken in deciding the response to the emissary. Had the priestess personally decided to reject that offer, or had she been given no part in the decision by the leaders behind the wall? Allana was also wondering whether Priestess Leanna would act to save the girl on the pyre, in the same way that she had saved herself in Arlais.

Allana now noticed Jarrett walking back towards their tent. As the giant duke arrived, he said, 'Are you sure that you want to watch this, Lana? I'm afraid that this is going to be an ugly spectacle.'

'They're going to burn her?' asked Allana. 'It's definite?'

'Almost certainly.'

'Then I'll stay.'

She felt a need to bear witness to this. Their shared experience in that dark fortress had given her a sense of twisted kinship with this unfortunate captive.

Soon after, a male officer of Aiduel's Guards climbed onto the raised platform, and he began to speak to the audience around him. Allana could not discern all of the words, but it sounded like a speech of condemnation.

Condemning her despite her innocence, Lana. As they would have condemned you.

The speaking officer was watched by thousands of Elannis and Berun soldiers, all of whom were stationed out of range of the walls. He was also observed by a large gathering of camp followers and by a further mass of figures on the ramparts of Septholme. While the man spoke, the trebuchets were not firing, and most of the spectators were quiet.

Allana could feel outrage and fury continuing to build within her as she watched the captive beginning to sob. The darkness inside her was becoming increasingly turbulent; memories of fear, of torture, were seething inside her, and she found herself grimacing. She moved a few paces back from Jarrett, such that he would not observe the cold expression of loathing which now settled onto her face.

The red-cloaked officer had ended his speech. He stepped down from the raised platform, leaving the girl alone and bound, with her body facing towards the walls of Septholme. Allana watched as two other Aiduel's Guards began to approach the pyre, both of them carrying flaming torches.

At that moment, she felt a surge of power from the woman Leanna, as if the priestess was attempting to do something. But there was no discernible reaction, no change in the environs of the pyre, and then the burst of energy was gone.

She's failed, Lana. But you're closer. You can stop this. You can stop them!

The thought and her resulting action came at the same time. She had spent months concealing what she truly was. Months of burying the horror of her captivity in the fortress, whilst trying in vain to pretend that trauma had never happened. For almost all of that time, she had been restraining the call of the darkness which her torture and abuse had helped to foster.

LUST. POWER. DOMINATION.

But this time, she reached deep into the dark core within her. She unleashed that blackness towards the two red-cloaked soldiers who were carrying the torches, and it poured forth from her in an invisible torrent.

Only Allana could see the trail of the darkness as it crossed the distance to the two male soldiers close to the pyre. It then swarmed around them like a mass of twisting tendrils, before both of the men started to scream in agony and horror as it entered and then assailed them.

One of these two red-cloaks dropped his flaming torch onto the floor, and then followed it down as he slumped to his knees.

However, the other held onto his, flailing it about himself while his free hand reached up to claw at his own face.

Allana continued to pour her inner darkness through this connection to the two men, preventing either of them from reaching and lighting the pyre, but she could see a reaction now from amongst the figures around them. The officer of Aiduel's Guards was running towards the standing soldier, and Allana realised that he meant to grab hold of the flaming torch to complete the task.

She allowed the tendrils of darkness to lash out, to encircle and penetrate this man in turn. Allowing him to share in the horror, and to join his colleagues in agonised screaming as he collapsed down onto his side.

Allana was resolved that they would all feel the consequences for their actions today, and she felt strong and fearless. This time, the presence of the woman Leanna was helping *her*. She wondered momentarily if the other woman could perceive and feel what was happening, and whether she understood it. Whether she recognised that there were others who could work… *miracles* and wonders. Different miracles.

The bound captive on the pyre was shrieking in panic now, as the three men writhed in tortured hysteria before her. Allana's gaze flicked to the young woman; Allana was going to save her. She would be her secret saviour. If anyone else tried to grab hold of those torches, she would stop them.

But then the figure on the platform shuddered abruptly. And again. Two arrows had sprouted from the captive's chest. Then a third arrow slammed into her, and a fourth. Allana's gaze switched to a cluster of red-cloaked bowmen, who had run in front of the still unlit pyre. Allana felt black despair. She was ready to lash out again as a fifth arrow impaled the prisoner, and the girl's head slumped forwards.

Make them pay, Lana! Make them all pay!

She reached deeper into the darkness, preparing herself to unleash something even worse. Something even more ruinous, which the presence of the woman Leanna was rendering more accessible. Allana steeled herself, readying-

She was interrupted as two large hands grabbed hold of her from behind, under the armpits. She was then being lifted and carried towards her tent. She turned her head, ready to unleash her fury on whomever it was, but she recoiled when she saw that Jarrett had taken hold of her.

'Get inside the tent!' he hissed. 'Your eyes!'

The surprise of his action and words caused her to break her connection with the three suffering men. Instantly, the darkness was dragged back into herself.

She realised with a sense of shock that she had been on the brink of unveiling herself to everyone there, in the same way that Leanna of Arlais had already revealed herself to the world.

In the moments before Allana was carried into the confines of her tent, she witnessed that the three Guards had ceased their hysterical screaming. Indeed, the one still holding his torch now managed to stagger forwards, and he touched the flame against the edge of the pyre.

The last thing that Allana saw before the tent flaps closed around her was the pyre blazing into life. Its burgeoning flames spread quickly, hungry to consume the slumped and motionless form of the innocent blonde-haired girl.

—

'Your eyes, Lana!' exclaimed Jarrett, when they were inside the tent. 'Something had happened to your eyes!'

'What?'

'They were golden! Shining and golden.'

'You're imagining it, Jarrett. It was a trick of the light, that's all.'

Her heart was pounding, and she could feel the echoing after-effects of her rage.

'You were involved Lana, I know it! The things that were

happening to those men. It wasn't being done by the girl on the pyre. It was *you*. I saw you!'

His voice was an anxious whisper, and he appeared to be on the edge of hysteria. His hand reached up to touch the statue of The Lord Aiduel On The Tree, which hung from his neck.

'She was a witch, Jarrett.' Allana tried to speak calmly, despite her own anger. 'You said yourself that she'd confessed to being a heretic and a witch. She must have used dark powers to attack those men, to defend herself.'

'Your eyes were glowing, Lana! I saw it!'

'No, they weren't. You're mistaken.'

'Stop lying to me!' he hissed. 'I saw it! But how? Please, promise me that you're not a heretic and a witch? Please!'

Allana's emotions were still churning from the events outside.

How dare he challenge you like this, Lana! Who does he think he is?

'How dare you accuse me of that!' she snapped, then swung her hand towards his face, attempting to slap him. He took a step back to avoid the blow, then caught hold of her wrist.

'What are you doing, Lana?'

His tone was a mixture of surprise and indignation. He kept a grip on her wrist, making no attempt to retaliate, but Allana attacked him again with her free hand, striking her palm hard against his cheek. He grabbed hold of her other wrist in response, and she could see that he was both shocked and upset by her aggression.

Allana could not help herself. Her rage was reignited, and she recognised then that the situation had gone too far between them. This was not an occasion where sweet words and apologies could atone for her actions. Nor could they return things to how they had been before. This required something more… *drastic*.

Since the day when they had met, Allana had used her abilities sparingly on Jarrett. Even then, they had only been employed to nudge him towards the course of action that she desired. However, after her fury at the deeds of Aiduel's Guards, she was in no mood for subtlety or nuance. No mood to try to finesse her way out of this situation with clever explanation.

Before Jarrett could take any further action, tendrils were ripping out of Allana's mind. Locking the giant duke into place, then surging into his soul and claiming possession.

You want me, Jarrett! You've so much desire for me that it consumes you! And you can continue to have me. But only if you give me whatever I want. Whenever I want. Whatever the cost. Now submit!

She had no patience for explanations or for asking for his understanding. She assailed him with the force of her will, first ordering him to release his hands, then forcing him to his knees.

Despite his attempts to resist, he obeyed the commands, and she could see his jaw clenching in anguish as he looked across at her. In this kneeling position, they were almost the same height. Allana reached out a hand to his neck, and she took hold of the statue of The Lord Aiduel On The Tree, lifting it in front of his chin.

'This is the last time that you'll accuse me or disapprove of me, Jarrett. No matter how far you rise, or what your precious Lord Aiduel tells you is right and wrong, you'll always obey me and serve me, and you'll never again challenge me. Or I'll do to you, what I did to your mother. Do you understand that?'

For a handful of seconds, he continued to stare at her with horror as if seeing a stranger, but his will soon shattered under the crush of darkness. And he nodded.

She then proceeded to tell him in whispers how things were going to be. As she did so, she recognised that it was not particularly nice to have to do something like this. However, as the events of the day had already proven, there are a lot of things in the world which are not nice. Indeed, some of those things might even be described as awful. Truly awful.

But anyway, she could reassure herself that he would not remember any of this, once she had finished with him.

—

Allana left the tent a short while later, in response to a tumult of noise from outside. Jarrett remained within, kneeling on the floor in a stunned daze. Allana was still feeling tense and agitated; the encounter with the duke had done nothing to diminish her earlier anger.

Her turbulent emotions were not soothed by her realisation that the pyre continued to blaze, although the body of its victim was no longer visible within the conflagration. Looking past the fire, it was clear to Allana that the armies of Elannis were massing for another assault on the town walls. Thousands of men were once again assembling, with large clusters forming around another battering ram and the two remaining siege towers. Allana peered towards the town, and she could see that the defending soldiers were gathering on the battlements in response.

This attack appeared to be imminent despite the fact that Leanna of Arlais was still inside the town. Allana assumed that the Elannis leaders wanted to test whether the priestess would act to stop their assault again, now that she was aware of the threat to the other captive women.

Within minutes, the assembled Elannis forces were starting to move forwards, with thousands of men advancing around the siege towers and battering ram. A barrage of arrows was soon raining down from the battlements, and Allana could also hear the creak of the Elannis trebuchets as they started to launch boulders in the opposite direction. The first of these hefty rocks crashed into the lower exterior of the town wall, shattering against it in a shower of rubble.

Allana wondered how the Angel of Arlais was going to react. Would the woman intervene again or would she walk away? Allana's answer came swiftly, as she felt the pull of power across her connection with the priestess, moments before a brilliant globe of light shone into life atop the wall. Allana witnessed this golden orb forming and spreading around the silhouetted form of a woman on the ramparts, who again had her arms raised high. Alongside that figure, captured in the same ball of light, was the smaller silhouette of a second woman.

Energy was now being drawn from Allana again, in increasing amounts. She had still been feeling agitated from the actions of Aiduel's Guards and her subjugation of Jarrett, and this violation reignited her fury.

How dare she do this again, Lana! How many more times will you allow her to do this to you?

More energy was being drawn from Allana. In the sky above the northern wall of Septholme, the cascade of radiant light was again beginning to spread and form, illuminating the land outside in a golden hue. The advance of the Elannis troops was becoming more hesitant, and a second boulder now arced above their ranks, which crashed into the shimmering barrier and deflected away.

Still more power was being taken from Allana, making her feel as if she should drop to her knees. And she believed that she could sense the contrasting emotion of the other woman, resonating across their connection of energy. This Priestess Leanna seemed… ecstatic, overjoyed, *exultant*.

She rejoices whilst you suffer, Lana! It is enough. No more!

At the moment when she thought this, she lashed out. She allowed her inner darkness to be released along the connection with the woman on the wall. Pouring it into the Angel of Arlais in a torrent, and assailing her with it.

Hurting the priestess. Hurting her as she had hurt Allana in the preceding days.

Allana could feel the sensations of shock and pain through their connection as her horror washed into the other. The woman had selfishly taken from Allana, but now she would be forced to receive what Allana chose to give.

She'll feed on you no more, Lana! She'll learn that this will be the last time!

Allana watched as the figure on the wall appeared to stagger, and the golden cascade above the town began to fail and fade. The cocoon of light which surrounded the priestess also seemed to dim, then disappear. The smaller accompanying female could be seen to move closer, and to place her hands upon the reeling Angel of Arlais.

After only moments, the barrier of light above the town was completely gone. There was a collective cheer from the soldiers of Elannis in response to this, and they renewed their advance towards the walls.

Allana resolved that she would soon cease her attack upon the priestess. The lesson had been taught, and the woman would never again have the temerity to think that she could use Allana for her own ends.

She is beaten, Lana. She is less than you. End this now.

That thought was interrupted as Allana felt a new presence. A *second* presence, of another who was like her. And not the one who was currently suffering on the ramparts of Septholme.

The sensation of this person came from the opposite direction. From somewhere to the north-east. Allana turned to face that way, although she sensed that the presence was still too far away for her to see. But whoever it was, they *shone*, even from a great distance. They radiated their magnificence.

It was definitely someone who was of a kind with Allana and with the priestess on the wall. And they were travelling towards Allana and Septholme.

Could it possibly be Arion? Could he be coming to her?

She felt excitement, despite the horrors of the day so far. If it was indeed Arion, she knew without hesitation that she would need to seek him out. Would need to meet with him again, after all this time. She would have to get to her horse and ride out of the encampment to find him, without any delay.

She finally ended her dark assault on Leanna of Arlais, and turned back for one last look at Septholme. The massed forces of Elannis, equipped with their ladders and siege towers, were drawing closer to the town wall.

On the ramparts, she could see the form of the priestess standing up straight again, supported by the smaller female figure at the woman's side.

She won't dare to use you again, Lana. She won't forget this lesson.

Allana watched as the men with siege ladders reached the walls, and the defending soldiers responded. Now that she had ceased her own attack, Allana started to will the woman Leanna to get away from that place. In just minutes, the top of that wall would be swarming with hostile attackers.

Allana was still thinking about this at the instant when a flying boulder arced across her peripheral vision and crashed onto the ramparts. Seemingly, almost upon the very place where the Angel of Arlais and her companion had been standing.

There was a booming noise, and debris from the battlements was churned into the air. Accompanying this, Allana felt a sudden agony in her legs, shooting down from her thighs to the tips of her toes. A pain which was pulsing through her connection with the other. It was beyond excruciating, as if all of the bones in her legs had been shattered at once. She groaned.

She looked up towards the wall, to the smashed ramparts where Leanna of Arlais and her companion had been standing. Now, no forms were visible. Indeed, the only remaining trace of the priestess was this agony which Allana could feel throughout the lower half of her body.

Allana needed to get away from here, needed to get herself out of distance of this madness and pain. And she knew exactly where she was going to go, and what she was going to do.

She would leave this encampment. She would take her horse and would ride to intercept the one who was coming towards her. The radiant person she could still feel, even now, amidst this pain in her legs. The one whose coming presence was helping her to endure this shared agony.

Allana staggered away from her tent, in the direction of the horse enclosure. Once she had placed distance between herself and the priestess, she hoped that she would also free herself of this pain.

She paused to take one last look at the northern wall, and to witness the massed battle now raging there.

This isn't your fault, Lana. She forced you to do this.

Leanna of Arlais had paid the price for her own choices and actions, and for her attacks on Allana. It was all the priestess's fault. Allana had simply been forced to defend herself against the other woman's violations. As such, she was entirely blameless.

Allana knew that the priestess might not live through such grievous injuries. Even if the woman did, she would no longer be able to protect Septholme from its attackers. Indeed, given the violence of the battle now taking place upon the wall, the town might fall today. Even if this precious Angel of Arlais lived through her wounds, and survived the battle, it seemed that she would be claimed by Aiduel's Guards.

Better her than you, Lana.

Allana turned away, then staggered on towards the horse enclosure, wincing despite her determination to ignore the agony in her lower half.

It was time at last for a reunion with Arion Sepian.

28

Corin

—

*Year of Our Lord,
After Ascension, 770AA*

Corin was waiting on the same dirt trail where he had intercepted the foul-mouthed Brune and his swaggering band of Kurakee, almost two moons earlier. Much had happened in that intervening time, but the threat of the Kurakee horde now loomed imminently. Less than a week remained until the festival of Spring's Heart, and Corin's scouts had reported that the Kurakee horde was just days away.

For the past two weeks, the swift horse-riders of the Qari had acted as the Chosen Alliance's eyes. From their reports, Corin estimated that between five and ten thousand enemy warriors were travelling towards the Chosen lands. Brune had made the claim that the Kurakee had conquered over eighty clans, so such numbers made sense.

By contrast, Corin knew that the ten clans which he had assembled could muster one thousand two hundred fighting men.

Three more northern clans had joined the Chosen Alliance in recent weeks, their decision to join accelerated by the shared threat from the barbaric Kurakee. Corin recognised that he was now directly responsible for all of the Chosen people; it was his job to keep them alive, and free from subjugation.

When Corin's weary and depleted party had returned from the north, weeks earlier, Corin had immediately summoned all of the leaders of the clans. Within days, a council had been organised inside the Clan Hall of the Borl village.

Addressing all of his chiefs and senior advisers, Corin had announced, 'The Kurakee have told us that they'll be coming. And we have no doubt now that they *are* coming, and in vast numbers. And perhaps they hope to find us on our knees, ready to give up our freedom and our people. But if that's the case, then the Kurakee are going to be disappointed. *Fatally* disappointed.

'I am returned from the north, now. While I was there, I found the entrance to the Land of the Gods. I spoke to the Gods there. And they shared their secrets with me, and allowed me to return. I'm still their Chosen, but I've come back with even more strength and power than I had before.

'Since my return, I've inspected the preparations which have been made to the lands around Karn, and I'm satisfied that we'll be ready for the Kurakee, when they come. Let no one be in any doubt. When the Kurakee arrive, we'll be waiting for them. And we'll fight them, and we'll destroy them!'

There had been unanimous support for Corin's stance. None of the leaders were prepared to accept the life that surrender to the Kurakee was likely to bring, for either themselves or for their clans.

Corin had also told them about the events in the far north, and he had described some of the expedition's incredible discoveries. He had used this information to give the chiefs confidence that his powers could protect their peoples. Indeed, he had outlined all of the resources and strategies which they could utilise to defeat the Kurakee.

He had not told them *everything* of his experiences in the north, of course, and much of it would remain concealed from them. In particular, he had withheld all of the details of his encounter and discoveries after touching the giant arch. The chiefs did not need to know about the revelations of the ghost.

Whilst on the return journey, Corin had thought extensively about those revelations. After the coming conflict was resolved, if he still lived, he might need to act upon some of the things which he had learned. However, the time for that would be later, after the Kurakee threat had been faced.

The preparations for the Kurakee horde's arrival had accelerated in the period after Corin's return. During the last fortnight, a migration of the peoples of the Chosen Alliance towards the lands of Karn had taken place. Thousands had travelled from the other villages of the north, transporting whatever food and livestock they were able to. Corin had no intention of letting the Kurakee descend upon and wipe out each settlement one at a time. The Chosen clans would face the Kurakee horde within the lands of the Karn, and Corin's people would be united for that battle.

Corin's thoughts about this were interrupted as he spotted the Kurakee vanguard appearing in the distance. Corin's Qari scouts had warned him that a warband was approaching, again numbering approximately eighty warriors. Corin had opted to intercept them here, on this same route to the south-east of Karn, which offered no view of the village.

Corin had brought one hundred warriors with him, a group which included fighters from each of the Chosen clans. Blackpaw also stood beside him, with claws extended.

Corin watched the Kurakee coming closer, and he recognised the corpulent form of Brune leading them. The Kurakee warriors were again moving with an arrogant swagger. Corin felt his anger rising, and he allowed himself to relish the emotion. He had thought much about the Kurakee since their first visit, and of the things which they had boasted of and threatened. Sacrificing the elderly.

Raping women and children. Breaking up families. Destroying and enslaving clans.

Last time, Corin had meekly accepted their threats and their insults. He had suggested that he was amenable to kneeling to them, a response which had been unpalatable but expedient. This time, his reaction would be different.

When the fat Brune was less than twenty paces away, he stopped. Corin could see that the Kurakee leader's gaze was sweeping across the assembled Chosen warriors. Brune then made a guttural noise. In response to that sound, each of the Kurakee readied the weapons that they were holding.

'You are in the lands of the Chosen,' announced Corin. 'State your business here.'

'You know our fucking business, boy,' replied Brune. 'We're here as the vanguard of the Kurakee horde, to check that our tributes are being prepared. And I expected to meet your head in a sack, not you in person on the road.'

'It's not Spring's Heart yet, Brune of the Kurakee,' said Corin. 'And I choose to keep my head on my shoulders, at least until then. But your check of our tributes? I'm afraid that won't be happening. We're not letting you pass.'

Corin watched as the fat warrior rolled his neck and then spat in a gesture of contempt. The Kurakee leader then started to shout, 'Know this! The Kurakee are com-'

Corin stopped him there, sending out tendrils to seize control of Brune's mind, and ordering the man to stop speaking.

'Be silent, you vile piece of shit,' Corin said, his voice suddenly cold. 'I've heard more than enough of the filth which spouts from you.'

Corin watched as the fat warrior started to gasp. The Kurakee leader was trying to get words out, and was failing. Brune then turned around to his fellow Kurakee and pointed towards his own mouth. Corin could perceive consternation amongst them that their foul mouthpiece had been silenced, and he observed a number of them taking a step forward, with weapons raised. In response, Corin could also hear weapons being readied by the Chosen warband. This was accompanied by a prolonged and menacing growl from Blackpaw.

Corin sent forth more tendrils from his mind, to start to take control of each member of the Kurakee group. Locking them in place, binding their limbs, and paralysing them. When over half of their party was controlled, he continued speaking.

'We've heard much about the Kurakee, Brune, and we don't need to know any more. We know that you are murderers. Rapists. Looters. Slavers. That you break up clans and families, and sacrifice the weak and the helpless. That you're like an evil wind, blowing foulness and death across these lands. But no more, Brune. The time of the Kurakee is to come to an end. And that end shall begin when we destroy every last man amongst your horde, at Spring's Heart. And so, Brune, I thank you. You and your brother Kurune have done me a great favour by bringing yourselves here, where I can kill all of you at once, rather than forcing me to have to travel to hunt you down.'

Corin could hear approving noises coming from the Chosen warriors behind him, as they watched the Kurakee group struggling in vain against Corin's control. In particular, there was satisfaction for all of those who had witnessed and been enraged by Brune's first arrogant approach, weeks earlier. By the time that Corin had finished these words, he had taken control of every member of the Kurakee warband.

'I need one of you alive to take a message back to Kurune,' he continued, 'and that's why I'm going to spare you, Brune. And this is my message, so listen carefully. The Chosen are ready for the Kurakee, and we're going to kill every last one of you evil bastards. And when the battle's over, I'm going to feed Kurune's corpse to my felrin.' Corin gestured towards Blackpaw. 'Who will enjoy eating him, and then shitting him out afterwards, into our village cesspit. Tell Kurune this; if he wants the north, then fucking come and get it. We'll be waiting for him at the village of Karn. Come fight me. Come fight the Chosen people. And find out what happens when he faces the Chosen of the Gods.'

Corin paused, preparing himself for what was about to come, before he continued.

'Brune. I want you to step forwards now, away from your warband.'

Corin transmitted the instruction to the fat warrior, who staggered closer to the Chosen warband, his limbs jerking under Corin's control.

'And now,' stated Corin, 'for the crimes of murder, and rape, and slavery, and human sacrifice, I condemn you all. For everyone but Brune, the sentence shall be death, delivered in a few moments by my warriors here, and Blackpaw. For you, Brune, the punishment shall be more forgiving, and you'll deliver it yourself. I'm going to make you drop your trousers, and then you're to use your axe to cut off your own cock. And then you can walk back to your brother, and offer it to him, as a gift from me. Just make sure that you pass my message onto him, as well.'

Corin felt satisfied to observe the horror in Brune's eyes as the obese man heard this. Corin then signalled for the assembled Chosen warriors to descend upon the remainder of the Kurakee. He allowed Brune and his clansmen to speak again in the moments of slaughter that followed.

And of the many noises of pain which then rang out across the plains of Karn, Brune's scream was perhaps the loudest of all.

—

Two days later, Corin was standing at the top of one of Karn's new watchtowers. He was facing southwards, peering into the distance. Alongside him was Clan Chief Munnik, who was facing in the same direction. Two newly-trained archers were also sharing the small space with them, and Corin was aware that he was being keenly observed by this latter pair.

There was no sign as yet of the Kurakee horde to the south, but nonetheless the lands around Karn were alive with activity. Hundreds of Chosen warriors were hastening around, making preparations for the battle which would arrive with the enemy on the next day. Weapons were being honed, stakes were being sharpened, and arrows were being distributed. Corin felt certain that many of the warriors would be sharing stories of past exploits, to help to overcome their collective nerves, or would be praying to the Gods for good fortune.

Corin's Qari scouts had been tracking the northward progress of the Kurakee, ever since the humiliation and emasculation of Brune. To Corin's relief, the Kurakee horde had ignored the village of the Anath altogether. Corin had already evacuated all of the Anath people and livestock, and had relocated their boats to Karn. However, he was still pleased that the Anath settlement had not been ransacked.

Prior to climbing this watchtower, Corin had been with the other Chosen leaders, confirming the final arrangements about where they would place their forces. Corin now pointed southwards, addressing his comments to Munnik.

'As I said earlier, we know that their horde is travelling alongside the Great Lake, as they move northwards. I expect them to approach Karn from the direct south, first appearing over that low ridge.'

'Exactly as we want,' stated Munnik.

'Yes. *Exactly* as we want. I feel as confident as I can be, Munnik. Everyone knows where they're meant to be and what their role is. We just have to hope that the Kurakee are the disorganised rabble that I think they are.'

'I think they will be,' replied Munnik. 'But more importantly, *we* are ready, Chief Corin. Ready and united to fight together as a single Chosen army. Our warriors will camp to the south of Karn tonight, and we'll be ready for them at dawn tomorrow.'

Corin nodded. He could see from this vantage point that Karn and its surrounding territory had been transformed since Brune had first delivered the Kurakee ultimatum. Prior to his expedition to the far north, Corin had given explicit instructions to Chief Munnik and to the other Karn leaders, and these had been implemented perfectly.

Inside Karn itself, the fortifications had been completed. Four watchtowers stood at each corner of the village, within the finished palisade wall, and internal high walkways connected them. On the day of the battle, these towers and walkways would be bristling with archers.

When Corin had been exposed to the visions of the Song in the far north, he had witnessed countless epic battles. He had shared in memories of many settlements which had been assailed and defeated by the tyrant Mella and his forces. But he had also viewed rarer instances of better fortified locations, where the defenders had successfully organised themselves and had survived. From these observations, Corin had gained many new ideas, some of which he had tried to implement in the weeks since he had returned.

One of those ideas was that of women fighting for the Chosen Alliance. Corin had witnessed this in the battles of the past; women standing alongside men, trained and armoured just as the menfolk were. It was a notion which had seemed preposterous to the clans, after generations of just the males killing each other. But faced with the Kurakee threat, and with Corin's encouragement that it had been revealed to him by the Gods, the enlistment of female fighters had been hastily and willingly adopted.

The watchtowers and palisade walls of Karn would now be held by the bravest and strongest women of the Chosen Alliance. Each of these new fighters had been provided with a bow, and a quiver full of arrows, items which had previously belonged to men. In just three weeks, over four hundred women had volunteered for this role, bolstering Corin's forces by a third. Corin hoped to keep this archery force out of direct melee, for there was insufficient armour and weaponry to equip them all properly for such combat, and they were untrained. However, he needed them to inflict pain on the enemy under a hail of arrows, and the women had embraced their role with enthusiasm and courage.

Indeed, two such volunteers were sharing the watchtower with Corin at this moment. One was a woman in her late-twenties, and the other was a girl in her teens.

'Do you both feel ready for the battle?' he asked, looking towards them.

The younger girl blushed, but the older woman replied boldly, in a Renni accent, 'Yes, Chosen. We promise that we're ready to fight, and to kill.'

Corin nodded in approval. 'Then we're lucky to have you alongside us. Remember, when the moment comes to fight, don't hesitate. Scream your bloodlust and fire on the enemy. Use all of your arrows before the battle's over. Every single Kurakee that you hit could save a Chosen life.' He was paraphrasing words which his father Akob had once said to him, many years ago.

Speaking to this pair reinforced to Corin just how much responsibility he now bore. Four hundred women would be here, and in immediate danger, during the coming fight. They would be dependent on the wisdom of his decisions, and they might pay the price for any mistakes which he made.

All of the remaining women, children and elderly of the Chosen clans had been evacuated to a camp many miles to the north of Karn, by the edges of the Great Forest. They were now protected by a small force comprised of other women and elderly men. If everything went wrong in the fight against the Kurakee, Corin had arranged for Qari scouts to ride to this camp and to notify everyone to flee for their lives. But he did not want to dwell too much upon that ghastly outcome.

He now turned to peer southwards again. In the fields to the south of Karn, the terrain had been transformed. Corin's people had worked to create a wide corridor of land which ran southwards from the village for several hundred metres. The intention was to channel Kurune's army along this north-south corridor.

This was to be achieved by way of hundreds of wooden stakes which had been planted at close intervals in the ground to the east, along the whole length of the corridor. Behind these waist-height and sharpened stakes, a ditch had also been dug, which was two metres wide and almost as deep.

At the point when Kurune's army would first encounter these stakes and the extended trench, there would be a gap of four hundred metres between these obstacles to the east, and the woodland bordering the Great Lake to the west. Corin hoped that Kurune would advance on towards Karn, without caution. By the time that the Kurakee horde had been funnelled northwards along this corridor for a few hundred metres, the gap would have narrowed to a quarter of its initial size. And at the end of the funnel, they would be in range of Corin's archers and would meet the Chosen front lines.

Corin wanted the obstacles to make it much more difficult for Kurune's superior numbers to flank and to overwhelm the Chosen forces. If Kurune was sensible, he would advance cautiously, he would surround Karn from all directions, and he would not allow his forces to be channelled in the way that Corin wanted them to be. But Corin was counting on the Kurakee leader being overconfident and impatient.

Despite this, Corin was intending to retain his small body of Qari horsemen as a mobile force, to impede any attempts to flank from the east or north. The Qari riders would be kept to the east of the long ditch, to be given freedom to manoeuvre. And if Kurune chose to send any warriors into the woodland to the west of the corridor, and through the woods beside the Great Lake, there would be another force waiting for them.

Corin had devised a number of other surprises and traps for the approaching enemy horde. The first of these were scattered around the thinnest part of the corridor. At that point, Corin's people had stacked close to forty piles of wood and hay, to act as obstacles for the Kurakee warriors as they approached. Each stack was at least as tall and wide across as the height of a man. Corin had a nasty plan for the use of these.

He knew that it was vital to seek out every possible dirty advantage in order to achieve victory. Tomorrow, they would be facing an enemy with a massive numerical superiority, and they would only win by being ruthless and fearless. And even then, it might not be enough.

'I thank you, Munnik, for all of this,' Corin finally said, gesturing towards the preparations. 'You've given us a chance.'

'Thank me tomorrow, Corin, after the battle,' said the older man. 'Thank me tomorrow.'

—

Late on the following morning, the Kurakee army appeared in sight to the south of Karn. At the moment when the line of thousands first became visible, as the enemy passed over a low and distant ridge, Corin was standing amongst his men in the front lines of the Chosen. Immediately, he could hear gasps and curses from some of those around him, as they began to fully appreciate the enormity of the enemy horde.

Corin was sharing that concern as he witnessed the Kurakee numbers for the first time. The horde stretched in an unbroken line across the entire width of the corridor between the woods and the trench, presenting a four hundred metre expanse of barbarous, axe-wielding warriors. Even from this distance, Corin could hear a repeated and ominous thud from their war-drums, and he could discern a war cry being shouted by thousands.

'Kurakee! Kurakee!'

Corin could perceive how the Kurakee had been able to overawe so many opponents. In the face of such a formidable threat, he believed that many clans would have elected to surrender and to suffer the consequences, without even attempting to fight.

'Let them tire themselves out with shouting,' he announced confidently, seeking to bolster the men around him. 'They haven't faced the Chosen people before, and the Gods are with us!'

The main body of the male Chosen forces had been lined up to bridge the narrowest point of the corridor, between the woods to the west and the ditch to the east. Corin was in the centre of this line, which was six ranks deep, and the warriors surrounding him were all wielding spears. In fact, the front three ranks were all armed with spears of varying lengths.

Corin had witnessed this tactic being used in his visions in the north, and he had married this with other ideas which he had developed after observing the Borl. Upon his return, he had ordered the production of several hundred spears, and today he would see if this new innovation would work.

Corin continued to watch as the Kurakee approached. He was satisfied to see that the enemy masses were allowing themselves to be funnelled along the narrowing corridor. As far as Corin could see, none of the Kurakee horde was attempting to climb past the stakes and through the ditch. Nor were any flanking into the woods. The enemy appeared too confident in their numbers to be concerned about tactical threats and nuances.

For once, Corin was not with Blackpaw, but he could see through the felrin's eyes, and he knew that the beast was ready for when its master called. Corin was instead surrounded by a number of Karn warriors, including Kernon, all of whom were holding shields. They had been told to protect Corin at all costs, including shielding him from arrows and from thrown weapons. It was possible that the enemy would recognise Corin as the Chosen leader, and then would try to target him once he unleashed his powers on them.

When the masses of enemy warriors had closed to within two hundred metres of the Chosen front line, Corin could see that the Kurakee were bunched closely together. Exactly as he wanted.

The din that the horde was making was deafening, however, and a chant was now booming from the enemy ranks of, 'The Kurakee are coming! The Kurakee are coming!'

Amongst this body of enemy troops, Corin spotted an extremely obese and heavily-bearded man. This figure was visible because he was reclining on a grand chair, which was being held up high above the heads of the surrounding Kurakee. Corin guessed that the man in the raised chair must be the Warlord Kurune.

Corin glared at the fat individual, making him a focal point for anger. It would be important for Corin to maintain control of himself today, to allow him to ruthlessly implement his plan. However, he was also well aware that embracing his fury would allow his powers to build.

The Kurakee leader was peering towards Corin's lines, and was looking entirely relaxed about the coming battle. As far as Corin knew, this was the individual who had led the Kurakee conquests of so many other clans. A man whose tribe had thrived on inflicting suffering and pain on countless victims. Someone whose people had delivered death, pillage, rape and sacrifice. And on top of that, this man wanted to destroy all of the good which Corin was building within the Chosen Alliance. He wanted to unravel everything that Corin had achieved, and to ravage Corin's people.

A god named Mella had also once devastated these lands, thousands of years earlier. Corin had been an appalled witness of that, though he could do nothing now to change what he had seen. However, he could do something about this new monster in the chair, who led the Kurakee.

Corin let all of these thoughts feed his anger, fuelling it. He could also feel the ferocious reaction to this within Blackpaw, some distance away, but the beast knew better than to cry out in response.

'Release flame arrows!' shouted Corin.

This call was repeated multiple times by the people around him. Within moments, flaming arrows were whistling over Corin's head, aiming at the various stacks of wood and hay in the space between the Chosen front line and the enemy. This was another tactic which Corin had witnessed in his visions in the north, albeit one used by Mella himself.

Corin watched with satisfaction as all of the targets caught fire. Flames erupted in multiple places on the ground between the

Chosen lines and the Kurakee, sending plumes of smoke into the air. The bunched masses of the horde would need to navigate through the obstacle of these fires, significantly restricting the space through which the enemy could charge.

'Lower spears!'

Again, Corin's cry was repeated multiple times across the whole of the line. Corin now moved himself back from the foremost ranks, and watched with satisfaction as the front three rows of Chosen spearmen lowered their weapons. This action had been drilled at length, with shortest spears at the front and longest at the back. There was now an unbroken line of spear-tips running along the entire length of the corridor mouth, from the ditch in the east to the woods in the west.

'Hold!'

This shout came from a number of Corin's chiefs and war leaders. Unlike so many other battles which Corin's people had been in, today's conflict would not begin with a mad forward charge. Corin had witnessed countless battles within his visions in the far north, and he knew that such a tactic would not work against a force of this size. Instead, his men were going to face the enemy charge from a stationary stance, with spears pointing forwards.

'Chosen!' shouted Corin. Within moments, a thousand voices had repeated the call, sending goosebumps along his back and neck.

In response to this, a prolonged scream of bloodlust echoed through the Kurakee ranks. Their war drums then thundered in unison, and the enemy horde started to charge.

The Battle of Karn was about to commence. It was time to fight.

29

Arion

—

Year of Our Lord,
After Ascension, 770AA

As Arion rode his horse along the narrow path through woodland, he felt a sense of satisfaction that he was finally nearing his goal. After a gruelling journey which had covered hundreds of miles across war-torn Andar, Septholme was at last just a handful of miles away.

By the Lord, I'm going to make it!

For the last two days, he had endured an arduous physical ordeal. He had been sleeping rough for just a handful of hours each night as he had circumvented Rednarron and its besieging army, and had finally crossed into Western Canasar. He had been spotted from afar and pursued at various times during the journey, and had been forced to stand and fight on two more occasions after flight had ceased to be an option. But he had survived his trials, each time more wearied. And he had continued onwards, ever onwards, towards his home.

He had heard occasional news about the plight of his province as he had travelled through it. Stories from local folk had confirmed the defeat of Gerrion's army, and the retreat of its surviving soldiers towards Septholme. Those same locals had uttered many curses about the treacherous forces of Berun, and about the pillaging by the army of Elannis as it had headed south through the region. Arion had also heard disturbing rumours about the imprisonment of women by Aiduel's Guards, for reasons unknown.

But at last, he was now near to his home, and his bloody odyssey was approaching its end. Ever since deserting from Sendar's army, he had been fixated on getting back to Septholme. To some extent, that objective had taken primacy over the much greater problem of what he was going to do when he arrived. But he would soon have to confront the daunting challenge of the latter.

For days on his solitary journey, he had been wondering about the condition of his home town, and whether it continued to stand firm against its attackers. If it still stood, he would need to find a way to get inside the town walls, even if there was a besieging army of thousands. Whichever way he was going to accomplish that, it would soon be the time for action.

Earlier, he had left the main coast road, having expected to run into blockades. He was approaching the town along a minor trail to its north-east, which he had discovered in his teenage years. This narrow path was barely wide enough for his sole remaining horse, and wound through woodland which was sufficiently dense to obscure Septholme from sight. The forest floor and the trail were dappled with sunbeams which shone through the canopy of leaves above.

So far, Arion had not encountered anyone hostile along this route. However, his horse was proceeding at a controlled trot, and he was watchful for blockades and ambushes as he progressed.

It was in this state of alertness that he first felt the presence of the *other*. It was unmistakeably another person like him, another *Illborn*, somewhere to the south-west in the direction of Septholme. He could feel their energy pulsing towards him across the distance between them.

Lord preserve us! How is this possible?

He reined in his horse, briefly savouring the sensation of the other's presence. As previously, it rejuvenated and revitalised him, allowing his fatigue to be disregarded. His heart was also pumping faster, beating vigorously in his chest.

He proceeded on cautiously, still feeling the presence, until he became certain that it was coming towards him. Travelling *fast* towards him, in a manner which suggested that the person must be riding. He spotted a small glade at the side of the trail, and he decided to steer his horse into there to wait.

The presence was still coming closer, and a question was replayed in Arion's mind; was it Leanna or Allana? He climbed down from his horse and tied its reins to a nearby branch. He then waited in a state of nervous agitation, with his hand moving unconsciously to the sword on his hip. He could feel the other drawing ever nearer, their presence pulsing ever brighter, each such pulse mirroring the pounding beat of his heart.

When she finally appeared on the trail beside the glade, she reined in her horse from a gallop, then smiled as she turned towards him. For Arion, it was as if the sun had burst forth out of the gloom of his memory, and was shining gloriously onto the present. The natural sunlight dappling the trail played across her face, and across the red velvet outfit which clung to her body. Arion was awestruck. He was breathless and mesmerised.

In the last year, he had held the memories of her beauty, and of his desire for her, tight to his chest. Almost obsessively. On countless occasions, he had recalled those final moments when he had left her alone on a country trail in the middle of the night. And he had tormented himself with the regret lurking in those memories, after he had thought her dead.

But until this moment of her reappearance, he had underestimated just how incomparably alluring she was, and how much he truly wanted her. Why he had been on the precipice of casting all other things aside for her. He was breathing heavily as her horse trotted into the clearing, and as she climbed down from the animal. When she then turned to face him, it was beyond question that she was the most desirable woman that he had ever met or would ever meet.

By the Lord, how can I have forgotten this? Forgotten her?

He could feel her aura enveloping him, swirling around him, as he had once felt it before. Enticing him, unsettling him, but making him feel vibrantly alive. Enflaming his senses.

There were things that he wanted to say, matters that he wanted to challenge her about. Had she been responsible for the letters which had dragged him to the other end of the country, and which had led to this prolonged ordeal? Had she ever had any intention of meeting him in Andarron? And why was she here, right now, in this place and at this time?

But even as he was thinking this, she stepped closer to him, until less than a foot in distance separated the two of them. Her eyes roved up and down his body, hunger in her gaze, and he could not help but stare in turn at her perfect form. Her thick dark hair was loose, some of it hanging forwards over one shoulder. He wanted to reach out and touch it as their eyes locked together.

'Allana…'

'Don't speak,' she said. 'I *knew* it was you. You look… so dishevelled… and delicious, Arion. And I can feel… your raw power. But no talk, this time. Do what I know you want to do. What we both want to do.'

Her accent was as drawling as he remembered, her tone low and seductive. She edged closer again, such that only inches separated their mouths.

'This… is not the time,' he protested, weakly. 'I am marr-… I must…'

He had to get to Septholme, to complete what he had travelled all this way to do. Back to his home and to Kalyane, before-

Her hand reached up and softly touched his neck, and her mouth moved closer again. As had happened once before, it seemed that there were whispers in his mind, urgent and insistent whispers, which were accompanied by arousing fragments of carnal visions.

Promises of sensual bliss. Despite the teetering resistance of his conscience and his sense of duty, he felt his body respond.

I want her. I need her.

'This *is* the time,' she said, her lips resting close to his neck, her chest now pressing into his. 'You won't ride off and leave me this time, Arion. And if not now, then when? I know that you've longed for this moment, as have I. Now do what you want to do, Arion, and give me what I want. What we both *need*. Take me, Arion. Possess me and let me possess you. Now, stop fighting this, and *fuck* me.'

His resistance and reluctance were shattered. His mouth pressed hard against hers, and his arms wrapped around her, crushing her against his body. She pressed her full form intimately into him and moaned, and he responded with a low guttural sound of his own.

Their hands were then roaming on the body of the other, their mouths locked together, with clothes being cast off hungrily in the desperate urgency of the moment. The vibrancy which emanated from her was embracing him, enveloping him in a sensual and powerful cocoon, which intermingled with his own aura as their bodies also melded together. The air was crackling around him, and coils of energy were encircling his limbs as he lowered her to the grassy forest floor, their forms still entwined.

He was close to ecstatic within this shared sensation of power and pleasure, which was beyond anything that he had ever experienced before.

Her hand was on his neck at the moment when he first entered her, and he heard her whisper a victorious, 'Yessss…'

And in what followed, as Allana dei Monis moaned beneath him, the rest of the world, and the people in it, were forgotten.

―

Afterwards, he was holding her in his arms. He was on his back, staring into the canopy of branches and leaves above, his breathing heavy from what had just taken place. She was on her side, her face buried into the hollow of his neck, and he could feel the delicious heat and shape of her body as it pressed close against him. His arm was around her, his hand on her hip.

His mind was reeling, feeling shocked by the frenzy which had just gripped him. There was an air of unreality about what had just occurred, as if the actions had been undertaken by a person other than himself. By someone who had been overcome by an all-consuming desire, and who had lost control of any rational thought. It was as if his lust had made him disregard who he was and why he had come to this place.

'That was amazing,' she purred, as her hand moved across his chest. 'It's never been like that before. Not even close.'

'Yes,' he whispered, and despite his sense of disorientation, he knew that she was right. He had never experienced anything remotely comparable. 'Amazing.'

'This is how it's meant to be,' she said, sounding softly triumphant. 'How it was always meant to be. I feel like… a goddess… and you my god… when I'm with you. In complete and utter bliss.'

He recognised the truth in her words, and his response was a grunt of acknowledgement. He squeezed his arm to press her closer against his body.

'You should never have left me, Arion.'

He still felt languorously dazed, but he realised that she was referring to the night of her escape.

'I… had to leave you that night,' he said. 'I had no choice.'

For a few moments, she was silent.

'You *did* have a choice,' she said, eventually. 'But I survived, and I'm alive, Arion. Very much alive, as I know you can feel. And I'm returned to you, and we're together again.'

He recognised a hint of reproach in her words, and whispered, 'I'm sorry.'

'And you married someone else, despite your promises to me.'

This time, he felt a tinge of annoyance that she was criticising him, however soft and alluring her tone of voice. But worse than that, submerged guilt surfaced within him at the mention of his marriage.

Lord preserve me. Kalyane. What have I just done?

'I was told that you were dead,' he responded, his tone not betraying his sudden rush of emotion. 'And I truly believed it.'

'It doesn't matter,' she said. 'I forgive you, and we're reunited now. And you'll leave her, because we belong together, and you're mine. My... love. I love you, Arion.'

'And I love you.'

His response came easily and felt sincere. However, even as he said the words, he could feel a part of himself awakening, as if gently emerging from a dream. The rational part of his mind was beginning to reassert itself, and the questions which had been troubling him since Andarron were returning with pressing insistence.

'How are you *here*, Allana?' he asked, after a few seconds. 'And *why* are you here?'

He could feel a sudden tension in her body, before she responded, 'I... came to find you.'

'But why now?'

'It... just seemed like the right time.'

He could hear an awkwardness in her voice, and her aura suddenly felt more... tempestuous.

'And the letters I received,' he continued, 'were they from you?'

There was a delay before she responded with a quiet, 'Yes.'

'Both of them? Including the letter inviting me to Andarron?'

'Yes.'

'Then, why weren't you there? I went to the tavern but you weren't there.'

'I... had to leave,' she said. 'There was danger.'

By the Lord, she's lying to me.

He gently prised her off his chest, then sat up, in order to see her face. 'That isn't true. You were never there.'

She raised herself on one arm, naked and arching her back. She looked so glorious that Arion felt tempted anew, despite his questions and doubts.

'Yes, I was,' she said. 'Please don't say that, Arion.'

'You were never there, Allana. I asked the innkeeper. Why are you lying to me?'

She stared into his eyes through lowered lashes, and she appeared crestfallen in reaction to his words.

'Please don't say that, Arion! Please don't call me a liar! Why are you being like this, after what we've just done? After how wonderful it was! Can't we just celebrate being here together, at last, and talk about our love, our future?'

'Our future?' He frowned at her, suddenly feeling as if his mind was casting off any lingering traces of enchantment. 'Not until I better understand the past, Allana. Not until you tell me the whole truth. You wrote a letter asking me to go to Andarron, to meet with you. And I did. But you lied, and you weren't there. Now, please tell me why you did it?'

'Because I wanted to protect you, that's why!' she snapped, and it sounded like she was on the brink of tears. 'Is that so wrong, wanting to protect you from this war? Wanting to get you away from here? I just wanted to do the right thing! For you, not for me! I have nothing to feel guilty about!'

He frowned again, feeling more and more confused. He started to gather his clothes, before standing and pulling his trousers back on.

'Then why are *you* here?' he asked. 'And why are you here right now? Why didn't *you* go to Andarron, like your letter said?'

'Stop asking me questions, Arion, as if I'm your prisoner to be interrogated!' There was a shrill quality to her voice as she said this. 'I've been interrogated before, and it was horrible, and I won't accept it from you! Why are you trying to ruin this, when we love each other?'

He was about to respond when he heard a voice from the woodland trail.

'Lady Allana? Is that you?'

Arion's chest was bare, and Allana was still completely naked, when a man on horseback emerged onto the trail beside the glade.

This individual appeared to be in his mid-twenties, with a boyishly young face, and he was wearing the tabard of a soldier of Berun.

Arion reached for his discarded sword and scabbard, and rose to his feet. He was ready to attack and kill if this stranger made any move against him, but he could also see that there was shock on the newcomer's face.

'My Lady?' said the man. 'What is this?'

'Stay there, Connar,' said Allana. 'Don't move.'

Arion noticed that her voice was suddenly deeper and more commanding. He observed as the soldier's wary expression was immediately transformed, with a dreamy, vacant look appearing on the man's face. This newcomer now seemed to be disregarding Arion's presence, and he was focusing his attention entirely upon Allana.

By the Lord! What did she just do?

'There's no need to feel threatened,' continued Allana.

Arion drew his sword from its scabbard.

'Lady Allana, he just called you,' he said. 'What does that mean?'

Allana did not look at him, but she murmured, 'It means nothing.'

'He's a soldier of Berun,' Arion persisted. 'How does he know you? And why does he call you "My Lady"?'

This time, Allana turned to regard him. There was irritation in her expression, and she hissed, 'I said, it means nothing!'

'And this thing that you seem to have done to him. Is that your power? Is that what you've done to me, too?'

'I didn't do that to you! It doesn't work the same on you, as on him! Don't pretend you didn't want me, Arion, as if it wasn't your choice.' She paused and took a deep breath. 'Please, please, Arion, just stop all of this nastiness!'

Arion stepped closer towards the Berun soldier. 'He's invading my land as part of a hostile army. This man is my enemy. You there, how do you know this woman?'

The man's gaze flashed towards Arion for just a moment, then returned to Allana, his expression looking besotted and full of desire. He did not answer the question.

'Whatever you're doing to him,' said Arion, addressing Allana, 'stop it and permit him to speak, or I'll kill him.'

Allana's brow furrowed in response, and Arion noticed that the man was geeing his horse in an attempt to ride away. Arion reacted instantly, moving towards the soldier in a blur of speed. He dragged the man down from his mount and slammed him hard against the ground.

Lord preserve me, I think that she ordered him to flee!

The soldier groaned as his back crunched against the floor. The daze in his eyes appeared to clear, and he looked up to find Arion leaning over him. One of Arion's hands closed around the man's throat.

'You're a soldier of Berun, yes?'

After asking the question, Arion briefly squeezed his hand tighter.

The soldier gasped, and looked terrified. 'Yes.'

'Where's your army?'

'At Septholme, besieging the town.'

Arion felt rage. 'Right now? Led by Duke Jarrett Berun?'

'Yes.'

By the Lord, I'll find him and I'll fucking rip him apart!

'And who is this woman to you?' said Arion, while pointing towards Allana. 'Why did you come looking for her?' The soldier tried to turn his head to face Allana, but Arion squeezed his neck again, and bellowed, 'Who is this woman?'

'Sh-she's Lady Allana, Duke Berun's w-wife-to-be.' The man was gasping the words. 'He's ordered me to guard her.'

'What?' said Arion, feeling stunned.

He turned his head towards Allana, somehow hoping that she would deny it. However, the mixture of discomfort and defiance visible on her face told him that the Berun soldier had spoken true.

'You're betrothed to Jarrett Berun?' Arion spluttered. A fury was continuing to build, that he was struggling to contain. '*What? How?* And you're here with... *him?* With his army?'

'Let me explain, Arion,' Allana replied. 'You married another wom-'

'Wait!' he interrupted, then turned to face the soldier. 'Does the town still stand? Speak true.'

'Y-yes, but only b-because the Angel was protecting it. But she fell today after the rock struck, and it seems like we'll take the walls now.'

'The Angel?'

'The Angel of Arlais.'

Arion turned towards Allana and shouted, 'Leanna's here! Why didn't you tell me any of this? Did you know that another one of our kind is near?'

Allana's face and bare chest were flushed, although whether it was from anger or from embarrassment, Arion could not be certain.

'Why should any of this matter?' she said, her voice low and imploring. 'Let's leave him and get away from here! Please Arion, we love each other, and I choose to be with *you*! I want to be with you. Let's leave, just you and me, before it's too late!'

'Just answer me!' he bellowed at her. 'Is Leanna of Arlais inside Septholme?'

'Yes!'

Arion addressed his next question to both Allana and to his captive. 'And what of Duke Gerrion Sepian? Does he still live?'

'Yes,' gasped the guard. 'He's a prisoner.'

Thank you, Lord!

'Where is he?'

'The fortress!' said the soldier. 'Aiduel's Guards' fortress, outside the town.'

Arion paused, trying to collect his thoughts, while his fingers were still clasped on the man's neck. There was almost too much information to take in here. He stared down at the Berun soldier, wondering whether there was any way that he could release this individual, this invader of his homeland. He was hesitant to kill someone who was co-operating with him, but this man was his enemy, and they were at war. After a few moments, he came to a reluctant decision.

'I'm sorry.' He wrapped his arm around the captive's neck, then wrenched the man's head sideways. There was a sharp crack, then Arion lowered the lifeless form to the ground.

With this done, he stood up and turned to face Allana again. She was still completely naked, and she seemed unperturbed by his action. A part of Arion could not fail to note once more just how flawlessly beautiful she was, but he wilfully resisted any stirrings of desire.

'Were you going to tell me any of this?' he asked her.

'No!'

'No? Why not?'

'Because it doesn't matter! We're together again! And we can be together now, Arion, like we should be.' Her voice was softer as she said these latter words. 'Nothing compares to the feeling when I'm with you, and I know you feel the same! Remember how blissful it was, being together today. We can have that every day, every night. Let's just leave here together, make a new life together, and forget about all of this. Please, Arion.'

'I don't think so,' he said, struggling to contain his disdain as he started to dress. 'Have you fucked Jarrett Berun? Is that who you're comparing me to? Or maybe it's my father? Or possibly some other duke?'

'Don't act all holy with me!' she replied. 'You haven't stayed celibate since you abandoned me, so why should I?'

'No, indeed, why should you?' he sneered.

'Don't look at me like that! You still want me, Arion. I know that you do.'

'Want you? Want you? How could I want *you*? You've been whoring yourself to Jarrett Berun!'

She took a step towards him after he had said that, with her hand raised as if to strike him. But then an expression of anguish appeared on her face, and she halted. She lowered her arm and took a deep breath.

'Don't you dare use that word on me, Arion,' she said, after a few moments. 'Don't you dare! Not you. And how can you have the gall to judge me? I'm not the one who's married. I had no idea that you'd come here. You're the faithless one!'

'I'm not faithless!' he said indignantly, though he recognised the truth in her words.

'Yes, you are! You married another woman, despite your promises to me, and now you've cheated on her, too! And you call me a whore, but you weren't criticising me when you were inside me, fucking me, Arion!'

'By the Lord, Allana, I see now how deluded I've been. And if I could take back this encounter, in fact *any* encounter with you, I would.'

'Don't say that, you don't-'

'I see you now for what you are,' he interrupted, as he buckled on his belt and scabbard. 'You sent me to Andarron at Jarrett Berun's bidding, didn't you? To get me away from here so he could invade my homeland. Lord, what a fool I've been for you, time and time again. Do you realise what you've done? My whole country invaded, my army destroyed, and me not here, and it's all because of *you*!'

'That's not true!'

'It *is* true. I'm leaving, and after today, I want nothing more to do with you. I'm going to free my brother, and I'm going to find Kalyane, Karienne, and Leanna. Three women in my life who are actually worth something! I love my wife, even despite… *this*. She's worth a hundred of you. And Leanna of Arlais is worth a thousand! If I never see you again, Allana, it'll still be one fucking time too many!'

He was fully dressed now. As he turned towards his horse and untied its reins, he suddenly realised that he was uncomfortable to have his back exposed to Allana. He turned his head so that he could see her in his peripheral vision.

'That's it,' she said, as he climbed into the saddle. She was starting to dress, her voice sounding on the edge of hysteria. 'Run away, and leave me here, like you always do. Go get yourself killed in

Septholme, and I'll be there to celebrate when Jarrett conquers your town, and puts your precious women in the dungeon! And makes me Duchess of Western Canasar! See if I care!'

He turned to face her as he geed his horse into motion, and he uttered the words, 'You fucking whore.'

For a second, the anger on her face was again replaced by distress, and he felt a moment of remorse for the venomous nature of his words. However, he was then riding away from her, his horse turning onto the trail towards Septholme, and she quickly disappeared from sight.

'Arion!'

Her final call sounded like a plea. But he did not look back.

As his horse galloped towards Septholme, Arion realised that he could hear the distant noises of battle. His senses had returned to complete alertness, and the agitation that his encounter with Allana had roused meant that he was now even more ready to fight. He was eager to release his anger upon the enemy.

He would have to decide what he was going to do before he reached the end of this woodland trail. Should he head straight for the town and try to find a way in, to help Kalyane? Or should he travel towards the fortress of Aiduel's Guards, to attempt to free his brother?

He could still feel the presence of Allana dei Monis as he rode towards the sounds of battle. He realised that she was also moving, somewhere behind him, tracking the same direction along the trail back towards the town.

By the Lord, I've been bewitched by her! How could I not have seen her for what she is, before now?

He was still reeling from the encounter. His infidelity with Allana was yet another stain on his honour, if indeed he had any remaining claim to such virtue after his actions of the last month. But without any doubt, it was one more deed for him to feel ashamed of.

He continued riding. Only then did he become aware of the pulsing of a second Illborn, in the distance to the south-west. This presence felt weak, lacking Leanna's usual vibrancy and radiance, but it had to be her. She was alive, despite the soldier's words.

Arion realised that with Leanna close by, and Allana seemingly following him, for the first time ever he was in the proximity of two other Illborn at the same time.

The air crackled around him as if in recognition of that fact, and he felt the resultant coils of energy encircling his limbs. Would he be even stronger now? More powerful and resilient? Even more capable of deeds on a battlefield which might once have seemed unimaginable? Certainly, the fatigue which he had carried with him across Rednar and Western Canasar was now forgotten, a trivial inconvenience.

He continued to urge his horse onwards, seeing the end of the trail looming up ahead. The town, the fortress and a now cacophonous battle were drawing close. Soon, the enemy would emerge into view. After that, there would be an awful reckoning, and a possible way to make reparation for some of his shameful deeds. A way to appease his guilt.

And one thing was absolutely certain. Many people were going to die today.

30

Leanna

—

Year of Our Lord,
After Ascension, 770AA

At first, all that she knew was pain. Agonising, stabbing, shattering, maddening pain. Spanning her entire lower half, as she floated in darkness.

'Lea...'

A quiet voice, a familiar voice, seeming to whisper to her, but she could focus only upon the unbearable agony.

'Lea...'

Was there a hand on her face? Memories, the last-second glimpse of a boulder looming, arcing towards her. Too late to react, too late to do anything. Amyss pushing her...

'Lea!'

The frail voice was louder this time, more insistent.

Leanna's eyelids drifted open, and the blue of a clear sky was revealed above her. She was lying on her back, facing upwards. There were alarming sounds all around, a chaotic din of screams and metal. Her mouth was dry, tasting of dust and blood, and the world around her seemed to be swirling. Amidst her confusion, she could not remember where she was. But from every direction, there were emotions of pain, horror and fear. Bombarding her, and threatening to become as overwhelming as the agony of her own injuries.

She opened her mouth to scream, but all that emerged was a whimper.

PAIN. DYING. WORRY.

Within the chorus of external suffering, this one call was nearer and more resonant than the others. Leanna recognised the intimate voice of this emotion, from one who was so familiar and loved. She wanted to reach out to it.

But she could not focus; her return to consciousness was bringing renewed awareness of the pain in her shattered legs. This time, she let out a full-throated and anguished scream.

Then a hand was touching her nose and cheek again. Turning her head to the right.

'Lea!'

And there was… Amyss, beside her. Lying on her side, facing Leanna, their faces just inches apart. Blood was on the mouth and chin of the petite priestess, and her eyes seemed glazed. Behind her, there was a broken battlement wall. They were on the ramparts.

'Amyss…' whispered Leanna. 'It hurts…'

Leanna began to feel a detachment from the reality of where she was, and from the horrific sounds and emotions that were all around her. The pain was beyond excruciating, and she desperately wanted to lapse into unconsciousness again. To pass into the escape of oblivion, and to hope that this overwhelming agony would go away. She looked back up at the sky, feeling an urge to close her eyes.

'Don't sleep! Heal yourself, Lea!'

The hand was still on Leanna's face. Fingers were on her mouth and nose and eyes. Annoying her, bothering her. Stopping her from closing her eyelids.

'Heal…?' she murmured.

'Heal yourself, Lea… please…'

Amyss's voice was growing fainter, seeming more distant. The hand slipped from Leanna's face and slid down to rest against her shoulder.

PAIN. DYING. SORROW.

From beside Leanna. Amyss was in terrible danger. Amyss was dying too.

Lord Aiduel. Help me…

Leanna closed her eyes as proper awareness was gradually returning to her. But this time, she resisted sleep and oblivion. She was beginning to remember more of who she was. Of what she was. And of what she could do?

Heal people. She was a healer.

And at this moment, she was in the utmost pain, on the brink of death and in extreme need of healing. As was her beloved Amyss.

DEVOTION. SACRIFICE. SALVATION.

The words whispered softly into Leanna's mind, without any accompanying roar of angels. But it was enough to sustain her, and to give her hope.

Lord Aiduel, please help me…

In the darkness behind her closed eyelids, she began to seek out the wounds within herself. And in mere instants, she could see them. Blackness throughout her legs; bones shattered, splintered, broken, jutting through torn flesh. It was a wretched mess, which pulsed with the chaos of her own internal agony.

She sought further, as her invisible and ethereal fingers reached towards the petite woman lying beside her. There was less external damage… but Amyss was fading away. Then Leanna found what she was searching for; there was a severed artery in one of Amyss's legs, and her lung had also been punctured. The lifeblood of the small priestess was bleeding out onto the stone surface of the battlements beneath her, as she lay beside Leanna. Amyss was mortally wounded. Perhaps they both were.

Leanna felt so weak… both from the injuries that she had sustained from the boulder… and from the terrible attack before that;

a very different type of pain and horror which had been inflicted on her by another. There was still a lingering temptation to sleep now, to drift off into darkness in order to escape this excruciating pain. But if she did that, she believed that she would die. And Amyss would die.

She therefore forced herself to fight against the seductive sanctuary of unconsciousness, and she concentrated upon her healing. She was striving to do something which she had never done before; to encompass more than one person within the focus of her powers, and also to turn The Lord's miracle of healing upon herself.

Lord Aiduel, please keep me awake. Please give me the strength to do this.

The ethereal fingers under Leanna's control began to seek out and address all of her and Amyss's injuries. She could feel the flesh in her lower half starting to repair, and could sense that her bones were knitting together. She opened her eyes a fraction, and witnessed that she was once again bathed in golden light. This radiance also encompassed the form of Amyss, as Leanna worked her healing upon the two of them.

She saw now that there were others standing around her. Blue-tabarded soldiers, some watching with awe, some facing outwards, but all seeming to be dedicated to protecting her.

Leanna turned her head towards Amyss. The other woman's eyes were closed, and she was not moving.

Leanna was close to exhaustion. As she lay within her cocoon of healing, she was concerned whether she would have the energy to complete this work. But she strove to continue to attack the darkness within her own body, and to repair the mortal wounds within Amyss's still form.

Leanna's eyes closed again. The pain in her lower limbs was at last beginning to ease, which was some small solace to be thankful for. However, the urge was renewed to fall back to sleep. To slide into oblivion and to let all of this fade away. But still she resisted, for as long as she possibly could.

LOVE. LOVE. GOODBYE.

The tender and frail emotions carried to Leanna with the faintest murmur. However, in their heartfelt nature they were like a clarion call which rang above all else on the horrific battlements. They gave Leanna the fortitude to carry on her work for just a few moments more, before it all became too much for her.

And they were the last thing that she thought about, before she lapsed back into unconsciousness.

—

When her eyes flickered back open, there was again confusion. She was being carried in someone's arms, down a series of steps, and her head was lolling gently. She could see the top of the battlements receding above her, and could hear the sounds of fierce battle still raging there.

The external cacophony of emotions, which had been close to overwhelming her, now seemed to be greatly diminished. Indeed, so did her access to her own powers, and the pain in her lower limbs was also gone.

Leanna felt disorientated, and turned her head to see who was carrying her. It was Caddin. The head of his hefty mace was visible over his shoulder, where he had attached it to his back. There were flecks of blood on his face and on the weapon.

'Caddin…'

They had reached the bottom of the steps, and she saw him regarding her with something approaching tenderness in his expression.

'Leanna.'

'What's happened?' she asked.

'The wall's being overrun, and I think the town's going to fall. I had to fight my way across the ramparts to get to you. I've got to get you out of this town, Leanna. Somehow.'

Leanna felt an abrupt wave of dizziness as she was held in his arms, and the world seemed to lurch around her. She squeezed her eyelids shut, trying to fend off the threat of nausea. Instead, memories returned to her of the events on the battlements, reminding her of the instants before the rock had hit.

The golden shield of light had been raised high above Septholme's walls. Leanna had been exulting in the moment, energised by the power which had been surging through her. In The Lord's name, it had been enabling her to prevent a resumption of bloodshed and death. And the woman Allana had been helping her, feeding her with energy.

Then sudden, unexpected darkness had arrived, writhing along the connection between Leanna and the other woman. Sensations of drowning, of burning. Emotions of envy, bitterness and fear. Horror mixed in with lust, power and pain. Leanna had been shocked by what the other one had been *pushing* into her, too stunned to act to defend herself, and she had not known how she would make such a defence anyway. She had staggered in anguish, her body and mind assailed as one, and the golden shield had faded and failed.

Amyss had run to her, holding her up, and had prevented her from falling under the force of the terrible assault. And eventually, the attack had ended. It had left Leanna feeling beleaguered and unsteady, but she not been prepared to abandon her goal.

She had taken a deep breath, readying herself, and had stood upright. She had been preparing to see whether she could renew the golden shield, in some form. Trying to find the power within to prevent the impending bloodbath.

Then a glimpse of movement. A large object looming in the sky above. Amyss pushing her...

Then pain. Darkness. And pain.

Amyss waking her. Insisting that Leanna was to stay awake and heal herself. And Leanna had started that healing, as her beloved companion had been bleeding to death beside her...

As this memory arrived, Leanna was beset with panic.

'Where's Amyss?' she asked. 'I said, where's Amyss?'

'I'm here, Lea.' It was a frail voice, but a recognisable one. Relief flooded into Leanna, washing over her alarm.

Lord Aiduel, thank you, thank you, thank you!

Leanna turned her head towards the sound. She saw the figure of a stocky Andar soldier nearby, who was holding the petite form of Amyss in his arms. There was still a red mark on Amyss's mouth and chin, and the lower part of her dress was heavily bloodstained. The red-headed woman was also very pale, as if she had lost a lot of blood.

'Put me down, Caddin,' said Leanna. 'Please. I think I can stand.'

In response, Caddin lowered her down gently onto her feet, although his arm remained wrapped around her back and under her armpit, to support her. Leanna started to shuffle towards Amyss, assisted by the burly man. She felt some astonishment that her legs seemed to be working fine, and there was no apparent discomfort in her lower limbs.

When she reached Amyss, she could see that the other priestess looked exhausted and dazed, with the petite woman's head rolling back onto the forearm of the soldier who was carrying her.

Amyss made a visible attempt to focus and said, 'Lea…'

Leanna placed her hands onto either side of her companion's face, and kissed her forehead. Once. Twice. Multiple times. Leanna could feel tears in her eyes.

'For a second,' she said, 'I thought…'

'I know,' replied Amyss, her voice still sounding weak. 'I thought the same.'

Lord Aiduel, thank you for saving her. For saving both of us.

From somewhere behind them, there was a thunderous crash as another boulder must have smashed into a building inside the town walls.

'Leanna!' said Caddin, interrupting Leanna's focus on Amyss. 'We have to go. Now! They'll be inside the walls soon.'

Leanna came back to her senses and to the urgency of the moment. The sounds of fighting from above seemed ever more vicious, reinforcing Caddin's concern.

'How much time do we have?' she asked.

'Not a lot,' he replied. 'Too many have made it onto the battlements. I need to try to get you both somewhere safe. I can't let you fall into the hands of Aiduel's Guards.'

As he mentioned that, Leanna remembered what the religious order had done to the poor young girl on the pyre, earlier that day. Leanna had tried but failed to prevent that murder, before sensing a separate, more disturbing intervention by the woman Allana. That latter attempt had been accompanied by another alarming sense of… *darkness* emanating from the other woman, a foulness which had been a precursor to what had later been inflicted on Leanna.

However, Allana's efforts had also failed. Leanna shuddered at the memory of the blonde-haired girl's awful death.

'But where can we go?' she asked. 'Should we return to the hospital?'

'No, it's too close to the wall,' said Sendromm. 'It'll be one of the first places to be overrun. Let's head towards the castle.'

'Very well.'

—

Their party started to move together, heading steadily away from the northern wall and its deadly melee, and deeper into Septholme. Caddin's left arm was around Leanna's back and waist, almost lifting her along, whilst his right hand now clutched his mace.

The soldier who was carrying Amyss followed behind them. On a couple of occasions, Leanna looked back, and it appeared that her companion had lapsed into sleep or unconsciousness.

They were soon moving through a maze of streets and alleyways, and Leanna was disorientated, but Caddin seemed to have a good sense of exactly where they were going. Their passing was observed by a number of townsfolk who were milling about outside, looking worried. However, many others appeared to be hunkering down indoors, in fear of what was to come.

Despite Leanna's recent agony, there was now no pain in her legs, and she seemed to be moving without any impediment. She believed that she had healed herself completely before passing out, although she had not yet dared to look upon the two limbs which had been shattered. Caddin's current support was more to help her to offset her lingering fatigue; she was still tired, though it was not remotely close to the exhaustion that she had felt immediately after waking.

As they moved onwards towards the castle, Leanna thought again about the actions of the woman Allana. Just when Leanna had been glorying in The Lord doing his work through her, with the shield of light raised high, the dark-haired woman had assaulted her with a terrible power. And this assault had caused the golden barrier to fail, resulting in the bloodshed and death which now threatened to cause the fall of the town.

Lord Aiduel, please forgive her for her actions today.

Despite this plea for forgiveness, Leanna was deeply troubled by what the other Illborn had done. She knew that she would need to think on it further, once her party was out of immediate danger.

As they continued to move through the town's winding streets, Caddin was regularly checking behind them for signs of threat. However, for now they were untroubled; even if the Elannis armies had captured the northern wall, it appeared that Leanna's group was well ahead of any such rampaging soldiers.

When their party finally reached the main thoroughfare which ran between the castle and the harbour, Caddin paused. Leanna watched as the burly man peered towards the seafront area for a few moments, before shaking his head and starting to walk up the road towards the castle atop the hill.

They had not climbed far when they noticed a body of two dozen riders coming towards them, from the direction of the castle. The approaching group appeared to be heading towards the waterfront.

Leanna and her companions moved to the side of the road. As the riders drew level, Leanna was startled to spot Lady Kalyane in the centre of the mounted party. The auburn-haired woman was wearing a padded riding jacket and trousers, with a shining breastplate covering her upper half. Arion's younger sister Karienne was beside her and was similarly attired.

'Lady Kalyane!' Leanna shouted. To her relief, the noblewoman glanced over and spotted her.

Kalyane reined in her horse, and called her party of riders to an immediate halt. Leanna noticed that a number of the riders were carrying small chests, of a type used to store valuables or money.

'Priestess Leanna, Caddin,' Kalyane said. 'By the Lord, I didn't expect to see you here. I'm glad that you're well.'

'We were about to return to the castle,' said Caddin.

'The northern wall is lost, is it not?' the auburn-haired woman asked. 'I was watching from the castle battlements.'

'It will fall, my Lady,' stated Caddin. 'Today, their numbers are too many. And Leanna's attempt to stop them failed.'

'I saw,' said Kalyane. 'The wall of light disappeared, and then the boulder hit. I thought that you were...' She looked across to the sleeping form of Amyss. 'How is she?'

Leanna felt tears returning to her eyes, and she was grateful when Caddin replied on her behalf.

'She was injured in the attack on the wall,' said the grey-bearded man. 'As was Leanna, and they're both exhausted. But they survived.'

A look of distress flashed across Kalyane's features, and she said, 'A lot of people are going to suffer death and injury today because of my stubbornness and my choices. Thank you for trying, at least, Priestess Leanna.'

Leanna tilted her head in acknowledgement of the words, but she did not feel as if she had achieved anything worthy of thanks. Indeed, the failure of her actions had almost resulted in Amyss's death.

'I'm surprised to see you out of the castle, my Lady,' said Caddin. 'Where are you going, if I may ask?'

'If the wall has fallen, then the town is lost to us,' replied Kalyane. 'And if the town's lost, then the castle won't survive a siege for long.

But I'm resolved that the Sepian House will not end here, on this day. I have the castle treasury, and I intend to get Karienne to safety. And then I'll find Arion. Our best chance now lies at the harbour.'

'Escape by sea?' queried Caddin. 'You plan to lower the chain across the harbour mouth? What about the Dei Magnun fleet?'

'I know the risks,' Kalyane replied, 'but what choice do we have now? Yes, it may allow their navy in. But we have ships in the harbour, including our galleon, with provisions already on board. If we can ready them quickly enough, it at least gives us a chance to try to escape through the naval blockade. A chance for us, and for as many of our people and soldiers who can accompany us as possible.'

Caddin frowned as he appeared to consider this. After a second, he said, 'Then may we please come with you, my Lady? If Priestess Leanna is in the town when Aiduel's Guards take over, she'll be killed.'

'Yes, of course. Follow us to the quayside. It will take time to lower the chain and to muster the necessary crews to prepare the ships. But if we need to fight our way out of here by sea, then we will.'

At the conclusion of their conversation, Kalyane gestured towards her lead rider, then she and her accompanying party continued their journey down the hill towards the waterfront.

Once all of the horses had passed by, Caddin stated, 'Come, we must follow them.'

Leanna nodded and began to walk alongside him, again moving with his support. The stocky soldier with Amyss in his arms was following behind them.

Leanna peered towards the harbour as they walked, although her view was obstructed by a number of tall buildings. She was now familiar with the sight of the twin towers at the end of the two thin peninsulas of land which extended out from the town. From this perspective, the metal chain which ran between those towers was hidden behind a line of ships in the harbour, which included the mighty Sepian galleon.

It appeared to Leanna that it would be no small task to separate those vessels, and to get them ready to sail out of that harbour mouth.

Also visible, half a mile out from shore, were the numerous masts and white sails of the Dei Magnun navy. If the Western Canasar ships were to escape, they would need to evade that enemy fleet. It felt like a desperate attempt.

'Caddin,' she said, 'is there no other way?'

'The town's surrounded, Leanna,' he replied, looking grim. 'There's no way out by land. Aiduel's Guards know that you're here, and they want you. We could try to find somewhere to hide, cut your hair short, and attempt to disguise you. But they're going to search everywhere until they get you. This seems like our best chance.' He paused, appearing to listen for a moment. 'Come on, we need to move faster. I can definitely hear fighting inside the walls now, to the north. This area might be overrun soon, too.'

She nodded again as they began to walk down the hill at a faster pace, with Caddin almost carrying her.

'What happened?' he asked. 'On the wall, to the barrier of light?'

'There's another like me,' she replied quietly, conscious of the soldier who was following them. 'Another Illborn. Outside of the walls. I think that she... attacked me.'

He looked alarmed. 'Another? A woman?'

'Yes.'

'And she attacked you? How?'

'With powers. I'm not exactly sure what she did, but it felt so... *dark*.'

'Dark powers?'

'Yes.'

He frowned, before asking, '*Evil* powers?'

Lord Aiduel, how can I answer that? At first, I thought that she was sad and needed my help.

'Evil? I... don't know,' she replied.

'Another?' he muttered again, sounding like he was thinking out loud. 'What if some of it's true? What if it's *her*?'

As he was saying this, Leanna felt a tug of sensation from somewhere to the north and east. It was like a faint tingling inside of her, a slight awakening of her senses, which she was sure were dulled by the proximity of Caddin and his medallions. She halted, then extricated herself from Caddin's grip.

'Caddin, please take your medallions away from me. Please, it's important. Quick.'

He looked confused but did as she said. He walked several paces away, until she could feel her powers re-emerging.

'Leanna,' said Caddin, his eyes scanning all around them while he clutched his mace, 'whatever you're doing, do it quick. The fighting's getting closer. Hurry.'

Leanna ignored him for a moment. She could now properly feel the return of the presence of the other, to the north east. She felt it as a quickening of her heart and as a resurgence of energy, overcoming some of the exhaustion which had been with her since her ordeal on the battlements. It seemed as if this presence was outside of the town, but was moving fast from north to south, and was coming closer.

Then she gasped, arching her back, as she felt a second external presence. *Another* person like her, from the same initial direction, who seemed to be travelling the same route as the first.

And with the arrival of this second presence, somehow forming a triangle of power between the three of them, the sensations of renewed energy in Leanna's body were magnified, many times over. Instantly, the shackles of exhaustion were cast off, and she felt wonderful. Rejuvenated, powerful and exhilarated.

There were three of the Illborn here. Leanna, the woman Allana, and one other. Leanna allowed herself to hope that the third was Arion. That even now, he was outside of the town and was seeking a way in.

'Leanna, come on!' ordered Caddin, with more urgency in his voice.

She nodded, and did as he said. She was able to move unaided now, heading quickly towards the Septholme harbour. She had to get to Kalyane and inform the noblewoman that she believed that Arion had returned. That he had come back to his home and to his family.

As they carried on towards the seafront, Leanna could feel the energy building within her body, bolstered by the presence of the other two Illborn. Her senses were returned to alertness, and she could now clearly hear the fighting which was taking place within the town. The attackers of Elannis had conquered the walls, and it sounded as if they were battling their way through the northern streets, swarming towards the castle and the quayside area.

Septholme was falling. Soon, it would be completely overrun.

But at the harbour, there was the desperate possibility of escape.

31

Allana

—

*Year of Our Lord,
After Ascension, 770AA*

As Allana rode her galloping horse back towards Septholme, following in the trail of Arion Sepian, she was feeling a sense of stunned bewilderment.

Everything had been *perfect*. They had been together again, and they had made love within a cocoon of their merging powers. The wonder of that experience had introduced her to a level of euphoric bliss beyond anything which she had imagined possible. Everything had been right, and everything had at last seemed simple. He was finally hers, and she was wholeheartedly his. All of her schemes alongside Jarrett, all of the events of the last few months, and all of her fears and panic; none of it had mattered anymore.

She and Arion had been together, and they had declared their love for each other. She had spoken those three words without any hesitation, knowing them to be true. And she had been prepared to forsake the status and privilege which Jarrett could offer her. She had been ready to ride away from this place with Arion, and to commit her entire future to him.

But then, for no apparent reason, he had turned against her and it had all gone wrong. The awful things that he had subsequently said, and the unfair accusations which he had made! As she drew closer to the edge of the woods, the thought of it was making her feel sick, upset and angry. Arion had called her a *fucking whore*. She shuddered as she remembered the moment when he had uttered those words with such disdain, before leaving her.

How dare he speak to you like that, Lana! How dare he use that word! How dare he hurt you, and be horrible to you, when you love him so much!

She recognised that she had also shouted awful things at Arion, but that had been completely excusable; she had only been trying to defend herself from his accusations and nastiness. But how could Arion have used such a malicious and insulting term, after she had opened up her heart to him, and had told him that she loved him?

And those other nasty things which he had said. That his wife Kalyane was worth a hundred of Allana, and Leanna of Arlais a *thousand*. Allana felt particular anger about the comparison to the woman Leanna, who everyone seemed to think was so perfect and superior.

She's not, Lana. You proved that you're better than her, when she got what she deserved! But anyway, how does Arion even know her?

As Allana re-emerged on horseback into the army encampment, she glanced towards Septholme's northern wall. There appeared to be an intermingled chaos of fighting there, all along the battlements. However, it seemed that yellow tabards were now outnumbering the blue of the defenders, and hundreds more Elannis soldiers were swarming onto the ramparts using ladders and the pair of siege towers.

As she rode further into the camp, Allana's attention was captured by the sensation of *two* other presences. Arion was to her south, and indeed he came back into view now. He was over two hundred metres ahead of her, riding fast towards the fortress of Aiduel's Guards. His horse had clearly galloped unimpeded through his enemy's encampment, before anyone had time to react.

And from inside the town of Septholme, the presence of Priestess Leanna had suddenly blossomed back into life, as if from nowhere.

She lives, Lana. And somehow, without pain. But how can that be possible?

Allana felt a triangle of energy forming between the three of them. It invigorated her, filling her with a previously unmatched sense of power. However, it also acted to further unsettle her troubled emotions. Her darkest ability, that inner pool of blackness from which she could draw power, suddenly seemed restless and even more accessible.

There were a handful of shouted challenges to Allana as she rode through the encampment, but she was able to make it to the far side without hindrance.

Arion was still travelling towards the fortress, and Allana believed that he was intending to free his brother. She recognised that she was still pursuing him in that direction, as mad as that seemed to her. But she was determined to catch him and to confront him. What precisely she would do or say to him, she did not know, but she could not allow his last words to her to be, 'You fucking whore.'

You'll change his mind if you face him again, Lana. He'll apologise, and he'll beg you for forgiveness! You can still be together!

The fortress now loomed ahead of her, squatting on its shallow hill with a wall of woodland behind. The bleak, grey walls seemed increasingly oppressive as she closed the distance towards it.

She witnessed the moment when Arion reached the entrance to the fortress, well ahead of her. He leapt from his horse with sword in hand, and Allana felt a burst of power emanating from him as he surged forward into the entranceway. Once again, he seemed to move at an unnatural speed, akin to when he had accosted Connar in the glade. Then he was gone from view.

Allana reined in her horse several metres from the fortress entrance, before dismounting. As she walked towards the open gateway, she could sense Arion's power pulsing from within the fortress grounds. She reached the entrance and paused, feeling repeated bursts of his energy.

Six dead Aiduel's Guards, four men and two women, were sprawled in the area inside and beyond the gateway. One man's head was a pulp, as if it had been slammed with force against a stone wall. Arion was not in sight.

Allana hesitated as she looked into the inner grounds of the fortress, noticing a slight trembling in her fingers. Had it suddenly become harder to breathe?

Why did he have to lead you here, of all places, Lana? Are you really going to follow him in there?

Despite her urgent need to pursue Arion, she was suddenly uncertain, and was unable to step forward into the grounds inside the fortress. With the darkness so tangibly within reach, she knew that she had a means to protect herself until she reunited with him. But could she find the courage to overcome her fear of this place? Or should she wait for him here?

Her heart was beating fast as she lingered in the shadows of the gateway, surrounded by the bodies of the murdered red-cloaks. She leaned to peer cautiously into the grounds beyond, and immediately spotted a further eight Aiduel's Guards. They were to her left, sprinting away from her, heading around the outside of the dour grey-stone building which was nearest to the fortress entrance.

The sounds of fierce fighting and occasional screams echoed from somewhere inside the compound, and these noises appeared to have drawn the attention of this group of red-cloaks. Allana felt certain that Arion was in that direction, and that he was carving a violent trail of death as he crossed the fortress grounds. It seemed that he was truly as deadly as had been suggested by the tales of Moss Ford.

What are you doing here, Lana?

Memories had begun to emerge in her mind, triggered by her return to this place. They had locked her inside a stinking cell somewhere within these fortress walls, with a hood on her head. They had interrogated her and threatened her. And she had been malnourished, mistreated and humiliated.

And they had tortured her. With water. With heat. With threats.

She had endured horrific suffering in this place. And even after her escape, she knew that the trauma of her captivity had continued to haunt her. Yes, she had fled to Berun, after killing Evelyn dei Laramin, but had she ever truly escaped from the horror of what had happened to her here?

But you've changed since they hurt you, Lana. You're so much more dangerous now. They should be fearing you!

Her experiences within this fortress had undoubtedly contributed to the unlocking of her darkest ability. She was no longer the defenceless girl who had once been condemned to suffer in this place. Indeed, she could feel her power whispering to her at this moment, fortifying her against the threat of panic, and tempting her…

She reached down deep into the turbulent darkness. Embracing it, and feeling its seductive corruption. Ready for whatever she might face, if she followed in Arion's footsteps. However, she was still unable to take that first step forwards out of the shadows of the gateway and into the terrible fortress.

'Help us!'

The desperate cry came from Allana's right, and was clearly a woman's voice. From the sounds of violence within the complex, it seemed that Arion had headed to the left, in the opposite direction to this call.

'Please, someone help us!' pleaded the unknown female again.

Allana wanted to continue to follow Arion. He was the reason why she had come to this place. However, after her own experiences here, it was difficult to ignore the despair which she could hear in the woman's voice.

After a moment of further indecision, she stepped forward to enter the fortress, and moved away to her right. She skirted around the outside of the stone building, remaining alert for further red-cloaked soldiers. When she turned the corner, she was shocked by what she saw.

The wooden cage ran alongside a fifteen-metre stretch of the fortress's southern wall. It jutted out perhaps four metres from that wall, comprised of lengthy, thick wooden stakes which were planted into the ground, with gaps of a few inches between each. The floor of the cage was comprised of grass and dirt, and there was a closed gate at the far end.

Inside this prison was a huddle of perhaps fifty captive women. They all appeared to be young, with blonde hair, dirty faces and weary expressions. One was slumped on the floor, pressed unmoving against the cage bars, although her eyes remained open in a vacant stare.

A young woman who was leaning against the nearest corner of the cage was the first to notice Allana, and she shouted, 'Help us, my Lady!'

Other faces now turned towards Allana, and multiple voices were raised, begging for help.

'Please help us, my Lady!'

'Free us, please! We haven't done anything wrong.'

The young woman who had spoken first made a gesture to quiet the others, then called, 'They're torturing us, my Lady! They're going to kill us!'

'Torturing you?' asked Allana, as she walked closer.

'Yes, my Lady,' responded the young captive. She was of a similar age to Allana, with piercing blue eyes and long, wheat-coloured hair. She was speaking rapidly, as if frightened that she would run out of time to release her words. 'They put a hood on our heads and take us to a room. Then they tie us down, and they scare us, and they drown us, and they-'

'Burn you,' finished Allana, the coldness of her voice masking her inner fury.

Dei Laramin has gone, Lana. But Aiduel's Guards have returned, and nothing here has changed. Jarrett has allowed them back into Andar, and look what they're already doing.

'Please save us, my Lady,' the woman continued. 'My name is Esme, and this is my younger sister Neome...'

Esme continued to speak, but Allana was finding it difficult to concentrate on the captive's words. She could still feel the reservoir of darkness frothing and churning within, calling to her in seductive tones. She knew that its power, its threat, was vastly enhanced by the nearby presence of Arion and the priestess Leanna. She felt poised on the brink of snapping, of submerging herself deep within that darkness.

'You! Get away from there! You can't be here!'

This aggressive shout came from a male voice. Allana turned to face the source, and saw seven Aiduel's Guards moving towards her. A hard-faced man appeared to lead this group, which comprised five men and two women.

As these red-cloaks approached, Allana could see a number of them glancing nervously towards the far side of the fortress complex, from which screams were still carrying. None of the seven seemed to be in a hurry to head towards that fight. Nor did they appear to be about to launch into an immediate attack against Allana; her richer attire must have given them pause.

However, Allana recognised the leader as he came closer. He was an officer, and she had encountered him twice before. As she readied herself to confront him, she was still feeling rage, and was continuing to embrace the darkness within.

Most of the women in the cage were now watching her.

These soldiers will obey you, Lana. Or they will suffer.

'I am Lady Allana, wife-to-be of Duke Jarrett Berun,' she declared, and her voice did not betray anything of the storm which was raging inside of her. 'You are torturing these women?'

She could see that the leader was uncertain about how he should treat her. She was an intruder here, but she had announced herself as nobility. The sounds of battle from within the complex also seemed to be unsettling the man.

'They are captives of Aiduel's Guards, my Lady,' said a bulky Guardswoman, who was standing at the shoulder of the officer. 'Self-confessed heretics. What we do with them is... Holy Church business.'

'*Our* business,' added the officer.

'Free them,' demanded Allana. 'By order of Duke Jarrett Berun, the future ruler of this land, I command you to free them.'

'Excuse me, my Lady?' said the man. 'He has no authority over-'

'I said, free them!' ordered Allana. The sudden ferocity in her voice was masking a trembling of her limbs, as she struggled to contain her anger.

She knew that she could coerce this officer using other methods, and could also take control of at least some of his colleagues. However, the call of her inner darkness was too compelling. She wanted to hurt these people, as their kind had once hurt her. And by hurting them, might she also purge herself of the traumas which this place had buried within her?

'Let them go,' she added, 'if you value your lives, and before whoever is attacking this place comes for you.'

'You can't order us about,' stated the officer, with more confidence this time. A moment later, he frowned before saying, 'Wait... I *know* you. You passed us in that village. And before that... By the Lord, I recognise you now! Nionia dei Pallere, Septholme Castle... you were a prisoner here... Lord, the one who esc-'

His hand was reaching to draw the sword from his scabbard at the instant when Allana released the darkness.

LUST. POWER. DOMINATION.

An invisible wave of corruption erupted from Allana, engulfing the party of Aiduel's Guards. It deluged them in a torrent of ruin, which washed around and through the seven red-cloaked figures. Their leader was the sergeant who Allana had once encountered by accident in Septholme Castle. The one whose later questions had led to Aiduel's Guards' interest in her, and to her subsequent imprisonment and torture. How befitting that he should be the recipient of her wrath on this day.

And there was boundless fury for Allana to unleash, accumulated by a succession of events; her failed attempt to stop the brutal execution of the young woman before Septholme's walls; her clash with and subjugation of Jarrett; her enraged response to the assault by the priestess Leanna; and finally, the humiliating rejection by Arion.

Then, in this place where she had suffered so much misery, she had come upon these imprisoned and tortured women. Following which, this sergeant had intended to attack *her*! It was all too much. She had passed her breaking point, gone *far* past it, and it was time for someone to pay a price on this day in a currency of horror.

The darkness had wrapped around the seven soldiers, and it was smothering them in its embrace. All of them were collapsed in various poses of distress, and each one had started to scream. Some had raised their hands to their eyes, in a vain attempt to shut out whatever horrors they were seeing and feeling.

Power surged through Allana, enhanced by the proximity of Arion and the woman Leanna. She used that power to tap ever deeper into the reservoir of darkness inside of herself, and to feed it into these seven victims, who were becoming unfortunate receptacles for all of the agonies which she had suffered in this fortress.

Make them pay, Lana! Make them all pay.

As she unleashed her rage upon the red-cloaked victims, there was a continuing accompaniment of the sounds of battle from inside the fortress complex. These noises were soon joined by cries of fear from some of the imprisoned women.

Allana recognised that almost everything that she had done before this had been conducted in the shadows, where others had either not seen or survived her actions. But today, she was unveiling her powers before an audience.

It's not just Leanna of Arlais who can work miracles, Lana.

She glanced towards the cage, and saw that many of the captive women had backed away from the bars. They were staring at her with gaping mouths, their expressions a mixture of fear and horror. Allana knew that these reactions were based purely on the visible suffering of the seven victims. She was certain that only she could perceive the swirling cloud of tendrils and darkness which was enveloping the red-cloaked soldiers.

Imagine their terror if they could see all that you can see, Lana.

She stepped closer to the nearest two guards. The bulky female soldier had now collapsed onto her side, with her legs tucked into her body. The sergeant was beside her, on his hands and knees.

Allana could remember what had happened with the dowager Sillene Berun, months earlier. The woman had been ruined and transformed, after Allana had gripped her flesh and had spread the corruption by touch. What would Allana's touch do now, with her power magnified by Arion and the priestess Leanna?

Arion Sepian was close by, inside the fortress. Arion, who had rejected and humiliated Allana, despite her declaration of love. Who had called her a *fucking whore*, after spending himself inside of her.

Allana's powers were also bolstered by the nearby presence of the Angel of Arlais, a woman who seemed to have placed herself ahead of Allana in Arion's affections and admiration. Who was worth *a thousand* of Allana!

The thought of the priestess added to Allana's fury. She leaned over the two Guards and laid a hand upon the neck of each of them, then let the ruin and corruption flow directly out along her fingertips. A burning smell immediately wafted up to Allana from where her fingers were pressed against their bare flesh.

Make them suffer, Lana! As they have chosen to make others suffer.

The two victims of this foul touch began to writhe and convulse on the floor, their cries of anguish becoming ever more tormented.

The captive women were also sounding more distressed and frightened. Allana glanced briefly towards the cage, and could see that all of the prisoners were now pressed against the far fortress wall, with the exception of the lone, vacant-eyed figure who was slumped on the floor against the bars.

Allana turned her attention and rage back to her two principal victims, these two *torturers*, and pressed her fingers more firmly against their flesh, causing both of them to scream again. There was a definite stench of burning and *corruption* in the air, coming from the places where she touched their skin. But she was too far gone to stop this. She *needed* this release, after the events of today. Needed to make somebody pay.

Then she felt the stirrings of the transformation within these two victims.

She kept her fingers in place, experiencing a righteous sense of satisfaction as she watched what was happening. The pair's bodies were twisting, breaking and stretching. She could see that ruinous changes were taking place within them; muscles swelling, arms extending, teeth and nails growing sharper. The clothes of these two victims began to tear, and armour straps were soon ripped apart, as the soldiers' bodies were morphing into something different. Something new. Something dark.

This was what had happened to Sillene Berun on that night long ago. Only this time, Allana was witnessing it all, and she was resolved to see it through. Let these two experience the feeling of being tortured, and humiliated, and broken inside. Let them share in the suffering which they had been so happy to inflict upon others. On these captive women. On Allana.

The bodies of the two continued to twist and stretch, as did their faces. Mouths and noses were becoming more elongated, and their facial features more feral. Their clothes and armour were completely torn away now, and shredded rags were falling to the ground, as their bodies swelled to a length and bulk far beyond what had been there before.

These changes were accompanied by further terrified reactions from the women in the cage, and Allana heard a frightened cry of, 'Witch!'

But she was set upon this course, and she was determined to see it to its conclusion. The ruin and corruption continued to pour into the two figures who had once been Aiduel's Guards, and it was close to completing its work. Nails were being transformed into claws, teeth into fangs. Thick hair was sprouting through the flesh across the head and body. Taking the transformation to a stage far beyond what had been done to Sillene Berun. Creating something new and horrific. Creating *beasts*. That belonged to Allana. That obeyed her. That would protect her, at all costs. That would *worship* her?

When she finally sensed that her work was complete, she released her hands from the two figures who were now prone before her. The corruption and ruin which had been flowing into their bodies now ceased, as did the torrent of darkness which had washed through and around the other five Guards.

The women in the cage had fallen quiet, resulting in silence in the immediate surrounding area. This gave prominence to the renewed sounds of fighting from the far side of the complex, and Allana could sense surges of energy which suggested that Arion was still active there.

However, her attention was on the two creatures. After a few moments, the two beastly figures began to climb to their feet, unwinding their limbs with a graceful and deadly elegance. Raising themselves up and standing at full height before Allana. They were both close to eight feet tall, towering above her. Golden eyes observed her, and elongated maws were slightly open to display sharp teeth and fangs.

She knew instinctively that these creatures now served her, and that she was their mistress. The individuals who had owned these bodies were no more, their minds shattered into these feral beasts. Monsters which would serve Allana, and only Allana.

You are like a goddess to these creatures, Lana.

She locked eyes with the beast which had been the sergeant, before focusing on the other five Aiduel's Guards, who all appeared to be collapsed and unconscious.

The creature seemed to understand without Allana needing to articulate her command. It sprang into action, followed moments afterwards by the second beast. Claws of the pair then stabbed down repeatedly into the five figures who had once been their colleagues, and blood sprayed up into the air and onto the monsters themselves.

The beasts turned to face Allana again, and she glanced towards the cage. The captive women inside were regarding her with horror, and none of them spoke. The creature which had been the sergeant then began to walk towards the wooden gate.

Rational thought was returning to Allana, and she was beginning to realise the implications of her actions being witnessed. The women in the cage had all seen what Allana was and what she was capable of. If they were to leave this place, they would be able to tell their story of the woman – the *witch* – who had done this. They would talk of it, and the tale of unnatural deeds might spread far and wide, and into dangerous ears.

And they had heard her speak her name.

What have you done, Lana? You've let them see this, and now they'll talk about you! They'll betray the secret of who you are and what you are!

She could try to threaten them into silence, as she had once threatened Nionia. But there was no realistic possibility that this many women would keep her secret in the long term. And if just a single one of them was interrogated again by Aiduel's Guards, they would tell of everything that had happened here.

Everyone would then know who Allana was. What she was. And she would be hunted again. She would lose *everything*.

They'll destroy your life, if they leave here, Lana.

She clenched her fists, feeling frustrated by her total loss of control in the midst of her fury. It was utterly stupid to have done this in front of an audience.

Why did you do this, Lana? Your actions here are going to force you to choose between their survival and yours.

As she was thinking this, the creature which had been the sergeant approached the wooden cage door, gripped it, and then ripped the frame off its hinges in an exertion of bestial strength. This resulted in a series of shrieks from the women in the cage, who clustered into the corner furthest away from the beast. The lone exception continued to be the vacant-eyed figure who was slumped on the floor by the bars.

Now that her rage was subsiding, Allana felt a moment of crisis, as if she was teetering at the edge of a precipice. She realised that she was trembling again. Her survival or theirs? Her or them? Was there any other choice?

She stared at the women, noting the terror in their expressions. None of them appeared grateful for what Allana had done to their captors. None of them seemed thankful that Allana had meted out the revenge which they were too weak to deliver themselves. None of them were in awe of the miraculous thing which she had just done.

No, all that she could see was fear, horror and disgust. Panicked eyes staring at her as if *she* was the monster.

The two beasts now entered the cage. They moved to a position inside the open doorway, standing upright and blocking the women's escape. Allana knew that the creatures were awaiting her instruction.

'Please, my Lady!' cried out a pleading voice.

Allana identified the source. It was the woman Esme. She was on the outside of the cluster of women, nearest to the monsters, shielding her sister with her own body.

'Please, my Lady, please spare us. Please let us go.'

Allana was still trembling as she said, 'I want to, I really do.' And she knew that she meant it. 'I only wanted to help you. To free you. But you all saw me. You saw what I can do.'

'Please. We… thank you, for killing the Guards. And we won't talk about this. None of us. Ever. We swear it, before The Lord. Please, spare us.'

The woman's voice was soft and imploring. Allana felt herself becoming increasingly torn. Could she dare to let them go?

'I don't know what to do,' she said, raising shaking hands up to the side of her head. She could feel tears forming in her eyes. 'I don't know what to do!'

'Just let us go, please,' said Esme. 'We won't say anything. We promise. Please, Lady Allana.'

Allana froze, her heart pounding after hearing those last two words. This one, at least, had taken note of her name. And how many others had done the same, now that it had been repeated?

Those ill-chosen words acted to finalise Allana's decision, and she averted her gaze from the woman.

This isn't your fault, Lana. They were going to die, anyway. None of this is your fault.

She had wanted to save them, she knew that, just like she had wanted to save the girl on the pyre. After first seeing these women, she had been determined to free them from the cage, to spare them a repeat of her own suffering. Her intentions had been good. But matters had spiralled out of control, all too quickly, and had gone too far for her to ever take back. She should never have followed Arion to this place.

But she could at least console herself that even if she had not come here, they had all been certain to die, anyway. Better a quick death than the horror of being burned alive on a pyre. In some ways, what she was about to do would be a kindness.

You'll be doing them a mercy, Lana, compared to the fire.

Her body was still trembling, more forcefully now. She did not want to be in this situation. She truly did not. But she was here, and she could not take back the actions and decisions, or the rage, which had led her to this moment. And there could be no avoiding the devastating choice which she now faced. Them or her. Her or them.

The darkness beneath the edge of the precipice was beckoning to her.

You will do whatever it takes to survive, Lana.

She looked up, and through her tears she met the gaze of the woman Esme.

'I'm sorry,' she said. 'I have no choice.'

Allana turned away, not wanting to see the woman's reaction, or to witness what was to come.

The instruction which followed was more a thought than an articulated word, but the creatures understood, and they acted upon it.

Kill them.

Allana was walking away from the cage, her mind falling into the midnight black of the abyss, when the screaming started.

—

The slaughter took surprisingly little time. Soon after, the two beasts returned to Allana's side.

She had wiped the tears from her eyes, but her emotions were overwhelming her, and she was continuing to shake. She was struggling to process what had just happened, and to control the darkness which she could feel swarming around and inside her, suffocating her.

You had no choice, Lana. It was your survival or theirs. Your survival or theirs. Your survival or theirs!

She was still lost in the spiral of these thoughts when she was disturbed by a familiar sensation, which was coming from the west of the fortress. Arising from within Septholme.

The woman Leanna was drawing on power. Drawing on a *lot* of power. Allana could feel it, surging and swelling, although it was not being taken from Allana herself, this time. But from another. From Arion.

Allana felt certain that the priestess was using Arion to do something. This sudden blaze of power in the west suggested that the woman was working some new miracle. Something else, no doubt, to make everyone adore her. True, she was not taking from Allana, but she *was* using Arion. The man who should belong to Allana, but who had instead rejected and humiliated her, and had told her that Leanna of Arlais was worth a thousand of her!

How dare she do that, Lana! How dare she use him, when he should be yours! She's going to take him from you. She must stop. She must stop!

Allana felt a renewal of the flame of her rage, and she looked up at the two creatures beside her. They would do whatever she asked of them, they had already proven that. They would do it without hesitation or question or conscience. And no one would ever know that the deed had been undertaken at Allana's instigation.

As she considered this, the memory of the recurring dream flashed into her mind. In particular, the latter parts of that dream, which she had only recently been able to recall after waking.

ONLY ONE CAN CLAIM THE POWER.

That is what the voice in the dream had said. Only one.

KILL THEM AND MAKE IT YOURS. KILL THEM ALL!

The Angel of Arlais was of a kind with Allana, and she possessed a vast power. Could the priestess have shared this same dream, and have heard these same words? Could she soon be readying herself to act against Allana?

Allana's instincts were telling her that the woman represented a genuine threat, and the priestess's actions in Septholme had proven that she could be a danger to Allana's very survival. Leanna of Arlais was too strong already, and she could not be allowed to continue to grow stronger. Could not be allowed to take Arion away from Allana.

Yes, it seemed that she was definitely a threat. But Allana had experience of dealing with threats, and of surviving them. Ronis dei Maranar had been a threat. As had Evelyn dei Laramin. And Sillene Berun. And even, at one time, Duke Conran Sepian. And they had all ultimately paid the price for being of danger to Allana dei Monis.

Allana could feel where the other woman was. The priestess's surge of power in the west was like a blazing beacon, precisely marking her location. And Allana could share that knowledge with the creatures beside her.

She paused for a moment, considering whether she was truly ready to take the action which had now formed in her mind. But what was one more death, in the context of today's horrific bloodshed?

The command, when she finally issued it, was delivered with conviction.

Kill her.

And the beasts raced away.

32

Corin

*Year of Our Lord,
After Ascension, 770AA*

The Kurakee masses started to close the distance towards the Chosen army's lines, their advance heralded by the war cries of thousands. Corin felt a chill of fear as he watched the dark wall of the enemy surging forwards. He could also sense the same reaction of concern from all of the warriors around him.

'Chosen!' shouted Corin again.

Within seconds, the cry was taken up by hundreds of his men, fortifying each of them against the approach of the horde.

'Chosen!'

The Kurakee were in amongst the flaming piles of wood in no time, large clusters of men navigating through the narrow channels between the fiery obstacles. Corin heard his senior warriors bellowing orders from behind him.

'Release arrows!'

From the walls and watchtowers of Karn, a hail of arrows flew over the top of Corin's lines. These missiles descended into the body of the advancing enemy, felling large numbers as the Kurakee wound between the obstacles. Many of the horde reacted by raising their shields above their heads, to offer some protection against this attack from the sky.

Although there was no return of arrow fire from within the Kurakee ranks, Corin's bodyguards now closed around him, surrounding him with shields. Corin could still see forwards, and he was anticipating the best moment to attack with his powers. When the enemy was less than sixty metres from the Chosen line, with a large mob of Kurakee massed between the fiery obstacles, Corin was ready to take action.

FEAR. CONTROL. ORDER.

He experienced time decelerating again, and he felt alive with power.

Prior to the battle, he had spent a significant amount of time considering the most effective ways to utilise his own powers. He appreciated that there were limits on the number of men that he could control; if the enemy were packed closely together, he estimated that he could lock over a hundred in place, giving his own men an advantage. This was a powerful tool, but against the awesome numerical superiority of the Kurakee, it would not be enough. As such, he had decided to adapt his tactics and to change the command that he would implant.

Multiple invisible tendrils now erupted from Corin's mind, and he began to seek out scores of victims from amongst the Kurakee. He broke their will with blunt force and implanted a simple instruction, before moving onto another victim.

INTO THE FIRE! SET YOURSELF ON FIRE!

Throughout the advancing horde, men who had suddenly lost control of their own will found themselves lurching towards the nearest pyre of wood and hay. To their own horror, they then threw themselves into it. By the time that their clothes, hair and skin were ablaze and melting, Corin had already moved onto another victim.

Within seconds, he had done this to over fifty of the enemy, then moments later to more than a hundred.

Fear spread through the ranks of the Kurakee as they witnessed fellow warriors being dragged into the fires against their apparent will. To add to their woes, once Corin had released his hold on each victim, many were then tearing themselves away from the stacks of flaming wood whilst still ablaze. They were then jostling against their fellow Kurakee, and were setting others on fire within the bottlenecks between the pyres. Agonised screams of burning men carried over the battlefield.

The fearsome Kurakee charge had lost its momentum. Within a minute, it had changed into a panicked mass of men clustered together, each trying to keep their distance from the pyres to avoid being the next person to be set alight. Adding to their confusion, a hail of arrows continued to descend down upon them, now finding more victims since there were fewer men holding up shields for protection.

Despite all of this, and despite Corin continuing to drag more men into the pyres which blazed across the battlefield, sheer weight of numbers was pushing the Kurakee mob forward towards Corin's line. The massed body of men to the rear of the Kurakee was still advancing, which would cause a crush unless those at the front also pushed on. Corin could see the Kurakee warlord gesticulating furiously in the distance, exhorting his troops to regroup and to advance. For now, the man was too far from Corin's power to be vulnerable.

Eventually, large numbers of Kurakee had broken through the obstacles of the pyres. Under a continuing barrage of arrow fire, they were assembling less than thirty metres from the stationary Chosen ranks. The spear-wall of Corin's front line remained in place. Corin was aware that his men would be bristling to launch themselves into a charge against the enemy, but they all understood why they could not.

'Hold!'

The instruction was issued by Corin's leaders along the front line, repeated several times. Corin knew that the order was not necessary, but it was for the benefit of the Kurakee.

Even as Corin was continuing to drag more men into the pyres behind them, the hundreds of Kurakee assembled at the front of the horde were now raising axes and shields. After releasing another chilling war cry, these warriors proceeded to charge headlong towards the Chosen defenders. They closed the remaining distance in seconds, directly towards the unbroken wall of spears. Twenty metres, ten metres, five metres…

And then the front ranks of the Kurakee disappeared, downwards.

The ditch in front of the Chosen line was over two metres wide and deep. It had taken weeks to dig it along the whole width of the corridor mouth. A lot more work had then gone into building the fragile, false surface which had been laid above it, and into planting the numerous wooden stakes which pointed upwards from its base.

Hundreds of the Kurakee disappeared into the extended trench in front of them before the momentum of their massed charge could be halted. The first and least fortunate of these were impaled on the sharpened stakes embedded in the pit floor, or suffered broken necks as they crashed against the walls of the ditch. Those following were slightly luckier, and some had their fall broken by landing on top of other Kurakee.

However, this fortune was short-lived, as Corin's spearmen immediately began to thrust downwards, impaling any man who was seen to stand. Within minutes, hundreds of Kurakee were dead in the ditch, in exchange for mere handfuls of Chosen casualties. Those Kurakee remaining on the other side of the lengthy pit were thwarted and frustrated, since they could not reach their enemy in order to fight, and some resorted to throwing weapons. However, yet more of the horde were still pushing forwards through the dangerous channels between the fires, causing even greater numbers to cluster on the edge of the trench.

Corin had continued to use his powers to drag Kurakee warriors into the fires as they passed, but now it was time to alter his focus. As he watched hundreds more of the enemy lined up at the side of the pit, where they were screaming and cursing at the largely untouched Chosen, Corin changed his command.

INTO THE PIT! JUMP! FALL! THROW YOURSELF IN!

Using all of his will and fury, within a matter of seconds this command was unleashed on dozens of waiting Kurakee. Each time, Corin forced his victims to throw themselves down into the pit below, where they became new casualties of the thrusting spears of the Chosen.

Corin guessed that the Kurakee must have lost over a thousand men by this point, whilst his own army had suffered barely any losses. However, the enemy still retained a vast numerical advantage, and yet more were emerging past the fires. Corin spotted some of the Kurakee forces organising themselves to go east and west, in an attempt to avoid the ditch into which so many had fallen. To the east of the Kurakee was the shallower north-south trench. Unlike the deep pit between the two armies' front lines, this smaller ditch was capable of being scaled. To the west were the woods which ran alongside the Great Lake.

Corin was relaxed about the threat of being flanked from the west, even while he watched scores of Kurakee disappearing into the treeline there. The east was more of a concern, where he could see warriors of the horde jumping down into the smaller north-south ditch, before scaling the far side.

'Pass the command! Concentrate archer fire on the eastern ditch. Kill them!'

Corin heard his order being repeated, and he was pleased to see many more arrows flying in that direction. He also observed with satisfaction that the Qari horsemen were charging against any of the enemy which emerged from that ditch.

Corin continued to employ his powers throughout this time. He was dragging more and more of the front ranks of the Kurakee into the pit between the front lines, where the Chosen spearmen then finished them off. Bodies were piling up at the bottom of the trench, its floor a ghastly and muddy pool of corpses and blood.

Corin closed his eyes for a moment, and then he was sharing Blackpaw's vision, seeing the scene in front of the felrin. Blackpaw was waiting in the woods to the west, concealed within the treeline near to the shores of the Great Lake. The beast was watching with tense hunger as a multitude of Kurakee were passing through the trees in front of it, as part of their efforts to approach Karn from the south-west. The creature was poised and ready.

Corin passed an instruction to his felrin. A few moments later, he was satisfied to hear Blackpaw's piercing shriek echoing out across the battlefield. The sound was audible even despite the surrounding cacophony of pain and battle. Corin saw a handful of enemy heads turn towards the western woods, in response to the noise. Hundreds more then reacted as a dreadful, sustained and much louder howl arose from that direction, only seconds after Blackpaw's call.

As this was going on, Corin looked again to the east. The Qari horsemen were attempting to run down any Kurakee who emerged from the eastern ditch, before the enemy could gather in force. However, the rising tide of horde numbers threatened to soon overwhelm the small group of riders.

'Marrix! Akob!' shouted Corin. 'Take your warriors to the east. Support the Qari! Hold our eastern flank!'

He heard this command being repeated, and he felt confident that the two war leaders of the Karn would see this fulfilled.

Then the screaming started from the woods to the west. It was hard to discern whether the screams were of terror, agony, or both. But they were clearly the cries of men, and Corin knew precisely what was causing them. As did every man and woman amongst the Chosen forces.

Corin shuddered. He understood that there are times and places to meet a felrin, and to have a hope of surviving against it. He had witnessed that, in his visions in the north. The best hope of survival arose from being high up on walls, above the beast, or in the midst of a phalanx of spears and shields. But in woods, amongst trees, where the creature could come at you from countless hidden directions, was not that place. And now was not that time. Corin could witness Blackpaw unleashing its savagery on the enemy, and through its eyes he could experience the carnage in the woods.

Then, through his own eyes, he saw many Kurakee warriors emerging back out of the treeline. They were running in desperation, some looking anxiously over their shoulders. A large number appeared to be without weapons, having ditched their equipment in their eagerness to flee. The majority of these warriors were running back towards the flaming pyres, and were heading into the blockage of the massed clusters of their clansmen, who were still pushing forwards. Others were running towards the ranks near the front ditch, forcing an even tighter crush there, and pushing greater numbers over the edge.

Then the cause of their frantic rout appeared, in pursuit of them. Felrin. Hundreds of felrin.

The creatures came forth out of the woods in a frenzy of savagery, hunting down and leaping upon the backs of the terrified warriors who were fleeing from them. Along a two hundred metre stretch of woodland, felrin emerged into the open flank of the Kurakee army and unleashed themselves upon it. The beasts were a startling mix of shades and colours; brown, grey, white and black. But the splattered colour of blood was common to them all.

The creatures had but one intent, embedded within them by their original creator. To kill. They would feed later, but for now their only focus was to kill one, then another, then another.

Corin had witnessed the charge of the felrin within his visions, when he had first listened to their Song. He had seen something like this before, played out in the mists of time. And he had also pictured a moment like this and had asked this of the beasts, on a later occasion of joining their Song.

And yet, even with this foresight, he found himself stunned by the carnage which was released upon the unprepared Kurakee. He could also sense the Chosen warriors around him recoiling in horror, but that was as nothing compared to the terror and panic which was washing through the Kurakee ranks.

The men of the Kurakee started to push against each other in their haste to escape, but they were packed too closely together, and most had no opportunity to get out of the way of the frenzy of death which was coming towards them. Corin added to their panic by continuing to force other men into the deadly trench or onto the flames of the fires.

Corin could feel Blackpaw's exhilaration as the creature savaged and slaughtered in the midst of its brethren. And he could also sense the collective emotion of all of the felrin as they fought for their new master. As they ravaged and killed on behalf of the one who had listened to their Song, and who had freed them.

It had been Corin's last act, before departing from the edifice in the north. He had spoken to the race of beasts again through the Song of the Felrin, and he had released them all from Mella's last command. He had set them free. But he had also asked them to come here, and he had promised them this day. Fight for him. Release their collective fury. Kill the Kurakee. And feed upon them.

And they had come.

The confidence and arrogance of the Kurakee was now shattered. Their drumbeats had fallen silent, and their war cries had been replaced by countless screams of terror and pain.

Corin's gaze swept across their ranks, seeking the man in the raised chair, the Warlord Kurune. And then he spotted his obese counterpart again, finally within range of Corin's threat. The Kurakee leader was near to the raging fires, still on his chair, trapped amongst a huddled mass of men. He appeared to be screaming commands at the warriors around him.

Corin formed an instruction in his mind, aimed at the men holding up the chair. He then watched in satisfaction as the Warlord Kurune, reputed murderer of thousands, was toppled sideways from his elevated position. The Kurakee leader plunged headfirst into a nearby pyre. His obese form was incinerated in seconds, witnessed by scores of his shocked followers.

And still the hundreds of felrin were ploughing through the Kurakee ranks, ravaging with both tooth and claw. It was time for Corin to finally crush the remaining will of the Kurakee.

As he had done once before, in the battle against the Renni, Corin blasted a message from his mind, speaking to all of his enemies on the battlefield.

I AM THE CHOSEN OF THE GODS, AND THE FELRIN FIGHT FOR ME! NOW RUN MURDERERS! RUN RAPISTS! RUN SLAVERS! RUN!

And they did. Every single man within the Kurakee army started to rout, in whatever direction they could. Anywhere to get away from the killing ditch and the fires, and most of all from the relentless wall of death which was the felrin horde.

The small number of escapees who made it across the eastern ditch were now met by the forces which Akob and Marrix had led there, and they were swiftly dispatched. However, most of the Kurakee fled to the south, towards the ridge from which they had first appeared. But in that direction, there would be no escape from death's remorseless pursuit.

Given what he had learned about the Kurakee, Corin knew that this horde of enemy warriors was beyond redemption. They had inflicted death and horror across countless lands to the south. As such, unlike with the Renni, Corin had no inclination today to show mercy or to attempt reconciliation.

There would be no surrender. No prisoners. No survivors amongst the enemy. Corin did not just intend to win the battle and to force them to retreat, for such mercy could allow the Kurakee to regroup. It might also enable them to continue their subjugation of the peoples of the south, and to possibly attack again in the future.

No, there would be no mercy. Corin intended to wipe them out. Every last one of them.

And something which no fleeing man is capable of doing, no matter how healthy or swift of foot, is to outrun a felrin. The instruction to Blackpaw had been very clear, and this had been shared with all of the other felrin through their Song.

Kill them all first. Feed later.

An army of thousands, like the Kurakee, takes a lot of killing. But when that army presents its back to creatures spawned by a god, and those creatures can end a life in a moment, the butchery took much less time to complete than Corin had expected. The beasts caught up with each of the Kurakee in turn and then dragged them down.

Blackpaw was a little more than two miles away when the last of the enemy horde fell beneath felrin teeth and claws. None had escaped.

That stretch of land was now littered with the bodies of thousands of Kurakee. Not all of these were dead, and the desperate cries of the wounded echoed across that killing ground.

Corin's face was grim. He scanned the area around him, looking for and finally locating Chief Munnik. There had been very few casualties amongst the Chosen army, but Munnik still looked appalled by what he had just witnessed, as did most of the men around Corin.

In order to be heard by as many as possible, Corin bellowed, 'We had to do this, otherwise they would have killed every person here. They would have taken our families as slaves! And raped and killed them, and sacrificed our elderly! Remember that!'

Later, he would speak to them all at length. He would use calmer words, which would be full of reassurance. But for now, there was still work to be done.

He gestured for Munnik to come closer, then pointed towards the fields of death which stretched before them. 'Get the ramps. Take your men over the ditch and seek out any wounded in those fields. Then kill them all. There are to be no survivors. Then get out of the way, so the felrin can feed.'

Munnik nodded, his face pale. He then started to shout instructions to his men.

'Kernon,' Corin said, turning to face his brother. 'The ditch. Get the spearmen and the longest spears. Again, no survivors.'

Kernon also nodded, staring at Corin with an expression which suggested horrified awe, before setting out to execute the instruction.

Corin took a deep breath, trying to control his emotions. He did not know whether to laugh or to cry, but he was fully aware that his actions on this day had resulted in the deaths of thousands of men. This knowledge would no doubt strike him harder, at some later point.

But his actions had been undertaken for the right reasons. He had destroyed an evil, a great source of fear, and had taken another massive step towards bringing peace and order to this land. And he had saved the lives of thousands more.

He could still sense Blackpaw in the distance, through their connection. The beast was surrounded by hundreds of its kin, and it was exultant at the killing spree which had just been undertaken. Corin could feel that elation pulsing from the felrin.

He could also feel the eyes of his people upon him. The urge to do something to release all of his tension and stress was just too great.

He leaned back his head and he closed his eyes. He then howled, as if releasing his bloodlust for the very first time. The sound lasted for seconds, and then was echoed by Blackpaw's own cry, which resounded across the fields from two miles away.

Moments later, the voices of two thousand other triumphant felrin and humans also joined their call.

33

Arion

—

*Year of Our Lord,
After Ascension, 770AA*

Arion wrenched open the wooden door at the corner of the long, single-storey building, and he peered into the gloomy corridor within. He believed that the prison cells of the fortress were contained within this grey stone structure, but there was nothing in sight before him to confirm that.

Only a handful of minutes had passed since he had entered the fortress grounds. His sword was raised in readiness, its blade bloodied from the killing which had been necessary to cross to this eastern part of the compound. Nineteen Aiduel's Guards had already fallen to violence; six red-cloaks at the main entrance had been quickly overwhelmed, five more had died as he had crossed the fortress, and a further eight had dared to assault him in front of the entrance to this building. This latter group had been cut down in a relentless blitz of deadly motion.

Arion knew that they had never stood a chance against him. At this moment, he was overflowing with energy, and he was infused with supernatural speed, strength and agility. He felt invincible.

'Gerrion!'

His shout echoed down the corridor. In reaction to this, he could hear warning calls ahead of him, spoken in Dei Magnun accents. But there was no reply from his brother.

Arion focused upon an open doorway to the immediate right of the entrance, from which there were sudden sounds of frantic activity. He was poised and ready as two red-cloaked soldiers emerged into the corridor, his blade slicing through them both before they had any chance to confront him.

He moved forwards into the building, checking rooms to either side as he progressed. However, his attention was focused on a closed door at the far end of the corridor. He could hear movement beyond there.

All of his abilities and senses were enhanced by the joint proximity of Leanna and Allana. He could still feel the latter, so close that she might even be within the fortress. He was certain that the dark-haired woman had pursued him.

By the Lord, what does she hope to achieve by following me here?

He frowned, then consciously pushed the thought away. He needed to focus on the task at hand.

He was now resolved as to what he would do today. After witnessing the northern wall being overrun, he realised that it might already be too late to save the town. He had therefore decided to free Gerrion from this fortress, and then he would find a way into Septholme, to seek out Kalyane, Karienne and Leanna. If the town was going to fall, he would get them all out, and they would escape from Western Canasar. But first, he needed to rescue his brother.

He swung open the door at the end of the corridor, and was immediately attacked by a further two Aiduel's Guards. One was directly ahead, a man who thrust his sword tip towards Arion's groin. The second lunged from beside the doorway, his knife stabbing forward. Both strikes were quick, but Arion's reactions were sufficient to thwart them. He parried the sword thrust, while his free hand slapped away the forearm holding the dagger.

He then barged through the doorway, grabbing hold of the knife attacker as he passed and throwing the man against his colleague. Both figures tumbled to the ground in a jumble of arms and legs. Arion followed behind them, the point of his sword ending their lives before they could regain their feet.

A third red-cloaked soldier was further down the stone corridor, beside an open door. As soon as this balding individual noted Arion's slaying of his colleagues, he fled through that doorway.

Arion heard the metallic sound of another door clanging shut as he pursued the balding man. He entered a cramped rectangular area, with what appeared to be four prison cells around the outside. Each had a closed metal door with bars on the upper part, which allowed a view of the cell inside.

'Gerrion!'

Again, there was no answer. Arion moved closer, looking into each of the cells in turn, without putting his face too close to the bars. On the third such attempt, he found what he wanted.

Gerrion was inside, standing against the far wall, with his hands bound before him. Arion's brother looked unkempt and weary, but he was alive. His dark eyes met Arion's, and an expression which hinted at relief appeared on the older brother's face.

Thank the Lord! I've found him!

However, two Aiduel's Guards were inside the small cell with Gerrion. The balding man was standing close to the cell door, with a sword in his hand. The other was a middle-aged man with a grizzled beard. This one was at the far wall, beside the young duke, and he was holding a long knife to Gerrion's neck.

'We've locked the door!' the balding Guard shouted, his voice wavering as he spoke in a thick Dei Magnun accent.

'Open it and release him,' said Arion, trying to keep his voice calm. He pushed against the door, testing whether the man had spoken true. 'I'll spare you.'

'No,' responded the bearded man. 'You've fucking killed everyone else. Now leave or I'll kill *him*.'

'No one else needs to die here,' stated Arion. 'Not the duke, not you. I just want Duke Sepian. Let him go, please.'

He was keeping the corridor in his peripheral vision, concerned that more of the red-cloaks would be arriving soon.

'He's our prisoner,' said the closer Guard. 'And there's a locked door between us. So, like we said, you need to go. If you try anything, we'll kill him.'

The bearded man pressed his blade against Gerrion's exposed throat, as if to support this point.

Arion glanced at the cell door. Its hinges were thick and appeared to be made of iron, as was the frame and the door itself. He was trying to assess whether he would be able to break into the cell. Energy was still coiling around his body, continuing to be bolstered by the presence of Allana and Leanna. However, he was still unsure whether he could move with sufficient speed and force.

'I'll spare you, I swear,' said Arion, and he sheathed his sword by way of emphasis. 'Just give me my brother, please.'

'Your brother?' said the bearded man. 'By the Lord, Barr, I think I know who this is.'

'Fuck, he's the Butcher of Moss Ford,' replied the one named Barr. He then shook his head. 'Forget it. No chance we're going to open this door. We'll wait for help to arrive.'

'Open the door, *please*, and I'll spare you,' implored Arion, while trying to maintain an external calm. However, he was tensing in preparation for what he was about to do.

Lord preserve us, what choice do I have? I have to get Gerrion out of here, and return to Septholme. Right now!

'No, we'll just stay in here, if it's all the same to-'

STRENGTH. VICTORY. GLORY.

Arion shot forwards in a blur of force, smashing shoulder-first into the cell door. The metal object was torn out of its frame as he impacted it, and it crashed backwards onto the closest Guard as Arion's momentum carried him through the doorway.

The world had slowed to a crawl around him as he cannoned into the room. Gerrion was just five paces away, and the older brother flinched in reaction to Arion's violent entrance. The bearded man also jerked backwards in response to the collapse of the door, and their combined movements caused a thin line of red to appear across Gerrion's neck.

Then Arion was upon the grizzled guard, with one hand gripping the fingers which held the knife, before tearing the weapon away. Arion's other fist smashed into the man's head, shattering his skull between knuckles and wall.

Arion twisted around to find the balding guard pinned beneath the heavy door. The man's sword had been cast away under the initial crushing impact. Arion reached down to the dazed soldier, took hold of his head, and yanked. A sharp crack announced that there were no more threats in the room.

By the Lord, he should have just opened the fucking door!

He turned back to Gerrion. For just a moment, the young duke's mouth turned upwards at the corners, suggesting happiness at their reunion. Arion felt an instant of joy, a recognition that at last he had done something right, something good.

But then he saw confusion appearing on Gerrion's face, and blood was blossoming on his brother's throat. Red liquid was emerging along the line cut by the jerking knife, which suddenly did not seem so thin. Gerrion's body started to collapse sideways, and only Arion's reactions prevented the elder sibling's head from crunching against the cell floor.

Arion found himself cradling his brother, and lowering him gently onto the ground. His eyes found Gerrion's, and there was fear there. A childlike uncertainty which he had never seen in his elder sibling, in all the time that they had known each other. Arion did not want to look at the wound on the neck, which was long and deep. Blood was seeping out.

Arion had moved too slowly, and the bearded man had cut Gerrion's neck. Arion's brother was mortally wounded.

Arion's actions had killed Gerrion.

'Ar-'

The word was started as a sigh by Duke Gerrion Sepian, but it was never completed.

'Gerr, I'm...'

I'm sorry. This is all my fault. Forgive me.

But the light had already gone from Gerrion's eyes.

―

A short time later, Arion was still staring down at the lifeless form of his older brother. He could feel a surge of power from somewhere close by, something which Allana must have been doing within the fortress. The sensation of this action felt dark, and somehow wrong, and he wondered whether he could hear a distant series of screams. However, at this moment, he did not care.

'He's here!'

The shout came from the corridor outside of the cells, and was followed by the thumping sound of approaching boots. More of the red-cloaked soldiers.

Arion inhaled deeply, then took one last moment to stare at his dead sibling. One last instant to say goodbye. He then drew his sword and stepped into the space outside of the cell.

Three Aiduel's Guards had already advanced into that small rectangular area, and more were in the corridor outside. They would be feeling confident that they had him trapped, and that he could be vanquished under weight of numbers. They would soon be taught the error of that belief.

Time crawled within Arion's world, and he could feel his power coiling, encircling each of his limbs with energy. The air about him was crackling in anticipation of an eruption of violence, and the darkness of whatever Allana was doing was a spiteful chorus in the background of his thoughts.

These red-cloaked soldiers had chosen to confine themselves in this compact space with him, and they would be the first to suffer vengeance for Gerrion's death.

Kill them! Kill them! Kill them! Kill them!

He exploded into the red-cloaks. In what followed, his anguish was released against them in a tide of blood and pain.

—

By the time that the killing had ended, and the screams of his opponents were no longer ringing in his ears, he was back outside in the central grounds of the fortress. There were dozens of corpses scattered about him. He wiped his sword, then sheathed it.

He was uncertain about how long he had been fighting, or precisely how many he had killed. However, he was covered in blood, and there was death everywhere around him. No one was attacking him anymore, and it seemed as if he had run out of adversaries to strike down.

By the Lord, I've failed again.

He had come here to save Gerrion, but his actions and choices had killed his elder brother. He had not been quick enough to break into the cell and reach his sibling, to prevent the killing blow. And if he had not chosen to attack this fortress, Gerrion would still be alive.

Arion began to wander back towards the main entrance, feeling dazed. Part of him was wondering whether to claim Gerrion's body, but that would involve retracing his footsteps through a stone-building which had been transformed into a charnel house. In any case, he needed a few moments to try to recover his senses.

As he was thinking about this, an immense power ignited from somewhere to the west. Within Septholme. He knew immediately that it must be the work of Leanna. Even from a great distance, he could perceive that she was blazing with energy, like a radiant sun. He could feel her reaching out to him, allowing his strength to bolster and fortify her, as he in turn was strengthened by her presence. He opened himself to her, to support her in whatever deed she was undertaking.

He continued to move forwards. After passing around the outside corner of a building, the main gates of the fortress came back into sight. Six further corpses were scattered there, his first victims in this place.

Arion realised then that he could still feel Allana, somewhere nearby, although her powers had now fallen dormant. He glanced around, and was relieved that the dark-haired woman was not in sight. He did not want another meeting with her here, and he felt uneasy that she had followed him.

The adulterous encounter in the forest was one more act for him to be ashamed of. He recognised that he had been overwhelmed with sudden desire, and had lost control of any rational thought. It was as if he had willingly allowed Allana dei Monis to enchant him, and to seduce him with her promise of exquisite carnal pleasure. For a period, he had seemed to forget who he was, and he had casually disregarded his urgent reasons for returning home.

But only in the aftermath of their mutual lust had the full extent of her manipulation of him become evident. *She* had written the letters. *She* had been responsible for coaxing him to Andarron, away from his family. And this had been done to support the traitorous cause of Jarrett Berun, his greatest rival, whom she was somehow betrothed to.

All of Arion's turmoil and distress during the last few weeks, all of the disasters resulting from his absence, it had been of her making. He knew that he himself was ultimately to blame for his own lack of judgement and honour, but *she* had instigated all of this.

By the Lord, keep her away from me, or I might do something else that I'll regret!

As he was thinking this, a pair of large, dark forms barrelled across the open space to his left, heading out through the fortress gateway. These shapes crossed his field of vision too rapidly to get a proper look at them, but what he glimpsed triggered an alarmed recognition.

They were exactly like the monstrous creatures which he had witnessed during his last prophetic vision; two massive beasts, covered in fur. Arion ran to the fortress entrance, and he could see the pair of monsters bounding on four legs towards the town. Their speed was incredible.

'I'm sorry, Arion.'

He was interrupted by these words, and glanced to his left to see that Allana had emerged around the opposite side of the building. She was standing with her hand on her hip, her lustrous hair hanging loose around her shoulders. Even after everything that had happened, it was difficult not to stare with hunger at her raw beauty. Difficult not to want her.

'I'm sorry for what I've done to you,' she continued, quickly, 'and if I could take it back, I would. Please don't leave.'

'I need to go, Allana. Now!'

'Don't go!' she urged. 'It's not too late to change your mind. I followed you here to say that. I love you and I want to be with you. We can still be together. Don't leave me.'

He tore his gaze away from her, and could see the beasts increasing their distance from him and from the fortress.

By the Lord, I need to go!

He could still feel Leanna's power surging in the west, from within the town. A realisation then struck him, and he felt sudden fear. Could Leanna be at the harbour? Her powers were like a blazing beacon which hailed her location. Could Allana feel the same?

Arion turned to look back at Allana, and said, 'Those beasts, are they connected to you?'

'No,' she replied, but he noticed that she averted her eyes while answering.

The memories of his vision were in his mind. The creatures descending upon the harbour area, killing as they raced through the streets of Septholme. A golden wall of light rising from the ocean.

'What have you done, Allana?' he asked her, his voice suddenly shrill. 'What have you done?'

She did not answer immediately, and her silence triggered him into action. He burst through the gateway, running in pursuit of the two beasts.

Leaving Allana dei Monis behind him, on her own in the grim, death-filled fortress.

—

As Arion sprinted out onto the open land beyond the fortress walls, he could see his untethered horse and one other galloping away, both too distant to be of any use to him. He therefore continued on foot, following the trail of the two monsters.

By the Lord, I have to catch them!

The beasts were in the distance, still visible ahead of him. They were bounding forwards on all fours directly towards the walls of Septholme, four hundred metres away, and to the steep cliffs on the eastern side of the town. If Arion had been any ordinary person, running in their wake, the creatures would have left him far behind. However, he was soon sprinting at a pace which no other person could have hoped to attain or maintain, moving faster even than the two creatures.

He witnessed the moment when the monsters passed over a line of Berun troops, who were maintaining the siege perimeter on this side of the town. There was agitated uproar amongst these soldiers as the two monsters hurtled over the top of them, before continuing on unimpeded towards the cliffs ahead.

Arion could still feel the blazing power of Leanna to the west, and he was certain now that she was the target of the beasts. In his prophetic vision, he had seen a wall of golden light arising in front of Septholme harbour, a miracle which he was now sure would be of Leanna's making.

He could also feel Allana to the east, receding from him. This time, she was not attempting to follow.

In this space between the two of them, Arion's powers were surging again. Even though Leanna was drawing upon his energy and vitality in whatever task she was undertaking, he was doing the same to her to maintain his velocity and stamina. They were both stronger as a result.

When he approached the Berun siege line, he leapt into the air as he came within five metres of the enemy soldiers, who were all still facing towards the creatures. He sailed high over the soldiers' heads, landing some ten metres past them with a crunch, then sprinted onwards without breaking his stride.

Lord preserve me!

The eastern cliffs of Septholme were now looming, and Arion could see the two monsters already scaling up the steep rockface. They were springing from outcrop to outcrop, using long, bestial arms and powerful hind legs. The beasts were ascending straight up the cliffs, headed for the walls at the top.

Arion pressed on in pursuit, willing himself to gain ground on the creatures. At the base of the cliffs, he leapt upwards instinctively, finding a hand and foothold then launching himself onwards once again, pursuing the beasts up the rock wall in a manner which no other man could have dared to attempt.

By the time that he reached the upper parts of the cliffs, he could see the beasts scaling onto the eastern ramparts of the town. The creatures howled as they reached this point, and then disappeared from sight. Arion willed himself up the latter sections of the cliff, urgently dragging himself upwards, before pulling himself onto the town's eastern battlements.

Despite his sense of urgency, he could not help but glance for a moment towards the northern quarter of Septholme, and he felt his stomach sink. The northern ramparts were now covered in a sea of yellow, with no visible traces of the blue tabards of Andar.

In the streets behind the north wall, a number of buildings were ablaze, and others were part-demolished, as if struck by boulders. The sounds of battle were carrying up to Arion's vantage point, and it seemed that there were still some pockets of fierce resistance in that area. However, it was clear that the town was lost, and Arion's arrival was too late to change that outcome.

He forced his attention away from that calamity and jumped off the far side of the battlements, determined to continue his pursuit of the creatures. He thudded down onto the street below before setting off running again, soon turning onto the main thoroughfare which ran between Septholme Castle and the waterfront. As he was sprinting downhill, he felt a moment of unsteadiness as everything finally came into focus from his prophetic vision.

Out at sea, a line of Dei Magnun warships had bows pointing in the direction of the harbour, and were seemingly travelling in that direction. But ahead of them, something ethereal and astonishing shimmered above the water; a golden wall of light, which sat above the ocean's churning surface beyond the harbour mouth, and which extended far to the north and south.

Leanna's power was still blazing, and Arion felt certain that she was responsible for what he was witnessing. He continued to run towards that miraculous sight, and he soon spotted one of the beasts again. It was still well ahead of him, bounding down the road towards the quayside area, and it was causing a chorus of shrieks from terrified townsfolk as it barrelled straight through them.

Lord preserve me, I must reach Leanna first!

Arion skirted a dead body as he sprinted down the hill. The corpse looked as if its throat had been ripped out, with fresh blood pooling around the gaping wound. Then Arion spotted the second of the monsters, which was also still ahead. This one was leaping from rooftop to rooftop, displaying unnatural agility, and its destination again seemed to be the harbour.

Arion continued to pound down the cobbled road, managing to dodge any civilians who were in his path. Now that he was lower in the town, the ethereal wall of light was even more imposing, covering the entire seafront outside of Septholme's harbour. The Dei Magnun fleet was drawing nearer, and it seemed that the lead ship would soon be passing into and through that golden, shimmering wall. Three other vessels were just a short distance behind.

Directly in front of Arion, the two creatures disappeared from sight as they entered the harbourside area. He had been closing on them, but they were still too far ahead of him. Two monstrous and chilling howls were released by the now unseen beasts, followed by a series of distinctly more human screams.

Arion turned the corner onto the quayside at the exact moment that the lead Dei Magnun ship crashed into the golden wall of light. The screeching sound of wood cracking and splintering was audible across the entire harbour area, and was quickly joined by three further such noises.

Time slowed to a crawl as Arion peered around the waterfront, his eyes taking in fragments of the events occurring there. The mouth of the harbour was unobstructed, and numerous Andar ships were sailing out through that channel into the ocean beyond. The lead vessels appeared to have steered south, sailing parallel with the shimmering wall of light.

The House of Sepian galleon, *Star of Canasar*, was the most prominent ship remaining in the harbour, and its canvas sails were billowing in apparent readiness for sail. Its bow was swaying in a high tide, and it was much closer to the quayside than would normally have been considered safe. Sailors were in the process of extending its gangplank towards the stone quay.

The waterfront area was crowded with townsfolk, who must have fled here in response to the impending fall of the town. These people were being held back from entering the stone quay by a line of blue-tabarded Andar soldiers. A panic was breaking out amongst these frantic citizens as they turned to face the terrible howling noises, and saw two creatures of nightmare charging towards them.

Beyond this foremost mass of people, and at the far end of the quay, was a figure which had to be Leanna. She was facing out to sea, enveloped in a radiant orb of light. Her shape was silhouetted within this brilliant globe, and her arms were raised to the sky. Arion could feel immense power pulsing from her as she maintained the shimmering golden wall.

Two other people were standing some distance apart from Leanna, one of whom was recognisable as Amyss. The small priestess was leaning against the side of a much larger man.

Arion was then both surprised and concerned to spot his wife and sister. Kalyane and Karienne were standing in the midst of a second, smaller group of Andar soldiers. They were halfway along the stone quay, close to the point where the galleon's gangplank was being extended.

As Arion continued to sprint forwards, dodging past people as he ran, he watched the two monsters scything through the crowd of townsfolk at the mouth of the quay. Bodies were being scattered in all directions as the creatures progressed, and the crowd was easily parted by the pair of ferocious beasts. The first, thin line of Andar soldiers charged forward in attack as the monsters closed, but Arion was dismayed to see the beasts crashing through them, leaving the row of defenders broken and reeling.

Arion was sprinting urgently between and sometimes leaping over the scattered mass of townsfolk. However, he was still not gaining sufficient ground as the creatures bounded onwards along the quay, closing towards the group which contained his sister and his wife. He could see now that Kalyane was wearing armour, and she looked brave as she shouted instructions to the soldiers around her, preparing for the approach of the monstrous creatures.

Arion was now on the quay itself, leaping over a cluster of sprawled bodies. He was getting closer to his wife, time edging forwards with painful sluggishness and clarity. For just an instant, he thought that Kalyane looked in his direction and saw his frantic pursuit of the looming beasts. Was it possible that she spotted him? Did she realise that he was returning to her, in the very place where they had parted weeks – *a lifetime* – before?

One of the charging beasts slammed into the middle of Kalyane and Karienne's group. Its arms and legs lashed out, sending people flying in all directions. To Arion's dismay, his wife seemed to collapse out of sight, whilst his sister was knocked backwards with two other people, all three of them plummeting off the edge of the quay. Arion heard a brief scream from Karienne, which was cut off as the girl crashed into the water below.

The second of the two monstrous creatures had leapt past this chaos, and now howled again as it bounded on towards the figures at the end of the quay.

Arion continued to sprint forwards, trying to close the distance to the nearest of the beasts, and to his endangered wife.

As he drew ever closer, he saw that the creature was raising itself into an upright position. As it did so, it dragged a smaller form up with it; a slender female, with long auburn hair, who the beast was gripping around the neck. Time seemed to cease as Arion pounded forwards, and he could only observe as Kalyane's hands reached up to desperately claw against the thick, fur-covered wrist which held her. Her legs were kicking as she was dangled above the ground, and as the beast reached across with its other paw to clutch the back of her head.

Arion was frantic. He was less than ten metres away when his wife's terrified gaze settled upon him. This time, there definitely was recognition. A meeting of their eyes. From her, a silent plea for help amidst her sudden terror.

Arion was therefore close enough to see the final look of shock on Kalyane's pretty face, at the moment when the beast snapped her neck.

His anguish was released in an unholy roar, a noise which reverberated across the entire quayside.

The creature was turning to face him, and was roaring in turn as it tossed Kalyane's limp form aside, when Arion launched himself against it.

34

Leanna

—

*Year of Our Lord,
After Ascension, 770AA*

After Leanna had arrived at the waterfront, events had escalated rapidly.

It had been no small task to pass through the hundreds of fearful townsfolk who had gathered there, but Caddin had used his imposing size to bully a path through the crowd. The line of soldiers guarding the landward end of the stone quay had then recognised the grey-bearded man and Leanna, and had allowed their party through.

Leanna had walked to the midpoint of the quay to join Lady Kalyane, Lady Karienne and a small group of loyal guards. She had then moved a few paces away from Caddin and his medallions, allowing her energy to be quickly renewed by the pulsing presence to the east of the other two Illborn.

In the minutes which had followed, she had waited and watched as dozens of sailors and soldiers had hurried to implement Kalyane's orders. In a short span of time, the ships in the harbour had been released, and the chain guarding the harbour mouth had been lowered. Amyss had awoken in the midst of this activity, and had leaned wearily against Caddin's side.

Leanna had started to dare to hope that escape might still be possible, a sentiment which had also clearly been shared by the gathered townsfolk. As the sounds of fighting within the town had grown closer, there had been a growing clamour to board one of the ships which were being readied.

However, the actions in preparation for an escape by sea had also been noticed by the Dei Magnun navy. A number of Kalyane's retainers had called out in agitation as the foreign ships had turned in formation and had begun to sail towards the town. In response, Leanna had walked to the end of the stone quay, as close to the sea outside of the harbour as she could possibly get. Caddin and Amyss had trailed behind her, remaining at a distance.

The sea breeze had been blowing through Leanna's loose hair as she had watched the Dei Magnun fleet approaching, closing the distance far too rapidly in comparison to the preparations in the harbour. Leanna had soon reached the conclusion that there would not be enough time for the ships of Septholme to escape, unless *she* intervened.

DEVOTION. SACRIFICE. SALVATION.

She had unleashed a blaze of power, this time leaning upon the strength of the one who she was sure was Arion. And with that power, she had created another transparent wall of radiant light, an impenetrable barrier which had spread slowly across the ocean outside the harbour, to the north and south.

Leanna had become cocooned within her own orb of brilliant light as she had done this, her deed visible to every person in the quayside area. She had again been exulting in the power of The Lord as He had worked His miracle through her, and as time had slowed down around her.

Some of the first ships to leave the harbour had begun to pass her by, loaded with evacuees. Despite the disasters of the day, Leanna had been aware that she was still doing some good and that she was helping to save lives.

She had also been able to feel an intimate connection with Arion, and she had sensed that he was travelling quickly towards her. However, the Dei Magnun navy had also continued to draw closer, sailing rapidly through the waves towards the shimmering wall of light, as if expecting their ships to simply pass through it.

Leanna had been bracing herself for that moment, readying for the impact of the fleet against the shield in the ocean, when she had first heard the howls.

—

In the moments after, Leanna watched as the four lead ships of the Dei Magnun navy sailed into the barrier of light.

At the northern battlements, slower moving objects had simply been pushed away. However, these massive warships were sailing at force directly into the shimmering wall. As such, when the bows of the vessels impacted head-on with the impenetrable light, they simply crumpled.

Announced by a screeching noise which carried across to the quayside, the prows tore and shattered, and wooden beams cracked and splintered. In just moments, the four ships were turned sideways along the shimmering barrier, and all were dipping in the ocean as seawater poured into their breached bows. The Dei Magnun ships further away were already changing direction in the water, desperately trying to avoid a similar fate.

Leanna could feel Arion's presence very near to her. As the power continued to course through her, she half-turned her body to look back towards the town.

There was sudden panic amongst the crowd at the waterfront. For a brief moment, Leanna wondered whether the Elannis army was descending upon the townsfolk, but she could see no signs of yellow tabards or of soldiers fighting.

Then the two monsters emerged into sight, as they smashed through a line of blue-clad soldiers who had been standing at the mouth of the quay. Blood sprayed into the air as the unnatural creatures crashed over and through that line of defence, and then bounded forwards on four limbs.

Lord Aiduel, what am I seeing?

There was no hesitation in the monstrous beasts as they hurtled onwards along the stone quay. Leanna's heart was beating fast, but she knew that she needed to focus on maintaining the barrier in the ocean.

Even now, more Andar ships were sailing through the harbour mouth, carrying evacuees from the town. And the House Sepian galleon was drawing alongside the place where Kalyane and Karienne were standing. This was the vessel that Leanna and her companions were also going to escape on. Leanna knew that she would need to keep the Dei Magnun navy at bay for a while longer.

In the decelerated world around her, Leanna was able to process all of this, and to watch with horror as one of the two creatures leaped into the centre of Kalyane's group, scattering bodies in all directions. However, Leanna's gaze was drawn to the second beast, as it charged along the remainder of the quay, directly towards her, Caddin and Amyss.

Leanna did not know how to intervene to help her companions, given the concentration and effort required to maintain the wall of light. She could only watch, feeling helpless, as Caddin pushed Amyss to the ground, grasped hold of his mace in two hands, and readied himself for the attack of the monster.

The beast closed towards Sendromm, initially charging straight for him, then shifting direction to dart past. Caddin displayed lightning-fast reactions, his mace crashing downwards at the passing monster. The weapon slammed into the creature's shoulder, knocking it off balance and sending its monstrous bulk careering towards the edge of the quay. For a brief moment, it seemed that the beast would tumble into the waters below. However, a long front limb snaked out, and claws caught on the edge of the quayside, leaving the monster dangling there.

Caddin rushed forwards to attack again, but he was too slow. The creature sprang upwards into his chest, sending him sprawling backwards, his body thudding to the ground close to where Amyss was crouching. Caddin had somehow maintained a hold on his mace, and Leanna saw him swinging it as the monster leaped towards him.

Leanna senses were hyper-alert as she watched all of this conflict playing out in slow-motion, and she was torn with indecision. She desperately wanted to help her companions. However, if she released the golden shield in the ocean, the Dei Magnun navy would be able to reach the harbour mouth.

Lord Aiduel, what must I do?

She then noticed that the second of the monsters had risen to its feet, and she was aghast when she spotted the auburn-haired woman who was struggling within the creature's grasp. But that emotion was as nothing compared to the horror that she felt as the beast casually snapped Lady Kalyane Sepian's neck, before casting the woman's body aside.

Lord Aiduel! Please, Lord, no!

Almost immediately afterwards, there were two deafening roars, and the creature which had committed the murder suddenly flew backwards, as if some mighty force had hammered into it.

Closer to Leanna, Caddin swung his mace from an exposed and horizontal position, in an attempt to thwart the nearest beast's leaping attack. The monster crashed away from him as the mace-head connected, although it seemed that its lengthy front claws had also raked across Caddin's body.

The creature landed in a place closer to the end of the quay, its rear limbs missing Amyss's head by just a fraction. It then turned to focus its golden eyes on Leanna, and launched itself towards her.

Caddin did not follow. Indeed, he seemed momentarily incapable of climbing to his feet. Leanna could see him rolling onto his side, watching with a look of pain and desperation as the creature charged towards her.

Time was still slowed down for Leanna as the monster approached. She could observe every element of the fur-covered beast clearly now; golden eyes, a long maw, sharp teeth, and limbs which were both long and thick. Everything about it felt... *wrong*, unnatural. Darkness swirled around it, visible only to Leanna. It was an abomination.

Lord Aiduel, make my thoughts and actions true, and deliver me from evil.

The beast leaped from three metres away. Its jaws were open and its forelimbs were stretched out towards her, with claws extended. Leanna flinched back, knowing that she had nowhere to go.

The creature crashed against Leanna's cocooning, radiant orb, and bounced backwards from the impact. It reacted immediately, raising itself onto its rear legs, and then it started to swipe against the barrier before it. From the beast's position of less than a metre away, howls of frenzied bloodlust were directed at Leanna, matching the fury which she could sense pulsing from inside the creature. Up close, she could clearly perceive a halo of darkness which surrounded the monster, and could see tendrils of that darkness attacking her orb of protective light.

Leanna's heart was pounding, and she strove to maintain her composure and concentration as the beast tried to break through to her. She knew that if her focus failed, the creature would be upon her.

Lord Aiduel, please help me!

Then Caddin was there, raising his mace to strike down at the creature from behind. He must have removed his medallions, because Leanna's powers were unaffected by his presence. The strike, which was aimed at the beast's head, was powerful and precise.

However, the creature's reactions were too fast. A thick forearm shot backwards and caught hold of the shaft of the descending mace, before wrenching it from Caddin's grip. The creature then backhanded Sendromm, slamming him onto the floor. It cast the mace aside, then lunged towards him, with an arm raised to kill.

But before this blow could land, another figure impacted the beast in an explosive flurry of movement, driving it away from Caddin. Leanna felt elation and relief as she realised that Arion was there, his close proximity evidenced by the sudden surge of energy within her body. The young noble and the monster fell to the floor, their limbs locked together in ferocious combat. Only Leanna could perceive that Arion's body was at the centre of a swirling vortex of rainbow colour, mixed in with the corrosive darkness of the beast's halo.

With the world slowed down around her, Leanna was able to properly appreciate the force and speed of the blows then exchanged between Arion and the creature, as the two rolled and struggled on the ground. The beast was striking at Arion with its claws, but somehow this did not result in a mortal wound. Instead, a multitude of small cuts were appearing on the surface of Arion's skin, through his shredded clothing.

Arion was initially punching the creature, to keep its maw away from him, but then his focus seemed to shift to grasping hold of its upper and lower jaws. Leanna could see that he was steadily forcing those jaws open, even as the creature's claws were trying to rake his flesh.

The struggle ended abruptly, with a wet tearing noise. Leanna realised that Arion had ripped the beast's jaws apart, to an almost vertical position. He had killed the creature with his bare hands.

Lord Aiduel, now I can see the powers that you have given to him.

Leanna watched as Arion threw the dead form aside. The monster's corpse slid off the edge of the quay and dropped into the waters below. When Arion stood, Leanna could see that he was covered almost head-to-toe in blood, only some of which appeared to be his own.

His expression was full of anguish, and he seemed to be on the verge of tears. However, he held out a hand to her, his forearm breaking through the edge of the golden orb as if the barrier was not there, and he said, 'Come, Leanna, we must get away from here.'

—

In the minutes that followed, Leanna made her way onto the Sepian galleon *Star of Canasar*, and moved forwards to the prow. Within the glorious energy of Arion's presence, immense power continued to flow through her, and she was maintaining the shimmering shield of light outside of the harbour.

The deck of the ship was crowded with other people. Caddin and Amyss were watching Leanna from a distance away, whilst slumped beside the main mast. Amyss was still exhausted from Leanna's earlier healing, while Caddin was suffering from multiple cuts and appeared to have a broken arm.

Leanna could see that Arion was standing at the stern of the ship, looking back across the quayside waters towards the town. Sailing crew of the vessel were bustling around him, readying the ship to cast off, but he appeared isolated and alone.

He was holding the body of his dead wife in his arms and was shouting, 'Karienne!'

At first, this call had been made with frantic enthusiasm, as if he still believed that he would hear a response from his missing sister, but he now sounded like a man without hope.

A number of townsfolk had been allowed onto the galleon by the surviving group of Andar soldiers. Following this, those few soldiers had also crossed onto the ship, and the gangplank had been withdrawn.

Hundreds of people had been unable to get onto any of the fleeing vessels, but had stayed in the waterfront area despite the terror caused by the attack of the beasts. Leanna now witnessed another ripple of panic running through this crowd, as yellow-clad soldiers of Elannis emerged from the surrounding streets. There was a surge of bodies onto the quay.

'Cast off!'

The shout was repeated by multiple of the vessel's sailors, even as some townsfolk were attempting to leap the distance from the quay to the ship.

The galleon was then pulling away, the last boat to leave the harbour. Leanna observed the shore for a few moments, feeling sombre as the conquering Elannis force spread out into the waterfront area, pushing the panicked crowds before them.

Lord Aiduel, please let them show mercy on the people of this town.

Her attention then returned to the waters ahead of her, as the ship passed through the harbour mouth and into the choppier sea beyond. The swaying galleon then turned to the left, being steered to follow the southerly route of the other escaping vessels.

Leanna turned to look towards the Dei Magnun navy, which was on the opposite side of the shimmering wall of light. The foreign fleet, which had seemed so formidable just a short time before, now appeared to be battered and broken. Four ships had crashed into the golden shield, all of which now appeared to be sinking. The undamaged remainder were near to the distressed vessels, and were retrieving stricken sailors from the ocean.

Leanna was determined to maintain the barrier for as long as she could, to give the evacuating ships the best possible chance of escape. However, her energy was finally beginning to diminish, even in Arion's presence. At some point, she would have to release the golden wall. After that, they would all find out whether the Dei Magnun fleet intended to pursue them.

Looking back towards land, Leanna could see the full outline of Septholme expanding into view as the Sepian galleon gradually extended its distance from the town. There were many fires visible now within the town walls. Leanna shuddered to think of the horrors which might follow that evening, if the armies of Elannis were allowed to run amok through Western Canasar's capital.

Eventually, she was too far away, and could no longer maintain the wall of light. She released it, exhaling heavily as she did so. She was relieved to observe that there were no immediate signs that the Dei Magnun ships were readying themselves to pursue.

Leanna's gaze then fell upon Arion, who had remained standing on the quarterdeck at the stern of the ship, and was facing away from her. He was holding his wife in his arms. Kalyane's head was slumped backwards over her husband's forearm, and her auburn hair was cascading down, almost touching the surface of the wooden deck below her.

For a brief moment, sunlight played in that hair, illuminating the lifeless form of the woman. But within seconds, shadow had returned.

—

It was late afternoon when Leanna first approached Arion. The Dei Magnun fleet had not pursued them, and their escaping flotilla of ships had travelled a long way south, following the Western Canasar coastline.

In the preceding hour, Leanna had moved amongst the crew and passengers of the vessel, healing anyone who was injured. She had also healed Caddin's wounds, and had left her two companions sitting together, with a sleeping Amyss leaning against the weary grey-bearded man.

Arion was still standing at the stern of the ship, holding the limp form of his wife. As Leanna moved closer to him, she noted that the emotions within his aura were as unreadable as ever. A vortex of colours raged around him, displaying every shade of the rainbow between darkness and light. However, as Leanna drew alongside him, she could see a tear running down his cheek.

Lord Aiduel, please ease his pain.

'Arion?'

He did not respond for several seconds, and continued to peer out from the rear of the ship. When he finally spoke, he stated, 'I've given the order to head to the island of Abass, Leanna.'

'Abass?'

'It's controlled by the Holy Orders, so it's neutral at least,' he said, in a matter-of-fact tone which was contradicted by the redness in his eyes. 'It might provide a refuge for a while, and it should take us away from the Dei Magnun navy. I doubt that there's a safe port anywhere on the southern coast of Andar, right now.'

She waited to see if he would say more, but he did not. After a few seconds, she reached out a hand and placed it onto his bicep.

'I'm so sorry, Arion.'

This time, he turned to her, then looked down at the still form of his wife. His cheeks were wet.

'I failed her, Leanna,' he said. 'I failed all of them. And now I've lost them.'

'It wasn't your fault, Arion. That... *creature*... it wasn't your fault.'

He gave a mirthless laugh. 'Wasn't it?' He drew in a deep breath and then added, 'I was too slow. Kalyane, Gerrion, Karienne. Too slow, to save any of them.'

Leanna felt confused. 'Gerrion?'

'He's dead. I tried to rescue him, but... instead, I caused someone to cut his throat. Then watched that... fucking thing, knock Karienne off the quay, and then... I was so close, as it snapped...'

He lowered his head to stare down again at the unmoving form of his wife, then released a sob which tore at Leanna's heart.

'I'm so sorry for your loss, Arion.'

She placed her hand around his back, hugging him, and rested her forehead against his upper arm.

He sobbed for over a minute after that. She remained silent as he cried, allowing him to release something of whatever was inside of him.

'I just realised,' he said, after his sobbing had ceased. 'I'm Duke Arion Sepian now. Duke of Western Canasar.' He barked another mirthless laugh. 'The duke of *nothing*. No, that's not right. Not nothing. I'm the duke of failure and of dishonour.'

'You're a good man, Arion,' Leanna replied. 'I can only imagine the pain that you're feeling after what's happened. But there's no dishonour in you.'

'Isn't there?'

'No. I see a good man before me. An honourable man. You returned to her, Arion. She always believed that you would, when others had given up hope. That... means something, surely? Something important to her. You're a good man, Arion. You did what you could to-'

'I betrayed her, Leanna.'

Leanna was bewildered, and she raised her forehead from his arm.

'Betrayed her?'

'I left her, left Septholme, to go to Andarron to seek out Allana dei Monis. Kalyane had no idea that was my real reason for leaving, because I lied to her. But it was, and it's why I left them all here, to face this disaster without me. And now I'm without family, Leanna. Without people. Without a home. And I'm without honour.'

Leanna did not know how to respond.

'And it's worse than that,' Arion continued. 'Earlier today, before returning to the town, I met Allana. And I lay with her.'

'No more, Arion,' said Leanna. 'Tell me no more. You're not respecting Kalyane, by talking of betrayal to me. Save it for another time.'

Leanna's voice had remained compassionate as she said this, but she was shocked and disappointed by his confession.

Lord Aiduel, please forgive his sin.

'And you can't remain standing here like this, with her, forever,' she added. 'She must be laid to rest, Arion.'

Her words seemed to register with him, and he turned towards her.

'Let's give her the Rite of Passing,' she continued, 'and send her soul onwards in the Grace of Aiduel. You've two ordained priestesses on this ship, Arion. Let us do something to honour Kalyane, and your brother and sister, and the many others who've passed on in these recent days.'

He looked down at her, his expression solemn. After a moment, he nodded.

She could see that his eyes were still bloodshot and wet. And she recognised that she could better understand his emotions now, despite her inability to use her powers on him.

Grief, sorrow and self-pity. These were all evident.

But most of all, there was guilt.

—

The Rite of Passing service took place later that day. The sun had started to set, colouring the clear sky with a pinkish hue, and the surrounding seas had calmed. Most of the passengers and crew of the galleon were gathered together on the main deck.

Arion was standing at the edge of the ship, again holding his wife's body in his arms. Kalyane had been wrapped within a sheet.

There was a respectful silence as the service began. Amyss had asked to lead it, and Leanna had gratefully ceded that role.

'Lord Aiduel, Saint Amena,' Amyss began, her demeanour as sombre as Leanna had ever seen. 'We gather before you to commend the safe passage to heaven of the souls who have left this life. They have passed from this world, in order that may you welcome them, Lord, in your everlasting Grace. And that you may let them reside with you in your own Place of Ascendance, forever a part of your eternal peace and benevolence.'

Amyss's words continued on from there. Sometime later, she read out a list of the names of any deceased who were related to the survivors on the vessel.

'We commend Lady Kalyane Sepian, Duke Gerrion Sepian, Lady Karienne Sepian…'

The list contained over thirty names. After finishing reading this, Amyss also added, 'And all others who have lost their lives in the battles for Septholme, Western Canasar and Andar. May they all pass on in your Grace, Lord, may their souls rest with you in eternal peace, and may they be standing behind you to welcome us when we in turn pass beyond.'

Leanna stepped forward at that point to commence the Holy Recitals. 'Lord Aiduel, make my thoughts and actions true, and…'

'Deliver me from evil,' responded the gathered audience.

'Let me stand tall and face the darkness…'

'As Aiduel faced the darkness on The Tree.'

The Holy Recitals continued on from there. After they had been finished, and after Amyss had concluded the remainder of the service, the petite priestess had one final ritual to perform.

'Accept this body into the… ocean, Lord,' she said, 'and watch over Lady Kalyane Sepian's soul, for all of eternity.'

She then nodded to Arion, and Leanna watched as the young noble released the body of his wife into the seas below.

—

Afterwards, Leanna was sitting with Amyss on the main deck. Their arms and shoulders were touching, and they were staring towards the setting sun in the west.

'We survived, Lea,' said Amyss, following which she yawned. After being awake and alert for the service, the petite woman was again struggling to resist sleep, and she tilted her head to rest it on Leanna's shoulder.

'We did,' said Leanna. 'How are you feeling?'

'Me? Tired. Sleepy. A little numb from everything that's happened. You?'

'I'm feeling sad, Amyss. Sad, and disappointed in myself. I don't like how the events at Septholme ended. For a while, I'd hoped… I could use my powers to stop the killing. But just like Arlais, things have ended so badly. I almost died. *You* almost died. And although we've managed to escape, so many others *did* die. I wish I could have done something more.'

'You did everything that you could,' said Amyss. 'No one could have done more.'

Lord Aiduel, I doubt that's true. I failed on the wall. And I fled whilst others were suffering. The powers that you've given to me still weren't enough to prevent the bloodshed.

'Coming so close to death today,' said Leanna, '*seeing* so much death today, it's brought things back into focus. Of what's important.'

Amyss placed a hand onto her arm. 'And what's important?'

'You. The people I love… *my parents*. I've been thinking about them while sitting here, on a ship sailing to a foreign land. I'm leaving Angall, and I don't even know if they're still alive, Amyss.'

There was silence for a few moments, and Leanna could feel a sudden fear pulsing inside her companion. However, despite that, Amyss said, 'I think that they are. And if you ever want to return to Arlais to try to find them, then I'll support you, Lea.'

'Thank you,' said Leanna. 'But it's not just that.'

'What else?' asked Amyss, as she stifled another yawn.

'I think… I can't keep ignoring what I am, Amyss. The things Caddin told us… what if they're true? My powers… are *growing*. I'm so much stronger than I was, even compared to the day at the pyre.'

'If you're becoming stronger, that's a good thing, Lea. You'll be able to heal more people. Protect more people.'

'But… I think Arion is getting stronger, too, and the woman Allana felt *very* powerful. According to Caddin, that's exactly what the Archlaw predicted, as part of the prophecy. That our powers would keep growing.'

'But we already said… the Archlaw might have *lied*, Lea.'

'He might have done,' said Leanna, 'but I think there's some truth in it. And more and more, I believe that there must be an important purpose for these powers. A purpose which has to be linked to the Gate.'

'I suspect you're right.'

'I think I am. But if that's the case, there's only one person who might be able to give me the whole truth about who I am and what the prophecy means.'

'One person? Lea, surely you don't mean…'

'Yes, I do mean that. The *Archlaw*, Amyss. He's the only one who knows what was actually written in that letter. If I'm ever to find answers, perhaps I-'

Leanna paused as she felt a diminishing in her powers which told her that Caddin was close by. She turned to face the burly man, who squatted down next to her. His mace was in his right hand.

'May I speak, please, Leanna?' he asked.

'Of course,' she said. 'What is it?'

He raised the mace and pointed the tip towards Arion Sepian, who had returned to stand at the stern of the ship.

'I was watching you with him earlier, and it made me uneasy,' Caddin said, keeping his voice low. 'And for good reason. I saw what he did today. I hadn't realised before, but I do now. He's one of you, isn't he? Another Illborn?'

'Yes,' she replied.

'Did you both know?'

Leanna and Amyss both nodded.

'He's dangerous,' said Caddin. 'Lethally quick and strong. Are you safe near him?'

'Yes,' said Leanna, without hesitation. 'I am. He's acted to save my life, twice now.' After a moment, she looked at the mace and added, 'Don't even *think* about doing anything to hurt him, Caddin.'

He frowned, then said, 'I won't, unless you tell me to. But I'll be watching him, Leanna. Very closely. And although he hasn't come close enough to me yet to notice the medallions, he will soon. And then he and I will no doubt be having a *conversation*. But for now, I'm more concerned about the *other* one you mentioned. The woman outside the walls.'

'Her name's Allana,' Leanna said. 'And yes, she's also worried me.'

'I think you're right to be worried after the events at the wall and the waterfront,' said Caddin. 'Just think. We've found two more of your kind. And you've told me that one of them has *dark* powers, and has used those powers to try to hurt you. And now I'm asking myself questions.'

'Questions?'

'Yes. After I murdered the boy, my fanatical belief in my mission also died. But now, I'm suddenly wavering again, and I'm asking myself; could the Archlaw's prophecy still be true? And if it is, could the real threat be this woman, *Allana*? And if that's the case, what do I – what do *we* – need to do about it?'

—

Later, Amyss had taken herself off to the tiny cabin below decks which had been allocated to the two priestesses. Despite being tired, Leanna was still feeling restless, and she felt a need to talk to Arion again before trying to sleep. He had remained at the stern of the ship, facing outwards as sunset was fading into darkness. Once again, as she approached, Leanna could see that his emotions were swirling in a confused kaleidoscope of colour.

His first words after she stood beside him were delivered in a calm tone, but they surprised her.

'I'm frightened by what I'm becoming, Leanna.'

'What do you mean?' she asked.

'What do I mean? Exactly what I said. These... powers. I'm getting stronger and stronger. More dangerous with every passing month.'

Leanna instantly recognised the similarities between Arion's words and her earlier conversation with Amyss.

'I kill so easily,' he continued. 'Without thought. At times, I feel so much... *rage*. They called me the Butcher of Moss Ford, Leanna, and I'm beginning to believe that they were right. I kill, and I kill, and I kill. And sometimes... I find that *I relish it.*'

'I don't believe that, Arion.'

'You may not, but I'm worried that I'm beginning to. I think about my actions of recent weeks, of so much violence and dishonour. So much harm to those around me. What makes me fit to have these powers, Leanna? Why were they given to me? And if I keep getting stronger, where will this end? What am I going to *become?*'

'You're a good man at heart, Arion,' she replied. 'I genuinely believe that. If you've made mistakes, I believe that you still have the decency to recognise them, like you're doing now, and to seek forgiveness and redemption. But only you can choose how you'll use your powers, if they continue to get stronger. It's for *you* to decide what you'll become.'

However, even as she was saying these words, Leanna was thinking again about Caddin's confession in Septholme Castle. About the mission which Caddin had been set upon two decades earlier, and the Archlaw's explanation for that mission...

'...the powers of the five Illborn will continue to grow... if you find the Gate and come into your full strength, you'll destroy the Holy Church and will drown the world in blood and war.'

She shivered as she felt a chill, and she took an involuntary step away from Arion. He was still looking outwards, and he did not appear to notice her sudden uncertainty. However, his next words unsettled her even more.

'I believe that Allana created those monsters, Leanna. I don't know how, but I first saw them near to her, and I believe that she had... *made them.*'

'What?'

'I think that she used her powers to create them, somehow.'

'How?'

'I don't know. But I *do* know that I've been infatuated with her for too long. And I can see now... there's a darkness at the heart of her. Something... *bitter*. But there's also power. A lot of power. I think that she made those creatures, and sent them after you.'

Leanna was momentarily lost for words, and another shiver passed through her. She could not forget the foul nature of the attack which Allana had unleashed against her on the northern wall, and the concerns raised by Caddin were at the forefront of her mind.

'I think that you may be right,' she said, finally. 'Earlier today, she did something else to try to hurt me. Though I don't understand why.'

Arion grimaced in response. Leanna looked out over the darkening sea, her mouth dry as she began to consider the wider implications of Arion's words and Allana's actions.

Lord Aiduel, what if Caddin is right? What if the Archlaw's prophecy is true?

She suddenly felt hesitant about sharing any details of what Caddin had disclosed to her in Septholme. In particular, she did not feel ready to reveal the burly man's words about the Gate.

'Anyway, perhaps you're right,' said Arion, after another period of silence. 'Perhaps I can still choose to control the person I'll become. I'll think about it more as we sail to Abass. And I'll also think more about my choices, after that.'

'Your choices?'

'Yes. My choices. I've lost everything, Leanna. And right now, I *feel* completely lost, too. What do I do now? Where do I go? I have so much uncertainty.'

'And what do you think you might do?'

'I'm not sure. I can try to find a way to return to Andar, to rejoin the army and the war, and attempt to reclaim my birthright. Or…'

'Or what?'

'Or, I can leave it all behind, to start again. And I can go to find my brother Delrin, in the Holy Land.'

—

That night, Leanna lay on her thin bunk below decks, in a pitch-black cabin. Amyss was sleeping on a separate bunk, and Leanna was alone with her thoughts.

She was dwelling on the momentous events and conversations of the preceding hours, days and weeks. She was also thinking about her own role in everything that had happened, and the responsibility that she bore for the suffering which she had witnessed.

She had been running and hiding for far too long. She recognised now that she had been too reluctant to accept that she might have a purpose, and a destiny, which extended far beyond the miracle of healing.

She had fled from Aiduel's Guards and from those other killers who were hunting for her, but death and misery had nonetheless overtaken her. And she had allowed herself to fall victim to the schemes of others, simply reacting to the headwind of events, and buffeted in different directions by the tragedy around her.

But no more.

Lord Aiduel, I cannot keep running out of fear. It's time for me to accept and to embrace what I am. It's time for me to understand the destiny and purpose which you have set out for me, Lord.

After Caddin's revelations in Septholme Castle, she now had a greater understanding of what she was. According to the Archlaw, she was prophesied to be one of a handful of *Illborn* who would destroy the Holy Church and would drown the world in blood and war, in a prophecy that was linked to the Gate of her dreams.

Much of what the Archlaw had revealed to Caddin had subsequently been proven to be correct, such that Leanna had to acknowledge that there was at least some truth in his words. And she also accepted that her destiny appeared to be intertwined with that of the other Illborn. With Arion, Allana and possibly one surviving other. However, such acceptance did not mean that everything else disclosed by the Archlaw was true.

She could *never* accept that she was meant to do evil. In Septholme, she had used her healing ability, and her new-found miraculous power, to attempt to do good. Even if she had failed, that did not distort or undermine her intent.

Lord Aiduel, I serve you, and I will never turn away from the faith and from good.

Taking her own words to Arion; it was for Leanna herself to decide how she would use her powers, if they continued to grow in strength. It was for *her* to choose what she would become, and what she would do. And she knew that she would never intentionally act to destroy the Holy Church or to drown the world in blood and war.

Indeed, she would do everything that she could to prevent such a terrible outcome, if it was the goal of another.

But to achieve this, she would need to take control of her own future, starting from the moment of her arrival in Abass. Never again could she allow herself to be directed by the decisions and actions of others.

In the darkness of the cabin, she could perceive that there were various pathways ahead of her, and choices to be made. One possible but dangerous destination was Sen Aiduel, where she might be able to find answers to unresolved mysteries; what was in the letter, what other secrets did the Archlaw hold, and why was she not meant to find the Gate of her dreams? Another potential destination, vastly more challenging, was Aiduel's Gate. A city cut-off from the world, where the ethereal archway itself might possibly reside?

Lord Aiduel, I am Leanna, the Angel of Arlais, and I now embrace and accept my destiny. Henceforth, I will march towards that destiny, rather than run away from my fears. With devotion to you and with sacrifice, Lord, I will deliver salvation.

With that recognition, she felt more at peace, and was at last ready to sleep. She then closed her eyes, wondering if the ethereal Gate and its hidden mysteries would once again appear to her within the depths of her dreams, as *Star of Canasar* sailed on through the night towards Abass.

35

Arion

—

*Year of Our Lord,
After Ascension, 770AA*

Sometime after his conversation with Leanna, Arion headed below decks to find his cramped ship cabin.

After he was tucked into his bunk, sleep was elusive. He stared into the darkness of the cabin with his eyes wide open, and thought about his family and his home. All gone. All dead, but for Delrin. All because of him.

Lord preserve me, if I could take it back, I would.

He remained like that for a long time, although no tears returned. The ship swayed and creaked around him, but even after he closed his eyes, for an extended period he could not find rest. Instead, his mind was circling repeatedly around the mistakes which he had made.

He knew that he could claim to be stronger and faster than any other man alive. He was blessed with incomparable physical powers. However, in the face of his poor choices, his strength had failed to deliver either victory or glory. Only defeat and shame lay in his recent wake. His homeland had been conquered and his family had been destroyed, and he had arrived too late to prevent either disaster.

And so it was that he lay in the dark, tortured by his regrets and his guilt. However, after several troubled hours had passed, fatigue eventually overcame him, and he descended into an uneasy sleep.

Once again, his slumber was to be disturbed by the torment of his recurring dream. But on this occasion, in the aftermath of the unleashing of vast powers in Septholme, something different was about to happen. Something new.

For on this night, he was finally going to witness all of the dream's hidden and shadowy recesses…

—

…And then he can see Him. In the Gate. Waiting. Watching. Golden, glowing, terrible, magnificent. He wants to kneel, to bow his head, to murmur his obeisance, but still silently he walks on. Closer, ever closer. So too do his companions.

The figure in the Gate moves His hand, a summoning gesture, and once again his body takes him forwards. And he can hear the clash of distant weapons, glorious ringing sounds given the shape of words.

STRENGTH. VICTORY. GLORY.

But then the gesture of His hand changes, and he is aware that something is wrong.

A single finger is raised. And he knows what he must do.

ONLY ONE CAN CLAIM THE POWER.

The voice erupts from the Gate like a relentless barrage of lightning, searing into the core of his very being.

KILL THEM TO MAKE IT YOURS. KILL THEM ALL!

He is paralysed, unable or unwilling to react to this devastating invitation to unimaginable power. But he watches as a shining companion responds; it twists in position, snatches something from the ground, and runs towards him.

After a fleeting struggle, in a bludgeoning of pain and betrayal, he is the first to die. And yet, his soul remains, trapped within the radiant, golden shadow of the Gate.

He bears witness as each of his other companions fall before the frenzied violence of this silent, blazing killer. Only one other fights back, desperately kicking and clawing and scratching. But they all die.

He observes their souls parting from their dying forms, and feels sorrow as each in turn is forced to remain, locked in place within the aura of the ethereal archway.

And at the end, he still watches the sole survivor, this triumphant murderer. This exultant avatar which strides forward, full of hunger. Into the Gate...

—

And this time, when Arion awoke, he remembered.

36

Allana

—

*Year of Our Lord,
After Ascension, 770AA*

Allana entered Septholme Castle alongside Jarrett, both of them riding on horseback in the midst of a company of Berun cavalry. Septholme had been conquered the previous day, but only now had Jarrett deemed it safe for the two of them to enter the town and to claim the castle.

Their cavalry procession passed through the main gates, unheralded. A handful of other soldiers of Berun were visible around the entrance and inside, interspersed with a few yellow-tabarded troops of Elannis. Otherwise, the courtyard of the castle was empty, without any retainers there to acknowledge their arrival. There was none of the lively bustle which Allana could remember from this place.

'Where is everyone, Jarrett?' she asked.

'The retainers of the castle are being held in the main hall, pending our arrival,' he said, in a dull tone. 'We'll summon them soon.'

'Oh, that makes sense. I'd expected… more people to greet us.'

Jarrett did not respond, but instead he seemed to wince, and he reached up to place a hand onto his chest. Allana frowned as she watched this.

He doesn't remember what you did to him, Lana. You don't need to worry about that.

She knew that Jarrett would have no recollection of how she had dominated him after their argument in the tent. Nonetheless, she was finding his mood since that clash to be of concern. He had seemed withdrawn for all of the prior evening, forgetting to pray, and his despondency had stretched into this morning. There was none of the sense of triumph that she had expected to see in him, after Septholme had finally been conquered.

Allana was also feeling a little subdued by the condition of the town, with a stench of death pervading Septholme's streets. After her party had travelled through the North Gate, they had passed a column of six carts laden with dead bodies. Those carts had been headed towards the funeral pyres which had been burning for hours, on the fields to the north. She had also seen a large group of Aiduel's Guards on one street, banging on doors and entering houses. The massacre in the fortress had seemingly done little to quell the aggression of the religious order.

'How are you feeling, Jarrett?' she asked.

'Fine,' he replied, but his hand had not moved from his chest. 'Let's get this over with, shall we? It's time to take control of our new castle.'

—

Sometime later, the Berun cavalry company had dismounted and had formed an armed square around the outside of the courtyard. The retainers of the castle were then led out.

Allana and Jarrett had remained on horseback, and were facing towards the confused procession of people who appeared from the direction of the castle's Great Hall. Allana was still feeling unsettled. She had lived in this place for a long time, and the surrounding walls and buildings were comfortably familiar. However, so much had changed since that day when Duke Conran Sepian had died.

Were you happy here, Lana? Did you feel safe here, while Conran was alive?

The castle retainers were being shepherded into the centre of the courtyard, within the square of Berun soldiers. Allana could remember daydreaming of this moment, of the precise instant when the castle staff would recognise her and would be in awe of just how far she had risen. However, as some of those staff looked up and focused upon her, the only expressions that she could see were either hostile or indifferent.

Amongst the retainers, Allana now recognised the face of Ami Randle, the Head of Household for the castle. Allana had once worked for the older woman, although their relationship had soured after Randle had called Allana a whore. Randle was staring directly at Allana, with an intense look of anger on her face. Allana met the woman's eyes for a few seconds, then looked away. She could feel her face flushing.

When all of the retainers were assembled outside, Jarrett began to speak.

'My name is Duke Jarrett Berun, and I am your new lord. The House of Sepian is dead, and their time as the rulers of Western Canasar has ended. The House of Berun rules here now. The sooner that you accept this as your new reality, the better it will be for all of you.'

Allana's gaze swept around the crowd, taking in the reaction to these words. She could see a mixture of dismay and timid resignation on most of the faces there.

'Later today, I'll hold a ceremony in the Great Hall,' continued Jarrett. 'One by one, you will kneel before me. Then, before The Lord, and on the Holy Book, you will swear loyalty and fealty to me and to House Berun. Anyone who refuses to do so will be cast out from here.

'You will also be required to swear your devotion and allegiance to the Holy Church as led by the Archlaw in Sen Aiduel. The days of the Imposter Church are over, and anyone seen to be practising the heretical devotions of that church will be handed over to Aiduel's Guards. Traditional services shall be reinstated, immediately.

'That is all for now. You will all continue to be held in the Great Hall until the ceremony is complete. After that, you may resume your duties here and prove your worth to your new master and mistress. But for now, you're dismissed.'

Jarrett waved a hand to notify his soldiers that he wanted the castle retainers to be led away.

However, before anyone could react, a female voice from within the castle staff called, 'What is *she* doing here?'

Allana recognised the common-sounding voice as that of Ami Randle. Jarrett was about to react with fury, but Allana spoke first.

'I am Lady Allana dei Monis, wife-to-be of Duke Jarrett Berun. I am the new lady of this castle, and you will all obey me and serve me. Including *you*.'

As Allana made this statement, there was a growing murmur of discontent from amongst a number of the retainers.

'You're a fucking whore, is what you are!' shouted Randle, the older woman's face turning red. 'It clearly wasn't enough that you spread your legs for Duke Conran, you treacherous little bitch, so now you've moved onto another one!'

Allana felt her face flushing red again.

How dare she speak to you like that, Lana! How dare the old hag say that!

She looked towards Jarrett, feeling outraged, and this time the duke did react. He signalled to a Berun officer, following which the soldier approached Randle, and casually back-handed his metal gauntlet into her face. The middle-aged woman collapsed, with blood spurting from her nose. The Berun officer then looked across at his duke. After receiving a confirmatory nod, he proceeded to repeatedly kick the unfortunate woman. Randle lifted her arms to try to protect her head, but she was quickly battered by the assault and was begging for mercy.

After a few seconds of this, Allana shouted, 'Enough!'

The officer paused, awaiting further instruction.

'Let's not start our time here with a murder, Jarrett,' Allana said, in a lower voice. 'There's been enough death already. Just throw her out of the castle. That's enough.'

Jarrett frowned, then said, 'Very well. Drag her outside of the castle and dump her there. And please, for the rest of you, let me be clear. If anyone chooses to disrespect or insult me, or my wife-to-be, or any other member of my family, they'll receive the same treatment. Now, would anyone else like to speak up?'

There was silence amongst the castle retainers.

'I thought not,' stated Jarrett. 'Think hard on my words before you're asked to swear allegiance.' He gestured again to his soldiers. 'If you are loyal to me, as these men are, and if you diligently observe the true faith, then you'll find me to be a fair master. Do otherwise and you'll feel my wrath. Now please, take them all away.'

Allana observed the departure of the castle retainers. She could hear some of the women sobbing, as the slumped form of a bloodied Ami Randle was dragged by the arms across the castle courtyard. Otherwise, there was silence.

Allana felt queasy and even more unsettled. Her homecoming to Septholme Castle had not provided the rapturous reception which she had once envisaged.

Not at all.

―

Later, Allana was alone inside the largest bedchamber in Septholme Castle. She was reclining on her side, on the bed.

She knew that she would not be disturbed for a while. Jarrett was inspecting the castle, and Allana had given instructions to her guards in the corridor outside that no one else was to interrupt her.

One of those guards had earlier informed her that her young officer, Connar, had been reported missing. She had feigned surprise, and had expressed hope that he would soon be found.

It was strange for Allana to be back in this room, and in this bed; it had once belonged to Duke Conran Sepian, and she had spent many nights with the duke here, as his lover. Indeed, as she lay on the mattress, Allana could remember falling to sleep in this bed whilst dreaming about becoming Conran's bride.

That had been before... *everything else* had happened. Before his death. Before her imprisonment in the fortress of Aiduel's Guards, and her dreadful torture. Before that terrible ordeal.

She realised that her body had started to tremble, and she felt as if she was on the verge of tears.

Must you suffer this again, Lana? Must you really be so weak?

She had come back to Septholme as part of a vast army, which had swept all before it. She was soon to become the duchess of both Berun and Western Canasar, and was to be married to a man who might become the most powerful in all of Andar. Indeed, she was well-placed to become the most powerful *woman*.

Added to that, she had confronted her nightmares. She had returned to that dark fortress where she had suffered so much trauma. And this time, *she* had been the one instilling terror. The red-cloaks of Aiduel's Guards had become *her* victims, the recipients of *her* horror. She had proven that she had nothing to fear from them.

But if all of this was true, then why was her body shaking? Why did she still feel breathless and unsafe? And why did it seem as if nothing had changed?

She recognised that the previous day had been truly awful. So much conflict and so much death. She had been filled with uncontrollable rage, an overflowing well of anger which she had struggled to control, and which had dragged her into reckless action.

The suffering which she had inflicted upon the red-cloaked soldiers had been terrible. In particular, the transformation of the two principal victims into beasts had been ghastly. But had they not all deserved it? They had each been complicit in the imprisonment and torture of the women in the cage, and they had been about to attack Allana. Those things justified what she had done to them.

But you did worse, Lana! You killed all those women!

With that thought, she huddled her knees in closer to her body. She could remember the screams that she had heard from the cage, as the monsters had been set loose upon the captives. Would she ever forget those desperate cries?

But it had not been her fault. It was *not* her fault. The awful situation had forced her to choose between their lives and her own. And faced with that decision, she knew that there had been no option other than to do what she had done.

If she had set those women free, and they had tried to escape, they would have been recaptured in no time at all. And then they would have been returned to their imprisonment and torture. They would have been trapped in that cage, and later burned on a pyre. She had to believe that she had done them a mercy, by ending their suffering and their lives so swiftly.

And if they had been recaptured, they would have exposed Allana for what she was and what she had done. They would have destroyed her life.

You had to take their lives, Lana. You had no choice. No choice! You have to survive, whatever the cost!

But as much as she was trying to convince herself of this, she could still hear those screams, and her body would not stop trembling. And how did that justification reconcile with her subsequent instruction to the monsters, to kill Leanna of Arlais?

Allana knew that her actions in respect of the woman Leanna had been impulsive and rash. Both attacking the priestess with darkness on the walls, and then ordering the creatures against her. But had Allana truly meant for the other woman to die?

She believed that she had. Leanna of Arlais felt like a rival, and Allana had an instinctive feeling that, one day in the future, there might be another reckoning between them. Allana's action with the beasts was justified by that threat.

You were acting to defend yourself, Lana. That's all.

It anyway seemed likely that the woman had survived any attack, if the stories about the golden barrier out at sea were true. And the priestess was gone now. Perhaps she was an evacuee on the flotilla of ships which had escaped from the harbour?

Arion was gone, too, most likely on the same ships.

They might be together, Lana, at this very moment.

The thought of that sickened her. Arion Sepian had rejected her twice more. Once in the forest, when everything had seemed so perfect, but then had turned into a nightmare. And then again in the fortress, after it had cost her so much to follow him there. He had chosen to discard her, after they had lain together, and she had proclaimed her love. He had callously cast her aside, after she had offered her life and her future to him. He had run away, towards Leanna of Arlais.

Perhaps that was why Allana was shaking?

She lay there, trying to quell the trembling of her body. Instead, the thought of Arion caused tears to come forth. It seemed that he had chosen his wife, and the woman Leanna, over her.

How could he do that to you, Lana? You were meant to be together!

She had supported Jarrett in his schemes for this war, in order to put herself into a position of power. Into a place where she would feel protected and secure, and could never again be imprisoned or tortured. And today was a culmination of their efforts, a day when she should have been full of triumphant emotions. But she did not feel that way.

Nor did she feel any safer, after her rage had brought her so close to exposing her abilities to the world. But worst of all, she recognised now that her schemes had caused her to lose the person whom she wanted above all others. The one who was most like her, who shared her powers and who she was meant to be with.

In hindsight, she realised that if she had simply written to Arion to declare her love and to ask him to come to Andarron, without any other machinations, he would have come. Indeed, he had travelled there to meet with her, despite his marriage. They would have made love together, as they had done in the forest, and afterwards they would have held each other and declared their undying passion, without any rancour or recrimination. They would have been together, and they could have spent a lifetime together.

Instead, she had ruined it. Ruined everything.

She started crying, her sobs contributing further to the shakes which were running through her body. And she recognised that their victory in Septholme did not possess a sweet taste. In fact, it was quite the opposite; it delivered a most bitter flavour.

—

Later, when a much more composed Allana re-emerged from her room, one of her guards notified her of an unexpected arrival at the castle. This person had begged for an audience with the new lady, and was being held in the castle courtyard, pending Allana's decision. When Allana heard the supplicant's name, she was intrigued and headed directly there.

The teenage girl was standing at the edge of the courtyard, looking bedraggled and miserable. Her eyes were red, as if she had been crying. Allana recognised the plain features immediately, despite a large bruise on the girl's left cheek, and she knew that this person was indeed who she had claimed to be.

Lady Karienne Sepian.

Allana strolled towards her, straightening her back and approaching with an air of authority, as was befitting of the new mistress of Septholme Castle.

'Yes, what is it that you want?' she asked. She noted the look of recognition and shock on the girl's face.

'My... my Lady.' Allana felt annoyed by the hesitation. 'I am Lady Karienne Sepian. This is my home. I came here because... I've nowhere else to go.'

'Correction. This *was* your home. House Sepian is no more, and this is now a castle of House Berun. Also, with the fall of your family, I believe that you're no longer a noble. Just *plain* Karienne.'

The corners of the girl's mouth turned down, and she appeared to be on the cusp of tears. 'Please, my Lady,' she said. 'I fell into the water at the harbour. I got so wet and cold, and I nearly drowned. But after I'd recovered, I found out that… they'd all left me. Please, I'm so cold and hungry, and I've nowhere else to go.'

Allana stared at the ordinary girl, with her homely features, who had lost her only claim to being anything other than mediocre. Allana was minded to cast her out onto the street. To discard her as if she was nothing and worthless, as Gerrion Sepian had once cast out Allana. But Jarrett would not be pleased that a member of the Sepian family was wandering free around the streets of Septholme, and therefore the girl could not be allowed to leave.

Allana also recognised that it might be useful leverage over Arion Sepian, to have possession of his younger sister. Only if it was ever necessary, of course.

How would he react if he knew that you have her, Lana? Would he dare to come back?

Karienne Sepian had no awareness of any of these thoughts, and all that she saw was a smile, as Allana came to a conclusion.

'Oh, don't you worry, Karienne,' Allana said, after a few moments. 'We won't send you away. We'll find you somewhere that's private and dry, where you can stay with us. For a long time.'

―

By the time that evening had arrived, Allana had rejoined Jarrett in the Great Hall. She had returned to being externally calm and assured, and there was no trace of the woman who had earlier been crying and trembling.

She had changed into more elegant clothing and was wearing a flowing dress which had been taken from the wardrobe of Lady

Kalyane Sepian. Allana derived a tinge of satisfaction from the fact that the garment was almost too tight around her bosom.

The ceremony in which the castle retainers had sworn allegiance had finished, without any further acts of disrespect. Allana and Jarrett were now seated beside each other at the head of the grand table, in the centre of the large room.

They had been joined in the Great Hall by Prince Markon El'Augustus. Jarrett was engaged in conversation with the royal prince, as the three of them indulged in a sumptuous evening meal.

Allana was listening intently, feeling relieved to sense that there was again desire stirring within Markon, whose eyes occasionally strayed onto her.

Two men of power, Lana. And they both want you.

However, an early topic of conversation grasped hold of her attention.

'I must inform you, Duke Berun, that Duke Gerrion Sepian is dead,' Prince Markon was saying. 'That news came as a shock to me, earlier today. He was murdered. And strangely enough, not by our own hand.'

'Dead?' repeated Jarrett.

'His throat was cut in his cell,' replied Markon. 'A nasty business. His murder appears to be part of an attack against and massacre of the garrison in the fortress, whilst we were taking the town.'

'Lord, I wasn't expecting to hear that,' stated Jarrett. 'May he rest in the Grace of Aiduel. I never liked him, but I didn't loathe him in the way that I hate his brother. You say that someone attacked the fortress?'

'Yes. No one's sure how, but upwards of eighty Aiduel's Guards had been installed there as a garrison, and *every last one of them was killed*. While not a single dead attacker was left behind.'

Allana felt a flush creeping onto her cheeks.

You mustn't look guilty or suspicious, Lana.

'Could it be rogue Andar soldiers?' she asked, admiring the calmness in her own voice.

'Possibly,' replied Markon. 'We think it's most likely local forces, but if so, they're a bunch of vicious bastards. They not only killed the garrison, they killed Sepian too. *And* all of the heretic women in the prison cage, in what sounds like an absolutely appalling massacre. They were all butchered.'

'Lord preserve us,' stated Jarrett.

'Well, almost all,' added Markon. 'One madwoman was found alive on the floor of the cage, under a pile of bodies, who I understand was rambling about a witch and her monsters. My men haven't been able to get anything sensible out of her yet, though.'

Upon hearing these words, a chill ran through Allana.

'Monsters?' said Jarrett. 'Haven't there been reports of monsters in the town, too?'

'That's right,' replied Markon. 'Strange stories from the harbour, from when those ships were escaping. I've asked a captain to investigate.'

'How peculiar,' commented Jarrett. 'But all in all, we've had a very strange week, first with miraculous walls of light, and now this. Momentous, but very strange. It seems that we're suddenly living in a world full of miracles and monsters.'

If only he knew what you know, Lana.

'It does,' said Markon. 'But even in the face of those events, think about what we've achieved. We're here, we're alive, and we've completed the first key objective in this war. That's worthy of celebration.'

He raised his glass of red wine.

Jarrett nodded, copying the gesture, and said, 'I'll drink to that. But how is the war going, otherwise? Have you received any further news from the west?'

'It's still patchy news rather than confirmed reports,' said Markon. 'Duke Orlen Condarr is dead, I know that much. He fell in battle to the armies of Andarron, led by the new Imposter King, Sendar Pavil. Such a shame that Prince Senneos didn't survive to claim the throne after his father's death. He and I had become friends, during my captivity, and I found him to be... *malleable*. His brother seems to be made of sterner stuff.'

'Sendar will be a difficult adversary,' stated Jarrett. 'He's a man to be taken seriously.'

'Trust me, we will,' stated Markon. 'Last that I heard, Pavil's army was advancing to confront our forces at Rednarron. There's been no further news, but that battle could prove to be decisive. My own forces will be decamping to march for Rednar tomorrow, however. We'll expect the army of Berun to hold Western Canasar from now on, Duke Jarrett, and to conquer and subdue the remaining towns, whilst we complete the conquest of Andar. Lord knows, holding this province shouldn't be difficult for you, given how comprehensively we've crushed their armies.'

'We'll hold Western Canasar, as we've agreed,' said Jarrett. He then paused, appearing to consider something, before adding, 'As you'll hopefully appreciate, from the day that we opened the Canas River bridges, I've kept faith with everything that was agreed between myself and your uncle. I trust that you have full understanding of our wider agreement, Your Highness?'

'I do, of course, and I recognise your good faith, Duke Berun,' stated Markon. 'Western Canasar would never have fallen so easily if we'd been forced to attack across the Canas River. And rest assured, Elannis will hold true to its promises. The province of Western Canasar is now yours, as was agreed with Lorrius, and we now regard you as a faithful ally of the empire. Govern this territory well, crush any remaining resistance, and suppress any attempt at revolt. And make sure that our supply lines remain open, as we conquer the remainder of Andar.'

'I will,' said Jarrett. 'And I have found the Imperial Family to be faithful and honourable allies, too. But what about the last of the conditions which I agreed with Prince Lorrius? I trust that I still have your support for this, Your Highness?'

Allana leaned forward to listen, feeling her heart beating in her chest. She could well remember her private meeting with Lorrius in Berun Castle, when she had compelled the Emperor's brother to accept and to support this last condition.

'You do,' said Markon. 'The agreement that you made with Lorrius and Archprime Kohn still stands, Duke Berun. Indeed, after the unfortunate death of Duke Condarr, the delivery of that agreement becomes less… *complicated.*' He paused.

'Go on, please, Your Highness,' said Jarrett, and Allana felt some relief to hear a return of enthusiasm to his voice.

'Therefore, when this war is concluded,' continued Markon, 'we all expect that Andar will become a vassal state of the Elannis Empire. Andar will continue to have its own monarch, although that person will of course be a vassal of my father and will swear loyalty to the Holy Church in Sen Aiduel.'

'That is, of course, all well understood,' said Jarrett.

'Such a person can never be a Pavil,' continued Markon, 'although it will be better if the people of Andar will be able to regard them as one of their own. And who could possibly be better for such a role than a proven ally, whose faith towards the one true Holy Church is unquestionable. Someone who's an important member of the Andar nobility, but who also has the blood of the Imperial Family flowing through his veins. I therefore support the decision, when this war is over, that you shall no longer merely be Duke Jarrett Berun.'

Allana waited for the prince to conclude, feeling building excitement.

'You will be King Jarrett, monarch of Andar, first of his line, and loyal vassal of His Imperial Majesty the Emperor.'

—

Later that night, Jarrett and Allana retired to the duke's chambers in Septholme Castle. Allana had decided to forgive Jarrett for his offences of the preceding day, and they made love together in the bed that she had spent so many previous nights in.

Afterwards, she fell asleep quickly. And sometime later, during that sleep, the recurring dream came to her for the first time since the dark events in the fortress.

When she jerked awake from her disturbed slumber, she realised immediately that something was different. She sat up, feeling shocked and horrified.

She could remember the entire dream. All of it. Every vivid and chilling moment, until the brutal end.

ONLY ONE CAN CLAIM THE POWER.

She had heard that terrible, thunderous voice again, and had witnessed everything that had followed. All of the violence. All of the death.

KILL THEM TO MAKE IT YOURS. KILL THEM ALL!

But she had been murdered in the dream. Brutally murdered, by one of her four shining companions. That was the dark truth which her mind had been concealing for so long. Which she had been prevented from holding onto, after awakening.

She had been dreaming of her own death.

She had seen it all, and had been the last to be killed. She had fought desperately to avoid that fate, struggling furiously against her assailant. Kicking and clawing and scratching, trying to hurt the blazing avatar who had killed her other companions. But her efforts had been in vain; the attacker had been too strong, and the end had been abrupt and vicious.

It wasn't you who died, Lana! It was someone else's death you were seeing. It wasn't you!

But try as she might to persuade herself that it had not been happening to her, she was not convinced. Now that she could remember its every secret, the dream seemed too real. Too tangible. As if she had indeed experienced it herself. Had lived it herself.

And if it was not her own death that she had witnessed, then whose was it?

You will never let anyone do that to you, Lana. Never!

The bitterness of watching the sole survivor – the *murderer* – walking into the Gate, exultant and triumphant, still lingered after waking. They had betrayed her, killed her, trapping her there. And then they had entered the Gate and had stolen the promised, *supreme* power which should have been hers. They had traded her life to claim it.

It made her feel furious. If there was such an almighty power to be claimed, and only one could take possession of it, then she would have to be that one.

And she would never allow herself to become a victim of murder, like the weakling which she had been in the dream. Not with the powers that she already had. Not with the means which she possessed to protect herself. If she had indeed been dreaming of her own death, then she would never allow a repeat of such a deed in her waking life.

She would find a way to survive. Always. If she deemed it necessary, that would include finding the Gate, wherever it was, and then claiming that power. And if anyone tried to get in her way as she was doing that, or if anyone tried to take it from her, or threaten her, she would deal with them. If required, she would *kill* them.

And *then* she would claim the power.

Whatever the cost.

37

Corin

—

*Year of Our Lord,
After Ascension, 770AA*

Corin walked at the forefront of hundreds of other Chosen men and women, all of whom were survivors of the Battle of Karn. As he led them, there was little conversation amongst the following mass of people. The majority walked in silence, as did Corin himself.

During the past day, he had noticed troubled expressions on the faces of many of those who had been in the midst of the events to the south of Karn. They were all now forever united by being party to the slaughter of the day before. All of them could claim that they had been part of the astounding victory, which had been delivered with little cost of life to their own people. However, they had also witnessed the carnage which had taken place, and Corin believed that many of them would carry those haunting images for their entire lives.

They were now travelling northwards from Karn. Corin's intention was to unite with the women, children and elderly who had been evacuated and who were now returning.

There was to be a celebratory feast tonight amongst the survivors of the ten clans which now formed the Chosen Alliance. It would be an event to embrace the common tradition of Spring's Heart, and would be one more act to bind them together.

The celebration would take place far northward of Karn, to remain out of sight of the killing grounds to the south. For the last day, the felrin horde had been feeding. Hundreds of felrin had been gorging themselves on the corpses of their victims, within those same grounds. Corin was able to communicate with the mass of the felrin through Blackpaw. For the moment, he knew that the beasts were content to accept his order to remain in the areas to the south, between those fields and the Great Lake. And to desist from attacking anything else.

What was to become of them after that was another question which he would soon need to resolve, though he knew that he could not allow hundreds of felrin to roam unchecked in the lands of man.

'I see a man who should walk tall and in glory, Chief Corin,' said Chief Munnik, who was walking behind Corin. 'A man who has saved his people. And yet he does not. He plods along with shoulders slumped and with heavy feet, as if he carries the tallest tree of the Great Forest upon his back.'

Corin looked around and he smiled wanly. 'I am weary, Munnik. And yesterday's scenes… I'll remember them, too.'

As they continued to walk, Munnik moved closer and put a hand onto Corin's shoulder. 'We'll all remember, Corin. No one who was there will forget yesterday. What we saw. What we survived. And what you did. You saved us all, Chosen.'

'Did I, Munnik? But at what cost?'

'A *necessary* cost. And one we would all choose to pay again, to follow you. We all now know that with you as our leader, we've become something more than we were before. Something stronger and better. I'd lay down my life for you, Chief Corin, as will so many others here. We know what you are. We know *who* you are.'

'And who am I, Munnik?' Corin asked, quietly. But he had

already guessed the answer. Yesterday evening, he had heard it being shouted by hundreds of Chosen warriors.

'You are Mella Reborn, Corin. We are all certain of that, now. We are led by a God, reborn. And for that we all thank the Gods!'

'Yes, thank the Gods.' Corin frowned as he said this. 'I carry many titles, Munnik. Perhaps too many.'

He had once been Corin of the Karn, known to most as Runt. After his banishment, he had become even less than that. Now, he was the Chosen of the Gods. Leader of the Chosen Alliance. Destroyer of the Kurakee. The God in the West. And there was no longer any doubt in the minds of his people that he was Mella Reborn.

Of all of these, it was the last which caused Corin the most discomfort. But given what had taken place, how could it be otherwise? Every one of his people had grown up hearing the stories of the Gods. They had all heard and in turn had told of how Mella had led a horde of felrin to battle the Outsiders. And yesterday, they had witnessed their own leader commanding hundreds of the beasts. Corin's horde of felrin had inflicted a devastating slaughter on the barbarous Kurakee, in a massacre which had delivered a resounding victory for the Chosen peoples.

Only Corin knew of the true nature of the one known as Mella, a man whose legacy had been the direct opposite of everything which Corin hoped to build. It was therefore not a name that would ever settle easily onto Corin's shoulders, but he must learn to accept it.

'And what now, Chief Corin?' asked Munnik. 'Now that the Kurakee are defeated, what comes next for the Chosen people?'

'I'll talk to everyone tonight, Munnik,' said Corin. 'It's time for me to address all of our people. I'll speak to them while they're gathered in one place and I'll tell them about our future.'

'And what will you say, Chosen?'

'I must find the right words to try to renew them, Munnik, and to inspire them.' Corin paused for a moment, considering what he was going to say next. 'First, I'll inform them that we've won a great victory, and I'll tell them to celebrate that. To be thankful for their homes, and their families, and their lives. And to rejoice.

'But I'll also let them know that our work isn't complete. I'll tell them that we have a duty, Munnik, to bring order to this land. To continue to build on what first started here, in the lands of the Karn and the Anath and the Borl. To secure order and a lasting peace, and to return these lands to what they once were.

'And I'll remind them that, while the Kurakee horde has been defeated, there will still be countless more clans across the lands to the south who are ruled by cruel Kurakee chiefs. Whose people have been given up to slavery and misery. Whose way of life has been destroyed. And there will be more Kurakee warriors, spread across those lands. We've chopped the head off the monster, but it breathes still.'

'And what would you have us do, Chief Corin?' asked Munnik.

'The Chosen Alliance will not end with ten clans, Munnik. We must free all of the clans to the south. We can destroy the Kurakee way, and teach *our* way to the people of those lands. We can unite all of the people of every land, under our control. In order, in peace, and free from fear.'

Corin's voice had risen in passion as he was saying this, and he was aware that others were listening to him as he walked ahead of them. After he had finished, he saw that Munnik was smiling.

'Before the Gods, I swear that if any other man said those words,' said the Borl chief, 'they'd be laughed at. Mocked as crazy and deluded. But when you say it, I hear my spirits soar to the sky, and I know that I stand alongside the greatest of men. One who I'm honoured to serve. I pledge my spear to you, Corin of the Karn, for as long as you may need it.'

'And I accept it, Munnik, and am thankful, yet again, that I stand shoulder to shoulder with great men like you.'

Munnik slapped Corin's upper arm in response to this. After that, they continued to trek onwards in silence. As they marched, Corin was further formulating the words that he would speak to the Chosen people. He was also beginning to think about how the Chosen Alliance would need to organise, to expand southwards. Munnik had been correct to observe that Corin carried a burden, and it was not one which was likely to lift anytime soon.

However, words in a speech and plans for the Alliance were not truly at the heart of Corin's mood. Indeed, now that the immediate threat of the Kurakee had been vanquished, he was once again able to consider other challenges and issues.

In particular, he could permit his thoughts to return to the events in the far north. Specifically, to the encounter at the ancient arch, and to the revelations which the presence had shared, and to the decision which Corin had made.

Even now, he could close his eyes and could vividly replay the last moments of that interaction in his mind. As if he was once again there, with his hand on the towering archway, bearing witness to the startling secrets of a ghost named Cillian…

…I remember you now. I'm starting to remember all of us, and I can see us, too. Now look…

In the aftermath of the ghost's words, a succession of images flashed into Corin's mind. Images which might have been visions, or memories, or both, but which he felt certain were outside of the here and now. And he witnessed a handful of strangers…

> *…the first was a skinny boy, with sandy-coloured hair. This youth was sitting at a wooden table, within a gloomy stone house. There were three others in the room with him, including a burly, grey-bearded man. Everyone else was watching the boy, whose face was contorted in apparent pain, with his eyes scrunched shut…*
>
> *…a slim and elegant young woman came into view, one whose golden-blonde hair fell long past her shoulders. She was*

standing within a blazing orb of brilliant light, on a stone structure which was surrounded by water. Her arms were raised to the sky, with palms facing upwards. She appeared both determined and exultant as immense power pulsed through her, achieving some unknown but almighty task…

…then there was a tall man, brown-haired and muscular, who was standing within a grim fortress. He was covered in blood, as was the weapon in his right hand. Around him lay scores of bodies, warriors in red cloaks who had been cut to pieces. It seemed as if the air was crackling around the man, energy coiling about his limbs, and there was no doubt that he had been the deliverer of these many deaths…

…and finally, there was a dark-haired woman, whose stunningly beautiful features were contorted in a rictus of fury. An aura of darkness was emerging from this woman, washing outwards, directed principally at the two victims who writhed in agony on the floor before her. This woman's actions reeked of past abominations, and something truly terrible was about to happen…

Corin gasped as he emerged from these visions, and he found himself recoiling from the last two of the four. Instinctively, he knew that all of these strangers were like him. That they were of his own kind, and that each of them possessed power. Immense power.

But was it a god-like power, equivalent to Corin's own? And could the dark-haired woman truly have been undertaking such a heinous act? Could these people be a threat to him?

ONE OF THEM IS A BOY. IS THAT YOU?
Yes, I think it was.
YOU ARE YOUNGER THAN THE OTHERS?
It… confuses me, too. But I think … it's the day I was murdered.
WHO MURDERED YOU?
There was anguish in the response.
The big man. He killed me. And Ma. And Da…

WHO ARE THE OTHERS, THE ONES YOU SHOWED ME?

You've forgotten them? Yes... I'd forgotten them, too. I can still only remember... parts, though I don't know how. But we were all children, and we were together. And for just the briefest of moments, I think we were happy.

A further image rushed into Corin's mind, and he was immersed within a vision which he sensed was much, *much* older...

> *...it was the same sandy-haired and skinny boy as before, the one who had been sitting in the gloomy room. However, this time the youth was reclining near to the edge of a cliff, which was high above an endless terrain covered in lifeless sand and rocks. And the boy's skin was darker, more tanned...*
>
> *...resting close beside this youth, there was a girl with piercing blue eyes and golden-blonde hair, which had been dirtied by layers of sand and dust. Her mouth was stretching into a beaming and radiant smile...*
>
> *...and near to the two of them, a heavily-built and handsome brown-haired boy. This youth was sitting alongside a petite and younger dark-haired girl, the latter child possessing a beautiful heart-shaped face and bloodied knees...*
>
> *...then all of them were laughing. Corin felt as if he was resting in the midst of them, looking around at the others, and he was laughing too...*

Corin was enthralled as he experienced this. He felt as if he was participating in it, was reliving it, and it hinted at long-forgotten relationships. However, the presence's next words dragged him back out of the experience.

I don't want to see... what comes after. I don't want to remember that. What he... what I? ... did...

Corin felt a sense of frustration as he tried to comprehend what he had just witnessed. The sandy-haired boy had been identical, but for his skin tone, across the two visions. But as for the others, had they all been younger versions of the people whom he had observed, just moments earlier?

It was hard to be certain, but he believed that they were indeed the same, witnessed at different times in their lives.

WE HAVE TALKED OF A GATE. I THOUGHT IT WOULD BE HERE, IN THE LANDS OF THE GODS, BUT IT'S NOT.

No. This isn't the Gate.

THEN WHERE IS IT?

I'm not sure. It was in my dreams, too. And I think the others dream of it. But I can feel it, connected to this place…

The Gate from Corin's recurring dream flashed into his mind, revealing the glorious ethereal archway at the end of the winding path on the mountain.

WHERE IS IT?

I can feel it, calling to us. Reach out with your mind…

Corin did as instructed, and indeed he could also now sense something. A distant flame of power, somehow connected to the ancient structure that his physical form was touching. And if the edifice where Mella's life had ended was now a dying candle, then this was a blazing sun. Far, far away.

I CAN FEEL IT TOO.

And alongside that recognition, there were more images; of lands of sand which stretched to the horizon, and of a fertile plateau which sat above that barren terrain, in the midst of mountains. And Corin knew that he was again being shown the place of that clifftop, where a group of children had long ago rested and laughed.

I think we have to go there. We must all go there. To make it right.

There was a hint of excitement and pleading in the boyish voice as it said this.

NO.

Corin had come to a decision, and his response was curt. It elicited another wearied sigh from the presence.

No?

YOU CANNOT STAY. I HAVE TO SAVE AGBETH.

I must stay.

YOU MUST LEAVE. GO BACK AND LEAVE AGBETH.

Please, no.

YOU MUST LEAVE. GO BACK AND LEAVE AGBETH.

No… you don't understand. You will need me… I don't know how. But I think you will die again, without me.

I DO UNDERSTAND. NOW LEAVE.

I… must stay…

Corin's patience with the ghost called Cillian was at an end. He had travelled to the far north for one principal purpose, which overrode all other priorities. All other considerations.

YOU MUST LEAVE HER! YOU MUST GO BACK TO WHERE YOU CAME FROM! NOW! I COMMAND YOU!

Every last shred of Corin's willpower was slammed into this order, reinforced by the traces of power which still lingered in the edifice. Immediately, he felt the presence being wrenched away from him.

There was a wailing cry, that of a child, as the ghost hurtled away from Corin. It plummeted downwards, as if being dragged by some violent force.

In moments, the presence was gone. But at the last instant, a final and frail whisper emerged from the distant depths.

Kellon… I'm so sorry, for what was done to you. For what was done to all of you.

Corin was still remembering this exchange when the sprawling band of evacuees appeared in sight.

These people, travelling from the north, already knew that they were safe from the Kurakee threat. Qari riders had reached them in the hours after the battle, and the evacuees had been told to return.

Nonetheless, Corin relished the thought of walking amongst them and of sharing the news of the victory himself. Today would be a counterbalance to the horror which he had inflicted upon the Kurakee. He would be able to look upon each of these people, and would know that they had survived and could live in peace and possible happiness, because of him.

As the distance between Corin's group and the evacuees closed, he spotted the person whom he had been looking for.

Agbeth.

Corin had insisted that she be one of the evacuees. He had not been prepared to risk her suffering further injuries during the battle, after everything that she had already been through.

She was at the front of the other group, moving slowly forwards with the same lopsided limp that was so wonderfully familiar to him. She was walking of her own volition, without any guiding hand on her arm.

And she was awake.

He grinned when she finally spotted him. She waved, and he started to run towards her.

At the edifice, Corin had chosen to force the ghost to leave Agbeth, and to return to the place from whence it had come. He had subsequently been overjoyed to realise that this decision and action had awoken his wife, and had made her whole again. Indeed, for all of the time since that fateful day at the ancient arch, she had been free of the dream-state. Living her life again, conscious and alert.

At first, during the journey back to Karn, accompanied by a small group of weary survivors and a horde of felrin, Corin had fretted that Agbeth's return to awareness would not last. His immediate joy at her recovery had also been tempered by the pending threat of the Kurakee.

But now, he was increasingly certain that the expulsion of the ghost had restored Agbeth to what she had been before the injury. And the Kurakee had been vanquished.

Corin's expedition to the north had therefore achieved even more than he could have hoped. He had saved his wife *and* his people.

He met her between the two large groups which were coming together. As Agbeth looked up at him, there were tears in her eyes.

'Corin. You did it.'

'Agbeth. Yes.'

And then they were hugging, her head pressed tight against his chest, and their arms were squeezing each other. For minutes afterwards, they remained like this, locked together. Hundreds of people passed around them as they embraced, people who in turn were searching for and reuniting with their loved ones. However, Corin and his wife were close to oblivious of the world around them, as his heart beat against her ear.

Corin held Agbeth in his arms, and all was as it should be. He felt like he never wanted to stop this embrace, and he knew that she shared the feeling as her arms were clasped tightly around him.

Of course, even in this moment, he could not completely disregard the visions and warnings of the ghost. He now understood that there were three other people in the world who were like him. And they were somehow linked together, he and these three strangers who also possessed powers. He felt as if he knew them, although he could not make sense of why he had seen them as children, on a clifftop, in a place where he had never been.

ONLY ONE CAN CLAIM THE POWER.

The thought of them again made him wonder whether they too had been haunted by the recurring dream. Had they also finally seen, and remembered, the end of that dream? Had they too heard the terrible, thunderous voice and experienced their own deaths?

Ever since the events at the edifice, Corin had seen and could recall every aspect of the dream, including his murder at the end. And he now believed that somewhere to the south, to the very *furthest* south in lands on the far side of a great ocean, there was a real place which held the beautiful, ethereal archway of his dreams. He believed that the Gate truly existed, and that it lay within an ancient desert city which bore the name of Aiduel's Gate.

It was a place which Corin had questioned the missionary Hellin about further, on their return journey. She had told him that the city had been closed off from the world for hundreds of years. It was said to sit atop a mighty cliff, and to possess walls which towered like the Great Forest, which none could breach. But Corin now believed that one day he must go there and that he must enter that place, even if it required him to scale those cliffs and to shatter those walls.

Gather them. Open the Gate. And claim the power.

He would gather the clans, he would open the Gate, and he would claim the power. He was resolved that this was his destiny, irrespective of any warnings of death which had been issued by the desperate ghost.

And if there was a power to be claimed, then he would claim it for the clans. He could not allow it to be taken by the others. In particular, he would not permit it to be possessed by the dark-haired woman who was walking in Mella's footsteps, or by the vicious male killer. He must reach it before them, and if they were to get in his way, then he would have to deal with them. His powers and his felrin would have to deal with them.

But matters of such import were concerns for a future day. For on this day, for the first time in a very long time, Corin's people were not threatened with war or subjugation, and his beloved wife was whole and was beside him.

In this moment, as he held Agbeth in his arms, in lands for which he had delivered peace, he felt contentment.

And once again, even if for just a short time, Corin of the Karn knew what it was to be happy.

Aftermath

Allana

—

Year of Our Lord,
After Ascension, 770AA

'And now, before The Lord Aiduel, I pronounce you husband and wife.'

Allana was smiling as she heard the priest speak these words, and as she kissed Jarrett afterwards.

There was little noise in reaction to this. The wedding was a quiet ceremony in the chapel of Septholme Castle, undertaken with little fuss before a small audience of soldiers and retainers. However, Allana could celebrate within. In the eyes of The Lord and the world they were wed, and she was bound her to her husband's future, and to his future title.

After Allana had heard Prince Markon's confirmation of how Jarrett's status was going to improve, she had taken the decision that it was time to marry. And it had required only a small amount of compulsion to encourage Jarrett to agree.

The bitterness which Allana had been feeling just a few days earlier had now been pushed down and within, hidden in a deep and dark cavern inside of herself. And today was a day for warm smiles.

'I love you, Lana,' said Jarrett.

In response, Allana beamed and then kissed him again.

In the end, her decision to marry had been an easy one. Arion Sepian had rejected her three times, and she would not give him an opportunity for a fourth such rejection. Anyway, she had not felt his presence for days, and he appeared to have abandoned Septholme and his home, perhaps never to return.

In contrast, she knew that Jarrett would never desert her. He was too besotted with her, and on that day in the tent in the encampment, she had revealed to him who was in charge when she had broken his will.

And unlike Arion, who had lost everything and was probably now a fugitive on the run, Jarrett could offer her a life of power and protection.

He was going to be the king.

And you will be his queen, Lana. Queen Allana, the most important woman in the whole of Andar. A beautiful and powerful queen who men will desire, and who women will desire to be.

And all of that, alongside a monarch who would be hers to command.

She smiled again, another beaming smile which she was sure would dazzle everyone within the chapel.

For Allana, on the outside at least, today was to be a day for rejoicing.

Epilogue

―

*Year of Our Lord,
The Year of Ascension*

―

Epilogue

Amena

—

*Year of Our Lord,
The Year of Ascension*

She was dying, and this time even Aiduel would not be able to save her.

She was slumped in bed within their home, this safe place which they had shared for the last fourteen years, ever since their return to Aiduel's Gate. She had been in a deep sleep, lost in aching dreams of younger days, of times when her limbs had been strong and supple. As her eyes drifted open, she guessed from the light playing across the ceiling that it was afternoon.

Recently, she had been sleeping more and more of the day away, her lungs coping better with slumber than with the waking hours. It would not be long now until she took her final rest, and her eyelids closed for the very last time. However, this did not fill her with grief. She was ready to leave her long life behind and to pass on.

But was *he* also ready for that moment?

Amena's head was resting on pillows, and she raised her neck slightly now, to look at her husband. He was seated with his back to her, working at his desk with quill in hand, writing on a parchment. He had been spending all of his time in here recently, despite her protestations, and the very nature of him meant that she was always cognizant of his presence, even when wearing her medallion.

He would be aware that she had awakened, but she knew that he would wait until she was less disorientated and was ready to speak.

'Aiduel.' The word was a croak, and for a moment she hated the frail, old woman that time had transformed her into.

He turned towards her, smiled, then walked to the bed. 'Mena.'

He lifted a cup to her mouth, and she took a sip of the cool water within. He then leaned forwards and kissed her softly on the lips.

Over sixty-five years had passed since they had first kissed, and then had lain together. That first night, under the desert stars, they had both been tanned, young and beautiful, and the promise of their future had seemed to stretch into eternity. And although such promises had proven to be a deception, and nothing could be eternal for her as it was for him, they had lived a life of meaning, and of happiness, for the many decades since then.

And they had accomplished deeds that would endure far beyond the mortal span of her years.

But, alas, time was both a liar *and* a thief. In those intervening years, she had aged and withered. She had become the tired, wrinkled crone who languished in this bed today, counting her final moments. He, on the other hand, still looked to be a man no older than thirty. His skin was unlined, and his smile was as captivating as it had ever been.

A man who had always been true to her. A good man.

'It will be soon,' she said, her voice a whisper. 'I have days. Possibly hours. That's all.'

She witnessed him grimacing, and she could see a redness in his eyes which suggested that he had been crying.

'I don't accept that,' he said. 'Let me try—'

'Be at peace with this, Aiduel.'

He reached out and took her hand, not meeting her eyes.

'You're troubled, my love,' she said. 'It's the dream, isn't it?'

He sighed, and replied, 'I'm trying to accept that you'll be gone, Mena. Trying to ready myself for what I know is coming. It's all that should matter.'

'But you're dreaming again, aren't you? Speak honestly.'

'Yes,' he said, quietly. 'I've dreamt it again. Over and over, as I kill them. It grows stronger.'

She pressed weak fingers against his palm and said, 'Please… try to put it aside, Aiduel. I've forgiven you. And if they'd seen the things that you've done, all the good you've done, *they* would forgive you, too.'

He did not answer, and his silence told her that yet again he had not truly accepted her absolution. He had confessed his sin to her many years before, but she worried that his guilt would endure long after she was gone.

'Please,' she continued, despite the words suddenly becoming harder to form. 'In the years ahead… think of the good that you can still do. Cherish the memories of… our life. But put *that* memory aside. Please.'

She saw then that he was weeping. She opened her arms, and he moved onto the bed, resting his head lightly against her chest. She began to stroke his hair, feeling worried for him.

'I don't know how I'll carry on without you, Mena.'

'Don't say that. You will. And it will be a great life.'

'I fear, though…'

'What do you fear, my love?'

'I fear… if I go on, without you beside me… my grief and my shame and my loneliness will drive me to… *change*, for the worse. You are the last of my Disciples, Mena. What if I cannot cope when you're gone, and I descend towards tyranny?'

'Don't say that, Aiduel. Please. No more of that, not now.' Her mouth and throat felt parched, and speech was becoming more difficult.

'I'm sorry,' he said. 'Let me talk of other things... of that day, beside the stream in the meadow. Let's remember...'

For a while longer, she listened as he talked of experiences from days long gone. She could feel her eyelids growing heavy as he did so.

However, she could sense that there was something else. Something unsaid.

'What... is... it?' She had to strain to form the words and to force the sound out.

'What?' he replied.

'What...?' Her mouth was too dry, and the sentence that she wanted to speak was unattainable.

What aren't you telling me? she thought. *Say it, please, before it's too late, and there's no one else to tell.*

There was silence for a number of seconds.

'I've found a way,' he murmured into her chest.

A way?

'A way to bring them back, Mena. To let them live again, if I surrender myself and my power to the Gate.'

To bring them back?

'I've seen it in a vision.'

What have you seen?

For a brief moment, an image flashed into her mind, and she knew that he was sharing his thoughts. *A familiar place, the city renamed Sen Aiduel. Above it, the sun was disappearing and the sky was turning black...*

'When the sky darkens above Sen Aiduel,' he whispered, his head resting against her weakening heart, 'the five of us shall return, born anew into woman without man, and blessed by the powers of the Gate. And next time, if I can gather them together, I think that...'

Amena did not hear the rest of his words. Sleep's doors had drifted open to her with an enticing welcome which could not be refused, and she slipped through gracefully and gratefully.

She would never again awaken.

THE ILLBORN SAGA WILL CONTINUE IN BOOK THREE OF THE SERIES...

Acknowledgements

Thank you for reading my two novels, and thank you to everyone who has supported *The Illborn Saga* so far.

If you have enjoyed reading my books (which I truly hope that you have), please leave reviews or ratings on Amazon and Goodreads, and please recommend my series to other people. Every single positive review, rating and recommendation makes an enormous contribution to growing the readership of *Illborn* and *Aiduel's Sin*, and is massively appreciated.

Thank you in particular to the wonderful group of readers and reviewers across the Instagram, Twitter and Booktube communities who have become ardent supporters of *Illborn*, and who have helped to lift an unknown self-published debut novel out of obscurity. You are too many to name individually, but I hope that you will know who you are and how grateful I am.

I would also like to thank the kind people who have acted as beta readers for the two books, including; Ben, Mark, Pat, Jennie, Dave, Jeremy, Tom and Caoimhe. Your input has been invaluable in improving both books significantly.

I also must say a massive thank you to my wonderful sister Kate (my personal cheerleader whenever I need my spirits lifting) and to my lovely wife Elaine, who has patiently edited every chapter in both enormous tomes (sometimes more than once!), and who can now confidently claim to have made me both a better person *and* a better writer.

Thank you again for reading my novels, and I hope that you will continue with the journey of the Illborn onto book three of *The Illborn Saga*.

Matador

For exclusive discounts on Matador titles,
sign up to our occasional newsletter at
troubador.co.uk/bookshop